Foundation Stone

The Library of Alabama Classics,
reprint editions of works important
to the history, literature, and culture of
Alabama, is dedicated to the memory of

RUCKER AGEE

whose pioneering work in the fields
of Alabama history and historical geography
continues to be the standard of
scholarly achievement.

Foundation Stone

LELLA WARREN

WITH AN INTRODUCTION BY
Nancy G. Anderson

THE UNIVERSITY OF ALABAMA PRESS

Published originally in 1940 by Alfred A. Knopf

This edition is printed from the Collins edition, which was published in London in 1941.

Manufactured in the United States of America

Library of Congress Cataloging-in-Publication Data

Warren, Lella.
Foundation stone.

I. Title.
PS3545.A7443F6 1986 813′.52 85-24498
ISBN 0-8173-0287-5
ISBN 0-8173-0288-3 (pbk.)

THIRD PRINTING 1990

CONTENTS

	Introduction by Nancy G. Anderson	vii
BOOK ONE	*The Home Place*	11
BOOK TWO	*Pioneering*	97
BOOK THREE	*The Land Yields*	215
BOOK FOUR	*The Cotton Snobs*	387
BOOK FIVE	*Cotton Militant*	473
BOOK SIX	*The Land Scarred*	533
BOOK SEVEN	*Rock Wall*	615

Lella Warren, 1899–1982

(Original Photograph: Will G. Murray;
Restoration: Jerry Morgan Medley)

INTRODUCTION

Nancy G. Anderson

To get all the facts—not only the incidents that lived in a family legend, but that vast quantity on the lay of the land a century ago, the way of the settlers and their Indian neighbors and all the rest of the thousand and one details which make up a vanished way of living.[1]

SO LELLA WARREN DESCRIBED her goal in writing *Foundation Stone* (Knopf, 1940). For the source material to achieve this goal, at the urging of her father, Warren turned to her Alabama heritage—the history of her birthplace and her family.

On 22 March 1899, Lella Warren was born in Clayton, Barbour County, Alabama, in the house in which her father had been born. Her parents—Benjamin Smart Warren and Lee Ella Underwood—were both descendants of pioneers who had been prominent in settling Alabama, especially Barbour County. Because of Dr. Warren's assignments with the United States Marine Hospital Service (a forerunner of the U.S. Public Health Service), the family moved away from Clayton when his older daughter was only a small child. Lella Warren spent much of her childhood at various Marine bases or quarantine stations. Later, her family settled in Washington, where her father became assistant surgeon general and medical director of the Middle Atlantic with the Public Health Service. The young daughter attended the prestigious Western High School in Washington and, as a member of a government official's family, enjoyed the social life of the nation's capital: leaving a card at the White House on New Year's Day, receiving engraved invitations from President and Mrs. Woodrow Wilson to parties at the White House, and attending teas and receptions with families of military officers, politicians, and diplomats.

But Dr. Warren never allowed his family to forget its Alabama heritage. As Lella Warren wrote in a 1977 Warren family history:

LELLA WARREN, ABOUT 1915
(Restoration: Jerry Morgan Medley)

Dr. Benjamin Smart Warren,
1871–1935,
Assistant Surgeon General,
U.S. Public Health Service
(Original Photograph:
© Bachrach;
Restoration: Jerry Morgan Medley)

". . . he made a habit of saving up his leave for two or three years at a time, so that he could take us back down home to be re-imbued with the spirit of our birthright." Often these "leisurely visits back down home" were summer-long stays in the home of Grandmother Warren, an independent woman who had full responsibility for her large family after the death of her husband, a prominent Clayton physician, in 1885. When Dr. Benjamin Warren had an assignment on which his family could not accompany him, he left his wife and children with his mother, his sister Weetie, and his brother Monroe in the old family home. On occasion, young Lella even attended school in Clayton's one-room, "plank" school until the family could be reunited in their more permanent home in Washington. In small-town Clayton, she and her brothers and sister,

LELLA WARREN, ABOUT 1917 (Restoration: Jerry Morgan Medley)

quickly recognized as "Ben Warren's children," were readily accepted into Clayton life each time they returned. Later in her life, she described these visits as her father's tests of whether his family's ". . . transplanted roots could still burrow back into native red clay and flourish."[2]

The origins of Lella Warren's writing career also lie in the influence of her father: when she got into trouble for confusing fact and fiction in tales that she took to school or told her brothers, Dr. Warren encouraged his daughter to write her stories in notebooks, early works that he read and discussed with her. Another stimulus to her writing career was a creative writing teacher at Western High, Margaret Bell Merrill, who recognized her student's potential and, to encourage her, sent one of her stories to William Rose Benét of *The Century Magazine*. Benét wrote

Warren on 2 October 1917, when she was only eighteen years old: "We have been very much interested in your story because it does seem real."

Lella Warren attended George Washington University for her undergraduate work, except for her sophomore year, which she spent at Goucher College. At Goucher, she knew Sara Haardt, about whom she wrote a descriptive blurb for one of Haardt's stories in *College Humor.* Because of finances, Warren returned to GWU, where she completed her degree in 1921. There in Robert Bolwell's class in advanced composition, she began work on what later became her first published novel, *A Touch of Earth* (Simon & Schuster, 1926).

Immediately after graduation from GWU, Warren married John Spanogle, an aviator-friend of her oldest brother. She spent the next few years balancing her obligations as wife of a research engineer and mother of their young daughter with a desire to write. If *A Touch of Earth* is "semi-autobiographical," as Warren described it,[3] the differences in the temperaments and interests of the heroine and her husband portray the cause of the Spanogles' divorce.

The success of her first novel enabled Warren to support herself and her daughter, through the early depression years and the first years after her divorce, as a short story writer for the "slick" magazines and as a journalist, especially for three Washington papers. In these works the young writer had not yet turned to Clayton or the ancestors of her father and mother—the Warrens, the Underwoods, and the Lawsons—for any substantial subject or setting; the South, as used in *A Touch of Earth* and several of the short stories, remains a vaguely suggested place of white verandas, scuppernong, and honeysuckle. Although she acknowledged merit in some of these early publications—particularly her articles about Charles Lindbergh and George Washington University, in retrospect she viewed most of these publications as "meaningless" and, even worse, a distraction from the books she really wanted to write.

Warren's letters and papers verify that, even as she was spending her energies on these short works, as early as April 1927 she was turning to the history of her family and birthplace and collecting ideas and materials for a novel about the "true South," the South that she and her father had known and loved and frequently discussed as a good subject for her writing. In a long, confessional letter to Stephen Vincent Benét requesting his permission to quote seven lines of *John Brown's Body* as the epigraph of her forthcoming novel, she described a summer day in 1928 as a turning point in her work on that novel. On that day as a friend read aloud from Benét's narrative, Warren found "a pattern" and "the backbone" for the "formless material" that she had been collecting about her ancestors and Alabama. In the letter to Benét, she goes on to describe her own reading of *John Brown's Body* and testing her reactions against her father's:

> Well, after I had finished reading your book, I took it to my father, and gave it to him. But I didn't point out anything in it to him. Still just as soon as he came to that passage [description of Elspeth Mackay] he told me how it was like his grandmother Warren. And from then on I tried to write about her, so that her book would be the right kind of thing to tell in detail about her life. . . .[4]

From these early stages in her work on *Foundation Stone*, Warren was using her father's memories and guidance.

There are numerous stories about the research and the writing in the years intervening between those first notes in 1927 and the release of the finished novel in 1940. In the early stages Warren wrote as many as 450 pages and burned hundreds, salvaging perhaps 35 pages. Her work was further interrupted by serious illness for two years in the early 1930s. She slowly recovered, and early in 1935 she read several sections of the planned novel to her father. According to Warren's account of this incident in the unpublished "Born Patriarch," the passage about the Warren family burying-ground in Clayton moved her father to tears: "Though of course it wasn't altogether my writing that made him cry; it was that I'd made him homesick. But at least I had done *that*. He said, 'A dream brought true.'" After hearing another passage about Clayton, he cautioned her about her writing: "'*Stick to it along the lines that we've discussed, that you know are right for you. Even if the money doesn't come in easily.*'" Only a few months after this incident, Dr. Warren died, and his daughter no longer had his counsel and guidance from their conversations as she followed him up and down the rows of the garden he tended so carefully in his retirement years in Washington. She never forgot his contributions to the novel that brought her recognition; when *Foundation Stone* was published—five years after his death—she inscribed a copy for him:

> This is Papa's copy of the book.
> He charged me to write
> about our kind of forebears.
> In it I hope that I have not
> only made another
> "Dream come true"
> but reincarnated the truth as
> he and I know it about our sort of South—

Sept. 9, 1940

The next day, near its close, she went where she had not gone for a long time, up to the family burying-ground (p. 386).

WARREN FAMILY BURYING-GROUND, CLAYTON, ALABAMA
(Original Photograph: Jerry Morgan Medley)

As Dr. Warren had warned her, the money did not come in easily. In 1936, she married Gerald Breckenridge, a young novelist-journalist; then there were two writers and her daughter Lee struggling to live on writers' incomes. Breckenridge's novel *Brief Kingdom* (Doubleday, 1936), dedicated to his wife, had been successful enough that his publishers gave him an advance on a novel about "present-day family life." In addition Warren was far enough into her work that she decided to send more than one hundred pages of the incomplete manuscript along with a synopsis of this book and outlines for two sequels to her agent, who submitted them to Alfred A. Knopf, Inc. Later Warren confessed that only five of those pages originally submitted survived into the final draft, and they were essentially wills and historical documents that could not be changed. One reader of an early draft, Carl Van Doren, urged Knopf to get the rights because this work would become "an American epic." As of 10 August 1936, Warren had a contract and began receiving monthly advances.

Since both Breckenridges were devoting full time to writing, after Breckenridge received his advance, they decided to move to Clayton early in 1936, where they moved into the Warren house with Warren's uncle Monroe. However anachronistic the two writers might have seemed in the old-fashioned Alabama town of about one thousand people, the townspeople quickly accepted them into the town's social life at the dance pavilion and the pool and tolerantly observed their writing routines: late rising each morning followed by long hours of writing through hot days and leisurely walks through Clayton during still-hot evenings as they discussed each day's writing. The year back in Clayton, even with the discomforts of living in the old homeplace that was now falling into disrepair, was crucial for Warren's research: proximity to Montgomery with its Department of Archives and History for Alabama history texts, maps, and newspapers; and to Clayton and Eufaula with Barbour County court records, wills, and deeds. By this point Warren had definitely chosen her great-grandmother Lucinda Ifort Warren as the unifying force of her novel, so she turned to relatives and friends for their diaries and memories of earlier days in Clayton and Eufaula and the stories—or legends—of the Warren, Underwood, and Lawson

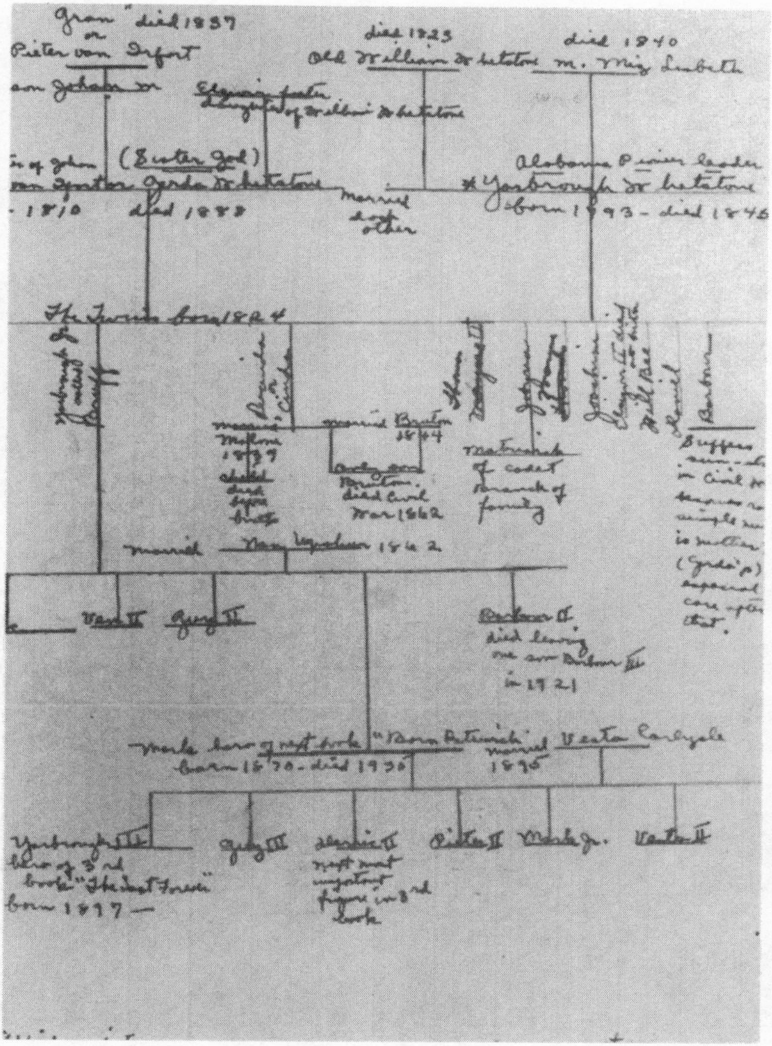

In her research notes, Lella Warren laid out the family tree of the fictional Whetstones, specifically designating her heroine as "Sister God," a working title for the novel.
(Photographed by Jerry Morgan Medley)

Tombstone of Lucinda Ifort Warren,
the inspiration for the character of Gerda van Ifort Whetstone,
Warren Family Burying-ground, Clayton, Alabama
(Original Photograph: Jerry Morgan Medley)

families. During this stay she renewed her friendship with Lewy Dorman (Ph.D., Vanderbilt), who became her historical consultant. Dorman, who had published *Party Politics in Alabama from 1850 through 1860*, was continuing his work on a history of Barbour County.

After spending most of 1936 in Clayton, the Breckenridges moved to New Orleans, where he had taken a job with a newspaper and she could do the research for her use of New Orleans and Tulane Medical School in *Foundation Stone* and *Whetstone Walls*. There, as Warren described in an unpublished short story, they lived from payday to payday—or advance to advance. On the acknowledgments page of *Foundation Stone*, she noted the contributions of Dorman and Breckenridge to her novel, even though she had divorced Gerald Breckenridge by the time the book was released (apparently the result of the strain of two writing careers in the marriage).

The Breckenridges' stay in Clayton in 1936 was Warren's last extended stay in her birthplace. During the next forty-five years she visited Clayton rarely. When she arrived there on her autograph tour for *Foundation Stone*, she went straight to the deserted Warren house and lit kerosene lamps. When she and her husband Buel W. Patch, an editor with Editorial Research Report, whom she married in August 1941, visited Clayton after the release of *Whetstone Walls* in 1952, they visited her great-grandmother's grave in the Warren family burying-ground, an important locale in *Foundation Stone*. Once she turned to her birthplace and family for her subject matter, she seldom turned to other subjects; it provided so much material that she was still writing about her family and birthplace when she died in 1982. But after the 1952 visit to a changing Clayton, she was content, as she described in a 1979 letter, ". . . to keep 'My Clayton' undemolished in my mind."

By March 1939, she had completed her novel. Then followed the months of editing and revising for a typed, final draft of 1,125 pages to become a 754-page published novel. Interest in *Foundation Stone* developed even before the book was released. As early as 21 June 1940, J. R. de la Torre Bueno, Jr. at Knopf wrote Warren that her editor, Bernard Smith, ". . . informs me that he has never in his experience seen such a demand from booksellers for advance copies of any new

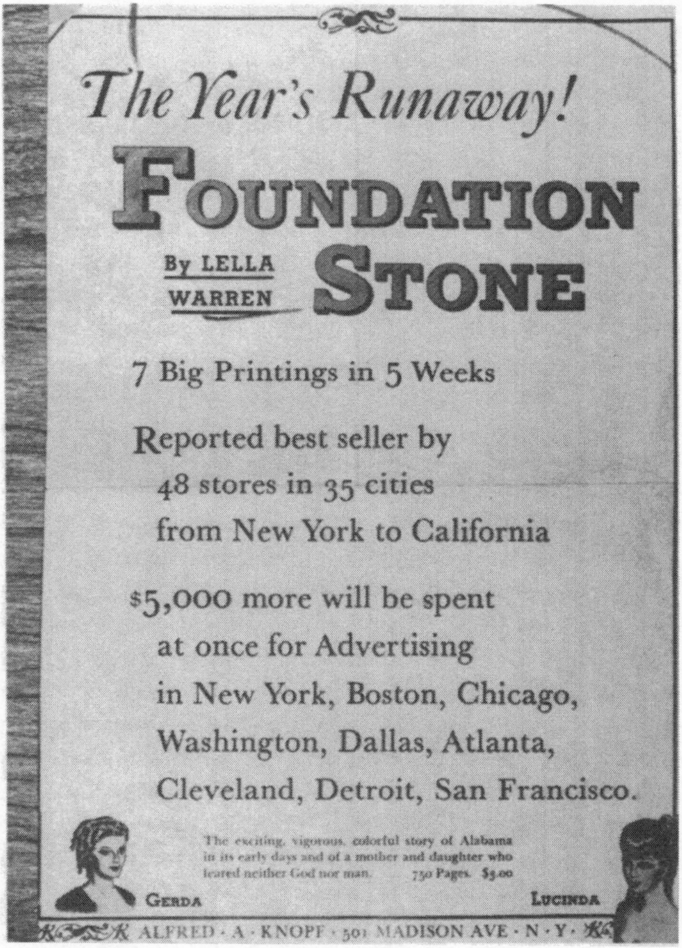

Lella Warren subscribed to the Romeike clipping service and put her clippings randomly in scrapbooks and large manila envelopes. This advertisement, from her collection, appeared in *Publishers Weekly* on 26 October 1940 and was for the book trade—wholesalers and book dealers. (Photographed by Jerry Morgan Medley)

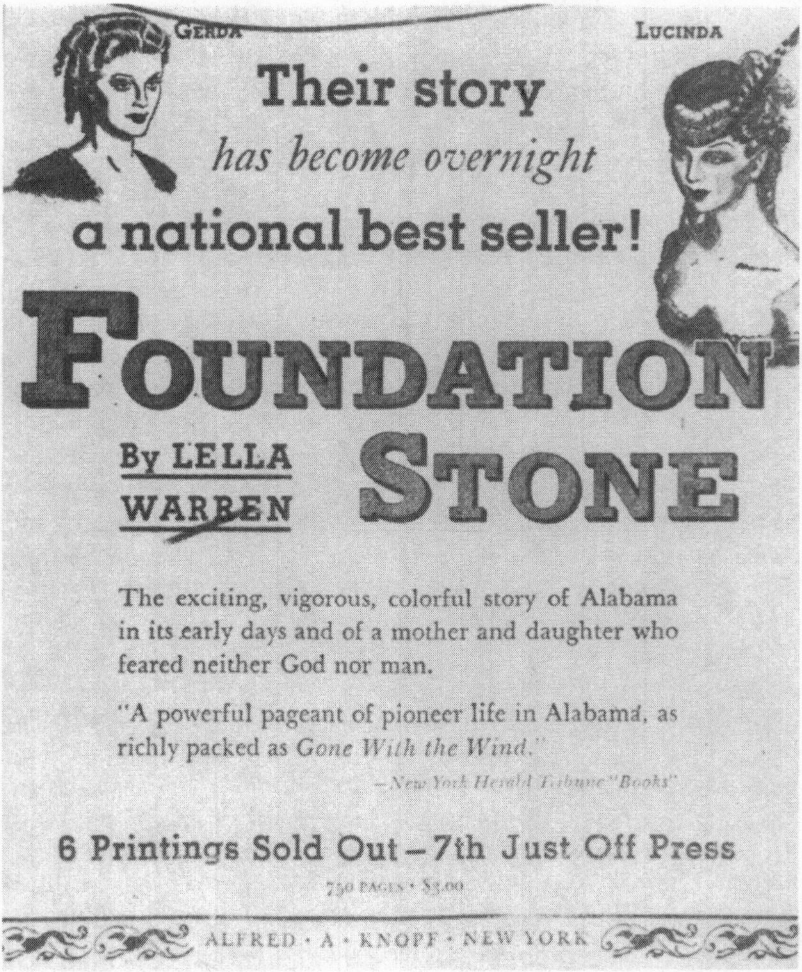

This advertisement appeared in the *New York Herald Tribune* on 28 October 1940 and was aimed at the reading public. (Reproduced from Lella Warren's clipping collection; Photographed by Jerry Morgan Medley)

novel as has come in for FOUNDATION STONE." Less than a week later, Smith himself wrote: "Mr. Knopf has selected FOUNDATION STONE for distribution to a little private book club we maintain called Friends of Borzoi Books." (This limited edition of 310 copies with an extra page reading "Friends of Borzoi Books" was signed by the author.) Early in July, Harold Matson, Warren's agent, wrote her about the novel's prospects and conservatively predicted: "People are beginning to talk about it and maybe there is a good chance it will do things despite all the competition like wars and so forth facing it."

Despite these predictions, Knopf apparently did not anticipate the extent of *Foundation Stone*'s success. The publishers planned a standard publicity campaign, particularly concentrated in the South, and a first printing of 7,250 copies; however, they ordered two more printings—8,500 additional copies—before the novel was released on 9 September 1940. By 13 October 1940, there were six printings totaling 30,750 copies. An advertisement in *The New York Times* on 17 October 1940 stated that the book was selling at the rate of 1,000 copies a day, and two days later *Publishers Weekly* noted that in one day Knopf had orders for 3,000 copies of *Foundation Stone*. By the end of 1940, more than 40,000 had been sold.

Such sales were obviously reflected in the best-seller lists: by 6 October 1940, *Foundation Stone* was fourth on the *New York Herald Tribune* list, and two weeks later it had climbed into second place after Struther's *Mrs. Miniver*. In *Publishers Weekly* of 23 November 1940, *Foundation Stone* was third after Hemingway's *For Whom the Bell Tolls* and *Mrs. Miniver*. It remained on the best-seller lists through the fall and winter of 1940 and 1941 and ultimately went through fourteen Knopf printings and a Grosset and Dunlap reprint. Rights for a Swedish translation were sold by Christmas 1940; there were also Portuguese (1941) and Danish (1947) translations, and there is some evidence that there was a pirated German translation.

The Collins edition in Great Britain came out in January 1941,[5] and 13,468 copies were sold, qualifying it as a best-seller in those days of the Blitz. The British edition reflects the austerity of those days in its small type (116 pages shorter than the American editions without any cuts in the text) and unadorned division pages. Warren attributed the success of the British edition to her themes of home and family, two things for which the British were fighting. In gratitude for the support of her overseas readers, she donated half of her British royalties to war relief agencies in England. *Omnibook* published a condensed version in the January 1941 issue. Several newspapers reported that major Hollywood studios, including David O. Selznick's, were bidding on rights to *Foundation Stone*, with offers ranging from $30,000 to $50,000; however, no movie contract ever materialized.

Reviewers around the country generally praised *Foundation Stone*. Edith H. Walton in *The New York Times Book Review* discussed, at some length, the effective combination of the themes of wilderness, plantation

Advertisements from Alfred A. Knopf frequently featured the firm's best-sellers together, as seen in this announcement from *The New York Times Book Review*, 6 October 1940. (Reproduced from Lella Warren's clipping collection; Photographed by Jerry Morgan Medley)

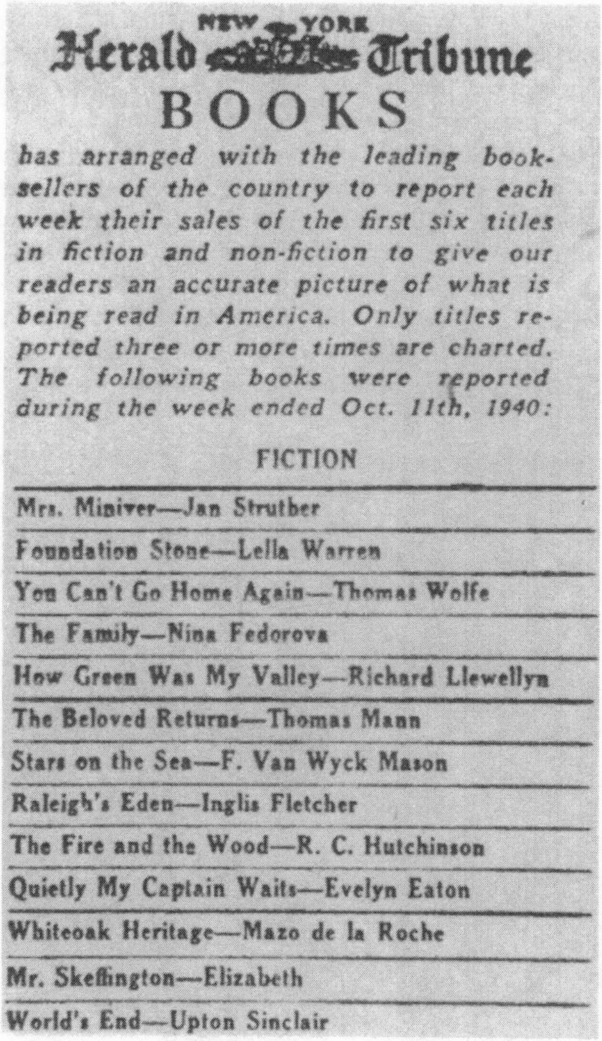

NEW YORK Herald Tribune

BOOKS

has arranged with the leading booksellers of the country to report each week their sales of the first six titles in fiction and non-fiction to give our readers an accurate picture of what is being read in America. Only titles reported three or more times are charted. The following books were reported during the week ended Oct. 11th, 1940:

FICTION

Mrs. Miniver—Jan Struther

Foundation Stone—Lella Warren

You Can't Go Home Again—Thomas Wolfe

The Family—Nina Fedorova

How Green Was My Valley—Richard Llewellyn

The Beloved Returns—Thomas Mann

Stars on the Sea—F. Van Wyck Mason

Raleigh's Eden—Inglis Fletcher

The Fire and the Wood—R. C. Hutchinson

Quietly My Captain Waits—Evelyn Eaton

Whiteoak Heritage—Mazo de la Roche

Mr. Skeffington—Elizabeth

World's End—Upton Sinclair

Detail from the best-seller list,
New York Herald Tribune Books, 20 October 1940, p. 23
(Reproduced from Lella Warren's clipping collection;
Photographed by Jerry Morgan Medley)

The dustjacket of the Brazilian Portuguese edition of *Foundation Stone* (Rio de Janeiro: Livraria José Olympia Editoria, 1941) was a pastel, textured rendering of the darker Knopf original. The literal translation of the title is "The Country House of the Wall of Stone."
(Reproduced from Lella Warren's personal copy of the book;
Photographed by Jerry Morgan Medley)

life, and Civil War, and summed up the novel as ". . . a book of scope and stature, easily one of the best of its kind."[6] Rose Feld, in the *New York Herald Tribune Books*, praised the novel for the way that research "is masterfully woven into the fabric of the tale."[7] The comparisons with *Gone with the Wind* were inevitable, and though Margaret Mitchell's work was favored in many reviews—especially in the South—*Foundation Stone* was praised for its broader scope. Of course, Northern reviewers also used this comparison, and some, like Lewis Gannett of the *Boston Transcript*, preferred *Foundation Stone*. Warren was once quoted as wanting to hear people in her home state say that "Georgia has Margaret Mitchell, but Alabama has Lella Warren." Because of their novels, Warren and Mitchell met and became friends, with Mitchell promoting *Foundation Stone* and even arranging the Patches' honeymoon to Sea Island, Georgia, in August 1941. Ralph McGill, another longtime Atlanta friend of Warren's, added his accolades in two columns devoted to Warren and her novel. Other critics compared the novel favorably with the works of Thomas Wolfe for treatment of time and John Galsworthy and Sigrid Undset for family sagas. At separate times, both in New York, Warren had met Galsworthy and Undset, and over coffee or tea they spent several hours discussing their respective family sagas. Several reviewers criticized the length of the novel and the number of characters, some suggesting that two or even three separate books would have been preferable. With her concern for presenting Alabama effectively, Warren must have been pleased with two reviews—significantly published in non-Southern newspapers. In the *Columbus* [Ohio] *Citizen*, John Webb stated that *Foundation Stone* is ". . . as virile as the red Alabama soil out of which sprang the cotton . . ."[8] and in the [Philadelphia] *Evening Public Ledger*, the novel was praised for presenting "a different Alabama from the one customarily found in novels."[9]

As these two reviewers acknowledged, Lella Warren told the story of her home state and of the sturdy, solid people who settled it. As the focus of this saga, she created the Whetstone family; their story covers much of the nineteenth century, from the early 1820s through the Civil War. Using the stories about her great-grandmother, she made fictional Gerda

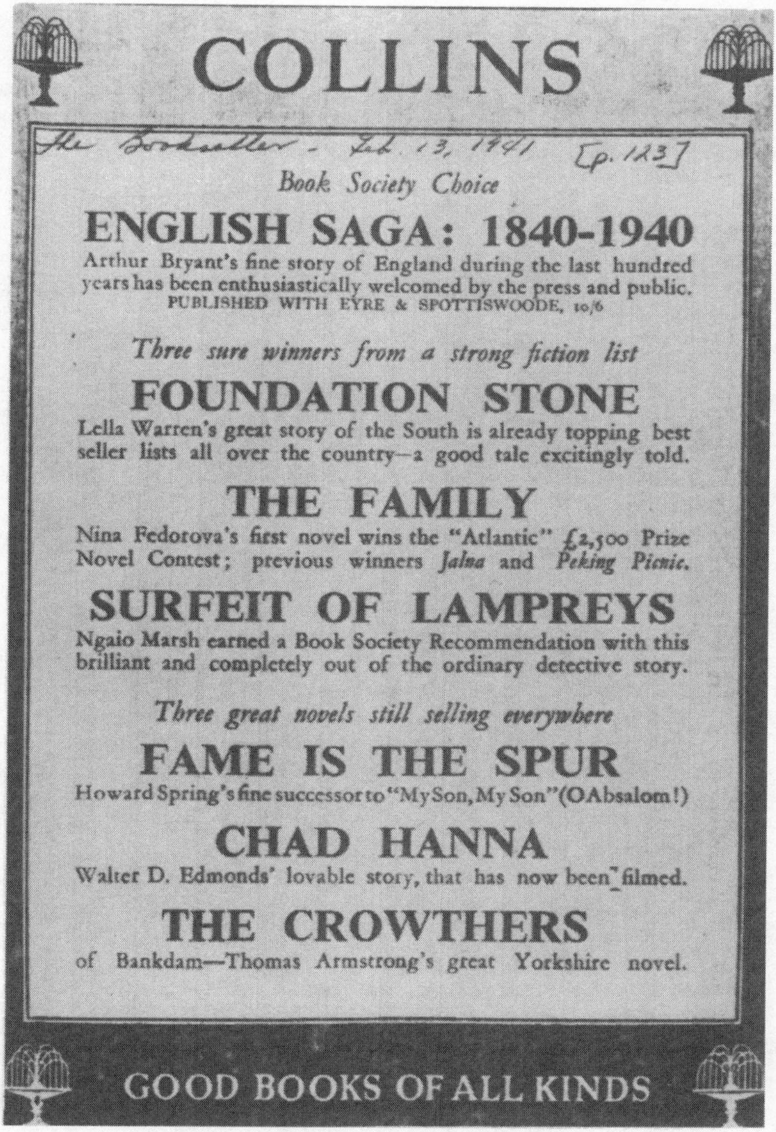

Advertisement, *The Bookseller*, 13 February 1941, p. 123
(Photographed by Jerry Morgan Medley)

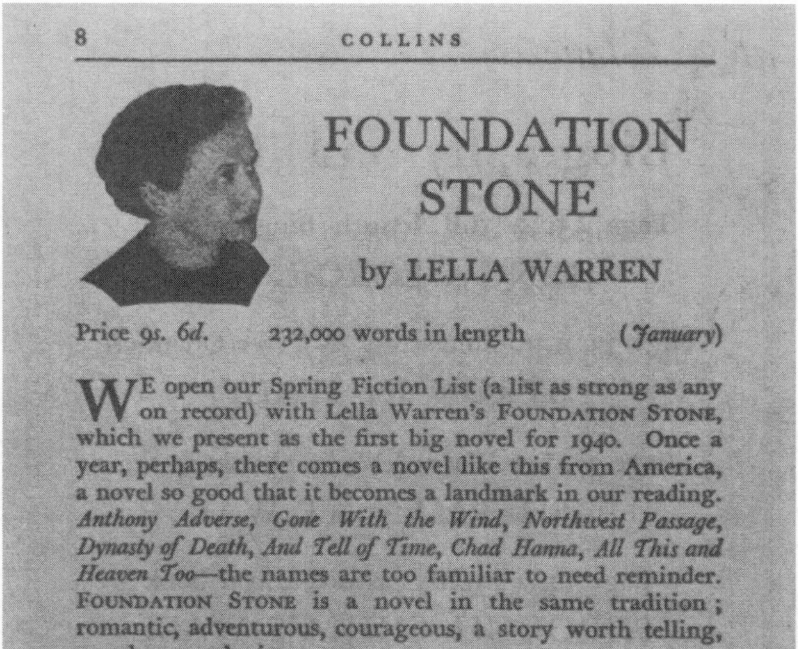

8 COLLINS

FOUNDATION STONE

by LELLA WARREN

Price 9*s.* 6*d.* 232,000 words in length (*January*)

WE open our Spring Fiction List (a list as strong as any on record) with Lella Warren's FOUNDATION STONE, which we present as the first big novel for 1940. Once a year, perhaps, there comes a novel like this from America, a novel so good that it becomes a landmark in our reading. *Anthony Adverse*, *Gone With the Wind*, *Northwest Passage*, *Dynasty of Death*, *And Tell of Time*, *Chad Hanna*, *All This and Heaven Too*—the names are too familiar to need reminder. FOUNDATION STONE is a novel in the same tradition; romantic, adventurous, courageous, a story worth telling, worth remembering.

FOUNDATION STONE takes us from the settled civilised splendours of South Carolina to the Alabama backwoods, from the Eighteen Twenties to the end of the civil war. It is the story of the Whetstone family, who lived boldly, hotly, and often dangerously. There is Yarbrough Whetstone, a typical Southern aristocrat. There is Gerda, his wife, a magnificent character who might be sister to Kristin Lavransdatter. As the strange flowering of their love there is their daughter, Lucinda Malone, the Scarlett O'Hara of this story.

FOUNDATION STONE is Lella Warren's first novel. She herself was born in Alabama, descended on both sides from pioneering families; so the background of this book is in her blood, and family legends have gone to the making of it. She has spent ten years of research and work on it.

Advertisement from "Collins Spring Books, 1941," p. 8
(Photographed by Jerry Morgan Medley)

van Ifort Whetstone the matriarch of this family. After Gerda's marriage to Yarbrough Whetstone in 1823, the family leaves the Home Place in South Carolina to seek richer land in the wilderness of Alabama. The Whetstones travel to southeastern Alabama with carefully selected household furnishings and slaves and settle near Yufala in an area that later would become Turber County, based on Warren's native Barbour County. Yarbrough and Gerda lead the other settlers in clearing the wilderness and establishing homes in this new land, and because of their determination and hard work, they prosper. Conflicts with the Indians, hardships of pioneering, and even the War Between the States cannot weaken this family; in fact, despite losses and suffering, these adversities strengthen the Whetstones even as Gerda and Yarbrough begin to turn their responsibilities over to their children, led by the oldest, twins Bruff and Lucinda. For all members of the Whetstone family, Turberville in Turber County remains the touchstone.

With this subject matter and setting, *Foundation Stone* could easily have become the stereotypical Southern novel of plantations, hoop skirts, magnolias, mint juleps, and contented slaves singing in beautiful white fields of cotton, but, given the charge from Dr. Warren, Lella Warren was determined to capture the "true South." To the opening pages of *Foundation Stone* with William Whetstone's hollering for a toddy on the porch of his South Carolina plantation home, the initial reaction might be that the book is the stereotype. But the author quickly establishes that this is a working plantation, where, unfortunately, the land is wearing out. Thus, after William Whetstone's death and the marriage of his son and heir to Gerda van Ifort, the Whetstones look to the wilderness of Alabama for a new beginning. Because she believed that the pioneering period in Alabama's history had not been effectively treated in fiction, Warren worked hard on that section of the novel and was proud of its final form. She did her research carefully, studying volumes of history for how the pioneers cleared the land and built shelters, what they planted and ate, how they prepared their food and wove the cloth. From diaries and letters she gleaned details about customs, social affairs, hunts, music, clothing, education—everything that went into the daily lives of those early settlers. The commentary in

The New York Times Book Review particularly noted the value of this section as an important background for the later prosperity and finally the Civil War. The experiences of frontier days serve Warren's characters well when the deprivations of the Civil War cause them to revert to their pioneer ways for necessities.

Nor did she allow her characters to become stereotypes: they are not good whites versus subservient blacks or virtuous Southerners versus villainous Yankees. Her whites represent all economic and social classes and include everyone from preacher to scoundrel; her blacks include the loyal friend and companion as well as the runaway slave; her Southerners can be scoundrelly and mean while the Yankees can be kind and sympathetic. With particular sensitivity, Warren portrayed the people of the Pine Barrens region outside of Turberville and the poverty and harshness of their lives. (She used the Pine Barrens again in *Whetstone Walls* and finally as the focus of the unpublished novel *This Nettle Danger*.) With family bonds as a unifying force, Warren controlled her numerous and varied characters, giving each one a unique personality; even the details of dialects and dress differ according to economic and social classes. The children of Gerda and Yarbrough reflect this diversity: from sturdy, hardworking Bruff to his impulsive and often irresponsible twin Lucinda to prissy Joby and perverted and cruel Wayne, not to mention five additional brothers and one half-brother.

Through the complexity of Gerda Whetstone, Warren not only demonstrates her skill at characterization but also foreshadows a significant concern of the later feminist movement: the sacrifice of identity for family and home.

> Then with a rush the years had swept down upon her, bringing the coif of wifehood, the bosom of motherhood, the gait of a mistress putting order into her household. The time had gone by deliberately, yet with no pause to break the hours apart, to permit her to garner her activities so they could be assimilated by the person of that early Gerda. Rather she had left off being so much the woman and had become a source of domestic simples and remedies for a family to follow until together they achieved a state of existence known as Home. . . .
>
> Yet now suddenly, as the pressure of the needs of others receded from her, she had an unreasonable eagerness to let her energies drain back from all these

diverse channels into one. She thought: "I shall have to learn to feel all over again!" [*Foundation Stone*, 330–31]

Warren's celebration of all of these Alabamians and their diversity—rich and poor, black and white—ushers the 1850s into a state that is beginning to prosper:

And what of the men who dwelt in this land, called her their mistress, and gave to this time its flavour, its tone, its shape, its reality?

They were not minted from any single well-worn stamp of high degree. Lordly and humble, they shifted and intermingled, until, without waiting for the passage of a single generation, they became a freshened breed, more vigorous than any of the stocks that went into the making. Virginians, New

Both Lella Warren and Rebecca Yancey Williams, author of *The Vanishing Virginia*, were on autograph tours during the fall of 1940. Here they are pictured at a meeting in Richmond, Virginia. (*The Richmond News Leader*, 30 November 1940; Reproduced from Lella Warren's clipping collection; Photographed by Jerry Morgan Medley)

A Davison's Christmas book supplement to *The* [Atlanta] *Constitution* (24 November 1940) featured articles by and about numerous popular writers such as Lella Warren, Helen Norris, Ralph McGill, and Inglis Fletcher. Pictured here at a Davison's luncheon are (left to right): Medora Field, Margaret Mitchell, Rebecca Yancey Williams, Raymond Kline, and Lella Warren. (Reproduced from Lella Warren's clipping collection; Photographed by Jerry Morgan Medley)

Englanders, Carolinians, Dutch, Scotch, and even the mercurial Irish strain, mingling in a common conquest, made a high-spirited, stubborn, ruthless race, building prosperity on the foundations of a wilderness. . . . Dashing, generous, crass perhaps, questioning, bombastic. But whatever else they were, they were not of a worn-out vintage of blue blood, past the best year for its consumption by life. [*Foundation Stone*, 389]

Through the lives of these characters, Warren created the drama, varying the tone, mood, and pace as she built suspense that led to a climax, even as she developed a new crisis. This action all takes place in a lush, sensuous natural setting that is more than backdrop: it is essential to the strength of the Whetstones.

In interviews about her work and publicity for her novel, Warren frequently reiterated her debt to her home state and her family. The success of the novel confirms her masterful weaving of historical and biographical details into the fabric of fiction. In recognition of her achievement, she was named a woman of the year—along with Margaret Mitchell, Marjorie Kinnan Rawlings, and others—by the Women's National Press Club, an award presented by Eleanor Roosevelt on 1 April 1941. She also received the George Washington University Alumni Award for Notable Achievement in Literature.

After the autograph tour, and the lecture circuit of 1940–41, Warren settled into twelve more years of research and writing on the sequel to *Foundation Stone*, *Whetstone Walls* (Appleton-Century-Crofts, 1952), with her husband "Dan" Patch as typist, editor, critic, and audience. In this novel, the second-generation Whetstones have followed their parents as leaders in Turber County and are now passing the tradition on to the third generation. Rob Whetstone becomes a doctor just as his father Bruff had done, but unlike his father, he wants "the higher goals of far-sighted medical science" instead of a medical practice over the red clay roads of Alabama. His brother Upshur chooses law and looks to the nation's capital, and so Whetstones begin to look beyond the boundaries of Alabama, just as their real-life counterparts had done.

The success of *Whetstone Walls* was limited, at least when compared with that of *Foundation Stone*. In her own comparison of the two novels, Warren laughingly noted that the later one had less sex and violence than its predecessor, perhaps explaining the difference in sales. However, a third printing was ordered before its release on 7 November 1952, and there was a fourth printing in December. Reviews in the large newspapers were favorable or mixed. Coleman Rosenberger, of the *New York Herald Tribune Book Review*, said *Whetstone Walls* was "fashioned slowly and painstakingly and affectionately."[10] Mary McGrory of the Washington *Sunday Star* criticized it for "a lack of suspense and a theme" but praised the book because Warren "gives life to her characters."[11] The short reviews nationwide were generally favorable, and *Whetstone Walls* was a best-seller in such diverse places as Indianapolis, Little Rock, and Los Angeles.

Whetstone Walls and two articles in 1952 and 1953 mark the end of Lella Warren's publishing career—but not the end of her writing. During the last thirty years of her life, as she saw herself becoming the matriarch of her family, particularly after the death of her mother in 1955 , she continued to write. In the tradition of her last two published novels, her unpublished autobiographical essays, short stories, and novels are generally about family loyalty and sense of place. At the time of her death, she had completed an "interlude" novel about some minor characters in *Whetstone Walls* and was well into her "big book," the last work in the Alabama trilogy. The third novel in the Whetstone saga tells, through the character of Rob Whetstone, the story of her father and his role in the founding of the U.S. Public Health Service. But wherever the Whetstones move, Alabama remains a part of their heritage, if only—as Warren described the Whetstone homeplace in her summary of the trilogy— ". . . as a haven to which to come for succor when beset, a shrine on which to lay their trophies in triumph."

Lella Warren's contributions to Alabama's literary history were recognized when *Foundation Stone* was first released and continue to be acknowledged today. Emily Sinclair Calcott, in her review of *Foundation Stone*, expressed the hope that " . . . other writers of fiction will follow her [Warren's] lead in working this rich mine of early Alabama history. . . . As a fictionalized account of a little known period of Southern history, it is a valuable contribution both in its own right and in the possible influence it may have on other writers."[12] Over forty years later, Harper Lee wrote: "In my opinion, Lella Warren was in the front rank of her generation of Southern writers; that her work is now virtually lost to us amounts to a crime. In a few novels Lella Warren came closer than anyone of her time to the truth of that special, elusive (and dying) American breed, the Southerner."[13]

Lella Warren died on 3 March 1982, in the Washington apartment in which she and her husband had lived for forty years. Just as the

Whetstones remain loyal to Alabama, so Lella Warren—despite moving away from her birthplace at an early age and living in the Washington area for most of her life—continued to think of herself as an Alabamian, as her father had: she never forgot her roots nor lost her soft Southern accent. Her description of her father (in the unpublished "Born Patriarch") can just as aptly be applied to herself: ". . . there were a few secret stubborn spots in Papa's soul that were part of the very core of him. And his love of Clayton was one."

Throughout her life she had great pride in her birthplace, and from 1927 on, she did meticulous research to capture that state—its history, its land, and the spirit of its people—in her fiction. As Warren wrote in an essay for the *New York Herald Tribune Book Review*, "I've drawn on my native elements for my main source materials—in writing about the Whetstone clan in my major books."[14]

But any evaluation of the writings of Lella Warren must acknowledge that this author did more than recast Alabama history in a readable, fictional form: she created believable, intriguing characters and told riveting stories. Her goal had been to use the history of Alabama, particularly Clayton and Barbour County, and the stories of her family as the background for an effective and memorable novel about the "true South." She achieved that goal, certainly in *Foundation Stone* and generally in all her writings from 1935 on, as she deftly wove all elements of good fiction—captivating people, compelling adventure, and vivid settings—into enthralling works.

NOTES

1. Press release from Alfred A. Knopf, 21 June 1940.
2. Lella Warren, "Lella Warren," *New York Herald Tribune Book Review*, 12 October 1952, p. 14.
3. Letter, Lella Warren to Nancy G. Anderson, 23 January 1979.
4. Letter, Lella Warren to Stephen Vincent Benét, 12 March [1940].
5. This Collins edition is the basis for this new edition. In addition to a few typographical errors resulting from new typesetting, the British text contains the errors from the Knopf edition that Warren corrected in the Grosset and

Dunlap reprint: p. 133, l. 5, "view" should be "viewed"; p. 160, l. 3, "niece" should be "cousin"; p. 237, l. 12, "Benjamin Harrison" should be "William H. Harrison." There are also the British spellings, hyphenations, and word divisions: i.e., "honour" and "flavour," "to-night," and "every one." Also in British tradition "Negro" is not capitalized except for typographical errors such as the one on p. 15, first line of the last paragraph.

6. Edith H. Walton, "A Spacious and Stirring Story of the Old South," *The New York Times Book Review*, 15 September 1940, p. 6.

7. Rose Feld, "Matriarch of an Ante-Bellum Plantation," *New York Herald Tribune Books*, 8 September 1940, p. 5.

8. John Webb, "Lengthy Southern Novel Has Fresh Setting," *Columbus* [Ohio] *Citizen*, 15 September 1940.

9. Aubrey L. Thomas, "Book of the Day," [Philadelphia] *Evening Public Ledger*, 9 September 1940.

10. Coleman Rosenberger, "The Fortunes of a Tangled Alabama Clan," *New York Herald Tribune Book Review*, 30 November 1952, p. 6.

11. Mary McGrory, Review of *Whetstone Walls*, *The* [Washington] *Sunday Star*, 16 November 1952, p. E7.

12. Emily Sinclair Calcott, Review of *Foundation Stone*, *The Alabama Historical Quarterly*, Fall 1940, pp. 293, 294.

13. Letter supporting NEH grant proposal, Harper Lee to Nancy G. Anderson, 14 September 1983.

14. Lella Warren, "Lella Warren," *New York Herald Tribune Book Review*, 12 October 1952, p. 14.

Foundation Stone

To the memory of my father

BENJAMIN SMART WARREN

of the United States Public Health Service

and to my daughter

LEE WARREN SPANOGLE

I dedicate this book

MAY 19, 1940

" But she held her word and she kept her troth,
Cleared the forest and tamed the wild
And gave the breast to the new-born child
While the painted Death went whooping by
—To die at last as she wished to die
In the fief built out of her blood and bone
With her heart for the Hall's foundation-stone."

FROM *John Brown's Body*
BY STEPHEN VINCENT BENÉT

Here I wish to make grateful acknowledgment to a number of people for their invaluable help during the long years in which this book was in the making:

To Professor Lewy Dorman of Hurtsboro, Alabama, who so generously shared his wealth of source material with me. To Professor Robert Bolwell of George Washington University, who gave me the benefit of constant literary criticism. To Gerald Breckenridge, author of Brief Kingdom *and* The Besieged, *who collaborated on many crucial chapters. To Dr. E. M. Townsend, U.S.P.H.S., who by his surgical skill saved my life.*

And to my mother, Lee Ella Warren, for her unflagging faith and devotion.

THE CHARACTERS *and situations in this work, other than historical ones, are wholly fictional and imaginary, and do not portray and are not intended to portray any actual persons or situations.*

BOOK ONE

The Home Place

CHAPTER ONE

William Whetstone hollered: "You, Bonapartt! You, Patt! One of you rapscallions fetch me my toddy." Then he settled himself into his porch chair on this summer day in South Carolina in the year 1823. Patt came a-running with a palm-leaf. Bonapartt, a grand piece of ebony, fetched the toddy, then departed after the first snort of approval. Patt stayed to fan the flies away from his master.

By the second swallow old William was hard at his noonday occupation of fretting over his slave-ridden plantations. Smart men, who could figure on paper, had it that there were more than a million blacks in the upper part of the South, with their number being doubled every twenty years. Some gainful toil had to be found for them. Cotton was the answer. But cotton, dammit, needed new land. Maybe this land, like himself, was failing. That thought riled him, and to gainsay his feebleness he snapped: "Here you, Patt, hand over that fan! You *draw* flies. Git!"

The brown boy skedaddled, chuckling. Whetstone went on mulling his troubles. New land? What would Yarbrough think of this matter of a migration to the South-west? Yarbrough was his favourite of all his eight living sons, though William did not approve of his being still unwed and without issue at the age of thirty. Still, Yarbrough would not mismanage his life, you could depend on that. He was as smart as they came, and no milksop to be scared of a risk. He'd ask Yarbrough's opinion when he came up to dinner.

At that very moment Yarbrough was down in the plantation office by the big gate, knocking his knuckles against the bottom of a column of figures in a day-book, pondering the same question of great plantations and numerous blacks that were not paying their way. The office was a mere frame box, scorching hot in spite of the grey flow of shadow washed across the floor by the trees outside. It was furnished with a few spraddle-legged chairs, a high desk with ledgers, and oddments such as a discarded top cape and some treasured dusty samples of Sea Island cotton.

The man Yarbrough was proportioned to a race at its zenith,

although for the moment he was too obscured by brooding to display his points. To-day his stewardship of his father's properties oppressed him.

"Old worn-out land," he mused, "what can I do about it?" He picked up one of the bolls of cotton and fondled it. "Cotton? But I've tried that here, and the crops were all sorry. Now they tell it that in the South-west—in Georgia, Alabama, Mississippi—the cotton springs up like weeds. Even the Indians grow it! If we went down there——" He smothered a chuckle at the thought of the roar of anger his father would most likely let out should he speak of galloping off to Alabama.

Slamming the ledger shut, he went outside. There he reared his shoulders back, achieving his own high stature again, while slips of sunshine coming through the leaves showed up the gleam customary to his coin-graven features.

From where he stood he surveyed the family home place.

There was the big gate giving entry from the highway, so long left wide open that it had rusted on its hinges and could no longer be closed. Right at hand was the shabby office where efforts and property were tallied against the profits. Beyond, after the drive had shirred away to one side, was a maze of yew and boxwood hedges coated in late-summer dust and broken by the bright pattern of his mother's rose-walks. Distant above it all tilted the house, tall and bluish white, somewhat askew because of ill-placed iron grille-work balconies. Yet it appeared beautiful to him, even as it teetered among its scrambled vines.

A homesickness swept through him at the bare idea of forsaking this place. Why, this land of theirs need never grow sterile! He could replenish it from his own abundant strength. He began advancing towards the house as if towards his beloved's bower. Upon reaching the maze he grasped at a yew branch and throttled it like a woman's wrist. But it gave back none of the resilience of vital flesh and tendon; instead it broke, brittle, scattering that scent of leaves that age in graveyards.

Up in the gallery, out of Yarbrough's sight, his father sloshed the last of his double toddy around in its cup fretfully. Desert these cherished holdings of his? he demanded of himself. No, by the Lord Harry! He, William, had seeded this land and harvested it many times over. Here he would rot if need be, or drop from the vine. . . .

So fuming, he drank a swig too much for noonday, and died, purple in the face, a palm-leaf in his hand. As good a way as any, facing out over his own broad acres.

2

While that was happening in a grille-trimmed gallery in South Carolina, in upper New York State in a Dutch kitchen a young girl was teasing a mulatto servant to be allowed to scrape a cake bowl. All ignorant of how profoundly her life was to be changed by that planter's death, Gerda van Ifort was tickling yellow Pokey in the ribs to win her way. Finally seizing the spoon, she began licking the spicy batter. "*Ul-lmn,* go-od!"

"You'se gettin' too old fo' such tricks," reproved Pokey. "Turnin' thirteén is plenty time you was a young lady."

"*Ll-um,*" the girl continued her lapping.

Gerda was the orphan granddaughter of Pieter van Ifort, a man of varied activities. Whenever he went down to the city of New York he visited with the Pauldings, the Irvings, and other men of letters of the day. At one time he had been a professor of sciences at old King's College, until his bluntness about the Deity had ended his tenure. In any case he was not cut out for anything so serene as a scholar, although he was a man far in advance of his times in the new fields of physics and physiology. Essentially he was a great blunderbuss of a man, Dutch-shrewd, and unhindered in his honesty towards living.

His only child, a son, had married a girl from the South, one Elzivir, a foster-daughter but no blood kin to William Whetstone. Upon marriage she had come north accompanied by her handmaiden, Pokey; upon the birth of Gerda she had died, apparently severing the thread connecting the two families, especially as her husband did not survive her by a month. Thus old Pieter, with Pokey's help, had been left to rear the child as best he could.

Pokey had not been one of the Whetstone Home Place Negroes; still, having been swapped to William by a Louisiana sugar-planter, she was versed in the intricate New Orleans etiquette of waiting on ladies. She could read and write a trifle, and her speech when she took the trouble came quite close to that of the whites. Yet she wore violet and yellow bandannas such as no house negro would assume, and occasionally used a string of curses common to the canebrakes. Then, queer cross-breed that she was, at other times she shouted frankly Anglo-Saxon ditties above the clatter of her pans, with such lines as:

His beard was red,
But his chest hair black,
When he u-umped a wench,
Tra-la-la-da smack.

Undoubtedly she had lapsed into an awful slattern up here with no mistress to make her toe the mark. Still, she bragged that she had never had any lice on her in all her born days. She had spells also of trying to raise Gerda as befitted a lady, scolding: "You ought to keep yo' muslins and ribbons in a chest with powder of orris root to give them a flucey smell. An' if you don' commence to be laced in, yo' figger'll run to belly."

Gerda, who was as tough as a grapevine, only shrugged and replied: "Before you talk so persnickety you'd better attend to ironing my pantalets, instead of leaving them rough-dried. A fine lady I make, scratching in public."

Usually, however, Pokey left Gerda comparatively free of the namby-pamby restrictions imposed upon girls in the 1820's. Also Pokey was a good companion. To-day, for instance, as soon as the cake-baking was finished she had packed up a snack and gone with Gerda back over to her favourite haunt by Mountain Lake.

This lake was no tiny patch of baby blue like a toy looking-glass in the doll villages of the feast of Saint Nicholas. It was a gigantic stretch of arrogant indigo for which the vast sweep of mountains made a suitable frame. There was no smooth beach approach, only a very little coarse pebbly sand that had been grated off the huge boulders at the water's edge. Gerda skipped small stones across the water for a while to test her aim and the flex of her wrist. After that there was the swimming.

The water was cold and pellucid and sweet. Gerda swam in it

naked, at which Pokey was scandalized. "S'posin' somebody pass by an' see yo' shame?"

"Pother! A body unknown in the water feels no shame."

The water slipped over her so smoothly that Gerda could feel her body expanding until it took up all the room inside of her, clear to the outside curves. "Pokey," she cried, "the water makes your body *fit* your skin, instead of being just an up-and-down little string at the centre like the wick of a candle. You ought to come on in too."

"Hush! You know I wouldn' go in washin' befo' nobody."

After her bathe Gerda lay on a big rock and let the sun and air dry her. She stretched on her back, her eyes drowning upwards into the sky. Suddenly she was seized with an impulsive assumption of power. The bigness of the lake and her body beside it wrapped in air, gave her a feeling of triumph over all creation. She thrust her arms into space like spears, and shouted: "Pokey, that's the sky they're sticking into, *my* hands. The *sky*!"

Pokey cackled gleefully: "I declare, you put me in mind of that tale that goes: Then the Lawd A'mighty leaned back on his yaller throne an' sez: 'Help yo'self to a nice-size kingdom and plenty of victuals, Sistah. An' help yo'self to a good big piece of high groun' to stomp an' holler on. Kase I'se the Lawd of this heah earth. An' you, Sistah God, is my fav'rit chile.' Yes'm, you acks jes' like that high-steppin' critter. Like Sistah God ownin' the earth."

Well, exulted Gerda, so she did feel like Sister God! Ruling a realm on high right this moment. Then abruptly she turned mortal again. She sat up on her rock, yawning so widely that she all but cracked her jaw-bone. "I'm hungry. My stomach is as hollow as your old gourd dipper."

Pokey began unwrapping their snack.

In such hit-or-miss fashion did Gerda live until she was thirteen, with Pokey for both duenna and servant, and Gran, as she called old Pieter, for guardian. Still a rambunctious child when it came to romping, she was yet full-developed: deep of bosom, high-coloured, vivid-eyed, a maid being swiftly prepared for womanhood. On that day though, as she munched on one tea cake after another, she had no way of knowing how soon she was to be done with this first burgeoning.

3

In the name of God Amen—
I William Whetstone of Egton District and the
State of South Carolina being in perfect helthe,
since & Memory do Constitute and Ordaine this
to be my last will and testament.
Signed this 4th day of April 1823
his
WILLIAM *x* WHETSTONE
mark

Thus read Squire Dakin, causing William Whetstone, now under the sod, to be once more present full force in the Long Room of his home. Unable to sign his name, he had yet been able to make his word law even after death. Descendant of a Cavalier who had come to America to escape the rule of Cromwell, he had ever the Cavalier attitude towards book learning. His royalist forebears had left poesy to the hired bards and delegated letters to the clergy, though for a while they had sent sons back to the England of the second Charles to sharpen their sword-play and smooth their manners. While there, some of them had picked up the trick of courtier verse, which was a pretty thing and pleased the ladies.

Since then, however, there had been a change of kings in England and a war for independence from all kings in America, so that practice had disappeared. His own sons had been lucky to con their lessons under Squire Dakin, while he himself had been too taken up with crops to scribble with a quill. He had simply ordered the squire to set down his wishes, hard and fast, as his family would hear.

They had put on the look of sanctimony usually kept for prayers, but with strain beneath the sanctimony.

His married sons and older daughters, having been amply provided for long since, were now ticked off with tokens such as fine gaming pieces and feather beds plumper than clouds.

His widow he treated with both generosity and the gallant scepticism due the woman of his own marital choice. *I Lend unto my beloved wife Lisbeth, in during her widowhood her cooke . . . her four skilled wenches . . . my neat stock of animals and fowls except as herein otherwise disposed. . . . Also the use of my Home Place and household furtherture* [*furniture*]. *And after her dicease or Marriage to be equally divided between my two children Yarbrough & Lucey.*

"Jealous-hided tartar, how he does go on!" murmured Miz Lisbeth, glancing down at her twittery old hands. The fingers were worn to wisps from being bleached to show off before company, after having been stained brown peeling fruit for the preserve kettles. "Now, pray tell, who'd ever look at me?"

"Many a one!" declared Yarbrough, crumpling one of those tuckered hands.

"Pooh, old things that can't chew clabber," said Miz Lisbeth disdainfully. "No, thank you! You'll have to see after me now, son."

"You *know*," he promised.

Next they heard how William had cut off his lazy black sheep Ruthven, or Ven as he was called, grandly with five shillings instead of the proverbial one shilling, and, *one body servant Cudge, withoute whose help it is my opinion that Ruthven would not stir out of bed till Kingdom Come.* Ven guffawed at that belittling, dribbling tobacco juice down his finely tucked shirt bosom. His sister Lucey attempted to wither him with one immaculate look, but he was gloating at his father's further charge that he be provided *with proper sustance such like as he has in my lifetime enjoyed.*

"Egad!" crowed Ven. "Now my throat won't parch."

"One bottle a day," retorted Lucey, "is a gracious plenty for you, sir."

"I've been a two-bottle man for more'n twenty years, and you'll make no ninny out of me now neither."

Lucey was no longer attending him, for she was being read out her own portion. *To my daughter Lucey who doth reside at the Home Place & is wedded to one Guy Hampley I leave the Cargill lands, 4 hands able, two negroe wenches, her tire-maiden and 12 fine geese for down plucking.*

To her foppish husband Guy an order for two new sets of pantaloons, hopeing to make him more a man. To her son Willy even if he do be taking after his father, 100 acres of the Chinquapin lands 3 helthy hands, the mare Netty he rides, and fifty £ sterling from my English funds to be expended on further schooling. To Lucey's daughter all the doll poppetts 5-£ can buy, 2 new frocks, her present fetch-it gel, a portion of sugar lumps. . . . Also half-share inheritance of her mother's holdings if she cease sucking on her thumb before the age of ten, she being now 8.

Momentarily Lucey was overlooking the slighting phrases while preening over the numerous benefactions bestowed upon herself and family. Then suddenly her fan-tail collapsed, bedraggling her pride, as she heard the next bequest.

To the heir of my beloved dead foster-daughter Elvizir van Ifort, I do leave the Frederick plantation entire, six hands, two wenches, stock sound in limb to be chosen by Yarbrough, and one featherbed. For now do I greatly regret that I never saw to Elvizir's welfare after she journeyed northerly. So do I hope her heir prospers in the enjoyment of the land I do bequeathe.

The entire group sat in silence for a space, realizing how old William had been bound to acknowledge all claims of all dependents as did most landed men of the South, even if the claim was slight and the burden heavy. Yet a number of them did not blame Lucey for resenting so handsome a bestowal upon an unknown child, that might otherwise have fallen to her children.

However, Squire Dakin's voice continued, and the bodies of all the listeners stiffened to hear what had been left to the real heir, Yarbrough.

To him was left the residue, including the choice plantations near the highway, the bulk of the stock, numerous hands, *my Mill stones that I have now ready cutt, my blacksmith tools, all the craft-trained negroes, also my two best house servants named Patt & Bonapartt, and the Grits mill—To him and his wife when he takes one—to them and their heirs Forever.*

The squire's voice ceased like a sermon. Someone sighed. It was everybody. The black boys moved the long-pole fans at the flies again. Miz Lisbeth pulled her fingers loose from Yarbrough's. "I'd better go see how they're preparing the supper," she remarked from force of habit.

Little Gracey thought she was supposed to cry as she had at Gran'pa's funeral, and so did.

CHAPTER TWO

ALTHOUGH Pieter van Ifort had known and pondered for well-nigh a week upon Gerda's inheritance, he had not as yet imparted the tidings to her. The Dutch did not bandy even the talk of property. First it must pass through a process of contemplation, before it took on the dimensions of a fact that could be set before others in speech. Then, too, the manner of its announcement must be suitably phlegmatic. To this procedure even the outspoken Pieter subscribed.

To-day, however, he deemed the time had come to divulge it, so he summoned Gerda. "Can you walk a piece without blowing like a porpoise?"

She only laughed, drawing in the air so filled with that cider richness that hangs over apple country in early autumn.

He then said: "So. We shall climb the summit to Winkler's. A fitting pilgrimage for the occasion." What occasion it was not her place to ask.

Winkler's was in the other direction from the Lake, and Gerda had never been there. It was the home of some Low Dutch, who kept a few stored supplies to trade to their neighbours and did a bit of innkeeping on the side for travellers. It was reached by a narrow path among the evergreens, where there was deep silence broken only by the scratching of the rock chipmunks, and Gran humming gutturally.

Gerda did not query him. He would speak in his own good time. Presently he did and it was, surprisingly, of her parents.

She knew little about her parents, for Gran was too hearty to dwell on their memory in sentimental detail. Now he said: "Never knew whether your father had any real ability. He didn't live long enough to show what he could accomplish. He had an explosion trying an experiment in physics to show I was wrong on a point. I remember his looking at me with the one eye he had left at the end, saying: 'Now *that* goes to prove my point.' Imagine boasting over blowing himself into bits! I, I potter some at science, but, *och*, give me life above everything. So few are the years of it to us in any case. And after that of what are we sure except a blackness? Yet he had plenty of sand, he! That I say. *En* so also had your mother, Elzivir, though no bulk to back it up. Now you, I think you will be a great oaf like the van Iforts, and breed sons as easy as calving."

In truth Gerda did resemble Gran in his robust zest. He eyed her approvingly. "No, I think your Southern heritage will not harm you. Holland has seen to that."

Somewhat baffled, Gerda wondered what her mother had to do with her more than usual. Even Pokey, when she was trying to teach her her manners, seldom mentioned the frail dead girl. Certainly Gerda was not going to let herself take after Elzivir by being sickly. She dropped the thought at the sight of Winkler's.

The outside of the hut, she saw, was covered with bark, and the sun smote it into a pumpkin glow against the gloom of the crouching cedars. Gerda picked a trickle of amber resin out of a crack and chewed on its spiciness with relish. Gran rapped on the raw panel with his walking-staff. The door was flung open by a woodsman in a leathern jacket and a toboggan cap. A gnarled dwarf was stoking a great oven, and a woman was coming in from a back door with two milk-pails hung from a wooden yoke over her shoulders. There was a girl, too, with a red kerchief knotted at her neck, swinging her feet over the edge of the deal table on which she was seated. Strings of dried herbs and good sausage hung from the rafters, and the whole interior was one of warm sepias that went with people who lived close to the broken brown of earth.

The older woman set her buckets down with a clatter. "Mijnheer van Ifort! But this is *goed*!" And there was a great hubbub.

A place was made for Gran, not too close to the oven; also a place for Gerda. The wench was addressed sharply, to bring Mijnheer some ale. But she did not move sharply; she went with a deliberate indolence, swaying as she walked. When at last she stood beside Gran with the beer, he looked at her quizzically and guffawed. "I'd like it better if you fetched my beer with more haste, Marta. I'm too old to be amused by the sway of your hips while you loaf over serving me."

Marta shrugged with lazy good nature. "It was not for you that I put my hips about, Mijnheer." And her eyes slid over towards the woodsman.

"*Neen?* But see that you hustle with the next draught." And Gran nipped her rounded form smartly.

She brought it. Then pulling a small comb out of her pocket, she leaned over the back of his chair and began combing his thick locks. Gran closed his eyes blissfully, at which Marta laughed. "So, I know what pleases the old men too, *hein*?"

She crossed her elbows up behind her head and hugged herself, at the same time stretching from the thighs. The woodsman studied her hips from over his whittling. On Marta's neck was a reddish diamond of skin made by the harshness of the mountain weather; and just as plain as if it had happened, Gerda could see the man's chin nuzzling down past it to the softer, whiter flesh below. Gerda thought that if she should stick her hand out in the air between those two she could have felt a surge like a tide.

Gran rose at that moment, tugged his beard, rapped his stick for Gerda. "It grows late. We must be on our way."

Outside, Gerda spoke up. "That Marta, she is no fool about knowing what it is she wants. 'Tis the woodsman."

"A buxom one, Marta!" chuckled Gran, then blew gustily into his beard. "I shall miss all these good folk with their thrift and their tidiness. I fear for my temper in dealing with a pack of negroes when we reach South Carolina."

"But, Gran—what do you say?" cried Gerda, who had heard nothing of all that.

Now he told her how she had inherited through her mother a plantation and some hands from old William Whetstone, and that they were to journey south shortly, to take it up.

"I? How much land?" asked Gerda, bursting with a sudden Dutch sense of possession. She had not thought of owning aught before, except a penny now and then or the apple she was munching. Now she wanted him to count up the land, and name for her each of the slaves. "And has Pokey been mine all this time? Yet *I* doing *her* bidding?" Was there a house on the plantation? No, nothing but quarters for the blacks. They, Gran and Gerda and Pokey, would stop with the Whetstones until they could determine what had best be done about a permanent abode for them.

Had he not said, though Gerda questioned him, that there was a feather bed left her, also? For her own? Then she would sleep on that one. And he could be sure she would give it a good plumping up each morning herself, not leave it to any lazy negro.

In the village she ran ahead to their house to break the news to Pokey. "Now you," she promised Pokey, "may be my serving-maid and do nothing but attend me."

"I don't know how I like that. I likes to cook."

Gerda stamped her foot. "You will do as I say! You can depend on that."

"Sho'!" snickered Pokey. "You remines me of my first mistis. She carry on jest like you." Pokey was mighty pleased at Gerda's sudden high-born notions. That night, holding the girl's bedtime candle, she said: "I'll make out somehow to flute you pant'lets from now on. So's you won't be put in the shade by them Whetstone gals. They was always a sashayin' lot."

"Most likely a pack of little feather-headed ninnies!" scoffed Gerda. She was not concerned with languishing about in frills. *She* was setting forth to be a real mistress of her own plantation, of that they could be sure!

2

Two nights before they started their southward journey there was a knock on their door. And when Gran swung a lanthorn to see who it was, why, it was Marta Winkler, with a shawl over her head and cheeks all puffed from crying. When she was once inside she hung on Gran's hand and wailed: "He *is* dead, Mijnheer. Dead! My Hans—a great tree fell on him. Ooo—let me go *mit* you. Away where not he was. *Och God*——" And again she was all shaken with sobs.

Gerda stared, dumbfounded. He had meant all that to Marta, that woodsman, like any other woodsman? There was something here . . . so big that it made her feel numb with ignorance, yet stirred by a portent of her own unplumbed womanhood.

Gran was putting Marta's cries in order. "You wish, then, to give us your services, in order to leave these parts? Well, that I think we can arrange. I would do as much for any of your family. And a white female travelling companion for Gerda would not come in amiss."

"*I'se* waitin' on Miss Gerda," mumbled Pokey, insulted.

"Silence! My pig's eye! Who is the master here? So-o, yes, a suitable arrangement, that one, Marta. And I have no doubt we will find ample use for you down there among all those slothful blacks."

"Huh!" snorted Pokey under her breath to Gerda. "That's the laziest woman, white *or* black. Outside the bed, *cooee*!" she tittered, in spite of Gran's thundercloud brow.

It was settled, though, that Marta was to come with them.

"She kin leastways comb the rats out of his hair," sniffed Pokey, "ef'n it don't wear her plumb out."

CHAPTER THREE

NEVER BEFORE had Gerda encountered such supreme courtesy as that in the welcome of Miz Lisbeth Whetstone. A tiny-boned woman, she showed the marks put upon her by the oft-repeated fecundity to which she had been ill suited. Simultaneously she displayed the pride that would countenance no acknowledgment of weakness. Her hands gave grace to greeting and an instant direction to the details of settling the arriving guests.

" My son Yarbrough," she informed them, " will regret not being on hand to welcome you, but urgent matters required his presence on the Cargill lands for a few days. Patt, watch those boys, they're joggling the boxes too much. Bonapartt, pour Mr. van Ifort a dram. Gerda, child, you don't take after your mother, except for something about the set of your throat. It holds your head so far above your shoulders. I am glad to see you have better health than she, and are tall." She smiled pleasantly at being forced to look up into this young girl's face.

Recognizing Pokey, she half-hugged the mulatto's shoulders, and the latter mumbled some belated condolence about her old master, William. Miz Lisbeth turned the scene off from any dolorous strain by giving her attention to settling Marta's station in the household. " I'll put you in the small room off the packing-closet. You spin and weave, I trust?"

" That gal," warned Pokey in a low tone, " needs to earn her keep. Don' go too easy on her." Gerda noticed how Miz Lisbeth reproved Pokey with a glance, while accepting the implications of her advice.

As they were shown to their rooms Gerda gazed about. Her main impression was one of space, and waste : of high ceilings and incessant windows showing far acres without, of looming dark-rubbed furniture and too many servants within, of wide halls giving into wider chambers, and of a plate with a large cake staling and forgotten on a tallboy.

Their first supper here was something to cause her to marvel, with its maze of rich dishes and the thirty people who sat down to it, including some visiting gentlemen who had never laid eyes on the Whetstones before, but who put up at the Home Place as a matter of course because they were transacting business in the vicinity. Out of the jumble of cousins Gerda could sort out only those who lived under this roof. There was Cousin Ven, who drank whisky instead of wine, and the sugar-coated Miss Lucey with her dapper consort, Mister Guy. They had two children, Gracey, who at eight was learning to faint, and fourteen-year-old Willy, who had asked her if they weren't "kissing kin" upon their meeting. Thereupon he had put his mouth, which was like some soft pouty fruit, against hers. *Faugh!* She could have spat. Breaking away, embarrassed before the company, she had glared at him, but his doting mother had simpered: "Now there, his young cousin has captured my Willy's heart at first glance."

Gerda had no fancy for either the boy or the girl, but, surveying their spindly frames, she decided she could be rid of their constant companionship by exploring the plantation at a great rate. They could never keep up her pace.

Shortly after supper, tired from her journeying, Gerda made her good-nights. Upstairs Pokey, who was waiting for her, opened the door cautiously to prevent any disturbance of the pallet laid along the door-sill. "Dat's where I'm s'posed to sleep, now I been turned into yo' servin'-maid. Still I cain't let my bones ache on a hard floor jes' yet. Takes time to usen myself to it again. So I rolled a quilt into a bolster an' put it to divide the bed in two. I can sleep good in the small half of it, an' same time if you feels scared in the night from strangeness, you kin reach ovah and touch Pokey."

"All right," agreed Gerda, so drowsy she didn't see how she could climb up the ladder into the bed.

2

When the rising-bell rang the next morning, Pokey, who should have been up and doing, grunted protestingly. Blindly she reached across the rolled quilt to jog Gerda awake, only to find the space empty. At that her sealed yellow lids flew open to discover her young mistress standing in a long window staring at the view of the side grounds.

"Come 'way from there, less'n somebody see you in yo' night shift."

Impatiently Gerda switched back into the privacy of mid-room. "Let's hurry about dressing," she exclaimed. "And for Heaven's sake don't wash my ears."

"I will so! This is the ver' one morning I ain't goin' to let you skip a thing. Think I'll let Miz Lisbeth catch me leavin' any wax in you ears?" With that she poured water and started the gruelling torture that made Gerda's ears feel as if they were being pulled out by the roots. It was finished only when Pokey was satisfied with the way the light shone through them in a clear pink. The rest of the dressing was comparatively easy since Gerda didn't consent to lacing. Within a short time they were both down in the dining-room waiting for the blessing, Gerda in her chair near Miz Lisbeth, and Pokey standing over where she could help serve them from the hot-bread table.

After Gerda had cleared her plate twice, she glanced at Miz Lisbeth eagerly. "May I be excused?"

"Certainly, child."

Gerda nearly dumped her chair over backwards in leaving. Even so, she found her cousins, Willy and Gracey, at her heels by the time she reached the pantry passage.

"You needn't," Gracey informed her prissily, "try to tease sweets out of Bonapartt right after breakfast."

Gerda stared her down. "Doesn't your sweet tooth ever give you a rest?" She didn't bother to go into her own fever for exploration.

Bonapartt was very affable about her curiosity even in the midst of directing the dishing up of a certain conserve for a special and testy guest. It pleased him to see how awed she was by the delicacies in his trust, and when she remarked: "We never had anything to compare to all this!" he opened up his choicest cupboards.

From his domain she went to peek into the busy kitchen, connected by an arcade to the house to ensure the dishes coming up piping hot. She had better sense than to enter it now and be underfoot; instead she went out into the dooryard. When Willy tried to assist her, she shrugged loose from the weaving touch of his hand on her elbow. "I dislike that."

"You're not bent on being amiable, are you, Cousin?" he asked, trying to tuck her arm into his palm once more.

Again she shook him loose and turned to look out over the place. There was so much for her to discover. How could she rid herself of these pests?

Then almost before the question could die in her mind, Willy was called by his tutor, and Gracey was approached by Dilsey, her little fetch-it piccaninny, who had all their dollies laid out for the day's pastime. "We're trading doll-babies to-day," announced Gracey. "Of course I always get the best of it, for Dilsey's very obedient." She smiled with sly condescension while the little darky grinned with pleased vanity in her own subservience.

"You two," said Gerda brusquely, "play your game as planned. I'm off for a walk." As they skittered into the arcade leading back to the house, she made her way down the yard. "I have a great deal to learn here," she told herself with a troubled mind, "if I'm to manage things right on my own place after a while. I wish I had known my mother now." Then she squared herself up. "Still, I can trust the van Ifort way. It will see me through." Oddly, she was not at all surprised at her own deepening preoccupation with production rather than with play. But then, she had ever matched her grip against the real thing, never trifled with the small.

Now, gazing about, she felt somewhat entranced, as if poised between two stages of her own existence. The slow lazy beauty of the season hung over the activity that teemed wherever she went. She wanted, childlike, to stop and pass the time in pleasure at half a dozen spots, where some expansive negro would have enjoyed showing off his or her lore. Yet something of the Dutch *vrouw* urged her on to inspect the whole system.

She widened her range to take in all the small houses pertaining to the various industries necessary to the maintenance of this sprawling estate. She overlooked nothing from the smoke-house to the carpenter shop, while her respect for Miz Lisbeth's diligence in keeping these departments running mounted sky-high. More and more she realized what an indomitable will that puny body housed. Late in the morning when she returned to the house, she felt almost weary, simply from observing what Miz Lisbeth had in her care.

In the back upper hall she chanced upon that lady, holding a forefinger to a puckered forehead, trying, so she said, to recall where she had stacked the last of the cut silk pieces for company quilts. "I can't seem to recollect a thing right off. My mind's been like a sieve since William passed."

"Miz Lisbeth," interrupted Gerda, "the wonder is that your mind can keep up with half of what it knows. I've just come from looking over the things you attend to. No man could manage all that."

"Pshaw!" Miz Lisbeth dismissed the credit dryly. "You're only a child, which makes what I tend to seem like a heap to you. But just you wait till you have a chance to learn what a man has to contend with, running the real labour of a plantation. You don't *know*. Why, honey, we women wouldn't be here to do our fretting over quilt-pieces and lard-tying and babies teething if 'tweren't for the way the men see to the land."

Her milk-blue eyes looked into a distance as yet unscanned by Gerda, and saw some old truth there. "Whenever you start thinking a woman's lot is a hard one, 'twouldn't hurt to ask yourself if man's isn't harder. Because he isn't thinking of just taking care of his own, the way a woman does. Why, child, he's thinking of how to keep a whole countryful of land fertile, and safe from savages."

Her tones died down from that unaccustomed ring of proclamation, and her mouth drooped back to its wonted frost-bitten persimmon texture. "My, I was taking on there, wasn't I? But don't you forget all I said."

Gerda promised her that she wouldn't.

3

After her rather solitary childhood, the girl was enjoying the genial activity of the Home Place. There was youthful companionship in plenty, and she found the cousins from the nearby plantations a jolly lot, although the two young Hampleys quickly became her bane. Gracey adopted such an air of resentful spite that Gerda dreaded the approach of the vain chit. Willy, however, with his sentimental attentions, was a worse trial. He was for ever following her about, catching her in corners, playing with her wrists, coaxing: "Aren't you at all fond of me, Cousin?" To which she replied gruffly: "You're no real kin of mine."

He continued to plague her, putting his cheek with its sticky feel of peach fuzz against hers, until finally on the third day she hoisted her knee and bumped him in the pit of the stomach. He went "Ouf!" and sulkily gave her a wide berth for the rest of that day.

"What he needs," she decided, "is a man to put him in his place instead of that mother spoiling him rotten. If only Gran weren't still standing on such ceremony, he'd bring him down to the size of his half-measure breeches. That's the only thing that I've noticed amiss about this place, the lack of a master to take charge. A big pity."

It was the very next day that Yarbrough Whetstone returned home. Gerda heard the yard darkies running along the drive shouting: "Marse Yarbrough, dar he!" At which Miz Lisbeth hastened to the gallery and stood working the rings on her fingers. He came up the steps quickly and she cried: "Son!" on a choked laugh. Then she fairly bubbled: "They've arrived, Elzivir's kin. So like your father in a beard. The grandparent, I mean."

"Miz Lisbeth, talk straight." He pinched her elbow fondly.

Patt was scuffling to keep any one else from taking hold of Yarbrough's saddle-bags, and mother and son entered behind the rumpus. Gerda ducked out of sight, where she could look her fill unhampered by courtesy.

He was tall, with a long rocking stride and a way of slinging his left arm to match it. He had eyes exceeding bright and darting, a smile that came not often, and a way of tracing his forefinger along the high bridge of his nose while he observed his surroundings. She judged him to be about thirty, showing some fish-net lines from weather and wind; also he was dusty. But she had never seen any one so much a man! Even hidden as she was, she felt some part of his energy reaching out and playing upon her, as if he were aware of the presence of some other forceful creature, of whom he must take good account. It was hard for her to refrain from crying out: "Here I am!" and go plunging forward to an immediate encounter.

As mother and son passed from sight Gerda unclenched her fists, that had been squeezed in delight. "So that," she concluded, "was why the family seemed aimless before? It lacked *him*?" She rushed upstairs then, to be, for the first time in her life, a great trial to Pokey about the nicety of her attire for supper.

"I hopes an' trusts," said Pokey sharply, "that you ain't deckin' yo'self out like this fo' that Willy-lily."

Gerda's answer was a scornful snort and a command to draw the unaccustomed lacings tighter till her cheeks flamed.

"It beats all how you done growed up lately," approved Pokey, braiding ribbons into Gerda's heavy hair. "Jes' 'peared to happen while I had my back turned."

Down in the Long Room Gerda found things far more festive than on the night of their arrival. In truth this seemed to be their real welcome, with the master here to give it. He and Gran were already becoming acquainted over glasses of amontillado, and Gerda waited composedly until they should take notice of her. It was but an instant before Yarbrough turned, saw her, and took a fresh clamp on his goblet. Gran batted his eyes at her metamorphosis, while Miz Lisbeth murmured: "This is Elzivir's child, Gerda."

"Child?" ejaculated Yarbrough, putting his glass away and reaching her side in a long step. He stood a space noting the wide firm sweep of her shoulders above her crimson gown, and how the level of her eyes was not girlishly far below his own; also that her gaze sought to establish candour between them, an acknowledgment that he as well as she felt urgently compelled. She had his virtual admission to that, though he said only: "Have they supplied you with every comfort?" To which she replied: "They have been most considerate."

Gracey made a sniff-face at Gerda's being treated thus importantly, while Willy ogled her again. Gerda merely stood on her dignity and kept them at a distance.

Every one behaved more formally at this supper, except Ven, who fussed at Cudge's insistence he use a silver snuffbox instead of his usual quid. Later during the music and talk Yarbrough thrice addressed himself to Gerda alone, while often his eyes were upon her, sombrely attentive. Once, even, he did not hear Miz Lisbeth when she spoke. She had to call: "Son!" a second time and touch his arm to make it known that she had spoken.

When Gerda judged it time for her to retire, she moved with as unflurried an air as if she had been in every court in Europe. Yarbrough walked beside her. At the foot of the stairs he took her hand, but studied it instead of bending over it. Its size was capable, as he remarked before he said: "You are not the daughter I expected of Elzivir."

"You are not," she returned, "what I expected of Miz Lisbeth."

"That's true," he chuckled, "but you should have seen my father."

"You have seen my grandfather. I am van Ifort."

"Well, don't say it as if you were spitting on the Whetstones," he warned her, not altogether in jest. "That will only serve to sharpen steel, for that name means something, Whetstone." Then his face relaxed and his eyes went over her warmly. "It is good to see a woman made as you are, to stand up to living. Believe me, I am glad I did not tarry away from home too long. Or did I? All those gentlemen in there have eyes."

"I was nothing to look at before," she said perversely. "You are but tricked by my best frock. And I've scarce been able to breathe in it all evening," she ended in sudden childish discomfort.

He laughed and, tweaking her cheek, sent her off as if to her nurse. But she knew, after she was once more free in a loose night-robe, that its folds wrapped someone now almost a woman.

4

The next morning Gerda was wakened by Gran in her room bawling at Pokey with characteristic bluntness. "Why did you not tell me she was thirteen? A man forgets such matters. But you, you ginger-faced one, you should have told me she was become grown. A fine kettle of fish we might have had, with me letting her run the woods over! Why, she might have got with a bush-child, for all of us!" Then he rounded on Gerda: "And I expect you know not a solitary thing about this woman business?"

"But yes, I do," Gerda contradicted him. "Pokey speaks up very plainly indeed to me, and then I have noticed the animals."

"Hobble-gobble!" He dismissed that. "I should have had some proper dame instruct you. However, go you to-day to Mistress Lucey and say—*och,* say that it is my request she instruct you in the duties and functions of a female."

"She'll think," murmured Pokey slyly, "that you means drop-the-handkerchief." And as soon as the door closed behind him she added: "I like to heah what Miss Lucey say. Mistah Guy he ain't yet positive that she got legs, under them petticoats."

Pokey had been unbelievably forthright with her charge, so that the girl was not at all in the dark. Directly after breakfast, however, Gerda went obediently to Miss Lucey, who was flustered out of her wits. It wound up by her telling Gerda some nonsense about a mother carrying her " babe in a cradle hung from her heart."

All Gerda could think of at that description was of a baby hanging in a breech-cloth suspended from the bottom tip of a gold heart-shaped locket. She laughed out loud, imagining an infant Gracey swinging from Cousin Lucey's gilt heart and becoming a little seasick.

" Gerda," reproved Cousin Lucey, " mirth is most unseemly now."

Gerda controlled herself until she was outside the door, then relieved her spirits by calling Willy to romp with her. He came pell-mell, glad of her unexpected favour. She did not smack him when he squeezed her about the waist in a tussle, for after Lucey's simpering she welcomed all tug and pull and jostle.

She came in none too tidy for dinner, and Yarbrough, who had not been present at breakfast, eyed her hard in her hoyden guise. After the meal he waited until she came by him in the narrow back passage, where they had to touch if he did not give aside. He closed a palm about her firm elbow, where the flesh was streaked with childish sweat. They could both feel the hot pattern of his fingers, and the danger up and down their bodies.

Then Bonapartt had to walk past them with a waiter-load of dishes.

5

A day or two later Miss Lucey screwed up her courage to go to Yarbrough concerning a plan she had formed, resulting from Gerda's visit to her that other morning. Yarbrough was down in his office where the womenfolk were not encouraged to come, but Lucey picked her finicky way into it.

" Do you mind stating your errand, sister?" he asked brusquely.

She hated to come to the point quickly, yet was afraid to disobey him. " It's concerning our young Cousin Gerda. Her grandfather has—hmm—given intimation he deems her of marriageable age. Now my Willy has quite lost his heart to her. Of course he needs a year or two of study at the University in Virginia before marrying. Still, don't you consider that a betrothal now would be very fitting?"

"You ask," Yarbrough's tone sharpened, "that I bespeak Gerda's hand for *your Willy*? Jupiter, what sort of match——?"

"A most suitable one. It would join her land to the portion for Willy, making a very handsome plantation. Still, it's the boy's feelings that sway me. He has his heart set on her. Will you then ask Cousin Pieter, on behalf of Willy? For Guy never puts a thing right."

"Enough! I will lay the matter before her guardian, since you ask it. But," his frown broke, "*Willy* for *Gerda*!" He yowled with laughter, and at Lucey's pout added: "Be off now, sugar." When he was rid of her, though, he fell into a brown study. Perhaps Lucey was right about that young pair, women were often sharper to see those things. Gerda, for all her ruddiness, might favour the lad. Perhaps the other evening when he thought he had arrested her fancy, perhaps she had been cozening him, to be sure of his approval as the head of the house. After all, her short thirteen years to his thirty must not be overlooked. He called a yard boy to fetch Patt.

"I want whisky," he told Patt. "And then my compliments to Mr. van Ifort, and ask if he could see me here in the office. Or any place that suits his convenience." He turned the whisky in the tumbler and gulped it.

Gran, when he came, was a trifle puzzled. "You would know something that I can tell you?"

Yarbrough kicked the cake of the stable lot off his boot and said tersely: "My sister, Mistress Lucey, desires me to ask your granddaughter's hand for her son, Willy."

"Hein?" Gran was startled. "My Gerda to marry with that treacle-mouth? Are you mad, man?"

Yarbrough eased up considerably at that, but repeated punctiliously: "My sister wished a betrothal for a year or so, while Willy finishes his schooling. Remember the lad will grow in time. Patt, that jug again."

Old Pieter was snorting, beyond the help of schnapps: "*Och,* I would sooner put Gerda to yoke in the fields and see some use come of her. Is it that you think matching one property with another near-lying property is wise? That I can understand very well. But Gerda and Sweet William! Put it before her, *Mijnheer,* if you wish. But me, I wash my hands of it!" Blundering from the door he hardly waited for Patt to lead the way back, and Patt took care to keep out of Marse Peter's path, as he told Pokey when later he let her know what was up.

Pokey in turn said to Gerda: "Such foolishness! You an' that milk-tooth Willy. All that's Miss Lucey's schemin'. Look sharp, though, else they mought get you in the small corner and marry you off to join plantations. White folks think such a heap about they land."

Without answering, Gerda left the house and went to lie on top of the scuppernong arbour, pondering bitterly, yanking off the few grapes that were left, mostly shrivelled like raisins. Then Willy, who had heard from his mother how Yarbrough had agreed to broach his suit, came in search of her. When he peered up at her through the tangled mat, she stared away from his direction. He tossed the late summer dust with the toe of his shoe, and asked: "You can't abide me, can you?"

"Oh, I could put up with you in a friendly way. Only no more!" she cut off short.

He touched his slight hand timorously to her bronzed fist. "You warm me, Cousin Gerda. You give me the feel of burrowing in fine brown dust, like a broody hen."

She was not hearing him at all. He took hold of her thumb spitefully, meaning to bite it to attract her attention, then her whole arm seemed so lax that he gave it up as being no use.

At that moment Pokey called to Gerda to come and be dressed in a fresh frock to go to Marse Yarbrough's office, but Gerda insisted on going as she was, in old hose and with no trim of lace showing on her pantalets. Patt, eaten up with curiosity, led her down.

At her entrance Yarbrough rose and spoke to her straightway. "My sister, Lucey, has requested that her son Willy's proposal for your hand be presented to you. Your grandparent has authorized me to make the suit. Does it please you?"

"Not in any way."

"Perhaps you have not considered well. Your plantations lie near together, and the number of hands you each have, while not sufficient separately, working together could——"

She saw a taste of grape-stain on her finger and sucked it indifferently.

"—make for profit. A betrothal of a year or more would give you time to learn your mind."

"I know my mind." A yellow jacket swooped down and stung her heel. She did not cry out, only stamped her heel hard to stop the throbbing, then stood solid within herself.

"What is it, Gerda? What is it that you are holding back from me?"

Sullenly she told him: "I mistook you for the master here, not the go-between to step aside for a whining lad."

At that he flung down the boll of cotton he had been worrying and took her unbound waist in his two hands. "Have a care of me!" he gave her warning, but she only lifted her whole body around in his direction.

When they stood back from each other once more, he jerked out: "I am no longer a very young man. And am a hateful creature when in a temper."

"I am not frightened of any man's temper."

The plum mist of late day was full in the windows. Patt still waited on a log, slapping mournfully at the bites on his legs. Then Gracey came mincing down the maze, calling: "Aunty Pheaby sent word that supper will spoil if you don't come on right away."

They went up to sit at a table, where tallow candles sputtered when the moths flew too close. Every one seemed in a jangle. Mister Guy spilled gravy. Gracey got the hiccups, and Gerda's appetite was completely gone. Gran rudely ignored the others and talked Low Dutch to Marta, who was at supper to-night because there was only the family and no second table. Presently Ven crooked a finger to his hovering Cudge. "Fetch her," he nodded towards Marta, "some ale from somewhere." She put her hand on her hip and gazed over it at him.

"Nev' mind," grinned Ven, "nev' mind *that* for me. I don't hanker for women."

Marta was blowing red in the face, when she spied Miz Lisbeth, who said reprovingly: "Please to pass me the salt." Marta sent it up from where she sat, below it.

Observing her coyness, Gerda stared at Marta with something like hatred for her fecklessness. What about her Hans? Did she not recall him? And the surge there had been between them, resembling this ocean tide of her own towards Yarbrough? Or was Marta plump for any man's picking?

Miz Lisbeth spoke again: "This elderberry jelly . . . bitter. What's that, Lucey? You say use geranium leaf to take away the rankle taste? My, *pee-yuky,* no ma'am! Well, I didn't mean to put you into such a swivvey . . . touchy to-night, ain't you, Lucey? And Willy looks jumpy too."

Gerda wondered if the old lady was gently masking malice, and she felt some apprehension about Miz Lisbeth's reception of Yarbrough's choice. Gerda wished they had settled her betrothal, for now she feared they might yet deem it wise to palm Willy off on her. She picked viciously at a curdle of tallow dripping from the candle. The biscuits were all crumbled now and they pushed chairs back. She went out on the porch. The gnats had set up a hum, the crickets were sharper, the bullfrogs deeper.

Then Yarbrough was standing beside her, and she became aware of the fact that her dress was dirtied. And wished it weren't.

6

Next morning Yarbrough had evidently spoken to Gran, for he announced at the breakfast table: "I have some news that may not be as pleasing to several of you as it is to me. Gerda has given me the great joy of consenting to marry me."

This announcement when it was exactly five days since they had first looked at each other!

Miz Lisbeth put her usual hand on Yarbrough's arm. Willy winced. Gracey looked pleased over her brother's predicament, but crestfallen at Gerda's importance. Pokey, secreting her grin, ceremoniously reached over Gerda's shoulder to serve her with a plate of chicken still smoking hot from the frying-pan. The sunlight filtered through the pod-vines on the side porch. She could hear the fowls squawking and knew they were putting down three-splayed prints in the back-yard dust.

Later, going out, Yarbrough held Gerda aside until the others had passed. "You will be wedded to me shortly. And you know I expect a *wife.*"

"A wife I want to be!" she answered, and stood back, ripe-cut at the bloom.

CHAPTER FOUR

GERDA had been married to Yarbrough close on to a month, and with Miz Lisbeth and Pokey to show her, she was fast learning the woman's end of running a plantation. Already she portioned out the rations to both the slave quarters and the big kitchen, for Miz Lisbeth had insisted that she take over this prerogative. "The sooner the negroes learn to mind you as the mistress, the better. I can't keep after them the way I used to." She sighed pleasantly.

The Home Place, Gerda soon realized, was cluttered with darkies of all ages. The small fry belonged to the white children as "fetch-it nigs," or were apprenticed to some older negro. The strapping wenches and bucks carried the burden of the labour. And the ancient ones ruled the roost over white and black alike, coddling or punishing, accepting their "gemmen's tempers and ladies' tanterums" as "jes' white folk's ways." Most of them shirked periodically, were easily sullen, as easily doubled up with belly laughter, and given to coaxing for trinkets. They all prayed like Christians, but planted heathen conjures in graveyard ground. A jumbled staff, decided Gerda, many of them skilled, yet all prone to hide slackness behind much bowing and scraping, and not one of them with the rogue-sharpened wits of Pokey.

To-day while Willy and Gracey had gone picnicking after persimmons brought on by an early frost, Gerda was in the weaving-house where the big sewing for the slaves was done twice a year. She was gravely measuring a piccaninny for one of the apron-shirts, that single garment the young ones wore, made of cotton in summer, of thicker stuff for winter. She had her hands full, not only with her sewing but with keeping Marta in order to prevent her making trouble among the negresses. The work, however, went steadily ahead, and at noon Gerda stayed behind a bit for the satisfaction of taking stock of the piles. "This beats persimmon-picnicking all hollow!" she crowed. Still, that did bring up a picture of Gracey and Willy larking along through the autumn woods; and recalled the

Mountain Lake, about which the peaks had reeled, troubled with purple through many Octobers. Suddenly she was homesick for the apple-smell and, yes, even for her old despised lesson slate.

At that moment Miss Lucey came teetering in. "Could you," she began, "tack up this place I snagged in my frill?"

"I'm not much hand at ruffles," said Gerda, "but maybe I can at least make it hold."

Lucey fidgeted during the stitching and kept shooting curious glances at Gerda. Obviously she had something on her mind, and as Gerda finished she came out with it in a rush. "I don't know what's come over Yarbrough! He paid court to girls before he went so daft over you, and he always remembered who and what he was. Yet now married, and with the best bedroom in the place, he takes you roaming in the fields! Like negroes!"

"You—*you*——" choked Gerda, mortified at having Yarbrough and herself spied upon.

"Don't deny it! Densey passed you all, by the wood pond."

"How dare you let a negro wench use our name so!" One hand looked as if it were going to strike Lucey in spite of everything; then Yarbrough's footsteps halted at the door-sill.

"Not that! Don't let go that way," he cautioned Gerda, taking down her hand. Then he turned to Lucey and snapped: "Pray, what have you been up to?"

"Why—why——" she stammered, unable to speak of such a thing as nuptial trysts to a man, but Gerda flung out: "She dared to speak of our being together in the woods, as if it were something shameful!"

Quite beside herself now, Lucey shrilled: "You've made a show of yourself! So that all our friends are scandalized and I——"

"They were at our marriage," Yarbrough growled. "Do they hold anything was amiss with the vows?"

"Heavens, no, but Gerda must learn how——"

"Learn only to please me," cut in her brother plainly. "I knew what I wanted and I took it." Then his laugh came on top of his anger, and he pulled Gerda to him so frankly that Lucey squealed: "Mercy!" and went scurrying out, not knowing what she might see if she stayed.

2

Gerda had been married to Yarbrough three months now as Christmas week was being ushered in. All the young slaves, who had been pairing off while the crops were being made, had permission from Yarbrough to marry now. Christmas Night was the favourite time for marrying, with the white folk present and the wedding veils starched by that troublesome Densey, who was yet the most skilled washerwoman. There was much running back and forth between the house and the quarters. Gerda alone was made to keep to her room out of the noise. For she was with child and, this being her first pregnancy, they all conspired to coddle her.

"It's a pack of tomfoolery!" she railed at Pokey. "And I specially wanted to see how Densey makes up the stiffening for the net."

"Miss Gerda, you cain't do that. It's bad luck for a woman to touch a weddin' veil whilst she's heavy."

Gerda scowled. Pokey had some conjure sign to stop everything she tried to do, yet Gerda was afraid to go counter to the omens.

This afternoon Lucey came into Gerda's room bringing Miz Lisbeth along, the latter carrying some very sheer white batiste. "Mother wants to know," Lucey said, "whether you would like this material for the christening layette? It came from Ireland and she's had it in her chest with rose leaves over twenty years. Smells sweet."

"Oh!" Gerda touched the soft, fine stuff awkwardly.

Miz Lisbeth peered at it indecisively herself. "You're welcome to it. But maybe—well, once I used to think I might use it to be buried in. Now it looks a little young for me, my black silk's better. Still, if you think this was charmed bad . . ."

"Not a mite of harm done," declared Pokey. "'Tain't ever had shears set to it with such a thought, has it now? An', anyhow, ain't dreams of funerals always bringin' good luck? It's weddin' dreams that are evil-spell for women that's carryin'."

Gerda scowled again.

Sensing ill temper, Miz Lisbeth sought to pacify Gerda. "Don't you see how pretty this goods will take to pin-tucking galore?"

At that Gerda spoke up obediently. "I've never seen the like of it." But she felt half-hearted about it. Then, hearing Gracey and a flock of girl cousins giggling in the upper hall, she called out: "Gracey, what are you up to?"

They sidled in, casting sly glances at her to see if they could notice anything peculiar about her figure yet. Knowing of their curiosity, Gerda turned full towards them to swing across the room under their gaze, so that they might see how staunch and unmarred her body appeared. Pokey shooed the girls out finally, and the two ladies followed. As the door closed, Gerda picked up a pincushion and hurled it bobbing all across the room. "I don't want to stay shut up here! As if I'd done something wrong," she shouted at Pokey. "I'm a woman and I'm married, and this is what a woman's *for*! So let me out of hiding!" She went stamping towards the door, with Pokey at her heels.

But just then the door burst open, and Yarbrough came striding in, shaking off the fine rain that was silver-furry on the locks of his hair like frost on blades of grass. "Jee-rusalem, this is nasty weather for Christmas. Hey, spit-back, what're you gnashing about now?" he grinned at Gerda. "Becomes her, whatever it is, doesn't it?" he demanded of Pokey, and began to pinch Gerda exploringly on the elbows, shoulders, and hips. "I'll wager it's a great bumpkin of a boy, the very first try."

Gerda laughed back at him. At his presence this room had become all at once the gayest place in the whole house.

"I'll brew you a punch," he offered, "if this slow-poke of yours will fetch the makings, and not try to stand me down that it'll curdle your milk a year from now."

"More likely put some body into both," exclaimed Pokey, leaving the room.

Yarbrough studied Gerda more closely. "Lucey's not been nagging at you again, has she?"

"Oh no, Lucey's been nice, and Miz Lisbeth brought me a present. It's just that I hate being kept out of things."

He made a place for her on his lap. "By George, I believe you've put on a stone's weight already," at which Gerda boxed his ears. They huddled their shoulders together, which shut them close. The firelight jumped up and down in warm bright daggers and her heart began to kick up with pleasure. She was to bear a child for him, for

Yarbrough Whetstone out of his manhood, and anything else that anybody was doing seemed dull by comparison.

3

The swelter of the July morning was already making the fields steamy when Miz Lisbeth came out of Gerda's chamber looking completely done in. "You can go in now," she told Yarbrough. "It all went as easy as one-two-three for Gerda."

"Praise God!" he said, which was an idea he seldom had. "Is it a boy?"

His mother merely motioned him into the room.

There Gerda looked up at him quite naturally, although he saw her hair was matted with sweat. "There!" she announced triumphantly. "I never do things by halves! Show him, Pokey." Pokey pulled the coverlet back from the burden on her arm. It was a boy and a girl, both lustily cross.

At the sight Yarbrough threw down the ball of handkerchief he'd been wadding across his forehead. "Damme, if you didn't do me proud!" And he rushed at Gerda where she lay, barely through with it all.

"Hold on!" warned Pokey, but Gerda laughed exultantly. Yarbrough caught himself in time and did not bump her bedstead. He held her very hard for a moment, though, and she was glad it was not with gentleness.

"Here," Gerda told Pokey presently, "put them down where he can see his whole family."

Someone peeped in at the door, and it turned out to be Lucey.

"Did you hear it was twins?" called Gerda.

"My, yes!" marvelled Lucey, glad to be let in. "Oh, what pretties!"

"Are they?" questioned Gerda eagerly. "I'm not much of a judge."

"Little beauties," said Lucey emphatically. "Both Gracey and Willy were too sallow."

Gerda thought: "Lucey's not half bad to me, since the babies started." Thought it rather tiredly, though, and Pokey lifted the babies away, saying: "Y'all have to get out now. An', Miss Lucey, please'm set little Pinky outside the door to keep folks away."

They departed in a murmur that buzzed down faint . . . fainter . . . to Gerda. The blinds were drawn and the room swam in green shade. She slept.

4

It was a good fall for Gerda. The twins thrived, since she needed no wet-nurse to help her suckle them. There was a merry snap to her eye and her step was light as she went from the kitchen to the quarters, seeing about the performance of tasks. Miz Lisbeth, looking on, murmured: "Seems to me I was more tuckered out after my first one came."

"Ho, but I'm as strong as an ox!" Gerda reminded her, almost jeering at her own strength. Indeed, she was brimful of life, as woman and a mother, and she but turned fourteen!

5

Thus the years rounded upon one another, until they had added up to three since she had married. Now she had had two more children, a sturdy quiet boy named Tom Two, and a shy baby girl christened Jobyna. Born separately, their advents were taken matter-of-factly. Since Gerda had pulled through so splendidly with twins, there seemed no need of making a big to-do over her bearing, as long as the others came as regular as clockwork. Gerda herself felt a lazy content after these confinements, rather than that first boastful rapture.

Her main concern each succeeding time had been to recover rapidly, knowing that the domestics took advantage of these occasions to slack up. Marta in particular was troublesome whenever Gerda was brought to bed. It was plain laziness, although Marta pretended that she, being white, did not relish taking orders from mulatto Pokey, who acted as Gerda's proxy at such times. On the other hand Pokey contended that Marta was a trollop, with her mind always on her belly or her buttocks. The phlegmatic flesh of the Dutch woman enraged the agile mulatto past endurance. "I wish that gal hadn't come knockin' on our door that night before we left New Yawk. Only brought trouble in her tracks."

"Oh, hoot!" laughed Gerda. "She's a sort of keepsake for Gran."

Gerda was fully recovered from her confinement with baby Joby now. This August morning she had been down to the cabins before breakfast to attend to a fracas two of the women had had over a man. So she sat down hungrily to her great cup of coffee and bowl of fresh-peeled figs, glad to be fit and presiding over the table once more. Miz Lisbeth had finished her hot water and light bread, which was all she now ate in the morning, and was gathering the petals scattered from the rose vase, for pot-pourri. Ven, nursing a whisky head, looked irked at her bird-pecking ways. Miss Lucey was spreading jelly for the girl twin Lucinda, who was her namesake and pet. Guy was planning future ball-gowns with Gracey, who at eleven tried to give herself the airs of a young lady of fashion. These two had reached the point of describing what Gracey's costume for her first Saint Cecilia Ball should be, when Miz Lisbeth interrupted them with a snicker.

"I wouldn't work myself into a swivvey over that just yet. Two, three more years of crops like the ones lately, and with Yarbrough's notes piling up against Cousin James in Charleston—well, Gracey, his wife won't favour asking you down under her sponsorship."

"Why, Granny," cried Gracey in tearful alarm, "if a girl can't attend the Saint Cecilia . . ."

"Is the ball," inquired Guy, "run according to usury?"

"Great sakes," sniffed Miz Lisbeth, pleased at the commotion she had stirred up, "I was only pointing out that money didn't grow on trees. At least 'tisn't growing in our fields as plentiful as it ought." Rising, she spilled her rose petals. As she left, Guy and Gracey tagged after, to pry further into Gracey's social fate.

After their departure Ven snuggled a toddy-glass in his fingers, asking: "Where's Yarbrough?" to which Gerda answered: "I don't know, and I specially want to see him."

"Here he comes," announced Lucey.

He came in without the usual spring in his step. Bonapartt brought his hot breakfast directly, and no one bothered him while he ate. When he'd had his fill he turned sideways in his chair and slung one leg over the arm. "Ven," he announced, "if you run short of cash from horse-betting from now on, don't count on me to advance you anything against the crop profits. Because the way it looks now, I can't bank on making much out of the crops this year. I swear I can't figure where we're heading at this rate!" He shook his head, as if to rid his mind of this worry before he spoke to Gerda. He put on a teasing look for her. "Out with it," he told her. "I can see something is sticking in your craw."

"What say?" Her thoughts came back with difficulty from that primary problem of crops. "Oh, yes, it's that wench Densey. She slipped into Eda's cabin last night and took up with Eda's man, Ruben. They like to've had a lime-chunking. Eda tried to throw some into Densey's eyes to blind her, but Densey ducked. I put Eda to helping up here, with Pokey to watch over her. And I'm going to have Densey whipped."

Ven took a chaw. "Densey's been mighty uppity ever since that year she went mixin' with those white boys."

Gerda clamped her jaws set, and her eyes took on a slow, cold look. People talked of such things up north and Pokey was a mulatto of course, but this was the first time she'd had to deal with *that*. The bottom gave way to her stomach, she felt like a sick pup.

Yarbrough spoke up sharply: "What's that, Ven? About Densey and white boys? You know I won't stand for . . ."

"Don't be hasty," Ven drawled. "I didn't say nothin' about anything on your places. I was referrin' to the time when Uncle Andrew's Drew came home bringing those young bloods from his college. Back when Densey used to belong to them."

Yarbrough was pressing Ven. "You're positive, though, that she hasn't been carrying on here?"

And Ven drawled: "You heard Gerda say it was a nigger man. Besides, who would it be? Women ain't much in my line, 'tain't likely Guy would be up to such, and Willy's away."

"Well, by Jupiter!" cried Yarbrough, banging his fist on the table, "*you* may think it's a joke, but I'm the one that has to see that these all-fired plantations are run right. And one thing I *won't* have is the white men spoiling the wenches, nor yet abusing them. Look at all the rumpus that was kicked up over at Uncle Andrew's."

"Didn't need to have been," said Ven dryly, "if young Drew'd just slapped the wench's mouth shut."

"I'll have to put Densey out in the fields a spell till she comes down off her high horse."

"How you talk, Yarbrough!" said Lucey impatiently. "Densey's the only real fine laundress we've got."

"Listen, Lucey," said Gerda, "I'll make Pokey use the fluting irons right, on your ruffles, if I have to stand over her with a stick." She would have promised anything to uphold Yarbrough's discipline, at a time when he was so troubled with graver matters. When the other two had left she sat staring at him earnestly, wanting him to go further into the subject of the poor yield of the land. He kept silent, though, shoving the heel of his palm against his forehead, and her domestic lore could not supply her with the words to question him intelligently. Finally she rose. "I'd better," she thought, "go and see that my own end of things is run right, but after this I must learn more about his. I'm beginning to catch on to what Miz Lisbeth meant about a man's lot."

She stroked his shoulder in passing and he hugged that hand an instant.

6

There was not so much company as usual right now, but at dinner time to-day Yarbrough brought two new arrivals up from his office. One was a Virginian named Towers, who usually stopped with the Whetstones every year on his way to a plantation in Louisiana. The other man was a stranger, a Mr. Malone, who lived mostly in Alabama. Yes, he told them, there were unfriendly Indians in the state, the Creeks. Still, the white people were taking up the land fast, flocking in. And such land! Why, even the Indians could grow cotton on it like wildfire. No telling what white men could do with it. As he expounded the future of Alabama, Yarbrough drummed on the table, doing figures in his head. Once he asked their guest how they sent their cotton to the markets.

"Down the rivers by steamboat," Malone replied. Then for Gracey's benefit he spoke of some of the things advertised by one of the dry-goods merchants up in Tuscumbia: luxuries including Florentine vestings, crêpe robes, and tortoiseshell combs. Oh, they weren't going to stay backwoods for ever.

The visitor now turned to old Pieter. "I purchased a mighty fine half-pipe of Holland gin from their wet-goods merchant not a week before leaving. I have some in my flask. Will you honour me by accepting it?"

Gran nodded eagerly. "That will be no hardship."

Gerda eyed their guest warily; he seemed bent on gaining the good-will of all. Presently he produced a letter which he'd been asked to deliver to Yarbrough from a friend of both travelling in Alabama. "There, Mr. Whetstone, you can read what a great country he thinks it, if you doubt my word."

Gerda continued to study Malone. He was indeed chock-full of his subject, Alabama and its cotton; but she mistrusted his Irish way of smoothly giving pleasure to each member of the family in turn. Why, he had even Miz Lisbeth bridling, and he glanced down Gerda's way more than often. She thought: "I like some vim he has, and then I don't."

Yarbrough had run through his letter and now was re-reading some parts of it aloud:

We had dinner at the home of a young chief named McKintosh, the son of that chief who was shot and quartered by his tribesmen who claimed he had betrayed them in a treaty with the whites. This younger McKintosh has two wives, one an Indian, one the white daughter of a planter from over in Georgia. She welcomed us like any planter's wife, which she indeed is, the family being possessed of upwards of seventy negroe slaves.

The country hereabouts is thickly populated with Creek Indians, all loathe to forsake their lands for more Westerly ones beyond the Red River. That can be readily understood, since much of it here is under cultivation for cotton, though on a more humble scale than that in more accessible parts.

I noted though that the Creeks were not civilized past thievery, though their Chiefs claim that that trick, as well as the drinking of whiskey, they learned from our race. However, I saw also that the men put the brunt of labor upon the women, which causes them early to look sullen and old.

The cotton here is beyond belief healthy, I have never seen a finer stand to the acre. But you can hardly credit me until you see it for yourself.

Yarbrough's voice stopped, though his eyes followed on down the page intently. Then he refolded the letter, and screwing his port-glass round and round in his hand, he fell into deep thought about Alabama and its fabulous yield. Seeing his preoccupation, Gerda stood, and moved to the door as a signal. The dining-room gradually cleared of every one else; still Yarbrough sat on with his ponderings.

On the piazza Malone came up to Gerda. "You would like my country, ma'am," he said. "It's a place fitted to call out all in you."

She went back a step, primly. "I'm sure this place here takes it out of me a plenty."

"Not you!" He eyed her boldly.

At the supper table the talk again turned on the question of the removal of the Indians from the coveted area. President Adams, all the gentlemen agreed, was shilly-shallying about the matter. He was a man of little gumption anyway. It made them wonder if Andrew Jackson, for all his championing of "the common man," might not have been the better choice. The Indian Wars had shown how he could settle the question.

After supper Yarbrough went down to his office alone, carrying his letter to brood over.

In the long twilight some of the larger cousins started a game of blind-man's-buff. Presently every one, even Gran and the tumbling twins, joined in, and Gerda was soon in the thick of it. Mr. Towers could twitter in a high treble that fooled the "blind man," but Malone thought it better sport to trip the seeker.

Finally Gerda, being "it," lost her bearings and stumbled away from her victims into the yew-hedge maze. All kept silence by conspiracy, to let her go farther astray. Malone, however, desiring to keep up the romping, bounded after her down one of the paths. When he stepped out in front of her suddenly, she collided into his arms, and he choked with laughter. Dazed and blindfolded, she fumbled with her hands to identify him. Finally she put her fingertips up, to trace out his nose. As she did this, he settled his arms more closely about her and pressed his features caressingly against her hand.

"Oh, she gasped in startled recognition, but before she could cry his name and pull away to proclaim him "it," there came a shoving of branches and Yarbrough's voice saying curtly: "Mr. Malone, I was in search of you in reference to some points in this letter. Now, though, I see I must ask you to wait for me at my office, not in my home."

Malone dropped his arm easily from its embrace of Gerda, and answered with a chuckle in his voice: "Anything you say, sir." Then his steps went away. From behind the blind of her handkerchief Gerda could hear Yarbrough's hard breathing; then *smack,* the hot slap of his palm clapped her cheek. She snatched the bandage from her eyes and flailed back at him, until he caught her hands.

"It was only a game!" she cried through tears of exasperation at how puny her strength became when matched against him. "You—you're hateful."

"That may be," he said flatly, steadying her down as he would a fractious colt. "But Malone has none too good a name among the ladies. Though I never thought *you* would act in such a way. Only, Lord, I forget what an untried babe you were when I married you. Yet you have hot blood running in you, as no one knows better than I. Now go to your room and bathe your face," he advised, brushing the tear-streaked red mark kindly.

Then he sighed. "There were a lot of questions I had wanted to put to that scamp, though, about the yield of the Alabama land. But never mind, he's such a braggart I couldn't take too much stock in his talk."

Gerda dug the ground with her slipper toe, regretting her ill-timed blunder that had obstructed her husband's agricultural discussions. "Are things so bad here on our lands, then?"

"Poorly, indeed," he admitted, but then he puffed his cheeks out with air and blew it forth with a sound as if he were pooh-poohing both his own crops and Malone's tall tales of Alabama in one breath. "Go wash your face like I told you."

An hour later from her window Gerda heard a carriage pull up, and peering out she saw Malone climb in with all his traps. Young Cousin Drew followed him, telling Ruben on the box to drive them over to Uncle Andrew's, where Malone would finish out his stop in Egton District. Later, when Yarbrough came up to their room, he loosened his neck-band with a yawn. "Well, I fixed that touchy point without making big trouble of it. 'Twasn't worth it. But let this be a lesson to you, my ficety one, now and for ever: No Whetstone will stand for a lally-gagging wife! Even if he has to break her neck apart himself!"

Gerda nodded, about to pop with pride in him.

CHAPTER FIVE

As another year passed, Gerda began to take on wifehood as a way of life, not as a garment in which some child masquerades, conscious of playing a game. She lay down on her bed at night with household matters measuring their way through her mind, rather than the quarter-hours that should have marked the darkness. She woke in the morning to observe whether it was a bright day for bleaching linen or a rainy day for piecing quilts. Now, too, she no longer gave an order with an air of adventure, but from habit.

In spite of her pride in being considered the mistress of the establishment she was grateful for any help received from her women kin, especially where it relieved her of attention to fine points. Miss Lucey, of all people, had proved a joy from the time of the twins' birth. She found in babies something even more dependent than herself; then Gerda's naming the girl, Lucinda, after her won Lucey completely. She rubbed their first difficult teeth through swollen gums on her silver thimble. She stood Lucinda in the corner for clipping the baby's hair to stuff a doll pillow with, and she switched Bruff, as they had nicknamed the boy twin who was Yarbrough's namesake, for fighting too much. Naturally the children wore her out at times, and then she was temporarily prostrated.

But on her well days she purely enjoyed them. The high point of her day came when, starchily dressed for the afternoon, they came to her room to learn curtsies and bows, and the Episcopal catechism. Afterwards the daylight would begin to die as they sat in a solemn little row, listening to the story about Aunt Lucey's Lace Fan, or Jug-Toe Tappum's Spell, and dusk came creeping sort of scary between the white curtains.

Then the supper bell would ring-a-ling-a-ling through the halls, at which they'd go scampering down to a dining-room that was full of light and noise and dozens of plates laid on a long table, and where there would be jabber-jabber.

Aunt Lucey often did not follow them, but sent word for a tray. This brought older members of the family wanting to know what was wrong. She didn't really wish any of them to stay, for she enjoyed her solitary hours looking over her jewels, touching her turquoise ear-rings, trying to remember some sensation of girlish anticipation.

When Lucey took to her bed regularly, nobody thought much of it, and she was careful to smother her cough in her pillow at night. Then one evening she came to supper again, wearing a satin dress as bright as light-green sugar cane, which caused them to forget to look to see if her face above it was peart. Directly after the meal she went back upstairs, and holding on to her poster bed she died, without even unlacing her corset-strings.

The next morning the children were told to tiptoe through the halls, and Gerda took Lucinda to gather all the early violets to sew on a little cardboard cross as something special from her namesake.

The whole district turned out in a cavalcade for the burying, with harnesses polished as if for a wedding, causing Miz Lisbeth to whisper to Gerda: "My, but Lucey would've been pleased!"

That evening shortly after dark they missed Lucinda, who showed up later lugging the violet cross. "I didn't want it to get rained on," she defended herself.

The grown people continued to sit in the Long Room, listening, without meaning to, for Lucey's vague distracting step that would not sound again in her room overhead. Miz Lisbeth, spying a scattering of flower petals on the floor where the casket had been set for the services, forgot herself as badly as Lucinda and stowed them thriftily in her handkerchief for her pot-pourri.

2

Willy did not return to his studies after his mother's funeral, but stayed on with his family, rather stunned. Death he had thought belonged to God and the old and had nothing to do with his mother, who was a small woman in ruffles. Still here was Miz Lisbeth portioning Lucey's trinkets out to the namesake Lucinda, and Gerda refusing sharply to accept them for her daughter. "Can't you let them alone for a while?" she had demanded.

Nice of Cousin Gerda not to want to claim them greedily for her child, thought Willy, yet he felt queer seeing Lucey's pretty belongings swathed in tissues, turning into ghostly keepsakes. Grieved as he was, however, Willy had small time to feel bad all by himself. That would have taken too many hours standing in her room alone, or hunting out the end of the gallery where she had used to smell the petunia scent, murmuring: "Ummn, it's thick to-night."

No. He wanted to do things like that, for they sweetened the ache. And he fully meant to do something of the sort every day, but someone else was usually hanging around at the time he would have chosen for special remembering. Then he had to say instead: "It's turning into summer, the mosquitoes are starting up."

Willy soon found that his main occupation was that of distracting his father from the lethargy of his widowerhood. The task became very trying when it required conversation, for they couldn't keep repeating over and over: "She seemed too young to die."

For a while they tried chess, but on the third day of their tournament Guy stammered: "I—I think I'll go look up Ven. He said he had something to tell me." Whereupon he went down where Ven was tossing quoits behind the stables.

Ven looked up in surprise, not having sent for Guy at all, but he invited him to join in. For an hour or so they pitched, sitting in low splint-bottomed chairs, with stable boys to pick up the horseshoes and Cudge to pour drams. At first Guy sipped cautiously, forgetting that Lucey was not here to nag, but shortly the drink made him feel that he would not have cared if she were. At supper that night he even spoke up to Yarbrough when the latter was dwelling again on the subject of poor crops. "You ought," stated Guy loudly, "to pull up stakes and go down where the land is worth while. To some place like Alabama or Mississippi."

Yarbrough stared at his rabbity brother-in-law as if the latter had gone daft. True, he had himself been dwelling on the idea of an Alabama migration for longer than any of them had guessed. Still it was not a notion to be taken up and acted upon lightly. Here in South Carolina they could always have comfort if not their present opulence, while down there devastation might wait. There was no gainsaying that such a move would take endless planning, the shrewdest disposal of present property, and terrible courage. For a man with a large household it meant a great wrench to leave an old established Home Place with its association in beauty, its assurance of safety, and its pillars bedded in all the tradition that was his heritage. To leave that and strike out into an unknown savage country was to cast a die more grave than the pitch of any stable-yard quoit.

Yarbrough rose and tramped out of his dining-room, into the open, across his land, to a space where he could think without the hindrance of house walls.

When the meal ended, Gerda wandered distraitly out into the maze, gazing in the direction of the office though she sensed that Yarbrough had not gone within doors. Presently she was joined in her walk by Willy, to whom she gave a kinder attention these days. This attitude had not come about solely because she was sorry for him, but because she had noticed him growing sharper in his perceptions, if not brawnier as a man. In fact nowadays she was always interested to hear his opinions, even if she disagreed.

To-night she caught him eyeing her speculatively before he asked: "Gerda, are you becoming too *laissez-faire*?"

"What are you driving at, with that silly French phrase?"

"I mean, are you content to let things simply jog along round you? Somehow you seem to have grown too confounded settled! I think you are losing your verve."

"What of it?" she demanded.

"This!" He darted a glance at her to see if his shot went home. "Your verve is your strongest appeal, your strongest hold over people. Even over Yarbrough."

She lifted her chest sharply at that. "You impudent one, to tell me how to behave to Yarbrough."

He merely whistled a bar, then murmured: "I never thought to see you grow dull. And I'll wager Yarbrough never did either."

They remained eyeing each other warily, for they both knew that he had weighed his remark after careful observation, and that she could not dismiss it lightly. Finally Gerda threw up her hands. "I do feel somehow stalemated here. And Yarbrough is in the dumps about the whole she-bang on the plantations. He doesn't know which way to turn."

"I thought so," nodded Willy, "and I hate to see you two in a treadmill. You two who were meant to progress." With that he strolled off.

Gerda stood nonplussed. Was she holding Yarbrough back, by

appearing lackadaisical? She had merely felt too ignorant to counsel him on the momentous matter of emigration. But if that was what he wanted, why, she would help him tooth and nail!

She had not meant to slump into casual ease on the Home Place. The Home Place had been to her a new province to explore, a set of exacting crafts to learn. Now, however, she held the skein of skill as mistress and mother secure between her fingers. Now there was something more awaiting her of wifehood, something larger concerned with growing to the stature of a person.

She must seek Yarbrough at once, and tell him that she had no fear of change, or chance, or any danger. A wilderness? What could be so dread about that, if the soil from which the jungle sprang be rich enough to reward his toil? A wilderness? What could frighten her in any dusky unknown country if Yarbrough led her there?

3

Striding through the soft summer dark, Yarbrough felt as if the damp air rising from his acres was the very breath of his earth's body. He slowed down to let it touch his cheek with its gentleness. He must not let its dear frailty betray him. The land was not the sovereign, it was the servant of man. He was here to populate the world, and the earth must answer his needs not yoke him like an ox.

This land his forebears had claimed, had used to their own ends, and learned to love fiercely. Some of them, his father among them, had fought a war to keep that claim. They had reminded a king of this, as they had back in England when in the thirteenth century King Edward had issued his writ of *quo warranto* to inquire into the titles by which his nobels held their lands. Then John, seventh Earl of Whetstone, had unsheathed his sword before the justices and declared: "Behold *my* warranty. *Gladio vici, gladio teneo, gladio tenebo.*" Which being translated meant: "By the sword I conquered, by the sword I hold it, by the sword I will hold it!"

Hence had come the family motto: *Tenebo, I Will Hold.* Hence also that tradition of wresting from the world lands and sustenance, though of late it had been done by that fabled plough hammered from the sword on the anvil of fortitude. Yet the family creed remained the same, that of holding all together come hell or high water.

Such for centuries had the Whetstones been, before ever they came to America. Call them raw invaders, call them royalists, call them patriarchs. The words changed, and the guise changed. The spirit remained. To take the savage land, to keep it, to protect therein their own. And if that fiefdom, that stronghold, went down before the tracks of Time and the world's new ways, to leave it. Go forth. Find and build anew!

CHAPTER SIX

ALL WINTER Yarbrough had pondered, all winter Gerda had endeavoured to show him how willing she was to seek new land, and all winter the watchword had been Alabama.

During the continuous discussion of the subject, the blowing hot and cold about migration, Yarbrough had kept up an incessant correspondence with men in the South-west who offered him the riches of a new world, and cousins in Charleston who were attempting to help him dispose of his portion of the old profitably; and there were not many buyers for nearly depleted plantations, even when a well-kept home and grist-mill were thrown in.

Day after day Yarbrough tramped over his nearest and dearest acres, the dirt quagging under his boots. He could hardly believe that this land would not yield at his command, it had succoured the Whetstones so long. Overlong, he knew, twisting the toe of his boot in some soil that would soon be a prey to weeds.

He returned to the office to tot up the assets he had in houses, furniture, and farming equipment, which Cousin James might credit against that spate of notes at the bank. He felt as bad as if he were selling off some of his best hands, he felt as if he were selling off members of his own family.

On that particular evening he tarried long enough to add up all the columns that he knew so well; then he set his seal to the bottom of the last one in red wax. "That's as binding as anything Cousin James might draw up, betwixt me and another party." Instantly he felt that swift clean state that comes upon a man when he decides. *Air filled his lungs, and light was full bright in his eyes even in the dark, while the going ahead was plain. He took the first few steps forward with a strong gait. He was man, he was master.*

It was later at night that Yarbrough became again his old self, jumbling in his mind about the figures on those sheets he was offering purchasers, recalling the soft outlines of the roof of his house, as seen when the moon was begging rain from the sky. . . . But then he reminded himself, this place would always be begging some mercy of nature. He shut his mind like a window against all soft entreaty from his loved home and took up the rest of the night by twisting in his sheets with worry for the future.

2

Finally one day as the last dreariness of winter lay slack across the land, Yarbrough came stamping in and hurled his cape off exuberantly. " By Heaven, I'm going to scout forth and see for myself! I'll never believe in his wonderful Alabama until I clap eyes on it, yet I'll hanker my heart out if I abide here unconvinced." Then he spun Gerda around on her heels. She tripped and they flumped in a laughing heap on the floor.

From there he ticked off what he would need most on such a preliminary expedition: two wagon-loads of farming implements and supplies, essential staple food, several of his sturdiest field-hands . . . a neighbour, John Screws, to accompany him; also the insistent Guy, perhaps Gran, who had taken up with the notion, and lastly Marta to cook for them and see to Gran's crotchets. Their goal would be that unbelievably rich land bordering the old Indian Line in the heart of the Creek country, for it was there that the great tracts could be obtained most profitably if one was not afraid of risk.

" A fig for the risk!" cried Gerda, who expected to go with the party. " I won't mind that."

Yarbrough leapt up. " But you can't come along on this first trip. What of the children, especially the tyke Wayne, who is ailing and cranky?"

" Why, Pokey's a better nurse by far than me."

Still Yarbrough shook his head as he leaned over and picked her up. He swept her skirts into place to make a proper cambric canopy. Then he told her gravely: " This is but an experiment, my trip. It may prove all wrong. Therefore while I am away things must go to our best advantage here, and there is no man I could call upon who could serve me so well in my absence as my wife. You, I know, will give a good account of your trust."

" That I will!" she declared, standing back from him in her tent of skirts, though oblivious now that she was a woman or anything other than a plain human, who, like him, wanted bread for their own and walls solid against destruction.

They regarded each other very clearly in the severe grey light of winter.

3

The expedition set forth from Yarbrough's office on a day that showed the first crack of spring. The faint rime of frost, not yet dispelled from the daybreak road, but put an edge of excitement on the adventure. And the two wagons in spite of their loads came up with a clatter and the halloo of their drivers. Shade was in charge of one and Tid of the other. All the negroes were up from the quarters to watch the lucky ones off and were hard put to it to disguise their envy in spite of calling out such gibes as: "Speck y'll be walkin' barefoot, 'stead of ridin', befo' dem Injuns git through wif you!"

"Slice 'em up! Dat's what we'll do to ol' Injuns!" bragged Shade. "Slice 'em up!"

Patt, looking as fresh as paint, was to ride behind Marse Yarbrough and wait on him as body servant, which was a great grief to Bonapartt. Now not even Bonapartt's silver waiter for passing the company decanter could pacify this jealousy.

Every house servant was present to say good luck, and the white children were all underfoot except for the baby and the querulously sick Wayne. Even Gracey was down, her childish curiosity getting the better of her young-lady elegance. Miz Lisbeth, however, had said her good-bye to Yarbrough in her own chamber, while it was still shadowed by night. "Take care, son," she had cautioned, then couldn't think of anything else to add. Her lips had puckered pitifully for a second, but he had quickly brushed her fine white hair back from her brow in a way that soothed her, reminding her: "Nothing's ever harmed me yet." To which she had agreed: "That's so." She knew worrying over Yarbrough was foolish. After he had gone down the steps, she fell into one of those light naps of the old and consequently did not hear the departure.

It made a great clamour. Gran boomed, children shrilled, Gerda directed Bonapartt to carry a pot of coffee around once more among the men after they had mounted, not overlooking their black attendants. Then she had an earnest talk with Marta about not slighting the camp cooking. "I'm depending on you, Marta. Gran Pieter is old, and all of them will feel exposure and strain. Be chary of the salt. Don't give it away with too free a hand, for it's a long way to salt stations."

Marta promised everything. She would see after those men. Men had ever been her job.

Cudge, watching the exodus, scratched his pate and inquired: "Marse Ven, how come we ain't goin' on dis frolic?"

Ven shrugged. "Because you and me, we're too worthless to spunk it out."

Willy held Bruff up to his father for some sort of command to the oldest born. Then the short line formed, and someone picked out a tune. The darkies pitched it surer, began to swell it into harmony. Shoulders swayed closer together, forming a phalanx before the Home Place, while melody was a charm to ward off evil from the travellers. Then a woman's voice made a burst of gold, better than the sun still missing from the sky. From the vanguard Yarbrough fanned his hat back at Gerda in salute, and she lifted her hand aloft. This day would open up a new spring, and a new road!

4

The first letter that Gerda had from Yarbrough was brought by a neighbour who had passed them. They had been gone but a week, so of course it told little.

"We keep well," wrote Yarbrough, "and your grandfather is as hearty as any of us. Marta's cooking is only tolerable." ("Drat the girl," thought Gerda.) "The roads so far are fair, and thick with migrants all in a high good humour over their prospects."

Gerda stared wistfully at the scrap of paper, seeing all those people jostling, thronging, on their way to a fine new land, and she not with them. "I was never cut out for a stay-at-home!" she cried, vexed.

Willy, who was standing by, touched her arm. "Our neighbour here is waiting, he has another message for you that Yarbrough sent by word of mouth."

The neighbour cleared his throat. " Mr. Whetstone charged me to present his compliments to Miz Lisbeth, and his deep love to you."

Gerda coloured at this, thinking that while she had been fuming she had forgotten Yarbrough would not be back home to-morrow by sundown, that she would have to be content with " word " from him, a thin thing after his harsh grip.

It was a long time before another letter came. Meanwhile Gerda had her hands full running the plantations. She had turned the domestic affairs over to Pokey, while she rode about overseeing the fields. Whenever she had to go to outlying ones such as the chinquapin lands, Willy rode with her, though she was not afraid to journey alone. " But," he pointed out, " you have to be gone from home overnight."

" Well, I'm not intending to sleep by the roadside," she laughed. " I'll be staying at the nearest cousin's house."

" Still, it's unseemly for a woman to come riding up alone on horseback, the way you do. Now, if only you'd pack a proper band-box and drive in a carriage——"

" Be that as it may, I'll be needing my own strong-winded horse to carry me about, to see if my hands are stirring their stumps in the fields. I'll be farming, not visiting."

Willy saw then that he might as well drop the subject. He rode along behind her, feeling like a stable boy.

She stopped at Uncle Andrew's that first time, and occupied the supper hour by talking with a man who knew a lot about the latest methods of fertilizing. That evening she paid no attention to the feminine chatter, but sat yawning from her day in the open, contented at the gain she would be able to show Yarbrough upon his return. Consequently, several days later when she was back home and received his next letter, she did not feel so envious of the travellers. It ran:

The roads are well-night impassable and we have had to lighten the loads, but have discarded none of your precious salt, since Marta impressed upon us your warning. Believe me her cooking tastes mighty good to us now. She proves to be of a brighter manner also, less sulky than at Egton, where mayhap she felt classed with the negro wenches.

Should we decide to come to the South-west, there are many things to consider, though the land as far as we have come into Georgia is all they claim for it. But the lack of conveniences, the trouble with the Indians, and the question of health must not be overlooked. The graves of members of families are near every house, and, my Gerda, I did not take you into my keeping to bury you early in a wild and lonely country.

After finishing this letter, Gerda looked all about her room with its comforts, thought of her secure nursery, her summer and winter kitchens, and the great ease of life they had here. Perhaps when Yarbrough returned, if they both worked hard with all their might and the new knowledge she had been learning about re-enriching land, perhaps they might be able to stay on here at the Home Place, safe.

Gerda's complacency did not last long, however, for some of the hands fell ill; consequently she was hard put to it in the fields. Then Pokey complained about impudence from the other house servants, and a general shirking, while Miz Lisbeth was now less than no help in the house. Everything went at sixes-and-sevens, until Gerda wished with heart and soul that Yarbrough were here, or she with Yarbrough.

Finally one day Willy caught her standing in a corner with her knuckles jammed against her mouth, chewing on them to keep from screaming her head off with loneliness for her husband. He said: "For shame! A great girl like you blubbering." She was supposed to laugh at this, but instead she snuffled: "G-go away."

Willy was with her also on the day the letter came that put her out of sorts. It contained a lot of the usual news about broken wagon axles and the game they had bagged. Then her eye fell on the next line:

Yesterday we fell in better luck. Our people were watering stock when a rosy-cheeked lass came tearing up on a bay mare and asked of Patt, "Is your master the one who sits so straight in his saddle? Then tell him to come after me. I live in that big house, and my father wants him and his friends to sup with us. Tell him to shine his buttons bright for me." Whipping her horse she then rode off laughing over her shoulder with great mischief.

These Georgia girls seem more free than our Gracey. That night this minx made a great show of pouting, upon learning I was no courting blade. But all the same after the meal she took a guitar and played an air directly at me, ogling me the while.

"You cannot stop the wind from blowing,
You cannot stop a heart from showing—
When it has been snared!"

"Why, the jade!" cried Gerda. "I'll snare her!" And crushing the paper, she tossed it hard upon the floor.

Willy watched her a moment while her breathing moved her ribs up and down. Then softly he retrieved the letter and scanned it further. "See here," he told her, "Yarbrough's bitten by jealousy too."

"What's that?" Gerda asked quickly, and he showed her:

Such a forward miss needs a sound spanking, which puts me in mind of the grave warning I gave you on a certain occasion concerning the likes of Mr. Malone. I am now far off, but I left not only my home in your keeping, but my honour. Have a care of it, my wife.

Gerda made a little noise of happiness in her throat, and Willy smiled upon her gently. He had a great admiration for her staunchness, a pity for her clumsy honesty, and fear for her unarmed heart. These emotions he felt deeply, and there was sincerity in the gestures of sentiment in which he clothed them, in the absence of any other beloved woman. He had always thought there would be one such some day. Only Gerda would not have done in any case, he told himself, smiling wryly at the poor figure he cut beside this woman full of splendid faults. He knew she was having hard going now, as the weeks of her husband's absence turned into months.

Yarbrough's journey was to have consumed four months, if they had no ill luck, without counting the time they were to spend in Alabama. Then Gran had fallen sick in Georgia, necessitating a long-drawn-out stop, and Yarbrough wrote worriedly of the delay. It was the end of the summer, and they had still to reach Alabama. Aside from looking over available land there, he meant to study the trade routes to the cotton markets, to go down to Mobile and to

Montgomery. For there was no sense in not seeing the whole view after coming so far and taking so long.

In one letter he told Gerda:

I sometimes wonder if I am the same man. All that was real before seems remote and dreamlike. I shut my eyes and cannot remember how many windows are across the front of our house, and the sound of your voice goes wrong when I try to hear it.

Gerda was moody for weeks after that, though she said nothing to any one. She simply walked a good deal more in the evenings, shooing the children away if they tagged after her. She was trying to rid herself of Yarbrough's "absence." She had some notion that she could destroy distance between Yarbrough's face and hers if she could only think out his features, but they would not fit together.

Willy saw her once shutting her eyes and smelling in the air as if she were trying to catch some scent that was missing. And Willy worried: "There's some feeling there, some intensity, that's passing out of human bounds."

Still she looked after the crop-gathering faithfully and did her mooning only in her spare time.

CHAPTER SEVEN

FAR AWAY from South Carolina and the Home Place day broke and showed the Chattahoochee River. Yarbrough, viewing its meandering width, yawned, stretched his legs to stand the straighter, and thought: "Well now, at least we'll soon see the last of Georgia. Over there that's *Alabama*!"

Every one in his little company scamped on breakfast, being eager to set foot on Alabama soil. They were somewhat delayed, however, for quite a collection of riders, wagons, and other vehicles were waiting in the churned-up mud by the river bank. So the sun was well up before their turn came for the Indian to ferry them across. All fell silent as they passed mid-stream. They had come a long way to reach this land.

As they arrived at the shore a hubbub went up. Two horses started kicking, and Patt bopped Shade on the mouth. Their group landed from the ferry-raft, slipping and sliding as best they could in the wet clay. Yarbrough's mount made the grade the most easily, straining its great shoulders. After that they went with little talk through the Creek settlement of Yufala. Only Guy said: "Huh, all Indian?"

For an hour they rode on, making about four miles through a forest of pines that now showed many lofty hickories and oaks as well. They came into a clearing and Yarbrough had his first vast view of the plateau. A vista stretched away into majesty. He felt dwarfed, yet also strangely like some lonely patriarch of old.

Then the small clearing was swallowed up by the blue-black of the trees, with the first slight red of the sumach showing.

Hour on hour they went riding deeper into that forest, the little band drawing closer together in the sombreness. At noon they ate some cold pone while riding, for nobody wanted to stop until they had crossed over the Indian Line. It was late when Yarbrough, who had been watching the trail closely for a sign that had been described to him, spoke sharply. "We're over it! That blazed tree back there by the pile of stones marked it."

They drifted along yet a little farther, to leave the boundary safely out of sight behind them. Then they clambered down stiffly and made camp for the night almost in silence.

Yarbrough went a little way apart and leaned against a tall tree-trunk, his arms folded to rest the sag of his weary shoulders. Through a gap he could glimpse a lift of sky. The trees seemed to roar up against it. Up! Everything seemed on high here. Not a single peak, but the whole land was held above the place where the earth had been before. It would take large men to set foot upon it and stay.

He turned away and came back towards their fire. "Well, it will be somewhere hereabouts—the land that will be ours."

The half-light fell through the trees. An owl hooted. Unknown creatures scuffed in the underbrush. It was the wilderness!

Then a mule nickered, and Marta, turning a hoe-cake in hot frying bacon grease, called: "Come for your supper."

Gran sighed: "*Och*, a woman is a comfort." To which they all agreed. And Yarbrough felt more like a man, less like Moses leading a lost tribe.

CHAPTER EIGHT

THE TIME CAME when Yarbrough returned home.

It had been raining all day, with the steady downpour of the last of the winter rains. The children were romping in the Long Room, because it was the only place with space enough to keep them from feeling cooped up. Every now and then Miz Lisbeth called out: "Take care!" when she thought they might break one of the more delicate chair-backs.

The room had lost some of its grace since Lucey had died. There were no flowers in water, and the mahogany was blurry, while the stuffing showed below the bottom of one sofa. A dog dozed on the hearth, Ven was paring an apple, and by the fireplace Gerda was relaxed in the great chair. She had had a hard day, down where the millstream was rising over its banks, and Pokey had gone to fetch her some ham and biscuit and a special compound of hot milk with rum. Meanwhile it felt good to Gerda to flop here with the scorch of the fire on her face, her hand tugging at the setter's ear, the children's voices humming . . . swinging nearly out of her sleepy hearing. . . . "Is that you, Pokey?" she murmured. "Just set the cup down."

Then violent arms were pulling her up out of her drowse, and a dream that lately had always broken off in distress seemed coming true. Yarbrough? Still in a half-stupor she clung, grabbing his sodden cape with both fists. "Yarbrough, don't wake me up! To be alone!"

She bent to smother her sob, and then tasted the acrid wet real wool across his shoulder. It *was* Yarbrough.

Her eyes sprang wide open upon the revelation of his face. There was a gloss over his eyes of tenderness at the sight of her.

Then suddenly all the others' voices drowned out hers in welcome to him, while she simply stood there. A dog snaffled the ham out of the plate of biscuits, and the rain came down like a mill-race outside the window, but Yarbrough was back!

2

Late that night Gerda and Yarbrough stood looking out of their bedroom at a watery moon which had at last broken through the clouds and was sailing high. He had talked himself out, for in spite of the weather the men of the family connection nearby had ridden over for supper to hear his news. He and Gran, accompanied only by Patt, had made the return trip. The others were staying down there, to break in the hands to the ways of working on that new land, also to watch out for bargains in possible property.

Yes, Yarbrough had told his kin, the land was rich beyond description, but some of the hardships were also "beyond description." The Indians were still troublesome, though the planters were looking to Jackson to put an end to that when he came into office. However, Yarbrough had indicated that he wanted time to discuss things with Gerda, to weigh every angle before he moved his family, lock, stock and barrel.

"Besides, my wife has given such good account of her stewardship here, perhaps I ought not to remove her from these plantations." He had raised his glass to Gerda, and she had been proud of his praising her before them all. Yet she'd had her fill of nursing this failing land.

All together the evening had been one mellow with old candlelight. Miz Lisbeth had worn her highest comb, which was soon tipped raffishly over one ear, and Gracey had looked exceedingly pretty. Yes, it was a pleasant celebration for fair, though Gerda had caught herself wanting the guests to leave or to retire. Now though, when finally she and Yarbrough were standing close, with herself straight in her white nightdress, she could only wait for him like any green girl, picking at the window-blinds with her calloused fingertips.

She heard Yarbrough say: "You've grown gaunt," and she replied sharply: "Well, a year of breaking my back over this sorry land would hardly soften me up like ripe peaches."

"So you're the same hot-headed spit-back, eh?" he laughed. "Well, you can quit being the man of the family now. And wash your face in buttermilk like Gracey. Though just you let me catch you at such folderol foolishness, and I'll fan you till you can't sit down." He had her close to him now.

"I am as tanned as shoe leather," she admitted ruefully, "and as stringy as dried corn-silk tassels."

"That's not the way I find you," he said, his arms roving up and down the firm curves of her body, while she held to him.

3

April was sending a soft push of air through the windows of the Long Room, freshening it after winter mustiness, and a bunch of jonquils reflected a brash yellow before the mantel mirror. To-day Gracey was trying to make them drink afternoon tea, for Ven had carried her with him to President Jackson's inauguration in Washington, and since she had returned home she had been showing off. A pot of tea, if you were tired or had missed a meal, was all right, Gerda thought; but at five o'clock with cakes and preserves it would only spoil your supper. More cousins had just now arrived, giving Gracey the opportunity to tell about the trip all over again. "We were entertained by some lovely people," she told them, "and I was invited twice to the English minister's house. I think the English charming, with such delightful customs." She sipped her tea self-consciously.

"President Jackson," cut in Ven dryly, "bid me to dinner. Showed me his pipes too. He has a great collection, with all sorts of fancy ones from every which place. Still he sticks to smokin' his same old corncob. Says his wife used to smoke one along with him."

Gerda glanced at Yarbrough, who was leaning abstractedly against the mantel. She would smoke a pipe with him, if he ever wanted that. She had never been so happy before in her life, not even as a bride or when the twins were born. Her cheeks were once more rounded out and her rich blood went pell-mell. She was a complete woman now, nearing twenty and trained in fulfilment. Also she had noticed a greater gravity in Yarbrough, something that mastered her, as was rightful.

Then Yarbrough was speaking eagerly to Ven, asking: "Tell me about the President's speech on the Indian removal from the Southwest."

"That's right," continued Ven, stealing Gracey's thunder further. "He made a speech about that on the 23rd of March. First he said some very Christian-sounding hog-wash about how we had to be kind to our poor red brothers. Then in the next breath he came right out and said that nobody could interfere with the states of Georgia and Alabama within their own limits. He said the Indians would have to behave or move out beyond the Red River. Well, there 'tis! You can pack your duds and go down and pick your spot for cotton-raising."

Everybody was interested in this subject except Gracey. She was sick to death of that same old thing, cotton. She preferred silk. As she pouted into her tepid teacup she was unaware that for once Gerda was approving what she had done to the Long Room with the bouquets of jonquils, feeling glad her dress was the same colour. For Yarbrough had leaned down to say: "You look as good as butter in that, I could eat you," and Gerda revelled in sitting there a cherished lady.

4

On this sweet May morning Gerda sat staring stubbornly at Gran and Yarbrough. A day ago she had told Yarbrough that their reunion was to result in another child. She had told him in greatest triumph that this halycon time was going to leave a signet of their love. He had been so perturbed, however, that she had questioned him. "Is it Alabama you're thinking off? Well, this needn't hold us up. We'll go when we're ready, in the summer as we had planned."

Dubiously he had shaken his head. "You can't imagine, Gerda, what a woeful hard trip it is."

She had paid scant attention to his forebodings though, and presently her joy had seemed to prevail. For Yarbrough had gripped her arms hard, exclaiming: "Nothing daunts you, does it? Well, the sap did run sweet, so I'll be bound the fruit will be fine." Yet his tone had been more one of amazement at her spirit than joy on his own part.

Now to-day he had come bringing Gran to their room, where the two of them sat as if in conclave before her. Gran had been booming at her in that voice of his: "Gerda, *mijne Liefste,* you cannot go into this wilderness of Alabama while with child. The way is too difficult! Strong as you are, it would take too great a toll of you. The rain—there seems always to be rain, until the wheels sink and cannot turn. Then every one must clamber out and toil ahead on foot. Also there are streams where there are no bridges, and hurricanes of wind." He broke off. Both men looked broodingly into their minds where hardships and other memories still hung heavy.

"You see what he says," Yarbrough told her. "True, I have counted upon migration a long time, but we are not compelled to go. Also I have large moneys invested here, amounts I cannot realize by quick sale if I leave. Much that I value must be left behind. While down there awaits rough living, wild country, and a hard road to reach it. Now, since you have told me this latest news, I don't see how we can tackle it. There are too many drawbacks, circumstances to which I do not wish to subject you."

Gerda opened her mouth, but Gran spoke first. "I tell you, in that barbaric land you will encounter only trouble and all manner of grief. I counsel you and your husband to remain here, and with your good Dutch thrift change the slothful ways of your slaves, make of these possessions a profit that any man would envy."

Abruptly Gerda jerked her head up. "What nonsense are you talking, the pair of you? What ails you? Advising that we abandon our long-contrived plans, after Yarbrough and I have lost a year apart? Fiddlesticks! You sound like two old crones." So she sat facing them, implacable.

Gran pulled his beard hopelessly. Yarbrough lifted his shoulders in a shrug, then let them fall. "Gerda," he said in a flat tone, "we are only trying to do our best, but I'll leave it up to you. Only think well, for I do believe with all my heart that you will be happier here."

She set her mouth. "We'll not stay here and rot, and have you turned from your purpose. As for me, I've always before been able to carry the burden of any child."

Gran heaved a windy sigh. Yarbrough mashed his palms against his temples as usual when wearied out. "Very well," he said. "The die is cast."

Still, somehow, there was no taste of victory for Gerda in his words.

CHAPTER NINE

THE PACKING was a hard, heart-wrenching task. Most of their wagon train would be needed to transport necessities like farming implements, cottonseed, food supplies, and small stock which they could not obtain for years to come in the new country. This meant they had to limit themselves to the most helpful pieces of furniture and a very few of their precious treasures.

The children for the most part could be easily persuaded to abandon anything too awkward. Bruff was quite happy at being allowed the rope swing that hung from the beech tree, but Lucinda was upset because she could not take the summer house where she and little black Pinky played paper dolls. Gerda pacified her by suggesting that she personally carry her dominecker hen in a basket. Gracey was the most troublesome, being insistent on packing all her party clothes. When Yarbrough remarked that she would have little use for ball gowns in the wilderness and might as well divide most of them among her cousins staying here, she flew into a great pet. She'd go without a stick of her furniture, she said, except her looking-glass, but she'd be switched if she'd toss away her pretty frocks in such fashion. Yarbrough told her levelly then that she could take whatever would fit into one trunk, but that more velvet and satin than that she would have to forgo.

Miz Lisbeth, strange to say, made no fuss whatever about leaving behind things she had loved and lived among for fifty years. She said simply: "They would look odd any place else and make me feel bad seeing them setting around every which way. But I would like to take my bed if it's not too much bother. I wouldn't sleep well in any other."

"You certainly can!" declared Yarbrough. "We can take one bedstead easily, and many feather tickings, also some of the tables and chests of drawers. Don't you want to help pick them out?"

"No, son, let Gerda do that. I'd like to take my best black silk, though I'm not counting on traipsing to as many parties as Gracey," she snickered. "Gerda knows what I want that for, to look right in my coffin. Then there's one more thing, my crystal candelabra. It's an awfully spraddly old thing, though, so I don't know whether I ought."

"Spraddly nothing!" cried Gerda. "It certainly shall go, and I'll wad it about with cotton to keep the pendants from breaking."

"Oh, those can be unhooked," explained Miz Lisbeth happily. And that was all she seemed concerned about, though in the few days that were left she went about touching old possessions gently.

They set out on a July morning. Yarbrough and Willy were at the nead, Yarbrough on his big stallion, Willy on a nervous mare. Close behind in the gig Gran and Ven followed, with a pillow apiece for the crick in their backs. The women and some of the children were in a great pudding-shaped carriage, where Gerda was nursing the youngest child and Miz Lisbeth nursing a slip of the red rose brought over from England. The older woman's faded eyes were looking back at the Home Place, at the gardens that would now run to seed and the ground holding her husband's grave. She was wondering if William would be angry with her for leaving him in this outlandish way. Gerda's mind, on the other hand, was pressing forward to the new adventure. She nudged Lucinda happily. "Isn't this fun?" she asked, and Lucinda bounced up and down joyously.

Behind the carriage came several wagons carrying Pokey and the other children, the house servants, and some husky women able to chop cotton. Next there was a dearborn, a sort of ambulance for the very aged and ailing negroes. Then came the loads of home furnishings. And after that the field-hands on mules and afoot, laughing and groaning and squabbling. Thus the Whetstones moved in a cavalcade, full strength towards Alabama, the stallion in the lead, the children's pony and the farm stock in the rear. Wagons full of white children and black slaves, feather beds, mahogany dressers, fans, peach preserves, seed corn, salt pork, and silver waiters. The belongings of a family of gentlefolk who would soon be seasoned by wind and rain and wildness into the tough grain of pioneers.

2

At first there was a feeling of a fête day in the carriage on the part of the twins. They could gaze out the side windows; they could demand that their mother have Ruben halt the carriage and hitch on the side steps to let them climb down after a drink of water; they could ask questions about the Indians, still far off. And best of all they were going somewhere!

Presently, however, the monotonous rolling, rolling, rolling began to wear on them. The woods still looked the same, like those back home, and their legs felt full of needles and pins, while Cousin Gracey flounced about, taking up more than her share of space. 'Bruff pushed her over with his elbow once and was slapped for that.

Then Miz Lisbeth began to talk to herself, as she often did in her own room, but it sounded funny out here, for she was not pretending she meant to speak to any of them. She commenced: "Dear me, can't remember if I pulled the west windows down . . . the rain'll ruin the Chesterfield sure tee-wydee . . . don't reckon it makes much difference . . . though Andrew might sell some of that stuff for us yet. . . ." She mumbled a little lower, then her voice picked up fresh volume: "Yes, that's the way 'twas, Andrew didn't mean to marry Eva . . . the porch was dark and he thought it was Nannie he was kissing . . . but if Andrew only knew, he got the best end of it anyhow . . . Nannie was as flat as a bed slat and had to pad. . . ." Miz Lisbeth laughed out loud at her own good company.

"Well, my William didn't know beforehand that I had to sleep with my head under a pillow either . . . to keep from being scared of the dark. . . . He used to get fit to be tied, arguing: 'It's dark under there too, ain't it?' But I'd say: 'I can't *see* that it's dark, though.' Then he'd curse the air blue. 'It's worse than sleeping with a corpse,' he'd declare. . . ." Miz Lisbeth droned on and on, oblivious of the others. She nodded and smiled to herself, or interrupted herself from time to time with a correction of her own reminiscences, while the carriage rolled and rolled, and still rolled on to her droning.

Presently the children lost track of what she was saying. They fidgeted and fussed. Yet *mumble, mumble, murmur,* Miz Lisbeth's voice continued, like water dripping in the spring-house, until Gerda thought she'd scream. She and Gracey eyed each other helplessly, wondering why they had not stopped the old lady in the first place. Now they were too embarrassed by her disclosures to speak up.

Then suddenly Bruff plucked a feather from Lucinda's dominecker hen, making it squawk, and Gerda's temper burst out gladly. "You little rascal, you'll be sorry for that!" Signalling Ruben to stop, she clambered out with Bruff. "Now, sir! You can just pick me a switch from that bush there, and I'll attend to you!"

She laid the whip on with a will, and he danced and yowled, though it did not really hurt much. He was simply glad to jump up and down freely. After Gerda had finished she mussed his hair affectionately and their impudent eyes crackled at each other. "For the Lord's sake," she whispered like a conspirator, "let's ask Miz Lisbeth questions as fast as she says a word after this. Then she can t swamp us in such a flow of talk again."

"Yes, ma'am. She's sure like an old mosquito buzzing."

Back inside they found Miz Lisbeth was now passing candied orange peel about, and soon every one was in high feather.

Off and on, though, for days, they had to take turns stopping her private monologue. Gracey grew to be the best at it, for she learned how to take the old lady's hand and by rubbing it gently from wrist to palm, over and over, soothe her into a doze. But when that happened, things were so dead quiet that the children thought the time would never end.

Weeks later, by the time they had entered northern Georgia, the children had taken to staying mostly in the wagon with Pokey. There they could have piccaninnies to play games with them and Pokey to tell them weird stories; though Aunty Pheaby, the cook, rebuked Pokey: "De Lawd's gwine to strike you dead some day, talkin' about conjures like dey wuz de Gospel."

"No, He won't," Pokey said easily, "'cause I soak my rat-tail charm in baptizin' water before I wear it to preachin'. Hi-yah!" She suddenly pointed back to the end of their train. "Look there! That's a wench-wagon, I'll be bound."

"A wench-wagon!" all the darkies took up the cry, and some of the bucks began to walk at a prance.

The wagon was drawn by a team of mules driven by a negro wearing an air of authority. Beside the team walked five wenches, and underneath covers in the wagon were stowed a lot of bastard piccaninnies belonging to the wenches. Their master was evidently banishing the women for bearing children outside the general plantation rule of monogamy. As usual they were on the look-out for courting, hoping they could take up with some buck along the way, and be bought by his master before ever reaching the slave market for which they were bound.

The wagon slacked into place just ahead of the Whetstone stock, but decently behind the dearborn. "Tryin' to keep out of sight for their carryin' on," observed Pokey, and all the negro women from the Home Place cast their eyes around to make sure of where their men were. Two of the strange wenches came sauntering up to the house servants' conveyance. One of them in spite of her work-gnarled feet was a pretty thing, with a shiny copper look and a slow smile without any sass to it. The other was a jibbery monkey who asked pertly: "Does y'all get meat twicet a week?"

"Twicet a day," Pokey told her, and the gal's mouth watered, but she declared: "You lies."

Pokey didn't stoop to answer this; she simply helped herself to a dip of her store-bought snuff.

"My gums is itchin' fo' some ob that," whined the monkey-face.

"Scratch 'em," advised Pokey, putting her box away calmly.

This exile, Lyddy, instantly rolled her eyes wildly. "Bettah give me snuff to stop my devil in me!" She gave a jerky motion with her half-raised hands, shucking her feet forward in a voodoo stir-step. The twins gawped.

"Marm," said the other strange negro girl in a soft Charleston accent, "I'd be pleased to walk the chillun a little piece forward to rest they legs."

"I'd be much obliged," agreed Pokey. "What's yo' name? Lessy? Well, Lessy," she leaned over and murmured softly, "see that spry brown boy walkin' beside the saddled mule? That's the master's body servant, an' he ain't tied to no woman. His name's Patt. Tell him Pokey sent you an' for him to help you entertain the chillun a spell, while we're goin' slow as a snail like this."

Half-way through the afternoon the cavalcade had to pitch a "stuck camp." This happened every now and then when the roads became too bad. To-day for hours Yarbrough had been having boys walk along behind the wheels, scraping the mud off with paddles. Twice the carriage had been mired and required half an hour to be hauled out. Now the dearborn was in too deep to be pulled out by animals already winded, so it seemed best to stop for the night.

While they were drawing the other vehicles off the road, Yarbrough eyed his creatures critically. "Do you notice," he asked Gerda, "that the hair has been worn off their legs by the mud, as smooth as if it had been shaved with a razor?"

"So it has," she agreed, "and Willy's mare looks very fretted from it. Better tell him to have his boy soothe her with some liniment."

The camp was springing up quickly. Already the tents that the ladies and children would sleep in were pitched, and Miz Lisbeth had been prevailed upon to lie down in one for a rest. A trestle had been set up and Pokey was spreading a white tablecloth on it, while Aunty Pheaby was cooking a bigger meal than usual. The occupants of the wench-wagon kept hanging around trying to be useful, in hopes of having a taste later of good victuals.

Yarbrough had gone down the stream to see if he could catch a good fry of fish. Gracey and Lucinda were poking about among the clumps of wild flowers after a bouquet for the "table," while Bruff was watching the motley procession of equipages that detoured around their mired dearborn. No planter went by with a carriage, but everything else did: Jersey wagons, buggies, horseback riders, and ox-carts. Then suddenly he called out excitedly: "Looka there, looka there!" causing his twin and Gracey to come hurrying up.

In truth it was the queerest turn-out of all the queer ones they had seen along the road. It was a sort of "brush sled." Two long sapling poles had been hitched at one end to the harness of a mule, while the other ends were left trailing on the ground. Across the poles had been woven pieces of brush, then the owner's goods loaded on top and tied to it. The owner himself, a toothless old codger, was ambling along beside it crying: "Giddy-ap, you son of Satan!" to the moth-eaten animal that looked as if it had never had any hell-fire in it in all its life.

Bruff and the girls burst into derisive laughter, but the man babbled on, in a good-natured, simple-minded singsong: "On my way to Mississippi—to git me niggers—where cotton grows in bolls—bigger than your fist—goin' to set in shade—an' watch cotton bust out—an' niggers sweat. Ain't never goin' turn my hand—to a Lord's blessed *thi-ing*—all the rest of my *da-ays*!"

"Shake, pardner," said Ven, who had come up from behind.

"Giddy-ap, you son of Satan," shrilled the man again, and the "sled" creaked uncertainly ahead. They all watched the outfit except Bruff, who had gone running off with a shout and a handspring. But just before the old man reached the bend of the road Bruff overtook him, panting. "Here's a measure of oats," he said, and the man took off his tattered hat to put the parcel in its crown for safe-keeping. "Thankee for the fodder."

"And I brought you a snack for yourself," added Bruff, "but hold it careful, for there's a half-pint cup of Uncle Ven's whisky in it. Drink it careful too, or it'll fry your gizzard."

The old fellow winked in a comradely way at six-year-old Bruff, who watched him out of sight, standing with his legs spread wide apart like his father's. "Jee-rusalem!" Bruff announced, proud of himself, and spat largely.

Pokey, coming to call him to supper, spoke sharply. "You know better than to ack like trash even in the woods."

"Aw, pshaw!" he replied brashly. "I'm a pioneer now."

The table gleamed very white in the dying light beneath the trees, and Gracey's flowers nestled in a bright splash at the centre. Miz Lisbeth asked the blessing, with birds making a silvery interruption. The pepper-hash went around in dishes served carefully. Little Lucinda looked up past the tree boughs as was her wont, to make a wish on the first star in the sky. Then two darkies came to hold light-wood splinter torches for them to see by, as the dusk thickened and the mysterious sounds of the wilderness increased outside their family circle.

That night the darkies were very gay, because of the addition of new company from the wench-wagon. The banjos twanged all hours, and there was the slap-slap of palms marking time for the dancers. Yarbrough remarked to Gerda: "We have a faithful lot. I never even think that some of them might run away while we're on the march."

"No," she agreed, "I'd as soon expect it of one of our children. In fact I would sooner expect Bruff or Lucinda to do so," she laughed.

3

The weeks now totalled two months since they had started the journey, which Yarbrough had taken slowly for Gerda's sake. Wherever they could, he had put up at some planter's home. At such times Gerda had been glad enough to lie on a wide smooth bed in a dim room, with the gentle sounds of a household filtering up to her, the shutting of a door or the sweep of a broom.

As they travelled farther down across the state of Georgia, after leaving Macon, Yarbrough began to point out the cruder differences in the newer homes. A stateliness was gone from their structure, yet the bare, unpainted boards looked cool, and plainer clothes felt right. The slacker manners, too, made them feel more at home than could any lavish hospitality.

One day during one of their stops Gerda, walking through the breeze-swept open centre hall that held the two halves of a saddle-bag house together, hoped that they might have one like it before long. Sitting down in the shade of the airy back porch that connected the dining-room with the house, she offered to help the mistress with her churning. "No," replied the other easily, "just rest yourself, child, and why don't you take your shoes off, to let that swelling out of your feet?"

Gratefully Gerda complied, for the added weight of child was growing uncomfortable. As she sat there rubbing the puffiness out of her ankles, seeing the wide shallow pans of milk that would be skimmed for cream, and the field pease waiting to be shelled, she felt that this hour was good and plain. It seemed to forecast for her the pattern that her days and ways would follow in Alabama.

4

From the moment they crossed the river into Alabama there was something about being in the Indian country that held the children spellbound. When they stopped at Yufala, the first real tribal settlement, they felt a pleased apprehension at the sight of warriors, with their heads shaved except for a bristly coxcomb down the centre.

Naturally, since he was feeling scary, Bruff did not mean to fight with the Indian boy, but the child had tried to steal Bruff's ground peanuts when he spilled them in the dirt, so there was nothing else to do but haul off and hit. It might have wound up in trouble for all had not Yarbrough make quick amends. When Gerda heard about Bruff's fight she but sighed tiredly, too weary to punish him. South Carolina and her old cocksure vigour seemed almost forgotten in the dim past, and the stretch of Creek country still ahead of them was something to toil through, by the skin of her teeth.

In the last hour before their arrival a storm was coming up. The great trees wrenched in their branches, there was a green light between earth and sky, and Gerda smelled danger. She was desperate with a dry fatigue, yet she could tell no one, for Yarbrough had gone into a deepening silence and Gran huddled, brooding. There was no lifting of spirits such as one might expect upon nearing the end of a long, hard journey. "It's the storm," she thought, but took no comfort from that explanation.

Before the rain broke she caught her first glimpse of the new "Whetstone plantation." It was a scattering of crude log huts in a stump-encircled clearing. Gerda descended awkwardly from the carriage and looked about. The bark, still on the brown logs, brought back the picture of an old afternoon hour belonging to the child who had once been happy in a hut by a Dutch oven.

Then the door of a cabin swung open, and Guy came hurrying forward to greet them, with Marta loitering after, carrying a baby under a year old in her arms. Guy cried out: "So you all are here at last!" People milled together, then eddied apart, until Gerda could see Marta clear—and the baby.

Gerda looked hard at the child, saw its Whetstone features one by one, and met its sharp dark eyes, which were Yarbrough's own. Then, turning abruptly, she cut short the look of guilt passing from Yarbrough to Marta. "It's his," Gerda thought numbly; "so *that* is the outcome of our year apart?"

She knew now why Gran had wanted to keep her away from Alabama. "But that would not have helped," she told herself wearily; "the thing was done. Moreover I could not let Yarbrough go back on this Alabama enterprise." She motioned Pokey to come with her, as slowly she went to her cabin without a word of any sort. Once inside she simply stood there, trapped in her own pregnant body. She turned one of her hands over and over, backward and forward, and back again, staring at its shape, yet not knowing what she saw. She could not call this pain. It was being filled up with something cold and solid. She knew not what to call it, because it was—nothing.

She let her hand drop.

Pokey touched her carefully. "They's waitin' supper."

Gerda tossed her bonnet aside and shoved her hair back behind her ears. She walked with even steps out, then across into the dinner cabin. At the foot of the trestle table she took her place opposite Yarbrough. And for the first time she, instead of Miz Lisbeth, raised her voice to ask the grace: "Accept our thanks, O Heavenly Father, for these and all Thy blessings." Then she began helping those at table to hominy grits.

CHAPTER TEN

Gerda was tired and found herself falling to sleep early in spite of her trouble. Just before she dropped off, her mind took in gratefully the up-flicker of the firelight on the cabin wall, the rain-fresh smell of bark. She stirred slightly to give her limbs one last comforting feel of the coarse homespun sheets. A firefly darted in at her window and circled like a spark. Well, she sighed, they were here, at last! Nothing else mattered much.

When she woke it was daybreak and she had slept the night through.

From under the dull blow of the night before, her spirits lifted again. Dressing quickly, she unbarred the door. When it swung open a fresh wind came in on her face. She stepped out. Everything was under a hush. Not another door in the cluster of cabins was open, for they were letting the travellers have their rest out. Not even the stock scuffed in their stall-pens as yet.

She made her way through the stumps towards a higher hummock of ground, overgrown with some sort of vine. It gave on a little gap between tall pine trees, where she stood filling her lungs. The leaves of the vine were coated with dew, making it shimmer like frost, and some berries were picked out bright against it here and there. The trees around were big-girthed, and shot high into the air. In the gap the sky showed white with the day that was waiting behind it. And the morning star hung very big and clear, about to set.

Gerda thought: "There's something free and new here, and this will be more *my* land because I helped to start it." The Home Place had already been shaped by other hands. It was only a trust, loaned to her for a short space. This would be hers, as much of it as she could put her mark upon.

She thought further: "I will have to take care of that matter of Marta's child. Still, that's only one thing. There are many things that I will have to look after, if we are to survive here, and many years to plan for. No one thing must use up more than its fair share of me. I must learn to proportion myself instead of depending always upon my vigour." Turning her steps down from the hummock, she was somehow not oppressed. This was a beginning!

The smoke was curling up in a blue twist from the kitchen chimney as she drew near the enclosure, where children were calling out and running about, eager with hunger.

2

It was right after breakfast that Yarbrough followed Gerda to a quiet place in the clearing. He said: "I want to try to tell you how it was."

But she said: "Don't, Yarbrough. I don't want any—any *notions* put into my mind, to fasten on. To turn over and over."

"But it was so everlasting lonely!" he burst out.

"Yes," she said steadily, "I know how lonely it was. I was lucky to have our house and everything in it to hold me true while you——"

He did not speak up to her. He did not say any of the things he might have said, about not being himself, or being strayed 'way off in a strange land. She waited long enough to give him a good chance to make any excuses that might ease his situation, but he kept quiet, only his face looked worn with regret. She laid her hand on his upper arm and smoothed it abstractedly. "You won't mind if I do what I see fit about—her?" she asked.

"No, you go ahead," he replied, granting her justice.

They stood a moment.

"Gerda," he said, "I've been wanting to tell you about it so long. You do believe it was mostly for your sake I didn't speak?"

She nodded. "You mustn't take it too hard now, though. It won't help us any. Oh—I must——" she broke off a second, then went on: "I must grow a little used to it before I get over it. But we——" She stopped. She didn't know how to say things about their marriage lasting for ever, so she finished: "We'll work it out somehow, you can depend on that!"

"I don't feel like a very fine fellow," he said bitterly. As she went away from him it was not with a heavy step, and she looked back to wave her hand before she lifted the latch of her cabin.

3

Directly she sent Pokey to summon Marta; then when Marta came, she faced her squarely. She would have no mercy on her own feelings or on Marta's. The other woman was looking defiant as Gerda said calmly: "Sit down while I settle this business." Marta saw then there was no use pretending.

Gerda looked out of the window for a moment, pondering over just the right way to put it. Then she turned and spoke: "I am to have the last say in this matter, because nobody paid any attention to my side of it before. I'm not preaching. A man's a man and his flesh gets the better of him sometimes. So too does a woman's. Well, all that junketing is over now. I am here to be a wife to my husband and to help him make a start. We'll have our hands full. There's nothing here for you except the hard lot of a woman with no settled standing. Up north maybe there might be another woodsman for you; and——" she paused, then continued: "he wouldn't have to know about this. You would stand a chance of marrying."

"But the child would give my secret away," objected Marta.

Gerda drew a good breath. "The child does not go. The child is a Whetstone and stays to be reared in his father's house." She saw the relief in Marta's face before the other had time to hide it.

"We-ell, I don't know——" began Marta, though Gerda knew that she was merely using cunning to be bribed the more dearly for giving up the child. Gerda had already seen there was no love between Marta and her offspring, that the woman seemed to consider it but an ill break after carefree indulgence. Aware of this, Gerda started to say something sharp, then held her tongue.

Presently she spoke slowly instead: "I think I shall call him Hans. I have never overcome feeling a pity for you about your betrothed, Hans. Also I will see to it that we spare you something for a dower, which I hope will help you to a match. I know another woodsman would not be a Hans to you. But then, you can make the best of it. Most of us have to, at some time or other before we're done." She stopped short. She had no wish to share with Marta, of all people, her thoughts about the makeshift measures required by even the best of marriages. Yet still it struck her that she had never felt a tide between man and woman resembling the pull that surged between her and Yarbrough except perhaps that she had once sensed while watching Marta and Hans together. She, for one, owed a fidelity to its power simply because of its strong influence upon her own full-passioned love of Yarbrough.

Marta might not be much of a woman, was feckless and lumpish. However, Gerda granted, Marta had had to " make things do " for six dreary years in an alien land; therefore Gerda promised again: " We will do our best for you," feeling that that best was very little.

They rose and walked together towards the door. There Marta looked at Gerda quickly. " You have been more patient with me than most women would. That I know for a fact." Then she hurried out of the cabin.

4

This first day had been an eventful one, much like a holiday, all told. Guy Hampley had shown Gerda and the twins over the place, explaining each strange pioneer method. They learned that though the work animals were kept in railed enclosures, the cattle and hogs were turned loose to fatten in the forest; and every few weeks one of them was driven up and killed for fresh meat, which the settlers shared with neighbours who had befriended them. When Gerda questioned the fact that no cotton had been planted this year, that all the cleared fields had been planted in corn, Guy explained: " Have to have corn the first years to live on. There's no grist-mill near, but Chokho has showed us how to pound meal by hand, finer than grits." Chokho was the friendly Indian squaw who helped Marta with the kitchen work.

At this reply Gerda murmured thoughtfully: " I can see where I have to learn a lot all over again down here, about how to keep a household."

" Yes, ma'am," Guy assured her, " and every time you turn around you'll find there's something else you had to leave back home that you would give your eye-teeth for. But you'll fix up something to take its place every time."

They were at this moment looking down into the tan-yard branch, where layers of hides were placed between layers of red oak leaves, soaking. They would make hats and clothes as well as shoes out of this home-tanned product, Guy informed them. Bruff instantly asked for a leather hat, and Lucinda stood perplexed, trying to think of something leathern she could demand. Yet she most certainly did not want shoes, for she had already made up her mind to run barefoot like Bruff and the little nigs. "Bet we don't have to dress for the afternoon hardly ever down here," she whispered to Bruff gleefully.

That evening all the women and children except Gracey congregated in the kitchen. The kitchen was a cabin at some distance from the others, connected by a plank wall with the dining-hall. There were no built-in brick ovens, only a tin one to place over the coals in the fireplace, and the baked fare it produced was often coarse and crude. Miz Lisbeth worked gingerly at her gums with her fingertips and thought what she would give if only she could have some fine white light bread once more.

Gerda was watching the squaw, Chokho, who did not like to dip into the winter's supply of ready-ground meal; she was pounding young gathered corn into sweet meal. Gerda was approving this thrift, and Aunty Pheaby was glowering at it. "I ain't nevah had to skimp along in no such po' folksy way befo'," she muttered. Her scorn was increased when she heard that even the white folks were going to have to make out with molasses in their coffee every day but Sunday. "Den how they goin' tell themselves from trash, ef'n they go usin' long sweetnin' like niggahs?" Yet here everybody else was, smiling and carrying on as if it were Christmas or crop barbecue doin's. Taking on over hearing they'd get bear's meat to eat some day. But she wasn't going to eat any such heathen flesh, if she had to feed on grits to her grave. She crept over and sat close beside Miz Lisbeth for comfort. Miz Lisbeth leaned down and whispered: "Kinder turns my stomach talking about eating bear's meat. But maybe you don't mind, I was told your granny was a cannibal."

"Don't say any such!" begged Aunty Pheaby, rolling her eyes.

The smells in the kitchen began to reek richly. The hams of the forest-fed shoats had been cured sweet, the cows here gave good butter, the Indian pudding was bubbling thickly under its browning crust. Gerda watched Chokho's immovable face and listened carefully to the low monosyllables she spoke as she used a spoon and a long one-tined fork. Pokey sat holding little Hans, while keeping the other children quiet. Marta lounged over a corner of the trestle-board, staring dreamily at the steam from the tea-kettle. Once she chuckled: "I heard Miss Gracey threw fits because she couldn't cart all her ball gowns down here." Gerda grinned back. "I dare say she'll find somewhere to wear them, if it's only to an Indian war-dance."

"Ssh," warned Miz Lisbeth, "be careful what you say before that redskin Chokho."

"Aw, she's only a Methodist," put in little Lucinda witheringly.

5

That night Gerda took time to examine how her cabin was made. It had puncheon floors, merely split logs with the flat sides turned up. The walls were of logs notched at the ends to join the corners together; the doors were nailed with wooden pins. There were solid board shutters that opened out at her windows, and the air coming in was clean with pine smell.

Pokey was helping her to undress. Gerda sat on the side of her bunk, plaiting her hair into a long heavy braid. "I'm going to like this country," she told Pokey, nodding her head. "But all the same, I'm glad it's to-night—instead of *last* night."

"I should hope you would be!" snapped Pokey. She didn't see why that gal Marta hadn't had her head busted open, didn't know what ailed Miss Gerda acting so milk-watery kind.

Gerda went over to look out the open window at the night, the way she did whenever she had liked the day just gone by. Some twigs crunched under a footstep. Yarbrough's voice spoke out of the shadow. "I came to tell you good-night. Do you feel all right?"

"Yes," she said, and laid her face against his cheek. It scraped hers, dearly.

6

A week later they heard of a wagon train leaving Columbus, Georgia, for the North, and it was decided that Marta should join it there and travel homeward to New York. Gerda had an idea in her head concerning Yarbrough, but she scarcely knew how to put it to him. He himself, however, came up to her and broached it: "Some one of our menfolks has to go with Marta to see her over that first dangerous lap of her journey. I was wondering if you would mind if I did that."

"I think you ought," she replied briefly.

"That's what I thought," he told her, relieved, and went out.

Pokey, who had been sorting clothes in the corner, looked up and said sharply: "That's foolishness!"

"No," said Gerda slowly, "it's only good sense."

"You means that ef he's still hankerin' after that gal, he'll get over it sent along with her, free as air?"

"Well, I do believe it's best to give a man enough rope, instead of tethering him so close to your side, if he wants to be footloose. Because then he'd only turn his grudge upon you for making him feel hobbled. Yet no, that was not the main thing I was considering." She stared at the shawl she was folding. "I just think he ought to do that much for Marta. It's only decent."

"Lawd save us!" ejaculated Pokey. "Now you do sound crazy! I tell you that hulk of a female ain't nothin' more than a roll in the brush."

"You're right, generally speaking," agreed Gerda quietly, "but she's a charge of ours. And I expect she's a human after all." She turned and walked away to close the subject.

The day Marta set off under Yarbrough's escort, with Gran going as far as Yufala with them, Gerda said to her: "I promise you I will take good care of little Hans. Better care than if he were my own."

"I know that," Marta answered, touching the child's hair with a sudden clumsy kindness. "He has been never much trouble," she finished.

The last Gerda saw of her she was staring too straight ahead to see the child again. Gerda started to run after her down the trail and hold her baby out to her to take. But Gerda did not follow her impulse. "I know the little thing is better off here," she told herself tiredly, "with its father."

7

During the night she felt very ill and sensed that something was amiss about that child of her own that she was carrying. Twice on the journey down she had all but lost it, and now she thought: "I feel I'll not bring this one to term." She lay awake, watching her own symptoms during the tedious drag of the hours, until, when day came, she called to Pokey: "Wake up, Pokey. We have something to do."

"I'se awake, Miss Gerda. I've been listenin' to you near 'bout all night. What you want?"

Gerda raised herself up carefully to put her feet over the edge of the bunk. "Something's gone wrong with this child! I can't carry it to its time. I don't want to be caught suddenly, so I want you to bring on labour. To-day."

"Miss Gerda, child! Not with Marse Yarbrough gone 'way for two weeks!"

Gerda answered slowly. "That's one reason—I want to get it over with. After Marta, it seems—as if I must endure this—by myself," she panted.

"We-ell, I don't blame you fo' not wantin' to take a favour from him," agreed Pokey.

Gerda made no answer until she caught breath enough between those early pains to say. "Now, Pokey, you go see to the children's eating their breakfast, while I take my time about cleaning up."

There was a ewer of water on a shelf by the wall and a dish of soap. She stripped off her nightdress and made a lather. As she scrubbed her body she took stock of it. For all her five children, it had been left fine and vigorous. Her bones were strong and well joined, the flesh lay on them cleanly, and she walked well and swingingly, so that even now smooth muscles held her shapely. She thought: "I've a good body. I don't want it to be ruined." She placed her hands on the swell of her belly, as if to shield it. The morning was bright outside. She wondered if she would see the night.

Presently Pokey brought her some milk, which she drank, though she had no taste for it. Next Pokey said: "I'm preparin' to make that brew now, and I 'spose you got the medicine chest heah, ain't you? With the quinine and castor oil?"

"Yes," said Gerda, measuring the first dose of the quinine.

Then she moved about, putting the cabin in order, spreading fresh sheets.

Two hours later Pokey went to work on her. One minute Gerda

was thinking: "I could stop her now, let Nature take her course, which might turn out—all right. I could stop her——" The next minute she was thinking, "Maybe—I've had myself slain, but it's too late now. We can only go ahead." A lightness took hold of her head that had nothing to do with the quinine.

Then it became nightfall, and still there were only light, nagging pains, no true labour. She had been able to get up and go to the supper table, to sit there talking, though she had eaten little. Then at last there was nothing to do but go to bed and wait for a delivery that did not come.

"Call me the first instant you needs me," Pokey cautioned her. "If I sleep a-tall it'll be with one eye open."

Occasionally Gerda dozed for a minute fitfully, only to be startled awake almost instantly. After a long while morning came. Then Pokey helped her over to wash her face and pretended that act was important. She did not ask about the pains now, for she could see they were not amounting to much.

The two went to the breakfast cabin, where Gerda had some coffee with white sugar, and Gracey twitted: "My, my, I thought we weren't any of us to be pampered." At which Miz Lisbeth said: "You *are* a trial, Gracey. Gerda, has it come on you?"

"Near 'bout," answered Gerda briefly, and Gracey flushed at her unintended rudeness.

After breakfast Pokey said: "I expect you better walk some. I'll come along beside you." After Gerda put on the easiest shoes she owned, Pokey took her arm to guide her. They found it was not over hot in the forest, where there were wide spaces between the tree-trunks, also a creek making a cool noise. Gerda thought: "It's pretty here. I'd hate to leave it, but I guess I'm in for it now, sure enough."

They trudged a long way, and when they neared their settlement again she told Pokey: "I think that did some good, stirred it up. But we had better ask Gran to help now, if he's back from Yufala."

"Yes'm," groaned Pokey, "an' he's goin' to blame me somethin' awful. I ought to've known better than to trifle with child-bearin'. If there was only some way to hold out without tellin' him!"

"Get him! And tell him *I'm* to blame!" Gerda managed to say through tight lips. "Only get him!" What did blame matter now when she might die! Providentially they came upon Gran immediately outside the forest. Gerda had to take hold of his hand and hang on for a moment, while she bent double. After that he picked her up and carried her the rest of the way. She was drenched with sweat when he laid her upon her bed. The sheets were comforting.

Pokey had mumbled the story in Gran's ear. Now he spoke sorrowfully: "Gerda, you would try to bend all things to your will, but the world is too old and large for your young hands."

Gerda did not hear what else he said. She was thinking how she wanted this world. To be in it! Wondering if she could have her way about only that *one* thing.

The rest of that day the pains came regularly, and she worked them hard, but after a few hours she made no further progress. Pokey tried to keep busy, to make it seem that there was something else she could do for Gerda, but Gran simply sat with his big old hands clasped, regarding them as if he expected no help from them. Once he said, more to himself than to Gerda: "I had thought that something would come like this, one day. I had a fear all your life that I would lead you amiss. Give you your head too much, because I did not wish to see you bound down."

Gerda wondered then whether she would rather have been herself, unhindered as she had been for these few years, or a weakling spinning out a long thin thread. Now she knew only one thing was true: *she wanted to be alive!*

Looking out of her window she saw some of their negroes coming up from milking the cows. It reminded her that the chores would go on without her, and she recalled how the family had soon learned to laugh over Lucey's little whims after her death, instead of having their eyes water with tears.

The pains kept clutching, but that was all. They accomplished nothing. Gran said finally: "Soon I will try to turn the child in the womb. Perhaps that will move things to a finish." That prospect at least gave Gerda the relief of something to count upon, some action.

Now the lights were lit in the other cabins; people came up and made a clatter at the yard wash-basin, children laughed and shrilled between the kitchen and the dining-hall. Then presently things quieted down for the evening meal, and Pokey went to bring Gran food.

When Pokey returned she reported that the older children wanted to kiss their mother good-night. Gerda thought Miz Lisbeth had put them up to the notion, deeming it a farewell, and when they came and reached for her face she too felt it might be that. She loved the twins then more than ever before.

"Gracey's trying to make us mind her," complained Bruff. "Can we tell her not to pick on us?"

"Yes!" said Gerda fiercely. "And," she called after them as they scampered from her into the night, "tell Aunty Pheaby to give you each a piece of bread and butter with sugar."

Now Gran had finished his meal, and having washed his hands he flexed the big knuckles carefully. "These old joints are stiff." He tried to smile, to reassure her before he had to hurt her. But Gerda lay still and held the sides of her bunk while he twisted at the tiny body hidden beneath the walls of her belly. When Gran rose up again his face showed nothing. Had he still felt life in the child, Gerda wondered. She tried to read something into his blank expression, but she could not tell and dared not ask.

"Try to take some rest," was all he said.

They put a shield over the one candle left burning, and he huddled himself heavily in his chair, while Pokey lay down on a pallet beside Gerda's bed.

The opium he administered had now put a dimness over Gerda's mind. She dreamed things . . . that they were back in South Carolina . . . that she was not pregnant . . . that she was, but that the birth was going easily . . . that it was all over and Yarbrough was here holding the child aloft in his arms, crying: "What a fine fellow!" Then she woke—and it was not yet over. A queer dreadful pain was ripping away at her insides. She called out: "Gran!" and tried to bear down on the pain properly. But it seemed not to go that way.

Quickly both Gran and Pokey worked over her, and Gran was pleading: "If only you could push *some* part of the child down, for us to reach! *Och!* The shoulder is now here!"

Then "Yarbrough, Yarbrough!" she cried out, and went down into blackness, but thinking: "I won't give up to it, I won't let it swallow me! Not death!"

She did not know after that what happened to her next, except that she thought she kept spading back the blackness as fast as it tumbled down upon her. Then there seemed to be a blank.

After a bit of that she opened her eyes and saw that the candle had gone out, that it was another day, and Pokey and Gran were standing looking down at her carefully.

"I'm alive," she whispered. "Will I stay alive?"

"You must keep very quiet," Gran warned her.

She felt pain all over, but this pain did not move. It was simply there, and she did not have to fight it as long as it remained motionless. They need not be fearful that *she* would move and stir it up. She asked nothing about the baby. She did not want to hear. She could feel Gran and Pokey sitting quite still beside her. Then she forgot it was broad day, because the last she had known there had been more left of the night.

The next time she spoke it was twilight. She could tell that by the mixture of half-sounds outside the cabin. "I hurt," she murmured plaintively.

"Yes, *liefste*," Gran agreed. "But never fear."

"I'm hot," she added.

Yes, they knew that. They wanted her to drink herb tea. They wanted her to drink more tea. And they had her head and shoulders propped up on a queerly high slant. They watched her closely always.

That night she slept more, and without dreams that tired her. When she woke in the dark middle of the night they were there with another cup of tea. Later still, when she woke and lay wide-eyed, Gran gave her more opium. She slept a long time after that before she woke again. When she did she could feel that she had rested somewhat, though she still had a fever and one of them, usually both, stayed by her all the time. They seemed to be giving her tea always. She drank it down as she was told. She knew she would have to try hard, and keep on trying harder, to live, for her belly was distended as tight as a drum, bigger than when she had carried the child in it. And that was wrong.

Night came again. And the day, and the tea, and they watching.

Then one night her forehead felt cooler. And Gran, putting his hand upon it, brought his fingers away moist. "She sweats!" he cried out to Pokey.

Gerda fell into a cool peace.

When the day broke once again, the cabin no longer seemed like some strange place. The two chairs had their right shape and the open window-shutter was not a windmill after all. Then she ventured to ask : " Was it a boy?"

" A little gal," Pokey told her, with pitying mouth, knowing how few girls the Whetstones had.

Gerda turned to the wall, to shut off hearing any more.

That day went by as an Indian-summer day would, lazy and yellow and slow, with a powdery look to the sunbeams that slanted through the window. She went to sleep that night as a person usually does, thinking in snatches, wanting to drop off, jerking back at the verge, then finally sleeping.

The next morning Pokey brought her some mush and milk and good black coffee. " I'll be getting up before long," announced Gerda.

" Bettah go slow," advised Pokey.

" What day will your master be home?" asked Gerda.

" Not till next week anyways."

" I'll be up to welcome him."

Pokey said : " Finish up your mush."

Yet, true to her word, Gerda was propped up in a chair when Yarbrough arrived. Yesterday she had been so eager to rise, then later, feeling shaky, was glad to be back in bed within a few minutes. Pokey had set her mouth grimly after that foolhardy attempt.

Yet now to-day Gerda was again in a chair by the doorway where she could act natural towards Yarbrough when next she saw him. She knew that if he felt he had used her too ill he would be uncomfortable around her. And " If I make him fester, he'll grow to hate me." So when he came up the path and into her room she looked up cheerfully, and in fact her joy at having him back overcame any rancour.

He held her close a long while before he muttered a question about her health.

" I'm doing fine," she said, pulling free.

He glanced over at the bed where the child should have lain, though Pokey had already told him of their loss. Then he went and stood in the doorway with his back to Gerda, his eyes staring outside. His shoulders moved once, then he braced them. He came back to her and reached down for her hand, which he held gently. She gazed through the door at the evening stealing up through the woods. There was nothing that could stop her now from feeling glad to be alive. Not even a hurt to her love. She looked up at him and he saw how her face was not sorry. At that his eyes crinkled a little at the edges, in the way they were used to when wrinkling from his smiling.

"I'm glad to be home!" he told her.

8

The baby of course had been buried several weeks, by Gran and Pokey without any ceremony. But to-day Miz Lisbeth came to Gerda and said: "I have that slip off our red rambler rose to set out, and there's enough warm weather left for it to take hold. I'd like to put it over Elzivir's grave. I thought we might call her Elzivir after your mother, since she must have some name."

Gerda stopped at her task, but kept silent. Yarbrough put his hand down on the back of Gerda's chair to show her he was there.

Miz Lisbeth went on: "Willy prays right pretty; he could say a prayer at the planting. And the rose would make a start for a garden."

"Or a start for a burying-ground," thought Yarbrough, and dropped his hand heavily away from Gerda's chair.

However, they did as Miz Lisbeth suggested. They marched in a line up to the little knoll where the young holly bushes grew. The berries were still green on them, not turned to orange even. Miz Lisbeth handed the flower-pot over to Willy, who tucked the tiny slip into the ground. "There!" she said when she was satisfied with his work.

He stayed on his knees with the garden spade in his hand while he prayed. Gerda would not look, but stared away over Yarbrough's arm that held her. When Willy said "Amen" and rose awkwardly, Yarbrough stepped over and put his hand down on the little mound; then, drawing it back, he wiped his eyes roughly, leaving dirt stains.

They all trooped downhill again, mud caking the soles of their shoes. It was nothing at all like Lucey's funeral procession of carriages. It hurt more.

BOOK TWO

Pioneering

CHAPTER ELEVEN

ONE DAY in early March they were sitting as usual in the kitchen, where the biggest fire blazed. Gracey was working at her embroidery, yanking the needle so hard that she snarled the floss. Finally the thread broke, and she put her head down on her arms to sob.

"Why, honey, what ails you?" asked Miz Lisbeth mildly.

Gracey raised streamy eyes. "*Embroidering*—embroidering *flowers* on *silk* in a *kitchen*!" Her voice shrilled up beyond control. "It's not what I was cut out for."

Gerda, standing over a pot, turned and put a hand on her cousin's shoulder. "We ought not to have brought you down here away from all your friends. It is a poor place for a girl."

"I had to come with my family. I'd have worn out my welcome with the cousins, but"—she prodded her eyes to dry them—"but don't they *ever* have any entertainment down here? Any fun?"

"Fun!" cried Bruff. "Why, there's more than you can shake a stick at!"

"Hush!" commanded Gerda, as she stood puzzling over the question. "There doesn't appear to be much in the way of social entertainment here, but I was thinking, Gracey, suppose the next time the men go on a wolf-hunt we have supper here first, with some dancing. Would you like that?"

"Oh," exclaimed Gracey quickly, "and could we ask the ladies to wear party clothes? Most of them have some fine things packed away."

"Well," hesitated Gerda, "the men won't exactly want to dress up before going hunting."

But Ven, warming himself in a corner, spoke up. "What's the difference? Let the men come any old way, like the backwoodsmen did at Jackson's inaugural reception at the White House, eh, Gracey? 'Twon't be the first time this gel's had her ruffles trod on."

"That's it!" exclaimed Gracey, squeezing her hands together in excitement. "We won't pay any attention to the men's apparel, but the ladies will come in fashion. Then we'll spread the best damask cloth, trestle table or no trestle, and have out the candelabra!"

"Now I declare, I'm glad I brought that old thing," murmured Miz Lisbeth, pleased.

"Do I have to dress up too?" asked Lucinda.

"Shucks," said Bruff, "I don't, because I'm a man."

"You're not any such thing!" Lucinda disagreed. "You're only seven years old, the same as me."

"Ain't nobody said you chillun was comin' to the party," Pokey reminded them.

"A-aw," they wailed. "We can, can't we, Ma'am?" they demanded of Gerda, calling her by that title which took the place of "Mother" with them.

"Of course you can come," promised their cousin Gracey happily. "I wouldn't let you miss the treat for the world."

"It's the wolf-hunt that is the treat," said Bruff. "That's what I don't want to miss."

Gerda eyed her son. She was about to tell him that his father would have to settle that question, when Guy Hampley came in. He had grown heartier down here and walked like a man. Now he addressed Bruff: "You're just the fine fellow I'm lookin' for."

"What you want me for?" demanded Bruff suspiciously. They had a way of making him tote wood now so that they could use the little negroes for harder chores.

"Oh," drawled Guy, "I was wonderin' how you'd like to make a meal-trip with me, startin' to-morrow. Your father says he can spare you."

"A meal-trip? Jumping Jehoshaphat, wouldn't I just!" shouted Bruff, turning a somersault since there wasn't room for a handspring. "Now what do you think of me?" he demanded triumphantly of Lucinda.

"But a meal-trip," she retorted, "is no wolf-hunt by a long sight."

A meal-trip was made by some man in the community every month over to Fort Gaines, where the nearest grist-mill was. One man at a time would drive over in an ox-cart from the community, picking up a bag of grain apiece from each neighbour, and bringing back the ground meal. Taking turns this way kept the people pretty well supplied with meal. That was a good thing, since pounding the corn with a hand pestle as Chokho and other Indians did was a slow business, and for a big crowd like the Whetstones it hardly produced enough to go around. At the prospect of such a jaunt Bruff was whooping it up. He guessed Lucinda couldn't taunt him with not being a man now.

"But you'll miss the pedlar's cart," she reminded him. They had heard that the first pedlar's cart of the spring was on its way.

"Maybe we'll pass it." He dismissed that without a qualm.

Lucinda stood regarding him fixedly. Boys had the best of it down here . . . meal-trips, and maybe wolf-hunts. Well, she was going to learn how to do every single solitary thing Bruff did, just as good or better. She turned from staring at Bruff to look pityingly at Gracey, who was patting her curls. "La-de-da!" Lucinda suddenly mocked her young lady cousin, and turned a somersault too, not caring that it showed her pantalets.

"You like to've upset my churn," complained Pokey, but said nothing about a little lady not being supposed to behave that way.

Six days later when Bruff arrived back home from Fort Gaines, he was greeted by a victorious Lucinda announcing: "I killed a snake, Bruff!" A rattler coming out from its winter hole, that scared Ma'am blue!"

Glumly he tugged a bag of new meal up into his arms. "Get out of my way," he ordered, trying to restore his male authority after hearing with envy of her dangerous encounter.

2

The household had many a set-back preparing for Gracey's party. It was early for wild flowers, and though the twins and thirteen-year-old Ronald MacDuff, the first white child born in Turber County, combed the forests and climbed the trees after flowering vines, their plunder looked scanty after the profusion of the Home Place gardens. There was nothing to do but finish it out with festoons of Spanish moss.

On the day of the party, however, young Ronald brought over a cluster of narcissus from his mother's cherished plot. "They're for you to wear," he told Gracey shyly; "they would look pretty in your hair."

Considering him a child, she hugged him enthusiastically for thanks.

"You're a precious!" she told him, as he stood with his eyes on the ground, getting his breath back.

"That's little to do for you," he replied finally, then slipped away with a silent tread like the Indians he'd been born among. From a little distance she heard him whistling bird-calls.

Miz Lisbeth had seen to arraying the dining-cabin. The damask was creamy under the weight of silver plate, and the candelabra spread regally with its wasteful fill of candles, while Gracey had to admit that the Spanish moss hung gracefully. The cabin across, connected by a runway, had been cleared for dancing and also decked with forest spoils. Dimly lit, it had a faint air of romance with Miss Lucey's cherished harpsichord showing yellowed ivory keys in the gloom.

An hour before the appointed time for the arrivals Lucinda set up a howl. "Can I come barefoot? I cain't get my feet into my slippers!" Her feet had not only grown since the migration, but spread from going barefoot or wearing brogans.

Miz Lisbeth stood over her with compressed lips. "Squeeze!" she commanded her granddaughter. "A lady can get her foot into any shoe, no matter how small."

"No, I cain't, I cain't! Ouch, it hurts. Ma'am," she appealed to Gerda, "don't let them cripple me."

Gerda jerked off the kid instruments of torture. "After all, we aren't Chinese!" she flared impatiently at Miz Lisbeth, as she rubbed Lucinda's swollen toes.

Gracey flopped down in exasperation at this hitch. "I was an idiot to think we could have things go right. We might as well give up." But then she bounced up again and hurried to her sleeping-cabin, from which she returned dangling a pair of her own sandals. "Here! Have Densey use a leather-needle to take these up at the heels to fit Lucinda. Then she can wear them pretty as you please."

"Oh!" Lucinda was entranced at the idea of a grown lady's dancing-shoes. "Can I have them for keeps?" But Gracey was gone; she could stand no more fuss now.

The first part of the party was pure frolic. The men had had only one toddy or so, which loosened their tongues with compliments to the ladies turned out in their disused finery. Everybody voted Gracey the prettiest one there, and she thrived on their generosity, discarding her habitual vanity until people remarked: "Why, she's not so airy after all. She acts as plain as hoe-cake." Gradually, as the colourful crowd dissolved into familiar faces, Gracey saw that there was no gentleman there worth noticing. They were the same ones who had shared meat with them at hog-killing time, borrowed their tools, and were married to some woman who made good butter. Or else they were working hard to send back home for a girl called sweetheart.

Gracey had danced lightly enough at twilight when the party first gathered, she had returned the toasts happily over the pound cake and the raisins. Now, however, she was perfectly willing to take her turn at playing the harpsichord, for she had no desire to be twirled about any longer by men musty in old hunting clothes.

Also the men were already drawing together in restless groups, and no one of them called for another dance tune. Finally Daniel MacDuff, who was a man with a strong voice, spoke up. "Well, men, we'd better be getting along. We've tracked down the wolves' den, and John Screws'll get tired waitin' there all by himself."

A babble of masculine agreement went up. One group shambled toward Gerda, another towards Gracey, to mumble good-bye, calling back to their own womenfolk not to sit up for them. They would be out all night by a campfire waiting for wolves to prowl, drinking whisky until they feared nothing, shouting down echoes in the big pine timber.

Gracey spoke her piece to them prettily. Let them go! She cared not a fig for any of them. Yet when the last one was gone she turned towards the window to stare out rebelliously into space, only the window-panes were made of greased paper, stopping her gaze. She looked at an opaque blankness instead of a night sky.

A moment later Miz Lisbeth called: "Won't you play us something, Gracey? The ladies would enjoy a tune while they're knitting." Docilely Gracey went to oblige them. She played and she played and she played, a river of tinkling sound, while the ladies sipped party tea and the boy, Ronald, turned her sheets of music.

CHAPTER TWELVE

SUMMER CAME with a lush heat such as Gerda had never felt even in her first Southern summer at the Home Place. Here it was tropical. Their small clearing was shut in by a dense wall of forest that required chopping with an axe to penetrate any great distance. Pines, hickories, sweet gum, and water oaks rose to heights well over a hundred feet, with Spanish-moss ropes lacing together the top branches and underbrush, choking out all air below, making their shade stifling rather than cool. Gnats and mosquitoes swarmed so thickly that the children, coming back from exploring the edge of the woods, were bitten and swollen like grotesque puff-balls, and Pokey had to rub them with camphor grease to keep them from scratching themselves raw. All grew heartily weary of the long-drawn-out endlessness of summer.

The corn in such fields as had been cleared, however, throve in the simmer of sun and the fall of rain, shooting up to enormous green heights, heavy with well-filled ears. Corn was their main crop these first pioneering years. It was eaten green as a vegetable, dried for winter use, pounded into hominy, grounded into meal, used for bartering, depended upon heavily, and despised passionately by Gracey and Miz Lisbeth.

Oddly enough, the cotton for which they had made this migration from an old and well-established ease into a hazardous discomfort was relegated to a minor place for the time being. There were as yet no markets nearby and no means of hauling it in quantities to other places where its value could have been realized. Therefore at first each family raised only enough for its domestic use on the plantation. Having no cotton gins here, the lint had to be picked off tediously by hand from the seed, the children helping. The seed was dumped into ditches to put it out of the way. There it made woolly grey piles that Lucinda, Bruff and the other children could jump in as Gerda had once done in haystacks up north in New York. Gracey, watching the other women at work over the seed-plucking, sniffed to Gerda: "I suppose you think I ought to contract asthma helping?"

"No, I'm not such a fool as to count on any such thing from you," grunted Gerda, dumping another bushel basket over where Lucinda could reach it.

Lucinda had spry fingers that could almost equal the stint of the best of the negro women. She had, in fact, a knack for almost all of the crude inventiveness involved in the ways down here. To her it was like taking a dare, vying against exciting odds which Bruff tauntingly declared too great for her.

Somehow the long summer ended languidly, in a slower buzzing of flies, a faint blue smokiness rising from the ground because of a deep-hidden chill there, in the ripening of the sugar cane and the grinding out of its juice under the painful golden hum of a swarm of yellow jackets. Yes, the summer ended with the corn in bins, a shed raised over the stock-pens, and the cotton lint flying up the active Lucinda's nose till she sneezed. Then the rains set in, in dead red-clay earnest.

2

Pokey, rising in the cold dark of a fall morning, felt her bones creak slightly and thought: "I ain't as young as I was once. Wondah jest how old I am. Near 'bout forty, I reckon." Then she made sure the children were all tucked under the warm quilts before she felt her way back along the plank walk towards the kitchen cabin. As she went she sniffed the air. There had been frost in the night, she could see the shimmer of it on the hen-coops. In the kitchen she helped herself to a fat pine splinter and held it to hearth embers to catch. There, that would make a fine torch. She blew on it a little to bring it up brighter. Gazing at its orange flame in the gloom, she was mesmerized by something that went back in her blood to a circle of fires in an even more brooding forest, on a continent she had never seen. She stared a spell, warmed in this drafty cabin by one piece of kindling-wood and her thoughts. "Bet I was one from de rulin' tribe. Fine steppin' they were, the king of this and the king of that! Only I don' know . . . for all they was so big, they didn't last out. Mostly died before they could be landed over here off the ships. My mammy tol' me. They wouldn' even eat whilst sailin', just moped. But I sho' ain't a puny woman."

She shook herself. Better be warming that milk for the young ones before they commenced to holler their heads off. She fastened her torchlight in a chink in the wall and was pouring milk into a pan when Aunty Pheaby came clattering in. At that sound, a cocoon that had been lying inert in a corner unrolled, and Chokho, the squaw, came out of it. Pokey had heard tell that Chokho was sister to the Chief Kochi Fixio, but it was hard to believe that about such a slow gruntin' creature. The squaw moved silently now, folding the blanket, looking neither to right nor left, studying only the task she was doing. When she had finished that, she set about the monotonous task of pounding corn into *sofka* with a pestle. No matter how many bags of meal and grits Guy brought back from Fort Gaines, Chokho still insisted on preparing some of this chief staple of the Indians.

While this was going on, Aunty Pheaby began cackling crossly at Pokey, of whom she was jealous because of the other's superior post in the family under Ma'am Gerda. "Messin' round my kitchen, huh? All time messin'! What you been into now?"

Pokey, still under the influence of voodoo memories, replied: "Wondah if Uncle Make is goin' to teach Cudge how to beat the tom-toms befo' he dies. Uncle Make's ailin' bad and won't last long."

"Conjure stuff!" snorted Aunty Pheaby.

"Call it that," retorted Pokey, "and take yo' chance on restin' easy in Baptist ground. But I want to have the tom-toms beat fo' me seven diff'rent nights of seven diff'rent weeks aftah *I* die. And Uncle Make's the only one that knows how, but he won't outlive me, to drum for me. So I'm worrit about who will. It's got to be somebody full black and with a *tribe* name, not a Christian one."

At that word "tribe," Chokho raised her square face above the wooden corn-trench. Her eyes were as opaque as ever, but she turned them intently from one black face to the other. She knew that nothing save ill could come of going against tribal laws, no matter what the white men told you.

Pokey did not let on that she was taking notice of the savage's stare. "White folks' ways is white folks' ways," she continued, "but I ain't nevah been so impudent as to try to set myself up with white folks at any table here, and I ain't positive the Lawd wants me crowdin' them at the Last Supper. Miz Lisbeth sho' wouldn't."

Aunty Pheaby knotted a puzzled brow. One minute she had been sure she had Pokey in a tight corner for talking like a heathen about voodoo, and the next instant Pokey reproved her for talking uppity about ol' Mistis. Looked like she never could get ahead of that Pokey. Aunty Pheaby began grumbling into her batter.

Chokho had gone back to pounding corn. Blacks knew nothing of the laws of a tribe, a people. To them it was the sound of a dance, a shout, an excuse to stop work and strike their feet on the ground. They did not know that if one stole, one had to have an ear cut off to satisfy the honour of the tribe. Chokho kept on with her pestle obdurately.

Pokey poured her warmed milk and marched out holding her lightwood splinter carefully so the resin would not drip into the milk. Aunty Pheaby, humming hymns, sliced ham and stirred up her egg-bread.

Outside, the noise from the stall-pens was at its height. The smallness of the cleared enclosure here made all the out-sheds stand close to the living-quarters. There was not the dignity of distance that there had been between hall and slave quarters in Egton, but there was a deal more knowledge of how work was progressing. Yarbrough passed by now on his way to the pens, pulling his shirt closer together at the throat, glancing about yawningly at the signs of weather in the sky overhead and the tracks of rabbits beneath his feet. He must tell Shade, the head of the lot-hands, which creatures to turn loose to-day to fatten on fallen acorns and berries, and which to holler up at evening, for killing in the next few weeks. Seeing her master, Aunty Pheaby knew she must hurry with his coffee. Everybody on the place was not privileged to drink coffee every day; most of them drank chicory except on Sundays. But not Marse Yarbrough. He had coffee fresh from the grinder, and strong enough to make the spoon stand up in it. She had better make haste or it wouldn't be as pizen-black as he demanded it.

Yarbrough lounged in his walk this morning. It tired him rising at daybreak rain or shine, and he often wished he could lie abed and let an overseer take the brunt of it, but the Whetstones had never believed that was the right way. "Farmin' cain't be done second-hand," old William Whetstone had warned him. So here he was, walking across a patch of ground that was no more than a chicken-run according to South Carolina standards. Chopping away a wilderness was a stubborn job, however, and people didn't bother about acres of space wasted in yards. They were glad enough if they could have planting-ground ready in time for the seed.

He stretched his arms wide in the air where the thin milkiness was dispersing. "Oh, hum!" He sagged on the top snake rail of the fence. Shade was belling the lead-creatures before turning them out. That would keep them together, in less danger from wild animals. Yarbrough shook his head, he was too dead on his feet to really pass judgment on the critters. His mouth tasted sour. Finishing his directions to Shade, he turned about and strode back towards the kitchen, wanting coffee.

In the kitchen he found Gerda, also still a little fogged by sleep, but with her hands and arms doing the proper things to some fuller's-earth paste which she was preparing to clean spots from woollen clothes. Although she gawped occasionally, her eyes darted about, seeing to it that Aunty Pheaby put the grease in the spider, yet didn't fry the stack of eggs too soon. Yarbrough looked at Gerda glumly; it almost made him dislike her to see how well she went about her duties, whether tired or no. Wasn't she human? Sometimes he doubted it, remembering how she had forgiven him about Marta without any fuss.

Presently the others trooped in. In the colder weather they ate breakfast in the kitchen because it warmed up quicker than the dining-cabin. They grabbed sturdy white ironstone plates piled with saugage and cornbread and fried sweet potatoes. The children all gobbled, except small Hans, who saved a bit of his most choice portion to tuck into his apron pocket for a morning munch.

As the white people began scraping back their chairs, there was a sandy slapping of bare soles on the outside step, and one by one the negroes who worked outdoors, but in the living-enclosure, sidled in. They ranged themselves silently round the walls, studying with marvelling eyes the broken scraps that remained on the family's plates. They knew they would not get them, for the pick of it all was claimed by Pokey or Aunty Pheaby, and the rest Patt would scrape up for the master's dogs. Still, it was a treat to see how white folk's victuals looked, lying on their plates.

Gerda, after giving one last direction to Chokho, followed Yarbrough out. "I'm going ahead," he told her, "with widening our trail into a decent wagon-road. I don't want us shut in fast this winter as we were last."

"You do get restless stuck in one place, don't you?" she commented.

"What of it?" he barked. He was out of sorts with her to-day.

"Nothing. I happened to notice, that's all. I expect I'd better be moving along to the loom. The MacDuffs and Lydia Screws are coming to help us weave to-day."

As she walked away she wondered at wifehood, and suddenly she kicked at a stone viciously with her brogan toe. She was sick and tired of keeping steady, when she was scarcely twenty-one. She stopped short on the threshold of the cabin and turned her back on it. She faced instead towards a sweet gum that flamed a savage red. Suppose *she* should scoot off into the woods and stay there the whole day fishing. She thought of the black silver of the cold streams. To take a day all alone, with no group of people to be managed and fed, shifted from chore to chore or pacified. Only herself, solitary in the air and the light and the breeze that smelled of hawberries!

However, she commanded her eyes away from the beckoning landscape and opened the door of the weaving-house. Then she spoke to Eda and Densey, who were propping the loom. "You have it twitched too far back," she told them, and set it right.

To-day when Gerda welcomed her closest neighbours to lend a hand at her loom, she knew that they looked forward with relish to spending the day with her. They were Lydia Screws, a witty pock-marked woman, meek Miz MacDuff, young Ronald's mother, who could spin a fine thread, and her two plain, capable daughters. When the group arrived in the Screwses' wagon, with Lydia driving the mules, everything was in readiness: the loom set, the spindles stacked with wads of lint, and in addition a bulk of thread already spun and awaiting the weavers.

Soon two wheels were humming, one under Miz MacDuff's deft fingers, the other under her daughter Eliza's. The children, black and white, were fetching and carrying, and Gerda took the lead in the weaving. This was serious business to start with, for the Whetstone loom was large and ample, and the shuttle had to go back and forth with a slow deliberate motion. It took all the women's attention, until presently they saw that the warp and woof were closing together squarely in a firm web. Then Gerda took her tongue from between her teeth and eased up the tension in her chest, while Lydia Screws whistled.

The two MacDuff girls raised their voices in a well-known spiritual, to set an easier rhythm for the weaving.

"*I washed—I wa-ashed,*
I washed in the river Jordan—
Jordan!
Knee-deep, knee-ee-deep,
But the Lord said:
That
Won't
Do!"

Pokey picked up the tune in a rich contralto under their lighter, white voices.

"*So I stepped, yes, Lawd, I ste-epped*
In
Up
To
My Neck!"

"But de Lawd"—Densey's voice was as deep as a baritone—

"*But de Lawd said:*
Dat
Won't
Do!"

Jubilee, Jubilee!" all the voices had taken hold of it now, with the *whir—whine—whir* of the spinning-wheels high above it, and the march of the shuttle from side to side until the walls rang back and the floor shook with the beat of the treadles.

"*So I ducked my* head
In the river Jordan,
And the Lord He said:
WELL
DONE!"

Aunty Pheaby and Eda brought the dinner over in a basket, and they trooped outside and ate it sitting around on stumps. Little Hans dropped his peach turnover in the sand and tried to brush it off clean. "Here," said Lucinda, "you can take mine," and she began stuffing it into his mouth. He was the only person she was ever known to give up so much as a smidgen to.

As the afternoon wore away, surprisingly Miz Lisbeth suggested: "Gerda, you can do as you please, but I've been thinking wouldn't it make more sense, with the boys running wild, to put them into apron-shirts like the piccaninnies? For this one year at least?"

Gerda stared at her mother-in-law. Could this be the former mistress of the Home Place with all her ceremony of rose pot-pourri? Could this be *Miz Lisbeth,* willing to turn her grandsons loose in nightshirts? Gerda laughed aloud with happy incredulity.

"What's so funny?" asked Miz Lisbeth querulously.

Gerda could only shake her head. "Nothin, and it's a fine idea. Only I'll be bound it won't be for just this one year. It will most likely last till they're fourteen, and grow into manhood and breeches!" Her eyes were dark with fun at the forecast of a planter's sons roaming the plantations attended each by his own little fetch-it nigger like small lords of creation, yet clad simply in homespun nightshirts and with dirty bare toes. "Wonder," she chuckled to herself, "if their bottoms will get cold."

3

Yarbrough had been at his back-breaking work of tree-felling all day. He had not been sitting idly on a horse directing a gang of negroes; instead, stripped to the waist, he had been hewing away at some of the tallest, hardest trunks. Now he chose one whose girth was tremendous, and with Patt on the other side to give him stroke for stroke, he made his axe ring against the mettle of hickory until his shoulders streamed sweat, and the great column of the tree between two deep notches was balanced on the hairline edge of a prism, yet still barely quivered. Then it shook in the sky, suddenly, ominously, and with a great black roar rent its way to the ground, wreaking havoc among the younger trees. Young Bruff cried: "Hi-ee!" as it plunged.

His father wiped an arm across his forehead and grinned down the length of the swath they had cut through the woods since morning. "We'll be down to the road in no time," he said, "if we don't have rainy weather. With our own road opened wide, we can get through the year round."

"I like to be able to rear loose from that squinched-in cabin lot myself," agreed Bruff.

The sun was taking on that pallid weakness of late afternoon when the woodchoppers heard hounds giving tongue. Yarbrough set his axe-head on the ground. "What's that?"

"Hawg-huntin'," said Patt.

"What? Not my hogs!"

"No, seh, I don' mean our *owned* hawgs that we turned loose. These is wild ones, and wild as a tiger. But they're tasty, an' when the brush dries out so folks kin git through the woods on horseback, white gen'lemen have had a heap a fun huntin' 'em down."

Guy broke in: "Likely you didn't notice it last year, Yarbrough, because none of your stand of land was clear enough for them to come close. But it's quite a sport, taking the place of fox-hunting, and this year that Mr. Malone has come in, with a pack of trained dogs!"

"Malone! Do you mean that scoundrel Jerard Malone, that I had to turn off the place back at Egton because of Gerda?"

"Jerard Malone," Guy informed him, "is one of the most powerful and landed settlers hereabouts, even though he doesn't live here the year round. He's an up-and-coming man."

"Bah, a blackguard! And if he sets foot on my land I'll open his head with this axe."

"Don't talk so fool-brash. We white folks have a sore enough time toughing it out in this jungle without flying at each other's throats. Leave the scalping to the Indians."

"It would pleasure me plenty," declared Yarbrough, "to see his crown lock dangling at a Creek's belt."

"Hush!" implored Guy. "No telling what savage ears are listening and will take you at your word." Then the little man assumed a dictatorial tone. "You'll make no bad blood against any white down here, Yarbrough Whetstone! For there's a *pioneer's code* that's stronger than any gentleman's who ever cocked a pistol. Keeping belly and soul together is a heap sight more important than any prancin' poppycock! *Huh!*" Guy gave him a final snort, so wrought up that he wasn't even scared of the tall man.

Yarbrough stood astounded, biting at the black traces of moustache above his lips, for the very name of Malone incensed him. Then precipitately the first of the hunted hogs flashed across his vision through the trees. They looked so little like hogs and so very like greyhounds with sharp thin backs and tall legs that he laughed aloud in spite of himself. He was still cinching the girth of his saddle involuntarily when Ven and Malone galloped up in the wild chase.

"Halloo!" greeted Malone as if they had parted on the best of terms, and Ven yelped: "We've flushed a regular covey of these hogs to-day. Better join in."

Yarbrough eyed Malone hostilely, taking his fingers away from the buckle he had just been snapping. "I don't believe that I care to ride with *your* pack, Mister Malone."

Malone dismounted, trampling through the fresh debris of twigs and loam. "Going to keep a spite worked up toward me till doomsday, Whetstone?"

"I think," remarked Yarbrough, his tone deadly cold, "that 'spite' is too light a word to apply to my feelings about our last encounter. *Enmity* is a more fitting term." He wound up his arm in a great swing to hit out, but Guy caught his fist before it landed on Malone, and Ven jumped off his horse, cackling: "Now if y'all cain't behave yourselves, you'd better have it out all fair. But no brawlin' like this. No such, please!"

Carefully Yarbrough removed his wrist from Guy's grasp, and eyed the red finger-marks on it resentfully. "You may name your weapons, Mister Malone."

"Oh, let it go by the board, can't you, Whetstone?" Malone ejaculated. "There's plenty for us to shoot at down here without picking on each other. You sweat me out!" Then his voice grew jovial. "You're scarcely a howling saint yourself, if I've heard right about you and the Dutch wench. Seems like the best-mannered of men find themselves with children from the wrong side of the blanket——"

This time it took both Ven and Guy to hold Yarbrough back, while Malone added in earnest haste: "If you still harbour ill will against me for tryin' to play tag with your wife when she was little more than a lass, believe me, I apologize. Humbly and fully."

"I accept *that*," Yarborough told him haughtily, since there was nothing else he could do that made any sense in a country where the survival of many depended upon the survival of the few strongest men. He still eyed Malone warily though, as a congenital adversary. And it cost his pride dear not to deal with the man as he felt he deserved.

Malone on the other hand was already making banter about their rival potency. "You're a fine fellow, but you're too stiff-necked. And there's no use in your thinkin' you're the only man that's walked the earth in breeches, even if the ladies are inclined to." He pounded Yarbrough on the back, and Yarbrough was hard put to it not to try again to throttle him.

"Come on, mount up," urged Ven, "before all the hogs run clear over beyond Pea River."

Yarbrough's zest for sport rose uppermost at that, and he was glad to have the point of honour about Malone off his chest so he could join in the chase. But he hoped the rascal broke his neck!

Now they were off pell-mell, bushes going down with a crackle beneath their horses' hoofs, low branches slapping against their jacket sleeves, for this last wild hog that they had sighted showed good sport, leading them a smart chase. Once when it was close-pressed it stood at bay and fought the dogs with sharp tusks, gouging one young, untrained hound badly. Yarbrough was so angry about the hurt little bitch that he wanted to put an end to the hog with a rifle ball, but Malone said: "No, just clip its ear with a shot to mark it; then that hog'll be yours even though it's turned loose. You don't need it for food just now, and it might give us another fine run some time."

"Confound it! You talk of hogs and food. Why, it's your dog that has put me to suffering," Yarbrough almost snarled, as he saw how the pup was lying on one side trying to move away from its hurt. He knelt down beside the injured animal. "Here, girl," he spoke to the little dog, pinching the gash in its flesh gently together with thumb and forefinger to check the bleeding. When he saw that wasn't much help, he lifted the small creature up in the crook of his arm. "If you don't mind I'll carry her home and swab it out. The rest of you come along in time for a swallow or so before supper."

However, they all chose to turn their horses in behind him straightway. As they rode, a noise like an Indian war-whoop fell upon their ears, but it was in truth a more peaceful sound. It was only Shade calling up the fattened domestic hogs. He had practised until he could keep up a shout lasting nearly an unbroken minute before lapsing into variations. Now it was *walla-wallahed* through the burnt-brown sky of after-evening, somehow making a pleasing if outlandish welcome.

4

Gerda had been seeing to it that the dining-cabin was ready for her weaving neighbours. A fire had taken the dankness out of it, and the plates were ranked up and down the long deal table. Then, hearing the unusual bustle of boots and voices, she hastened to tell Aunty Pheaby to make ready for an even larger crowd. In the kitchen she found that Lucinda had made an unholy mess, trying to learn how to mould bullets in the bullet mould. Little spraddles of lead were all over one end of the largest kitchen table.

"I'll punish you later for this," cried Gerda, jerking Lucinda so roughly that one of the child's fingers was dabbed by a molten splash. Lucinda whooshed in her breath and poked the finger quickly into lard to stop its blistering. No use howling now, for she could see that Ma'am Gerda was on a tear.

"Dish up some brandied Egton figs, Aunty Pheaby, as well as the new wild-plum and blackberry jam," Gerda ordered, trying to scare up something fit for company after a heavy day of weaving.

As she hurried back to the dining-cabin she thought she heard a voice like that Malone man's, but was positive nothing could induce Yarbrough to tolerate him here. Then, bless her soul, as she came up she saw Yarbrough urging his guests in: "Step in, step in. Supper's nearly ready. I'll be back as soon as I attend to this dog." And Gerda actually caught sight of Malone again, there and as large as life! She saw his face too, big and red, bursting with a jocose lust for living, and she remembered all about him, including the trouble he had nearly caused.

Still, he was Yarbrough's guest now, so Gerda went forward with a hand held out. "Welcome. You see we did come to take our chances in this country after all."

"I see you did indeed!" Malone answered heartily, his eyes sizing up her ripening as Gerda went kitchenward again. They would, she knew, be wanting food quickly after downing the drams Ven was offering. As she hastened preparations she puzzled over the fact that she didn't like the man Malone exactly, yet something curdled in her mind at the bare idea that he might take no special notice of her after that passage among the yew hedges in Egton.

At supper, between huge mouthfuls, Malone plied Gracey with foolish sayings, until the poor girl could scarcely pick at her food. The table talk broke up when Miz Lisbeth said she was sure this was all very pleasant, but would they kindly excuse her, and Yarbrough remarked that he must see how the hurt dog was resting.

"You can keep her if you'd like to," said Malone, "and save me the trouble of shootin' her."

Yarbrough winced at that idea and went to where the animal lay wrapped warm by the fire. He wondered about the chill that would come on her wound later when the fire died. Feeling her lick his fingers with a feeble little tongue, he decided: "The devil, I'll take her in bed where I can see she doesn't catch cold." He went off to tuck her in a spare bunk he would occupy in the men's cabin, not wanting to disturb Gerda's rest with the poor thing's whimpering. "*Foolish* is what I'll name her. Little foolish dog attacking a boar's tusks." As he spoke, the dog cocked one bright half-slit of an eye at her new master.

Back in the dining-cabin Malone was now growing restive under Gracey's responsive coyness. Why, he wondered, didn't the gel have sense enough to let a man be, while his food settled? Then he looked across the room at Gerda, who was frankly resting after all her day's weaving and the heavy food. That chit of a Gracey ought to take a leaf out of Gerda's book. At precisely that moment Gerda struggled to her feet, knocking her chair over in sheer fatigue. "Your pardon, gentlemen, but I have some things to attend to," she mumbled, and went towards the door, out into the air black with another chill night. She looked up at the sky cut across by an angle of her cabin roof, but the only thought she had was that she wished she were in bed.

Before she was able to move far towards her haven, a step came up behind her that had the heavy sound of Jerard Malone's. Earlier she might have felt pleased at his seeking her out; now her exhaustion was too thick. She moved off, keeping in the shadows where he would fail to find her. Once she heard him lurch rather close to her, mutter an oath, then call: "Mistress Gerda, don't play cat-and-mouse with me!"

But in another second she was safe in her cabin. Pulling the covers of her bunk down, she crawled in, letting her face go unwashed and wearing her shift for a nightgown. This was rest indeed.

Somewhere in a corner of her mind she wondered whether she felt pleased because Malone had tried to follow her or angry at his presumption.

Then *bang, bang, bang* came the sound of someone knocking on her door. Why, the fool, making a racket that would raise the roof! Well, let him try to break that strong latch off. He would find soon enough that he was barred out here.

CHAPTER THIRTEEN

Naturally Gerda could scarcely be very religious, reared under Gran's tutelage and given into the keeping of the none too devout male line of Whetstones. She had always gone more or less automatically to the plantation chapel that Miz Lisbeth had opened every fourth Sunday in the month, back in Egton district. She had kept respectfully still, only shifting a foot if it went to sleep, and her voice did not fail in the responses.

Those phrases sent her home in a pleasant daze of noble thought and Sabbath sensuousness, able to take the lethargy of the day as it came and to face Monday a little spryer because of having laved her energies in the stagnant backwaters of ritual. But church-going was quite a different proposition down here in Alabama.

The raw country was not always congenial to the suave Episcopal clergy, but it suited well the hard-bitten breed of itinerant preachers and circuit-riders. During the week they farmed or shod horses like all the other men, and on Sundays preached to congregations tired like themselves from heavy toil. Pioneers wanted immediate personal answers to their prayers, not a far-off echo of eternity. They wanted comfort, as rough and warm as worsted, to wrap around their hearts, shutting out fear.

Brother John Upshur was one of these circuit-riders, jogging along on his mule with one change of clothes and a few doses of calomel in his saddle-bags in case he was needed for doctoring too. It was a mild November day with a sulky dampness settling down and the sunlight seeping late through the fronds of the tree branches, the kind of day he liked, homely. Also he knew there would be a vociferous welcome for him at the Whetstones', where he was to stay. This was only Friday and he would not be preaching until Sunday. He had been sitting up with the dying and was tired. They had buried the body right away because it was unseasonably warm.

John Upshur could remember the first burying he had attended. It had been his brother's and the coffin had been a tree-trunk hollowed out with the help of some neighbouring Indians. Soon after they had buried it, the bushes had grown up over it so thick that before the summer was gone, even his mother had forgotten exactly where it was.

Well, these times were not so hard as those, though they had seemed to get along better with the Indians then than lately. But here he was, almost at the Whetstone Stand. The sun had spread over the evening sky as if a turkey gobbler's wing had brushed it. Still the wilderness and its dangers lay just behind that fringe of grey trees whenever the light should be gone.

Almost as soon as he dismounted, Gran van Ifort swung the door open and bellowed: "*Och,* come in, come in. And warm yourself with something other than the fire." And as he entered, Lucinda grabbed his arm, yelling: "I've saved a dried peach stone for you to carve a monkey for me with your knife. Pokey says if I can come by it holy from you and wear it next to my bare skin, it'll forfend me from hair-falling fever and warts, and make me the catch of the county."

"Aw," jeered Bruff, "a girl's not the *catch* of a county, a man is that; you'd have to be a belle."

"I *won't* be a belle! Gracey tries to be one and I wouldn't be a chalk-and-water priss like her on any account!"

After supper he hunched over the peach stone under the light and fretted at it with his knife painstakingly. As the tiny gargoyle began to grow under the knicks he was making, Lucinda exclaimed: "It looks like Pokey!" and was spanked by Marm Pokey for sassiness.

They went to bed early and Upshur was glad, tuckered out as he was. Next morning, though, he was up early and joined Shade at the stall-pens to lend a hand with some ailing stock; then he walked up the yard and met Gerda by a hen-coop. "Fine fat hens," he told her. "They must lay good-sized eggs."

"They do," she agreed, grinning. "Aunty Pheaby tells it on me that I won't let her have any for cooking. Says the only way she gets them is to crack some a little bit, so they're no good for hatching, and that then I pass them over to her for the kitchen use."

"Well, I expect your fowls are better fed than ours. We can't spare much corn. Della's a pretty good hand with chickens, but they're bound to be scraggly if they have to scratch for every blessed thing." He looked at the plump fowls, without covetousness.

" How is Mistress Della?" asked Gerda, recalling that poker-thin woman.

" Why, she's a good deal pearter since the fall season broke her fever." He thought what a pity it was he had only one strong negro to work in their fields, and that half-grown coloured girl to help his wife. For Miz Della came from finer folk than he did; she had stacks of china too good to touch, that had been her grandmother's in England. Howsomever, that didn't do her much good here. A setting of prime eggs and a fine fat hen would have been more good to her than anything, except some flesh on her bones.

At this juncture his worries were cut short by Lucinda dragging little Hans across the yard. " Ma'am, he wet himself again, but I managed to change him by myself 'cause neither Lessie nor Pokey were anywhere about."

" There, I'm proud of you," Gerda told her. " But I'll have to wear him out with a switch if he doesn't stop such baby tricks. Hans, boy, you're too big for that."

2

Sunday morning Upshur came to breakfast glum because he could eat only a cold meal, since a preacher was supposed to partake of nothing that required work on the Sabbath. He sat drinking milk from the day before, trying to be thankful that it was not summer, when it would have turned sour. His palate jerked when Gran Pieter blew on his hot coffee and sputtered: *" Zeer goed !"* as the crusty black smell of the brew went up Upshur's nose, and he could feel his Adam's apple work in his throat, longing for a taste of it. He hastily finished scraping his breakfast plate and quit the table.

The preaching took place under a brush arbour. It was thick enough overhead to shut out a lot of bad weather, and there were split-log seats for most of the people. Nobody drove up in carriages. In fact, the roads being what they were, the Whetstone carriage was growing mouldy in its cracks from disuse. Gerda sometimes doubted if it could any longer roll so far as a rod. They went in a Jersey wagon, with the men on horseback or on a mule. And each time a different negress minded the children. Before meeting, Lessie, who was tending them to-day, gave each of the smaller ones a sugar-tit made of old linen dipped in syrup, to suck on during the sermon. As this was no church with a slave gallery, Lessie sat at the end of the row, where she could keep her eye out against any mischief.

Gerda sat in her place fairly quietly, although she shifted now and then. What a fine day it had turned out to be, after the sky had burst out in bright blue! These spirituals were like breakdown tunes, which they could almost shout.

John Upshur took for his text some words that commanded respect: *But other fell into good ground and brought forth fruit, some an hundredfold.* Most circuit-riders in the pulpit revelled in fire and brimstone, but Upshur was more concerned with their health and the care of their land. He was standing stock-still, not ranting and flinging his arms about. Once in a while, at most, he rubbed his hands against the sides of his breeches, the way a man does before he takes hold of a job. But that was all. He spoke quietly. "It may be that you came to hark to me to-day expecting a warning. Or it may be that you look to me for a prophecy. I am afraid I have no grand words for you, not having been called into the high court of His Majesty. Yet there is enough wonder close at hand for me. I rise up of a morning and I dip me a gourdful of water, and while I stand there swallowing it, I see the mists ravelling away from the tree-tops, uncovering the day!"

Thus Upshur went on, telling them about the very things they knew, small things concerning smell and taste, and the driblets of rain through leaves. When he had made their senses take hold of their daily living, he led them on through the unrolling of seasons, through the bareness and the budding, the long summer sunlight, into the deep purple they felt before the long fall closed down over the wet winter. . . . Before they knew it they almost recovered from feeling worn out after wrestling with the rigours of their pioneering life. They were suddenly swashbuckling their way through the forest. And God was a Giant Planter, with a yearlong picking season and a cotton field as wide as all creation!

Gerda studied the man as he stood there, with the light streaking through the brush arbour over his head, making a comical pattern over his eyes and nose. He wasn't much to look at, but he made her feel that this land down here was worth all grimness, all sacrifice, even the horror of the Creeks lurking beyond the old Indian Line.

They ate as usual that day, enjoying all the rich Sunday dishes, until even Yarbrough undid the thong of his belt. After the meal Brother Upshur packed his things. As he was leaving, Gerda followed him out to the chicken-run, over its pock-marked earth that the hens had left. They both breathed the raspy smell of decay the fowl-droppings caused. Gerda had a feed of corn in her apron, and both were thinking of Miss Della's scraggly chickens. Abruptly Gerda asked if he could carry home a setting of eggs in a croker-sack, that and one broody hen. "It would give your wife a fine start on laying hens next year," she told him.

He took them gratefully, and as he went out to his mule she could hear his tongue clucking gently.

CHAPTER FOURTEEN

YARBROUGH came in earlier than usual one afternoon in March '32 and pulled his boots off with a profound sigh of relief. "Well," he said, flexing the cramp out of his toes, "they've signed that new Treaty of Removal with the Creeks."

"At last!" exclaimed Gerda thankfully.

"Yes, sir! The Indians can now take their choice of selling their lands and moving west in nations, or they can stay here and become ordinary citizens of Alabama. The whites, though, are forbidden to take up Indian land till the Government makes a survey, and those on it now have to move off as soon as they gather their crops."

"Hum? Do you think they will?" asked Gerda.

"Have to, the Government says so," he replied.

"Well, then, I'm glad we're not on the wrong side of the Indian Line, where all our work would go to waste, and I hope no greedy fools stir up trouble, trying to buy in ahead of the rest." As her husband stretched himself on the bunk, Gerda threw a quilt over him absently. She was thinking how good it would be to shut off that Indian worry, for although their own relations with them were friendly, partly because of Chokho's devotion, constant reports of trouble between other whites and the Creeks kept coming to their attention. Therefore a small nagging worry had hung always in the back of her mind, to fret her when everything else was going right.

She could not blame the Indians for being hard to handle when it was so plain that they were getting the little end of the horn. Besides, the Creeks were not the roving type of tribe. They were a farming people who loved their lands. True, the poorer ones were a shiftless lot, dirty and thieving, but then the down-and-out specimen of any race was never any great shakes. And there were plenty of hard-working ones who tilled fine fields of cotton as well as corn, owned snug houses and even some negro slaves. These slaves, or their forebears rather, had been given to the Indians by the British for service in the British King's forces against the Colonies, and as a result they were called King's Gifts. King's Gift negroes were unusually courteous and well-behaved, a great asset to their owners. No wonder the well-established Creek chiefs and their relatives wanted to hang on to their houses and good acres, since they were cotton-planters and slave-owners, and this was *their* land. To them the whites were new-come usurpers. Gerda felt guilty at dispossessing them, even while she was rejoicing at her own imminent release from anxiety.

When presently she went into the kitchen, the first thing she noticed was that Chokho's facial expression appeared more still than ever before. Gerda tried to make little remarks to brighten the squaw up, but it did no good. Chokho's face stayed shut.

That night everybody came in excited over the treaty, and Ven kept shoving his jug at first one man and then another. He even wanted to mix a mild toddy for Bruff, but Gerda slapped Bruff's hands when the little boy reached for it. "Aw, Ma'am," the child cried, "I had a swallow once from Mr. MacDuff when I felt frozen, and it didn't do me any harm."

"But this is no freezing weather," retorted Gerda shortly. There were times when she worried about Bruff, the way the men spoiled him, and the rough life here gave him so much leeway. Presently, however, they all became absorbed in discussion of the treaty, and that worry slipped her mind, while she watched Yarbrough in his home-tanned moccasins there at the head of the table, looking sleepy and satisfied at the prospects for the state.

2

Somewhat later that spring Yarbrough made the trip to Tuscaloosa, which was then the state capital, to hear the farewell of ancient Chief Yufala to the Legislature. When he saw how comfortable some of the Tuscaloosa homes were, he thought: "I should have brought Gracey along. She's pining for just such a sight." Gracey was now seventeen and likely to be an old maid at this rate. Funny she could not catch a beau, as pretty as she was and with gels so scarce! But somehow she had taken off on the wrong foot down here. The *la-de-das* that attracted men back in South Carolina were a nuisance in this harder country. He thought of Gerda and her robust splendour, with a warm rush under his ribs.

As he tethered his horse near the Capitol he admired its dome and high columns, feeling state-proud and no longer like a Carolinian. An Alabamian was lustier, tougher, clumsier, realer. Had dreams, but dealt with facts first. This gave Yarbrough a great sense of power in his shoulders as he jostled around among his friends. It made him call out greetings in a hearty voice that caused other men to shout back.

"We're up to something big!" he told himself. "Nothing can stop us! What a domain we are building down in this country!" And, as he viewed their total aim, hardship seemed no more than a jaunty cape, to be worn for a short length on a journey towards a desired goal.

Presently the members of the legislative body took their places and spectators arranged themselves for the ceremony of convening and opening the day's session, which was soon begun and ended. After that, in the presence of that assembly of weather-beaten settlers, of prancing adventurers, of dour Scotch-Irish and arrogant ex-Virginians and Carolinians, of predominantly Nordic, self-appointed God's-anointed white men, came the stately Chief Yufala. He studied the faces of men who must have seemed to him mere blundering boys, for all their victory over his race and his acres. Then he spoke. With what irony we cannot know, not being of the race that was stilled into a bronze immobility the better to bear annihilation.

"I come, my brother chiefs, to see the great House of Alabama and the men who make the laws, and to say farewell in brotherly kindness before I go to the Far West, where my people are now going. In times gone I have thought that the white men wished to bring burden and ache of heart upon my people by driving them from their homes and yoking them with laws they did not understand. But I have now become satisfied that they are not unfriendly toward us, but that they wish us well. In these lands of Alabama which have belonged to my forefathers their bones lie buried. I do not believe that our Great Father means to harm his red children. We leave behind our goodwill to the people of Alabama who build the great houses, and to the men who make the laws. This is all I have to say. I come to speak farewell to the wise men . . . and to wish them peace and gladness in the country which my forefathers owned, and which I now part from to go to other homes in the West. I leave the graves of my fathers, for the Indian fires are going out . . . are almost gone . . . and new fires are lighting yonder for us."

As soon as the chief's voice had finished sounding, Yarbrough left the Capitol. He was thinking of the great hazards that man must encounter in removing a whole tribe into a totally unsettled realm. He was at once grateful for his own more limited responsibility and shamed at the part he and his kind were playing in the eviction called the Treaty of Cession. His steps pounded slowly.

3

One evening in the summer following that spring, the Whetstones had a supper marred by a disagreeable occurrence. The meal had started much as usual when of a sudden Chokho, who was passing some boiled greens, went in a swooping half-circle around Guy, giving him no chance to help himself to the dish. He had his hand all but lifted to take the spoon and looked foolish when she skipped him.

Yarbrough growled: "What's all this, Chokho? Mister Guy didn't say he didn't care for greens." At this admonition Chokho set the pot and spoon down without a word and went out of the cabin. That was the last they saw of her, so she must have kept on going.

Gerda, who had jumped up and peered out of the door after her, said: "She's heading for the road that leads away from our land." Then they all stared at Guy, who had a sheepish look on his face which made Yarbrough grip his fork with the handle boring down into the table.

"Now what have you been up to?" he demanded of his brother-in-law.

"Well, you don't think I'm going to be a ninny all my days, do you? I'm dead tired of being ordered about by another man on a plantation that doesn't belong to me, so I've gone and bought one of my own."

Yarbrough had some trouble drawing out of Guy exactly what he had done, but gradually Guy explained. Jerard Malone had advised him to do what plenty of others were doing, to move in and squat on some of the new land and not wait as the treaty directed. Consequently Guy had staked himself out a good claim of the best land, only it had turned out that it belonged to Chokho. "That's the reason she's having fits," he finished, "but I'll attend to her, for I won't back down before any squaw that waits on me at table. Not by a long shot!"

"But she *didn't* wait on you this time!" gibed Lucinda.

Yarbrough cut in worriedly: "You realize she is a *chief's* sister? I don't know what to say about it to you, Guy; you're usually more than cautious. It looks bad, coming from you right now. Those provisions of the treaty were especially aimed at keeping the whites from taking up land too fast and causing reprisals from the Creeks."

Guy, however, was not listening to Yarbrough. He was talking excitedly himself: "Why, this way I get it for next to nothing! You just wait and see."

"That's not what I'm talking about," persisted Yarbrough. "What's bothering me now is what kind of hornet's nest you have stirred up. Think of what will be said by Chief Kochi Fixio, her brother, when Chokho reaches home with her tale."

"Lord Almighty, who's going to pay any attention to her?"

"You know very well," explained Yarbrough wearily, "that they think of her as a princess."

"Well, I can take care of any Indian princess!" chuckled Guy. "You just hoe your own row. I'm going to be hoein' mine from now on."

That night after Yarbrough and Gerda had retired to their own cabin, Gerda had to speak to Yarbrough three times before he heard her. He was sitting there on the edge of his bunk, plucking at the wrinkles that were coming into his forehead, and scarcely answered her questions in the end. The last words he spoke to her before sleeping were: "I will have to see what I can do to straighten it out. I know Chief Kochi Fixio fairly well and he's a sensible man."

Gerda thought: "Oh, Lord, just when I was beginning to think I could rest easy about Indian trouble, Guy, who has never been anything much, causes trouble. It's a shame."

The upshot of it was that Yarbrough set out a few days later for Chief Kochi Fixio's plantation near the Yufala Indian settlement, taking Bruff with him for company. He wanted someone to whom he could talk to on the ride, but thought it best not to have another grown man who might make things worse by some ill-advised remark to the chief. It was not that Yarbrough was very peace-loving. He was far too stormy-natured for that. Yet he had come down here to Alabama in order to have plenty of the good things of life, and he did not intend to be cheated of them by any crack-pot schemes connived by the Malones and the Guys. He had found the life here unimaginably harder than any one could picture it beforehand. The only way to straighten that out was by pushing ahead with the land-settling stage, and he was sure Malone had the wrong idea in supporting land-grabbing. That would but set them back in the long run.

Riding along, Yarbrough came to the conclusion that he knew the nature of the Indian chief better than any sly, timid Guy or blustering Irish Malone ever could. There was something of an old form of living which he held in common with that Creek leader: a weightiness of silence when fuss and fume would be trying, yet sudden sharp cruelty when hard put to it by anger, also a muteness about trouble and honour towards dependents. All this resulted in a slow steeping in a sense of power that was bad for any man unless he could back it up with an equally measured wisdom at a time of crisis. The chief could, Yarbrough had heard, but he was not quite sure he could vouch for himself even though he had been able to require respect from every one about him, as far back as he could remember.

He and Bruff arrived at Kochi Fixio's plantation a brief while after noon. It was situated a short distance back of the village over which the chief ruled. The village was near a creek that fed into the Chattahoochee and most of the houses were small cabins made of hewn logs, with sheds on each side. The Indians, so Yarbrough told Bruff, slept under these sheds in the open air in the summer-time, and Bruff saw that the roofs of the cabins were made of skins and bark, and the doors so small that only one person at a time could enter. Some of the less thrifty Indians in other settlements they had passed had cruder huts made entirely of pine bark, but these people had decent-looking places, with tended gardens and rows of corn. And, Yarbrough told Bruff, many of them had blankets for their pallets as well as sleeping-mats made from sugar-cane stalks.

When they came near the end of the village a young warrior stepped out and lifted a hand in salute. He implied that he would show them to the chief's grounds. There was a log gate closed across the road that led to the house, and a very shrivelled old Indian squatted beside it guarding the entry, his eyes beady from gazing into the sun. He did not stir in any way after seeing that they had a proper escort. Shortly after they entered the gate Bruff noticed a little boy who had a blow-gun with him. Bruff knew that you could shoot a corkscrew-shaped arrow out of such a blow-gun, made of hollow cane, and that it could kill a human or a bird. He sighed enviously as the boy darted between the trees and out of sight.

One of the things different from on a white plantation was that much of the stock was quartered along the front way, and there were logs piled near the yard gate. Still, the yard was pretty, having in it gaudy crêpe myrtle bushes, some second-blooming honeysuckle, and red trumpet-vines. Also there was a cool porch shading the open hall, making it quite the finest place Bruff had seen in Alabama. A negro boy had gone cutting round the corner of the house as soon as he saw them approach, to announce their arrival. Consequently, as they reached the two hitching-post trees at the side of the porch, Chief Kochi Fixio was already there, waiting for them. "You are well-come," he told them, raising his arm.

Yarbrough thought: "The old buzzard has been waiting for me," but he kept his face as imperturbable as that of his host.

The chief's two full-blooded Indian wives were nowhere to be seen, but the one known as Amah Letoh, who was reputed to be one-quarter white, came out on the piazza now, smiling easily at little Bruff, saying: "The children are down by the chinaberry trees, carrying on some games. Would you care to join them there? Here Plug," she called, and a negro boy came round the corner of the house. "Lead the young master to where the young chief is playing." Her eyes snapped at Bruff so brightly that he felt sure she was sending him to have some real fun. She had a way of standing easily on her moccasined heels that gave the idea she was glad about something. Yarbrough looked at her curiously, noticing that she did not hood her eyes as squaws did. Instead she gave him back his glance freely. Yarbrough turned again to Kochi Fixio, who was waiting ceremoniously, and said: "I have come on a matter I do not like."

Kochi Fixio motioned him to the side of the piazza where chairs stood in the shade. "There is more cool here than elsewhere," he suggested.

His wife went away silently, then came back with a servant bearing a pitcher of pomegranate nectar, which had been chilled from hanging in the spring. As she poured some in Yarbrough's gourd, her beads swung out and all but touched him. She looked down at them, then to his eyes again, and he caught a scent as of dried petals of Cherokee roses from her garments. He wondered how this old, lined chief had been able to take such a girl to wed. She left them some small sweet-corn cakes wrapped in green corn-shucks, tied with grass, and Yarbrough found them to be the best of refreshments.

He perceived now, what he had always heard, that Kochi Fixio was truly a planter. Kochi Fixio might be a chief, with a tribe of redskins and a haunt of warpath tunes; still he was a planter, worrying over crop yields and slaves and the price of cotton. Thus understandingly these two men sat there talking about how fine this land was for cotton, if they could only transport it to the markets more readily. They spoke of corn and what a godsend it was for everyday living. They also spoke of the hunting here. They did not speak of Guy and his chicanery, however.

Yarbrough could not discern whether his host's avoidance of that subject was due to a willingness to overlook that matter, or to a deeper-rooted resentment than even he had feared, at a slight put upon the tribe. Eventually Yarbrough broached the point himself. " I came to speak about the matter of your sister's land. I know my brother-in-law has acted far from right, but I will try to make good for him One of my neighbours paid two hundred dollars for the same amount of land, some three hundred and twenty-five acres. I will give you twenty-five more dollars than that."

Kochi Fixio continued drawing away at his pipe, and Yarbrough waited. When the other still did not answer, he felt himself growing angry and thought he had better strike a bargain before his temper burst beyond bounds. He hoped the Creek was not trying to make more out of this fix than was necessary. As long as the Treaty of Cession was signed, and they would all be moving west like Chief Yufala's people, there was no sense in any one's kicking up dust for nothing. Yarbrough felt that he had made a fair offer, to keep both sides out of trouble, and he was not going to sit around forever while some old Indian sucked on a pipe. " What do you say?" he demanded sharply.

" *I* do not say," droned Kochi Fixio. " My sister, Chokho, has gone out of my tribe into yours. And since she has chosen to go with her land and belong to the man Hampley in wedlock, I cannot stay it now."

"Do you mean to tell me," ejaculated Yarbrough, "that Guy Hampley has married the squaw, Chokho?"

"The Princess Chokho," his host corrected him, "has this day made the choice of going with her land. I believe it has come into the possession of your kinsman."

"Jehoshaphat!" Yarbrough spat on the porch before he could control himself. Then Guy had outsmarted them all? Yarbrough could scarcely take it in, and he was glad of the Indian's silence, in which his own stunned mind could try to gain its bearings. Dimly he felt that he had been an awful fool, coming here with all his grand talk of righting a wrong and settling a crisis, as one chief to another, while that tricky little Guy had already appeased the tribe and was in possession of much good land to boot.

For the present its sting did not penetrate too far, as he sat there on the piazza sipping nectar, watching the Creek planter's stable-hands driving up the cows. Shortly after that the darky Plug came to announce to them with great dignity that supper was ready. At the table Plug stood behind his chief's chair as Bonapartt had stood behind Yarbrough's at the Home Place. Children sat sedately in rows up and down a table covered with a coarse but white cloth. At the foot presided the mistress, with deep graciousness, for all the snap that her huckleberry eyes gave when they chanced on Yarbrough.

He thought: "How homesick they will be for this place with its peace and plenty, as they make their way into a hostile land! When I left my home, at least it was voluntary; I was not forced out by other men."

CHAPTER FIFTEEN

GRACEY's humiliation when she heard of her father's marriage to the squaw was really piteous, and she and Willy both elected to stay on with the Whetstones. "I couldn't bear going to live in a wigwam," she cried when Guy diffidently approached her on the subject.

"'Tain't exactly a wigwam. It's a good cabin, with a tight roof of skins. And, honey, you could have one of these here King's Gift negroes to wait on you." Gracey's hysteria at the idea of a roof of skins barely let her hear his proffered bribe of a King's Gift. He had retreated deeply disappointed, for his main idea in acquiring that tract of prize land was to set up his own family home. Chokho knew her place, she would not have expected to eat with his white family. None of the Indian women who'd been a party to a mixed marriage did, and they stayed out of sight when company came. Why, Gracey would have been the real mistress, and very shortly she would have had a fine plantation to queen it over, one that would catch the eye of some of the young blades trooping in. As it was now, people had the mistaken idea that she was a poor relation of Yarbrough's.

In spite of an inward cringing, Willy had taken the situation lightly, cynically amused at Guy's belated independence of action. He also pointed out the fact that Guy could now be a lot of use to the other white men as a "linkster," as they called the interpreters. "He might," he said, "act as a general go-between in some of the disputes that are coming up, since he buried the tomahawk so neatly on his own score."

"Yes," agreed Yarbrough sourly, "we are going to need some go-betweens all right, if many more of our people pull such sharp tricks to get Indian land. They won't all have squaws handy to fix it."

"True enough," laughed Willy, "but Father has a way with the Indians. I'll wager you he never has to carry a gun to his fields while he's farming, the way most of the white men are obliged to who live above the Indian Line."

"Most likely he won't go out in the fields at all, now that he has a squaw he can work," said Miz Lisbeth tartly, and that was the only word she said about it, scandalized though she was by his defection from Lucey's memory.

All in all, the family accepted this alliance like other inconveniences of pioneering they had to endure. It grated on most of them, but, as Gerda view it, it was nothing to lie down and die about. She felt sorry for the lonely absurd figure Guy cut when he had his traps collected and was standing in the yard stuttering over his leave-taking. Whereas he had meant to depart grandly, as a landholder and his own master for the first time in his life, he appeared as an ineffectual stray, traipsing timidly into exile. Yarbrough not only consented to let Bruff accompany him for a visit, but made Guy a gift of a bottle of old spirits and a horn of the scarce, precious gunpowder. He would rest easier, knowing of that latter protection for his first-born son, in case there was trouble.

Once clear of Whetstone Stand, Guy's spirits rebounded and he and Bruff felt tootin'. The boy was so excited over the adventure of going to stay for a while in the heart of the Creek country that he was quite beside himself. "Hi-yook!" he shouted now and then at the top of his lungs, and when they passed any one he waved his leather cap with a flourish, feeling superior to them because they were going back in the safer direction.

2

Now the December drizzle had turned to a downpour that made the yard a mess of crimson mud, and the trees soughed, lashing their grey moss ropes about like shrouds. Inside the kitchen cabin the children were stringing popcorn to festoon the holly Christmas tree, while Gracey was covering a cardboard star with some silver foil she had brought out of her trunk. The tree would be a gay sight with its own red berries and some bright bows of coloured ribbons that Lucinda no longer wore. There would be no Charleston toys this year, but they scorned such foolish knick-knacks now, with so many exciting things fashioned as the Indians had taught them, things that could be of real use down here. In addition Bruff had been promised a long-rifle of his own, now that he had developed into a good shot by practising with Guy's. As for sweets, they were going to have the fun of a syrup-candy pulling this very night, with even the new baby, Will Bee, sticking his fingers in, and Hans as usual probably getting tangled up in his twist of taffy until Lucinda could start it right and ropy for him.

Densey was ironing everybody's best clothes for Christmas Day, including petticoats for Lucinda and ruffled shirts for the boys to wear with their Sunday breeches. She used the "hot iron" instead of the ordinary flat-irons that sat on the hearth all the time. The hot iron was kept as shining as silver and had a little door on the top of its back for live coals to keep its temperature even. Densey kept it in a chamois bag as preciously as Bonapartt did the silver plate. She held up one of Lucinda's top petticoats now, and it stood out in snowy curlicues like a wedding cake.

"Surely I'll have admiration made over me in that!" remarked Lucinda, thinking of the gentlemen visitors who would pinch her cheek and say: "I'll wait for you to grow up, missy," following that with a kiss smelling of tobacco and bay rum and spirits. They always laughed in a surprised way when she did not wriggle out of their hugs coyly, but squeezed them around the neck and retorted: "All right, now don't you go back on your promise."

Recently Miz Lisbeth had pronounced sharply: "I think Cinda's too big to sit on men's laps; she's going on nine, and one to ripen even earlier than you, Gerda."

It was not at all unusual for the older members of any family, North or South, to deem girls to be of the betrothal age by the time they were ten, and to sanction marriage for them in their earliest teens, as in Gerda's case. The settling of raw land and incessant child-bearing took such toll of the women that grown men were often forced to turn to the most vigorous of the very young girls. Miz Lisbeth knew it was well when such men as her husband and her son found one who could endure to the limits of their own life span, though she knew herself to have been no such active match for her William as Gerda was proving to be for Yarbrough. In line with this view she was not frowning upon Lucinda's rapid maturing; rather she recognized the force there and felt it dangerous to let it proceed haphazardly. Formalist that she was, she had no intention of allowing this young *partie* to some potential desirable match to be jeopardized by laxness of supervision in the wilderness.

Now she studied the girl dryly, and little of what was taking place in that missy's mind escaped the astute old lady. She might not know the precise details of what occupied Lucinda's inner attention, yet she could follow the general trend and try to plan for the girl's protection and subsequent proper fulfilment.

At this juncture Lucinda herself was recollecting how she had happened to be in the empty passage between dining-cabin and kitchen and had put her mouth up in leave-taking of Mr. Malone. Though she still claimed the protection of being a child, he had wrapped her with him under his cape and kissed her like a woman. They had stood warm and close in the shadow, and there had seemed to be no more to the world than this dark corner under his cape.

She had been scared, during the next thunderstorm, wondering if God would strike her dead for her brazenness. Still, she continued to think about it at night, before she fell asleep. Now, though, she shook such thoughts out of her head; she felt uncomfortable remembering things like that in the kitchen among the family. To distract herself she peered out the only glass window they had anywhere on the place. Ma'am Gerda had said it was but common sense to put the glass in the kitchen, where they could see what was going on through it, though Gracey whined to have it in the dining-cabin for show. The rain was coming down so heavily that it made the daylight almost dark. Lucinda could barely discern the turkey gobbler that was to be killed for Christmas dinner huddled under his coop trying to keep dry. Foolish thing, trying to protect himself, when he'd be dead quick enough anyway. Then she started speculating about whether a sick turkey was fit to kill and eat.

Gerda, passing the window, saw the blurred shape of a figure on horseback coming round the big cedar tree. "Great mercy! Somebody's swum over to see us!" Now she could see it was Guy, who hitched his horse under the little lean-to instead of putting it away in the shed-pen. Yarbrough, who had been drying himself out, welcomed Guy with gusto, and the two were soon drinking hot rum, their clothes steaming acridly before the fire.

Guy glanced timidly at Gracey. "That's mighty pretty that you're making there, daughter," he told her. She merely sniffed and went on with the next point of the star, refusing to treat this rusty man who lived with an Indian squaw as her meticulous father who had once been dotingly particular about the sheen of her curls for the Saint Cecilia Ball.

Bruff was planted in front of Guy, begging. "You're goin' to stay a spell, ain't you, Uncle Guy? If you wait till after Christmas Day I'll go back with you again."

"Not this time, sonny. I'm not going toward—er—home. I'm carrying a message through the county. That's what I came here for, to bring the message to your father."

"What? What is it?" they all asked at once.

"Well, y'all know, of course, that we've been organized into Turber County by an act of the Legislature day before yesterday. Yarbrough here was one of the main ones to push that act through." Guy looked from one to another of the group. "So it seems your papa could about take his pick of being any big mucky-muck of a county officer that he wants, and he'll have to be at least foreman of the Grand Jury or I miss my guess. The main thing right now is, they want him to superintend the building of the courthouse, in what's going to be the town square of the county seat to be named Turberville."

"A town here? Turberville is it to be called? A courthouse? A county seat?" they gabbled.

"Yes, old man Loshum has deeded thirty acres of his land for it, about two miles away, and Yarbrough's to superintend the courthouse. And me, I'm to build the jail."

"That's natural enough," grinned Ven, "each to his own kind;" but Guy didn't mind the twitting reference to the shady way he had taken title to his land.

"I'll make it a good strong jail, then, that they can't break into as well as out of, seein' as you think I'll be an inmate."

Yarbrough was drumming dreamily on the table. He had worked patiently towards making this county take shape, and he had hated leaving Tuscaloosa before the thing was actually signed and sealed. Now he felt gratified, having Guy's tidings of the demand for his further leadership. They had set things to humming, all right. Before long they would have roads to the river, and boats going down to the cotton ports. Before long they would be raising cotton in earnest! *Cotton!* It was a creed, it was a toast, it was a way of life!

Through his preoccupation he heard Gerda say: "I expect Guy's in a hurry for something to eat, if he's to continue his trip. Aunty

Pheaby, dish it up right on this table. Children, pick your mess up."

They ate intently, all feeling they had to help Guy make haste to spread his tidings, and wondering just how much this new town would mean. Gracey kept saying to herself that a town would mean a social hall, and a hall would mean carriages and balls and silks again! She did not consider how useful her wizened little parent was endeavouring to be in placating Indians, that white men might rear halls to resound to future fiddling for reels.

When Guy rose to leave, all the men clustered about him, and Gran clapped him on his shoulder. "A jack rabbit you are, my good Guy, always on the jump."

Yarbrough said to him simply: "This was good news indeed. And don't think I don't know that you were the one able to persuade old Loshum to deed that land to the town, simply because he has a lot in common with you, with his Indian kinfolks."

Guy pinkened and twitched his scraggly little moustache. "Sho! Loshum was already minded to do it, I didn't have to coax."

"Here, I'll see you mounted," offered Willy, and throwing Gerda's yard sack over his shoulders he followed his father, the rain plastering his pomaded hair down like a drowned rat's.

3

It may have been the freshening air that made Yarbrough do the impetuous thing that he perpetrated early in the year. The wind that day was one of those raw sweet ones that seemed to come from blowing over a place not dull with winter, to come perhaps from over a sea beach. Work on the courthouse had been coming along fine, with the negroes singing at the top of their lungs, swinging their arms with a will, grinning when he told this one to take care in notching the ends of a log to join them, or that one to step up smarter with those four-foot hand-hewn boards he and John Screws had cut from the virgin oaks by the creek. Consequently when Malone came clattering past and reined in with a shout, Yarbrough had brandished his arm back in an equally swaggering salute, not to be outdone by the other. "Where you headed for?" he shouted against the wind.

"To Sparta to the land-office sale, to buy myself a batch of the best purple black land around here. And dirt cheap in more ways than one." He winked. "You ought to go there and catch up on what's happening hereabouts."

Yarbrough studied him through narrow, squinted eyes. The man was up to tricks as usual, totally unscrupulous. Still, when Malone drawled: "Fixin' a place to try me in for stealin'?" the colour whipped up in Yarbrough's face and he jeered back: "Oh, you're too slick for us ever to lay hands on, Malone," and he laughed aloud, suddenly not giving a hoot about Malone's questionable ways. Not on a day like this, with that wind blowing recklessly.

Almost before Malone was out of sight, Yarbrough directed: "Shade, I want you to take charge. I'm going to Sparta too, on a piece of business." Within an hour he had stopped by home, left word of his whereabouts, and was giving his stallion the spur to make up for lost time. As he pounded along, kicking up flecks of drying mud, he whistled *Boots and Saddles,* snatching at vines that slapped past, and cocking an eye up at the scud of clouds in the wash-blueing spring sky.

By fast riding and only a short stop overnight he made John Rutsey's, the land agent's place, by noon next day. Quite a good sized crowd of settlers were congregated, taking pulls from whisky-flasks, while skulking about among them were several Indians with a furtiveness creeping through their habitual blank masks. One of these, in spite of his regalia to-day, looked familiar to Yarbrough. He also caught sight of Guy sidling about on the edge of things, looking harried. Most of these men, however, were the rankest strangers, newcomers who had a rapacious look, a restlessness ill checked. Not the men he could count on to help set up a good county government. He glanced about for Malone and saw him over at one side evidently giving orders to that plaguingly familiar Indian, who in turn was nodding with a look of cunning in his eyes.

So? Yarbrough had it now! That was a "trickster" Indian. Rascally whites who wanted to obtain fine Indian land for next to nothing bribed no-account Indians to disguise themselves in strange garb and come to sales pretending to own the land in question. Then the white men bought it from them for low prices, most of the money being later returned to the buyer, the Indian keeping only a portion as a bribe for his services. A scurvy practice, and sure to cause trouble in the end with the rightful Creek owners who had been thus cheated out of their property. Some of the sharper of these trickster Indians appeared again and again as fake owners, by dressing differently to change their appearance. That was why this one's attire perplexed Yarbrough; it was not his accustomed clothing. Well, Yarbrough had known from the outset that Malone was up to no good, but now he'd be switched if he was going to let him carry out this swindle. For the moment Yarbrough had no idea how to stop him. But he would somehow, because his blood was boiling at the thought of having trouble brewed that would slow the community's progress. He was committed heart and soul to this matter of establishing a tremendously productive cotton county now, and, by George, he would see it through!

"Sir," he hailed a man near him who had just taken a swallow from a bottle, "would you mind accommodating me with a nip of that?"

"Not a-tall." The man's grin showed yellow teeth. Yarbrough opened up his gullet and let nearly a quarter pint drop down it. His palate was scorched, yet he never turned a hair, and the man's eyes bulged at the sight. "You drink like you learnt in Texas."

Yarbrough settled his shoulders. "No, sir, and that was my first to-day. I had to catch up." He could feel his blood working up steam as he looked about again for Malone. Rutsey was now mounted on a stump with another man nearby holding a sheaf of parchments that were land patents. Malone was close to them, laughing and going on as if at a barbecue. Yarbrough turned back to his new acquaintance. "Mind if I have another swig?"

"Just finish it up, 'twon't do me no good after you take another like that," chuckled the man.

Yarbrough didn't gulp it all; he saved some in case of later need. Looking about with this heat singing in him, he saw everything doubly bright. The light danced on the puddles, shoulders were cut out sharp, voices rang with laughter like dinner bells, and the whole roistering group seemed to be in on some big joke. A grin broke out on his own face as he started shoving his way deeper into the crowd.

The sale commenced and the land began to be knocked down prodigally by the section or half-section, not in any cautious little parcels of eighty acres as he had bought his first batches of holdings. No, these men were out to cut throats, to grab while the grabbing was good, and their faces had the wayward challenge of gamblers one saw on river boats plunging fortunes on the turn of a card. Except they were all winning here, with very little risk. Their trickster Indian pawns were well trained and the land agent was in the know. Only Guy seemed at odds with the trend, frowning anxiously, shaking his head disapprovingly. Since Guy had been living among the Creeks he saw their side of things and tried to take their part, but he might as well have tried to stop a spring flood as this barefaced sacrifice of the Creeks' lands to these invading whites.

Now and then there was a sharp flurry of hard words when two men crossed each other's path trying to secure the same land, but a few hurried low remarks settled the matter and the man who retreated was always next up to claim a choice piece offered in compromise. Yarbrough listened to the drone of description as Rutsey read out: "Pine barren," "Pine barren," "Pine barren," which he knew was a confounded lie. The land Rutsey was bounding, by creek and oak and cross-road trails, was rich and tillable, yet going for a song as "Pine barren." Finally Yarbrough could stand it no longer, thinking how he had paid high prices, patch by patch, for his land. And he knew what to do with land, too, once he owned it! He would not be swapping it off later like these thieves, nor putting it under the supervision of half-way overseers. It would remain his, to clear, to plant, to nurse, to love with something deep down in his soul.

Now he saw that Malone had signalled to that disguised Indian, and the latter had stepped forward at the description read from one particular patent. It was a whole section of the finest land in the county and lay directly between the courthouse and Whetstone Stand. There was no holding Yarbrough back now. He knocked through the crowd and caught Guy's arm. Now in a flash it came over him who that Indian trickster was. It was one of Chokho's kinsmen, sure to lose an ear or a hand if his knavery came to her brother Chief Kochi Fixio's knowledge. Oh, this was great luck for his purpose!

Yarbrough whispered fiercely to Guy. Guy demurred at first, but Yarbrough had heard Malone make his bid, confidently, and Yarbrough snarled at Guy: "I've put up with you and your squaws and all your tomfoolery; now I want that land! You mosey over to the scalawag Indian and fix him proper so he won't play into Malone's hands, or else I'll wring your neck like an old rooster's!" His face miserable with conflict, Guy threaded his way to the Indian, making no commotion for Malone to notice.

Rutsey was about to repeat Malone's offer and close the sale when Yarbrough called out ten dollars more in a voice that struck across the spring air with a clang Malone started, and jerked his head about; anger rushed red into his jowls. He gaped a moment unbelieving, as if half-looking for Yarbrough to take his bid back, but Yarbrough stared him down. The other upped the price five dollars. But Yarbrough could see what was happening behind Malone's back. Guy was speaking in sign language to his squaw wife's kinsman, and the Indian's face suddenly took on self-defence like a scum. Yarbrough observed that and bid once more and finally, adding a paltry five dollars to the indecently low purchase-price of that rich tract of land. Then the Indian motioned to Rutsey, and before Malone could grasp what was taking place, the redskin had scrawled his mark on the parchment, and Yarbrough had gained title to a plantation that would yield him cotton galore before the decade was out.

Malone blundered through the group that separated him from his opponent, his hands working, his blood-vessels knotting at his temples, but Yarbrough, prancing with elation and whisky, threw an arm across Malone's shoulder in mock conviviality. "Calm down, calm down! Remember what you said about white men not wasting gunpowder on each other?"

"*Awrk!*" Malone yanked a vicious chew off his plug of imported tobacco. He knew that this time he'd had one chalked up against him. Yarbrough dropped his pseudo-fraternal arm away from the other's shoulder then and moved to where his horse was tethered. He was standing nuzzling its nose in his hand and grinning when Guy sidled up.

"Uh, Yarbrough, that wasn't the smartest thing you ever did by a long shot."

"You don't always ask my advice about your actions," replied Yarbrough. "S'posing you let me manage mine."

"Yeah,' persisted Guy feebly, "but you made me interfere in this." His voice trailed off unhappily.

"Never you mind," Yarbrough assured him, "this is my bargain and I'll pay for it. Nobody, not even Malone, saw you putting the sign on that trickster, so you can rest easy."

"I don't know," muttered Guy, "whether any of us will be restin' very easy in our beds if many more such sharp trades are pulled on the Creeks."

"Ho, so the pot's calling the kettle black now?" chuckled Yarbrough, leaping on his horse. "What of your own sharp bargain?"

"But," mumbled Guy, "in the end it turned out I didn't take a thing away from Chokho." And as Yarbrough cantered off Guy shivered a trifle in the damp spring air. This land was not yet theirs. Not by a good sight. It would take more than a few measly dollars to possess it, there would be a blood price put upon it before the true Indian owners gave up their home-settlements, their tilled fields of cotton and corn.

CHAPTER SIXTEEN

By summer time Yarbrough had completed the courthouse, set cater-corner in the north-eastern part of the future square. He felt proud of the one-room structure, measuring twenty by twenty, of round logs unharmed by any broadaxe, as he was fond of boasting. There was one window at the far end and a door at the near one, while the forms for the juror's box had been planed tolerably smooth with his own jealously guarded plane. The building would be ready for the spring session next March, but Yarbrough had grown so proud of it that he was forever coming back and adding some further finishing touch. He liked to stand there by himself, now that the others were gone, and stare into the rich oaken gloom of this room of justice, to wonder what wrongs would be righted there, what echoes the years would raise, then muffle in the silent death of the past.

Standing there in that cool hewn shade, he thought: "Lord, I hate to grow old," and turning, came back into the full noonday blaze, to watch Guy still sweating and fuming over the irksome progress of his jail. Poor Guy, whatever his ability to fraternize with Indians, had not the knack of working negroes in gangs, and flurried them into mistakes that caused set-backs. "I'd better go lend him a hand," decided Yarbrough. That was how he came to be still tracking into town on construction work when November came. Continuing his heavy labour for so long a stretch had worn him down, so that he was dead asleep that dire night when Pokey came frantically to rouse her mistress. "Miz Gerda, Miz Gerda, fo' the Lawd's sake, come whilst they's still time!"

"One of the children's sick," was Gerda's first hazy thought, while Pokey, clutching at her mistress's nightdress, would scarcely let her wrap a shawl about her shoulders. "It's the end! It's the end!" she was crying; then instead of leading Gerda across the passage to the children's quarters, she steered her out under the sky where the most unearthly sight of doom was taking place. The stars were raining down in such vast numbers as to illuminate the heavens! It was the most awful and sublime sight any human being could imagine, with thousands, maybe millions, of meteors plunging directly towards the earth. Occasionally one of tremendous size would shoot towards them, leaving a serpentine trail of light in its wake for the space of five minutes or more.

Gerda's knees knocked together like washing bat-sticks, and her mouth was drawn hollow and dry in one swoop, with needles of fright tormenting the roof of it.

The clearing was in a wild uproar. The blacks were rushing back and forth not knowing in which direction to flee. Occasionally some of them would grow tired of running and drop down on their knees, giving up in prayer, but in a moment they would regain their strength and struggle to their feet, to rush either for cover or for freedom. The night was a shout of sins and a screech of repentance. Gerda herself grabbed Pokey by the arm and shoved her to her knees, scrambling down beside her, mumbling: *"Almighty and most merciful Father, we have erred and strayed from Thy ways*, but Jumping Christmas, Pokey, He can't hear any such namby-pamby piffle as that above all this yowling. Lord A'mighty, Pokey, what must we *do*?"

"Bettah not take His name in vain, leastways. He's sho' set against that."

Gerda stayed wringing her hands for a moment in a helpless frenzy, then "Yarbrough," she thought, "Yarbrough could take care of me!" She went tearing back inside to shake and shake him by the shoulders. "Yarbrough, Yarbrough! The world's coming to an end! It'll be on fire any minute! The stars have already commenced to fall down on top of us from heaven!"

He stared at her in a stupor. "What's caught fire? Not the stall-sheds?"

"The world, you fool!" she yelled, then babbled: "Oh, forgive me, Lord, I didn't mean to call my brother a fool; besides, he ain't my brother." Then to Yarbrough again, pulling off his bed covers: "Get up, get up and save us."

He struggled to his feet and followed her out to where the blazing meteors still showered, showing no signs of abating. Gran and the other whites had been roused now and were collected in the yard, the children cowering about Lessie's tremulous skirts. Hans was speaking accusingly to Lucinda: "You told me to steal that brown sugar for you and now I haven't got time to get forgaved!"

Gran put his hand down on the child's head. " Ask Miz Lisbeth to take you and the other little ones into her chamber and hear your confession of sins."

Miz Lisbeth, the only other calm one in the group, turned her hoar-frost-white face toward him. " Do you think that I can serve instead of one of His ministers?"

" *Och,* verily," answered Gran, standing there in his great beard with that hail of stars behind his head, quoting her own ritual for her benefit: *" Almighty God, who hast given thee grace at this time with one accord to make thy common supplications, and dost promise that when two or three are gathered together in His name, He will grant their requests."*

" I had forgot," the old lady said. " Come," and, holding little Will Bee and Hans by the hand, she led the children all serenely towards her cabin.

" Do you wish to follow her," Gran asked Gerda, " and take what comfort you can in prayer?"

" No! And for God's sake stop talking like the Lord come in wrath to judge the quick and the dead! He'll get here fast enough anyway." Her gaze shuddered back to the skies.

Gran let out a bellyful of laughter. " Surely, *liefste,* you do not fear this natural phenomenon! It's naught but some atmospheric disturbance, perchance caused by the sudden change from excessive sultry warmth to cold and frost."

She looked at him askance. " I've seen sudden frosts before, but they never set the sky on fire. Besides, why were *you* quoting the Scripture to Miz Lisbeth so solemn, if that's all 'tis?"

" Her faith is her possession, not mine to filch from her in her time of need. And, moreover, I like not brawling children." He stalked away, leaving Gerda staring after his unscathed calm resentfully.

Yarbrough, who had been scanning the heavens with lively curiosity, turned now. " I reckon I'll be getting back to bed."

" To bed?" she exclaimed unbelievingly.

" Yes. I'm bone-tired and I'll have a sweet time rounding up any negroes to work on that jail to-morrow after all this scariness."

So Yarbrough thought he would be working to-morrow? That laid a calm over her turmoil for a moment, but when he had gone in she remained shivering. The meteors kept ranging through the air in the direction of the east, until wan and pale the sun came up and obscured them. The day had come somehow, and the world was still here, though the dawn was as pallid as a ghost. Gerda wondered if God were spying down upon the havoc He had wrought, biding but a little while, staying His destroying hand for one short span.

She saw her darkies, eerie and shadowy, move away toward their quarters, a drone of relieved mumbling going up from them. Then Gerda went in out of the cold, wondering how she was to accomplish the day's tasks with the poor aid of that distrait and wearied band. Well, it was all up with her if the world did come suddenly to an end, because even now she could not feel any true surge of salvation. She felt the same as ever, drawn to Yarbrough, partial to the twins, impatient with Gracey, and a trifle musty from not having washed yet. At that thought she began laying out coarse fresh clothes and filled a basin to scrub herself from top to toe. Once more clean from the skin out to her starched calico, she went to see that the children were bathed and fed, although her performance of these ordinary duties had the perfunctory bravery of mien that surrounds a funeral. She endeavoured, however, to answer the children's questions in a sprightly way that would make them forget they might be right next door to the Hereafter. Bruff and Lucinda, she noticed, were beginning fidget and whisper together restively with their usual tendency towards mischief, and Bruff muttered to his twin: "I don't much like that part in the Bible about not eating in heaven."

"Goose, it didn't say we won't eat; it just said: 'There shall be no hunger there.' That prob'ly means you can have even third helpings."

Bruff still looked doubtful. "Anyway it sounds kinda like the whole place is a big fancy church. But there ain't anywhere else to go, except to the bad place, and I don't want to be set on fire. I don't see what was the matter with staying right here on earth for a good spell longer." He stared at his brogans gloomily. "I was getting to be a prime shot with my new long-rifle too."

Lucinda simply could not sit still any longer. "Let's ask Ma'am to excuse us." Once they were outside she surveyed the sky. "Looks like any other day to me," she announced. "I tell you, there's no use sitting there praying, praying, praying right up to the last minute. We've had our sins forgiven, as near as we can tell, so if we're careful not to commit any more, I can't see anything to stop our going chinquapin-hunting."

As they started across the clearing towards the forest edge, she said abruptly: "It's funny, but I still feel exactly like myself. You'd think you'd commence to feel either awful good if you were going to heaven, or awful bad if you were going to hell. I only feel excited."

"I know," he agreed. "I keep looking down at myself to see if I can see through me yet, like a ghost."

"I want my halo shaped like a crown," planned Lucinda grandly.

Gerda saw their slight figures vanish into the pockets of darkness between tall tree-trunks, and noticing how the light seemed to spring away from everything it touched—the ground, the shed, the sides of cabins—then return to the sky, where it shaded into a transparent shine, she thought: "I ought to call those children back." She started after them, but in doing so, saw Splayfoot Ike crouched behind a bush at the corner of the smoke-house, hugging one of her fresh-killed hogs clumsily in his arms. Why, the thieving ghoul, stealing even on Judgment Day!

"Ike!" she yelled angrily, and he dropped the carcass, stumbling over it. The sight of that fine pork sprawled in the dirt with this twisted, deformed black trampling over it made rage spout out of her. She tore a branch from the bush and laid into the craven Ike with a ferociously strong zest. She had never whipped a male slave before, except the little fetch-it niggers, and those only with slight peach-tree switches; yet now it never entered her head to wait for Yarbrough to perform this office. No, she laid the lashes on like the master of a galley, with a slicing strength. "There!" she ended. "That will teach you not to break into my smoke-house, kingdom come or no kingdom come!" He was yowling and all but licking his welts, which stood out, a livid violet, on his saffron skin. Stalking back to the kitchen, she felt the comfortable warmth of anger in place of the clammy fear of those last hours.

By evening everything was in a pleasant bustle. The twins had brought in quite a fall of chinquapins and were cracking them open with their teeth, removing the shells for the younger children. Miz Lisbeth was sopping some bread in syrup, eating it with greedy relish, not caring a fig now for the sustenance of prayer, and Gracey had her hair arranged in a new becoming way. Gerda called out to Aunty

Pheaby: "We'll cut one of those pound cakes even if 'tisn't ripened enough with the rum sponge yet."

There was a loud racket in the yard and all the men seemed to enter at once, Gran from his cabin, where he had been reading in calm retreat all day, Yarbrough from "town," pleased at seeing his household cheerful, and Willy and Ven like cocks o' the walk after several days spent at the Judson racetrack. "Lawse a' mussy!" hiccupped Ven. "You should have heard the screechin' and carryin' on there at the meteor fallin'!"

"We had plenty of screeching here," Gerda informed him.

"I don't mean just niggers and children. These were hardened criminals blabbin' like babies. Why, a thief confessed to the fact that he had been planning to rob the bank."

"I hope," declared Miz Lisbeth with spirit, "they clapped the thievin' rascal in jail so we all rest easy in our beds."

"Worrying about what you have tucked in your stocking, eh, Granny?" teased Willy, tickling her about the chin.

Ven gave Bruff a dram on the sly, and Lucinda began pilfering Willy's pockets for sweets, which he brought back from every trip. Everybody's spirits skyrocketed in release from fear. Nobody scolded the children for gobbling, and presently they were all comparing notes on the biggest whopper of a sin that had worried each one.

Gran watched the group quizzically. Death and God had been vanquished by safety. The Lord had to keep sorry company indeed, be an intimate of fear and disease and destruction. Gran rose and sought the out-of-doors. Presently the door opened again behind him, letting a slant of light fall across the dark; then he recognized Gerda's footsteps approaching. She reached out for one of his great old hands and hugged the knuckles, then she raised her eyes to the sky arched above them from forest rim to forest rim. She heard the creature snufflings the stock made in the pens; she smelled the yard dirt. She saw one or two stars drop to earth, making a golden scratch for an instant across the night. Then she spoke: "The stars and the sun, the coming and going of daylight and dark, the days passing by into seasons, that's about God enough for me, the Thing I'll go by."

He laid his other hand on top of hers. "A great wonder, this world."

CHAPTER SEVENTEEN

LIFE WAS MOVING ON and pioneers were turning into settlers, who now spoke of the things they needed above bare food and shelter. In the spring of 1834 the first circuit court was held in Yarbrough's courthouse. *Came the Attorneys and came a jury of good and lawful men,* as the verdicts later read, *and of this court was Duncan MacDuff the honourable Judge and Yarbrough Whetstone foreman of the grand jurors.* Yarbrough liked that first day of oaths and ceremony within the walls he had reared, and comported himself with such solemnity when he and other men were eating dinner at the Loshums' that Ven snickered: "Anybody'd think you were partaking of the Communion with that long face."

Well, let Ven poke fun all he pleased, that wouldn't hackle him. Let Ven get excited over horse-racing, if he liked child's play. For himself, Yarbrough was occupied with a riskier game, hacking into raw land after an El Dorado. A downy white one, stretching acre upon thousands of acres! To be baled up and bartered beyond the seas, for silks and brandy and beaver hats, for power and pleasure and a living legend! He broke off his thoughts and stacked his fork full of turnip greens. They might not have achieved much of his dream of grandeur here as yet, but they surely had victuals that a hungry man could appreciate.

"The next step is a post office, I reckon," remarked Duncan MacDuff.

"Yes, sir," agreed Yarbrough, "we need a post office at the county seat, though young Jake Votaw is giving us good service riding that mail route to Sparta. What we need most now is a school." It was his conviction that Bruff and the other boys of the community needed discipline, to overcome the idea that life in Alabama was a protracted picnic. He might do the first hard work of clearing the way for his offspring himself, but there would be other hard times for them to meet later. Building up a state would continue for a long time to involve a gamble, and drudgery, and danger, requiring a hardening of the sense of mercy towards those who stood in the way. His generation could not foresee all the ways they would have to travel to gain their goal, and their heirs needed plenty of seasoning to become sons who could stand by, strong and ready.

Yarbrough consulted Gran a number of times on the subject of educational plans, for the old man had given the children some spasmodic instruction in the past few years, but his intellect was too far advanced to be reduced to the elementary level the children required. He suggested now that, since there were other nearby planters in the same quandary as Yarbrough, the latter might sound them out on the matter of their subscribing together to pay a teacher. The tutor could take over Guy's abandoned cabin, which, being remote from the main group, would serve well for the schoolhouse.

" So it would, so it would, with a little repairing," Yarbrough agreed and went to have a look. It was over a half-mile from the main clearing, with the underbrush choking up around it again; a nearly lost bridle-path led into one corner of its yard. The warped door swung loosely open, and the clay that had filled the crevices between the round logs had dried and fallen away, leaving many cracks where both air and light penetrated. There was no window, yet Yarbrough believed they would need none, with that swinging door and those filtering cracks. Some hornets had nested in one corner; twigs and leaves had been strewn across the floor by unchecked winds. As he surveyed it, however, he measured how they could build desks around the four walls with wooden brackets supporting them, and forms of split logs to seat scholars.

The place would of course require a tutor's desk and chair. Yarbrough had a small desk from his old Egton office that he could spare, and Gerda had an odd chair that now only served to prop a door. It could be mended and she could use the broken churn for a prop instead.

He knew of eight of his neighbours whom he felt tolerably sure would join him in subscribing to guarantee a fee for a schoolmaster; and sons of less well-to-do men could come for a small rate per head. Girls? He'd have to talk to Gerda about that. He thought it might be better if Gracey and the MacDuff sisters would undertake to teach some of the gentler arts, though perhaps the tutor might have time to drill them for an occasional hour in simple sums, and in French. Yarbrough did not hold with cramming girls' heads full of book learning; besides, his object behind this undertaking was to shape men. It must be a male domain, a "college" where boys' minds were schooled and broadened into manhood's outlook and judgment. Lost in such contemplation, he experienced again, as when standing in the court-house doorway, that feeling of looking deep into decades of founding.

He poked his riding-whip gingerly at the hornets' nest, to find that it was deserted. "I wonder if I am becoming too much like a deacon," he asked himself, and feeling the need of breaking bounds, struck out towards the Indian Chief Kochi Fixio's.

He had seen the chief's wife, Amah Letoh, several times when community considerations took him to that plantation, but he had scarcely exchanged a word with her though he had known whenever her dark eyes rested upon him. Now as he rode, he was well aware of Kochi Fixio's absence in the West, where he was making ready new lands for his people. In all likelihood she would follow shortly, and before she went, Yarbrough desired to satisfy his wonder about that deep glance of hers that betrayed some forbidden interest in him.

Once Yarbrough reined in sharply, with a mind to turn back, asking of his errant impulse: "Could a fancy like this bring down my beginning realm about my ears? Not for any stray brightness would I send even a tremor through its growing structure." But a gust of dogwood petals flickered down a shaft of air and Yarbrough laughed aloud, continuing towards Yufala.

As usual at Kochi Fixio's plantation the negro yard boy heralded Yarbrough's coming, but this time instead of the chief he found Amah Letoh standing on the top step. The dance was gone from her eyes now; her tone was singsong with formality. "There is no fit welcome for you, since my husband travels abroad, seeking new lands."

"I know that he is away," said Yarbrough unflinchingly. "Still I come."

"I fear we can do you no honour here this day," she replied steadily, and swung on one silent heel, withdrawing into the dusk of her hallway. "Good travelling," she added in courtesy over her shoulder.

But Yarbrough came into the hall and stood over her so close that he all but touched her strands of beads. "You have been looking into my eyes a long time, Amah Letoh. You must know what you wish to find there."

She tried to keep her response subdued, but brightness broke through.

At that signal he pulled her to him, nearer the wall. The feel of the soft-dressed buckskin was more sensuous than he could bear. When she tried to murmur: " You, do you know our tribal laws and what comes of this?" he only answered roughly: " I bring different laws here!" and half-pushed her through her chamber door. When she lay on the couch her face showed itself to be brighter than he could look at straight. So he hid his face in her tawny, naked shoulder, trying it with his teeth, almost bitterly.

Later when he came away from her house the farewell words of old Chief Yufala beat upon his ears: *for the Indian fires are going out . . . are almost gone. . . .* He thought: " We've been as close as creation, she and I, yet I may never see her again."

2

In the days that followed, Yarbrough was oppressed by a sense of being under some unnatural spell that kept his hand tied, holding him back from those undertakings he had set for himself. He seemed to be lost in a half-world between the everyday one and some not quite glimpsed enchanted land. So listless was he, in spite of dogged efforts to bestir himself, that he had to rely on Gran to speak up for him in the meetings attendant upon starting the school. Gradually, however, as the days wore into weeks, his eerie detachment waned. He was able finally to touch a table and feel the grain of the wood, to scuff his boot heel in the ground and know he was stirring dirt, to hear voices and not confuse them with echoes. Then one fine day he worked his shoulder muscles about hard and in relief he exclaimed to himself: " Whew! That was a close shave. Goes to show that white men had better stick to their own kind!"

That evening he told stories to the children, permitting them to clamber all over him, as he did when in a playful mood. They felt perfectly at ease with him at such times. Jobyna, his only daughter besides Lucinda, was a shy plain child with an abundance of quiet brown hair behind which she tried to stay in constant hiding. Lucinda on the contrary was sharply the child of her parents' most headlong traits, sensuous, violent, direct, imperious, honest to the point of being disconcerting, and undeviatingly self-centred. She loved Bruff with the peculiar closeness of a congenial twin, yet was eternally in competition with him. She felt only the quick careless impulse of a blood tie towards the other children, with the exception of Hans. For him she had a special protectiveness, almost as if she as her father's deputy were trying to make up for a wrong Yarbrough had done to an inferior. So spontaneously kind was she to the half-waif Hans, and so fierce a champion that he never knew the difference between her defence of him and love. He was her only weak spot, but few people dared to trade on even that.

Yarbrough indulged Lucinda in many ways that he denied all his other children, even Bruff, whom he was training as his successor.

To-night she was taunting her twin about the boy's educational prospects. "Thank Heaven, I haven't to be cooped up in any old school. I can learn all I need from Pokey. She works charms to make men pine for me; then I scrub my gums with salt to keep my teeth white, and step light if there's fiddling. I don't have to fret over any old verbs. Bruff, you probably'll have to pinch your toes into brogans all summer."

Bruff scowled. He was fretted enough, without her rubbing it in. Other things were more important to him than school so far, things like snaring rabbits, gigging frogs, shooting partridge. Now he wondered what was to become of all his accomplishments if he had to spend the good daylight in that dusky old cabin, listening to a fussy man parsing Latin.

He need not have been so worried, for when the tutor, Danley Bruton, arrived, he was a far cry from Bruff's notion of a schoolmaster. To start with, he was young with an inquisitive brightness about his face, and a disarming air of knowing some joke on himself. He was quite respectful to Gran and Yarbrough as they attempted to tell him the plans for the school, but his eyes were jumping from one child to another and all about the kitchen. In the midst of one of Gran's most dignified sentences he went over to where Aunty Pheaby was cooking. "So that's hoe-cake?" he inquired interestedly.

"No, suh, dat's cawn pone."

He broke off a hot bit and put it in his mouth to taste, then spat it back in his palm quickly, blowing to cool the burn in his mouth.

He had been born in England, though he'd been in America some years and thought it all great fun. Yarbrough glanced at Gran a little nonplussed.. "Do you think he's much of a scholar?" he asked.

"*Och,* yes! His letters are of the best. And he has the inquiring mind that a good scholar always must have."

Danley was questioning Lucinda now. "How many of you young girls do I instruct?"

"Not me!" she told him. "They think Gracey can teach me to be a lady, but I won't be scrimped into any such nancified mould as that either. Why, I'm 'most as tall as you are," she exclaimed in sudden delighted discovery. "You're right runty."

"You're a rare one for trouble, aren't you?" he asked.

3

It took some time to put the cabin in readiness for classes, and there were some who thought they should have postponed school until fall, but the outcome was that the children were to meet and practise schoolroom ways somewhat before the July heat became unbearable for study. Finally one May Monday at eight o'clock school was called. The other boys of the community eyed Bruton with the same mistrust the Whetstone lads had felt at first and later lost. The group was restless and ready to bait him, but it was hard to find an opening. Immediately after roll-call he questioned them about their hobbies and dislikes, showing so keen an interest that they were soon answering lickety-split. They scarcely noticed it when he had some one of them change his seat to another place in the forms. They did not realize that he was thus grouping them roughly into classes, with regard to apparent aptitude rather than age.

Just as he was about to open one of the books on his desk, Will Bee, considered too young for schooling, came scampering into the room and up to Bruff without so much as a by-your-leave. "Bruff! Bruff!" he shrilled. "I've found a bee tree, and they're going to cut it down. Hurry!"

The whole school was instantly on its feet, yelling: "Where? Which way? Who's going to chop it?"

"Shade 'n Patt." Will Bee was tugging Bruff towards the door.

Danley rapped his ferrule on his desk, and the sound startled the boys into order. "Are you chaps willing," he asked, "to forgo your afternoon's exercise for a week to make up for this, if I give you a recess?"

They all assented quickly, and surrounded him in comradely fashion to show the way.

Patt and Shade were waiting, each carrying an axe, a bundle of loose cotton to make a smoke with, and a " gum " or square box to hive the swarm in after they found the honey. The boys lighted a fire while the negroes commenced chopping the tree. Danley had never seen such fast steady work; almost before he knew it the notches were meeting and the trunk had crashed to the ground.

A couple of hours later all the boys, surfeited with the sweet, obediently trailed along after Danley back to the schoolhouse. The green feeling of the forest shade enveloped them. " What a place to inspire you!" thought Bruton. " Now if I can only keep them from looking on me as a jailer." When they were once more seated he stood up at his desk in the darkening room and picked up his volume of Homer. " We shan't start with sums to-day. That would be too dull after our excitement. I'm sure I could not keep *my* mind on them. No, we shall start with heroes. With men who had courage, like your fathers, to tackle the unknown, with men who faced daily what you are facing, danger and maybe the sudden end of your lives."

The boys stirred. That was right, there were the Indians. They hadn't thought of them before as much but folks who knew more about corn than anybody else, yet this was a wilderness, after all. They straightened out of their slouches feeling a vicarious bravery, as Danley Bruton's voice went on: " I do not know what toll this conquest of a new land will take of you, but when the numbers begin to fall from your ranks, remember with the heroes of times past: 'Thus the gods wrought! They spun the thread of death for some, that others in the time to come might have a song!' " Then he laid Homer down and opened the Greek primer.

4

Clearing new ground was a task that went on intermittently but steadily, until the ring of axes was as familiar a sound as the whir of insects or the caw of birds. The wild canebrakes as well as the trees had to be cleared to make room for the coming of cotton, so Yarbrough made a holiday sport of canebrake burnings for his negroes at crop-barbecue time. It was a pastime that appealed to the negro love of the spectacular, and they held the celebration on a patch of ground near the biggest brake, where the largest cane had grown so old it would pop the more noisily when burned

All day long the barbecue had been going on, the joints of meat turning on their spits over the slow hickory coals. All day long they had laughed and quarrelled, courted and prayed, and now that night had fallen the white folks had come to see the fun. Yarbrough was to touch off the bonfire for them with a special ceremonial torch. Bonapartt took the brand from Cudge, who now knew how to beat the tom-toms, and had laid an old dark spell on its resinous flame. Then Bonapartt passed it thrice up and thrice across in front of Yarbrough's face, before he tendered it into his master's hand. Yarbrough received it and held it high. Their great round eyes stared at him white in the flare. "You have done me proud this year!" he declared to his people, and flung the blazing torch far into the brake. For an instant there was a dry hissing, and then, *boom-bong, bop,* the cane began to explode! It was a sound like the cannon of opposing armies, and the negroes yelled wildly before laughter broke through them like a surge of black water.

Yarbrough stood indulgently watching them dancing and leaping in the play of the flame. "Just children," he said, feeling very wise and tired. Then, at that moment of Yarbrough's sense of patriarchal fulfilment, Guy came up to him with a look of strain on his face and spoke in a queer low voice. "Will you step aside with me? I have same bad tidings."

With foreboding pumping his heart heavily, Yarbrough led him to where they were somewhat removed from the sounds of mock battle. There Guy told him slowly: "Amah Letoh, the chief's wife, is dead."

"Amah Letoh?" Yarbrough's voice groped through the unreality of the thought of that secretly pulsing body being inert in death. "No!"

"Yes, she died by her own hand because she had brought dishonour upon her tribe."

Yarbrough gazed down at his own two hands, seeing their guilt for her slaying.

Unhappily Guy cleared his throat. "I have another messenger here with me, a *linklater* of their own blood. Naturally I refused to speak such words to you from any Indian, chief or no. Will you listen to him?"

Yarbrough nodded abstractedly, with grief for Amah Letoh still a drug in his veins. Then a figure slid out of its obscurity and faced him in blank composure.

"I come to you from my kinsman Kochi Fixio, but not from him as a man wronged by another. That personal stigma my kinswoman, Amah Letoh, removed by the stroke of her well-directed hand. I come to you as speaker between two chiefs. My own chief, Kochi Fixio, as you well know, meant to depart from this his forefathers' home in amity. He had wrought with you, and the lawmakers of your state Alabama, in all accord for the cession to you of those lands. He forbore to bear spite against much chicanery on the part of white usurpers. He held not bitterness against your kinsman Guy. Since that one was able to make decent restitution for the bad-faith purchase of the Princess Chokho's lands through a trickster. He realized also that in truth, such conniving tricksters were a blame that could be laid at his own door, since he as their ruler had failed to control their knavery.

"Now he bids me tell you in sorrowful anger, that for the ravishing of his leader's honour and his leader's power he counts nothing of any avail. Save the destruction by him and his warriors of that enemy's strength who invaded his stronghold. The end by death of the white encroachment upon the Creek domains.

"The day is not yet appointed when he will strike. Years may pass before the accomplishing of his purpose. But mark well his warning! It comes from his own lips. His purpose is to be your undoing, and that of your people. The chief has spoken."

The *linklater* slid from sight, and Yarbrough stood with the burden not only of the betrayal of a woman who had put herself in his hands and of a fair-dealing man who had treated with him peaceably, but, above and beyond all, of the knowledge that he had placed in danger those of his own blood to whom he was unalterably bound. Grim grew his face at his own treachery. But there was no bending to fear in him; he had no faintest idea of how a white man would go about backing down. Let Kochi Fixio, or any other chief of all the Creek nation, speak.

After the battle had been joined and the carnage cleared, they would see who *stayed* upon this land! Bad as was the trouble he had caused his people, his sole purpose now was to lead them out of it. Whatever human lapses he had indulged in, in the end he could not fall, for he was supported from within by the iron-rod backbone of the true leader. Now he took a vow, as he strode towards the barbecue pits with the rapacious appetite of a challenged man: "*My sons, and their sons, and those of generations beyond their time, will still hold Whetstone Stand!*"

CHAPTER EIGHTEEN

GRADUALLY Yarbrough's remorse became more concerned with his having been guilty of a second defection from Gerda than with any other aspect of his erring. "She's had to put up with a lot from me," he told himself with compunction. "Not just my lally-gagging, but a hard life down here. The least I could do is to build her a decent house, to make the work easier for her." Then he fell to thinking how a bigger, more permanent house would also reinforce his dynasty, which he had endangered so foolhardily on a careless day. Yes, a good strong house that could stand for a century or more was what they needed. He decided to build it on that rise above the rock wall he had constructed to keep the soil from washing away, after he had felled too many trees in one spot. The rock wall place—by Gad, that was what he would call it, the Rock Wall Place at Whetstone Stand! He slapped his palm down on the kitchen table, making the knives and plates jump. "This fall," he announced, "and winter too, we're all, old and young, black and white, to cut timber every spare moment. For we're building us a real house this coming spring! I must get that job out of our way so I can attend to raising cotton."

"A house?" cried everyone, but Gerda's voice sounded over the rest. "I want a double-pen one, like the one where we stopped one night in Georgia on our way here. Remember that centre hall, open clear through, bringing a breath of air even on the hottest days. I never will forget the fine time I had there——" She broke off abruptly, recalling the baby she had been carrying then, so gladly, and the end that had come to it. Suddenly barbarous grief jabbed at her, and her stomach sickened. She chewed at her lips until she felt the raw skin sting. Then her woe was gone abruptly, though she felt the raw skin weak and had to reach for Ven's toddy-glass for a swallow. Knowing Yarbrough's eyes followed everything she did, she straightened her mouth into its usual calm. It was a long while since she had felt such a seizure of sorrow over that lost infant.

The others were talking at a great rate about what they wanted the house to have. Gracey was speaking up for a parlour for her harpsichord, with glass windows throughout. Then she switched her attention to her niece Lucinda, remarking: "And I'd better be instructing you about manners in earnest if we're to have a proper house." But Lucinda stamped her foot. "I won't have you pestering me more than you already do. I'll be able to hold my own along with you any day. You're no great shakes of a belle!"

Yarbrough chuckled, glad of any excuse to laugh even if at his daughter's impudence. He spoiled Lucinda in any case, seeing in her all of Gerda's young spirit unharmed by any wrong he had done her.

Gerda, however, drew her brows into a frown. She too could see her own most wilful traits in this turbulent daughter of hers, and though secretly she doted on Lucinda's vibrancy, she wondered where it would carry her. The girl had a way of drawing people warmly to her for a share in her laughter. The girl had a way of making even her anger break into colour and daring sound. The girl was brave with that unconcern of one who feels her own desires to be unquestioned for ultimate fulfilment. Gerda, watching her now, did not so much fear that the world and time might bring hurt to her daughter as that her daughter, showing no ruth, might hurt others beyond repair.

2

In the spring Yarbrough was able to enjoy his house-building to the full, as befitted this thing that constituted the cornerstone of his new estate. Before the winter was half over he had had the yard space cleared, and piles of timber ready-cut to draw upon. The neighbours helped him in the construction with a will, since it was the first sizable house for quite a distance around.

One day at the edge of the woods he saw a skulking Indian figure, and some fear nagged at him, telling him that it was one from Kochi Fixio's now hostile tribe. The next instant he realized it was probably merely that trickster scalawag from the land sales and meant only that Jerard Malone was back in the county to see his planting done.

Yarbrough's second guess was right, for soon after breakfast Malone himself came riding up to the new house-site shouting at the top of his lungs, bringing presents he'd picked up in Richmond or Savannah during the winter. In his relief from the thought of Indian trouble, Yarbrough was glad to see Malone and enjoyed hearing him exclaiming: "Blood of the saints! What a fine house that is you're throwing up, here in the bowels of the forest!"

Patt at his master's cordial command drew the corn-cob stopper out of a jug of whisky on the ground and poured some into two gourds for the gentlemen to drink to the house. And Malone and Yarbrough stood grinning together out of sheer pleasure at the way they were making this country knuckle under. Slinking Indians were forgotten. This was going to be a big year, the start of a big time! Why, they would even grow a few bales of cotton to export this season. Yarbrough felt like giving a shout of triumph. Then Malone wiped his mouth. "I'll mosey on to your cabins now to give the children and women-folks these gewgaws I brought."

"Do that. They'll be tickled. But I must stick here with these neighbours who're lending me a hand."

Shortly Malone came upon Gerda spreading cloth to bleach. She was regarding the expanse of creamy cloth with satisfaction, computing that they would have enough white cloth to do them proud in their new place.

"Good day," called Malone. "Have you any welcome for me?"

She turned quickly, a laugh rising. "As I live and breathe it's our big absentee planter! Welcome back. It's high time you came, if you don't want your crops to lag."

He held one of her hands, trying to smooth out the water-puckers from her pinkened finger-tips. "I told you this was the right country for you, Ma'am Gerda. You always looked to be bursting out of your seams, back there in that prim-laid Carolina garden."

She laughed again. "This does suit me," she declared.

He studied her face with open interest. "You take on measure as you go along, to meet whatever comes up. Still you don't seem to grow any older."

"Lordy," she exclaimed, "I feel like a granny loads of times. But not to-day, in this weather."

"Are you twenty-five as yet?" he asked.

"Just!" she answered. "And that really isn't so old, is it?"

He let out a shout of mirth; then quieting down, he said: "But you stand up to whatever happens to you, with no trace in you of the flibberty-gibbet. You must not ever have seemed a girly girl like Miss Gracey, nor can I imagine your withering into an old lady like Miz Lisbeth. You'll be a woman from start to finish." He still had her hand and now he bent it at the wrist until it hurt. "Come up yonder with me." He pulled her after him out of the clearing, out of sight from the cabins. There he took hold of her around the waist so hard that her calico was crushed. "Look here, you know what I want. You're a lot better than me, but still you're a lot like me. Yarbrough's like us too, we're all the same stripe, grabbing for what we want, and I want you. Now you can't feel hoity-toity at me about this, because you don't blame me, and neither could Yarbrough call the kettle black, though he'd choke the tongue out of my head if he heard me say this."

He stopped speaking and caught her closer under the crouch of his bulky shoulders. With an effort she put him back from her. She liked this man with her body in some quick simple way, but she remembered with a thud that she was with child again. She shook her calico folds of skirt straight. "I'm sorry, but that's all there is to that."

He stood there, grape-coloured in the face, his mouth making a whistling noise to get his breath back. Finally he spoke: "Have it your way. I know when I'm licked. Now I'll be off to see the children." As Gerda watched him leave she knew full well he would never seek her out alone again. She sat down on a half-rotted log to think over her knowledge of herself. It was not virtue that had stopped her. It was not even her feeling for Yarbrough, though she could never do away with his hold over her. It was the old inexorable breeding-rule that the woman kept all other men's seed away from one man's fruit.

Still, she was glad that Malone had wanted her so urgently that he had spoken out. It made her spread her shoulders now and shake off some of the hardships of this forest living. It exhilarated her like fresh air, and she found herself walking with a springy step, the burden of the child within her lightened as if by a renewed youth of hers.

The day they finally put the house under roof was a great day for them all, with the whole community gathering at the Whetstones'. The neighbour women brought special delicacies to add to the feast, and gifts of bright new quilts, feather pillows, or other house-warming offerings they had been fashioning during the winter. All this morning, ever since the first white-feather streak showed in the sky, teams had been pulling up and unhitching near the stall-pens. Soon the old cabin clearing looked like a camp-meeting hitching-place. Across the fences the presents spread and flapped: quilts patterned in Rose of Sharon, Log Cabin, Star and Moon, or May Basket, pillow cases edged with tatting, tablecloths with their hems fastened down with Italian drawn-work, and finally a runner of pale-blue satin worked out in strawberries by Miz MacDuff to throw over Gracey's harpsichord.

Soon Ronald stopped beside Gracey, bowing in the manner his mother had taught him. "I will be pleased to lay out your flower garden for you any time you say, Miss Gracey. I put the spring bulbs out last fall, when your uncle first spoke of building. Do you notice how some of them are now blooming?" he asked shyly. "Next year they'll be a sight to behold."

The morning passed quickly, the men working with a flourish, closing over the last gap in the roof, shouting and challenging back and forth. Bruff and the other young boys were running their legs off, acting as apprentice helpers. No one seemed to grow tired, but all became brisker and brisker as the hours moved towards noon. Ven was kept busy serving whisky from his jug to the workers, with plenty of cool spring water to wash down its fieriness, and plugs of tobacco for them to try their jaw muscles on as they banged away with their hammers. The clangour and shouts rose like a wave breaking up against the sky. Now and then someone caterwauled:

"Hallelujah! Here I come.
Hallelujah! Beat the drum!"

Bruff ran his legs off fetching tools and materials and whisky, sneaking a swallow once in a while as he passed behind a pomegranate bush. He hated the way it varnished the inside of his throat, but he liked the way it shot up his spunk till he could outdo all the other boy helpers. Then suddenly on one of his journeys after a hatchet his feet slowed up and dragged. He didn't see any sense in rushing his legs off any more. The sun was hot enough to bake your insides, and the budding cape jasmine gave up a smell like the spice in fruit cake. It made him drowsy. He walked away from its puddingy aroma; still the world of trees went around and around him in a moving bowl, which he could not stop from spinning. He staggered back and fell sprawling, jarring a shoulder as he hit the ground.

A girl's voice screamed, that ninny Gracey's, and Miz Lydia Screws pronounced him " Drunk."

All during dinner Gracey kept trying to avoid young Ronald and to attract Malone to her side. She waited on Malone with the choicest plates of food. She even managed once, in bending over him with a plate, to snarl a curl in one of his buttons, but he merely untangled it and went on eating. Perhaps she could have borne his indifference if she had not seen his eyes continually following Lucinda. In Gracey's opinion the girl looked a sight. She was dressed in a faded red calico without any white frills and was wearing moccasins, of all the outlandish things.

To-day might be the first time Gracey had noticed Malone paying attention to Lucinda, but it had been going on all spring. The day he had returned from his winter sojourn and had been rebuffed by Ma'am Gerda, he had hauled out the usual toys for the younger girl; then abruptly he had come out of his thunder-mood, ejaculating: " Why, bless me, you are a fine figure of a lass! I wonder if you would like one of these trinkets I intended for Miss Gracey."

Lucinda had appraised them. " Much obliged, sir, I believe not. I'm not at all on the same order as Cousin Gracey."

At that remark he had sat down on a wall-bench much amused. " You must tell me what would suit your taste, so then the next time I can bring you something to make up for this oversight."

She had begun counting on her fingers. " I'll tell you. I want a gun like Bruff's, to learn to be as good a shot as he is. Some charges of powder, which is as scarce as hen's teeth around here. Then I'd like to own some silver spurs, though I track around in moccasins mostly instead of boots."

After that, almost every time he dropped over to Whetstone Stand, he singled her out for some special favour, and she greeted him with zest, shoving the other young ones aside to hang on his arm, squeezing it close to her side. Once recently, when stopping his horse at a curve of their cart-road out of sight of the clearing, he had come upon her and, picking her up, placed her before him on his saddle. There she had lain so intently still that he had a sharp feeling in his chest which he could hardly bear. A wagon coming over the road had put a stop to that scene. Consequently to-day he looked forward with jerky impatience to seeing her alone.

Now he saw the red flash of her frock swinging off towards the woods and he followed after. He found her leaning against a tree, whistling easily at an answering bird, but she turned her head at his approach and moved over to make room for him to lean against the trunk beside her. He found himself saying, before he thought: "You know, some day you're going to be mine for keeps! I'll be speaking for you to your father to-day."

"No," she contradicted him, "not any time soon."

"Why so?" he asked belligerently. "Your mother was wed at thirteen."

She stared at him as cool as a cucumber. "Because I'm going to do all the things I've always promised myself I'd do. I want another few years of tearing around like a wild Indian, and then I have my mouth all set for being a 'toast-in-seven-counties.' Though I won't go about it in Gracey's *pee-yuky* way. I'll stand them on their heads, I promise you!"

In spite of himself Malone felt his admiring curiosity aroused. "A belle and a sharpshooter, eh? The two don't mix."

"They do in my case," she told him. "If any one treads on my toes I'll settle the squabble myself, though I won't be touchy about my name being called out by men in their cups, if it's in praise."

He stared at her amazed. "Upon my soul, I believe you mean what you say! You'd order pistols for two and coffee for one, then shoot the rascal down as neat as a pin, drinking your coffee later with relish." Tears of mirth spirted from the corners of his eyes. "Well, that's all the more reason why I must have you for myself in the end, do you hear?"

She stretched her neck back and her eyes bored into his like gimlets. "I'll agree to that, in the end, if you will promise to give me all the leeway I want for a few years."

"All right, you can have your courting, my vixen," he consented, "and welcome. You can lead all the fine dandies and pulling boot-lickers a brisk chase! I won't stand in your way, for you're right about having to cut your eye-teeth. But get this into your head: You're to be *mine* in the end!"

Then suddenly he clenched her chin with his fingers till the nails pinched in. "I want some proof that you're coming into my keeping some day. I want it now." He tugged at one of her braids. "Take down your hair for me, to show me that you're not trifling."

She looked at him, gauging her power over his excitement. "I'll pledge nothing without some signet from you."

"Here!" He thrust a hand into his waistcoat. "Keep this timepiece within your reach. It will signfy that I am always at your call." He held the bauble up, and as he did so the watch chimed the quarter-hour. Lucinda's face rippled with childish pleasure. "Can I have it for my own?" she demanded.

"It's yours," he answered, thrusting it at her. Once more he caught one of her braids where it was bound at the back of her head. "Loosen your hair!" he told her. "That's the thing I want to see." She reached up and began pulling the plaits apart. Untwisted, the braids shook free and fell down as thick as a cape almost to her hips. At the sight he drew in his chest as if at a blow, then one of his hands went out to feel that mantle.

Gerda, passing that way rather wearily, worn out from the day's excitement and Bruff's fall from grace, saw Lucinda rewinding her long, thick hair and noticed that the girl's bodice was crumpled. Still Malone's eyes were the bright ones of a man whose desire is unfulfilled.

"What's all this?" she demanded bluntly nevertheless.

Although they both started at her voice, neither of them seemed taken aback. She could not help laughing out. "This is a pretty time for me to be raising Hail Columbia about anybody's deportment. Maybe I ought to call your father, Lucinda. But I can scarce ask him to take up an insult to his daughter where he let it slide about his wife."

"It's no insult to me, Ma'am," interrupted Lucinda, "because Mr. Malone wanted to bespeak Papa for my hand to-day. I told him he'd have to bide my time." She skewered the last pin into her braids, then hooked her arm about her mother's waist. "You can't blame me for taking after you, Ma'am, can you, in growing up so fast? Nor for liking *him*. Only I'm going to have my free fun first that you missed, before any man alive gets me all dragged out, having babies and curing hog meat."

"You talk brash enough now," sniffed Gerda.

"Wait and see!" challenged Lucinda.

They all three moved out from under the tree. The afternoon light was falling in narrow slats across the ground, showing how far advanced was the day. Gerda said, because she felt she should: "I would charge you, sir, to bring no harm down upon my daughter's head, except I don't think Lucinda is in danger from any one but herself."

She separated from them then, following the path up to the knoll where grew a few garden flowers and the red rambler rose that covered Elzivir's tiny grave. Gerda pulled up some clumps of weeds that were choking the bush, thinking that she would have to transplant a shoot of the rose to the front yard. The holly bushes had grown into good-sized young trees and were blooming early with that constant sifting, sifting, falling of starlike blossoms that made a fragrant whispering rain. The sweet, pointed flowerets pelted over her face, snagged in her hair, and made her ache in some gentle way that she did not mind.

She stood there over that almost flat mound of Elzivir's grave and she felt not sorrow now so much as beauty. She sat down a moment and, slowly picking holly petals out of her hair, mused: "You cannot actually hurt from memory, any more than you can love as you first did when you were young, by recalling the colour of the dress you wore then. A little while ago, last year even, the pain was still lasting and I could feel it. But it has given me its last bad-gripping twinge. Now I fear new troubles that have not even cut into me yet, that bear names not decided upon: Bruff's, or Lucinda's or Hans's. . . ." She knew that this thing that used to tear her about her lost baby was stilled now. It did not make her struggle to draw away from its clutch. Rather she cherished it like something sweet to smell, to keep apart, the way the rare unlearned fragrance of holly blossoms is treasured . . . because she felt that if she lost its keenness altogether, some part of her would be gone, like her youth. Yet already she knew it had gone, that eagerness to lunge against pain.

Gerda rose and went down the slope. Half-way Yarbrough met her. "Here," he told her, "let me straighten you out." He brushed the flower trash out of her hair, while she leaned her heavy weight on the arm he gave her.

"This day is beginning to tell on my feet," she complained. "I'll be glad to rest in my new home till this child is birthed."

"Come along with me, I want to show you something." He led

her up to the house-site among the crisp shavings and scraps of bark, then hoisted her laboriously into the front part of the hall-way. She looked overhead and saw how their roof was tight-closed over them. It made her feel sheltered against weather, and Indian hate, and the blood in the veins of their offspring, which they could not turn into quiet channels.

CHAPTER NINETEEN

In the space of one year the skinned logs of the Rock Wall Place had weathered, till the house looked suitably settled among its water oaks, cedars, and horse-chestnut trees. The wide yard was a fair sight though there was no turf of lawn; instead of being planted with grass, which would not have thrived under the great trees' shade, its smooth expanse of plain earth was swept as clean as a whistle every day by piccaninnies wielding brush yard-brooms. The bottom of every tree was girdled with fresh whitewash and two large stumps had been left like gate-posts at the end for the front walk where wide fieldstone steps went down through Yarbrough's retaining wall. Young Ronald MacDuff had circled these stumps with a ring of snowdrops, then inside that another border of flag lilies to bloom later. Starting from the stumps, the path was edged on each side with ranks of jonquils and narcissus, and later native shrubs and flowers would burst into profuse bloom all over the yard. Right now the wistaria was putting forth its lavender tassels.

A piazza had been built across the front of the house, deep enough to shelter the loom that Gerda had placed there where she could conveniently take a turn at the shuttle in spare moments, making her web grow without even noticing she had been at work on it. As for the rest of the porch furniture, there was a chest to catch plunder, and a number of chairs, cowhide ones and others with bottoms made of corn-shuck ropes. Trestle tables were still in evidence in the rear part of the house, but Bonapartt, who could find little use for himself as a major-domo down here, was turning into a first-rate cabinet-maker. The walnut wood on their place had proved to be fine-grained, rich material; and Bonapartt, who had seasoned some of it carefully, was joining it into chests of drawers, a dining-table, and a secretary that compared favourably with the mahogany one they had left in Egton.

To Gracey's delight the right-hand front room had been set aside for a parlour, with her harpsichord and Miz Lisbeth's candelabra queening it over the most choice of Bonapartt's products. The bedrooms were rather sparsely furnished, Miz Lisbeth having the only tester bed brought from South Carolina. In each of the other sleeping-chambers at least one home-made poster bed had been built into a corner, the walls supplying the head-board and the support of one side. They were little more than a larger refinement of the old cabin bunks; but with pillows in great starched squares, and intricately patterned quilts spread over them, they had an ample, impressive air. There were also cots with frames laced together with leather thongs, in a row in one room for the boys. In addition there were stacks of quilts in a corner of each room, which could be shaken down into pallets for the children if a large number of guests were on hand. A rocker or two, a looking-glass, and small three-cornered washstands showed that the prevailing simplicity, unpretentious as it was, still had come a step beyond the pioneer cabin stage.

The main part of the house had an L-shaped passage connecting it at the rear with the dining-room and kitchen. There was a roof over it, though the sides had not been closed in. Attached to it was a locked storeroom holding provisions to supplement those of the smoke-house. Gerda carried the keys in a bunch at her waist, sleeping with them under her pillow at night. There in the ell, as they called that angled back hall, Gerda supervised her domestic industries. Strings of yarbs and red peppers hung overhead. Bundles of sage, mother-wort, and summer savoury were ranged on a shelf, also reptile-oil liniment for bruises, cucumber ointment for Gracey's freckles, sweet clover and dried jasmine to go among the sheets, and all manner of nauseous doses Pokey kept ready for the children's sick-spells. There were always baskets of beans and black-eyed peas drying, and peach halves and figs as well. Here were the churns, the crocks of new buttermilk, the shallow pans of sweet milk, waiting to be carried to the cool of the spring-house. Pats of fresh butter were waiting to be stamped with the four-leaf clover that Gerda used as her mark. Here the first spring kale and the last fall collard greens waited to be picked over. Here the negro women were measured for a bright new Easter calico, and gossip about Miz MacDuff's heart-spells was swapped for news of the latest betrothal. Here was the source of food and medicine and advice, and here was Gerda's brusque snort of laughter. Here, in fact, beat the pulse of the plantation household.

Outside in the fields were the arteries that pumped the blood into that pulse and allowed Gerda's several domestic enterprises to exist.

Out there was beginning to appear an ample stretch of tilled land, where the seed of cotton was being set in rich earth. What the yearly produce would be none could say, yet Yarbrough felt himself to be entering into his own as a cotton-planter, instead of a makeshift corn-farmer.

Turberville had been growing rapidly since it had become the county seat. It had courthouse, jail, post office, and postmaster. It had a warehouse and gin, and its first hotel, also a well-travelled road to the new river-port near Yufala, where in spite of the neighbouring Indian village the whites were settling thickly. From Yufala steamboats took the cotton to Apalachicola, and from there it was shipped off to world markets. Now Turber County was no longer buried in the wilderness, and there would be great times coming for Turber men, as their fields whitened acre by acre, year after year.

2

Gracey took every occasion she could to visit friends in the growing port of Yufala, for with a sawmill handy, the people there were rapidly erecting a number of imposing frame houses. They would rather eat coarse home-parched corn, and use the water-power of their mill to produce smooth boards, than live in log cabins. Gerda scorned such foolishness, but Gracey admired the fine houses overlooking the river from the bluff, with benches built out in front beneath the trees, where Yufala ladies sat of an afternoon with their sewing, watching the boats moving downstream.

At the intersection of Riverside Drive and Broad Street a two-story hotel had been built, the downstairs of which was an eating and drinking establishment. Upstairs the room used for gaming by the men was planned for occasional balls also, which gave the building its title of Social Hall, and Gracey was waiting with impatience for a levee to be held there, so she could go and shine. So far it had been only an amusement resort for the men of the family, as many of its frequenters were of a low type who drank heavily and used their bowie knives easily.

Ven, with Willy in tow, was often seen along the main street of Yufala, where the owners of fast horses hereabouts raced them, while the stores stopped business, and customers wagered on the outcome.

To-day Ven was loitering in front of the hotel, feeling out of sorts, having lost on a nag before dinner. This afternoon they were going to run off some green two-year olds. On visits to Guy's place he had watched a filly belonging to Neboh, that no-account trickster kinsman of Chokho's. Ven didn't know where the sneak-thief might have stolen her, but he was willing to bet any amount he could lay his hands on that she would win, though he was feeling edgy after his last dram in the post-noonday heat of a nearby tropical April. She out to win, but something told him that Jerard Malone and Neboh had hatched up a scheme he wouldn't like.

The men began wandering out of the hotel, picking their teeth, easing their belts. Willy was dusting his coat sleeves, wondering why he tracked around with Ven when all this hobnobbing bored him; yet he preferred this to the welter of striving, physical exertion under Yarbrough. To-day he sought out Ven, saying: "They're giving a ball soon, in the upstairs Social Hall. One fit for ladies."

Ven grunted. "Spare that. Can you tell me if you've heard anything being cooked up about Neboh's filly?" But Willy had not.

The race was the usual sort, with poor pickings running first, while a few small boys bet ground-peas against one another. Then suddenly, before Ven was ready for it, the two-year-olds started. And there he was caught, with nothing he could do except jog his nearest neighbour in the ribs and clap a dollar between palms, calling his terms.

There was nothing much out-of-the-way about the race, however, except that the filly, who had showed her heels to the field at the start, suddenly towards the end stumbled in a queer sideways fashion. She recovered, but the race was lost to her in that manœuvre and Ven smelt trickery in it. He had lost no great sum of money, but he could not abide cheating. Immediately he made his way to the lot where the horses were kept and discovered Malone pocketing a big stake of money on the second-rater that had won. Ven jerked past him to where Neboh was standing. He put his hand in his pockets first and spat on the ground; then he pulled his bowie knife from his belt and whetted it with more spit. "Turn round," he ordered Neboh.

Neboh did not move.

"Very well," said Ven, reaching over Neboh's shoulder. He picked up the Indian's lank war-lock and with three swift strokes sawed it off, then dropped it in the dirt. "Next time it'll be your throat," he warned, putting his bowie knife back in place.

Guy, who was hovering near with Willy, said: "Ven, you ought not to've done that. We're going to have sure-enough trouble with those Creeks as 'tis, if we don't watch out."

Ven frowned. "You will all please come have drinks with me now," he invited, dourly regarding Malone, who had ruined the race.

Over the drinks Willy broached the subject of the ball once more. "I intend to urge Yarbrough to make an occasion of it—to drive up here in the old carriage. I think the affair will warrant it."

The morning after that, the Whetstone family lingered about the breakfast table. Perhaps it was only the warm sun, but Gerda was reminded of the leisurely breakfasting back at the Home Place, and she was not surprised to see Miz Lisbeth, out of old habit, reaching forth to pick at the flower petals shattering over the tablecloth. Then little Jobyna went and stared through the windows to see if there were any sign of plums ripening, though the blossoms were hardly gone.

Presently Willy put down his fork precisely and said: "There's to be a levee at the Social Hall at Yufala."

At his words Gracey gasped: "A ball, with some music besides fiddling?"

Lucinda, looking down regretfully at her waist which she had refused to keep laced properly, saw it could never be pinched small enough in time for the ball, no matter how tight she drew the draw-strings. As she began to grumble Ma'am Gerda said: "Hush, you're too young to go anyway." Then she added to the table at large: "It's too bad most of us have let our clothes and looks go to pieces, but, Willy, you and Ven can accompany Gracey. She'll make a good showing for the family."

Yarbrough interrupted: "I'm not certain it's a proper place for Gracey to appear, with all that gambling and drinking going on downstairs."

Then Willy cut in: "True, but all the best families will be there, and I think ours should be represented at the first function hereabouts. Moreover *I* can take care of my sister."

"I am so, big enough to go!" cut in Lucinda obstreperously. "I can just see how I'll look in that raspberry satin, Ma'am, that you saved out of your wedding chest for me!"

"Well, you'll not show your face at this gathering," decreed Gerda as she beckoned Gracey to come with her, to look over the gown situation. .She was studying how her sheer cream silk shawl with the fringe would go with Gracey's opal-tinted gauze, when Willy pushed the door open. " Scheming like any match-making mamma, eh, Cousin Gerda?" he twitted.

" Get out of here," snapped Gerda, " while I'm showing Gracey how to dress."

But Willy kept a finger in the crack of her door. " You wouldn't change your mind and come and tread a measure with me, would you, Cousin Gerda?"

She sniffed. " You won't miss me, you've learned how to sit placid enough on the bluff helping the Melburne chit throw pebbles at the river steamers. Now could you be a help to me and go feed my chicka-biddies their soft mash?" With reluctance he went to the fowl yard.

3

The day of the ball Gracey looked lovelier than she ever had in her life. Miz Lisbeth's seed-pearl ear-rings were tossing at her ears, and her curls were built up in a golden fleece. The whole family including the house servants gathered to do her tribute. Miz Lisbeth neglected to remark: " Pretty is as pretty does," and her old eyes watered fondly instead. Yarbrough expressed what they were all feeling: " Gracey, you look very like your mother, sugar!" And they all stood recalling the faint sweet ghost of Miss Lucey for a moment, with Willy wishing he could cry with his head in somebody's lap, and Danley Bruton sorry to be present at this intimacy of their recollections.

Lucinda, dark and jealous in a corner, said spitefully: " Well, Gracey, don't waggle your fan so much, it makes you look as frantic as a hen flapping her wings after she's laid an egg."

In reproof for that rudeness Ven thumped Cinda on the head before he finished blowing his nose, then offered Gracey his arm stiff-jointedly.

Gracey felt slightly foolish going out by daylight in her evening finery, and wondered if she should have gone to stay at Melburne's in Yufala, where she could have appeared thus gowned after proper dark. However she preferred the idea of arriving at the ball in the Whetstone family carriage beneath the gaze of people who had not seen her before that day, uninteresting in her daytime percale.

As the old carriage creaked along, rusty in spite of the many greasings Ruben had given its axles, she sat in her corner and mused. Later, when Willy opened the willow hamper and offered food, she could scarcely nibble a chicken wing. While they rolled on, the trees grew darker and the sky russet; then suddenly, as she was gazing into the amber light, night blotted it up, and in the plush dark of the carriage her flounces frothed out mothy from beneath her cashmere wrap. She turned then and saw that her three escorts appeared to be fine gentlemen with their tucked shirt bosoms. She began to hum a tune, of which Willy caught up the refrain:

Stars go astray
While last of the day
Fades . . .
In glades. . . .

At the party Gracey came instantly into her own and Nettie Melburne cried: "I'm happy that you're to be my overnight visitor, because all the gentlemen will be attentive to me just to gain the good graces of my guest." And it was true. For the instant Gracey entered the dancing-saloon the young dandies besought her for measures enough to fill her whole evening. Still she did not promise her favours too lavishly, not yet having spied Jerard Malone. She meant to dance some figures with him. In her effervescent generosity at being so besought, however, she granted one too many to young Ronald MacDuff, and saw the boy from then on watching her constantly in thin young pride.

Willy also kept his eye on his sister, since she seemed to be spraying gaiety about foolishly. Later, when he saw her walk to the upper porch with that tardy arrival Jerard Malone, he slipped into the shadows to watch them. He heard Malone ask: "Where's the rest of the Whetstone party keeping itself?"

"Why, we are all in plain sight," she answered.

"I haven't laid eyes on Yarbrough, or on Mistress Gerda, or on Lucinda."

"That child? Why, she would be entirely out of place here!"

Malone laughed raucously at this. "You fail to give your young cousin her due."

"Your interest in Lucinda is remarkable," Gracey sniffed. "You need to overcome the foolish notion you have about that chit. Lucinda would be poison for any man, especially you. What you need is somebody who could be sweet to you, at trying times."

With liquor and disappointment making him harsh, Jerard broke in: "I don't want a sugar-stick lady. I despise lace drawers!"

Gracey almost pitched off balance at that crudeness of expression. Her heels squeeched, trying to steady themselves. Then she found that he had departed and she could press her hot face into the cool of evening. She did not hear Willy's stealthy departure from the shadow, and could not know how thankful he was that no discovery had put upon him the obligation to fight over his sister's provoking foolishness.

Willy had not been gone very long when young Ronald came searching for her, worried at the notion of such a weakly little thing being out on the porch with Malone. At Ronald's approach she whirled about, tucking a last tear away in the lace of her handkerchief, feeling very charming in doing so. Ronald did not mention his promised dance; instead he placed himself in front of her and ducked a little bow. "I have but just this instant past asked permission of your brother to address you. Anyway, I want you to marry me! I'll try to make you see it my way if it takes all the rest of my life!" He touched her elbow, as if in childish fear that she might leave him. Gradually it penetrated to her distraught mind that here was at least a *gentleman* wanting her for his *wife!*

She did not look at him clearly, but put an image in his place, the one she imagined on starlit nights, and she said to that image: "Sir, it is an honour you pay me. I can say this much, you may take hope."

After she had persuaded him to leave her she recalled the fact that his nose was aristocratic, and presently she forgot that it was only Ronald MacDuff.

4

The next evening, when Gracey and her escorts returned home to the Stand, she discovered that news both of her fêting and of her conquest of Ronald had preceded her. Ronald had already presented himself to Yarbrough as well as Willy and asked permission to court her. In spite of her few years' seniority no one thought it unsuitable, probably because she was so tiny and immature. Miz Lisbeth said astutely: "The match will suit you, missy, considering him and his flower-planting. I know there were times when I used to think your grandpa would wear me out with his bully-ragging. You had best thank your lucky stars you're getting someone who'll want to carry you around on a down cushion."

"Aw," scoffed Lucinda at Gracey, "why don't you get yourself somebody full-size? Why, I could lick the stuffings out of Ronnie, and I'm just a girl."

Gracey rounded on Lucinda like a virago, recalling the part the girl had played in her having to accept this suit as a last resort after Jerard's scorning. "Hold your tongue! No one asked your opinion, you pert piece! No *gentleman* would ask for you, the way you scuff about, as common as a wench!"

"Pooh, I could cut you out in five seconds with any one that really needed to wear breeches."

At that Gerda herself reached over and pulled Lucinda's hair sharply. "Hush up!" she told her daughter.

By then, however, Gracey's attention had been diverted, for Miz Lisbeth was fumbling in her pocket for a little fold of paper on which she kept her precious possessions listed. "You can keep those seed pearls I lent you. Let them be an engagement present, and I'll scare up the fan that was meant to go with them. My necklace I gave to Andrew's chit. A pity, for she has a neck as stringy as a moulting pullet's. Still, I'll tell you what! I'll trade Gerda my best set of Spode plates if she will agree to give me back that biggest sapphire."

"Oooh!" Gracey grabbed the old lady tight, suddenly no longer disappointed that Ronald was such a sapling youth, since she was being hailed with jewels.

At the supper table she heard only the pleasant chatter that was directed at her. She paid no attention to Yarbrough, looking grave over Willy's account of how the Indian Neboh had been caught skulking about once more, waiting for Ven to go out off-guard, and of how Neboh had been trounced and sent about his business. All that had nothing to do with her; besides, Indians were always up to some mischief. She never liked to hear the subject come up, for fear someone might mention her father's name in connection with Chokho.

She left the table as soon as she could and went to her room to prink. Ronald had left word that he would ride over this evening for his answer from her. Touching her face with rice powder, she knew that her reply would be yes. She slipped out of the house to be by herself, to seek the right mood. The weather had changed, the wind stirring Ronald's flower-beds held rain in its passing. The whitewashed tree-trunks gleamed at her. She smelled some damp flowers and thought: "It's all coming out right for me, in spite of everything that made me feel just a ninny around Gerda and Yarbrough. I'll ask him to build me a house with two-story columns! And I'll use silver forks instead of bone-handle ones." Her musings had dismissed the wilderness as if it were a thing of the past.

CHAPTER TWENTY

No ONE had given Guy a thought in connection with Gracey's betrothal. Nevertheless Guy had heard of it before sundown on the day after it took place and began cudgelling his brain over a proper dowry for her. A week elapsed before he could make the trip to see her, for he was taken up with more pressing matters. Sporadic hostilities on the part of the Creeks were increasing, until Guy knew what Yarbrough feared to be a fact : the pattern of Kochi Fixio's vengeance was beginning to be traceable. Yarbrough, ever on the alert, had urged higher governmental authorities to lend a hand to the county in deporting large numbers of the remaining Indians by boat, in hopes of so depleting the tribes that little actual warfare would be possible later. Since Guy had influence with many of them, Yarbrough had asked his aid.

Guy insisted upon telling Chokho of his intentions to render such services, being punctilious to preserve the dignity of her own customs. Following his announcement he sat with her over the pot-fire for the better part of an hour, to allow her the required space of silence to ponder her reply. At the end of that time she had raised herself from her posture of sitting on her shins, and stood calmly, her arms snuggled across the worn fringes of her doeskin jacket. "A man obeys the counsel of his tribe." Then she had simply moved aside for him to pass by on his way to the undertaking.

The task Guy had let himself in for was not a bit to his liking. It was no easy matter to induce even the most peaceable of the Creeks to embark on a trip down the Chattahoochee, for they were an agricultural people rather than a traipsing tribe. They were accustomed to doing little travelling, and that not often by canoes on creeks, much less by strange big boats down large streams of water. This was the first time most of them had ever set foot on a river steamer, and they huddled in groups, cringing at every jerk and start of the boat's paddles. They feared that the Evil River One, which had so often spoiled their growing corn with floods, was now waiting, a monster, to suck them down. Losing their stolid quiet, women wailed, children screeched, and some silly maidens lifted a reedy note of lament. The packet sounded like a vessel of death, passing between banks where pines bent like black brooms beneath an oncoming storm.

Guy had walked his pony most of the way back from this distasteful errand of overseeing the embarkation, and while dawdling along an Indian wood trace he noticed a faint sound, like some creature of the grass trying to catch its breath. His eyes focused on the spot from which the sound had come. He went over to it. Stooping above a small crouched figure, he was presently able to make out an Indian girl with eyes as blank as window-panes from fear. When he spoke to her in Chokho's tongue, she answered him a few broken phrases at a time: "I could not be taken into the River One's maw. So I fled here. Now the wolves may tear me. Yet here would I rather stay than risk that River One!"

He lifted her to her feet and set about taking her with him. When they finally arrived back at his place, Guy found that Chokho knew her. After the squaw had fed and bedded the child down, she told Guy, in what was a lengthy speech for her: "Ailsey would make a good serving-maid for your daughter. She knows how to wash laces, and work their broken patterns together again with a fine needle. She is well trained in gentle ways, for her kin once served the ladies of the Vine and Olive Colony, from that country you call France."

Well, yes, Guy thought, puffed with pride like a bullfrog, he could add this Ailsey to his daughter's dowry.

The next morning he made good time to Whetstone Stand and found Gracey on the front porch trying to string up some moon vines to shade the hot west end. She was already playing at being the lady of a plantation while waiting for the time to wed. Yet, being partial to the fuss and feathers of courting-time, she had set the day over a year off.

Guy cleared his throat. "Daughter—err-a—Gracey."

She turned around reluctantly. "Did you wish to speak to me?"

He decided: "I'll be Jimminied if I'll be put off in this high-handed way." Then he said aloud: "Nobody bothered mentionin' to me that you've been bespoke in marriage. All the same, I thought I might take some notice of it. I've a nice piece of land down near here. Maybe you and Ron might like to cultivate it—that is, if you ain't scared of the boogies getting you on it. There are some Indian burial-mounds there, you know. But if you two are smart you can make plenty of bales to the acre."

"You would have to speak to Ronald about that. I don't understand such matters." Gracey had brightened at his first mention of a gift, but lost interest upon hearing it was just more wild land. She waited with a perfunctory smile plastered over her mouth. Her eyes strayed from the wild blue lupin flowers eating up the new fields across the road, back down to the fine stitches in her lawn apron pocket.

Guy, seeing that he hadn't made much of a hit with her by giving her something substantial, now threw in the lagniappe. "Then I'm fetching you over a lace-laundress pretty soon, who'll make you a fine serving-maid as well, since your Dilsey died. Better than those cornfield wenches Gerda palms off on everybody but herself. This Ailsey's folks were trained by the Vine and Olive Colony ladies."

He stood there teetering on the sun-washed porch boards, flecking his brier switch at his leggings with the same gesture he had used in touching his riding-whip to his shined boots back in Egton. Gracey remembered forlornly those old days of his dandyhood. Her glance escaped down towards the road, half-expecting some cavalier she had never seen to come galloping up, his speedy horse's hoofs squirting mud. Then she remembered that she was now promised to marry a callow youth, and coming back to actual circumstances, she recalled that her father had offered her a domestic prize, so she replied: "Have Ailsey brought over here soon, and I'll try her out."

Guy dropped the brier switch forgetting all his disappointment. "Here, sugar," he told her, "here's something *she*—your mother—would want you to have at a time like this." Diffidently he handed her a wad of tissue paper that smelled musty. As Gracey picked the worn shreds of tissue apart, Lucey's tiny courtship locket of turquoise slipped out. She lifted it gently to twirl on its gold-thread chain.

After having bestowed his blessing, Guy went hastening away, for he had the feeling that there was something urging him back towards Yufala and the deep Indian country. He did not even look in at the ell and explain to Gerda that he wasn't staying to dinner. His "twitchiness" about the Creeks was returning unabated. As he led his pony down the road, he looked back and studied the Rock Wall Place. The porch was firm, with the centre hall making a clear shaft through its middle. It looked safe, yet Guy's chin quivered. "No telling what's safe, or what's coming," he whispered.

The road faded off into the trees so that he nearly missed its turns in his abstraction, it being that time of day when it is hard to see clearly, that half-light called "blind man's holiday." So Guy was startled when an Indian stepped out into his path, and wondered if maybe his time had come. Then he saw it was one of Chokho's charges and was relieved. The Indian said: "I came to tell you that a number of our people, feeling too wronged, have attacked the stage that passes Turberville and set fire to it. Chokho fears you cannot come in safety alone, so I was sent to lead you by a hidden way."

His message delivered, the Indian stepped back. Guy knew he was expected to say some wise thing, but he was unable to act like a chief. His toes squirmed in his stirrups as he wondered how he would manage in the fighting that was bound to come. He had to stand by Chokho, yet he was from a leading South Carolina family. At that thought he raised his hand in a sign of dismissal to the warrior and said: "No! I go ahead down this road. I have no fear." Then he rode forward where the shadows were deep and black across his way.

2

In spite of the fact that Guy arrived back on his own property without mishap, he was not lulled into any delusion of security. Nor did either he or Yarbrough relax their vigilance, knowing that Kochi Fixio inevitably meant to carry the contest between the races to the point of extermination of one breed or the other. Still, for a space the Indians, with their subtle ability to torture, ceased their more flagrant outrages, contenting themselves with minor reminders of the feud until a majority of the more hopeful settlers were convinced that they were to be left in peace. The work in their fields progressed, the women finished their spring sewing, and even the lighter social life was resumed, with emphasis upon courting.

Gracey had gone to Yufala to stay with Nettie Melburne for the May Day festivities to be held on the morrow. Both were expecting to take part in the figure about the maypole, weaving bright ribbons into a rainbow pattern. This evening they could scarce contain themselves and walked excitedly up and down the path along the bluff not caring that their frock hems were becoming soiled with dust. They kept prattling: "We'll make them simply perish!" or "We'll be having a cotillion club in Turber County before you can say Jack Rabbit!" not realizing that they were using backwoods colloquialisms to express future elegance.

Now they had come to the curve that gave the broadest view of the river, where the steamboat *Minnie B* was casting off, not yet trying to get up speed because it would have to stop just down below at McCabe's landing. People were hanging easily over the railing waving to friends on shore, not caring to go down into the dining-saloon for supper until after dark. A girl was tilting her parasol at a gentleman who was trying to peep beneath. This was the sweetest time of day on the river. Two little barques were tip-tilting about in the wash of the *Minnie B,* while the lights of the steamer began to prick out its shape against the grey phalanx of the Georgia shore.

Then suddenly this still clear hour was punctured by the *pop-pop-pop* of rifles, and dirty cotton twists of smoke began to drift in the wake of the noise. Gracey and Nettie instantly fell flat to keep out of the way of the shooting, though they were in no real danger. They lay there so long that they could feel their ribs scraping against the hard dirt of the path. Gracey tried, from their hiding-place, to see what was going on. She could make out a rush of curious passengers towards the steamer rail overlooking the Alabama bank. Then she saw where a figure or two had slumped against neighbours as if falling. And now the passengers were surging down into the saloon, except for a few gentlemen who remained to discharge pistols in the direction from which the firing had come. In answer to that, more rifles barked, and the *Minnie B,* which had been trying stubbornly to go ahead, now chunked uncertainly this way and that. The firing at her increased, until the steamer gave up progress and eased back to the Alabama landing. All the little shore craft were now out of sight in the coves.

Up on the bluff Nettie and Gracey were rising, but still shrunk together. "That," gulped Nettie, "was the *Indians* fighting white folks!"

"'Twas indeed!" gasped Gracey. "And they actually stopped the river travel!"

"Let's g-go in!" choked Nettie.

They scurried across the stretch between bluff and house and burst into the Melburne door, to find Nettie's mother hobbled in by the frightened servants. The girls sank down on the tarry-bench, their hearts fluttering like bits of paper. Miz Melburne and the servants thought that maybe the girls had been nearly killed by those shots, and Gracey and Nettie let them think so. Nettie's mother was sending for glasses of scuppernong wine when Captain Melburne came in, fit to be tied because the Creeks had been plundering his outer plantations, had stolen two of his best brood-mares, and set fire to his corncribs also. Nettie and Gracey began to chatter at him about how they'd been mixed up in the river firing, but he looked at them with eyes as stony as marbles for their presumption in interrupting him with prattle about mere fireworks on the river. He was telling them about a thousand dollars' worth of damage that those savages had done to his outlying property! Also another stagecoach, the one to Montgomery, had been burned.

Every one cowered and the girls began to tremble again at the implication in the sight of those passengers keeling over on the deck of the steamer. Gracey began to wish she were back home, farther away from the Indian settlements, where she could have the comfort of Yarbrough's and Gerda's familiar faces.

Strange things were all very well when they meant a holiday, but she scarcely thought about the abandoned May party the next morning when Willy and Ronald came to fetch her home. Ronald rode devotedly close to her, as if by this he could afford her some extra protection. His drawn face appeared a good deal older, and his few words were sharp with anxiety rather than timid with any wish to please her. She kept taking side glimpses at him, thinking that this intense stranger might some day even make her love him.

When they drew up safe and sound at Rock Wall she was relieved. By supper time, when she smelt the richness of syrup pudding baking, the idea of danger appeared ridiculous and she began to regret the maypole dance. "Somebody at Yufala ought to have had gumption enough to see that it wasn't called off! Why, just think of all those wreaths of flowers we wore our fingers raw weaving!"

"Lady Dainty, you don't say!" jeered Lucinda, but her father cut her short. Then Yarbrough addressed his niece in waning patience. "Gracey, you had better thank your stars that trouble was delayed long enough to remove you from harm's way; for you may be sure a powder-keg has been set off, though I can't predict when the main explosion will come. Nor which of us will live to tell the tale. But your pleasant life may well be marred beyond recognition."

"Oh, please don't scare me blue in the face!" Gracey pleaded, pressing the turquoise locket like a talisman that could ensure her safety with its accompanying luxuries.

3

One Saturday shortly after that the family was gathered in the ell, the men and older children cleaning firearms. The twins were helping Yarbrough, each bragging about being brave if attacked by Indians, while Jobyna was huddling near Gerda's skirts. Suddenly Jerard Malone entered without making much preliminary noise. Small Joby jumped screeching, before she saw it was a white man.

Without any greeting Malone swept his arm around to indicate their collection of weapons. "I'll wager you'll be putting those to sharp use before another sun goes down. Did you know that Dennisville has been burned by the Indians?"

"Dennisville burned?" demanded Yarbrough, aghast. "Why, that's not a stone's throw from Guy's place!"

"Where's my father?" cried Willy quickly. "Is he——"

"Guy's safe, and most of the rest of the whites saved their skins, because Guy's squaw warned him. But they had to scat over into Georgia for the present, though I think Guy has a hiding-hole for himself on this side. One that Chokho picked. Anyway, Dennisville proper is a mound of ashes. Now we know that Kochi Fixio is really starting on the warpath!"

Yarbrough dragged a black-greased hand across his forehead and then his eyelids. *"Kochi Fixio,"* he muttered. "Malone, do you mean the old chief himself?"

"Yes, though he hasn't batted his eye yet. In fact no white man has seen him lately close enough to watch him bat an eye. He's been near 'bout as invisible as one of their great spirits since his return from the West. All the same, his orders are working among them like yeast. Why do you suppose he let you and the Government transport a lot of his helpless folks away? To get them out of the ruckus, of course. And why do you suppose he favours Guy? Partly because he and Chokho, Indian-like, can't turn on a friend. But partly again," Malone lowered his voice for Yarbrough's sole hearing, "because he considers Guy might be a link of information for the Creeks' benefit, if they act sly enough.. And who can equal an Indian at slyness? Oh, that old fox is still feeling his way quietly. But don't overlook that he has dug his tomahawk out from under the cotton patch. And sharpened it up bright!"

Grimly Yarbrough studied the gun he had been cleaning. "I'll be ready for him!" he replied.

Then Malone's voice boomed cheerily to the whole room. "Guess where most of my scary negroes are quartered, now that they're hiding from the Indians. In the gin-house at Turberville. The bins of cotton-seed make prime beds, though I'll admit I itch considerably to-day from that sweaty lint."

"It strikes me," Miz Lisbeth spoke up sharply, "that somebody could have put at least you up properly, sir."

"God's truth, and many offered," he reassured her, "only I figured I'd better stay with my skittish outfit the first night. To-day my overseer has his spunk back, so if you all can accommodate me here I'll be much obliged." His eyes followed Lucinda, but she was too excited over the Indian uprising to cast glances at any man.

"I think," decided Yarbrough finally, "that we men had better divide the night into watches and take turns standing guard."

"You'd best call me out for the last spell of the dark, then," said Ven, "when my head's getting the best of me after the whisky has worn off and I cain't sleep anyway."

"And let me," cried Bruff, "sit with Uncle Ven to jog him if he starts to drop off to sleep."

"Better sit with him," remarked Miz Lisbeth, "to see that he don't jog up the bottle too often."

Lucinda shot a thwarted, envious look at her boy twin. Malone, noticing this, guyed her with the remark: "Lucinda, do you want to keep me company while I'm doing my watch?"

4

The next day was so perfect a May Sunday, with flowers blooming plentifully in sunshine, that fear receded again. Every one went bustling about in his Sunday best, shaking down skirts or setting stocks more trimly. Brother Upshur was to preach over at the Turberville church, and the first all-day preaching of the year, with dinner on the grounds, was to be a picnic occasion. The Whetstone turn-out made a fine appearance; the men's mounts cavorted and even the wagon mule-team lifted hoofs with a frisky air. The coachman, Ruben, rolled his eyes about very uppity whenever any neighbour came alongside. He knew how to drive, even if they gave him billy-goats hitched to a stump.

At the church, people talked a good deal less about the Indian scare than might have been expected, and when the services started, Brother Upshur gave out the more rejoicing hymns. They were singing with gusto when they heard a great *buckety-buckety-buck* out in the churchyard, a sound as if a horse were about to gallop up the steps into the church. The rider must have sprung from the saddle directly on to the porch, for in an instant they all saw Guy Hampley rushing down the aisle towards the pulpit with his hat still on.

Brother Upshur leaned over to hear what he had to say, then held up his hand to silence what singing had not dwindled away. Guy hopped up beside the preacher and faced the congregation; his breath whipped out his words: "The Indians have now fallen on the town of Roanoke over in Georgia and massacred all its inhabitants! Besides burning the town to the ground! They're on their way to Yufala now. After that, if they do away with Yufala, you will be the next to be slaughtered! The folks at Yufala have rolled the drums and rung the bells to assemble all. They've picked a spot and are building a stockade. I came down here—to ask your help!" He ended on a gasp.

A rush of guttural anger went around the room. Every throat rumbled. Every man eyed his neighbour in shared outrage at the Creeks' bloodthirstiness, for these settlers of Turber County had come to build homes, not to wage warfare. But if the Creeks were going to slaughter even women and children, these men would fight. Then John Upshur raised his preacher's voice over them all. "I move we men go out in the churchyard, where we can hold council how best to give our neighbouring settlement aid. The ladies please rest themselves in here."

The men drained out of the pews, crowding the doorway in their eagerness. Outside they sought the fence of the burying-plot to lean against while they talked. The sun had warmed its palings, and a sweet-shrub was giving out its nectar smell, but no one noticed that. They turned to Upshur as their spokesman, since he was their parson and they were used to listening to him. He put it to them quickly. They were all to see their families home, or into safe-keeping at some neighbour's if they lived too far. They were to appoint a few of the older men like Gran van Ifort to select some trusted darkies to guard the homes. Then every able-bodied man was to collect all available firearms and other weapons and reassemble at Turberville by one o'clock. From there they were to march in a band to Yufala to render such assistance as was in their power.

When Upshur had finished, Duncan MacDuff spoke up: "We'll need a captain and," he chuckled, "we're used to following Brother Upshur except on gambling days, so it strikes me we'd better choose him captain."

But John demurred. "I haven't any grudge against the Creeks myself, I'd hate to shoot at them. Why, I've had them for neighbours ever since I can remember." He was recalling the comfort they had given his mother, hollowing out a small coffin for his brother from a log.

At that point Malone suggested practically: "Whetstone's our man. He's the head of a family as big as a regiment." In a moment the ayes had it, and Yarbrough was elected captain. As they were dispersing Malone winked at him. "Now you two chief bulls can lock horns for fair."

By one o'clock a hundred men had assembled in Turberville to set out for Yufala, and by hastening, the company arrived there before sundown. They were in time to help move the women and children inside the stockade. The inhabitants, one and all, had worked with such a will that the rude fortifications stood completed. Now every one was hurrying about, bringing in firewood, bedding, cornmeal, and bacon. The visitors were soon lending a hand with the chores, until somehow it all began to seem like a big frolic. Nettie Melburne started making eyes at Danley Bruton, trying to annex him. He followed about amiably, doing this or that task she set him until she assumed she was making quite a conquest. Then he spoke in a curiously detached tone that disconcerted her: "It's odd, but people elsewhere never think of planters and their families as having to fight Indians from behind stockades. I myself had the idea before I came down here that all that was over long ago with Captain John Smith, ending in the Pocahontas romance. I pictured Southerners as sitting perpetually on verandas, gazing at magnolia trees, sipping juleps from silver goblets." He broke off with a short laugh. "Instead I find the young lords of the manor running around in homespun nightshirts for their only costume, and the ladies smoking corn-cob pipes if they choose, while they feed the chickens."

Nettie stood stock-still, spilling syrup out of a pitcher so that it ran in treacly brown threads down her dress. "Well, I never! I'll have you know my mother never smoked a pipe in all her life!"

He bowed ironically. "No doubt she follows the more refined practice of dipping snuff," and he walked away leaving her mortified, because her mother did dip snuff.

Afterwards Danley was half-ashamed for not staying and explaining how he admired, with all his heart, these robust people he had found inhabiting the lower South. He liked their crassness, their joviality, their pig-headed self-interest that begot bravery. But the girl Nettie was such a goose. She, like Gracey, was ineffectual on this soil fertilized for the Gerdas of the time.

That night, after the townspeople had posted sentries at every corner of the stockade, they built a bonfire, and when the food had settled and the whisky lifted the men's spirits again, they took advantage of the custom of ending the Sabbath at sundown. Two fiddlers were picked to spell each other out, and presently they were all dancing, not the stately mazurkas and the gavottes of their Social Hall, but rousing back-country square dances that chucked up a dust. The laughter of the young people went bounding about the enclosure as freely as their bouncing bodies. Laughter was a fortress, Indian-fighting was a picnic, and to-morrow would come the main show in the big tent.

True, they did not sleep much that night, but that was because of excitement rather than anxiety. Girls giggled confidences, boys swapped tall lies about their bravery, and now and then some older man snored in a short doze near the campfire. Presently morning came in with a puny colour and a smell of coffee breaking the air with its pungency. Somehow to-day there was no feeling of Indians being in the woods yonder. It was merely a May Monday with roosters crowing all over the deserted town, arrogantly angry at their unaccustomed hunger. So after breakfast one of the women rose, saying: "Who'll come along as a guard with me to feed my fowls and milk my cows?"

5

That was how the threatened attack on Yufala petered out. The men from down below the Line stayed on for several days, scouring the woods for signs of a hostile approach, trying to talk themselves into believing that any minute now they would hear a war-whoop. But nothing sharper sounded than the rattle of a woodpecker drilling into a tree-trunk. First Upshur, then Yarbrough, then all the others agreed there was no sense in lolling around underfoot, eating their heads off. Group by group they departed, trying to discuss weather and crops to conceal their childish disappointment at being cheated out of a rousing fight.

Once back home, they were not regarded as returning heroes, but more like pedlars with gossip from a neighbouring community. Nor did the women expect them to sit all day recounting it, not while weeds were springing up and negroes were chopping the cotton carelessly.

Yarbrough and the others went about their work somewhat distractedly, interrupting routine duties to build small stockades here and there, or to post look-outs. Summer came and went, with fall following on towards Christmas. Now and then just as they were about to forget the danger and to take pride in their cotton, growing as tall as spruce shrubs, word would come of some single fresh atrocity. Immediately all the men would grow feverish with desire for action that would settle the issue, but they could never locate the enemy. Exactly where the Indians were hiding no one knew, not even Guy. When he had returned to his place after the May scare, he had found all those of his household, save Ailsey, gone. He was able to read the sign-message Chokho had left on a stone. It said Farewell. What else it meant he could not divine.

He had stayed on his own stand of land for a good while after that, but it seemed mournful and deserted with only his negroes in the fields and Ailsey to cook for him. So his habit soon became to visit a good deal at the Whetstone Stand, trying to make up to Gracey.

She had little time for him, though, because with the abatement of open concerted hostilities she was occupied gathering her trousseau. She went to see Miz MacDuff often, since that lady suited her taste, with her aches, her *sal volatile,* and her worry about the texture of her hands. The only trouble with these visits was that Miz Lydia Screws was there a lot too, and put Gracey's teeth on edge. She would ask: "Waitin' for Ronnie to cut his milk teeth, eh? Well, that's right, for I can't picture you as playing nursemaid." Or another time she'd shake her head and say: "I declare I don't see what you two get married for. You could just as easy hold hands and pull the petals off a daisy right out in the front yard in plain sight. You don't need to hide under the cover for that." Then if Gracey jumped up furious and pink, Miz Lydia would add innocently: "But I expect you do want to have your own little doll dishes to play with, don't you, honey?"

Gracey would come home from such encounters thoroughly out of sorts, pouting at Yarbrough and Willy, pinching her serving-maid, and simply spoiling for a quarrel with Lucinda or Gerda. She got that quarrel full tilt with Gerda one day soon after Christmas. A number of the children were down with castor oil after over-stuffing, the negroes were again off the good behaviour they had displayed before gift-giving time, and the rain on the windows was enough to pound the brains out of your head. Besides, the crops had been short because of the neglect they had suffered during the recent Indian threat. Consequently when Gracey finally whined her umpteenth complaint, Gerda, who had a dipper of water in her hands, threw it into the girl's face. Then she picked up a plate and sent it skimming across the room, where it crashed against the wall and a splinter of it cut Hans's cheek. He sucked in his breath in terror, and Gerda, seeing fear of her in the eyes of this boy she had heretofore carefully guarded, only felt a more ghastly rage. She began to pound the heel of one brogan on the floor like a tom-tom, straining her apron between her fists until with a screech it tore apart in ribbons.

Gran's hand came down on her shoulders and held firm, until she heaved into stillness. "It is, I think," he said, "this war with the

Creeks which does not come off that betrays our nerves. Still you of all people cannot turn loose a wild beast in your household." His voice was a stern command. She moved around dazedly and sat down on a chair. Lucinda was already holding Hans's forehead against her skirt. "Come," Gerda told them, "bring me some water and I'll bandage it." The boy came, still holding close to Cinda for protection, and Gerda lifted him kindly into her lap, kissing him, big as he was. Then he rested against her bosom, comforted.

Gran added in his more natural tone: "It has been a hard year, *liefste,* and tedious with the suspense of withheld fear."

The domestics began picking up the litter made by Gerda's fit, and presently the supper bell rang. Those present went in to the meal, but Yarbrough was not there, nor Willy, nor Guy, nor Danley Bruton, and the whole meal passed with their plates still turned down. Finally, when yawns were beginning to dull the worry over their absence, the awaited noise sounded and the men entered highly excited.

There had been an open Indian skirmish at last! Just when they'd thought the alarums were over. It had taken place at Martin's field, with Walter Peterson killed, Bowen's arm hurt badly, and two or three others wounded, while the Indians had got off without a casualty.

"You mean they whipped the whites?" demanded Bruff unbelievingly.

"Surprised us, son," snapped Yarbrough, "that's all. This was just the start." He then added heavily: "We stayed to help bury Peterson. He was a good neighbour."

"And now what?" wondered Gerda silently. Well, now they would at least be rid of this fuming till all grew sick, this living that was not worth living.

"Call me," commanded Yarbrough, "at four in the morning. There's going to be hell popping before we can catch forty winks."

CHAPTER TWENTY-ONE

VERY RAPIDLY the white men rallied at Yufala, forming into two companies, one under Yarbrough, the other under Malone's captaincy. There they awaited impatiently the arrival of a troop of Georgians coming to their aid from across the river. The Georgians had taken the burning of Roanoke to heart and ever since had been all for stamping the Creeks off the face of the earth. While waiting, Yarbrough called for a volunteer to post himself a short distance upstream to scout out any Indians who might try to take the reinforcing troops by surprise, and Ven piped up: "I'm your man. I've fished in that spot between horse-races for the past three years." Yarbrough eyed him dubiously, but since the younger men hung back out of respect for Ven's seniority, there was nothing to do but to take him up on his offer.

Slapping his big back pockets to make sure his bottles were there, Ven chuckled to his fool heeny-mount, which he was riding since he could not bring himself to expose his beloved blooded horse to the danger of bullets. He'd be almighty glad to get off by himself and sit down out of this rumpus for a spell of sipping and chewing. Shortly he found the place he wanted, with the swash of the water sounding restful; there he leaned back against an oak trunk and before he knew it had dropped into a doze. Presently there was a sound like pebbles being chucked through his dreams and he jumped unsteadily to his feet, cocking his gun foolishly. A grunting laugh overhead caused him to glance up, where he saw that scalawag called Chief Billy Bowlegs lying on a limb dropping acorns at him.

"You old good-for-nothin'," Ven hailed him joyfully, "what you doin' roostin' up there?" They had drunk together many a time and the pseudo-chief would sell his soul for fire-water.

"Up high so see Georgia troops go by," Bowlegs leered. "They think they can sneak, but make bigger noise than herd of frightened deer. Soon they discover no use to try fight Creeks, who can creep as soft as lizard changing colour."

Ven scratched his head. He knew there was some trickery behind

Bowlegs's exposing his presence; either that or the rascal was parched for spirits. Ven studied the proposition. Did the wily Creeks expect him to make tracks for his comrades and frighten them with tall tales of the Indians' superior numbers and prowess, so they would retreat, avoiding a real battle, and the Georgia military would return home, leaving Turber County to the mercy of the warriors striking from ambush Indian-style? Or were the Creeks actually strong enough to win in an open encounter? He couldn't tell. But Ven was certain of two things: he wasn't going to carry any tale of false scare to the whites, and on the other hand if there was going to be a bloody onslaught he, for one, was not going to be caught in it! He was only thankful he had enough whisky to see him through to safety in Georgia, and to try out first a trick of his own which he hoped would settle Bowlegs's usefulness to his tribe.

He spat out his cud and washed his mouth out with whisky; then he raised the bottle again to his lips for a longer drag. He could almost hear Billy's mouth water, but Ven smacked the cork into his bottle and restored it to his pocket. There was a quick scraping sound as Bowlegs came shinnying down the tree. He hit the dirt with a smack of his moccasins almost loud enough to come from brogans. Ven started walking towards his heeny, with Bowlegs following right after him. Ven swung about, hitching angular shoulders in pretended surprise. Without any racial dignity Bowlegs gulped: "Have you fire-water to spare?"

Ven held the bottle up and measured its contents against the light. "I reckon I can spare you a mite." He waited until the Indian had swallowed three hard slugs and the warmth was beginning to curl up his throat; then Ven continued: "Sure as shootin' you better tell your folks to *git*! For we're makin' hash out of any that stay too long. We have scads of sure-enough soldiers to help us, with fine firearms, and we're well set up behind stockades." Two could play at this game of swapping lies, thought Ven. "It seems like a pack of foolishness to me for your folks not to git, while the gittin's good. What say?"

Bowlegs, who would rather pass the time drinking than doing anything else, agreed eagerly, lest he be deprived of his share of the bottle. He need not have feared, for Ven, with an expert's hand, went about plying him with it to the point of stupor. Finally leaving Bowlegs sprawled out, Ven sought a half-breed who would ferry him across the

Chattahoochee on a raft. He landed on the other side with the combined feeling that he had pulled a smart trick, serving the white troops well, and that he was likewise released from personally participating in a fracas he did not relish at his age. Now he decided he could salve his conscience by finding a suitably safe place to be used as a refuge for the women and children of Turber County. He did not hold with their staying in Alabama with so much shooting going on.

He was able the same day to send back word to Yarbrough:

I left the Indian befuddled, also worried about how we would chop them to pieces. I now wait to receive any of the women and children you might see fit to send over for safe-keeping. I trust you have not any of you met with mishaps, but better send the women along before it proves too late. So hurry them along.

Your Aff'ct bro.
Ven.

Yarbrough, upon receipt of the epistle, was badly mortified to think that any brother of his should prove so cowardly as practically to desert, but Willy laughed heartily, vowing it was a smart trick. Gran combed his beard judiciously and remarked solemnly: "That Ven is wiser than I at my years, old fool that I am to embroil myself with shot and powder. How I long to sit in a chimney corner with my forefinger between a book! But, *wat drommel*! How can one meditate like a philosopher with the buckshot biting his breeches?"

2

Shortly after that news came that seventy-five warriors were advancing by way of the swamp towards Upshur's Bridge over Pea River. Messengers were sent in all directions to warn people of the danger of Indian depredations, while John Upshur, man of peace, spent the rest of the night moulding bullets, listening unhappily to the hissing sound as the little peas of lead hit the water.

Soon after dawn the whites assembled. Before light they approached the swamp. Then dismay clutched! For two huge fallen white oaks were locked in mammoth union, strong breastworks before their foe.

Entrenched the Indians waited, while the white men scurried. Where was shelter for taking aim? Where their targets' hearts? How pierce through oak to flesh? *And confound these swamp vapours!*

Before they knew what happened the whites were drawn into lagoon warfare, at which the Creeks excelled. In the end the companies rallied, made a haphazard charge, but did it sprawling in muddy ignominy.

Then the Indians, because of lost equipment, retreated downswamp into the next county, leaving the whites chagrined at letting the enemy slip from their grasp. Slowly the men in the three companies departed to various nearby plantations for a brief respite, carrying their wounded and wondering silently what was coming next. . . .

They had not long to wait, for soon indications came that a second and much larger band of Indians was moving down Pea River Swamp. They could be tracked by the trail of burned houses and pillaging left in their wake, and their bold-faced plundering stirred the county to a fever-heat. Yarbrough, with twenty-odd men called the Turber Rangers, pursued them far enough to ascertain where they too would be likely to make camp in the swamp. Then he scattered his Rangers to secure all possible reinforcements. He knew that the Creeks were lulled into a temporary sense of security because some United States troops who had been aiding the settlers had dropped back into another county. And he counted upon this lull to attend to the removal of the women and children into the safety of Georgia.

Fagged from scouring the countryside for volunteers, he turned towards home to settle the question of his own household's removal with Gerda. He found Gran on the front porch sniffing the air angrily and growling in his throat, having just been given a vivid description by Willy of the havoc wrought to the houses, fields, and livestock of their friends. Gran's Dutch respect for property had been gouged too far. "Fire and blood, *och,* I hate them! To be burned in my bed I will not suffer! A gun I will get also, and go as blood-thirsty as that savagery which I deplore, until this menace is scourged from our countryside and I can sleep sound once more at night."

Sombrely Yarbrough reviewed the paradox called up by Gran Pieter's words. "It's a bad, mixed-up question," he finally granted. "We settlers of Turber County didn't make the migration down here with the thought of carnage. We only wanted to build homes. Then we ran into the fact that we had to despoil the Creeks of theirs to set up our own. Some of us tried to act decent most of the time, but few of us were blameless clear through. Lord knows, not I! Yet when the Indians commenced to retaliate with acts of mutilation against the helpless, we couldn't stomach that! Our race likes to fight it out between men. And yet—I wonder, if a time ever should come when the only way to keep our own women and children safe was to bash theirs, wouldn't we do that same horrible thing?"

He rocked his whole body, stretching his arms wide to untwist his muscles. "But, Jehoshaphat, I do wish we could manage it without pounding other humans to pieces! Still, we're in the mess now. And it's devil take the hindmost in getting out of it."

Suddenly he felt embarrassed by Gran's attentive scrutiny. "Sorry for my speechifying," he mumbled, "but I do like happy times, and knowing I've done fair by those I care about, also by those below or beholden to me. Sir, I'd lop off my arm at the shoulder to gain that end in peace, but looks like that won't do it now. There seems no way out but the letting of blood. Let's hope for God's mercy."

Yarbrough braced a hand on old van Ifort's shoulder and steered their way through the hall. "It's too late to bother about the rights and the wrongs of it. We're into it up to our necks and have to finish it. So come with me, I need your help with Gerda. For we're obliged to send the women and children over to Bro' Ven in Georgia, to remove them from this mess. And I doubt if Gerda will take it well."

Gran blew out his lips. "Now the sparks will fly!"

Gerda was at the foot of the back steps whipping all the children who had been ill-behaved that day. The two men stopped, out of her sight, to watch while she attended to this duty. She had them, black and white, lined up in two rows from the top to the bottom step. As each one's turn came, she plucked the offender off the bottom step, and the ones behind moved down a step. She told the culprit for what he was being punished, and asked if he was sorry. If he said no she laid on five extra licks, but if he said yes when she knew he was not sorry, she laid on ten extra. In each instance after the thrashing she reached in one pocket for a lump of brown sugar and in the other for a handful of pecans, reminding them not to crack them with their teeth. She called these "comfort snacks," and usually saved a lump of sugar to suck on to soothe herself. Now when she had finished she sat down, reaching for a couple of the littlest children to hug. Knowing she was to bear yet another child so very soon, the switching to-day caused her to wonder what was the use of breeding babies to beat.

When the two men called to her she stood up clumsily. And when they led her off into the big bedroom she knew at once it was something serious. Yarbrough came to the point at once. "There's another large band of Creeks over in Pea Swamp. The worst yet. We've rallied three companies and we're out to put a finish to them, since living can't continue in this fashion." He stopped and searched her face for help to tell her. "Gerda, you must go, you and the other neighbouring women and children—over into Georgia to Ven."

She pulled up out of the rocker, trying to hold her bulging body straight. "And leave you here to the Lord knows what massacre?" Yarbrough tried to put a calming hand upon her, but she twisted free. "No! I can see you have all taken the bit in your teeth and are going to fight till there's not a man left if need be. I can tell when you've been riding with the devil in the saddle, tell without even seeing your eyes walling. And, Yarbrough, you haven't a spark of common sense at such times! You need me to hold you down then, and take care of you."

"But don't you see?" cried Yarbrough, with desperation like gall in his mouth because he knew his recklessness had brought them much harm. "You can't tell me that you have to stay here in danger, to lick my wounds and bind me up like a swaddled infant! Do you think me a man or——"

Gran came lumbering between them. First he pulled Yarbrough's brandishing arms down, then he said: "Go to my chamber, my son, and leave this child to her *groot vader* to permit him to remind her of the precept of obedience to the husband, which she has forgotten since you bestowed upon her too much authority."

Yarbrough yanked his arm free. "Thank you kindly, sir, but I can manage this." He turned to Gerda and directed her to seat herself quietly, whereupon Gran left them to themselves.

"Now see here, Gerda! Once you sat in the place of Fate and took from us our unborn child. You did us then a greater wrong even than the one I had done you, I do believe. For you took from me by that dangerous, lone, forced childbirth part of my male spirit. Now you have to give back to me an equal portion of your woman's obedience. Not that you subtracted too much from my manhood, and not that your reward will turn out to be joy and peace. For I may be gone out of life by to-morrow night. But as long as I do live after this, you cannot thwart me and ever expect me to husband you again! Learn this once and for all, I am the *master* here, and *no woman,* not even you, can destroy me!"

He dropped his angry declamation then and put a kind hand on her shoulder. "Now I want you to rest through the night, since you have a hard journey ahead to-morrow. To a place where you can bear this tenth child of ours in safety."

"Yes, that's right," agreed Gerda almost dreamily, still spellbound by his dictates. Then with his help she pulled off her clumsy shoes and moved in a slow duck-walk caused by her heavy state over to the bed. There she lay down feeling sheltered by him even on the verge of danger.

3

The women and children of the community collected at Whetstone Stand next day to leave from there. Very early, before they arrived, Ronald rode over to spend a while with Gracey. She was wearing her grey riding-habit, not that she would mount a horse, but because she felt the plume curling around her hat gave her a look of appropriate dash. At the end, when Ronald came and led her away by the hand down where his snowdrops were shaking their white bells among green blades, she forgot her looks for a bit and saw him. In the odd light of a day that kept breaking from the overcast sky to rosy sunshine through clouds, his face had a silver edge, the nostrils pinched fine by a master hand at delicacy, and his hair crisp like frost.

He plucked one of the snowdrop bells and studied how each point of petal was delicately edged with a green stitching. Then he spoke plainly about something that was a conviction to him. "I am trying to do my share of this scrapping to make things ready for our home. I wish we were man and wife; that would be something to help me. I'm not a very good shot, because my wrists jerk when I get worked up. Still I was not born down here in the wilderness for nothing. I can step as quiet as any Indian, so I'm to scout out the lay of their camp, for our men. Your uncle Yarbrough says they couldn't do without my eyes."

He flung the snowdrop down impatiently. " I don't amount to much, and folks used to laugh at me because I played with rag babies so long. But ever since I first heard your laugh I liked its pitch, as if you're going to strangle on mirth. And I love the sweet smell your hands make in the air, after every fresh washing." He was half-scared to do it, but he put his arms around her little shoulder-blades, which were folded over like chicken wings, and he caught her lips in a quick kiss. They did not either one exactly care for the kiss, but they liked the moment after it, of knowing they had actually caressed. Then, in another instant they were feeling foolish at having to look at each other, and wishing someone would call them so they could separate. When no one did, he offered his arm and led her towards the wagons. She noticed how much taller he now was than she, in spite of his younger years.

All that day as Gracey jogged over the rutty road, she was looking at pictures of her own dreams, laid up against the dark wall of the pines they passed. She was thinking: " I didn't expect it to come about this way, with a boy I've seen playing in a creek, but I've fallen into love. . . . And it tastes sweet as sugar."

CHAPTER TWENTY-TWO

In the porridge-thick gloom of the spring nightfall the three companies encamped in spots close to Pea River. There they discussed their tactics in guarded tones while they munched their cold supper snacks. "The idea—eh, Whetstone?" asked Malone—"is that my bunch attacks and draws off a lot of the warriors by a pretended retreat. Then while they're away, your company and the Georgia militia fall on the Indian camp."

"That's it. Then as the warriors straggle back, you close in from your side and we from ours, combining forces to crush them into surrender, and to departing for good and all."

"A feasible plan," remarked Upshur dryly, "except you can't count on what the Indians will do."

Gran grumbled an agreement, yet since neither of the older men had any better plan to offer, they made no move to balk this one. Soon preparations for light sleep and early rising were made.

Before the night even began to wear thin, Ronald's mind snapped open, alert, calling him to his scouting trip. As he rolled out of his blanket, his father, Big Duncan, reached over and chucked him on the shoulder. "Countin' on you, son," he grunted; then the older man was wadded down in slumber once more. Ronald began moving out of the clump of men with the sour smell of their breathing too thick. He worked his way along, the wet earth oozing beneath his stomach. Four of his senses were receiving messages from the surrounding clammy atmosphere, but as yet he was not taxing his sight greatly in this density.

Slowly while he moved, a furl of mist began to uncurl, then gradually the whole fog started peeling off in layers and he knew he must hurry. For this day was going to break fine and clear after the long rains. Just as the true dawn came he reached a spot from where he could see the strip of higher ground in the centre of the swamp where the Creeks were encamped. He knew it to be the last and most deliberately desperate stronghold of the Creek Nation. He knew that Chief Kochi Fixio was established there with a diminished but fanatic retinue. Not that there was anything warlike about the scene, but the due regard for dignity that always surrounded the chief, even when he was unseen, was very evident to Ronald's native-born eye.

At the moment they seemed resting a bit in the belief that the rains had made the roads impassable for white men on horseback. Fighting seemed apparently the farthest thing from their minds for this hour. Young squaws were preparing *sofka* as usual, with several children tending the cook-fires. No trace of Kochi Fixio's actual presence was discernible, and the warriors were seated smoking easily, while some of the tribe's dogs were frisking about uncautioned to keep quiet.

Ronald wished with all his heart that he could simply go over and share their meal as he had so often done in his recent childhood. But he was not there to taste the contents of their cook-pots. Having spied out their situation, he turned about to creep back towards his own side, a talebearer.

As soon as he had regained his own camp and given the gist of his findings, Malone ordered his group into the saddle. Ronald, hearing how rambustiously they started out, tried to caution them that they could never take Indians by surprise that way, but they were already gone beyond his call.

Could he have followed their progress he would have seen his fears realized. By the time Malone's men came scrabbling to their chosen point of attack and tethered their mounts with much tromping and smothered ejaculation, the Creeks were more than forewarned. With their habitual cunning they drew the company down from the solid ground, and soon the whites were once more fighting at a disadvantage.

"Here, you!" Malone hollered at his companions. "Get out of this muck! And tole these crocodiles out after us. Get 'em on dry land, or we don't stand a chance. Now wallow out!"

They scrambled out, with the men mad clear through, both at the Creeks and at Malone's order to retreat. Jerard was dog-bent on carrying out the tactics planned with Yarbrough. As they slithered up the banks, however, the Indians were following too agilely, and before Malone knew what was happening, his company was retreating in earnest, with two hundred warriors at their heels. Forgetting all about their secreted horses, they were lighting out for the safe town of Monticello as fast as their own legs could carry them.

"At this rate," cursed Malone from where he had stopped unseen,

" those varmints of Creeks will soon have them routed and be back to fight Yarbrough's pack."

At that moment Guy signalled him from under a low branch, where he was holding their horses quiet. " I sent Willy tracking around edgewise, to see how that rout toward Monticello goes. Now we had better make haste back to warn Yarbrough, because I don't believe those warriors'll be long returning."

" No, by Bob!" snorted Malone. " What pine-knot chunks we were! Thinking we could stumble up and scare them away with a mite of gunpowder."

As they rode toward camp he was surly, while Guy was pensive. Guy felt that Chokho, who had been ever dutiful to him, was somewhere in the swamp they were intent upon besieging. Which side would win in this encounter was for the moment dubious; yet he knew of no way to protect her if, as he hoped in his deepest insides, his own kind were to survive in this country.

2

Meanwhile Yarbrough, back at their original vantage point, had tried to launch his own attack as decisively as planned. He had taken careful heed not only of every word Ronald had reported, but of the unspoken cautions the lad had tried to convey when he declared: " It smacks to me of Kochi Fixio, in all his might! For, sir, though they looked at rest, they looked also in readiness somehow. Ready for anything, and hardly afraid of what we could do to them. I can't make myself plain."

" On the contrary you make it very plain," replied Yarbrough. " They will be fighting to the end." He rubbed one fist in the palm of the other. " But we will be fighting for victory!"

Now feeling that the right amount of time had been allowed for Malone's decoying manœuvres, he set forth with his contingent. At Upshur's Bridge he left twenty men to cut off any possible strategic retreat of the Indians; then his main force moved ahead. The deep mud soon sucked almost as bad as quicksand, trying to swallow clear to the horses' shins. For a while Yarbrough tried to curb his irritation and hearten his followers to endure the inconvenience, until it dawned on him that this mush was a grave military obstacle.

Then he hauled his mount almost head-on into his band. "You can see the short way is ruined. We must go clear around by Prince's Mill. Takes longer, but it's surer. Now let's rowel ourselves as well as our horses to hurry." His voice rasped like a saw, and they went careering about in the changed direction.

Thus they missed Malone and Guy bringing warning, though what good that would have done is hard to say. Because of the mud they were unable to hold to any compact formation, and because of their long ride, hampered by mud, the Creeks had ample time to prepare for the conflict.

Surveying the awaiting scene, Yarbrough's face drew into narrow, wary lines. He felt something too quiet in the air. It was too peaceful. There was no flurry of warriors either departing in chase of Malone or returning. The campfires had been snuffed out. Dogs and children must have been hidden under damp bush-growth, and the squaws had so packed the wigwams away that they could not be distinguished from the shadows.

Yet Yarbrough could scarcely believe in that deceptive serenity. Suddenly, overpoweringly, he wanted to hurl a blow that would shatter its dreamlike quality. For somewhere in that pearly place was a man who would finish him, unless he could discover that man and, swapping wound for wound, demolish him, despite his immutable aboriginal endurance. Now the hour was knelled when Yarbrough must prove his own worth as a leader to his people!

In that marsh he could not see one thing solid, yet he picked up his gun with stroking, anticipatory fingers, and aiming it as deliberately as if at visible game, *fired!*

The noise of battle followed in his trail.

Pell-mell his men fell into blundering line, without either strategy or reinforcements. And the stillness of the swamp was giving up a myriad warriors, creatures who were moving in a familiar element, with a slippery way of balancing to and fro on the spongy bottom, while the whites stumbled clumsily, encumbered by their heavy clothing, that quickly became soggy. All was a bedlam of lithe Creeks and bashing militia.

The Indians, though short of firearms, could yet use their arrows and blow-guns with skill, as well as their knives and hatchets. The whites, betrayed into the lagoon as before, were attempting to fight like their foes, from behind trees or any other shelter. Each white man had twenty-four cartridges that could blow an inch-wide hole through a human, and their flintlock muskets were serviceable, though they kicked, badly bruising the shoulder, and the powder, when it flashed in the pan, exploded up into their own eyes.

Yarbrough himself, headed into a strong wind, felt it singeing his brows and lashes until his eyes smarted and he could scarcely see. He could soon tell, however, that the Creeks were trying to flank them. By making his men extend their line from the river to the lagoon he stopped that. Then the two ragged wings of his troops began to rally and advance in a semicircle, with the idea of closing in on the Indian stronghold as planned.

Every one was now fighting desperately, and Yarbrough looked about to see how his men were doing. John Screws must have run out of ammunition, for he was slashing at an Indian with a bowie knife. While others wavered, Gran was planted stolidly, taking deliberate aim and bringing down something each time. Big Duncan was laughing fiercely as if the fight gave him pleasure, but the kick of the flintlock was beginning to tell on poor Ronald. At the same instant both the boy's father and Yarbrough noticed that fact. They saw him fire once more very slowly and uncertainly, as if he could hardly manage the effort. Then they saw the gun fall from his hold, and one arm hang paralyzed, useless, while with the other hand he tried to reach over and rub the numbed shoulder. Thus he stood, all by himself, cut out sharply for a target against a clear space.

Both men went towards him with the idea of bringing him to shelter, but while they were toiling towards him, a shot took him off. He slanted over into the mire, and when they raised him they could tell he was already dead, with his unhardened boy's features comical with mud.

"He was my only one," mumbled Duncan, "and nothin' to compare to your young studs. Still he behaved right smart, for a chicken-livered one." He was trying to rub Ronnie's face clean and drag him behind a log.

Right on top of that Yarbrough saw Gran go crashing down like a tree-trunk, and when Yarbrough gained his side the old man snarled: "Me, I will be all right, if this accurst fight is soon finished and I'm moved to a dry spot."

"Well, we'll put an end to them now!" vowed Yarbrough. "Since I've witnessed Ronald killed and you hurt, it drives me wild! They may've trained themselves to sit around in stone-faced council dignity, but they take to savage blood-sucking mighty fast! Well, by glory, if they're foxes out to wring our chickens' necks, we'll let them slake their blood-thirst with the taste of their own!" He bolted away, feeling his thighs being throttled by the swamp, yet lurching on through the sucking mud. Anger incensed him to an acute point that led him unerringly to a slightly raised level. Looking up he saw Kochi Fixio at last!

The chief, with the soft wool of his night-blanket still drawn over his ancient shoulders, was almost as grey as the swamp that strove to hide him. His face was horrid with a pattern of paint not allowed to any other. Now he lifted from a half-hidden attendant his flamboyant head-dress and placed it upon his head, his eyes overshooting Yarbrough's stare as if not deigning to meet it. Yet Yarbrough noted something else: that the claws of his old hands sought their accustomed clasp about his elbows almost as if to keep them from shaking. And Yarbrough felt a swift scorn for all the chief's paraphernalia.

Yarbrough threw his head up, winking back the watering of his eyes beneath his scorched brows, and he called out: "Will you come down to fight it out with me?" Holding his naked eyeballs in a steady stare was agony, and the red rims of his lids seemed to sear anew. Yet he kept that gaze clamped open, because it encircled the world that he was claiming!

Obliquely across his shoulder an arrow whanged and buried its head in fallen Gran Pieter's leg. Then a Hades was surrounding them, in which Yarbrough could not forget the sight of young Ronald's scalp being taken and tucked away in a savage's clout belt. After that he went as wild as any Indian on the warpath. With a yell he rallied the whites into a berserk charge, causing them to fall on the warriors so fiercely that, in a short space, most of the Creeks were killed or mortally wounded. Then the two companies swarmed forward to lay waste the camp.

Yarbrough, again facing Kochi Fixio, suddenly clambered far enough up the bank to reach the chief and pull him half-way down. There against the slippery bank he demanded once more a fair fight between themselves.

He got no answer.

The old man fell back lifeless from the sheer exhaustion of senility. And Yarbrough knew the odd bereavement of the fighter deprived of his foe before they could come to grips.

He had trouble raising Kochi Fixio and laying him out decently. After that he had to rescue the headpiece of dyed feathers and try to arrange it on the chief's poor skull. Next he raked the limbs into a dignified pose.

Immediately after that Yarbrough knew they had won! That gave him little joy, watching over this particular cadaver. And it was hard to retain composure when forced to view the result of their carnage. It was impossible to tell the number of slain, with bodies floating so thickly on the water. There were more than a hundred and fifty that Yarbrough himself counted, bumping against one another as the flooded waters washed them downstream. Suddenly Yarbrough saw the face of one of them and felt his belly retch. It was Chokho, her face set in final quietude.

He could recall her patiently pounding out cornmeal to feed his household.

3

That was a bad night for Yarbrough. He wondered where Guy was and how he could tell him about Chokho. He thought of Amah Letoh, as if her dark lovely face too had floated down that water. Then he thought of Gerda and wondered whether her time had come upon her away from him once again.

He wondered how much he might have done to prevent the Creek War if he had not given way briefly to passion for a woman of an alien race. But then he thought how the greater force within him had been his passion for possession, unquestioned by any rival people, this rich growing land. He tried to put together the things that had happened, to bring some sort of order out of events, to divine some meaning that would send him on. To-night, however, he could only sit baffled by his own blunders, rubbing his fingers over the place where his brows had been.

CHAPTER TWENTY-THREE

They sat for the most part in silence there in Gran's chamber where Death was the biggest presence among them all. Gangrene had set in, in his wounded limb, because of lack of proper attention in time, and now there was no hope. They had all seen death before, but not by slow torture like this. The worst of it was that the massive old man did not want to die. He was as angry as a bull, gazing balefully around at their faces.

There was Willy, who stayed over by a window, frankly looking out of it instead of at Gran. He was wondering wretchedly how long before the stench of decay would force him to be sick, in spite of the camphor he had on his handkerchief to sniff. Guy was slumped listlessly in a chair thinking of Chokho in her numb dignity, being knocked about in river water. There was Yarbrough standing at the foot of the bed, one hand holding the post, twisting, twisting it without halt, as if he would wring its neck. Yet his face was under leaden control.

And there at the head of the bed was John Upshur, who had been trying for an hour or more to find some Bible comfort for Gran. But the old tartar had roared hoarsely in what was left of his voice: "You know I do not believe in any mythology! And of all of them I would last choose your milk-and-water brand of turning the other cheek. Liefer would I go to pit my muscles against those great blond lummoxes in Valhalla, or to drink schnapps with the wastrels on Olympus." A chuckle almost came into his words, but then he thrashed his shoulders about again. "I—*I* could have treated this wound myself if I had been put in a dry place and given the medicines I needed. And yet again I could have instructed that poor harassed doctor where and how to cut off the rotting limb had he had the instruments. I, and I alone, had the knowledge to save myself. Yet must I, with those things locked in this brain because I had not the use of my body, rattle with one last whiff of air, then go into that cave of nothingness which I know awaits me! And you, John Upshur, because you cannot heal my body with surgery, try to appease me with the fantasy that my brain can put on a new garment with wings and soar up to lounge on clouds. Wings!

My pig's eye, even a child could tell that man had fashioned that lie, not seeing how else he could sail up into the air without wings like a fowl. *Och! Spirit?* I know better than you do, sir, by what addition of blood and bone and nerves we arrive at the total of Self. And I call that self by no indecisive word, 'spirit,' which answers no poor human's question, only wraps it in the soft veil of stupidity."

The old man choked for breath and took fistfuls of covers in his clutch, at which the air about him reeked afresh with his stench. When he spoke again it was in a duller tone. "I have naught against you, John Upshur; in fact I know you for a practical man on most counts, and respect you for that. But hold your tongue when it comes to offering me the thin air of spiritual survival, for what I ask is a sound warm body, a bowl of potato soup steaming beneath my nose, and the thumping of my old gnarled walking-stick as I make my way across the yard to look closer at a red bird flashing from branch to branch of the water oak. . . ."

His voice trailed off in a dream . . . his listeners felt him lose his whole bright world in one beaten sigh. There were a few more hours allotted to him, but he had, at that instant, let go of the wide creation that five senses bound for a man. Joy was gone, and lust, and even anger now, and all the things that, quickening, set man apart in the temporary godhood of those that breathe!

CHAPTER TWENTY-FOUR

OUT IN THE LOT the next evening Yarbrough helped Upshur mount. The latter said: "I'll not do him the wrong of staying to say prayers over him," and Yarbrough agreed: "No, a Christian burial would only make a mock of him. He preached his own sermon better than you or any other could. Still, I thank you. You are a great comfort as a neighbour."

A neighbour, mused John Upshur, as his mule Minnie ambled on through the still night. That was about the size of it. He was a good neighbour and a farmer. Gran had torn the scales from his eyes. He was not a man of the Gospel who could bring exaltation to people. Like Gran, he cared most deeply for what he knew to be actually here. The earthy things were the good things—the seed, the soil, the crops, the dumb creatures. He, John, was not excitable enough to rock people into repentance and salvation. He had best till his acres and leave the preaching henceforth to prophets whose souls almost shook their forgotten bodies to pieces. "Souls?" He was sorry he had used that word so soon after Gran's farewell; it seemed to show no respect for the old man's greatness. "Not," he murmured, baring his head and looking up at the sky where his God was, "not that I mean any irreverence to You, O Lord. Amen."

The night was very gentle for March.

2

Over in Georgia the women of the Whetstone family knew nothing of the deaths that had affected them. Kindly neighbours, for once, managed to hold their tongues about news they longed to talk over with those concerned. Mister Ven had made it plain that they would be risking Miz Gerda's life if they tormented her with so grievous a loss as that of the old man who had been both father and mother to her. "And her God A'mighty too, I expect," he added, not caring how he shocked them as long as they held their tongues. Gracey, too, he protected from all gossip that would bring her news of Ronald's end, for he saw pityingly how lightly she stepped these days in her new-found happiness of romance. Time enough for calamity, he argued, when they were safe under their own roof again.

Yarbrough arrived the day before Gerda's confinement and was a great strength for her to lean upon. The child was born with no trouble at all, and had an impudent look from the first hour. "He puts me in mind of Bruff a little," remarked Yarbrough. "He does at that," agreed Gerda, then added: "Let's name him Turber after the county, as long as he came into the world just as we made the county really our own."

"A good idea!" cried Yarbrough. "It'll be a name he can be proud of."

"Yes, but let me tell you the county will be proud of him too, one day!" declared Gerda, very pleased with her last son, the child of her common sense and her readjustment to her husband. Turber was proof to her that her and Yarbrough's marriage could not be rent apart by any careless blunder. Many a day she would rise up to joint endeavour with Yarbrough, many a night would close with their shoulders touching, their hearts in comfortable content. She had long been a sturdy partner in his undertaking, but when the time had come for her to be just a wife, she had made herself exactly that—a woman. When she reached home she would tell Gran how right Yarbrough had been in his insistence upon her subservience to his wiser will in seeking safety in Georgia. And Gran would be proud of her helpful deportment there.

3

It was fine and fair the afternoon the women arrived home, and the yard was fresh swept. Irises were in bloom. On the porch the house servants, who had come ahead, waited in fresh head-cloths. Gerda looked about for Gran, she wanted his deep bearlike hug and his guttural endearment, *liefste*.

Yarbrough and Guy and Willy led Gerda and Gracey into the parlour, where a tray of scuppernong wine was handy, and Pokey stood just outside the door. Then Yarbrough told them, while Gerda faced him straight, and Willy held Gracey fast. At his words the girl's voice went up and up in a breaking, rippling laugh. That was the last sound Gerda heard as she went out of that room into her grandfather's.

She could not believe its *emptiness forever*. She could not believe that his voice was gone, with all its wise words, nor his great mouth gobbling food or gulping ale, nor his beard with his fingers plunging into it as he wrestled with some problem of philosophy or maybe with mere churlish temper. Nor could she give up his laughter rumbling out of the cave of his belly. She flicked her fingers open and shut helplessly. They were now minus a rudder that she had gripped all her life, and she was in terror lest her boat be sent spinning headlong.

Pokey's voice called gently outside the door: "Miz Gerda, they needs you wif Miss Gracey." Gerda came out of the room, and put one arm out to hold on to Pokey, who was all she had left of her childhood with Gran. Then, "Chile," sobbed Pokey, "I'se done lost my marster!" causing Gerda to give her a look of astonishment. She had not thought of the awful bereavement of the slave.

"What," she asked Pokey finally, "what did you come to tell me?"

"Miss Gracey's took with fits. Cain't nobody do nothin' with her. I thought," stammered Pokey, "maybe this time you could manage her."

Gerda made haste to the parlour, from which shrieks and jabbering were coming, one on top of the other. Gracey was a piteous spectacle. She was seated, or rather held, on the sofa between Willy and Yarbrough, and what she was saying was largely unintelligible. One moment she was murmuring in a broken-hearted tone of her love for Ronald, the next she was shrieking spitefully that she was not going to part with the jewels and other gifts that had been bestowed upon her in prospect of her marriage. "Yes, and," she turned to her father, "you can just trot me out that lace-laundress you promised me!" Then she broke into tears of disappointment over the bridal lace, so useless to her now. When she caught sight of Gerda she reached out a hand in appeal. "Make them let me go out by Ronald's flower-beds. They won't—and I'll choke to death in here!"

Gerda took the girl's hand, smoothing it. "Of course you can go out there. You don't mind if Gerda comes along, do you?" The girl eyed her suspiciously, but Gerda added: "I have to have air too."

"You? But you've no sorrow, you have a husband. Gran was old—old."

"Yes, he was the oldest, and Ronald the youngest. Neither one of them had any business dying the way they did." Gerda raised Gracey to her feet and led her to the door. Part way down the path to the circular bed she said: "I'll go this way now, where I can look at the holly trees. You call me if you want me." Then she went over in a shadow near the side fence, where she could keep an eye on the girl without Gracey's knowing she was being watched. Gerda hoped Gracey would not try anything foolish, because she herself was not yet strong enough to run after her. Gracey seemed woefully upset. Something she had cherished in her own way had been taken from her. And it was not solely because she was being cheated out of wifehood, to be an old maid for life, that Gracey felt so bereft. Of this Gerda felt certain, remembering how the other's face had lighted up lately in Georgia whenever they spoke of returning home to their menfolk.

Now she saw that Gracey had paused by the pale ruffled circle the irises made in the twilight. She kept holding out her hands to fondle their blooms, then dropping her fingers uncertainly. Now suddenly after a sly look around she reached down, pulled off her shoes and stockings, and, bracing one hand against the stump, felt of the flowers with the sole of first one foot, then the other. After doing this for a short while, with her face thrown back oddly, she put on her stockings and began to pace in a ring around the plot. This went on for some minutes until Gerda began to fear for the effect this rigmarole was having on her. Casually Gerda moved in Gracey's direction. Just as the girl stopped and teetered a moment to regain her balance from dizziness, Gerda reached her side and braced her. She said matter-of-factly: "Remember you always did get seasick from swinging." They both laughed a little self-consciously, Gracey adding: "Yes, didn't I? Such a goose."

Then she stooped and picked up her shoes unconcernedly. "Come on, I'd better go back in and tell them my news while they're all there together." She seemed quite self-possessed as they approached the house, except that she remarked, irrelevantly Gerda thought at the time: "I heard over in Georgia that Brother Upshur had quit the pulpit." At the doorway of the parlour she took stock of the family group within; then she entered and sat on the sofa. "Could I have that wine now? I'm sorry I carried on so, but it was a worse shock than you all knew. You see Ronald and I were married secretly by Brother Upshur the day we left, and I'm his widow."

There was a dead silence. Willy darted an incredulous look at his sister, and Yarbrough knew without question that Upshur had been too remote to be accessible to the young pair that day of leavetaking.

Miz Lisbeth rose and came over to her granddaughter and put a withered kiss upon her forehead like some secret seal of their order of widowhood. "You'll be better off lying down while you're grieving this way. By the time you're able to be up and about, Gerda and I will have dyed your weeds for you. Willy, you'd better ride over to the MacDuffs' and give them a message from your sister to tell them how 'tis."

Every one sighed with relief. Miz Lisbeth was right. It was best to take the easiest way out, by pretending to believe Gracey's sham. And Ronald would have wished them to humour her. As the room emptied of all but Gerda and Yarbrough, he chuckled, "I declare, she's a smart piece, picking on Upshur, who isn't a preacher now, who won't have to call her out in meeting for the sin of a lie. All the same I'll ride over there first thing and ask him to do us the favour of keeping it to himself that he didn't perform the ceremony."

In her room Gracey lay with the sheet pulled up smooth under her chin. She was in a lazy half-stupor. Her own disappointment in Ronald's knobby knees, her own arrested virginity of emotion, had made her remain single until it was too late. Yet she was not accusing herself. She was blaming Yarbrough, who had early put the bloom of wifehood upon Gerda; blaming Gerda, who had always outshone her in the eyes of men like Malone, who could not even have Gerda; and most bitterly and finally she was blaming Lucinda with her quick-ripening sensuousness—Lucinda, who was shoving her off stage into the limbo of things gone dry and faded.

"All the samey," she thought with satisfaction, "I fixed them! I called this turn!"

In this wise Gracey drifted off to sleep, not knowing that for all her pettiness she was going to ache for years to come for a boy who had never husbanded her, and feel bereft whenever scentless snowdrops made flakes of bloom at the tips of green grass stems.

BOOK THREE

The Land Yields

CHAPTER TWENTY-FIVE

WITH THE CREEK QUESTION settled, the county had passed a peaceful winter. The last two years had been prime ones for cotton, and the settlers resented not having had their rightful share of profit, owing to the Indian-fighting. However, they had worked hard since then to make up for lost time and were ready for an early planting. At Whetstone Stand they had cleared more new ground, broken mules, and moved the field negroes to freshly built cabins. Yarbrough believed in changing his field-hands into new quarters every few years, since the accumulation of filth in corners caused disease. The cabins where his domestic servants were quartered had been scrubbed with lye and newly whitewashed. They had board instead of dirt floors and need not be abandoned periodically. That type of trained house negro had a pride in keeping up appearances, and their abodes were called " yard cabins," because each one was permitted a fenced-in space for growing flowers and cultivating garden " sass " and other vegetables.

The cooking for the field-hands was done by a special cook with her two helpers, at a food-shed near the quarters, in order to let the females take their midday rest instead of fretting over cook-pots until they were no good for other work. Care was taken to reduce the stint of chopping and picking of the child-bearing women; and the tiniest piccaninnies, just learning to work in the fields, always helped only their own mothers, in order not to be taxed beyond their strength before they could grow into fine strapping hands.

Another precaution taken in the " sickly season " of the summer was to have a wide swath of a path cleared around the edges of the fields, to keep the negroes who went out before the dew had dried from having their bare feet drenched and coming down with the " ground itch," an ailment which made their feet swell evilly with a sort of poison, and often left the negro of little account for any hard work ever after that.

In general Yarbrough was beginning to shape up his plantation and make things run in fair order, although he still had to contend with a deal of shirking, which, when it actually endangered his crop output, made him mad as hops.

One hot May morning he was late for breakfast after having been out since the crack of dawn. Coming in he found the others still dawdling over plates littered with plum pits and fragments of ham. "Wait," he told those who started to rise, "I'm going to make a proposition to you all after I eat." He tackled a stack of batter cakes and his eternal hot sausage. When part of his second cup of coffee was cooling in its saucer, he said: "This year I have one of the best stands of cotton I've ever seen. And what do you think is about to happen to it? 'Sore shin,' that's what! Sore shin from nothing but careless darkies chopping too close to the stalks while they're still tender. And, by the Lord Harry, I won't have it! I mean to provide some sort of white supervision over every last one of my fields. It don't matter how young the person is, as long as he's white that'll jack up the hands. Now I want all of you children, except the two babies, to come out to the fields. And Ven and Danley there too. You can each and every one superintend a stretch, and chop hard yourselves while you're at it."

He swung to his feet. "I'll pay each one of you who does his share fair wages in bales you save me. Now come ahead. Yes, you, Lucinda, and Jobyna. You'll thank me this winter when you jingle those silver dollars." At the door he turned back to Gerda. "Have their dinner sent up to them in the fields." He knew they liked any kind of picnic. The negroes would go back to the shed as usual for their meal, as it was a great relief to them to stretch their backs walking after stooping so long over their hoes. On the other hand it was smart to win enthusiasm from his own brood by playing on their sense of fun.

The Whetstone children trooped out to the fields as their father had commanded. The twins charged ahead first as always. After them followed stocky Tom Two, the pallid Joby, then the sly-eyed Wayne, unliked by any of his brothers or sisters. Next in line was Joachim, fine to look at but empty-headed, and caring for nothing save his own looks and personal adornment, for which he would stoop to any trick.

Then came Hans, who was their brother, so they were always told, but something hung over him, holding the younger children back from any easy friendship with him. Both Papa and Ma'am Gerda seemed to favour him, and Bruff was never hard on him, while

Lucinda would rend anybody to pieces who troubled him. All that resulted in setting Hans apart in their minds, though they couldn't tell why. He hadn't the commanding dash that showed in Bruff's very bones, and certainly he was not handsome like Joachim. Yet now, before he was quite ten years old, his physique attracted their attention. He was overgrown for one thing, and had a thatch of corn-tassel hair above his dark eyes, distressed behind curled lashes. That widening curl of his lashes was the only sign of excitement that ever showed in his face, though he could not yet control well the sudden stumblings of his fine but over-big body. He tried not to draw attention to himself, which may have been one other reason why his younger half-brothers were inclined to sheer off from him.

Next after Hans romped Will Bee, accompanied by his quiet shadow, Daniel. Pell-mell they all strung out at their father's heels, eager to play a new game that would have silver prizes.

This day went by for the Whetstone children as did many others in a steady succession after that. The whole season seemed to run into this one single slow day which became their memory of that summer. Bruff worked in a way that counted. The next three, Tom Two, Wayne, and Joachim, made a mulish sort of team, but Hans worked doggedly trying to copy Bruff and made a very creditable showing. He took a special pride in these acres because it was a privilege to him to be one of Yarbrough's sons. Every now and then he raised himself up to rest the knots in his shoulders and cast a sharp eye over his row of negroes. Before he bent over his stint again his eyes searched out the area of sky circled by the trees they called theirs. His thoughts were not put into any grand words, but they went as deep as the roots of the biggest water oak.

Danley Bruton did his share well, working thoroughly if automatically, while his mind made plans for the academy he was going to open one day. He chuckled to himself: "I'll teach them that Cæsar and Cicero are something more than the names of black servants." He struck his hoe in triumphant iambics.

The two girls were doing bravely, Jobyna acting a trifle smug over her neat progress, and Lucinda erratic but as rapid as chain-lightning. Every now and then she flung some taunt back at her smaller sister, who merely compressed her lips and went on taking good care with each separate plant. Only once did Joby answer Cinda back. "Don't forget the fable of the hare and the tortoise, Miss Quick-Biggety."

"Be a tortoise for all I care," retorted the other; "go creeping along hidden under a shell, seeing nothing. I'd rather be the hare who went lickety-split all over the earth. What's winning a race if you have to keep your snout to the ground all the way? Who cares about reaching a certain old tree-stump first?"

"*They* care," said Jobyna stubbornly, pointing towards the rows of negroes working their heads off. The hands were striving for the prize, a silver quarter of a dollar Yarbrough had placed on a stump at the far end of each big field. The hand who finished his rows first won the quarter, to spend any way he chose. And the scarcity of actual money in their lives made the blacks work with a will for that white coin blinking in the sun.

But Lucinda had already veered away from that topic, her attention caught by something else. At this stage of cultivation each male hand usually had some half-grown wench working just behind him, fining up the soil in the wake of his heavier strokes. Lucinda had early noticed that big Ruben, their former coachman, was always partnered by yellow Rache, a sassy piece who had started cutting her eyes about at the bucks almost before she had lost her milk teeth. At this instant Lucinda saw Ruben, who'd dropped his hoe, lean down to pick it up and in doing so squeeze Rache's bare ankle with a lingering upward motion. Cinda nudged Joby. "Fur will fly if those two keep that up till Densey hears tell of it."

"Densey?" repeated Joby, bewildered. "But *Eda* is Ruben's *wife*."

"Ho, me," chuckled Cinda, "what a baby you are! Don't you know that Ruben has had Densey for his woman too, for years?"

They ceased their bickering, however, in the rush for the dinner baskets, which were being brought up. The children sat under a white oak that spread a hoop of shade near the edge of the field. They tore at the crusty fried chicken with their teeth, the little boys fighting over the drumsticks. They drank buttermilk rich in golden globules, they ate pound cake smeared with fig preserves. And when it was over they lay back on the ground for a lulling nap, feeling grass blades tickling their necks and ants skittering across outflung hands, while the oak leaves drooped overhead and the whole world lay ripe from its consummation with the sun.

In the afternoon the work went a bit slower and a deal quieter, yet it did not stop until the late clouds made purple splotches over the dark-green plants. Then whites and blacks began straying in groups toward the house or the quarters, trailing their hoes, stretching, looking forward to the night's rest more than to anything else. Thus the summer passed to the steady beat of heat and labour, until the first blossoms showed at the bottom of the plants, white as dogwood for a single day before changing to bright rose like hibiscus, making way in the end for the young green bolls.

2

This was a lazy day and Yarbrough and Jerard Malone were sitting on the front steps below Gerda's loom, yawning and exchanging plantation gossip like the friends they had become while fighting their common enemy the Indian. Yarbrough had given his hands a short holiday before picking-time, to raise their spirits and working vim afterwards. He was also enjoying this let-down himself, lounging there, every now and then reaching down to pull a tick out of the ear of his dog, Little Foolish II, the offspring of the hurt hound Malone had once given him. The bitch looked up at him with humble adoration, even while wincing from the tick-picking.

Malone, watching the dog and master, finally remarked: "It beats all how you ever get anything out of either your beasts or your blacks, when you're so soft-hearted. They'll get the upper hand if you're not manful enough to deal them out some healthy whippings regularly."

"My dogs," Yarbrough pointed out, "hunt well, my mules plough steady, and my hands keep the weeds chopped out fair enough. Then why should I be for ever frailin' my critters as you recommend?"

Malone ruffled his shock of grizzled, curly hair perplexedly. "You do seem to make out better than I do in spite of all my big holdings. I wonder if my trouble is having to hire overseers. Yet I must have them, what with plantations here and yonder all over three states. Look here at this letter from Dicks, my man here. It's what brought me home."

Yarbrough spread out the letter carefully and read its ill-spelt contents:

Dere Mr. Malone:

I am giting coten chopped as fast as culd be expekt. But it semes ower hands cant stay helthy, 5 down all last week with chill and fever. I wisht the three girls you purchest lately had bin full growen womin. These girls are to young for any use to wife any of your men and you have enuf small girls for your young boys. That last hand you purchest has got no toes on right foot. Had coten stuffed in his brogan by the trader to foole you. If trader is come-atible you should sue as he was meant to be sound. Any waye I look for you shortly.

Yr. Obdt'nt Servant,
Josiah Dicks.

"Well, I don't know," commented Yarbrough. "This trying to farm second-hand never works well; you have to see for yourself what negroes are up to. I don't turn my back on them long at a time. Whipping's necessary sometimes, but I think my way of partly babying them and keeping sharp track of them prevents more mischief than punishment does." He relaxed against the steps and stared down the half-S that bent towards the ivy-twined gate-stumps, listening to Gerda weaving above him on the porch, and rubbing his dog's coat with the toe of his boot.

It was after the men had cleared off the steps that Gerda grew tired of the steady motion of weaving. Her eyes strayed from her work to the far corners of the yard where shrivelled clusters of fallen chinaberries had not been swept up. Some lazy piccaninny had slighted the task, but she felt too worn out to bother. She hadn't had any energy to spare lately. The fume of the Indian War, the grief about Gran, the care of the baby Turber, and the fretting that Gracey caused with her peculiar "widowhood" combined to drain Gerda's strength. She rose in the mornings only half-rested, ready to fly out at any one who crossed her, then dropping any outburst of temper because it seemed scarcely worth the trouble to see it through.

Now she secured the end of the web and wiped her palms of their sweat. She hitched her chair about to face away from the house and its domestic litter, then leaned her forehead on her propped elbows to shut her eyes with the blessed feeling that if she opened them she would be looking at the country, not at any task that needed her. The sun began to go down across the front of her right shoulder, making a yellow dance over her closed lids. That felt pleasant—the alternate falling of flakes of light, then patches of slate dark, shutting her into a solitude. It was so seldom that she was alone that she sometimes wondered vaguely what she was like, whether she was really a person at all, or just a network of hands and feet, and a tongue directing people who were real persons.

A plank in the hall creaked under a step, then stopped, and she knew it was Pokey waiting with some question that needed her attention. Still Gerda sat on, her eyes obdurately shut, refusing to ask what the trouble was. Next she heard Pokey walking about on the porch, picking up scissors here, a fly-fan there, putting them in their proper places and breathing righteous complaints at every stoop. Finally Pokey's dutifulness won and Gerda opened her eyes. She saw that the lovely shuttling of light and dark had stilled into the single tone of twilight, but she had no time now to be soothed by it. She asked: "What is it?"

Pokey upon hearing the tired voice switched her attitude. "Nevah mind. I'll see 'bout it fo' you. It just has to do with that young Rache, who been foolin' roun' Ruben till Densey's out to take the hide off'n her, let alone what his Eda'll do when she heahs about it."

Soggily Gerda's brain refused to worry. Tom-catting went on among the negroes the same as breathing and eating. Right now she was too tired to try to keep them yoked properly. She stood up, kicking over her chair behind her, her face straining up in all its angles against the fading sky. "I won't be pestered, I tell you I *won't*! Let them all claw each other's gizzards out! Only—don't bother me!"

Pokey smoothed her arm. "There now, Miz Gerda, catch yo' breath. Then you bettah go rest in bed."

"I think I will go rest. You tell Miz Lisbeth to sit in my place at the supper table. And you see to jerking up Rache. After all, you ought to be able to manage her best since you're both mulattoes." Listlessly she moved towards her room, with Pokey calling after her that she had better take a purgative.

3

Here in her whitewashed cabin behind its bouquet of crape-myrtle bushes Pokey had collected all the contradictory things that she treasured. It was a spruce enough place to look at, rather jaunty in its trimmings of white folk's cast-off finery, but it had that stench of bacon grease, brewed chicory, and purloined perfume that hangs like a sweet decay over the habitat of the mulatto. It had the smell of cunning.

Here in this cabin Pokey called on the mat any wench who was getting out of hand, yet did not warrant Gerda's direct attention. While waiting for the troublesome Rache, Pokey had removed her shoes and sat scratching the sole of first one tan foot then the other. She loved that indulgence and hated to quit it even to go to sleep. To-night the gesture was more reflective and sensuous, for she was studying how best to handle Rache. Perhaps she would appeal to her vanity in her light skin, coax her into despising dark Ruben.

The hour had settled down almost into full night before Pokey heard the girl's shiftless step outside. "Come in heah directly," she ordered her. "An' don't try to make out like you don't know what I'm goin' to quarrel about."

The girl snickered nervously, at the same time trying to switch her shoulders airily to show she wasn't scared. All the same she had taken care to dress in her best to come before Marm Pokey, who now reached out an autocratic hand to examine her top petticoat. "Hmph, Miss Gracey give you that befo' the lace was half wore out. I expeck you done begged it away from her. Bettah not let me hear of you doin' such, else I'll tie your wool up by switches to a low-branch tree till you have to screech yo' head off."

"No, Marm, dat I won't." Rache backed away, hugging an arm over her threatened head at the bare idea of pain.

Pokey took out her snuff brush and flavoured her gums with it, then reared her turbaned head majestically. "I ain't mincin' matters with you, 'cause Miz Gerda's plumb outdone with you, and she tol' me to read you the riot ack. I'm tellin' you the long and the short of it—*keep away from Ruben*, an' his women."

"You means," ejaculated Rache, "dat Densey kin have a cleah track wid Eda's man, whilst I hab to step out de way? Well, befo' God, I'll tell Eda——"

"You'll do no such thing. Don't you know that, spite of all the long talk Eda an' Densey do, they been joggin' along about ten years with Ruben between 'em? Sometimes Densey sticks in Eda's craw, but Eda ain't never choked to death on Densey yet. Ain't liable to neither, long as Densey does her washin' for her, an' flutes up her Sunday best clothes till the edges is crisp enough to cut your fingah. An' nobody else besides me an' the white folks ever gets any of Densey's flutin', 'ceptin' Eda. Then, who you think nursed Densey's brat through the croup? Jes' Eda. 'Cause she hadn't any mind to let any chile of Ruben's die, even if Densey was the ma. Now I'm warnin' you, don't monkey with Eda and Densey less you want to run into a buzz saw. They's some things you is too flighty to understand and that's family ways 'mongst women and men; it's a sight more than courtin'. Better keep your skirts clear of the whole Ruben mess."

Rache stared sulkily at her toes squirming about on the planks. She felt herself almost beaten, yet was too vain to give up any man she had cast her eye upon. "Ruben," she mumbled, "ef'n Ruben feels like lookin' fo' some fresh meat, ain't nothin' them two old sows kin do 'cept hang up on the rack an' let him pass on by." She preened her skirts.

Pokey could see that the girl had the streak of fycetiness that came from her white blood; consequently she tried a new tack. "It beats me why a bright yaller gal like you will take up with a shuffle-foot, coal-black man."

"You don't know dis black man," chuckled Rache; "he kin court you to a cinder."

Pokey ignored this. "Gettin' along in age too, Ruben, an' fat as a tub of lard. I don't see why you don't aim for some nice light-brown buck who looks purty when he's slicked up for Sunday."

But Rache hunched one shoulder up. "Aftah I gets my fill of coal-black men, I ain't goin' to kill time on molasses-coloured in-betweens. When that day comes I'll get me a pure *white* man, in a feathah bed!"

"Git!" shouted Pokey wrathfully. "Git clear out a heah with your trash-talkin', blue-gummed mouth!" She hurled a china shaving-mug after Rache. It smashed into smithereens and lay with its cherished gaudy-painted roses in bits on the door-sill. Pokey eyed them mournfully. It had missed aim, and she had failed Miz Gerda, besides losing favour in her own eyes for not giving that gal her come-uppance. Slippery little eel! With her bottom lip in a sad pout Pokey took to scratching her soles again with a regular, slow scraping.

It was two days later when Densey met up with Rache over the wash-pots in the laundry yard. Densey seldom left her indoor work of ironing ruffles to come near this common wash. But to-day while Rache was poking corn-cobs under the black belly of the pot, Densey strode up truculently, her arms swinging like flails and her great jaw-bones set with menace. She stood half a foot taller than Rache, and Rache quaked, for she was a coward, mischievous enough on the sly, but craven if caught. Now she tried to busy herself by stirring the wash-stick in the blue-white bubble of clothes. But Densey knocked her hand loose, so that the stick sent a spurt of hot suds up to scald Rache's wrist. Next Densey yanked her about by one scrawny shoulder. "Looka heah, you pullet! You stop flappin' yoah pin feathahs at me an' Eda's Ruben! You heah me?"

"Your *and* Eda's!" cackled Rache, her teeth chattering through the impudence of her words. "That's a mighty funny way to call a man. How Eda like that?"

"A heap sight bettah than she goin' to like the sound of your name hitched to his. Now if you wants the cool of a good, deep, black grave jes' you go on courtin' Ruben, an' you'll be chokin' on dirt befo' you kin say Jack Robinson!" With that she crunched the girl's shoulder in one more shattering grip, then spun her out of the path so she could stalk away.

Long after Densey had disappeared Rache huddled near the pot rubbing her bruises, pondering sullenly on revenge. As time elapsed her fear dimmed till she became defiant once more. That woman wasn't going to scare her out of her pleasures with Ruben. The girl walled her eyes and hugged her abdomen recalling them, wanting to be with him right away. Presently she could restrain herself no longer, so she went to seek him out where she knew he would be sprawled in a thicket, dozing out his noonday rest. He opened lazy pleased eyes at her and with one sweep of his big arms pulled her down astraddle him. She laughed on a wild note.

Rache did not know that Densey had marked the path she had taken, and that Densey was even now trudging towards Eda's cabin with the news.

When Densey came to the door she found Eda piecing together bright calico patches.. She had hoarded these scraps for years, going without any new piece-made winter petticoat to save them. Now she had enough for a full-size quilt like the ones Miz Gerda spread on the white folks' beds. Maybe, she planned, some day Ruben would carpenter up a bed in a corner of their cabin; then he could rest easier than he did on the pallet, and that would make him sleep at home more. She looked up when Densey's shadow fell in the door, and held out a sprigged scrap. "Do you mind dat frock of Miss Gracey's? You always starched it till it set out lak a bowl." Eda chuckled happily at owning even a smidgin' of such finery.

Then when Densey paid no attention to her chatter, she asked: "What's distractin' you, Densey? 'Tain't yo' young 'un?"

"'Tain't any of Ruben's chillun he's got *so far* that's botherin' me. No, it's myself. I ain't what I used to be. We womenfolks gits old befo' our time, whilst a man is good as long as he can chaw."

Eda asked sharply: "What you talkin' about? What's Ruben up to that's aggravatin' *you*?"

"Devilment," said Densey shortly. "An' neithah of us can hinder him. He's aftah that yaller Rache. Been pinchin' at her shape evah since she commencet to git one. Now they's took to actin' serious, down by the branch that cuts through the big gully. If it wa'n't her, it'd be the nex' young 'un with a shiny eye. And, man alive, I hates knowin' I'm licked as a woman! That I'm no mo' use at night-time, jes' good fo' the day's work."

But Eda was not hearing her now. Eda cared only for one thing, Ruben. For having him come home in the end to this cabin, to let her wash his feet and put him to bed, to rest easy, so he was fit to hoe next day, without his breaking down before those hooting bucks that had been born to field labour, whilst he had been raised to sit on a coachman's box. Densey had made her mad many a time, but Ruben had had no notion of quitting her for Densey, who couldn't take care of him like herself.

Now Eda rose, dumping her lap full of quilt pieces on the pallet, and began searching for her Sunday brogans. She felt she wanted the strength shoes gave her step. "Where you say they is? Down by the big gully branch?"

Densey stared at Eda, her own eyes still glazed by self-pity, then suddenly a spark of live hate shot up in them. "Yes, they's in the gully. An' Rache done sassed all around about you'n me bein' old and shrivelled. How you like that? An' him slightin' us now he's wore us down wid his grind to old bones ready fo' de soap-an'-lye pile."

The two women faced each other over their rack and ruin. They knew the sunken spots that made their bodies grotesque now, as they knew the faint trace of ripening that was beginning to soften Rache's green young frame. Eda wrapped her thin arms into the cover of her apron, while she and Densey joined forces in a glance. Then Eda unrolled her arms again and stuck them down at her sides determinedly. "I'm goin' to cut me a good stout switch an' lay it on dat gal's hide till she holler fo' mercy out of both sides of her mouth!"

Eda struck out down the path that led towards the gully, her arms and legs both swinging stiffly, like sticks of kindling-wood dressed in faded cotton. There was no more of a woman to the eye than that; she was a scarecrow topped by a sunbonnet.

Rache and Ruben were lying a little spent, and still half-athwart each other, one of her legs flung out escaping his bulk like the leg of a baked ginger-cookie doll. Her hair, which was not short wool, made a black mat behind her catlike small face. Her eyes were shut, so she did not see Eda coming downhill upon them. The first she knew of that third presence was a rumble like thunder from Ruben as he bolted off the ground and smacked at Eda and her upraised switch, sending her into a dizzy whirl.

Rache scrambled up then, clutching her discarded garments in a bunch in front of her stripped body. Before Eda's spinning gaze Rache was nevertheless clipped out clear, her breasts small pointed spikes showing up against her young chest. And Ruben was a thick-hocked man who could wallow in comfort at home, yet plunge into the woods for pleasure whenever he chose! Something burst like purple pulp in Eda's head, and she began to bat her way through it, towards that sassy piece with the nimble yellow shins. She meant to claw a stripe from Rache's eyes clean down her cheeks, with a good dig at the teats, and make raw meat of those little thighs!

She couldn't see the dark baffled look on Ruben's face brew up into a storm of anger as he saw her dried fingers reaching out to make ribbons of Rache's sound girl-flesh. She did not hear the noise like a boat-whistle in his throat, as her nails sank in a jab into one steepled breast. Then suddenly she did see his eyes rolling in lurid yellow balls in their sockets as he towered over her, lifting a great field-stone! Was that Ruben? If it was, she could stop his blow by yelling out his name—*Rube*—but the stone had caught her smack over the lips and stopped the word, stopped her world for good.

Ruben sat on a log beside the branch, his loose hands dropped between his black knees. Long ago Rache had skittered off home to the quarters. Ruben did not look in the direction where Eda's body lay now, with the mouth like a blackberry pie. And he did not make any move to hide.

He was still sitting there when Bruff and Danley Bruton came crackling through the underbrush. "What's your trouble?" asked Bruton, not seeing Eda as yet; but Bruff, with a quicker eye outdoors, saw, and hurried over to Eda, though his throat was gulpy. "You did this?" he demanded of Ruben.

The black man lifted a face full of stupor. He tried to turn and look at Eda, hoping that he could find her alive and everything all right again. But he knew what a smeared mess would be there, so he could not look.

Bruff stood for a moment. "We had better go tell my father," he decided aloud.

"Don't you think," suggested Danley, "that we ought to give Ruben a chance to escape? Before your father is forced to punish him? Heaven knows what he will feel he has to do to the poor devil for a thing like this."

Bruff backed off shocked. "Push a negro into running away? Man, you don't know what you're talking about!"

Ruben's own face broke into horror at Danley's suggestion. "You all wouldn' make me be no runaway with dawgs at my heels? Not me, please, Marse Bruff! If you turns me loose I might get took by nigger-stealers, and they'll sell a nigger to ol' Satan hisself. Or ef'n they thinks they's liable to be cotched up with, they'll kill me an' bury my parts! Lawd Jesus, *don'* turn me *loose*!"

Danley's dumbfounded voice questioned Bruff. "You mean he might actually meet such a fate?"

"Why, they do, over and over again. A runaway slave's life isn't worth a picayune, and plenty of rascals are willing to risk that for profit. You can't turn your negroes loose to shift for themselves—just to get out of settling a mess. Here, get up, you!" he ordered Ruben.

" We'll take you up to Marse Yarbrough. I'll tell him to send back for—for poor Eda."

Ruben rose, with some hoisting by Bruff. They had to tug him to start him walking, and his feet moved even then like clods.

4

The next evening Yarbrough and Gerda were bidding farewell to Malone, who had called over about their trouble. He was going to Mobile in a few days and had offered to take Ruben down to the block-house there, to see that he was sold into good hands, since Yarbrough felt he could not keep the black man here and maintain order among the others.

" I told you," half-laughed Malone, " that you ought to whip 'em more."

Yarbrough shrugged dispiritedly. " That's still not the answer."

Gerda said : " It all came about because I was slack and told Pokey to tend to Rache's mischief instead of settling it myself."

" No," objected Yarbrough, " you can't put your finger on any one thing and say that that is what's wrong with the way we handle them. Their nature simply gets beyond us sometimes, together with this job of owning and working them——" He broke off. The care of negroes was a constant responsibility, and an owner couldn't shuck it off.

Malone spoke again as they moved out of Gerda's earshot. " I reckon you'd just as soon get rid of that Rache too, wouldn't you? I'll pay you a fair price for her "

" It's a bargain," agreed Yarbrough.

" I need her, in case any of my friends from New Orleans are staying with me and feel the need of a wench. Of course they're partial to quadroons and octaroons, but mulattoes are next best."

Yarbrough's face was disgusted, but he didn't feel smart enough right now to offer any advice concerning negroes. He merely answered the other's good-night tiredly.

CHAPTER TWENTY-SIX

THE FIELDS had quit showing much bloom now. The green bolls had ripened, then burst into a snowstorm of white, and Yarbrough walked with an exultant whistle sounding between his teeth. Every one from the house was busy in the fields except Miz Lisbeth, Gracey, and Pokey. Gerda gave Pokey directions about such simple fare as could be easily prepared, then set off early in the day with her own croker-sack slung over her shoulder to join in the picking race. Now although every one laughed often on an excited note, they did not tarry to talk, but plucked, plucked, plucked the downy breasts of the cotton from their brown-parched bolls. Every member of the household was intent on making as near to a bale for himself or herself as possible, while the darkies caught the contagion of energy. The pall that had hung over them for a while after Eda's slaying was lifted. Arms shot out from bush to sack, from bush to sack. At the cotton-house the loads were weighed scrupulously, each white seeing his pounds mount and mount towards that coveted bale; each negro seeing the score rise until the trade Marse Yarbrough had promised to allow at the Screws' store went beyond the thought of tobacco and snuff and took on the prospect of a bolt of bright calico or a knife with a blue-sharp blade.

Yarbrough praised one and all heartily these days, as he swaggered over the floor of his new gin-house. He was going to make he couldn't tell how many bales to the acre! And all with a fine creamy strand that put him in mind of Sea Island cotton, as tender and soft as silk.

He was so impatient to move his first worth-while Alabama crop to the markets that he decided not to hold it until later for possible higher prices. He had so large a quantity that his total profit was bound to be big. However, he couldn't bring himself to risk sending it alone down the shallow early-fall rivers with their treacherous shoals, so he planned to accompany it himself. Feeling more like a planter than he had since he left South Carolina, he took Patt along to wait on him, to carry his pistol case with the pistols shined up like silver spoons, and to hold his wallet with small change, with which to tip people who were considered beneath a master's notice. On board the packet Yarbrough had only one regret, that the Rock Wall Place had no river landing of its own to know the salute of the steamers' whistles. Still Yarbrough preferred his own choice of the land he had bought, deeper back in the county where the soil had looked richer to him.

The packet was for ever stopping at landings, either for cargoes or for wood for fuelling, making its progress slow. Luckily the river was swollen with early rains so that there was little danger of running aground. Yarbrough enjoyed himself, talking prices with other men over their victuals, or jesting with them over cards in the bright glare of the saloon's wick-lard lamps. Afterwards before turning in he had a last cigar on the deck, with river banks looming by him dark and unknown. He could not sleep very well at night, though, for his nostrils twitched constantly with the fear of smelling smoke from a fire in the cotton holds. However, they arrived at Apalachicola without mishap and from there he took another boat to New Orleans, having decided to go the whole hog and travel to the larger market. The Petit firm of big cotton factors were distant kin of Miz Lisbeth's, consequently he felt he could do better dealing with them in person.

In New Orleans he put up at the new Exchange Hotel, with its marble columns and bathing-establishment where water was piped in from the streets. He reminded himself to tell Gerda about that, and to describe to Miz Lisbeth the great crystal chandeliers hung with thousands of glass pendants. He found, much to his annoyance, that he had to waste a certain amount of time in social amenities with the Petit family connection before he could bargain, and wished he had brought Willy along to attend to that doo-lollying. After a few days of backing and filling he put on his plainest suit and went to Cousin Baptiste's office, located next to one of their warehouses, and blurted out: "Now let's stop beating about the bush and agree on what you will give me a pound for my cotton."

Cousin Baptiste raised veined womanish hands, then let them drop deprecatingly. "Cotton has done so well this year that it is about to become a glut on the market."

Yarbrough met that chitter-chatter with a blunt statement: "Then I'll haul my bales clear back to Turber, if I can't get terms that suit me!" And he meant it. Too much had gone into this first big crop:

a pleasant home back in Egton, left to rot with its mahogany contents, hard months over trackless ways, faith broken with Gerda and restored only by the slow cure of joint toil, chicanery against other knaves, and soil wet not only with rain but with the blood of Indian squaws. He did not like to remember all of this, so he bulged his bottom lip out stubbornly and stood his ground until Cousin Baptiste gave way with a hesitant sigh.

The deal concluded, Yarbrough went to the racetrack, where he built up the amount of the children's profits amazingly. After that he took another turn through his hotel's splendours, though personally he was tired of the whole ornate she-bang. When he set foot on the home-going packet at Apalachicola, he stowed his small change in his own pockets and sent Patt off to dice with the negro roustabouts below. He chuckled mildly at all the old habits of the waited-upon dandy he had once cultivated. He felt as if he had walked out of that self and left it behind, as he might have left a room to which he would never return.

The boat hove to at Yufala at the end of a day when brick-coloured sunset was filling the sky above the browned trees. There were friends in the houses all along the Bluff, who called out invitations for him to take supper and spend the night, but he could hardly wait to get home as it was. He loved every foot of the way, every stumble the strange livery-stable horse made in the holes that dipped suddenly in patches of shadow cast by the moon. It was the sugar moon at its full, big and round and gold as an orange. When he neared his own land he could smell how the air was juicy from days on end of cane-grinding. He dismounted quietly at the gate-stumps and sat down on the Rock Wall to take a look at it.

He could make out Gerda with the baby, Turber, in her apron lap, leaning back against one of the squat wooden pillars, her face a little blank in the white moonlight. Other figures were blurred below her on the steps. The children were playing hop-toad tag, their feet ringing on the pounded dirt of the yard. From somewhere back at the quarters came a negro whoop and the pluck of a banjo.

Yarbrough felt the untrammelled wideness of their manner of living, the open hall, the broad unhedged yard, the sprawling fields, the uncounted hogs, the tiered forests, the whole wasteful rush of bold men gorging their fill upon harvests and game, heat and storms, slaves and might. Trying to take the kingdom of God and set their seals upon it, sworn to with red wax on parchment before the land-office agents from Sparta to the Golden Gate!

Thus Yarbrough stood and savoured these early plundering years, not caring for any time beyond when there might be the luxury of rest. He belonged *now*, in the days of trail-blazing. A little chill ran over him like a graveyard wind. When the rawness had gone out of the land he would be—not here. He thought: "I shall lie among our hollies first." He could not picture this grappling, tumbling country as ever being weeded out, to grow the prim flowers of graciousness. And yet—something stopped his heart like a clock—for he saw that these early Alabama years were all but gone by. And he could not hold them back in his grip.

He tethered the horse to a stump and walked up the path. Then the children came at him in a clamour, and Gerda rose up under the awkward weight of the sleeping Turber. "So you are back? I thought I saw someone in the shadow down there, but then you didn't budge again." They squeezed the baby awake between them in their embrace, after which she turned towards the children. "One of you fetch your father a dipper of cane juice."

Hans brought it, toeing in carefully in order not to slosh it. Yarbrough sat down to quaff its icy sweetness, so purely luscious, like nothing else except the heart of all things that come to fruit.

The sugar moon was bowling down behind the clouds.

CHAPTER TWENTY-SEVEN

THAT WINTER Bruff was promoted from the childhood apron-shirt to trousers, and the finely tailored suits and waistcoats ordered by Yarbrough in New Orleans came packed as carefully as a lady's bonnet. There were linen shirts and stocks too, and glossy boots which Bruff eyed dubiously.

"Don't worry," his father reassured him, "they won't pinch half as much as new brogans. It's the soft thin leather they're made of that gives 'em that small look."

"All the same," insisted Bruff, "I'll get Tom Two to break 'em in for me." Then he saw that Yarbrough was holding forward a great gold watch, saying: "Take it, son, it's yours."

Bruff reached, half-scared of dropping the precious treasure. His father showed him where his name and birth date were engraved inside the case. "You can put your son's name in there one day and pass it on to him," Yarbrough said.

"He won't get it till I'm dead and gone!" declared Bruff possessively. The watch made him into a man, and no mistake! That prevented him from hugging his father around the neck.

2

In 1839, the year the bottom dropped out of the cotton market, Miz Lisbeth faded off into death, as gently as she had moved about in life. There was no pain and no fear on her part. She knew she was simply going where she could be reunited to her William, in something like a marriage service, only performed by the Lord instead of a minister. William would be as vigorous as when he was young, but he would look like the ruddy white-haired tyrant she had grown used to back in Egton, while she expected to be as young-looking as a girl, with soft tow tresses and a deft step. Her children left behind were all grown and in good hands, though she had forgotten who some of them were married to back in South Carolina. Still they were all right, as far as she knew, and the others she'd be glad to see up Yonder. Especially Lucey, with whom she could gossip mildly about the others' doings through pleasant afternoons resting on clouds as soft as this old feather bed. . . . Her thin lips puckered around the smile of old age as she went to sleep. She did not wake again next morning into this bustling log plantation house when the rising-bell rang.

3

In spite of the heavy depression throughout the nation, Turber County was prospering and many of the local fortunes were being founded. People were building finer frame houses, with polished oaken floors instead of the double-pen log ones with puncheon floors. They were also ordering carriages again, to be drawn by fine pairs of horses, instead of jogging everywhere in mule wagons or on horseback.

Turberville as a thriving county seat was passing ordinances against allowing cows and hogs to roam its three streets, and it had a real store of its own now to boast of. John Screws had put up a shed not far from the courthouse where the street turned into the Yufala Road. He had built wide doors that swung back like those of a stable, permitting the passers-by to see into the cool brown cave. Inside he had salt and white sugar and spices, cotton and even silk yard goods, as well as Irish linen for gentlemen's shirts, and fine-milled flour, brandy from France, also pink clumps of rock candy for children to suck in their jaws. John Screws's son, Nat, knew how to sort and show these things to people who came wandering in during Court Week. They were always asked to sit down, and in hot weather to have a glass of cold spring water, often with a section of precious lemon squeezed into it.

At the same time Yufala continued to thrive as a river port for shipping cotton, and crops were hauled there by mules and oxen from as far around as seventy-five miles. Guy saw the need of a bank and, having hoarded much of his money, came and made a proposition to Captain Melburne at Yufala. The upshot was that they set up a concern with Melburne as president, Guy as treasurer, and Willy as clerk. Willy was not averse to spending most of his days looking polite, with his parted hair and clean hands, passing out money. Guy chewing his quid was in the background to make sure that Willy did not sympathetically count out too much because people needed it.

It was along about then that the new Academy enrolled a hundred and fifty students, male and female, and Danley Bruton, who was its head, showed eyes glowing like jack o' lanterns with pride. He still spent the week-ends with the Whetstones, for in addition to having Bruff at his school as a regular pupil he was tutoring him in special studies to prepare him for the Medical College in New Orleans.

This was the year that saw the first attempt at a county newspaper, one which waged a bitter battle against the Whig candidate for president, Benjamin Harrison. This was also the year of the Harrison Freshet, a flood which they named after that same candidate and blamed him for, since he was the butt in these days of all their ill-will. The flood rose so high above the river banks that boats accustomed to go down the river under the bridge now had to steer around over the Georgia fields. After the flood had subsided and the planks of the bridge dried off once more, this year saw the start of the custom of eloping to the bridge, so many young couples escaping parents bent on balking the matches being wed there that it became known as the Marrying Bridge. And it was that year that Jobyna Whetstone, at fourteen, commenced to eat her heart out because no one paid any attention to her, with Lucinda around.

Lucinda gloated over the smitten victims she had collected, just as she had told Jerard Malone she would. There was Tewks Johnston, who broke his wrist trying to jump a ditch and snatch a kiss from her. There was Ace Willoughby, who carried what he thought was a lover's knot made out of her hair, but which was really a strand from a colt's tail she had palmed off on him. There was a widower in search of a wife younger than his children, and there was even a husband of one unsuspecting little thing who made eyes at Lucinda on the sly. There was, she jeered to herself, a whole pack of idiots who spoke reverently about Pure Women, but always hot-footed it after any girl they thought might cut the cake. They liked her, she concluded, because she was a vixen, yet with a good family name. What they wanted was a sinner in a saint's bed.

On one particular afternoon Lucinda came in out of the fall wind that was stripping the leaves from the trees, with her hair wet from a gust of rain, and her new riding-habit shabby from the way she had abused it. She went stamping agitatedly back to the dining-room, where Gracey was sitting in a small splint rocker in her widow's weeds. Gracey looked up from her hemstitching and went *Tch, tch!* at the sight of the fresh stains on Lucinda's habit. "You look more like a ragamuffin than the daughter of a well-to-do planter."

Cinda grinned with a queer pleasure she took in her extravagance, then her face hardened as she eyed Gracey's funereal garb. That was such a sham. It was Gracey's way of trying to pilfer the prizes from life without going through the heat of the contest. Under cover of her macabre masquerade, which was perforce accepted as the truth by the county, Gracey pried into matrons' talk of morning sickness, sneered at girls who were turning into honest spinsters, and moistened her lips furtively if she accidentally overheard some man's coarse jest. She gave her younger cousin the creeps, attired in her musty false black.

The girl's face must have shown some of her revulsion, for Gracey pursed her mouth in disapproval, remarking: "You needn't look so mad at me because I chided you about ruining your habit. What have you been up to, pray, to get in such a state?"

Lucinda picked up a pecan, cracked it with her teeth, ate the white meat, and dropped the hull on the sideboard; then she went out, whistling defiantly.

Outside in the ell Lucinda ran into Joby and Ma'am Gerda. Her mother took her roughly by the shoulder. "Is it true what Joby tells me? That you caused Thad Pinckney to try to drown himself?"

"I didn't do any such thing! Thad was just dog-drunk and happened to fall in the river after he quarrelled with me to-day. 'Twouldn't have been any great loss if he had drowned. Who pulled him out, anyway? I ran for help, but when I got back I could see tracks on the bank where he'd been dragged out all safe."

"C. D. Melburne saved him," chided Joby. "And Thad kept saying he didn't want to live, with you tormenting him so. Everybody is gabbing his head off about you."

"Blubbering sot, that's what Thad is, and I'll thank him not to come whining after me. And I won't have him thrown up to me like a corpse all the rest of my days, either! You spying tattler!"

Gerda shook her daughter by the shoulders and gave her a brutal, hard slap on one cheek. "You aggravate the very soul out of me!" With a sweep of the arm she propelled Lucinda into the girls' room, jouncing her across to land on the bed. "Now here you'll stay without a mouthful of food until you can behave like a human being! If it weren't that your father was so silly about you, I'd tan you good." Gerda gave the girl another box with her fist, then shut the door and bolted it behind her.

Cinda sat where she had been dumped on her bed, gritting her teeth in a high pitch of anger at being so humbled. "I'll get back at Ma'am somehow!" she swore. "I'll cut up some dido that she'll *never* forget!" Then she lunged back and lay on the quilt, forgetting everything but her tiredness after a day replete with scenes. Presently she was asleep, breathing with a delicate hiss.

When she woke, night had fallen and the room was chill because no fire had been lighted. She was stiff too, having lain crooked in the same position so long. She rose grumpily and began to pound on the door for someone to come with a kindling knot. It was Jobyna who finally answered, and poked the torch quickly through a small crack, saying: "Take it," then slammed the door again, as if she were afraid a witch were inside and might jump out to grab her. Lucinda laughed jeeringly at the other. "Scared of her own shadow, the little ninny. I'll think of a way to settle her book. Hmm. . . . I'll get even with that stuffy C. D. Melburne that she's always casting sheep's eyes at. I'll——" Suddenly Cinda spun about in glee, for an idea had come to her of how to get even with her mother also. Through Jobyna, that was the way! By persuading the girl to make a fool of herself over C. D.!

Lucinda now drew forth a tin box she kept hidden with a secret store of food, to enjoy here in her room, and as she ate, sitting cross-legged before her cheerful crackling blaze, she planned the prank that would upset Ma'am Gerda. The fire spit and snapped as she threw some of the sausage skin into it. "A lot of good it does to try to make *me* do without my supper!" she jeered, shaking her fist in the direction of the dining-room.

When Jobyna came in timidly to bed, she found Lucinda cheerfully sorting through ribbons and trinkets, putting many of the more delicately hued ones in a separate pile. Joby's eyes fastened on an apple-green satin sash that she had always coveted, until presently

Lucinda, who caught her admiring glance, lifted the ribbon and shook its glistening loops out. "Not my style," she said, and began to wind it into a roll. After that she turned her attention to some ear-bobs of seed pearls, all the time watching Joby slyly and thinking: "What she can see in C. D. Melburne I can't understand. I wouldn't shake a stick at him, though he's always trying to show off to me. He only sweet-talks Joby when I snub him, hoping to make me mad. Pouf!" She topped the pile of gew-gaws with a curled baby-blue ostrich tip and shoved it all towards her sister's side of the bed. "Here, take it. None of that stuff suits me, and 'twould set you off in fine style."

Jobyna half-reached out a hand to claim the pretties, then drew it back sharply, suspicious. "Don't tease me, Cinda. You know I can't—take a joke good." Her face puckered beneath her quaint smooth braids.

Lucinda had a moment's twinge for the deviltry she was up to, but she went ahead. "Take 'em, goose, they're cluttering up my chest."

"Ooh!" Jobyna was down on the floor now, her arms spread in a yearning embrace over the trifles. "You're awful good to me sometimes, sister," she said, ashamed of the almost constant resentment she felt towards Cinda. "I'm sorry about to-day."

"Shucks, that's nothing," returned the other gruffly, then added carelessly: "You ought to be more fixy, now that you're turning fourteen and boys like C. D. Melburne are beginning to take a shine to you."

"Who said C. D. Melburne had taken a shine to *me*?" demanded Joby.

"Why, every one knows that he's distracted about you, he talks it all around. He sighs like a stump-sucking mule every time I mention your name when we're dancing a figure. He says more nice things about you. But I'd better keep 'em to myself, or Ma'am will get me for putting notions into your head."

"Why, how can she say you're putting notions into my head, when I'm already as old as she was when you were born?"

"You're such a baby all the same, I'll catch the mischief again if she hears I started you to thinking——"

"Lucinda, I give you my word of honour I won't tattle on you any more! And if you don't tell me what compliments he flattered me with I'll know you're just fooling."

Lucinda laughed up her sleeve at that; then abruptly she leaned over and whispered into Joby's ear, which began to tingle pleasantly at the honeyed words.

Joby wriggled delightedly, "Called me pretty as a pink, did he? Well, his eyesight must be failing him. And all that other is stuff and nonsense. Or maybe he thought he *had* to say something nice about me to you, because I'm your sister."

"Pooh, most men don't feel called upon to sing any other girl's praises to me."

"I expect not," conceded Joby eagerly.

"Come on, let's get to bed. I'm tired as a hunting dog after the day I've had." Lucinda yanked off her clothes, leaving them in a huddle on the floor as usual. But to-night after Joby had laid her own primly over a chair, she picked Cinda's up carefully and examined the stains trampled into the fabric. "I can take that out for you, I believe," she offered.

"Don't bother," yawned Cinda, "I'll only get more on it to-morrow." Joby stood scraping at it anxiously with one small finger-nail, her face placid with a new sisterly affection.

In the middle of the next morning Yarbrough came and unlocked Lucinda's door. She was sitting by the window looking indifferent, thinking it would be Ma'am and wanting to appear insolent and unperturbed. When she saw it was her father, however, she rushed at him. "Take me with you up to Yufala to the Melburnes'. I heard you yelling you were going there, and I don't think I can stand Gracey shaking her head over me to-day about Thad Pinckney's ducking."

"Well, have yourself a bite while I see about the horses."

She was too smart to risk going back to the dining-room, for fear Gerda would forbid the jaunt. Besides, she had already stuffed herself on an odd assortment of food in her room, so Yarbrough found her waiting for him down by the gate. "You look mighty perky in that habit," he complimented her as they cantered along.

Glancing down at it, she saw that Joby had kept her word; the stains were all sponged away, the nap steamed up fresh. "Must have done that while I was still sleeping," Cinda decided lightly, and gave it not another thought. Or rather that set her off on a tangent about Joby and C. D. and the mischief she was cooking up. Her malice gave her a sparkle that Yarbrough enjoyed.

In the evening when they returned home she avoided Ma'am and Bruff, escaping by entertaining the younger children with her capers. Hans, her complete slave as usual, stuck as close as a burr and she encouraged him with kindness, for she was going to need his help to carry out her plans. When finally she went to her room Jobyna sprang up. "Did you see C. D. at dinner time to-day, and did he say anything about me?"

"I surely did see him," Cinda answered, "and I have a most important message for you." She went over and peeped out the door to make sure no one was listening, then she came back and spoke in low hurried tones to the younger girl. When Lucinda had finished her speech, Jobyna sat transfixed, her eyes like a china doll's. On and on she sat, her breath coming and going through a little round *O* of a mouth, her hands clasped like those of a baby saying its prayers.

"Well," asked Cinda sharply after a bit, "are you going to agree to it?"

"Oh, yes!" whispered Joby with a soft kissing little sound.

4

Two nights later when the girls stole out of the house Joby was hesitant with fright and misgivings. "S'pose Hans isn't waiting for us with the horses?"

"He will be all right! Hans would cut off his hand for me."

"But—but," protested Joby, "it seems to me like C. D. should have come for me, so we could elope *together*."

"Silly, he has to *stay* there at the Marrying Bridge with the preacher, else the preacher's likely to scoot if he sees any of our kinfolks. But of course if you're a fraidy-cat and don't want to marry C. D.——"

"Oh, no," whimpered Joby, "I didn't mean that. Only I feel scared of the night. Then I always counted on being married with a bouquet and a lot of refreshments and all."

"Pooh!" scoffed Lucinda. "A runaway match is lots more exciting."

Joby said nothing further then, yet she had never relished excitement, even hanging back when company came until they quit the hugging and hollering "Howdy?" Now she was greatly relieved when she saw Hans with the three horses waiting in the bend. Somehow having any one as steady as Hans along, even if he wasn't even twelve, made her feel they were not doing anything outlandish, anything for which they would catch Hail Columbia from Ma'am later.

Once, though, as the horses made their way at a trot, Hans asked Lucinda in a low voice: "Do you think we're doing the right thing? We could still turn back and all be in our beds before any one caught on." But Lucinda only shook her head and said: *"Ssh!"*

The black trees went by as the horses' hoofs clapped along, and the Mile Hill presently came into view, then slid by. Before they knew it, they were slowing their mounts into a soft padded stepping that would not rouse the streets of Yufala. They hid the horses at the top of the Plank Road that led down to the bridge, and Lucinda ordered Hans to stay with them until she whistled; then she pulled Jobyna swiftly down the walk. In the shadow at the far end of the bridge the scary little preacher was waiting with the lanky raw-boned C. D. Melburne. The latter came prancing awkwardly up to the girls and tried to snatch Lucinda's hand.

"Wait a minute," she told him, then spoke to Joby. "Stand here a second, I must speak to C. D." The younger girl stood like some stupefied calf while Lucinda whisked C. D. out of earshot.

Again he made a reach for Cinda's hands, but she side-stepped him. "What's ailing you?" he asked querulously. "Aren't you going to be my lawful wife in just a few shakes?"

"What, *me*?" she gasped in great pretended surprise. Then, feigning distress, she hurried on: "Oh, C. D., you didn't speak plain! You said you'd give your soul if Mr. Whetstone's *fairest* daughter would marry you. And any one can see *I'm* as dark as a crow. Then when I told you that I knew 'the girl in question' cared for you, I meant Joby. Why, poor thing, she's been eating her heart out for you for years."

"Jobyna?" he ejaculated. "Why, the thought of marrying her never occurred——"

"Hush! You don't want her to hear you. And let me tell you something, you're a lucky good-for-nothing to have her look your way! Why, she already knows more than I'll ever learn about housekeeping and cake-making."

"Don't like cake much, gives me heartburn," he objected sullenly.

"She's a good nurse too for the sick."

"Don't like women fussing over me with wet cloths and gruel."

Lucinda stamped her foot. "You'll like what you get, sir! And I'll thank you not to be throwing off on my sister. If you think you're going to make talk about her, by having her go traipsing back home after this, you're mighty much mistaken! Hans is waiting right up there by the horses, and if I say the word he'll drill you through with a bullet as clean as a whistle. The Whetstones are the best shots around here; they'd all fight among themselves for the next chance at you if he missed aim."

C. D. looked about despairingly. He felt hoaxed, yet he knew the truth of what she said. No young girl could go riding back home unwed close to daybreak after such an escapade as this, and the man in the case could hardly expect to get off unscathed, since, no matter how innocent the jaunt had been, her name would be mud afterwards.

Ruthlessly Lucinda pressed her advantage. "Besides, you couldn't do that to the poor trusting little thing. Why, she's been going around singing at the top of her lungs ever since I brought her your message. Even begging me for trinkets to deck herself for you."

C. D. cleared his throat miserably. "I reckon," he stammered, "there's no other way. Still, I'll always think hard of you for leading me on, sugar."

"I didn't lead you on! You simply didn't talk plain. And save your 'sugar' for her." She marched back over to Joby, then whistled for Hans.

There on a creaky wooden bridge with the dark water sloshing mournfully below, Jobyna, bewildered and cringing from her own daring, was married to a stalling man who had never before made up his own mind to do any deed. Lucinda grinned into her hood, thinking: "Now Ma'am *will* be in a sweet temper, and over her little goody-good." Hans was very quiet, not liking any of it.

When the preacher's words had come to a whining end and he'd departed, pocketing his dollar, C. D. looked from Jobyna to Lucinda nonplussed. "Now where in time can we go? Mamma's got the house all locked up for the night."

"There's the hotel, stupid," replied Lucinda. "They'll let you in if you haven't got the smallpox."

"No, Mamma would have fits if any of her kin stayed at a hotel with her house right in the same town."

"Then," gibed Lucinda, "you might go on over into Georgia."

"Yes," put in Hans for the first time, "we could leave a letter from you under your parents' door. That way Jobyna and you would miss the first blow-up. I can tell you I hate to think of how things are going to pop at Rock Wall. It'll be all right when they're used to the idea, but not right now."

Lucinda, ready with everything, fished out a piece of paper and a charcoal stick. "Joby left her note where Ma'am will find it at her place at the breakfast table. Now you word yours." She turned around to her sister while C. D. was scratching away. "You look peaked, Joby," she told her, rather kindly now, pinching the other's cheek. "Come on, get your dander up. You have your heart's desire, make the most of it."

Joby looked at her wanly. "Please, Cinda, don't let them make me come home until every one stops fussing."

At that, swiftly, surprising even herself, Lucinda leaned down and kissed her sister. "I won't, honey. Besides they *can't* make a married woman come home. You just be happy now, do you hear?" Presently she and Hans left the two of them standing there uncertainly on the planks of the bridge.

Jobyna lifted her face to C. D. wondering why her husband did not kiss her. He looked down at the helpless white spot the face made, then clumsily he bent over her. "Don't take on like you'd lost your last friend. Cry-babies make me see red." He found her little girl's cheek cool and smooth.

On the road back to Turberville Lucinda hinted in jerky phrases at how she had schemed to bring this elopement about, to be greeted by a dead silence from Hans. She hardly knew how to take that, from her Hans! By the time they were in sight of home it came over her that her prank had turned out far too solemnly, and she began to wonder exactly whom she had tricked after all.

She came to breakfast late the next morning, having overslept after her night's journey, and she found Ma'am alone, seated at the foot of the table with Jobyna's note still before her. "Come here, daughter," Gerda ordered, and Lucinda obeyed. Gerda in her chair looked down at the note a long time as if in search of a way to deal with its problem. Finally she raised her eyes and Lucinda noticed, somewhat with awe, that there was no flash of anger in them, but a sombre pity. Her mother's broad forehead seemed to widen and the dark surfaces of her eyes also, until it appeared to Lucinda that the whole breadth of the room was encompassed in that judging gaze.

At last Gerda spoke. "I know the whole story. I asked Hans. Perhaps something will move C. D. to be good to Jobyna, though I doubt that. Your making him feel a dupe would sour a better man than one of C. D.'s measly nature. I hope your overweening wilfulness is satisfied, now that you have played a sorry game with the whole of your sister's life."

She was silent once more, for so long that Lucinda thought she must have finished. Still the daughter could not move from beneath that heavy regard. Finally Gerda continued: "I wish that you could be frightened at what you have done to those two, and cry. Then perhaps I would know how to reach through to you, by comforting." She rose up and her full height was tremendous, but her eyes appeared blind now, as if she had lost her way at some turning of motherhood and could not grope to the right goal. "You may go now. Nothing I can say will help you. No one can. What a—*pity*!"

Barefooted and in her calico wrapper, just as she had come in for breakfast, Lucinda went out to the bins in the cotton-house where the seed was stored. She climbed into the woolly grey piles trying to bury herself there, to weep. She pulled her hair loose to hide under. Sick with a lead feeling in her stomach, it seemed to her as if this day, early as it was, was turning dark with the end of everything.

About an hour later she heard a muffled shuffling in the billows of seed beside her and, peering out from her hair, she saw Hans moving close to her, his lips quivering. "Cinda, I hated to tell on you. But Ma'am is—kinder like a part of God. I had to give her the truth."

Lucinda reached out and locked a little finger in his. "Never mind."

At that he crowded down and put both his arms around her tight. "Oh, Cinda!" he cried in a tortured voice. "I love you more than the whole world, and I can't bear having helped to hurt you."

"I'm bad, it doesn't matter."

"Yes, it does!" He grabbed her more fiercely and buried his cheek in her neck under her ear where his lips could feel her warmest skin. Her hair was dripping all over them both, in a tangle. She slithered about a bit so that he could hold her better, and put one of her own arms across the back of his faded shirt. He could feel the careless tenderness of her caress as if the cotton shirt were not there. "Cinda, nobody in the world matters to me but you. I love you as if you were—everybody that I could ever love!"

She stayed still and let him kiss her neck where his mouth lay. She liked it, here in these soft depths, hidden from all remorse, with only Hans's worship and his nuzzling animal nearness. "Let's go to sleep, I'm dead from last night. Let's sleep here all day out of sight, until they get worried about where we are."

"All right," whispered Hans.

CHAPTER TWENTY-EIGHT

A DAY OR TWO LATER Lucinda went chinquapin-hunting by herself, feeling unable to bear any one's company but Hans's these days, and he was busy picking at the top crop that was the last of the season's yield of the cotton plants. She wandered the woods all day alone, wishing passionately that she could go away somewhere, away from all the reproach around her. If it didn't let up she'd—she didn't know what!

She was seated on the edge of a bank washing the dust off her feet and nibbling chinquapins dispiritedly, when Jerard Malone found her. Taking a place beside her, he lifted her over into his lap without further ado. "I've come from speaking to your father and hearing about your latest performance. Now he agrees with me that it's high time you married me. I've let you have your fling as I promised, and you've kept your end of our old agreement. We've had some right sweet cuddles sometimes, though I swear I don't believe you care a continental who it is next to you long as it's a man with his blood up hot about you! Anyway I'd be taking too great a risk letting you run wild longer. I don't know even now whether I'm getting you first-hand or not. But no matter, I'll take charge of you from now on!"

Provokingly she laughed into his face. "Ho, you think you can put a bit in my mouth and pull me up short. You're mighty much mistaken. Why, we will be fire and brimstone together!"

"That'll suit me fine; then we can make some real hell pop."

She scanned his urgent face with rising excitement. Marrying him now would mean such a furore of getting together the trousseau, planning, and entertainments that no one could continue to chide her, the heroine of the hour. It would mean her immediate release from repentance. "Have your way then!" she exclaimed. "I always meant to marry you some day, and this is a good time for the bang-up."

He rolled her over so that the dry leaves scratched her as he embraced her tenderly. "For keeps, now?" he muttered.

2

It was drawing near Christmas and Lucinda's wedding clothes were being finished. Since she refused to have any of her underclothes made from the home-loomed cotton, John Screws had been commissioned to order bolts of the finest-drawn linen. As for frocks she was partial to velvet for winter wear, so lengths and lengths in all rich colours—bottle-green, maroon, rust, deep blue, and mulberry—had been imported for her costumes. Stroking the cloth, Cinda suddenly exclaimed: "I'm not ever again going to wear anything but velvet in the winter time, not with all the money Jerard Malone has. No, siree, nothing but dull velveteen for daytime, and the shiny kind for Sundays and frolics. It feels as thick and smooth as cream, and my eyes snap black enough to set it off. I'll be the lady in velvet now, for all my born days!"

"Mighty fine you'll look, churning in a velvet frock," remarked Gerda tartly.

"Churning? If you think I'm going to touch a churn, with the Malone negroes so plentiful that Jerard doesn't even know them all by sight, and has to make his house ones wear a white apron, *man* and woman, and his field ones wear a green kerchief around their necks so he'll know them—if you think——"

"Take care," warned Gerda, "that you don't blow up and bust after you're married to your Irish immigrant who owns so much black meat."

"Why, Miz Gerda," teased Yarbrough, who had come in silently, "you sound like Gracey a-talking blue blood." He twigged first her ear, then Cinda's. "I'll buy her the velvet now, and after she's married I don't doubt Malone will spread it down for her to walk on." Then he went out, taking his wife with him.

Lucinda picked up a sweet pomegranate that had dried out its skin in a bowl near her fire. With one rip of her teeth she had a clump of its ruby seeds in her mouth. She sucked it swiftly, swallowing the juice, then spat the sick ricy-looking kernels on the floor for her maid Pinky to clean up. Outside in the open hall she heard a flutter, then Jobyna's voice chirping away. She still didn't care to see much of Joby, so she kept quiet, hoping her sister would pass by the door, but she came in timidly.

"Take your wraps off," Lucinda then told her, "and come over here by the fire. You always look so frost-bitten."

Joby gave her a half-scared smile. "The wind blew bad on the Mile Hill and C. D. wouldn't stop to let me wrap up again good."

"How do you like it, living up there with the hominy-grits family?"

"I don't see why you call the Melburnes such a peculiar name."

"Because they remind me of a puddle of butter melting in a pile of mush," explained Lucinda cheerfully.

Joby sat picking at her fingertips, attempting no further conversation until Lucinda demanded: "What are you so downhearted about? What's wrong?"

Joby shook out her skirts irritably. "Nothing's wrong. At least I can't help it! C. D. just——" She bit her lip and tried to shunt her eyes away from Cinda's, but the other stared her down, forcing Joby's words to come in a rush. "I *love* C. D. He knows that, he ought not to be mad at me. But, Cinda, I'm not good and grown up yet. I can't help *that.* I will be some day, only he won't give me time." She bunched her mouth like a baby about to cry.

"Can't you grit your teeth and bear it? Pretend, until you learn to like it."

"No, that's not it," protested Joby, furiously pink. "I'd be glad to act that way, but I was too slow catching on. Now he doesn't give me a chance to act *any* way!" she ended in agony.

Lucinda whistled. "You mean he's given up acting like a husband without giving you a fair try? That won't do, at least not until you have a baby to show for your trouble." She began to study, narrowing her eyes to shut out any distraction. Suddenly she banged one fist into the other palm. "I tell you what! He thinks he's the only man you ever had a chance at, and that you're such a little-biddy no one will look at you. Now listen, there are going to be scads of men here for the wedding. Lots of regular dandies from all over the South that Jerard has known. They won't know at first that you're married and they'll start paying you compliments. Well, you let 'em, and play right back up to them."

"Oh, I couldn't! That would be wrong!"

"Wrong, my foot! Don't talk like Gracey. You aren't out to set your cap for a beau, but you've a husband who's gone cold-roast on you in the first few weeks, and you have to do something about it! Stop moping and twiddling your thumbs; I'll have Pinky fix you so fancy you'll turn all their heads, C. D.'s along with the rest."

"Honest and truly?" implored Jobyna, seeking any solution. "And can I sleep in here with you when the house becomes crowded, so he won't have to see my hair wrapped up in curling rags?"

"You certainly can," agreed Lucinda, feeling so truly sorry for her sister that she had to bend and stir up the fire with a dried stalk of old sugar cane to hide her softening. The smell of supper seeping through the crack under the door was a welcome relief, for she didn't know how to act with Joby after such intimate talk.

3

More and more, after Malone began to hope to marry Lucinda, he had made his Turber plantation his headquarters, leaving his properties in other states in the hands of overseers, while adding to the luxury of the two-story mansion he had built here in an evergreen grove on a high knoll. He called it Top Hill, and it was reached by an almost heart-shaped drive whose tip ended at an imposing entrance gate. The house was built of rich-coloured bricks, made of red clay from his own excavations, then hardened and baked in cypress moulds in his kiln. Laid with cream mortar, they gave the house an appearance as softly bright as old tapestry. The doorway, approached by a high flight of marble steps, had a fine Georgian fanlight over it, and inside he had sacrificed some of his choicest hardwoods to lay floors as slick as glass. In the little parlour, giving into the dining-room, the floor was covered with a bright flowered velvet carpet; but across the hall, where folding doors could turn the two capacious rooms into one fine large ballroom, he had only scattered white fur rugs and some small figured ones that had come in by the China trade to Boston. Heavy mahogany and elaborate rosewood, such as few people in Turber County owned in any great degree as yet, completed the air of grandeur started by the Carrara marble mantel and the girandole mirror. He had installed crystal chandeliers too since his betrothal, the ones in the Little Parlour having lard boats with wicks in them, but the ones in the Big Drawing-room burning candles. It made Lucinda feel like crowing triumphantly, for there was no other mansion in the county to compare with the place of which she was shortly to be mistress.

Nettie Melburne had suddenly become all honey and pie, in hopes of being named a bridesmaid and appearing in a romantic light to catch the eye of Nat Screws. Cinda couldn't abide him, though she was very fond of his sharp-tongued mother; but Nat was a bag of bluster, and Cinda had heard Miz Lydia Screws say frankly: "I must have been scared by a wind-storm just before I had him." Braggart that he was, he was suited to the show-off Nettie. Lucinda maliciously asked the latter to attend her, then chose a deep rose for her to wear that turned poor Nettie chalky, while it would set Lucinda herself off splendidly.

Presents now began pouring in on Lucinda from all sides. The groom's personal gift was about a teacupful of diamonds, to be set as she pleased. She had them made into a high haughty collar and ear-rings that were like cartwheels against the finely turned ears she never covered. Malone then sent for more stones for a pair of barbaric wristlet cuffs.

A week before the wedding, which was to take place on New Year's Eve, Bruff arrived home from New Orleans, where he had been taking examinations to enter the Medical College at mid-term. He appeared very much the eldest son of the house, with his hair cut according to the city style and Pint scraping and grinning behind him with his boxes. But Bruff dropped his dignity with a bang at the sight of his twin and rushed at her. "Wait till you see what *I* brought you! Whew, it's cut me down to the bare-board for all next term. But it will put your eyes out!" He pulled her by the arm back to the boys' room. In the dimness neither of them noticed Hans in a corner by the clothes-press curtains. Bruff hurried Lucinda over to the fireplace, where the blaze lighted things up. "Look!" Out of a box he swung a great ruby cross, dangling from a studded chain, blood-red like wine caught in ice!

"Goede hemel!" gasped the girl, reverting to their Grandfather Pieter's Dutch. "Rubies! Red! My colour! I've been given heaps of jewellery lately, but that's my pick of them all. Only——" She broke off, then both of them burst out laughing at the same time, as twins will, at the thought of his giving her a *cross*.

"I don't blame you," grinned Bruff when they had subsided a bit, "it is enough to make you split your sides laughing, my giving *you* such a sacred piece. Only it hasn't any Jesus on it. Besides it is your favourite colour."

"Oh, it's a beauty!" She hugged it to her as another woman might have hugged a baby.

"Glad it pleases you. Now I must go back to Papa and Ma'am and tell them the good news about my schooling. I'll be a doctor, dosing you with calomel, before you know it." He pranced out.

Seated on the edge of the nearest bed, Lucinda spilled the chain back and forth in her hands to watch the lights darting. She had been there for several moments before she heard someone trying to creep out of the room behind her back and, turning, saw Hans. "Hans, come see," she called, but he continued backing off. "Come look," she insisted. This time he came sidling over, but his eyes shifted away from the cross quickly, as if one look had hurt him. His face was compressed, his arms were rigid, yet quivering nervously.

"Why, whatever is the matter?" she cried, tossing the jewels aside and putting an arm around his waist.

"You and Bruff, and the fun you have between you, and all the fine presents everybody but me can give you. I love you more than all the rest put together—yet all I can give you is just an old nothing that I made myself!" He broke into a torrent of sobs such as he had never vented in childhood.

"Hush," she told him. "Hush up and show it to me. Everything you make is pretty as can be, and you know it!"

His sobs calmed down at her command and he brought out his offering. It was a small hand-carved chest to hold her many jewels. The wood was of sweet cedar that had been treated in the curing until it had a colour of the sunset rose that streaked their skies, and gave out a bouquet like pungent old brandy. It was lined with carefully matched doeskin, softer than any velvet from any foreign loom.

"O-oh!" Lucinda held it very carefully in her hands, fingering the soft bed he had wrought for her jewels. "Didn't you know that somehow I like things from here, from our trees and land, the best?" She looked up at him, her eyes dark with remembering her feeling for those earliest shoes tanned by their own tan-yard stream, for her turkey eggs to use as coins in trading with the pedlar, for the unbalked freedom she had gained out of the wilderness.

He searched her eyes until he saw that her thanks were true, then he sighed: "I'm glad."

She placed both arms around him and drew him down to lean beside her on the quilt. He lay for a moment content, then he choked: "I don't want you to marry Malone and leave me. He's too old and his neck's red."

"Here now," she chided with a laugh, "don't go acting up over nothing. You'll be coming over to visit me, and I'll surprise you with all sorts of goodies, with no one to make you stop gobbling."

"I don't want goodies. I want you *here,* where I can see you every day, and know you're right up the hall at night."

"Now, now," she scolded, rubbing her nose against his forehead to make him laugh. But his eyes remained turned solemnly downward where he could see the first wee crack that showed the beginning of her young bosom. He knew that none of the things she promised would make him happy. He could not help it that he had put her in the middle of his life. It had all happened back before ever he could remember. But at least he would not trouble her now, when she wanted everything gay. He could do that for her. Besides, she was going to kiss him in just one more minute.

4

The next day the rest of the visiting wedding guests arrived, as many as possible being put up at the Rock Wall Place, the rest being quartered at neighbouring plantations. By nightfall all of them with their local hosts had collected at Whetstone Stand for a welcoming supper and dancing. Gracey, arranging branches of holly with bowls of winter narcissus and Christmas roses in the parlour, stopped sharply right after she had lighted the tapers in the candelabra; she had noticed, as if for the first time, the way the flames danced like stars in the glass window-panes. There had been no glass to shine for her, in that crude cabin where she had given her pitiful little party. She recalled how her eyes had been blocked by greasy paper windows when the girl she had been had wanted to stare out at a vista of dreams. . . . A girl? She was not that any more. Yet she was nothing else, neither wife nor widow. "I might as well not be in the world," she mewed. She had never meant anything to any one, except to a boy who was a ghost. "I'm little better than a ghost myself. I was never much more than a dream I had of myself."

She sniffed absently at the narcissus, a habit she had formed in memory of Ronald, then went to see whose bowknots she could help tie in place. She ended by helping Joby, for every one was swamping Lucinda with aid. Gracey did very well by the younger sister, who resembled her more, though Joby had smooth bands of hair and a gentle quiet instead of Gracey's old frothy curliness. When the prinking was finished and Joby entered the parlour, she was so sweet to look at that even Malone remarked: "You look like a sprig of posies. Come here and meet my groomsman, Armand Petit. He's a distant cousin of yours, over in New Orleans."

Joby came glowing, to meet the man Petit, who was a sallow dandy with a spoiled damson-coloured mouth. She was flattered at the way his eyes lighted up at her. She could not know that he was thinking to himself: "Ah, *une jolie fille,* and virgin—what, *Madame* Melburne? But *non,*" he continued ruminating, "I know the virgin look when I see it, *moi.*" Skilfully he drew her aside, perceiving her shyness to be genuine, and encouraged her to talk of the things she had done as a child here, so short a time ago, which he found quite touching. She wound up her recital with the time at year-before-last's cane-grinding when the yellow jackets had stung her until she puffed up with poison. "My eyes were shut and I looked like a pincushion!" She was laughing now, quite at ease with this dashing stranger.

Petit was regarding her with increasing delight at her naïveté, for he rarely met with it in so pure a form. Even the most carefully guarded *jeune filles* in Louisiana were at least of the lush Latin form and temperament. This girl was the most untouched thing he had ever seen. Yet since she was the wife of that sour gangling Melburne youth, Petit need not have quite the scruples he would have been forced to employ had she been completely *vierge.*

Joby, feeling his interest, though not its quality, decided with a toss of her chin that she *would* take Cinda's advice. Surely when C. D. saw such a beau as this at her heels, he would have to retract some of his gibes at her feminine ineptness. Then she blushed at having thought of Mr. Petit in connection with the intimacies of her domestic extremity. Petit was enchanted with the blush.

No one thought of cautioning Joby, for by now everything was in a hullabaloo of conviviality. Yarbrough was occupied welcoming guests, and Gerda was in the dining-room overseeing last-minute preparations. If any one else observed Joby's sudden vivacity, he or she put it down to married life's brightening her up. When the company went out to where the tables were laid in dining-room and ell, such a gorging of food commenced that shortly all ordinary sharpness of observation was lulled. Joby, drinking her first imported wine, as befitted a matron, began to feel a warm pride in the darkening glances from Petit's eyes.

Therefore when shortly after the meal he discovered her outside the ell fanning herself to cool off, she made very little struggle as he put his arm about her. In fact before she knew it she was tucking her head against his shirt bosom, because she wanted a place to rest it from its swimming feeling. "Wine," she murmured, "I reckon you have to grow used to it gradually."

He was employing his lips against the nape of her neck very suavely, so as not to startle her before she should become used to their touch and like it; presently he could feel her hold very still, aware of his caress, hesitating, finally giving up to enjoyment of it. For rather a brief space they continued this knowledgeable indulgence in delicate sensuousness. To Joby, slight as it was, it was an admission of almost complete surrender to anything else he would have of her. Deeming, as she did, even a kiss wrong in a married woman, she knew no gradations in sin. She felt as she stood there under the soft stroking of his lips that she was simply this man's, at his bidding whenever he chose.

He was too clever to pursue his advantage now; he guided her up the steps into the light. He well knew the value of postponing the hour, until she had been tantalized out of any belated retreat into virtue. His guess was right, for as often as his gaze found her, it found also a quaint look of adoration in her eyes. She seemed to have completely forgotten her husband, whom Petit noticed squinting at her suspiciously. Armand himself kept a wary eye out, for though used to coping with shrewder men than this gawk, he had seldom met a surlier nature. Consequently when in the figure of a dance Joby kept lifting her face ardently to his, he gazed over her head. At the end of the music she refused to take her hand away from his, and said artlessly: "I'm all hot again, from the dancing, and I had another cup of wine. Oughtn't I to walk in the air some more?"

He was weighing discretion against his pleasure in her candour, when he saw C. D., ugly with whisky, shoving towards them. Armand tried to release her hand, which merely made it worse, for she resisted his attempt openly, clinging hard as her husband stepped up. C. D. had nothing to say to Petit, being too cowardly to confront a man. His vindictiveness was all directed at this girl who had been nothing but a disappointment to him in their marriage. "Come along with me." He freed her hand from Armand's with a snap of the wrist, then stalked out with her, unnoticed by any of the jostling crowd save the man who had caused the trouble.

C. D. marched his wife into Cinda's room; then, making sure it was empty, latched it from within. "Stand still," he commanded thickly, "right here in front of me. You and your goody-good ways, shrinking from me, your husband! Likely you've been staving me off because of him, or someone else you've never told me about. Well, take this and this, and this, and *this*!" Batting his hands back and forth, he slapped both her cheeks till her ears rang, and the room caved in black around her as she slid to the floor. She sensed him tugging at her clothes, then felt the crush of his body, and heard his coarse mutter: *"Agh!"* She fainted after that.

She did not hear when he stepped outside the door and found Petit guarding the way. "I think," said the latter, "you will answer to me for this, and not to her father. I am to blame for giving her a false appearance of indiscretion." Then he struck C. D. across the mouth. "Nor will there be any further encounter of a duel between you and me, to permit you to avenge that slap. One can insult only a gentleman, and *moi,* I fight only with men!" He walked haughtily away.

Inside the room after a bit Joby came to consciousness and began to rub her elbows where they had been bruised. "Now C. D. will have something to hold against me sure enough," she moaned. "About Mr. Petit."

5

The morning of Lucinda's wedding day Gerda was up by four o'clock ready to launch the last go-round of preparations. When she was ready in her grey wool wrapper to leave the room, she paused a moment by the door and stared at the mountain Yarbrough made under the bedclothes. It seemed queer that *they* had a daughter about to wed, for in spite of all her useful womanhood she had never discarded a feeling of the youth she had given into Yarbrough's keeping.

Then shaking off her unseemly thoughts, she stepped kitchenward. All the house negroes were gathered, wide awake and prancing. This wedding was the greatest thing that had happened since coming to Alabama.

The wedding fruit cake, as black and rich as dirt, had been made long ago and ripened with brandy; then yesterday it had been cloaked in a white frosting that almost blinded the beholder. The lighter cakes had been baked at their proper times, the hams boiled in cider and one special bridal one in wine. Last night Aunty Pheaby had sat up half the night to bring them out of the ovens in a final becloved outer crust of succulence. The turkeys were ready for their turn now, stuffed with onion-savoured egg-bread; and the yams and rice would soon be under way, while the imported store delicacies were waiting for Gerda's own attention.

Breakfast and all other eating before the evening wedding feast would be done picnic fashion from one trestle in a far corner of the ell, while Gracey and Willy, with Bonapartt, would shortly be decking the dining-room table in all the glory of the old Egton silver and napery. Right now the bustle was in the kitchen, where the usual churning and butter-making must be carried on through all this stir, since the ell had to be kept spruce in looks.

Late in the morning Gerda was worn to a frazzle and went outside to stand by a fig tree for breath. Its bare branches made jerky lines like knuckles against the dim winter colour of the sky. She was so tired that when Lucinda came up to her she looked at her dully, with no thought of any especial interest in the girl this day. Then Lucinda put a hand on her arm and said: "Ma'am, maybe I won't be such a bother to you after this. You can let Jerard do the worrying."

"No," said Gerda, collecting her faculties slowly, "parents aren't rid of their children upon marrying them off. That but adds more people to their responsibility. I do hope, though, that you keep your head better after this. It won't land you anywhere, cavorting so. Yet

I suppose, to tell the truth, I could have run hog-wild too if I hadn't been harnessed so early."

The girl studied the side of her mother's face covertly. They must have even looked very alike once, except that her own features had a little finer bone because of a streak from Yarbrough's more inbred race. Lucinda followed the other's glance over a dip to the far crests of the holly trees on the burying ground where little Elzivir's grave was. She had the notion that Gerda retained that small mount as some intact core of personal living that she never shared with any one.

Ma'am was a fine mother, but Ma'am was mostly a lot of daily rules that the household followed, while Gerda was—Lucinda stopped there as she always had stopped, before that richer-hued picture of the woman, Gerda. Suddenly to-day it came over her that she pulled up short before intimate investigation of Gerda because of the rivalry she felt for that woman, so like her in passionate demands upon life. They were both drastic powers turned loose in the land. "The only difference," Lucinda admitted inwardly, "is that she flows in deep channels towards some place, while I lay waste the land, flooding all over it."

Her face clouded. Wasn't that because there had never been *enough* for her to do here, enough that really needed her doing? Gerda being so like her, and having the priority, had pre-empted those things for her own domain. "There's no place for me in our family here, following so close on her heels. There's only room for one ruling woman at a time. Maybe though—maybe over where I will be the mistress, I will take on purpose."

Lucinda would have been surprised had she known how closely her mother's thoughts were following her own, that Gerda was even now adding to them, wondering if the girl had been allowed to run loose so long that she could never be hitched to pull a load. And if so, how much of that blame must she, Gerda, shoulder? In a few hours she and Yarbrough would be facing each other down the length of their board, in one of those fatal moments of the tallying up of their deeds by life. She wondered how straight she could meet Yarbrough's gaze, when she knew that now the scales were being tipped, holding this daughter's future.

Her attention was jerked back to the present by Cinda's earnest voice. The girl was trying to give her, not an easy promise of good behaviour, but an acknowledgment of the deep blood common to them both. "Ma'am, you *do* understand how I need Jerard Malone? Something so strong that no young lad can supply it. It takes a man for it, to make you feel like a woman. When you married a grown man you must have needed the same."

Gerda stopped her. At the bare mention of Yarbrough's wooing and wedding she put both her hands out before her and cut out a cone of air that made a privacy, into which no one could intrude upon those past lovers.

Thereupon Lucinda left her. "There! She pushed me out of her way again. She might have helped me to be a better person, by giving up a bit of herself to me once in a while. But no. Yet she was smart not to do so, for if she'd given a little, I would have taken a lot more. She couldn't risk that. She was right in looking after herself. And, oh, I don't care much! Because I enjoy being myself, just the way I am! It's the other folks I'm hard on. *Shoot a duck!*" she exclaimed cheerfully, and, picking up a fallen acorn, shied it down the side yard towards the Rock Wall steps.

6

Two little negro girls had broom-swept the front yard, and a negro boy was squatted by the entrance to the hall to wipe off the shoes of the guests to prevent tracks through the house. In the parlour Gracey with Ronald's mother had been working all afternoon, fashioning an altar between the two front windows. Miz Lisbeth's faded needlepoint *prie-dieu* had been placed under an arch of flowers, with a thick rag rug folded beneath it to prevent it from slipping. The fire on the hearth was not yet lit, for fear it would wilt the flowers.

In her room Lucinda was being garbed for her bridal. Gerda was not there yet, being busy in the back of the house, but Marm Pokey was present to superintend things, very stiff in her plum sateen, her white turban as swollen as a wash-basket. Densey was jealously guarding the heirloom veil that was enthroned on the largest bed like the shroud of a queen. Pinky, down on her knees, was trying to smooth the gossamer stockings up her young mistress's legs without twitching them sideways, and Joby was merely watching, trying not to muss her own attire.

Lucinda stretched her arms, trying to feel more awake after her hour's nap. Pinky had washed her off in a new wooden tub before the fire, with some of that bought cake-soap that had a cologne scent. It made her smell so sweet that she had sniffed under her armpits at the flesh-fragrance of a pleasant new cleanliness. "Feel like a heifer having its coat chalked down for selling," she grumbled good-naturedly.

"Don't talk such trash!" reproved Pokey.

Lucinda allowed her kid slippers with their winding satin straps to be adjusted on her feet. Standing up, she moved her ankles about to see if she could bear those new little blocks of heels that the French were decreeing should hoist the feet off the ground. "Kinder teetery, but it gives you a nice light feeling." She began to spin about on them.

"Watch out!" cautioned Joby, "or you'll have splinters digging into your toes. Those things are no more than foot-gloves."

Lucinda paused and stood still in her chemise, waiting for the rest of her underclothes, and Pinky put up her young mistress's wrists to drop the fluted underskirts over her in wide circles. Presently the bride stood ready for them to adjust the gown and veil, but still her mother had not appeared. Pokey and Joby went to the two chairs with the plank across their seats and a pile of feather pillows beneath it on the floor; they raised the sheet that had been propped over the deep cream thistle-brocaded gown, and Lucinda stooped and slid into it.

"Better call Miz Gerda to watch it's fastened right," said Pokey, at which Joby scampered away. She came back accompanied by Ma'am in her party garnet-red, with her hair looking splendid drawn back in the high polish that came from sweat. "Go ahead," Gerda commanded, and Pokey and Joby settled the satin smoothly about Lucinda's brawny shoulders and gathered the waist in tight till the skirt flaunted out over the hips. Lucinda gazed into the long looking-glass that Gracey had loaned her, and saw how magnificently the train fanned out behind her, how her bosom was nearly bursting with arrogant pride below her sunburned collar-bones. *"Ma'am?"* she cried, throwing out both palms for some token that the other thought she was pretty to behold, but Gerda was giving her attention to the next task, saying: "The veil now, Densey."

Densey lifted the delicate thing that had come so many years and so many miles in Miz Lisbeth's care and placed it over Lucinda's face. The girl, feeling the frail responsibility of the lace, turned gingerly to peer into the glass once more. She could not see very clearly from under that white drift. With her eyes dimmed, she wanted to cry somewhere, on a certain breast . . . but Ma'am was gone!

Pokey, peeking out the bedroom door, whispered: "Marse Yarbrough's ready," and Joby scuttled down the hall to signal Nettie. Then Pokey pulled the door open wider and motioned to Pinky to straighten the train. Lucinda saw Yarbrough come out of his room very erect, as if he hoped the kill would be over quick. She went towards him and he looked down in her face hard as he drew her hand through his arm, then muttered: "He'll treat you right. He knows I'll kill him with my bare hands if he don't!" She brushed her veiled head against her father's shoulder a moment. Pinky turned her train again, then she was in the parlour, where the guests crowded back to make an aisle for her to Malone at the altar. She could see Gracey at the spinet paying more attention to her finger rings than to the notes she struck from the keys. *She could not find her mother anywhere.*

Afterwards she learned that Gerda had been called to the kitchen because a hound had plundered the extra hams. Ma'am had not seen her married! "But then she didn't see Joby married either, thanks to me," Lucinda reminded herself wryly. However, the fact that Gerda had been missing set her off on a tear. She kissed all the men back who saluted the bride, she answered toasts in rhymes with a ribald suggestion that kept the male guests in a gale of merriment. Nor did she care when she heard ripples of comment stirring around her. *All very well to be in high spirits, bu-ut that Lucinda's a captain. How Gerda Whetstone ever had such a daughter*—such talk only egged her on.

Malone watched her with shocked face; she was clear out of his control. He had not bargained for such a rampage as this, and he fingered her veil uneasily. "You don't have to let 'em in on all our nuptial secrets just for the fun of it," he growled, but she twitched away from him and capped the last drunken toast with an *outré* witticism. *Whew!* He mopped his forehead.

The bad part really came when she tried to pull herself together after the cake-cutting to go and be gracious to the women who had drifted into the company chamber to see her display of household gifts. Lucinda had taken none of the interest in these that she had in the jewels and other articles of personal adornment; perhaps because she knew that Jerard had furnished their home in a way to answer every conceivable need. Then she knew too little of household routine to appreciate such gifts. Now she appeared in a very poor light, trying to feign interest in something she but slightly understood and cared for not at all. She might have carried it off, however, if Gracey had not perpetually buzzed at her elbow, endeavouring to coach her in a pretty speech for each gift, within the hearing of the donor.

"For Heaven's sake," Lucinda implored her nervously once, "don't nag me like a gadfly! I'll thank them all, in good time."

"Still," hissed Gracey, "they want to hear you take notice of their presents now. It sets them up so!"

Lucinda glanced around despairingly. Such droves of women! Each one self-conscious about some one particular donation, something each had given her, not so much because any of them liked her as because they were competing with each other in bestowing gifts and meant, one and all, to outshine the others. She felt they were buzzards circling about her.

Thank the Lord the men were beginning to drift in, herded away from the punch bowl by some women patrollers no doubt. Armand Petit was flattering a half-dozen grandmothers at once, but Jerard wore a hang-dog air and did not manage to push through to her side. Her father, though he remained near the doorway, kept affectionate and encouraging eyes upon her as if he and she were enjoying a huge joke that the others were too stupid to catch. If only these women wouldn't press her so, with hollow praise of gifts not their own, with pretended slurs for theirs, which she must quickly deny. If only Gracey hadn't kept going *s-s-s-s-s-s* in her ear!

Finally Cinda caught Joby by the wrist in passing. "Where's Ma'am? I've been married an hour and not clapped eyes on her except for one minute at the time of the first toast. Has she disappeared from the face of the earth?"

"Oh, she's starting the serving of the second table."

"I see," said Lucinda flatly, "housekeeping as usual."

Gracey had raised her voice a peg to cover the rising noise of the now crowded room. "And this—this hand-painted bowl and pitcher and—hmm, set—Ronald's mother did for you herself. Painted it all by hand! Isn't it *lovely*!"

Lucinda focused on the china atrocity and, not knowing she spoke aloud, ejaculated: "Lord a' mercy! It looks like some of that cast-off stuff in Pokey's cabin!" She slapped her hand against it as if to push it out of sight, and the pitcher wobbled back and forth in the basin with a grating sound: *Aruch—aruch!—Crsh.*

Every one gasped, then the room was hollow with horror, for Lucinda had broken a code as holy to them as hospitality: *A giver was sacred, a gift had an invisible altar in any home.* And Lucinda was—an outlaw.

Yarbrough came shouldering through the accusing ring, with Bonapartt behind him. He took his daughter's hand in his as if nothing were amiss. Then he turned to the company, claiming their attention. "In the presence of you who have honoured my daughter's marriage with your attendance, it is only fitting that I should make my own gift, along with the rest of you, to her domestic comfort. I have here a tried and true servant, whose talents have had little outlet in our crude life at Whetstone Stand. I propose to give him this day to my daughter, Lucinda, to serve her as major-domo in that new home of hers called Top Hill. She will be in sad need of someone who understands both her and her tangents, as well as the intricacies of social intercourse and conduct. As you have just witnessed, she is not so richly endowed as most of you with that womanly instinct for grace. But Bonapartt, I'll warrant, will be an able tutor." He chuckled and a relieved laugh followed his throughout the room, changing Lucinda's black blunder into a childish slip. Next he turned to the Punch-proud negro. "Bonapartt, I rely upon you to make Miss Lucinda mind her manners from now on. And I entrust you with her every welfare."

Lucinda, with her head up to match her father's, came forward and took Bonapartt's hand. "Now," she said gladly, "I know I'll toe the mark!" Bonapartt patted her on the head the way he had used to when she was a little girl begging sugar.

Gerda came in at the door at that instant, trying to understand what it was all about; but Lucinda no longer needed her mother, her father had pulled her through. From the parlour, high and thin, came the screech of the fiddlers tuning up.

CHAPTER TWENTY-NINE

With a mixture of feelings, Lucinda set out on her wedding trip by boat to New Orleans. She wanted to do honour to her new estate as a planter's lady, thus pleasing both husband and parents, yet the conflicting scenes of her bridal day were still causing an upheaval in her emotions. By turns she was resolved to deport herself in a fashion deserving commendation of all three of these important relatives, and by turns she nourished resentment against first Ma'am, then Jerard.

As the journey progressed, the restrictions put upon women while travelling by packet grew irksome. Ladies were allowed to join the gentlemen in the saloon only at meal times. The rest of her time she had her choice of pacing the cramped deck with Malone in the disagreeably raw air, or of being confined to the ladies' cabin, since there were no private accommodations for married pairs. She had for company in the cabin a sickly woman with a whiny baby, and a churlish Englishwoman who objected to American men's use of tobacco. Lucinda preferred playing Jacob's-ladder with Pinky to the society of either of the others.

The one exciting part of the trip down the river was the night the packet caught on fire. The blaze was splendidly garish for a while and there was the threat of damage to the cotton in the holds. But before the danger amounted to much, a providential rain poured, quenching the fire.

She regretted that they stayed a scant twenty-four hours in the jovial atmosphere of Mobile, yet at the same time she was eager to rush on to New Orleans and its renowned gaiety. After she arrived there, however, and recovered from her initial admiration of the lace-grille balconies and the fastidious elegance of the ladies' costumes, she quickly became restive. For the pleasures galore she'd heard of, the theatres, racetrack, and gaming-houses, were all prohibited her as a lady of good family. In short order she found the private entertainments in her honour tame to the point of boredom, because of their excessive mannerliness. At first she liked peacocking about in her finery, catching the murmur of the men; at first, too, she was piqued by the Creole sauces on the food. Then, in no time, her stomach turned at the sight of the incessant insidious spices. And as for the admiration she excited, it was all so fenced off by custom from any real impact with her person that it retained no more meaning for her than an echo.

Malone for his part was so blind-proud of displaying her that he did not realize she was eaten up with curiosity to see the more colourful aspects of the city. Also he assumed that Lucinda, being from the corresponding class in Alabama, would slip into the ways of the aristocracy here as easily as she donned a suitable gown for one of their parties. He reckoned without the impatience of folderol engendered by her pioneer childhood, and without her exuberant vitality.

She stood the formality of the Creoles until all expectancy of any real fun in their circles was exhausted; then she kicked over the traces one afternoon after a series of stiff duty-calls. "I *won't* eat any more shrimp jambalaya at Cousin Marthe's, nor play peekaboo behind a fan at Madame Duret's!"

She scuffed out of her footwear and began ripping off her confining calling-costume without any regard for the modesty required of a bride in the joint presence of her husband and her serving-maid. Jerard devoted his apparent attention to his cigar, while Pinky recovered Lucinda's shoulders. Impatiently the young mistress shoved her aside and continued:

"I am not going to that old musicale to-night either. Music gives me the twitches. Do you know what I want to do, Jerard? Put on that dark plum velvet with its cape and a thick veil no one can see through. Then have you take me to a gaming-place, where I can see some *life*!"

"That's out of the question," Jerard protested violently. "Why, Cinda, do you have any idea what kind of women frequent such places? No man ever yet took his wife to one."

"*Oh, potato mush!* No one would be able to recognize me as your precious *wife* behind that veil." First she started to flounce away from him in a temper, then instead she brushed the cigar out of his hand and ordered Pinky to leave. "There, that's better," she declared, insinuating her scantily clad person into his arms. "Let them think I am a cast-off light-o'-love that you're trying to pacify." She put her eyes up close to his, making his vision swim. "Try me out for your light-o'-love," she coaxed, "for one evening in public. If you do, I'll vow you won't want to trade me off later in private for any you have ever dallied with." Her shoulder was stirring against his chest, sending messages to his bumping heart. He yielded.

Some hours later when Lucinda was ready, Malone thought that she did indeed look like some mysterious woman out of a man's past. Her veil was so thick he could hardly have told there was a face behind it, except for the little puffing her breath made against it and the faint moist light where her eyes shone. The rôle induced in her a brooding silence, the glitter of her diamond clasps alone bringing her sombre figure to life.

Beneath her cloak, though, she had never been more avid for adventure, and for adventure that was far-fetched and strange and suited to this exotic city. Something she could carry home and cherish all hidden for years upon years. She pressed her hand upon Jerard's arm. "Let's pretend to-night that we're not ourselves. Let's do something we can never forget, yet daren't think of very often afterwards. Something that, when we do recall it—will always carry us far away from the humdrum."

She waited for him to put his far hand over hers, to sign to her that he understood her search that led her to the depths of passion, to the extremes of danger. He *must* feel how she longed to hold some hour apart as enfolding a measure of dark splendour in which she might die—and never care.

She held, and held, and held his arm, *hard*.

But the carriage drew up, and only then did Jerard give her his hand to assist her in alighting.

As soon as Lucinda entered the gaming-room the excitement of chance began to stimulate her, while her eyes scurried everywhere, taking in the bizarre scene. The guarded glances that followed her produced a fervid glow that turned her thoughts from her reverie in the carriage and induced a contrasting mischief. "If I weren't a wife," she thought, "what a swath I could cut here!"

At first Malone kept a jealous watch over her, but eventually, after a tour of the gaming-tables, he took his station at one where the stakes ran high. He was famous for his skill, so that spot drew instant attention and for a space Lucinda watched his play admiringly. He had an uncanny awareness of every gesture, every expression, or every overdone lack of expression on the part of his opponents. This gave him mastery over the shifting situation about the table, put Luck at his elbow. Lucinda could see power expanding in his chest as he won not only dollars but a sense of the submission of these other men's faculties to his. She admired him enormously for it.

Yet she had not pleaded to be brought here to pass the time as a mere spectator of his prowess at the gaming-table. Even while regretting perversely her recent moment of softened exposure in the carriage, she still sought some happening of the evening in which she might at least share a part.

Nudging Malone, she informed him that she intended to walk about and observe the adjoining rooms. Preoccupied, he gave his consent. The fixtures of gilt and brocade took her attention to begin with, but shortly she was more interested in the people. There were of course a good number of men such as she was more or less accustomed to, except that they seemed on somewhat different, more rakish behaviour here, although many of them were still talking cotton prices sensibly. Then there were freaks in breeches at whom she and Bruff would have laughed their heads off at home. It was mainly those of that category that presumed to peer at her noticeably as she passed. The women she deemed really rare specimens. Some were half-way pretty, few were half-way clean, and all seemed to be tricked out in things as gaudy as house negresses' scrap-bag petticoats. "Marm Pokey," she murmured to herself, "would say that they're trying to act like 'something blooming on the bush when they ain't nothin' out of the dirt'!"

Unconsciously she commenced snatching her own skirts aside whenever one of them came close. It did not take her long for this gesture to stir up a ripple of antagonism, which but made her pull aside even more. Her teeth started gritting and she wondered how soon she could suggest to Jerard that they leave, without having him twit her for losing her spunk.

At that juncture she decided to seat herself at one of the small far tables and refresh herself with a glass of wine. She had barely sipped it when a young man paused nearby and, bowing rather diffidently, spoke in a voice like those from over in Mississippi. "Do you object if I sit down, mam'selle? My name is Bones, and I know Mr. Malone to bow to at our cotton factor's."

She let him sit down, not overlooking his calling her *mam'selle,* and thinking how easily she was passing for Jerard's light-o'-love. Yet in spite of the fact that he ordered himself brandy and regarded her intently, he seemed ill at ease and almost determinedly respectful. Or if he were not quite treating her with respect, he was treating her with an almost trying delicacy that puzzled her. She decided to get to the bottom of it.

After young Bones had a swallow, he repeated that he was slightly acquainted with Mr. Malone. "Though he may not recall me by name."

"Don't worry, M'sieur Bones," pattered Lucinda, feeling very Orleanist behind her veil, "he will recognize you, even if your name is another, by *daylight* and *elsewhere*."

He started up, boyishly perturbed. "That is my own name, Carter Bones, and I have no need to hide away from it just because I gamble a little."

Then, recalling his pretence of worldliness, he pulled himself back down into his chair and smiled across the table. "Believe me, I wouldn't offer a false name to a man like your protector, and besides what occurs within these walls is never permitted to be noised about outside. So you needn't think that your protected days are over simply because Mr. Malone has recently made such a desirable match." He was leaning towards her in friendly earnest now. "You need never fear his wife will be allowed to interfere, so long as *you* can keep the secret."

Lucinda leaned back in her chair to laugh better. It did strike her as funny to have this young blade thus reassuring *her*. She could hear him clearing his throat and pointing out that, after all, gentlemen did not make such gifts of jewels as gleamed upon her to any one not in permanent favour. She might have laughed louder at this had not two wantons lurched against their table just then. Instinctively she turned to call them down as she would have done any blundering wench at home.

But her escort begged softly: "Please don't make them notice you the more. White girls in these places can't help resentin' you more sheltered octoroons."

"What in all blazes of kindling-wood do you mean?" gasped Lucinda, jumping up, ready to whack the very table to smithereens.

Before she could answer, the two women moved still closer to her and the smaller one remarked in a doubtful tone: "Do you reckon she really is one? Tall for one. Wonder if she has blue gums."

While Lucinda's vocal powers were lost in anger, the larger one sneered: "Cain't you tell she's octoroon without peerin' in her mouth like a horse's? Why's she holdin' off from us so uppity? So's she won't have her *gentle* trainin' ruffled by *us*!" The harlot's voice rose shrilly. "Makes me hoppin' the way octoroon niggers is treated so careful by their protectors! Taught by convent Sisters to play music and embroider. Like—like some little white gal whose pa is a big planter. While we have to fend for ourselves, and ain't thought fit for her to come amongst. And why's she all wrapped up in that veil?"

She swung around at young Bones. "You know the real reason. Not to keep us white whores from getting mad at a nigger mixin' with us. No! To keep strange men from the treat, the *great* treat of beholdin' her charms! I feel like I could tear it——" She made a swipe of her arm towards Lucinda's veil.

Bones leapt between. "You harm one hair!" he threatened, his eyes glaring at the rowdy, and the back of his arm acting as a shelter in front of Lucinda's face.

Almost simultaneously Malone, who had heard the end of the coarse tirade, reached the group. He grabbed Lucinda aside from the fray, and taking hold of the two harlots, he flung them into the ready hands of the two attendants. "Throw this filth out where it came from, on the dung-heap."

The last Lucinda saw of them was a grotesque flying of heels and ankles as the prostitutes tried to regain their balance after being ejected, their hair awry above shame-mottled faces. Her stomach sickened at the spectacle of such gross female subservience to men.

Curtly Jerard was bowing to Bones, saying: "Your face is familiar from seeing you at my cotton factor's, the Petit firm. I rely upon you to keep this dark. It was a great piece of folly on my part to give in to my wife's whim and fetch her here even thus disguised. You will understand of course, sir, that you must wait for a suitable circumstance in which you may be presented to her properly, since her incognito *must not be destroyed*." The two men bowed over this formality, while Lucinda recoiled with incredulous hauteur at having her true identity revealed, with whatever reservations, in such surroundings.

She departed, marching stiffly ahead of Malone.

When they were in their carriage again, Malone tried to coddle her into a pleasanter frame of mind, but she could not bear to be touched at the moment. She sat cold and upright, frigid with race pride and the denial of any dubiety of lineage, even though it had been cast not at her true self but at a shrouded unknown figure. Now she was filled with a still hatred not only of those purblind daughters of joy, but of Malone and Carter Bones too, since they had witnessed an insult, however oblique, being dealt to her. If she could have, at that moment she would have destroyed both of them in order to obliterate any human being who had viewed her catastrophe and knew her name.

Once, while they rode, she recalled how she had felt in this carriage an hour ago, spellbound at going towards something adventurous to keep for ever.

She had to shut that out now, groaning over what she had got to take the place of the happiness she had held in her heart for a moment.

Her anger would gradually subside, but it would leave behind it a residue of poison to work in her mind from time to time, transferring her own inadvertent shame to Jerard, until at moments she would despise this husband who had allowed her to fall into an equivocal position, even though one of her own making. She sat in her own corner, and Malone kept to his own side, holding to the lurch-strap, pondering heavily upon her unpredictability.

2

The isolation from Jerard on the boats during their return trip lessened Cinda's perverse feeling of repulsion rapidly; also he was such good-natured company when they took their short turns on deck in the new milder air that she soon felt herself enjoying being with him again. By the morning after their arrival home and after a good night's sleep in a soft bed her entire good humour returned with a rush. She was awake the moment she opened her eyes, eager to be up to inspect her new possessions. "Glory!" she snickered to herself, "this bed is as big as a front yard. I'd break my neck if I tried to get out of it without using these bedside steps." When she had clambered down, the soles of her feet felt the warmth of rich carpeting; at home they had only home-made rag rugs scattered rather sparsely. This chamber's furnishings included a variety of pieces specially designed to cater to her feminine vanity. There were more looking-glasses in this single room than she had ever seen in a whole house before. Had she but known it, Jerard wanted the pleasure of watching his young wife's posturings from many angles. At this very instant he was peering at her from his slothful half-doze, while she swung lithely about in her night-robe examining things. Presently his uxorious spying was rewarded by seeing her ignore her adjoining dressing-room and drop her gown in a white rim on the floor about her feet. Swiftly she scrambled into one of her plainest morning frocks, then twisted her hair in its night braid on top her head, without combing it out. In another moment she was gone helter-skelter out of the room, leaving him to the middle-aged luxury of a second morning nap.

She did not stay to study the inside of her mansion now, for the day was too fine outdoors and she had not been able to run loose for so long. More chilliness would come before February was past, but to-day everything trembled with spring. The bulbs in their rock-bordered beds showed a fine lot of blooms, a fuzz was softening the gum trees, and up over a back hillock she could see the first peep of mustard greens. She could not see the cotton fields from here, since Malone had all that cut off from view by a grove of woods left circling the back of the place. Cotton fields meant work, his house meant pleasure and rest. Therefore the quarters of the hands, the gin, the whole hum of his crop industry was shut off from the fainter buzz of domestic duties in vegetable patch, spring-house, and flower-beds.

From the outset this section had had a somewhat more extravagant attitude than that of the rest of the county. It was made up mainly of large holdings of absentee owners, who were concerned solely with the wealth attendant upon its cotton production; and except in rare instances they were not active like Yarbrough and his kind in organizing county government or improving local community conditions. When, like Malone, some few of them did build a home there, their wealth enabled them to import enough luxury from abroad to live in the manner of feudal lords. They were not pioneers but seigneurs, taking their tithes from the labour of their black serfs, a rather flamboyant symbol of the splendour one could attain to in the realm of King Cotton. As they represented the goal towards which most whites in the South were directing their energies, their interests, even though their status was exceptional, guided to a great degree the policies, the destiny, of the section. It was small wonder that Yarbrough urged Malone to attend their local meetings, to exert his influence to overcome the obstacles that the general run of citizens in the community had to face. Yarbrough hoped since this new family alliance to use Malone's weight to good advantage.

To-day his daughter, roaming about the yards of her new home, recalled faintly her early memory of their South Carolina lavishness. She was not yet aware of the underlying slackness that always crept into negro labour where master and mistress kept no close watch; she was merely thankful that she would not have to drudge like Ma'am, harder than any slave on all the Whetstone holdings! In her ramblings she had come around finally to the front of the house, and after mounting the flight of white stone steps the door was flung open for her by Bonapartt, beaming at his reinstatement in his former glory.

Malone had to be away the greater part of his first day at home, checking up on what had transpired during his absence, so after breakfast he had said to Lucinda: "Puddin', I'll eat dinner at whichever place I'm nearest at noon, but I'll be expectin' a royal welcome from you in the evenin'."

"I'll give it to you!" she cried, leaping off the ground and swinging from his shoulders in a hug, her fine animal spirits restored by her before-breakfast exercise. In addition she was so tickled at actually being mistress of so grand an establishment, at being able to indulge her whims without parental restraint, that she felt kindly towards him for bestowing the prize. After he departed she told Bonapartt to bring her more batter-cakes and syrup. She ate till the sweet cloyed, requiring a bite of bacon to kill the taste. Then she wandered through the rooms, examining the furnishings. She did not bother to go near the kitchen, for she had met the cook and other domestics, including her family's former sassy mulatto wench Rache, when they had all been lined up to greet her last night. Now she could leave their supervision to Bonapartt. She had located the ready-food pantry, should a sudden appetite assail her, and there her interest in the culinary department ended.

She was primarily concerned with the great double drawing-room, where she could give lively parties, and with the chambers upstairs, where she could accommodate innumerable guests. She particularly admired the vast mirror that filled the space at the far end of the double drawing-room. She began to pirouette in dance steps before it; then, noticing what a jaybird she looked in her hastily donned garments, she collapsed into a homesick child. She ordered her fast new mare saddled, and within no time at all she was cantering towards the Rock Wall Place and her rabble of kinfolks.

Of course they were through with dinner before she drew rein, but they welcomed her vociferously and in half a shake she was gnawing cold fried chicken while telling them of the sights of New Orleans in return for local news. She clean forgot the royal welcome she had promised Jerard and was washing her hands to sit down to supper with them later when he came clattering up, having learned she was here. Every one thought they were foolish not to stay for the meal, but Malone had looked forward to this first real evening under his own rooftree, so he bundled his bride off. Lucinda enjoyed the canter home as she did anything carried out on impulse. They sang at the top of their lungs, slapping their horses on the rumps occasionally to hurry them. Back at their own place they found Bonapartt had had all the candles lit in welcome and was waiting with a decanter of brandy to warm them after the night's chill. Malone poured some for Lucinda as well as himself, and she swallowed, trying not to let her face contort as much as her throat did. She preferred the sweet home scuppernong wine, yet she was set up over having a husband with whom to have a trot, and presently she decided she liked the warm glow it gave her inside and the lift it put in her feet.

"Tell Bonapartt not to let supper spoil, while I go dress up for you," she called, running upstairs to wake Pinky, nodding on the stool in the dressing-alcove. Pinky jumped with a scared "Hooch!" and Lucinda made her duck her head in the clean slop-jar full of water, to come to her senses. After that she had a good scrub herself, and scented up with some of the New Orleans perfume. She had her hair dressed fit to kill, with a high jewelled comb, but decided she would not wear either necklace or bracelets, as they pinched in embraces. She descended to her husband in grand style, the very devil twinkling in her eyes.

3

Lucinda found some new excitement in each new day. She had that sense of daring that comes at a few turnings in life when one feels changed into an entirely new person, into a fortunate stranger whose lot is legendary. In time she might grow accustomed to this new character, lose its strong flavour, or she might slip back into the attitudes of yesterday, but right now she was being swept on by newness and curiosity.

At last she even ventured into the kitchen to watch Mammy Lizzie and renew her childish fondness for tasting. Suddenly one day she felt she must cook some dish herself, to surprise Jerard. She would bake a cake, watching it emerge step by step from sugar and flour and plums into a structure whole and complete. The urge to create something was upon her. All one morning she toiled, half-vexed by Mammy's constant advice, half-frightened by the fear of failure. Finally the cake was in the pan in the oven; then she seated herself nearby to keep guard, not trusting even that static stage of baking to any one else. She looked like a child waiting for some spell to change a planted stick into a Christmas tree, but after a long dull time her miracle was accomplished and she brought forth her cake.

In doing so she gripped the hot pan in her bare hands, and before she could land it on the table both palms were ridged with horrible burns. Mammy frantically pressed the seared members into a pat of butter; still, blisters rose in inch-wide welts that made Cinda gasp.

"Marse'll scalp me!" wailed Mammy as the whole kitchen tribe clustered about, offering remedies which maddened Cinda, who could only bite her lips to keep from screaming. Then her eyes, darting nervously about, lighted on the cake someone had remembered to turn out on the sweating-board. It rose in majesty. "Look!" she gloated in spite of her burns, "I made that all myself!"

That evening, with her hands bandaged into white paws, she

waited eagerly for Jerard to come home and have his treat. But when he saw her hands he was aghast and stormed out into the kitchen to raise merry and particular hell with Mammy Lizzie for letting such an accident occur. Lucinda went tagging after him, telling him that he was crazy, that her own foolishness had caused it all. She was more ashamed of her clumsiness, the flaw in her perfect performance, than anything else, now that the throbbing of her palms was less intense.

He turned around and gathered her up as if he hoped that would keep her out of harm's way. "What would I do without you? If anything really had happened to you! Makes me scared to leave you in the morning, if they don't see after you better."

"Oh, *pouf*!" she laughed. "You needn't think you can put me back under a mammy nurse again!"

He ate three pieces of the cake for supper. Afterwards they roamed into the yard in the listless spring twilight. They could feel the tickle of the scent from shedding catalpa blossoms up their noses. "Better have them chopped down," he remarked. A last year's dried cone fell from a pine with a flop. They stood admiring the white flight of their front steps up to the arching fanlight. "I hope it all suits you, puddin'," he said anxiously. She pawed his shoulder with a grateful bandaged pat.

CHAPTER THIRTY

Every one at Whetstone Stand had been glad to have Lucinda back from her trip, popping in on them whenever Jerard was off on an extended round of his plantations. Her younger brothers looked on her visits as a treat, since they had always acknowledged the twins' rule over their young kingdom. And an odd assortment of subjects they made. Tom Two was as stocky and good-natured as ever, but Wayne was so increasingly odd and secretive that he was a trial to his companions, who frequently left him out of their games. Joachim was generally popular in spite of his rapidly developing bad habit of pilfering things from the others. When caught, he laughed as if it were a big joke on himself, saying: "Sho', take it back! Don't know what I wanted with that old thing anyhow." Will Bee and Daniel, who were less than two years apart, were now almost as inseparable as the twins had been, Will Bee being the leader, Daniel the follower. Hans continued to comport himself as a squire in the service of his half-brothers and like a serf, if need be, for Lucinda. The baby Turber, now five years old, was everybody's pet. He was the most beautiful of them all, having a brightness of expression that even the handsome Joachim lacked. Still, Turber could not quite come up to the twins' overshadowing racial arrogance, though his pert tongue was always making glib sallies that brought laughs. Ma'am Gerda was easier on him than she had ever been on the older ones, inclining to make light of his mischievous pranks. Since his nature was essentially sweet, she found him little real trouble, more a source of merriment for them all. Pokey was the one person who could withstand his blandishments, and never hesitated to jerk him up whenever she felt he needed it. He seldom was able to outwit her, and that gave him the greatest respect for her; consequently Gerda usually left his disciplining to Pokey, retaining for herself the enjoyment of his bright moods.

The boys in general were fond of going over to Top Hill to spend the day. There they were waited on hand and foot and could call for anything they wanted to feast on. Usually they came home from these junkets heavy-eyed and needing a good dose of purgative, all except Hans. Gerda noticed after the second or third time that he came back subdued, unhilarious, yet with his stomach in good order. When she remarked upon this, Turber exclaimed: "No wonder he hasn't any bellyache, he hardly touched his plate. And Cinda's feelings were hurt too. Why, she even offered him her best brandied peaches, and all he said was: 'No'm, I thank you, ma'am.' Calling Cinda *ma'am*!" Turber ended in disgust.

"It's a shame and a pity some of the rest of you don't have any manners," returned Gerda. "Well, Hans, you can trot along to the wash-basin. No need of dosing you." She watched him thoughtfully as he went out to the stoop where the water-buckets were.

She had observed how he drooped after his idol Lucinda had departed on her wedding trip; and often she had heard him tiptoeing into the girl's empty room to stand there a while. In a fortnight or so he seemed more like himself, except that whenever Lucinda's name was mentioned he stopped whatever he was doing to listen intently until the remark was finished. The day of Lucinda's first pell-mell visit home, Gerda had seen how pitifully glad he was to see her, not demanding her attention like Turber and Will Bee, but simply staying close to her and occasionally reaching out to touch a fold of her skirt. Yet now, when Gerda had expected him to be the most eager to visit at Top Hill, he had been oddly reluctant to go, and came back with no joyous reports. It bothered Gerda.

When she had made the last of the bilious ones swallow their doses, and given them all a twist of lemon peel to chew on, she went out to find the boy. He was standing resting the weight of his palms on the rim of a bucket. Gerda, sitting down on the old "punishing-step," said simply: "Tell Ma'am."

He yanked his shoulders straight as if trying to shake off some burden. "I don't believe I know how."

She watched him a moment, then asked: "Is it because you don't like Jerard Malone that you won't eat their food?"

He nodded. "Sort of."

"That's the right way to act, then," she commended him. "But he's never treated you mean, and your sister does care for him, so I can't exactly see why."

He let go of the bucket rim. "I can't explain why. Only I *feel* it's not to turn out right. Cinda doesn't *love* him. It's all on account of that great big house, and the finger rings, and his hundred and more negroes." He quit. What was the use? He couldn't make clear what it was that he felt in his bones had gone wrong for Lucinda. Besides, the real ache was all his own, one he had to keep to himself. He patted Ma'am on top of the head and went in to bed.

Gerda did not let him know she was keeping an eye on him after that, but she did, growing more anxious as she saw how sombre he was becoming. "More like a man than a boy," she mused. "Maybe we ought not to treat him too much like a boy."

That started an idea which she studied over for several days before she broached it to Yarbrough. Finally she spoke to him one evening, when they were strolling outdoors, discussing the clearing of another tract of land. "Yarbrough," she began firmly because she didn't know how he would take it, "I've been turning over something in my mind that you ought to see to. It's about Hans. He's going on fifteen now, and as big and heavy as a man. Steady too. It's my opinion that he'd make that stretch of new land yield a good crop if you put him in charge of it. I mean if you gave it to him *outright,* signed and sealed!"

Yarbrough stared at her in amazement. "Give that young whelp a hundred and twenty acres! For him to have the whole say about, to let it go to rack and ruin, or to sell if he took a notion? Are you out of your senses?"

"No. He won't do any such flighty thing," she cried hotly, "and you know it. He has a real love for farming. But the thing is: you owe it to him! If you deed it over to him now, while you're here to help show him how, he'll make a fine thing of it. Besides, then no one can ever question his title to it later, whereas if you willed it to him, there's a chance that someone might do him out of it, without legal proof that he's your legal son."

An awkward silence fell. It was a long while since they had last spoken of that old trouble, or even thought of it. Gerda could see Yarbrough working his mouth and chin, and hoped he did not think she was chiding him after all these years. When he spoke, however, he said: "I'll do it. I'll see to it to-morrow. You're a fine woman, Gerda, to forgive all." He pulled her into his arms, his lips tracing the frame of her face which they knew so well. The air moved against their foreheads. It was the first caress they had exchanged in the open in many a year.

Ten days later Will Bee came riding up at noon with the mail he'd picked up at the post office, and handed his father a heavy envelope that showed the land-office mark. Yarbrough took it carefully, then said to Hans: "Go fetch your mother."

Will Bee called to the yard boy to take his horse; he wanted to stay to see what was happening. The other boys sat up where they were sprawling on the porch floor. Gracey lifted her skirts, then flumped them down again expectantly. The April sun was heavier than usual with noon heat and the buzz of flies, the smell of turnips for dinner came richly on the air, a chicken cawed in one quick spasm over a new egg. Then Hans came down the cool open hall behind Ma'am Gerda.

Yarbrough stood up and opened the packet. He unfolded the parchment, then looking squarely at Hans read: "To all to whom these Presents shall come, Greeting," and there in the heat of the day, while the lavender chinaberry blossoms shattered down making a sweet faded mess in the yard, Yarbrough made it known that his *son*, Hans, was now "the sole possessor and *owner*" of one hundred and twenty acres of fertile cotton land!

As he ended, Yarbrough handed the parchment with its bright red seal into Hans's keeping. "All I ask is for you to do the best you can with the land, son." The red blob went up and down before Hans's dazed eyes, and Gerda touched him at the elbow to steady him. He pulled his eyes away from the dancing spot the seal made and looked straight into his father's eyes. "Thank you, sir. Oh, Ma'am, look! I have something all my own now!" He stood there holding his world in his hands.

2

It seemed to Gerda that she no more than had Hans straightened out before she was worrying over what sort of pickle Joby was in. She had never felt easy about her younger daughter's trumped-up marriage, and ever since Lucinda's wedding had noticed the girl had been scared of her own shadow. Gerda didn't like the looks of it one bit, yet she felt it best to bide her time. Always she let her children thrash things out for themselves as far as possible. Outspoken as she was about things she could see with her eyes or hold with her hands, she had a great reticence about mauling people's feelings out loud, except as a last extremity.

However, when one Sunday she and Yarbrough stopped by at the Melburnes' in Yufala before driving on to see Guy and were told by a shifty-eyed C. D. that Joby was napping and could not be disturbed, she decided she would make it her business at the earliest opportunity to find out what was up that could keep this child from coming down to greet her parents. The chance came all too soon. Only a few days later the young pair drove over to the Rock Wall place, and C. D. let Joby down at the gate, with some remark which made her shake her head at him frantically. After he drove off in the direction of the Screws', where he had business, Joby stood trying to stop the shivering that was shaking her thin frame.

Gerda called to her in welcome and went with her to lay off her bonnet in what had been the girls' room. She noticed how yearningly Joby looked around at its familiar furnishings, touching a pincushion on the chest of drawers. "I remember," she half-laughed, "when I made that for Cinda for Christmas, and she thought it was tacky. You had to make her keep it there and use it."

They moved out into the ell and Gerda started churning while Joby took out a bit of fine sewing, which her mother noted, however, was not a baby garment. The dasher went up and down in the churn with a brisk *swish-clap* as Gerda hummed the tune *Come, Butter, Come* that was supposed to hasten the butter. Densey brought a crispy pile of fine ironing in from the laundry and laid it out for Pokey to sort. Pokey carried it away to various rooms, then Aunty Pheaby stood a moment in the door of the kitchen grinning and gumming her snuff. A little gal walked by the back opening with an apron full of garden sass to be picked over. The May flies darted through, in one door then out the other, in zooming arcs.

"It's so peaceful here," choked Joby suddenly, "so safe—from harm." She put her fingers up and began to cry through them, her sobs jerking her like a jumping-jack. At that Gerda gathered her up like a baby, removing Joby's silver thimble so she wouldn't gouge her eyes. "What's the matter, Joby girl? What's the matter?" She rocked her back and forth until Joby caught her breath enough to speak; then it all came out in a gasping rush.

"He hates me because he says I'm *bad*! He won't let me in the bed with him, without beating me first. And that hurts so—that then if—then the other hurts too. More than I can bear! So he rails at me for that. Says it shows I don't love—him. Oh," she wailed, "I wish I were *dead*!"

Gerda's eyes were transfixed with horror. She could not credit the thing she had heard, that such a thing could touch her child! Slowly she lowered her gaze to the girl crumpled by shame in her arms, and rocked her gently over her own heavy heart. She knew that she must somehow show the level plain of safety to this one who had been trodden down and tortured.

"I'll tell you," she began to plan quietly, "we'll bathe your face and let you lie down for a good rest so you can enjoy your dinner. I'll have Aunty Pheaby make you a special little chicken pie with nothing but white meat. Then after dinner you put on one of your old calico play dresses I keep in your press, and Hans will show you what he's doing about clearing his fields. Then Will Bee can show you all the new calves and baby chicks. You're going to stay here a spell, till you feel right. *I* will see C. D. when he comes by, and tell him. I'll fix it all, and I'll guarantee that when you do go back he'll never raise so much as his little finger against you again!" She managed to say it all fairly gently.

After leading Joby into her room, she tucked her between smooth, cool sheets. Presently in spite of her sorrows Joby felt her eyes closing; then Turber's laugh somewhere and the creak of a well-chain sent her into a pleasant sleep.

It was half-dark before Gerda heard C. D.'s gig clipping up the road where she had been waiting for him. She had been there at this fork for nearly an hour to be sure to catch him before he drove up to the yard. "C. D., stop!" she called loudly, and he hauled his horse up. Startled, he jumped down and came over to her, a spasm of apprehension going over him as he saw his mother-in-law's eyes.

"Stand right there," she commanded, "off of *our* ground. I don't want you on it ever again, till I've finished. Then if you disobey the law I'm laying down, you'll never set foot on our land again and leave it alive! Joby's father wouldn't let you go now if he knew. This once

I'll settle it. A woman can handle a coward like you!" She paused to let this sink in. "I know what's been going on between you and Jobyna, and I won't have my child used like that! *Do you hear?*" she thundered. "If you ever raise a hand again, if you ever draw one breath against her that's lacking in decency and respect, I'll see to it that the *white* men around here swing you in the wind! And to make sure you don't forget my words, I'm going to wear your worthless hide raw now. Take off your coat!"

Quaking, he tried to dodge away, but she caught his sleeve and ripped the garment off. Then she came down upon him with the lash. The strokes of the whip swung down so rapidly and relentlessly that his cries were choked off hoarsely in his throat. Still the whip whistled down on him, until finally he stumbled, fell, and rolled over. Only then did Gerda stop. She kicked a spurt of dust into his face. "Don't come back here till I send for you. I have some thinking to do before I let my child under the same roof with a swine like you. Now go!"

She spat every now and then as she walked away from him, unable to rid herself of the taste of swill in her mouth. She went and drank a lot of well-water.

That night at the supper table she studied Joby carefully. It seemed a shame to let the little thing go back to him, yet Gerda knew he had learned his lesson. He might be snarly and mean-spoken from time to time, but there would be no more bodily risk for Jobyna now that C. D. knew he had been found out. Besides, Gerda reckoned, marriage was marriage, even the poor makeshift kind. And this daughter seemed to be shaped for patient endurance. Gerda was suddenly struck by the look of Miz Lisbeth that was coming over Joby there under the lamplight. "Maybe," she thought hopefully, "she'll gain some of Miz Lisbeth's serenity out of this, by and by."

3

When Bruff came home from New Orleans at the end of his first term of medical school, he found after the first flush of welcome that he was rather out of touch with the others' interests. Hans was wrapped up in his own "plantation," while the other boys were all hired out to Yarbrough on a percentage-of-bale basis. Other years

Bruff would have been more absorbed than any of them in making a fine yield, but now he was serving a new deity, Science, and there was not room enough in him for two big loyalties at this stage of his youth.

Only Ven with his cowhide chair tipped up against the trunk of the water oak in the far front yard seemed to welcome the lad's company, and even he was more interested in hearing about the horses at the Metairie Track than in the study of anatomy. "Don't relish talking about my entrails, 'cause all I can see in my mind's eye is those of a hog. I'd rather keep clothes on a human being."

Bruff fumed about the place until Gerda cried out crossly: "For land's sake, what makes you snicker and stomp like a mule in its stall? It seems to me there's enough to do around this place to keep anybody busy, yet you haven't turned your hand to do a lick since you came home."

"Plenty of others to do dirt grubbing!" answered Bruff. "That's all any one thinks about around here. A lot you all care if a person is interested in what goes on inside the human body."

"Very little but devilment," she responded tartly, "from what I've seen." Then she relented. "I'll tell you what. You ought to ride over and see Brother—I mean John Upshur. While he was a preacher he had to minister to ailing bodies as much as to souls. And after Gran died, well, he's been taken up a lot with scientific things," she ended briefly.

So it came about that Bruff rode over and found Upshur's place surprisingly comfortable-looking. Now that John was putting all his energy into farming, he was prospering, as was many another small farmer in this country. Starting out with one mule-team and one negro, plus a tract of rich virgin soil and his own energy, he was in a fair way to become well-to-do overnight. He now had a dozen hale field-hands, sound livestock, and so much land that his farm had become a plantation. In place of the rough cabin he had built a comfortable frame house with some fine key-moulding for decoration around under the eaves. Also he had a horse and gig to drive to church on Sunday. Whether it was Miz Della's release from drudgery that had improved her health or not, the fact remained that in her late forties she had suddenly given birth to a daughter. To-day the baby lay in a cradle on the porch under its mother's eye as Bruff came up.

"Why, how do you do these days, Master Bruff?" exclaimed Miz

Della as she recognized him. "Mr. Upshur will be glad to see you. Could you watch her while I call him?"

Bruff stood looking down on the girl mite in the cradle. Although she was a tiny scrap compared to the husky babies of the Whetstone clan, she seemed oddly much less of an infant. There was something precise in feature, intent in the dark eyes, that gave the impression of her being already a complete and self-sufficient entity. When suddenly she yawned, raising a delicate creamy fist to hide the yawn as if bound by some courtesy, he laughed out loud. After that she turned her regard away from him as if to dismiss him. He called out to Miz Della, who was returning: "I declare, I think your baby already knows her own mind, and she's made it up to think that I'm very small potatoes." He sat down chuckling to wait for his host's appearance.

They made him stay to dinner, and afterwards Upshur took him out under the spring-house shed, where Bruff found himself telling the other how at a loss he felt at home this summer. "I don't want to become all wound-up in the crops and weather, because I have to keep my mind dead-set on the big thing I'm tackling now, medicine."

Upshur nodded. "A good way to be. You'll never amount to anything if you scatter yourself. My trouble before was that I was divided in two, trying to preach when I was meant for farming." He tipped his head back and looked up at the threads of light showing through the shed roof. "I do pretty well now, labouring in this kind of vineyard, and I don't believe the Lord minds."

It was late in the afternoon when Bruff rose to go. "I'd like to come often, if I don't stop you from your work."

"You won't bother me," the other answered. "You could walk along beside me while I'm chopping my row."

Thus it came about that Bruff did a fine turn-of-work on Upshur's land that year; for he found himself chopping down the opposite row from John as they discussed the problems of the human body. Miz Della's Sal laid a plate regularly for him at their dinner table, and afterwards he would rest before going to the fields again, usually where he could joggle the baby Nan's cradle, sometimes teaching the mite to coo almost like bird-calls. He could not help noticing that here in the shade of this quiet household there was more peace than he had ever seen before, and that no one raised a voice.

CHAPTER THIRTY-ONE

MORE AND MORE now that the children were older and the household work had passed its crudest pioneer stage, Gerda began accompanying Yarbrough on his early morning rounds of the plantations; or sometimes taking over the circuit of fields close by, while he rode to more distant ones. She liked it best when they jogged along together, where the dew was still making a lustre on the purple-red earth, the air coming cool off the cotton plants. As they rode they discussed the merits of the different strains of cotton with which he had experimented. All the time they talked, they kept their eyes sharpened for anything that might be wrong in their present crops or creatures.

Whatever the state of things that Gerda and Yarbrough found, riding together or singly, they mulled it over afterwards at the breakfast table when the children had been shooed off to their tasks. Pokey then brought in a fresh pan of biscuits that had been held back for last-minute baking and scalding coffee to take the ache out of their bones. Gerda liked sharing the actual tending to the plantation with Yarbrough, for she had acquired a strong taste for it back when she had had to run their places in South Carolina. Only the exigencies of making their home take root in the wilderness had kept her so tied to the hearth instead of the earth. Even then, liking the outdoors best, she had often found time to slip away for a little hunting or fishing and had remarked the progress of their tilling as she passed by. Thus she was now able to keep close touch with their fields, and their flourishing became an obsession with her.

It was she who pounced on a stray sentence of Yarbrough's one morning, to the effect that they would gain ground if some of the men who were close friends hereabouts would meet occasionally and put their problems before the group for joint discussion. "Probably sounds foolish," said Yarbrough, "but I was thinking that if our own two heads are better than one, a dozen minds ought to be that much better."

"And why not?" she encouraged him. "We used to help each other raising rooftrees, and hauling meal from the Fort Gaines grist-mill. I don't see why we should let up now. If we met in a group, all could put forth their ideas and try out the likely ones to see which worked out best. Then you might learn where to write to other planters who are making a study of agricultural ways."

"That's right," he responded, "and I know one of the very men who'd be glad to answer a lot of our questions. He's called Martin Philips. He doesn't put on any airs, so what he'd tell us would be practical. Calls his place Log Hall. He farms."

"Isn't he the one that said he was just trying to ferret out the best plan of growing, and he didn't care whether science or tomfoolery furnished the principles?"

"That's the very one, Gerda. He makes some right funny mistakes, I'll have to allow, with his fooling around. Fed cottonseed to his pigs and killed a lot of them, but then he turned right around and used it for fertilizer, which was a great success. Anyway, he's up and doing." Yarbrough was pacing the floor along the length of the table now. "I tell you what, I'll ride around right away and see how many neighbours we can muster up to meet here to-night, to talk over planting-methods."

"Yes, bid them to supper, and they can stay the night, those that have too far to ride afterwards."

"You've made me hit on something!" he cried, pulling at one of her ear-bobs in his jubilation. Then he was off, feeling more frisky than he had since the Indian War.

That evening there was a round dozen gathered about the cleared table after supper. Gerda could hear that they set to in earnest, for now and then one voice rose above another till the words carried out to her. From these scraps of conversation it sounded as if they were making sense, not just tickled at a new game to play. Their discussion continued unbroken until the hour was so late she was forced to signal Yarbrough. Then she and Pokey and Lucinda, who had accompanied Malone over, carried food in to the men, who looked up absently, as if they wondered what women were doing there. Gerda chuckled, but Lucinda said snappishly: "Why on earth do you give a party for them to talk crops? Land knows they talk nothing else, from dawn till dark. I'm sick to death of the word *cotton*!"

"You'd be sick to death of starvation if it weren't for cotton," her mother reminded her. "Why, you all over in your section hardly raise enough corn for meal, have to buy it and syrup most the year round. If you didn't have your profits from cotton you'd be in a pretty quandary."

"Well, I don't care where the grits and sugar come from, the money always comes from somewhere. But I would care plenty to go on a junket to Mobile. We hardly saw the place last time, and I'd think a man who's hardly been married six months could find time to take his wife off for some pleasure."

2

Lucinda grew proportionately more restive as Malone grew increasingly absorbed in the agricultural projects of the county. She had not entirely lost a recurring distaste for contact with him, which centred on the New Orleans gaming-house episode; yet the moment he was inclined to let his interest in other things crowd in upon his infatuation for her she resented it. Besides she had always thought of Jerard as a sort of King Midas, who by a touch of his hand could produce all the prizes of the world for her delight. It had never occurred to her that this jocular man, who had poked fun at her father for his grave concern over the running of Whetstone Stand, ever had to sweat himself or knit his brows to gain his golden results. Now she saw him continually figuring over how many hands to how many acres would produce so many bales; watching him thumbing the stem of his wineglass of an evening, worrying over the gullies that were ripping open his land. She was also piqued to find that often when she joined him after her night's toilet was finished, her hair brushed silky, her nightgown in sweet folds about her, he was already an inert form slumbering under the covers—leaving her to lie there beside him outraged at her inviolate state.

One night it struck her to wonder how old he was, and it came over her that he was almost as old as Ma'am's young father would have been had he lived. She began to pity herself then somewhat for having a husband as old as a grandfather. Contrarily, now she longed for the company of the youths she had so scorned last year before her marriage.

Meanwhile Malone found her restlessness as trying as she did his growing stolidness. All he asked when he came in after making an arduous round of his plantations was to be allowed to slump in the wide chair before his office desk, perhaps to nod a bit. He usually pretended to doze if he heard her racketing about in the hall outside. Once he saw her passing through in a bright-striped dress that jarred his eyes. She held a sort of long supple switch looped like a rope and was skipping it. "Lordy," he groaned, "how awful young she is!"

It was shortly after this that Malone went with Yarbrough to see Martin Philips at Log Hall. Lucinda stayed at Rock Wall during his absence. The young people were putting a gala end to their summer there. The older boys were beginning to take an interest in girl visitors, and there were several including pretty, giddy Lutie Caraway, whom Tom Two and Joachim fought over. The number of local beaux was supplemented by Joe Walthall, a fellow-student of Bruff's, and Page McHugh, who was to assist Danley in teaching this fall.

The place had never been given over quite so completely to the young folk's pleasure before, as they had most of them been either too young or too hard at work in the cotton fields. This year every one seemed to wish them joy in their frolics. Gerda, concerned about diverting Joby, and unable to think of either of her daughters as grown married women, treated them as leniently as their company. She also often mounted her own horse to join them on a ride after a basket of giant peaches from the far orchards, and she could fish better than any of them as well as fry the catch for them right there on the bank.

Bruff's earlier discontent with Rock Wall had vanished. He delighted in organizing possum-hunts, knowing that that free-for-all sport was a fine sample of the county's entertainment, with its tumbling through the brush, the intent sniffing of the dogs, the scare about snakes, then at last the raucous yelping about the trunk of a tree, and the two stalled live coals of the possum's eyes high up in the top.

It was a fine summer that none of them would ever forget.

One night, seated in the sulky dark when there was no moon, Lucinda, finding herself next to Page McHugh in the group, let her breath go gustily at the same time as his, for they were both feeling the same youthful thing. There was a way that the sky covered everything, even the highest tree-tops. It was full of more stars than it could hold, so that some were wasting away into a fine silvery powder.

It made them feel like hugging the whole night close, to keep it from ever getting away from them.

As the days passed by after that, Page waited on Lucinda at every turn. When they were peeling white heath peaches for Gerda's pickling, he dropped his ribbons of peel into the same scrap-pan as hers; he sat beside her at table; and his horse always followed hers when they rode over the dusty road to Turberville after the mail. Once when she was glancing through a letter that she had just received from Malone, Page whipped his mount up and shot ahead out of sight round a dark-blue bend of pines. He moped the rest of that day, while Danley regarded him acutely.

Before many more days passed, all the young people noticed his constant attendance upon Cinda. The girls whispered, Hans spent the whole day over in his fields alone, and Bruff told Danley that he wished his father or Jerard would come home and take Lucinda in hand.

Danley worried, because he had brought McHugh here, yet concluded dryly: "If Page hadn't happened along, Cinda would have picked on someone else." However, he finally decided he had better speak to her, since she was the only one who could stop the whole performance. After biding his time for a day or two, he followed her on a solitary walk and overtook her where she was leaning over a fence by a path through the pine woods. She was popping at some late May apple pods and looked so innocently occupied that Danley felt foolish about his mission. He leaned beside her against the fence nevertheless.

"Cinda," he began without preface, "why in thunderation did you have to start poor Page to acting the fool? He's new down here and, as a teacher, needs the good opinion of the people, and you've set him off on quite the wrong foot."

She turned to him as if waiting docilely for him to continue. This threw him off guard, as he needed some resistance from her against which to pit the strength of his arguments. He ended a trifle lamely: "He doesn't mean a farthing to you."

She let that pass unanswered, as if it hardly merited a reply. Danley was becoming exasperated now, thrusting his face nearer to hers in the hopes of annoying her. But she leaned forward to meet his outthrust features till it seemed to him that their very breath was mixed together. He stepped back quickly with a ringing in his ears and stood quiet until his eyes focused on the pine needles on the ground. Then he said: "I suppose it was scarcely my place to upbraid you, but I feel a responsibility for the lad. My apologies." He walked off swiftly, his legs set in a stiff-kneed stride.

She stood there with her eyes twinkling. "Oho, my fine young gentleman and scholar! So you've taken your nose out of a book long enough to notice me at last? All you've ever done is scold me, but I'll warrant you'd rather have kissed me then than ferruled me!"

A very few days, however, sufficed to show Lucinda that she would not be able to inveigle Danley into any further passages; in fact she began almost to doubt that he had shown such a sharp response to her nearness that day in the pine shade. Presently the house party palled and she packed up her traps in disgust, saying that Jerard would be home shortly and would expect her there to welcome him. Some of the party lifted their eyebrows at this belated display of wifely devotion, Page groaned, Bruff and Danley sighed with relief, and Gerda merely gave her a tin of her special beaten biscuit, a favourite delicacy with Malone.

Once back at Top Hill Lucinda found its rooms echoing and empty, but she took a perverse pleasure in stalking majestically about through its shadowy grandeur. In her solitude she would pass hours on end, her eyes straying with pleased sensuousness from one polished highlight to another, while her ears listened to the night sounds and silences outside. During this time she was feeling her emotions, which had been churned up by the thought of this man or that, gathering into a great whirlpool that soon would have to burst forth through some outlet. Her recent anger and pettishness at Jerard were being washed away by the force of her urgent and growing need as a woman. She felt that she was waiting spellbound for his return. . . .

The night he did arrive, she had already retired upstairs when she heard the clump of his boots on the veranda. She ran out to the head of the stairs. He first waved his hat, then threw it up for her to catch. After that he came charging up the steps behind it and grabbed her off her feet as if he were going to eat her alive. Once inside their chamber he told her to stand off so he could feast his eyes, while he began loosening his stock, coat, watch-chain, and waistcoat. When he sat down on her slipper chair to remove his boots, she squatted before him and began tugging at one.

" Better get Busto for that," he began, but just then it came off with a jerk that landed her flat on her back. He dropped down beside her to help himself to a few good kisses. She lay there laughing at him. " Your bristles tickle my face," she told him.

Then they both scrambled to their feet. She walked over to where their front blinds were open and stepped out on the upper gallery. The moon had come full again, and as she turned back to where he was waiting she took care to stand before one of the long windows while she slid her top-robe off. The nightdress beneath amounted to nothing, showing itself only as a faint gauzy shadow over her limbs. She climbed the steps to their bed. On the top one she looked down at him and scooped a kiss off the inside of her elbow to throw at him, then followed it by a leap that landed her in his arms. He seized her, feeling through the linen thinness she wore.

She thought as he held her that the mocking-bird was singing very far off to-night, or else her blood was pounding in her ears to the point of deafness.

CHAPTER THIRTY-TWO

Lucinda had been wondering carelessly for several weeks what ailed her, when one morning the moment she rose she became ill and had to hasten to her wash-stand jar. After her stomach settled down again, she exclaimed in high chagrin: "So *that's* what's the matter with me! Going to have a baby before I can turn around good!" She made her hands into fists and began to pound them together to keep time to her angry thoughts. She'd swell up like a watermelon, then have to go through pains worse than fire and brimstone. All for the sake of having a puking, squirmy baby that would never give her a moment's peace from then on. She'd be tied down as fast as all the women in Christendom. She didn't want to be that way. She wanted to walk around alone in her own body. To rise up or lie down at her own sweet will, unintruded upon by any second being. And later, the thought of any pursed little mouth tugging at her for food—why, she knew she'd slap it sure as shooting!

She stood up with angry swiftness, only to feel her diaphragm heave warningly. Already she was under another being's control. Dressing hastily, she went in search of Jerard to tell him and vent some of her spleen on him for bringing her to this pass. He was just leaving the breakfast table, smoking one of his fine cigars, and the smell of it made her queasy. "Put that thing out," she cried desperately. "Bonapartt, take it out in the yard and bury it."

Jerard stared at her dumbfounded. "What on earth ails you?"

"The worst possible! I'm in a family way."

"Puddin'!" he reached out to sweep her into a joyful embrace. "That's prime!" But she shoved him off.

"Oh, *you* can blat and brag about it, and carry on like a stud horse, but *you* don't have to foal it. It's anything but prime for me."

But he was beside himself with pride. He and Cinda had been married going on a year, and he had begun to wonder lately if he'd let himself grow too old before marrying, if he would learn the bitter taste of irony as he went to his grave without an heir, recalling all the seed he had wasted where no fruit could be culled. Now it was a triumph to have this robust young wife whom he adored come to him with such tidings! He swung his arms wide, his shoulders almost bursting out of their seams. "Tell me what you want for a present. Anything your heart desires! Maybe a brand-new carriage, eh? The easiest-riding turnout money can buy, and silver on the harness. How'll you like that?"

"I don't give a rap," she cut short his jubilant rantings, "about any fancy new carriage. I hate poking along on wheels. I like galloping on my mare Milly."

"Well, we sure tee-wydee can't have any more of that now. You all might be killed."

"'You *all*,'" she mocked. "There 'tis already, I can't be treated like just myself. No, I'm a whole litter! If you're going to drool around like that, you'd better get out before I yell."

Cowed by her, because of a sort of divinity she had taken on as his child's mother, he tiptoed away grinning foolishly. Before the day was half over he had spread the news to her family and, she supposed, to half the rest of the county. Usually such matters were kept secret as long as possible, from every one except the wife's close kin, but Malone was never close-mouthed; now he let loose his braggadocio full force.

Gerda, who seldom left her own place except for infrequent churchgoing, came in bonneted state, with Pokey looking properly lugubrious behind her. Cinda was sitting on the front steps watching the October colouring that had come to the country and inhaling the fresh air which she needed.

"You look well enough," observed her mother, "but I didn't expect anything else."

"I don't *feel* well," declared Lucinda. "I feel dreadful, I can tell you."

"I done bring some cures fo' you' mornin' sickness," announced Pokey, "and some other tricks that'll help you, sho'."

"I won't take any of that slop!"

"Now quiet down," Gerda told her. "You've got to behave yourself while you're in this condition, and we want to leave you a few old remedies that'll give you a lot of comfort off and on."

"Then," said Cinda in a hard voice, "Pokey can take them up and put 'em in my dressing-room. Pinky can show her where. I'm not promising, though, that I'll take the old stuff. That's one thing, at least, I'm not a child now, so you can't hold my nose and pour doses down me." She turned her eyes back to the sky; she had no use for anything right now except space and fresh air.

2

As the weeks went by and her attacks of nausea became both more acute and more lingering instead of lessening, and as her kin, all except Hans, took to discussing her coming baby in preference to herself, Lucinda's resentment fermented. She felt that some sorry hoax was being played upon her, and that for once in her life she could not gather her wits together to turn the tables. She enjoyed no one's company, feeling too sour and dull to think that she could attract the usual attention from any of the entertaining young men; and she avoided the company of women like the plague since all they wanted to do was to mouth over her condition. She hoped she would never have to hear that word again, after this was over. She grew horror-stricken at the possibility of begetting children one after another as Ma'am had. Why, that would mean spending her life in a succession of illnesses. She couldn't bear it! She *knew*!

The colours had gone out of the hills, and the dun colour of early December had settled over the landscape. Her house began to take on that mouldy smell that would pervade it for the winter wherever the orange scorch of the fires did not reach to dry it out. She was standing before her bedroom hearth trying to clear that damp stench out of her nose, when suddenly the stink of some fallen dead ashes went up her nostrils and twisted at her unsteady stomach. She barely made the slop-jar in time.

When she was free of her heaving once more, she raised herself up and looked around with wild belligerence. Morning sickness, *bah*! This was early afternoon, and the sixth time to-day she had rid her stomach of its contents. Rid herself of everything save that one thing that was the cause of all her misery! Well, by Heaven she'd have a fling at that too. Something was wrong. You weren't meant to suffer this deadly illness every hour of the day, and for this long. It probably wouldn't take much to jog the incubus loose.

She flung off her crumpled wrapper, plunged her face and arms into water, sticking her arms right down in the pitcher up to the elbows. Then she grabbed her riding-habit from where it had been hanging useless so long. She was glad to see that it still fitted her, that she was as lithe as a coach whip and not yet a droop-bellied sow. She hurried down the stairs and out to the stable lot to order Milly saddled in person, for fear if she sent the message Tid might tell Jerard.

Once out on the open road, after she had let the mare loose in the speed of an arrow, she began to forget the purpose that had brought her there. Whirling this way past her, the drab woods looked mauve-veiled in the ground mist rising after the rain, and over in the direction of Pike County the sun had burst through like a ripe peach. The mud beneath the mare's hoofs went *sqush-clop, sqush-clop*, and the road measured off into a mile.

Now she had forgotten completely why she had come and, filling her lungs with the sun-shot fog, was about to burst out singing when a pain grabbed her in a spasmodic hold. She glanced about a little wildly, thinking of leaping down to safety and stillness, when she recalled what she wanted to happen. Grimly she clutched at the bridle, letting Milly out still faster. Now the woods passed her crazily, and a buzzing was starting up in her ears like a swarm of mosquitoes. Suddenly another pain like a giant hand caught her at the middle; it brought her up standing on her foot in the stirrup. Then it took such a long arching time to happen, yet was over in a second. She soared from her stirrup and went out into loose space. In the end she came banging down with a wet breaking of bush, and it was quite a while before she knew anything, except that hot tongs were clutching her. She tried to grab some branches of brush and pull her face forward into their wet rootiness, but the tongs grabbed her until she was numb, and she lolled over. Their grip broke then, and some dam within her burst; she felt she was being swept away, but was too weak to wonder where. The dripping from the bushes kept her partly conscious. . . .

The last time she regained consciousness Dr. Caraway and, she thought, Bruff were down beside her opening a satchel. Then she was in the new carriage with Jerard kneeling beside the seat to hold her head steady. She could not see how his face looked. But the carriage rode easy, not that she could feel it, but she could see how the boughs outside scarcely dipped.

The slow ride went on with once in a while a halt when Dr. Caraway felt her pulse, with Bruff's face stuck right there over his shoulders, though she knew her twin was away in New Orleans at school. After a while they were before the steps of her veranda. She couldn't tell how many people lifted her, except that it wasn't bad—only pleasant little tugs and a long swaying feeling as she was moved up the steps and the inner stairway on a quilt pallet. They laid her down on a low cot.

3

After it was all over, she must have gone to sleep, for the night passed in some weird fashion, with all sorts of people who could never possibly have entered her chamber coming towards her and receding. When she finally woke in the morning it was to find Gerda and Pinky sponging her forehead, and to see that it was quite an ordinary world, with her alive in it. Dr. Caraway was actually there, but they insisted that Bruff was still away at school. She lowered her lids to turn it all over in her mind. Presently she lifted them to make the statement: "I'm not going to have that baby now."

"No. A pity," said Dr. Caraway, but she moved her hands to place them in a contented caress on her empty belly.

The day passed unusually still. What was missing? She frowned but would doze before she could think. After night fell, when Gerda was sitting alone with her, she realized what the lack was. "Where's Jerard? You'd think he might come see how I am."

"You've done for him, almost worse than you have for yourself," droned Gerda. "He's not a real young man any more and can't count on making every lick tell towards fatherhood. Besides, you've put yourself in the way of likely not being able to have children after this foolishness. Reckon he's about ready to give up. That's what you've done for him." Lucinda saw that she was not the one for whom Gerda felt sorry, in however much pain she herself lay.

4

All of Top Hill was filled with a leaden atmosphere. The master and mistress eyed each other so sullenly that the servants skulked about their tasks almost furtively, and even Bonapartt had lost some of his bearing. The others were acting up badly and yellow Rache made so much disturbance that Lucinda had to order Mr. Dicks to administer what was deemed a moderate correction of six lashes. After that the girl grew so violent that the other girls in the yard begged to be allowed to eat in the hands' kitchen for fear she would poison them at the house as she threatened. Lucinda had Dicks remove Rache to the hands' quarters instead, to do heavy work as punishment. She chanced to see the girl shake her fist up at the house when leaving, but was too listless to attend to punishing that.

The house itself no longer seemed grand, for all its splendid furnishings. In fact, they only succeeded in making it oppressively funereal. Lucinda took no interest in overcoming this, nothing was worth doing. Jerard had been drinking steadily, until from morning till night he was in a haze. Lucinda observed this contemptuously and more or less indifferently. To-day he was in such a half-stupor that he had not gone about any of his plantation business at all and had chosen the Little Parlour, where she was, to slouch and snore in. Lucinda had been standing by the window trying to make up her mind to take a walk in spite of the dreary day, when she discerned a figure on horseback entering the drive and knew it was Yarbrough by the way he sat his stallion. She rushed out and flung the door open to wait for him on the veranda.

"How goes it, missy?" he asked as he greeted her with a hug. "I'm glad to see you racing around again, only don't go too fast. I wonder if you could send one of the boys to call Jerard in."

"No need to do that," she sniffed. "He's been too drunk to go out all to-day."

Yarbrough frowned. "I don't like that. 'Tisn't like Malone. I can hardly blame him, though."

"I don't see why not. He ought to be man enough to face trouble. Now I suppose even you are siding with him against me."

Yarbrough shook his head sombrely. "I'd never side against you. Only 'tisn't so simple to decide which way is *for* you." They were in the house now and he saw how grim the room looked, with the furniture not polished, no flowers to brighten it, and the fire sunk to a grey choked mass. In the midst of it Malone looked the picture of dejection, sunk in his drunken drowse, but Yarbrough went over to him and clapped him on the shoulder jovially. "A pretty howdy-do of a welcome, with you not even awake."

Malone jumped. "Eh, what?" A good-natured grin started to spread from ear to ear; then, remembering how and why he had fallen asleep, he drooped. But he pulled himself together enough to call: "Bonapartt! Bonapartt! Cinda, where in creation is that darky? You don't keep track of 'em at all."

Bonapartt appeared, grinning at his former master, carrying a tray he'd rubbed up hastily the instant he had descried Yarbrough's approach from far off. It had everything on it, from whisky and lemon to a platter of sausage sizzling enough to make even Yarbrough's eyes water. Bonapartt went around lighting lard wick boats to chase the early shadows out of the corners, and a boy soon had the fire blazing freshly. Bonapartt lingered a moment himself to watch Marse Yarbrough relish his sausage and hear him banter and laugh. That was the way folks were meant to sound. When Marse give him to Miss Lucinda, he'd never thought he was coming to any old graveyard like this had turned out to be. He'd expected feasts and reels and carriages driving up all day long. Cackling at Marse Yarbrough, he made tracks back to his pantry.

In the Little Parlour the restraint lifted for a space, while the three braced themselves with the refreshment; but presently Malone caught Yarbrough's concerned eye upon him as he mixed a fourth toddy, and Lucinda switched right out of the room. Malone swallowed the toddy defiantly in one swift gulp. "Puts heart into a man. Or takes the feelin' out of his heart till he can't tell how bad he's hurt, I don't know which 'tis."

Yarbrough overlooked this. "I came over to tell you that we've missed you at our agricultural meetings, and that we'll be needing your help again now that planting's starting up."

"You don't mean to tell me," protested Malone, "that you think I ought to go running around to meetings again, with Lucinda so dead set against them and having little enough use for me now as it is!"

"There are some things a man has to tend to, no matter what," declared Yarbrough. "Lucinda might as well learn that now as later. I dote on the child, and I was scared plumb foolish while she was so bad off. I'll admit it didn't make me feel very kindly towards you there for a while. But if she had only used patience and taken things easy it might not have occurred." He broke off. He could hardly make himself clear about how, as a father, he had felt a fierce anger at any man's putting his daughter in a state where she could risk such danger, yet how, as a man, he held the primitive belief that the male should be left free to provide food. He stumped his cigar out in a dish. "I reckon I'd better not stay around for supper. I might speak out of turn to her about what she did; then the fat would be in the fire for fair." He thwacked the other on the back again, to show that they were men together, having to put up with women's notional ways. "What I want you to do," he wound up, "is to come help us out, like you used to."

Malone straightened up gratefully. "I'll pull myself together, I promise you. I may be pretty no-account this season; still, I'll do my best."

Trotting his horse down the driveway, Yarbrough mused. Maybe it had been a mistake for any one as spoiled as Cinda to marry any one as wealthy as Malone. She might have been worth her salt if she'd had to help some poor man along. But, pshaw, if she had been in poverty he would never have stood by and not helped them over the bad places. She was his precious, and he'd always liked her bat-crazy didos. He counted on his sons to show what stuff the Whetstones were made of, only how would that make the girls wind up? Lucinda was a big bother.

Upstairs from her dressing-room window Lucinda watched him ride off. There, her father didn't even care to stay for one meal in this tomb! Well, she couldn't blame him, she'd like to leave it too and ride over to Rock Wall, where there was some life. Then she whirled about angrily. No, by all that was holy! She wouldn't have to run with her tongue hanging out, to beg for fun and laughter from other people's homes. She'd have it here! She'd make the place shine with brightness and ring with shouts! She'd show this mansion what it was meant for, if she made the walls fall doing it!

Lucinda was in the saddle again!

CHAPTER THIRTY-THREE

MALONE fell in with Lucinda's plans for a big house party fairly enthusiastically. He had kept his promise to Yarbrough to pull himself together and was appearing regularly at the agricultural meetings again. He was still drinking rather steadily, but he carried his liquor with gravity, and when he did any heavy drinking at night, he usually did it shut up in his office under the pretence of working over his accounts. To hide this closet sipping, he was more than amiable to Lucinda otherwise. Now when she proposed her party to him he said lavishly: "Get everything by the barrel, puddin'. Oysters, pickled mackerel, oranges." He thought that maybe her interest in pleasure meant she would stop holding herself off from him. In her excitement she did pause often and pinch his ear in sheer exuberance, or call him the dancing bear again, her old term of affection.

The house was cleaned from top to bottom and aired out with bags of lavender and pomander oranges hanging in the windows while they were open, to freshen the smell. She had a large upper chamber put in order for the younger girls, and a smaller but more private one for several of the older matrons she felt she could count upon coming. Another large room was prepared for the more crotchety older gentlemen, but the young blades were to be quartered at the nearby overseer's place. The extra upper chambers were put at the disposal of special guests from greater distances.

She sent Bonapartt in the carriage, with Tid on the box, to deliver the invitations, which were lettered in gold on heavy vellum, the like of which had never been used in the county before.

The day the guests arrived, some stable boy stood constantly by the horse block, with Tid in the background to give directions. A serving-maid kept her post on the lowest step where the carriages drove up, ready with *sal volatile* in case any lady felt faint after her trip. Malone was on the top step and Lucinda at the door, with Pinky behind her to direct the guests to their rooms, and Bonapartt to see that they had immediate refreshment to restore them.

The whole tone of the occasion was like that back in the Carolinas, and unconsciously the guests used less of their salty pioneer talk, while Gracey pressed Lucinda's hand happily. "This is the way it *should* be. You deserve a crown for starting them off in the right direction." Cinda smiled thanks, but thought to herself that she would set them a lead they would never catch up to.

By noon people were arriving thick and fast, including even Bruff, come all the way from New Orleans, and Gerda, who could stay only a few days away from Whetstone Stand. "I hope," she said to her daughter, "that you haven't put me to sleep in a room with a lot of parroting women. They give me the itch when they've no work to keep them in order."

By two o'clock they had all arrived and were ready to sit down to a big welcoming dinner. There was to be a dance in the drawing-room that evening, but this was a time for resting their feet, for hearing news from every corner of the county, learning the names of the newborn and the size of estates left by those who had passed on. Malone, his drinks carefully spaced all day, looked more like the man he used to be; and he gazed with pride down the mile of table to where Lucinda sat, the picture of wife and hostess that he had always planned her to be. March outside had brought new weather after a bad winter, and a fresh lease of life. He lifted his glass high and toasted gladly: "To Mistress Malone!"

That afternoon the men roamed over the grounds and stables or smoked lazily in Jerard's office, while upstairs the women gossiped or inspected each other's wardrobe. Lucinda kept her door open in case any of them might want something from her, but she was in her dressing-alcove, out of view, having Pinky rub her shoulders with arnica, for they ached easily since her accident. She was beginning to feel rested later when Hans called her name from the threshold. Pinky flurriedly threw a robe over her mistress's shoulders, but she remarked: "Pinky, you know he's seen me in a shift many a time."

"You wa'n't no gemman's wife den," objected Pinky.

"Well, get along out," said Hans, "so I can tell her how fine *my* plantation is coming on. Miss Cinda's not the only person who has come into land and grown up this past year." Pinky departed and he pulled the screen before the alcove to cut off any further visitors.

"Hans, I think it's fine the way you've taken hold of your place.

Papa's so proud of you. Talks about you these days heaps more than he does about Bruff."

He flushed. "It *is* making something out of me, I believe. I'm not afraid to walk up to anything now and tackle it." He looked down at her. "Tell me, are you happier? That's what I came to see about. Everybody's saying so and your face looks more proud now, instead of mad. Still, I want to be sure."

She put her hand up on his arm. "I'm trying it out this way, Hans, because I thought I might at least get more fun out of it than from fighting or moping. I'm always going to have my fun in everything!"

He saw from her excited eyes how final that was. She did not change, only changed the things she did, as she tried one adventure after another. Her beauty, though, had altered to something more aware of itself, more carefully tended. He could not keep his eyes from being drawn away from her eyes down to her mouth, then dropping to fasten on her neck. It was whiter.

He lifted his eyes and turned them out the window to a beech tree, shaking its pink new blossom-like leaves against a half-green sky. He had all he could ask, this moment with her near, and the parting day outside.

"Well——" he moved aside the screen to leave, satisfied.

2

That night the house was as bright as a Christmas tree, with ranks and ranks of white tapers between terraced masses of blooms. Lucinda was queenly in green *glacé* that looked like spring seen through ice. Very few people could take their eyes off her for long, and Malone was struggling not to become maudlin over her. The musicians had been brought all the way from New Orleans, and played with a measured ornateness that kept the company in a pattern of bows and compliments, a state of patrician behaviour. Yarbrough smiled at Gerda, much gratified at the becoming elegance their eldest daughter had evoked.

Guy and Ven, standing watching the dancing, sighed reminiscently for Egton. Ven said: "I never was much hand out on the floor, but, damme, I did like having my drams poured out of a fine decanter."

"I liked all this in those days," replied Guy. "Lucey set such store by it. She married me for my dancing manners. I can tell you I'd hate to have her see the way I live now, though I'm worth twenty times over what I used to be. Funny." His face was puzzled, recalling the nonentity he had been when he used to walk the chalk-line, and the man of consequence he had become by breaking caste rules. He felt he could answer to his Maker with a clear conscience, yet if Lucey came along while he was standing there before the throne, he'd hang his head in mortification. Being proper seemed better around her than being powerful.

Lutie Caraway was the next-prettiest girl on the floor after Lucinda, and she was all spiced up with the mischief of flirting with Nettie's beau, Nat. Not that she liked the tiresome profit-talking galoot, but she liked to put Nettie's fur up. Nettie was trying to retaliate by annexing new suitors, including Page McHugh. "Just as if," giggled Lutie, "Cinda couldn't come along and take him away with a crook of her finger." He paid no attention to any one except his hostess and spent his evening trying to be on hand when she had any favour to grant any one, so Nettie gave up.

Upstairs Gracey was standing before a mirror, flicking out her heliotrope skirt. Gracey, after six years, had finally ventured out of black, upon hearing that there would be a number of eligible gentlemen of suitable age at the house party. She had put her mind on Dr. Gadsdenn, of whom Bruff spoke so highly, since she judged that a widower would be easier prey than a man skilled in fending off matrimony.

She started rather guiltily out of her reverie as Nettie Melburne entered; then when she caught the trend of the girl's vicious resentment at the dearth of attention to her, she drew back rigidly into herself. Didn't the goose know that she shouldn't admit aloud that she wasn't sought after? Didn't she know you must hide the thought, stifle the fact? Fool other people with brightness, lie to yourself, and at the thought of a possible suitor, pray till you nearly went crazy with the singsong petition: *and-let-him-love-me-for-ever-and-ever*? Gracey turned and fled from the room, more to escape her own hysterical thoughts than the other girl's yammering.

At the foot of the stairway she ran into Danley Bruton, who asked her to be his partner in the grand march forming for supper. His attention built up the colour in her cheeks. She did not know that he was wondering if she were at last coming out of her self-sealed sepulchre. Poor thing, he thought, she had a right to live a little before she died. Then his eyes were switched ahead to the line of march about the ballroom, every one being paired off with someone he either didn't want or couldn't have, so that there was no telling what might break loose!

Late that night Malone slept almost as he had fallen on his bed, worn out with his own hospitality. Lucinda lay awake a moment or two smiling. She was going to have all the fun! And call the tunes. In the young ladies' chamber that night Joby dreamed girlishly a little while of a dim memory of Armand Petit. And Gracey lay on her bed feeling smothered by all the virginal breathing filling the room about her. She shivered, wondering if he, a doctor, would be able to discover that she and Ronald had not been—that her virgin breath belonged in this soft whispering chorus. . . .

3

Next morning after breakfast was finished Lucinda rang on her water-glass to attract their attention. "Between now and dinner time," she announced, "which won't be until three——"

"Never want to see any more food," grunted Ven, hugging his toddy glass fondly. "It clogs me up."

"Will you hush?" laughed Cinda. "Anyhow, between now and dinner we're all going to join in a magpie-hunt."

"Those pests?" objected Ven. "They're not fit to eat."

Lucinda cried out: "*Will* you let me go on? I'll explain what I mean. You all know how magpies steal trash for their nests, or even steal other birds' nests? Well, the notion behind this hunt is for you to pick up a lot of odds and ends of no-account things that I have listed and bring them back here. Only, these lists don't name the actual things, but are written in conundrums. You have to guess the answers first before you know what to look for. Now you draw for partners, and after you're paired off you're on your honour not to give any other pair help. The couple that gets back first with the most things wins. They'll be given prizes, and let me tell you the prizes are nothing to be sneezed at. Then those two will be crowned king and queen of the house party to-night at the charades, and their word will be law for the rest of the visit. Now ready, *go*!"

As they went trooping out the house shortly, she watched them a moment, then turned to pick up her cape and follow. But Malone, who had been gazing at her warmly while she preened before them, caught her back by the arm, his hand seeking the flesh under the sleeve. "Where're you going, Cinda?"

"Why, to catch up with first one, then another of the couples to see how they're making out. It'll be a holy show."

He began pulling her towards the stairway, in a way that made her feel she might not be able to manage him. He was mumbling: "Sugar, you don't want to play *children's* games. Come on upstairs with me while the house is empty."

"No, you're crazy. I want to go watch the fun."

"Yes, you do!" he jeered. "You want an excuse to lallygag with that Page McHugh whippersnapper."

She gave him a push that sent him, unsteady as he was from his morning drinks, grabbing at the newel post. In a hurry to overtake the others, she didn't see ugly frustration swamping his face.

The magpie-hunt went on hilariously for over two hours, until Joby and Danley Bruton, who had not been delayed by any dalliance with each other, arrived back first. The mud-splashed, raggle-taggle band that collected laughed and shouted: "Long live Queen Joby! Long live King Danley!" They opened their prizes, to discover for Danley a beauty of a new gun, for Joby a bolt of brocaded satin shot with gold thread. Every one else's mouth watered.

Lucinda looked at them gloatingly. "In the palm of my hand, that's where I have the whole parcel of them." Her father came up to her and gave her a terrific squeeze. "You're the real queen, precious. No one else can hold a candle to you."

"Ssh," warned Ma'am Gerda quietly, glancing at Joby. "You'll spoil that child's pleasure. Don't forget she's your flesh and blood too."

"But this one is more than flesh and blood to me. A man's first little daughter is his eternal weakness."

"You spoke the truth there," interrupted Malone. "You're blind on the side you're supposed to see Cinda's faults with. You've spoiled her rotten——"

"Take care," Yarbrough warned him. "I don't want to have any hard words with you, here and now."

Ma'am Gerda grinned at them. "I'd kinder like to see you two have a fight out some day. You've been threatening it over fifteen years, till it's become a pet notion." They laughed sheepishly and moved towards the bottles on the buffet, Yarbrough steadying Jerard's steps. Gerda felt a little sorry for Cinda with a husband who could not measure up to her father.

Joby was standing near a window where the shafts of light fell, having Gracey drape folds of the brocade over her to show how it became her. Dr. Gadsdenn who had been watching Gracey ply the folds, glanced at her curls, remarking: "You always hear people talk about spun-gold hair, but I never saw it before yours, Miss Gracey." Gracey spilt the silk at that and bumped Joby's knees stooping to gather it up.

Lutie Caraway put a hand out in a little dab like a kitten's paw to touch Nat Screws' arm. Nettie saw it, and her eyes glinted viciously as she came towards them. Danley Bruton glanced about apprehensively at the various storm centres, recalling ironically how he had been so pleased with their violent natures and strong wills when he first came among them. "But I was an outsider then; now I'm in the thick of the most riotous pack." Page McHugh was drawing closer to Lucinda, his eyes growing so dark that only a tiny rim of grey iris showed around the edge of his widened black pupils. Hans stayed moodily on a seat by the mantel, rubbing a setter dog with his boot-toe.

4

That evening the charades went gaily at first, though with a touch too much of witty tension here and there and an acute awareness of criss-crossed situations. By the time two hours had elapsed, Nettie was as ruffled as a setting hen at Lutie, Gracey was in a trance-like state because Dr. Gadsdenn had posed on bended knee before her in a tableau, and Lucinda had Page all but gibbering. Malone was going first to his office for a dram, then out to holler at some of the negroes, and next into the drawing-room to make some rude gibe at Cinda: "Why don't you play statues? You could be the goddess of love, all barefooted?" or "Tell them to guess who I am! They've all seen clowns, or dancing bears." She ignored his sarcasm and continued putting her guests through their paces.

Danley Bruton drew a big sigh as his group, of which she was a member, dispersed to rid themselves of their costumes. He meant to tell her to slow up before she had reason to be sorry. He caught up with her in the half-passage off the back sitting-room, which they were using for dressing, and took both her wrists tight. "Lucinda," he begged, "please come down off your high horse! You're riding head on, into God knows what!"

"Danley," she mimicked, "please come down off your judgment bench. You're spoiling the frolic."

"Cinda, listen." He put his cheek once, very gently, against hers. "You know it's all because I care for you that I'm for ever scolding you. This is no jest; poor Page has lost his head, and your husband is beside himself, if ever I saw a man that way! Girl, listen to me." He smoothed her cheek again.

Then a step rapped up to them, halted, and Page's voice came in sharp pain: "Ah, so that's it, is it? It's you two——" Involuntarily he put a hand forward to try to claim one of Cinda's shoulders, but Danley kept his hold on her wrists, trying to pull her in his direction. This left Cinda locked closely between them, just as a stumble of steps was heard and Malone came upon them with a lurch.

"I thought I'd find some such ruckus!" he growled like a bull. Befuddled, he could see only that his wife was being fondled by two men. He knocked their hands off her, scarcely knowing who the owners were. "You!" he said hoarsely, choking, to Lucinda. "Treating *me* like I was a beast. But of all the women I've ever had, white or black, you're the worst. And I made you my *wife*! Yet you couldn't even let me keep my child. Well, by God, I'll make no difference from now on between you and the other slu——"

Danley clapped a hand over his mouth before he could call her the word. Malone, twisting to free his mouth, glared with mad, bleared eyes and broke free. Then he looked Lucinda up and down, seeing her contempt and feeling how she was destroying first this part of him, then that. She was not a woman; she was an evil spell! He gasped: "A fine *white* lady, eh? Well, deliver me from them!" Turning, he went down the passage and out the door. They heard his steps, stamping like some animal in a pen, cross the yard towards the negro quarters.

5

Strained and almost shamefaced, the house party dissolved itself late the next day, all wondering, no one quite liking to ask, where their host had disappeared. Lucinda, cold-faced, stood in the hallway receiving their rather muffled farewells. Each member of her family tried to gain an instant alone with her, to ask if she wished any service or wanted any of them to stay with her for solace, but they could not penetrate her barrier. Gerda, going last, looked her daughter long and full in the face; then, knowing that they could not meet on any common ground, since each one held to her own, she departed. She saw none of the road all the sorrowful way home.

When the last person was gone and the house echoed with emptiness, Lucinda sat down in a chair, her head raised, studying the ceiling as if she were listening to some counsel. Then nodding her head once in decision, she called Bonapartt's name. "Send the overseer Dicks to me." Bonapartt went with the one word: "Yas'm." She waited in the same chair, her head raised, her face closed against everything except that thing she seemed to have heard spoken.

When Dicks came, his face serious, she arose. "Got your whip? Follow me." She led in a steady, unfaltering tramp, as if she had mapped out the path long ago. It led over to their secondary plantation where the hands were. The walk was long, some two miles. Coming out of cleared new ground where the stumps stuck up raw, she said: "It's the second cabin there, isn't it?" But her question needed no reply.

She went over, her shoes thudding heavily, the man following behind her woodenly. At the cabin of the wench Rache she paused and took one half-step aside. "Knock," she ordered. Dicks thumped with his whip handle. The mulatto opened it waveringly, her peering face patchy with terror, her mouth working as if in St. Vitus's dance.

Lucinda marched past her to the crude web bed from which Jerard was trying to rise out of a sprawling position. His face was breaking to pieces with a horror that made Rache's seem childish. When he was fairly steady on his feet, Lucinda said: "Tell her she's to be sold into Louisiana, for work in the canebrakes." She waited, and finally Malone nodded at the wench, who then began to have a sort of chill. Work in the canebrakes was one of the cruellest labours known to the whole black race.

"Now here!" said Lucinda next, and Dicks surrendered the whip which he knew she wanted. She poked it into her husband's hand and, jerking her head in the direction of his negress paramour, announced: "Whip her."

Lucinda walked to the door and waited with her back turned while he did. When the blows had fallen long enough to satisfy her, she looked back at the heap the girl made on the dirt floor. "That's enough."

She walked through the door and started her trudge homeward. She heard Malone stumbling along behind her, his breath coming in anguished gusts. He kept up with her somehow until they reached the edge of their back-yard grounds, then she heard him tumble down. She did not look back, so she did not know how long he lay there.

The next morning Bonapartt brought her a message from him, a scraggly line: "I had to leave the place, where I had become so loathsome, even to myself." She sat tapping the note against her teeth.

CHAPTER THIRTY-FOUR

TWO MONTHS went by and Cinda had no other word from Jerard. She stayed stuck at home to escape questioning by the curious, but several times her father rode over and catechized her on her husband's whereabouts. She shook her head. "I don't know."

Yarbrough scowled. "A pretty come-off!"

Lucinda merely stared back at him with a set expression. The strain was growing bad for her, yet she would not admit it. She had long ago dismissed her repugnance against Jerard. It had gone, once she vented her spleen on Rache. Now she was driven by a desire for his presence, for his voice ringing out in his side-bursting laugh, for the sight of the big full veins on the back of his hands.

Then on a certain May day when the insects were beginning to set up a hot, scratchy chirring in the long grass beyond the fences, word came. She had been pacing from the Little Parlour out to the front door, straining to see down the drive, as if her gaze could force Jerard to appear on the scene through the gate. It was shortly after noon, when she had made her twelfth trip to search the driveway, that the errand darky came bringing the post containing a letter from Bruff. The instant she opened it, Jerard's name jumped up from the page. She went inside to sit down while she read. Her twin wrote worriedly that he had seen Malone there in New Orleans quite by accident, that he had been ill with fever and was as yellow as mustard. There was none of his former fleshiness about him, his face showed the skin sagged into dry plaits across bony features. It was hard to see how he kept alive. Bruff knew it was none of his affair, but he was deeply concerned about them both and felt that Cinda should hasten there to fetch her husband home. He thought he had better warn her, though, that when her name had been mentioned, Jerard had shut up like a clam. However, she must bear in mind that he was a very sick man and make allowances.

Almost before she read her brother's closing salutation she was calling Pinky to help her pack. Dubious about how Jerard would receive her, she took no one into her confidence, instructed Bonapartt merely to state that she had gone to New Orleans, if any one inquired. She had her small trunk strapped and down in the lower hall by evening; she went to bed early to make the next day's departure come more quickly. Sick of inaction, she felt greatly relieved next noon, when she was riding down their drive in her carriage. Immediately outside the gate the errand boy met them with a more recent post that had a letter in Jerard's own hand. She told Tid to hold the horses quiet while she read.

He wrote:

I have made a great mess of things since we parted, lost one of my Mississippi plantations gambling in addition to everything else. Suppose by now Bruff has informed you he saw me. At first I was sorry he ran across me, but now feel it was for the best according to the plan I am undertaking. I am disposing of all my holdings away from Turber and sending you part of the profits. The Turber plantations I leave to you Free and Clear. Your father will help you to run them to an Advantage. And Dicks is trusty.

Divorce is out of the question in our part of the Country but I will see to it that you are rid of my Hulk. I am going to Texas. Maybe out there I can start anew, it is my only chance. I propose to change my name so that none will know me there and those back home never hear of me again. I will see to it that word and Proof is sent back to cause me to be accounted Legally Dead right away. I might as well be at the rate I am going. Don't fret, there will never be any question raised about my Decease after my Proof arrives, and I will be better off trying it this way. Do not try to track me down as I will make away with myself if you succeed which I doubt you can. I have not the Will Power to be a man around you and you need a mighty strong man to control both you and himself. Please try to think of me kindly. we had many sweet times as well as the bad ones together, and I will never forget you burning your hands baking that cake for me.

God Bless you and Watch over you.

yr. Former Husband,

J. Malone.

The words began to jiggle before her eyes, and the trees did also when she looked in their direction. "Tid," she said, choked up, "turn around. And drive back." When she alighted at her veranda Pinky and Tid felt scared at the expression on her face, but she made them leave her alone. Marse Jerard must be bad sick, they thought.

Lucinda went to her room and climbed the steps of their big bed. There she buried her head in it and tried to pray right, so it would bring him back.

2

Several unreal weeks went by, with the servants feeling in their bones that something was wrong, when the "proofs," the trumped-up messages of Jerard's death came, together with a few keepsakes. Lucinda studied them, as if trying to wring some clue to her husband's whereabouts from them, but they persisted in their silence. She locked them in a drawer.

They could not have a funeral, of course, but the family, convinced he was dead, thought that she ought to have services and a stone put up to his memory in a little plot Yarbrough had noticed that Malone had favoured. That it was a hard place to keep the blackberry brambles back from was all that Lucinda knew about it. The day the services were held, she stood so still she could not even feel her breath coming and going while the prayer-book words were falling. When the minister was ready to say *Amen* she wanted to stop him by crying: *No.* But he had said it, that word which hid her marriage away under a stone. She turned desperately and caught sight of Gracey wearing her weeds again for to-day. Cinda almost laughed with a bitter humour at being in a plight so like Gracey's—the victim of a spurious widowhood! She heard her father calling her brave, when it was simply that under the blank of Jerard's absence lay the fact that he was still in the same world.

During the first stretch of time after that Lucinda stayed at Rock Wall Place, because there she could forget that Jerard was not over home at Top Hill. She could feel that she might drive into the Court-house Square any day and see him tethering his horse near the saloon, or calling to John Screws to send out some barrels of flour. She could not believe that he truly meant he would never come back. Presently he would surely tire of travelling, decide he had taught her her lesson, and come home. But when one evening she caught herself walking down the S-path pretending that she was going to meet him, coming to pay one of his courting-time calls, she stopped stock-still. "I'm getting as bad as Gracey, making believe. That's enough of that! After all, he's alive and I'm alive, and we'll not have any more of this foolish imagining!"

She went back to the porch where the family was sitting and announced that she was going home to Top Hill. At first her father was up in the air at the idea of her living there alone, but Gerda pointed out: "Yarbrough, you haven't any right to make her give up her own home. After all, the Indians are gone, and she has Pinky and Mammy Lizzie and Bonapartt, with Mr. Dicks right close by."

Hans volunteered: "I'll ride over every week to see if I can lend a hand."

Once back, it took quite a bit of work to put Lucinda's place in good order again, so that the sunlight came in at breakfast, a cool shade lay over the rooms in the afternoon, and the fusty smell of a deserted house was banished. All the while she was superintending these things, she was trying to clarify some thought about herself in relation to Jerard, and herself in relation to Gracey. She would stand still right in the middle of a room whose floor was being rubbed with wax, and ponder.

Finally one day she went out on the front steps since there was nothing there that would distract her thoughts. She shook out the cloth she'd been gathering trash in and let it droop beside her skirts. Her mind ran on. She had gone through a decent observance of tribute to Jerard's memory, to avoid shocking the neighbourhood; yet the fact remained that he was *not* dead and she was *not* widowed. She would not conduct herself as such, except that she felt his absence too deeply to indulge in any levity in connection with him. As a protest on the side of his aliveness she now intended to behave as naturally as she could. And somehow, she felt, she must make some definite effort to help Gracey out of the fog she had been sucked into at the time of Ronald's death. Lucinda had the conviction that if she could win Gracey back to a normal life, then neither she nor Gracey, nor any woman whose life had not gone quite right, would be so at the mercy of those flickering shadows that other people encouraged them to draw over their strong personal grief. Yes, she would get to work on Gracey's case right away.

Accordingly she rode over to Rock Wall next day to invite Gracey to accompany her to Blue Springs for the last of the season.

Lucinda found her cousin drying her treasured unused engagement china on old fine lawn. "I want you," Cinda said, "to go with me to Blue Springs as my guest. I need a change. Your admirer Dr. Gadsdenn recommended it for me when he passed through on his way there himself, and promised to keep an eye on us if we came."

"Dr. Gadsdenn? I doubt if he'd thank you for calling him *my* admirer."

"Oh, yes, he would! In fact he urged the Springs for me twice as hard after I mentioned inviting you. How soon can you be ready? By Monday?"

3

They had been at the watering-resort over two weeks and Cinda felt that their stay had benefited them both. She was not oppressed, felt comfortable, was sleeping well, and had Gracey's manœuvres to watch for diversion. Adam Gadsdenn had made his intentions about Gracey very plain from the moment of their arrival, and squired Gracey on every possible occasion. Still something Cinda could not fathom led her cousin to treat the doctor to a good dose of coquettish evasion. Cinda was amused by her tactics, while hoping Gracey would not carry them too far and put the man clear off the track. But there seemed little danger of that, for whenever he could not be with Gracey, he was singing her praises to Lucinda, who could think of no husband better suited to cope with Gracey and her quirks than this kindly doctor. She was impatient to see the romance brought to a happy conclusion, and proud of having had a finger in the pie.

One day Lucinda had forgone her nap, to hear him weigh his chances of success in his suit. He said confusedly: "Eh—er—you understand the hopes I entertain of making your cousin my wife? Would it be too bold to proffer my hand with your sanction, instead of waiting to bespeak her from her father or yours?"

Lucinda stood up, feeling him a little too uncomfortably close.

"I'm sure the match will be most acceptable to our family, and I will speak in your favour at home."

That evening Lucinda scurried about, helping Pinky to deck out Gracey for the impending romantic event. It was understood, though not mentioned, that the doctor would address her before the evening was over. Lucinda urged the other to put on the mauve gauze that took on a pinkish cast under the lights, and she would not let her wear the black velvet bands on her wrists or throat. Instead she sent Pinky to pick a cluster of flowers to pin on Gracey's shoulders; and when Pinky returned with some waxen spikes of tuberoses she cried out exasperated: "Do you think we're trying to lay out a corpse?" She sent her back to fetch some roses. The whole lot she made into burgeoning bouquets and fastened them on her cousin with her own vivid emerald clasp.

Gracey backed off pleased with the vision she cast in the mirror and let Pinky give her the India shawl. She went down the stairs thinking how tiny her slipper-toes looked, pointing delicately.

The doctor was waiting for her in the raw-raftered hallway they called the reception-room. They were to listen to some selections on violin and pianoforte, termed by the guests a musicale, at which most of them would sit uneasily, eyes roaming out where the fireflies sparkled against the pines. Gracey settled her flounces in a way that, in spite of the harshness of the lard lamps' light and the creak of the splint chairs, gave her an air of as much ease as if she had been seated on a satin sofa. She kept her profile towards the doctor.

When the chairs scraped back at the conclusion of the programme, Dr. Gadsdenn pulled the fringes of Gracey's shawl free from the puckering splinters of her chair and led her purposefully past the people who wanted to stop and chat. Outside, Gracey kept putting her fingers up to her hair while she was being almost hauled across the veranda and down the creaking steps. The path in the dark was knobby beneath her slippers, forcing her to step limpingly. She pulled back with her elbow, complaining: "I can't see!"

The doctor paused penitently, and they walked on in a gingerly fashion. The path was only about as wide as a shoe-tongue, and the bench he led her towards was damp with wet bark. She thought how this was the end of her ruffles' crispness as she sat down, but she supposed she would not mind this once. She had dressed and come with him in the spirit of being wooed and of having a happiness offered her that many another woman would envy. Adam Gadsdenn was a man that would please even Gerda, even Lucinda. There would never be any need to make excuses for him, to pretend that he was something other than himself. What he was was complete.

Yet she sat here with her knuckles knotted nervously in the fringe of her shawl at her throat. Then she made them let go, feeling the fringe twist loose, and laid her hands carefully in her lap to show her best sapphire ring. He reached down for the left one. "Miss Gracey, you must know that I want you to do me the honour of becoming my wife. I scarcely know how to tell you what joy that would bring me."

All she could think despairingly was: "But I *can't*! And I could have married him so easily if I had not fooled them all with that fib about being Ronald's wife! Or I might have married him even so if he weren't a doctor. But he would *know* that I was never Ronald's!"

She rose from the damp seat and stood like a pale switch of plum-tree bloom before him. "You must understand that I feel greatly honoured, Dr. Gadsdenn. But my life in that way was over when my—husband—I cannot—*cannot* marry you!" She turned and fled up the path, her heels digging into the dirt, her hair tangling in her face. She clawed the door open as if this kind man following had become some sinister beast, as if his touch would bring death and sure destruction. Gaining her room, she all but fell back against the pine door to shut it. Her eyes, mad and hunted, went darting about to make sure that she was safe, that no man's face was at the dark windows.

Lucinda jumped out of her bed and came over to take her by the shoulders. "What's the matter? You look out of your wits!"

Gracey gasped: "He asked me to marry him. But I got away. I got away from him in time!"

4

Lucinda decided she had better take Gracey home by the early coach next morning and stayed up most of the night helping Pinky to pack while Gracey lay in a rigid stupor on the bed. When it came to dressing for the journey, Gracey was so acquiescent that she reminded Cinda of some docile sick child. But once safely in the coach, she began to shed her tractability and to assume again her habit of trying to dictate their conduct by virtue of being the elder. The first move she made was to drop murmured words here and there, meant to convey that her refusal of Gadsdenn had been based upon a widow's faithfulness to Ronald's memory.

Lucinda thought she had better let the wild thing she had glimpsed last night stay caged in Gracey's eyes, even if it did mean seeing her cousin smothered in a veil of dead sentiment and reverent hypocrisy.

That night at Rock Wall she noticed how Gracey, by having refused so desirable a suitor, had gained a curious elegance she had not possessed before. She spoke to Danley Bruton in an almost regal tone. "I understand that you have had trouble engaging an instructress to teach your young female pupils the pianoforte, embroidery, and deportment. I have decided to offer you my services if, of course, I am permitted to pass upon the social fitness of those admitted to my tutelage." She was standing behind her chair, about to excuse herself from the supper table, and held herself so straight that she appeared stately.

Danley replied: "Thank you very much. You take quite a load off my mind."

Bruff said: "Whew!" after she had left. "What airs!" Cinda crumbled a biscuit.

Later she went in search of Gracey to make sure she was all right. Opening her door a crack, quietly without meaning to be stealthy, she came upon the other unaware, pirouetting before her glass. Gracey was stripped except for a lace shawl and all the rings she could stack on her fingers. In slippers stained from the dirt of the Blue Springs path and decorated with clusters of honeysuckle, she darted and turned, half-chanting to her reflection:

Love—my love—
Pret-ty—as a pink!

crooning it over and over again. Then suddenly she broke off and went up close to the glass. "They won't ever catch on to you now! Not a solitary soul!" She patted her hand over the image of one bare breast in the mirror.

Lucinda closed the door silently and went outdoors into the air. She stared down at a crack in the step. How could Gracey be split into two people, one of them better controlled than ever, and one as crazy as a loon?

"Lordy," she vowed, "I'll marry again, no matter what sort of sin it is!"

CHAPTER THIRTY-FIVE

WILLY was in his counting-house taking stock of his profits on the Cotton Exchange for the past season. He had started speculating in cotton quite by chance. When he first took up his position in his father's bank he had gone about his duties in a dilatory way, paying more attention to aping the appearance of a Richmond banker or a New Orleans cotton factor than to the intricacies of finance. Gradually the rôle grew upon him until he found himself cultivating the acumen as well as the airs of his models, studying the vagaries of the market so closely that he could offer shrewd advice as to when to hold back a crop and when to sell.

Gerda, whenever she came up as far as Yufala to see Joby, liked to visit with him in the trim precincts of his office. It reminded her slightly of the one Gran had had for his studies on a street of the clean Dutch town where she had been born. She could look about the carefully brushed floor, at speckless desk and chairs, at the shiny window-panes with a pot of geranium on the sill below, half-expecting to hear the woodcutters come laughing and slapping one another's back in a great hurrah, down a narrow street where the air was still chilled from mountain snows. It made her rise from her chair with a swing to walk eagerly about the room, examining a ledger and a quill pen as if they had some new and exciting significance. She picked up the pen and, dabbing it in ink, began writing her name: *Gerda van Ifort,* before she noticed what she was putting down. She laughed out loud at that, which brought Willy to see what the joke was. "But, do you know"—he tapped the signature—"you do seem more like *her* to-day, and not one speck like Ma'am Whetstone."

She grinned back at him. "It's the truth that I don't feel a bit Ma'amish to-day. There's something about the Dutch neatness of your office that makes me remember how it was to be that van Ifort brat. Another thing, when I first knew you, you were a little the older and never let me forget it. After I married Yarbrough, though, I was the mistress of the place. Now in here you're smarter about figures and business than I am, so once again I don't feel so biggety around you."

She reached out and drummed on a polished pane.

He remembered how miserable he had felt over her betrothal to Yarbrough. He looked at her standing there in an oblong of clear light and saw how keen with youngness the bones of her face were, how springy her shoulders, how her waist was girdled by its own muscles, giving the hips below a swing, keeping her limbs held in a nice balance. He brushed the back of his hands over his face to rouse his eyes from their dreaming stare. There was no use letting her touch the tender spots again.

2

It was the dinner hour at the Academy, and Lucinda, who had come on a visit to Gracey, was sharing the meal, which was a jolly one. The older girls and boys looked forward to this hour of give-and-take talk with their headmaster. They spoke of fishing and hunting, they twitted any pair that was casting sheep's eyes at one another, but their main interest was in Danley. They tried to trip him up on some point about the classics, in the speciously literal manner of youth; they argued with him about the virtues of the Episcopal and the Baptist God; they asked him curious questions about England and kings; but they thought they knew all about Yankees and didn't want to listen to his say about them.

Lucinda saw all this, as would any visitor to the Academy, but she perceived something else as well: the number of girls who had lost their plastic young hearts to him. They were of all types, pretty and plain, either enthralled in complete hero-worship or merely holding him up as an ideal for their current beau to emulate. The one that Cinda had displaced when she came to table was a special case, however. She had barely eaten a mouthful after she had been moved down the board out of Danley's radius, but the few she did take she gulped so hungrily that Lucinda could guess at the years of undernourishment on grits and salt pork the child had endured before coming here to this more ample fare. Lucinda could not help studying the girl whenever the latter was not scowling at her. "Danley had better have a care about that one," she concluded, "or he'll have a sorry mess on his hands." However, she was distracted from the morbid worship displayed in the girl's face presently by some hilarity nearer her.

Late that afternoon Danley joined her for an hour's talk about the news from the Stand. Little by little as they sat in the visiting-parlour their words dropped off into silences; they had lived so long under the same roof they felt no call to crowd out a quiet with useless words.

Danley remarked after an easy silence: "You've improved."

"That's praise indeed, since you've come to be so plied with feminine worship."

"Oh, that?" He glanced sidewise at her. "It's not easy to manage girls at the gushing age."

"But the one I'd look out for is that one who looks like a thunder-cloud."

"Sara? Yes, she's a care. I want to help her to prepare to earn an independent living, but—this is a caddish thing to say—but there are times when I can barely stoop over her shoulder to correct a problem, her clothes smell so sour from being cast-offs." He glanced at Lucinda, abashed at his squeamishness.

"You take the cake, Danley!" she laughed. "Smell, not morals, protects that poor girl."

"I hadn't thought of it that way, but now I do have to admit that the reason I'm always helping little Dolly Walthour in and out of her hood is because her hair is as fresh as rain."

"Which," asked Cinda, "is Dolly?"

"The real young one that squeals behind her two hands."

"Oh, that one?" Lucinda was about to dismiss her, but Danley added, chuckling: "She squealed the one time I kissed her. It rather dropped me flat—gave her the odds after all."

"You kiss them?" demanded Lucinda.

"Why, yes, a few of them I have," he admitted, remembering how their young excitement had touched him—their rather groping little gestures and their eager breaking away, to rush, he felt ruefully certain, and confide his indiscretion to their mates. He had worried about these infrequent episodes causing some unruliness in the school at large, but things had continued to run smoothly. And when a girl brushed too close over his study chair, her hair tickling his neck, he couldn't control all of his impulses. Accordingly he addressed Lucinda stiffly. "I'm not precisely a mummy."

"So I am discovering," she remarked, "though you always took good care to keep the schoolmaster pretty well uppermost around me." She studied him with brightening eyes, and he tried to stare her down, which resulted in their looks clashing, then locking. He leaned over and twisted her far shoulder towards him. She did not flinch.

"Do you care," he demanded, "how I feel, and about whom?" His eyes probed hers, back into the thoughts behind their glossiness, trying to get at that matter about Jerard. He had been part of the scene that had sent the man away, and he had never inwardly accepted the news of his death, which others had taken for granted. Now he would not let her drop her glance from his searching, even for a second in which she might dissemble. He had no wish to make her break any covenant of silence she had formed with her husband, but he wanted her to grasp by some sign his complete if undetailed knowledge. "I understand your situation," he said slowly at last. "But your life must continue. Are you ever going to make, and act upon, a decision?"

"I am going," she replied, thinking of her own denunciation of the idea of any dubious widowhood, "to take a step, when I am ready. Shortly. When a full year is up, I will put off all signs of mourning, no matter how the county tongues wag."

"But I," he reminded her, "will be the one to *know* that that year will be as long as five in this case. It would all come to the same impasse."

Suddenly she said recklessly, scorning any subterfuge of silence such as that which encased Gracey: "You mean that you and I will know full well that any step I was contemplating about a man——"

"About *me*," he put in quickly. Though he had never mentioned it before, he intended now that she should understand he meant to claim her, whether or no. "Our so-called marriage vows will bind nevertheless. I doubt if you will ever escape me," he challenged her, "however *un*binding the ceremony."

"I will still be the lawful wife of Jerard Malone," she taunted him, "no matter to what pact we agree."

He pulled her waist close against his. "Since you were never cut out for wifehood, I think you will like our terms."

Her eyes went pitch-dark with excitement as she thought: "I am a wanton for fair!" She liked the sensation that, if Jerard could come to the door there and signal her, she would follow him miles into the wilds of Texas, and yet that she was this instant enjoying matching her power with this man. "I want to match feelings with more men before I die!"

She buried her face inside his coat sleeve, letting loose a low chuckle, for no other marriage could have caught her fancy so, after the full force of her union with Malone. No other except just this one, with an edge all about it of intrigue. She stretched one ankle out backward and felt the high arch of her instep flexing. She was *alive* all right!

3

Joby sat on the rustic bench built around the trunk of the water oak on the bluff. Below her the river was coffee colour, and the bushes sprang fresh green out of banks after the rain. Her feet felt a little damp through her soles, but she was going to stay out here in the calm of the day that was slipping away over water. She had discovered that she managed life better if she did some of the little things she wanted to instead of hanging on C. D.'s peculiarities. She had gained the courage to move in her own quiet way from the memory of how Armand had felt tender concern for her. It gave her a proud grace of bearing that exacted a certain deference even from C. D. She did not try to test it beyond its limit, but occasionally she chose to say: "*I* think *I* shall go over to Tuscaloosa and pay your Cousin Bet a visit, while I select some new dress patterns." Or "C. D., I'd take it as a great favour if you did *not* bring Thad Pinckney around when he is in his cups." And she went to Tuscaloosa, or Thad did not come, as the case might be. Nor was there any fuss raised, perhaps because she was always particularly gracious to C. D. after carrying some trifling point of her own. She might bring him a new beaver hat from Tuscaloosa, showing him how to brush his hair in a flourish at the temples beneath its brim, remarking: "I'd hate to have a bald husband like Nettie's Nat will become." Then she'd touch his shock of hair as if it were some live pet, sending little scallops of pleasure through his scalp.

He really began to eye her with favour after she put Nettie in her place. He and Nettie had always bickered and backbitten, each being jealous of the other's gaining some extra indulgence from their parents; and after Nettie finally married the prosperous Nat, it irked C. D.'s very soul to see her set up in her own ménage. He and Joby had continued to live with his parents under the testy dominance of the Captain and the perpetual nagging of Miz Melburne. C. D.'s bullying of Joby had been partially the result of never having been able to call himself his own master. Now Nettie's newly acquired independence galled him till he caught himself wishing that her fast-trotting carriage bays would run away and break her neck.

Usually Joby paid small attention to his ranting against his sister, merely pasting a commiserating smile on her face and allowing him to run on until he talked himself out. But yesterday Nettie had made the mistake of flicking Joby on the raw. Joby and C. D. had been idling on the veranda with Nettie, waiting for Nat to come and fetch her. Nettie had exhausted her boasting about her newest possessions and found Joby inattentive.

"Didn't you hear," reiterated Nettie, "that I had one serving-maid that never goes barefooted, not even in the kitchen?"

"She'll get corns," predicted Joby indifferently.

"Oh, you needn't try to take the wind out of my sails!"

"I couldn't," remarked Joby, "with Nat to puff them up with his bluster."

"You're just jealous because I have everything my heart was set on. And because I had a *decent-length* courtship that proved my beau wanted to win me. Not just to grab anything that came handy in the shuffle."

C. D. turned livid at this mention of his peculiar marriage, but Joby said blandly: "Then how do you account for Nat's being so cut-up the night Lutie Caraway sent him a note with a rosebud instead of running away with him to Columbus? His mother said he was so out of his head the next day that he gave away two extra pounds of sugar because he couldn't weigh right." Joby looked at Nettie pleasantly, as if, now that that was settled, they could talk about something else. But Nettie flew into the house to finish out her wait, promising herself that Nat would pay a pretty penny for this withheld folly about Lutie.

Meanwhile C. D. touched Joby's hand diffidently. "You certainly told her off good and smart."

She patted his hand back. "Well, she needn't think she can poke fun at us."

In their bedroom later at night he had tried his best to be gentle—bringing her a glass of water with a spoonful of brandy afterwards, saying: "Here, this will brace you up. I'll try—to be easier next time."

She had swallowed the brandy and it had helped, had made her drowsy enough to sleep instead of lying quivering. Once when she had roused fitfully, he had asked: "Want anything? Can I get anything for you?"

Now she sat and watched the tan river turn pewter as dark came over it, and her bones grew little marrows of chill inside them. "Poor C. D.," she thought, "it's too bad about our wrong start. Now he can't seem to get on the right track, hard as he tries." She was sorry about that, for she was fairly happy these days. Just not having quarrels was all she asked. Almost.

CHAPTER THIRTY-SIX

It was but nine o'clock in the morning, yet Gerda was through her household work, and that stumped her. She couldn't believe there wasn't something else she had to do, something she had forgotten. She stood in the ell and scratched one shoe-toe over a board that was wearing rough; a sorry piece of timber it had turned out to be, among all the sound. She passed her palm impatiently over first her chin, then her forehead, trying to recollect what it was she had left out this morning. But she could call off all the things she'd tended to, and nothing seemed missing. She stepped back to the kitchen door and called over her shoulder: "Pokey, Aunty Pheaby, is there anything you want me to see to?"

"Nothin' a-tall, Miz Gerda," Pokey spoke up for them.

"Umm. . . . You know I told Caney to sort the elderberry blossoms for the bitter wine. She's got fingers that wouldn't brush dust off a moth." Gerda still stood uncertainly, eyeing them over her shoulder a little suspiciously, as if she thought maybe they wanted to get her out of the way in order to talk quarter doings that they disliked to have her to hear. But Pokey said cheerfully: "I'm gwine to the spring-house direckly to see if they're chillin' that whippin' cream right. You can forget your frettin' and run along."

Gerda took a sauntering step or two back up the ell, then went into the front hall because there was nothing for her to do back there. She passed the chambers, all swept and aired, and saw that the youngest house gal had even stuck some jonquils in a stiff yellow cuff on the parlour table. She went out on the porch, feeling good for a moment to think of how everything was set just so behind her. After she had stood there a little while, long enough to let her eyes drift over the trees and down into the cup of the lower sky, then up into the bowl of it far beyond, she brought her gaze back dutifully to hunt for small untidy things on the porch floor. There weren't any. Out of habit she started to move towards her low rocker, where she always took her rest when she could get time for it, but when she reached it she merely touched the ladder-back and started the chair rollicking to and fro. She didn't want to sit in it, she wanted to be *doing*.

Her eyes, darting, caught sight of some everlasting fallen chinaberry blossoms in a heap skipped over by the broom of the yard darky. Her skirts made a scurrying sound as she hurried over, catching up the porch broom, which was handy. She swung her elbows in scythe-like sweeps as she cleared the mess, and watched the clean-scratched path her broom straws left. She was doing a good job of it! Then a breeze riffled, and a pelt of lavender blossoms came down to clutter the ground again.

She flung the broom from her, so that the handle jumped three times. " What a goose I am, simply killing time! I never thought I'd see a day with *nothing to do*!" It was like being halted in her tracks. Stopped in her orbit! She looked around almost fearfully, as if she expected creation to fall apart.

Slowly she rolled down the grey calico sleeves of her work-dress.

Gerda and Turber went fishing together all the rest of that day, with a dinner snack in a basket.

" Did you put in plenty of chicken gizzards for me?" he asked.

" A plenty, but you needn't think you can pig them all up from me."

" Not if I get the extra one, if they come out uneven?"

" We'll see," she grumbled, while he did a hop, laughing impudently. He was never scared stiff of sassing Ma'am like her other younger children.

It was just the right sort of day for fishing. The sun came down out of the sky as sweet as honey, yet there was a breeze lifting the leaves up in layers. They came to the pasture where the colts were.

" See that tar-black one?" asked Gerda. " I'm going to break him for myself."

" Papa won't let *you* break a colt," he scoffed.

" We'll see about that. I need a stallion to carry me; mares are either too poky or too twitchy."

They walked on, their fishing-poles over their shoulders, slashing the air.

After their dinner they fished some more. The catch lay like silver plopped in the wooden bucket which they had set in the shade. Earlier they had trolled the running part of the stream, but later they had finished up where the branch widened out to look like a small millpond. Now Gerda sat on the bank watching Turber cavorting in the water. He had begged so hard to swim that though she felt a rawness behind the sunshine, she had given in. He had taken her sunbonnet and held it over himself to reach the water decently, then hurled it back at her, shouting with laughter. But her face had worn only dry grins, for she was wishing she were a child like him, or a child such as she had used to be.

She recalled how she had made Pokey tramp clear up to the Mountain Lake with her . . . she remembered the blue cool shock of the water and its skylike immensity. She felt the pebbly grating of the rocks, and how her body had reached out and filled up itself until it touched the water all over. She had never before felt quite so *whole*. Like more than a person, like the reason there was a world, built in a ball around her. She had dived, deep in a globe of pure element, without any objects, not even a weed stalk to strike through that infinity.

Then she had come back up out of the water and stood naked with her head bent back for her eyes to hold the sky. And the universe had been in her chest, bursting apart her breast-bones!

When she and Turber reached home that evening, the family was at the supper-table, and Will Bee sprang up angrily to light into Turber. "When I traded you my good fishing-pole, I was supposed to get your guinea hen, Peck. Then when I went to fetch her into my coop, I found that a weasel had sucked her neck and she's been dead two days!"

"But it was Peck just the same," chuckled Turber.

"You're a cheater!" hollered Will Bee, diving after him. Turber ducked and Gerda staved off Will Bee. But instead of taking Will Bee's side fairly, she laughed too. "That'll teach you to look sharper, Will, next time you make a trade." Yarbrough whistled in astonishment at this from Gerda the just. He saw that she had her hair in a wet plait down behind her shoulders and that her cheeks were as bright as peaches.

2

It became difficult for people to keep up with Gerda's whereabouts, and Pokey, who had to take the load of the responsibility when her mistress was missing, began to be exasperated, but Gerda didn't let that worry her. Hadn't Pokey complained of her behaviour constantly back in those other carefree days? Well then, her grumbling merely struck the right note. When Gerda played truant from her household she often let the graceless Turber come along, but more frequently she set out alone. She was rediscovering herself.

To-day she should by rights have been seeing to the jam to be made from the small yellow plums that had come early, but she had remarked carelessly to Pokey and Aunty Pheaby: "You two could make the stuff in your sleep. Why should I parboil myself over it? I'd rather be outdoors."

"S'posin' we was all to go on picnics all the time? What would become of things?" demanded Pokey with asperity.

"I don't care! It's my turn to run loose now!" replied Gerda. "I've stuck at my knitting long enough." She flung out of the house.

The dirt was gold to-day beneath her feet, making such a glare that it was easier to look right up at the sky with its sun. Then shortly that blue grew too dazzling also. It was a relief to feel the shade close over her as she entered the woods. She took off her shoes so her toes could press into the sweet dampness of the grapevine path.

She was wondering. . . .

There had been this girl, Gerda van Ifort, going at life with a reckless rush. She had been so sure what it was like then—to be herself. She had known exactly how her tongue curled at the taste of apple-juice. She had felt the shape of the land she looked out upon from behind the sockets of her eyes; it had not escaped from her gaze into any blur of other people's activities. She had been able to take hold of a tree limb and receive the message from the grooves of its bark through her fingers, up her arms to her elbows, so that a tree was something she knew, vital with its own living. She had been aware of how her hair and neck and other members added up into the single body that was *Gerda,* who felt these responses to *things.*

Then with a rush the years had swept down upon her, bringing the coif of wifehood, the bosom of motherhood, the gait of a mistress putting order into her household. The time had gone by deliberately, yet with no pause to break the hours apart, to permit her to garner her activities so they could be assimilated by the person of that early Gerda. Rather she had left off being so much the woman and had become a source of domestic simples and remedies for a family to follow until together they achieved a state of existence known as Home.

She had been engulfed by no resentment at this. It was a thing she had wanted to do: to meet both danger and tedium with strength, to weld parts into a whole, to feel that days and nights, age and birth, revolved at her behest into a succession of time and feeling that made up Living.

Yet now suddenly, as the pressure of the needs of others receded from her, she had an unreasonable eagerness to let her energies drain back from all these diverse channels into one. She thought: "I shall have to learn to feel all over again!" Or not so much to feel as to distil the various senses of her feelings into a real consciousness. Not a vague state of light, as different from a general state of darkness that was death, but a leading up of many sharp strains of *knowing* into one blinding-bright point where shone her own being.

3

The year was now up since services had been held in memory of Jerard Malone, and one summer's day Lucinda had ridden over to see Gerda and apprise her of her and Danley's plans. But when she came into the ell Pokey said in a disgruntled tone: "Yo' ma ain't here, as usual. She's gone off in direction of de millpond." Lucinda set out for there. Walking through the woods that blanketed the rise leading to the pond, she was aware of how dead and airless it was; then when she came out suddenly into the hole of yellow sunshine where the pond was, everything shot forward, clear and unprotected. Lucinda stopped.

For there on a jutting stone in the centre of the pool was Gerda, all stark for swimming! She must have been in the water before, as her body was glistening. Lucinda tried to look away. Ma'am should be a person in a calico wrapper, with a face and hands and shoes, but not a torso. The sight of her mother's body was almost a blow. Yet even while Lucinda was repelled by the impact of it, she was also hypnotized by its splendour.

Gerda was standing planted on feet that were large but shapely, their arches making a fine cave beneath them. Her legs went up as sturdy as tree-trunks, and her waist was supple, above hips as smoothly rounded as melons. Her breasts were cupped high on her chest, and her neck arched up proudly into the familiar firm chin. Somehow those known features, seen above that unknown body, had a different cast, as if this woman inhabited a distant world where one spoke in a strange tongue that left an Olympian bell-sound in the air.

Lucinda withdrew into the woods once more with silent haste; she was too awed to approach Gerda now. Yet she was also shaken with shame at being female, for she felt as if all womanhood, in the person of her mother, had been disclosed to a gaping world. She would have to go and walk about their familiar yard, listen for something simple like dogs barking, to reassure herself. "I'll be as bad as Gracey if I don't watch out," she told herself sardonically. It was a good thing Danley was about to cut short her unnatural celibacy.

4

Lucinda and Danley took their vows quietly in the visitors' parlour of his Academy before a few relatives, both of them feeling a greater obligation because of their underlying freedom, to which their guests were not privy. There was no collation afterwards except a round of toasts in home-made wine. Then the pair drove to Top Hill, where they were to make their home, and where Danley was to open the new Bruton Academy, which he and Lucinda had decided upon as the solution for combining his career and her property.

They planned to have the girl pupils sleep in two or three large bedrooms in the mansion itself, while the boys would be quartered in the unused overseer's house in charge of the junior master, who was no longer Page McHugh. The main schoolroom, a slightly improved version of the log "college" where Danley had first tutored the young Whetstones, had to be constructed during the remainder of the warm weather. Even so they could not hope to open the term until late October, and they pressed the family and all available neighbours into service on the building. Although it would be cotton-picking-time shortly, enough people came to assist them to give the undertaking the same air of a protracted frolic that had prevailed when the Rock Wall house was being raised. Lucinda was in her element as hostess, and this time she was not over-keyed by the presence of conflicting cross-currents as she had been at that fateful house party, for she was under no great emotional strain with Danley. He was an amiable companion by day, sweeping everybody along at an enthusiastic pace with his contagious energy.

Though the schoolhouse perforce had to be rustic, he had it set in a grove, and said to Cinda: "If we train vines over it and spare the dogwood, it will be as pretty as a summer-house, which will please the young ladies of the smitten age."

She answered: "You should have listed among the accomplishments to be taught young ladies that they could receive instruction in the art of coquetry from you in your summer-house."

"Well, take care that you leave all that to me. If I catch you trying to teach the lads the companion art of courtship, I'll throttle you." He ended by laughing brazenly into her eyes. That was one of the things about him that pleased her most, his personal effrontery of her. She liked his baiting of her senses as contrasted with his constant scholarly endeavours. Also she admitted his canniness about trifles, such as the vines pleasing prospective patrons. His versatility stirred her.

He was yet another man at night when he became her lover. Then his face became sharp-shadowed, the contours pinched by the fierceness of his desire. His light voice dropped low until it startled her from his throat. The man's true station in life was that of lover. Even his feeling for the ring of poetry and the clash of ancient heroes had risen from his sighting Eros beckoning between the lines. It was an urge to let loose this god's power in the breasts of the young that made him try to drive the golden classic arrow deep into their senses. And the feeling that he gave to Lucinda and made her share with him had about it much of the keenness that had marked the games in which Greek girls and boys had vied. It made Lucinda exult to herself: "How young I am! How imperishable!"

In the mornings afterwards, when she moved about her room, attending to her attire, she walked with a quick spring and was careful not to stand and muse: "Jerard looked thus out of that window," or "Jerard sat always in that chair." For she had given herself over to living newly, not to remembering Jerard.

There was only one person whom she felt had a more abundant life than herself, and that was Gerda. She seldom thought of Gerda as her mother now, for the woman had become too vivid since that day when she had seen all of her. Gerda broke through her clothes with a quick stride of limbs, but more than that, her moods burst out of the accustomed mould of her face and showed the woman in flux—doing or laughing or arguing in a way that stirred the very atmosphere with her force.

To-day, in October, Gerda was seated on a log where the chips were flying, watching the final whirl of activity attendant upon the completion of Danley's schoolhouse. The cool had come earlier this year; some of the leaves were curling up yellow, and others were sprigs of red. Frost was a long way off, but she felt as if it were already there, the air was cut with such a tang. Her eyes were on Tom Two and Joachim, who were matching themselves against each other splitting logs for puncheon desks.

Gerda thought: "They don't like each other the way they used to. A pity, for they were thick as cream before, and it was Wayne neither of them could abide. It must be that little Lutie chit that has come between them. I expect she'll marry Tom Two, though she has a leaning towards Joachim. Wish he could get the best of that weakness of his, pilfering. There's never a grain of sense to the things he thieves, except when it's wearing finery." She shook her head disapprovingly, but eyed his big brown beauty leniently.

Just then there was a pounding across the ground behind her, and Will Bee and Turber came up, heading a troop of boys including three new lads in the county who had just been entered at the Academy. They were followed by the new-comers' father, a leathery, witty man named David Walthour. Turber yelled: "These ones here won't believe that you're a good shot with a rifle. They said they never heard of a lady who could shoot sharp. And you'll have to show 'em else I'll have to fight with all three of them."

"Ho!" exclaimed Gerda, who liked to display her shooting prowess. "That's easy. Let's all go to the stable door where the knot-holes are plentiful, and I'll show them how I 'thread the needle.'" They followed in her wake. "Turber," she ordered, "you'd better duck in and make sure the stock are all safe out of the way in their stalls."

He scunnied through a little dog-door and told one of Tid's piccaninnies to keep the animals out of range. Then he hurried back to see the fun. The excited boys were all jogging about Gerda. She picked up Will Bee's rifle and slid its slick barrel down between her fingers, then tested the feel of its stock against her shoulder. "I could do better with my own, but this'll do." She cradled her cheek against the worn wood of the stock for a second and sighted several imaginary targets. Everything became quiet so you could feel the wall of pines in back of the scene. Then she pulled the trigger and the gun exploded, the bullet whistling as clean through a small knot-hole as it had through the rest of the air.

"Whew!" cried the strange boys and the man.

"Go," Gerda told Will Bee, "and dig that lead out of the plank where it's bedded in the back wall of the stable. We can't waste lead for fun even yet." The new boys gaped respectfully. Walthour looked out over the country, then back at her as if comparing the two. "You resemble Alabama," he said finally.

She said nothing; she knew that. Malone had told her long ago. Glancing up, she saw Yarbrough riding into the lot on his horse and hurried forward to meet him. He dismounted, very dusty and more tired than she had seen him since the thick of cotton-picking. "What's the matter?" she inquired.

"Nothing, I'm just dogged out." He tried to give her a smile, but his lips were tuckered too. "Who's that? Oh, Walthour. He's taken up a fine piece of land not far from us." He moved over to meet his new neighbour.

Walthour offered his hand heartily. "I'm well satisfied that we came down here. Only I had no idea what surprises awaited us. This mansion here, with its school attached, and then your daughter here," he motioned to Gerda, "who was entertaining us with her marksmanship."

A hoot of laughter went up from Will Bee and Turber. "Papa's daughter, oh glory!" Yarbrough added his own shout of merriment. Walthour gave them all a dumbfounded stare.

Finally Gerda's words broke through the hubbub: "I'm Mistress Bruton's mother, and this gentleman's wife."

Walthour flushed, but Yarbrough chuckled. "Well, sir, I don't blame you for taking me for her father. As a matter of fact, I'm old enough."

Gerda interrupted: "No, the trouble is I've never behaved myself like a lady, rollicking or ranting around with the boys, until the kindest thing a person could say is that I'm not old enough to know better. Either that or half-witted."

Both men cut her short. Walthour said: "You can't be very old." And Yarbrough squeezed her fingers in a quick interlocking of his own. "You'd better stay young for both of us, I feel so mortal tired."

Gerda's glance hurried over each of his features, noting the strain at the corners of his eyes and an uncertain shape to his mouth as if he didn't know whether to hold it grim against fatigue or let it rest easy. "If you'll excuse us, Mr. Walthour, I'll make my husband go up and rest. He's had a hard day." They moved off together, and Gerda was glad when they gained the side yard where the falling shadows lay across their movements, obscuring them somewhat from sight. She could feel Yarbrough leaning against her arm.

The next evening when she saw he still did not look rested, although he had stayed still all day, she began to question him. "Are you sure nothing has gone wrong over at Rock Wall? Hadn't I better go back and tend to my end of things? I've been playing truant quite a while."

"No," he said, "there's nothing wrong. Pokey is managing the household and the quarters fine. And the crops were bigger than I expected. It's just—I don't know what's come over me." He lifted his hands, then dropped them listlessly. He thought of his fields boiling over with white, the way they had been but a short time back. Yet when he searched for the pride this had always evoked in him, it simply was not there. This gave him a curiously hollow feeling, rather as if his spirit had departed from his body, leaving a dry shell.

"I don't seem to have any gumption left," he told her. "I'm weary, weary. I never felt this way before in my life." He stared at the wall as if its blankness sufficed. His shoulders slumped, his whole frame seemed oppressed by lethargy. Gerda knelt down beside him swiftly, taking one of his leaden hands between her two pulsing ones, as if to pour her own vitality into him. When he spoke again, his tone was still one of despair: "I can't make out what ails me. Here I've bent my whole life towards this end, worked you like an ox, tried to shape a state for my purpose, sweated, slept, eaten, lived, killed even, to gain this victory of cotton! And here we are, the whole country coming out of depression and hard times, and here I am at my peak! I ought to want to sing and shout. But all I feel"—a tired breath went out of him—"is a hundred years old."

"Drat that man Walthour for his clumsy mistake," thought Gerda, "calling him my father." But this went deeper than that. She rose and moved around the edge of the room till she gained a window. Carefully she looked out of it instead of at him as she spoke, tentatively. "Maybe if we went on a little trip, perhaps back up in the hill country, it might do you good. If you could forget about the plantation for a while—I've stopped thinking about it every waking minute myself, and I feel as rambunctious as a colt. It might help you too, to leave things behind. You know you haven't really rested for twenty years."

He glanced at her, startled. "*Twenty?* Why, you're right! We'll go!" He held out his hand as if to seal a pact.

5

They set out next day on horseback, with a few garments in their saddle-bags, and their rifles for hunting. They had no special destination, except that it was not to be the home of any of their friends, where Yarbrough would be taxed with discussion of the problems of ruling over many acres and several score of humans. They simply headed north and west, into that section where plainer folk lived in a humbler way. They enjoyed their progress. There was the rattle of nuts falling; there was that most aged smell in the world, the scent from the caked leaf-mould reeking up like incense; there was air thinned out by the oncoming leanness of winter, until it shot through the lungs more swiftly; there was the sunlight thrusting through the trees in pale gold lances. . . .

They stopped the first night with a lone man in a hut and lean-to. He was too taciturn and they were too tired to exchange more than civilities. They slept like logs in the shakedown beds he provided, and ate heartily of the coarse breakfast. The damp was still seeping up from the ground as they rode off, with a slat-ribbed hound trying to make up its mind whether to follow them.

This day was much the same as the one before, except that the trail became more rocky and something about the set of the trees did not look familiar. They did not feel that the forest here was a kindly shield for comfortable plantation homes; the small cabins they came upon abruptly in the density looked as if they could be wrenched loose from their perches with one quick twist of storm wind. Still they were made comfortable enough each night in one of them, and each day Gerda noted how Yarbrough trotted his mount more briskly when they set out.

Then one day they came upon a wider stretch of clearing where some woman had kept tended a Cherokee rose. Under the house between the pillars on which it was built, the ground was swept as clear as the yard; and the two lone shade trees left standing were girdled with whitewash. As they dismounted, a woman in a starched sunbonnet came from around back, with an apron full of eggs. She greeted them with an open smile, more cordial than they had received from most of these dour hill people. Yarbrough asked if they could pass a night and a day or so there. As he spoke, several children came out one by one and drifted into a staring row, the littlest sucking its fingers. The woman, who said her name was Maria Somers and that her husband was called Jacob, told them she'd be proud to have them stop as long as they pleased. "You've come lucky too. We've just killed a hog, and our fall turnips have sprouted a nice mess of greens. Also our sweet potatoes seem to've sugared down earlier this year because of the cool."

Gerda noticed how there was more of an *r* rolling through the woman's speech, up here nearer the Tennessee line.

Maria showed them into the good room, which was much like the one Gerda had had in her first wilderness cabin, except that it had a wide two-poster built-in bed like their own present one instead of bunks. There was a stack of fine patchwork quilts piled in one corner, and Gerda went over to lift their edges and peer at their patterns. Maria coloured with pleasure at her praise. "I used to be a seamstress at a big house near Chattanooga before I married Jacob and we emigrated down here."

Yarbrough put down his saddle-bags and went back out on the narrow slanting porch, his eyes instinctively searching out the fields over behind a thin line of trees. When Gerda joined him, he had dropped down on a seat, his hands linked laxly between his knees. "This air up here is a lot easier to breathe," he told her, drawing some more into his lungs.

The hills were beginning to pile up in blue masses beneath a no-coloured sky. The shadows quit showing in clear outlines across the yard, as the whole ground became grey. The life of the little farm was reduced to such simple ways that there was only a mild stir as evening chores came on. The children slipped about, gathering up the downy biddies that had strayed, tucking them under the wings of a few sleepy, clucking hens. The several critters in the pens were easily milked or fed, and the sounds from the kitchen were unflurried. Gerda went to see if she could help, and Yarbrough, spying the man who must be Jacob coming across the field with a mule, went to meet him.

Supper was not so silent as most that they had shared along the way. The children, overcoming their shyness, became pert and bright-spoken, while the parents were still lively with youth. Maria had not a whine in her, and Jacob was eager to tell about the great things he expected to do with this patch of land as his boys grew old enough to help. His problems were so simple that Yarbrough could give him advice easily, without straining himself. Gerda helped clear away, but Maria dwelt little on household tasks; instead she wanted to hear what kind of gowns the ladies were wearing nowadays, about the mail-coaches that ran so frequently from Columbus to Montgomery, and the carriages the rich folks were able to ride in again, now that the roads were better. "Jacob was a teamster, but I think he's caught on to farming real good. No telling how far he'll go."

"Indeed there isn't," agreed Yarbrough from over Gerda's shoulder, and Maria flushed as if she had been commended by her former employer. Yarbrough took Gerda's arm. "Come on out, you two, to the porch. The sugar moon's up again, and Jacob's getting out his fiddle to give us a tune."

The four of them grouped on the steps, Jacob tucking his fiddle against his ribs. The children sat in a row back along the wall like five small cotton-tail rabbits, the youngest already beginning to nod. Jacob played sassy things at first, his fingers seeming to pick nonsense out of the strings. The children gurgled with the fun of it, and his foot kept tapping; but presently his time began to lag, and he waited between pieces. The oldest child pulled the youngest up by its armpits and dragged her back inside. There was a shuffling of bare soles over boards, a whimper, and one clear treble: " 'Night, Mammy and Pappy." Maria reached back and caught the last straggler around its knees for an embrace, then let it go. There were snuffles from inside the family room, and a thumping on pallets. Yarbrough and Jacob were holding still, with that removed air of waiting which men take on when women and the young are disturbing the hour.

Presently quiet dropped down over them. Below the bottom step in the yard the moon had put the print of the nearest tree—clear. Jacob lifted his fiddle, this time under his chin violin-wise, and began to play something soft. Yarbrough leaned forward intently, trying to name the song to himself. He could not place the melody, except that it went back before his sister Lucey had married, and it was both shy and provoking. He half-hummed:

Blue-thin was the light,
Gone was the night—

He could recall no more of it. He only knew that long ago when he was a lad he had stood with his shoulders pressed narrowly back against one of the columns of the gallery of the Home Place and heard this one song teasing the night air—rising, then fading—eluding him when most he had sought to capture its vagrant beauty. He had stood with his spine shuddering against that pillar, in an ecstasy of frustration that the young know for a promise, and vowed: " I shall win *her* some day, her and the moon!" And not known whom he meant, or why, except some wild frail thing that cannot come save out of the icy crust of youth, covering an emptiness not yet filled by the plenitude of ripening years, the acres squared off into harvests, the woman holding the child in her womb, the house weighted down by its roof. . . .

He turned to look at Gerda with the deep resentment of one betrayed by her fecundity, but he did not find such a Gerda. He saw instead a silhouetted Gerda pinioned against a rough-hewn post of this shanty porch. He saw from the lift of her head that she, too, was seeking for something missed. And he could tell that Jacob was trying to draw song out with his bow to keep that skirted shadow there, in the light cast up by the moon.

In their room they did not light the candle, so bright it was. They moved wraith-like. Yarbrough leaned out the window and said softly: "Are we finding something we had forgotten—together—too late?"

She answered: "The thing is that we have found it." She had not ever dreamed in so minor a key as he. Her desires had come upon her with a quick, importunate rush, and he had been there almost before she had burst out of the pod of girlhood, to garner the fruit from her. She had not lingered over her flowering, treasuring so faint a thing as fragrance.

She said now: "This is so beautiful," and meant their release into a spot in a wood where they could have each other, man and woman.

But he pushed his face far out into the night softness. There were yearnings he wished to share, there was a splendour he felt she embodied, there were regrets shading off into dim corners of his being, there was something he would never finish because he had never truly started it save in his fancy.

He shivered a little and returned to where she stood. She put a hand up to his shoulder and he could feel the drag of passion in it.

6

They slept deeply. Usually they woke only after the sun was well up. They tried not to trouble their hosts, but they kept themselves apart from any real concern with the industries of the little farm. Gerda lent a nimble hand in the kitchen yet never corrected the makeshift methods Maria employed. And Yarbrough, while he shared his planting lore, never went into the late, almost plucked fields. Their real concern was to watch tranquilly, while day came up and night went down.

One dawn Gerda felt a splinter of light prick her eyelids and she wakened. She went over to the open-shuttered window. The mist was curling off the ground in silver plumes, showing the earth in spots of mauve and purple dirt beneath. The sky was flattened down so low that the clouds were pressed out into long elliptical gull-wings. Then as she watched, Gerda saw the wings blur slightly and become an oval lake of light. The gold mellowed into primrose. The silveriness began to condense into grey pipe-smoke that dispersed, showing bushes. The magic phantoms dissolved into an earth with a sky overhead, country with trees growing out of it, and the weather that they would have next day.

She crept back into bed, where the sheets had grown a little cold, thinking that she sheltered something carved inside of her by the daybreak.

Most days they walked a great deal through the woods together. They rooted out strange plants with their fingers, to discover what they were and how they grew. They built their own barbecue pit of round stones and cooked many a midday meal of wild hare. They never asked each other questions about how they felt. Yarbrough had some sad thing he could not define living within him, which he would have to face when he went back. Yet he and Gerda kept hoping that they were undoing all his trouble by relaxing deep into this autumn season. A day came every now and then when he stood aside from himself and reckoned up things: the sharp tick of moments of delight, the slow swing of hours of rest, the drift of contemplation. He wondered how lasting was their healing.

Still he washed his face in a cold basin in the morning, ate large meals from a scoured table, watched hens pecking across the yard after fallen sunflower seed, and did not mention this sense of fatigue that was creeping up beside him, becoming his constant companion.

Gerda sent him off many days alone, to lie belly-down beside a stream gulping water that ran up his nose, or to roll over on rusty pine needles until they stuck through his jacket and scratched. Little discomforts that he had not noticed as a boy irked him now and spoiled outdoor freedom, when she was not there to fend for his comfort. But often he willed himself to lie still and make a cove of his hand to blow a partridge call, *pee-whoo, whoo,* and wait for it to fall down from the sky again.

When he came back to the house she always had something ready to rest him.

7

Their last evening ended in a fiddling-contest and dance, with all the folks from miles around gathered there. They used the hard level yard to dance on, and the dust pounded up in a bright powder in the lightwood torchlight. Most of the fiddlers jigged their tunes, but every now and then Jacob sent a sweet crying note through it all. Then Gerda, catching it, stopped stamping her heels and glided for a moment, or stood still with her skirts clenched up in her hands, searching out Yarbrough.

He had started treading the measures called, but he soon grew too tired and went to lean against a tree, watching. Gerda seemed to him to shoot about in the dance. But finally her billowing skirts began to droop, and she wove her way towards him. " I don't want to hurt their feelings, but I'm tired to death," she claimed. " Maybe we could say good-night."

He lounged a step or two forward, holding her elbow. " Good-night, all. My wife and I have to be up early and off on a long day's journey. So if you will excuse us we will retire." No one paid much attention to them, out of the screech of the fiddles and the hum-in-the-head of whisky; still Yarbrough thought Maria and Jacob might recall it to-morrow and appreciate this show of manners. He led Gerda up the badly-placed teetering front steps and pushed open their door into a little hollow of removed quiet. She stood in the centre for a moment, regaining her breath and her balance from the dancing. Then she pulled off her frock and her kirtle and almost dived into the bed. He followed swiftly and discovered he was no longer tired.

She placed her palms against his chest and bent her head back so that he could see the white of her teeth. The sight of her was that of a strange woman. He closed his eyes and took her, in a sightless hour—a blind space in time, such as men disavow by day.

But when the blindness had dissolved, he lost his victory, the mystery faded from his feeling, the woman was his wife, ready to share sleep with him in a quilt-covered bed.

He turned and hid his face in the pillow away from her, desolate.

CHAPTER THIRTY-SEVEN

After their return home Yarbrough and Gerda adopted an evening custom of stopping in their own room in front of the fire before supper while Gerda drank a glass of wine, Yarbrough one of brandy. They sat cosily watching the sky outside turn a dashing crimson. Nowadays the mist no longer drifted, but lay like fallen ash over the earth. They talked little of plantation problems, for all activities were slowing down with the approach of the idle winter season. They simply lazed pleasantly until Pokey came in to tell them that supper was ready and they heard the trample of their family walking down the ell.

The table was always alive with banter and quarrelsomeness, and some new crisis was for ever cropping up among the young ones. To-night Turber came and squeezed into the hook of Yarbrough's elbow. "The puppies didn't live, not a one of them. And Foolish II is in a bad way herself. Shade says she's too old."

"By Jupiter!" raged Yarbrough, dumping over his chair as he rose, "I told you and Shade both to keep Foolish shut up when she was in heat! I'm glad the blasted puppies didn't live, to wear her out with suckling." He was off in a furore, to nurse his pet past her danger. Unobtrusive Daniel righted his father's overturned chair.

Gerda glanced around at her family, trying to become used to their looks after her absence, not feeling very settled as yet. Joby and C. D. were here this evening, Joby immaculate in her increasing daintiness, and accepting small services from C. D. as if she were now accustomed to them, which was a good sign to Gerda. Ven, she noticed, kept worrying his knuckles with the clasp of his other hand, glancing out the side window as if he expected a messenger. Gerda tried to recall what horses were racing, and she hoped he hadn't wagered so much that it would make Yarbrough mad if he had to pull Ven out of the hole again.

The meal was all but over when Yarbrough came treading back exhausted, and glowering at Turber. "She'll probably pull through this time, but I'm laying down the law to you; you'll rue the day if you ever take a risk with her again."

"I won't," whimpered Turber, adding artfully: "but she always has such pretty puppies."

"Humph!" grunted Yarbrough. He had an unreasoning fondness for the bitch, who clung to his heels like a shadow, particularly of late. Outsiders were amazed at her comprehension where her master was concerned, but the family took it for granted and were merely aggravated by stumbling over her so often whenever they approached Yarbrough. Gerda was the only one Foolish II gave way before, and that was with an air of injured but forbearing courtesy.

Yarbrough was not allowed even now to finish his delayed meal in peace, for some bickering among the older boys broke out. Wayne said nastily to Tom Two: "Don't let Joachim fool you this time. He can't say that he thought your best ruffled shirt was something no-account, and that he didn't think you wanted to keep it. Do you know what he did with it? Before he tore it to try to make it look old and raggedy? He wore it over courting Lutie Caraway! Trying to cut you out with her! That's what he did."

Tom Two made a guggling sound and grabbed at Joachim's shoulder, but Joachim only smiled his blazing smile that meant danger and, ignoring Tom's hold, slapped Wayne backward out of his chair with his free hand.

Yarbrough thundered: "Silence! Or I'll tan-hide every last one of you! Now, Tom, tell me what the trouble is. I want the straight of it."

Tom Two told him in terse defensive tones about Joachim's purloining his best shirt, while Joachim scarcely seemed to heed what was being said for staring down Wayne, that shifty trouble-maker.

"So," ejaculated Yarbrough, laughing unexpectedly, "it all comes down to that pretty copper-headed gel, eh? Well, I can't settle the real dispute, that depends on who's the gamer man of you two. But I *can* see to it that Joachim eats crow for spoiling your good shirt in a trick against you, Tom. I'll tell you what, he'll have to wear his nightshirt tucked in his breeches, instead of a linen shirt, for a fortnight, to teach him to leave your things hanging in the press."

The other boys all howled with glee, but Gerda felt sorry for the peacock Joachim, whose outstanding virtue as a child had been his great regard for spruceness. She even knew that it must have caused him a pang when he desecrated Tom's good shirt by rending it in an attempt to cover up his guilt. She hoped to trounce Wayne for tattling.

With a scuffling back of chairs they rose and wandered into the closed-off angle of the ell where the fireplace was. Gerda supposed she ought to busy herself with some sitting-task, but idleness was too pleasant, so she continued to sit and study the others. C. D. was respectfully drawing Yarbrough into a discussion of the latest politics and their bearing on cotton. Hans was talking to Joachim in a corner, trying to divert the culprit's mind from his punishment. Hans, though as honest as broad daylight himself, had always taken Joachim's part against any condemnation. "It's easy for you all," he had once declared portentously, "to cry shame at him, because you just don't happen to want what he does. But if you wanted it, well, that would be a horse of another colour, I'll warrant. I know the Whetstones when they go after something they think they can't have." One way or another, she mused now, her boys were always sticking up for some one of their flock. That was the way things should be with brothers, even if squabbles did have to break out among them like a rash now and then.

It was not much later when a wind seemed to blow in at the side doorway, and Willy entered, caped and cold. He stood calling their attention sharply to focus on him. "I've done it! I've done it for you, Ven—made you a modest fortune on the Cotton Exchange. Now if you won't throw it away, you'll have a competence for the balance of your days!"

Ven let loose his long-tortured knuckles. "My luck held? I mean, my luck *turned*?" His eyes commenced to run water down his parched old cheeks.

Yarbrough looked at Willy, who nodded confirmation; then Yarbrough walked over and gave Ven a punch in the chest. "You rich old gander, you won't forget me when the cotton-worm spoils my crops, will you?"

"I'll remember you in my will, you young varmint," cackled Ven, grappling Yarbrough's arm in rough and youthful affection.

Willy turned to Gerda for his share of credit in Ven's triumph. She had jumped to her feet jubilantly, crying: "Willy, let me touch you for luck!" She shook a fold of his cape hard. "To think I used to turn up my nose at you for a ninny!"

"I know you did," he laughed, showing his precise girlish teeth. "I used to want to poke your eyes out too, because you fairly spat on me when I tried to kiss you."

"Oh, you were an awful sneak in those days, calling me cousin to excuse your trifling." They laughed together unashamedly. He touched first her forehead, then her chin with his lightly brushing fingertip. "You're throwing off even more sparks now, than you did in those days, *cousin*. Better take care or you'll have Yarbrough challenging all us menfolk to duels. I hear Walthour's daughter didn't like her papa's praise of you either. As for me, you know there isn't a girl I think can hold a candle to you."

Gerda looked him over, his chiselled miniature features, his taut small body that yet carried itself with the swagger of gallantry and something else not so easy to place, an air of decision perhaps, newly come by since his financial success. She could feel a little sparkle going over her at his words of praise. Yarbrough came up to them, his mouth genial over Ven's good fortune; but immediately he sensed some excitement between them that dissipated its tension as he joined them. He moved listlessly away, announcing: "I'm going to bed as soon as I have a look at Foolish. Willy, Gerda will see that you have a fire laid in your old room. I'm tired. This day has been trying."

While he was at the stables Gerda shooed them all off to bed, to quiet the house, that he might not be disturbed when he retired. She must have fallen asleep herself in a light cat-nap, for she failed to hear him come into their room, though she roused when she felt him there. The fire had been allowed to dwindle to one orange coal, as the night had turned muggy. He moved about almost stealthily, as if not wishing to attract her attention. After he had undressed he stood by the window, his arms braced against the sash, his profile showing in the greeny-white light of the new moon. "Lordy," his voice mused in a baffled way to no one. She did not let him know she was awake, when he sank down on his side of the bed. She could sense him staring off into the shadows from over his edge of it. They lay there for hours, the room, the very bed, cut in two, to allow their separate questionings to diverge in directions that could not meet in the same gloom.

2

The leaves were scurrying before a whistling wind the day Bruff came home for the last Christmas holiday of his years of medical schooling. The great oaks bent their upper boughs, and birds flapped in a helpless disarray before the blast in the sky. It all made Bruff feel fine, tired as he had become of the palmettos and exotic warmth of Louisiana, homesick for something more lusty. When the rig he had hired a seat in drew up before Rock Wall, he jumped out, with Pint tumbling down from behind, to wrestle with his boxes. The dust was blowing in whirlpools across the unusual dryness of the yard, and Bruff could see the ruddy leap of firelight on the front window-panes. "Ma'am, Papa! Boys, you rascals!" He bounded up the steps into the hallway, his brothers all coming at him at once, with Pokey trying to part them in order to make way for Ma'am Gerda to greet him. "Where's Papa?" he asked.

"He's in our room," Gerda told him. He followed her in, and for the first time was welcomed by his father seated instead of on his feet. Bruff's developing professional eye examined him. Never a fleshy man, Yarbrough now looked gaunt, and his summer's tan had been bleached away by a pallor Bruff did not like. However, Yarbrough's eyes snapped with pleasure at greeting his firstborn, and the grip of his hand was as powerful as ever. "I've been mighty poorly with a cold and a pesky cough. We didn't write you because we knew you'd be here soon."

Bruff drew a breath of childlike relief instantly. A cold could make a man peaked, and no mistake. He sat down and began rattling away with news and questions. How was Danley's Academy doing? How quick could he see Lucinda? And Joby too? Supper time, that was fine. The whole shebang would be here for Christmas, with a house party afterwards at Top Hill lasting through New Year's! In his honour? Well now, that was a lot of trouble for Cinda to put herself to.

After supper they crowded into the parlour, though every now and then one of the younger boys would sneak out to set off an early Christmas firecracker. Joby played carols and the negroes came hanging about the doorways to join in, their voices sustaining the airs with rich rolling chords.

The next few days went by fast, with a smell of spice and of corn popping. The boys shot down mistletoe out of the tall oaks and brought it in to be nailed overhead in pearly clusters like fairy grapes, to cause much kissing and teasing. Christmas Day itself came with a heavy coating of frost and a clash of ringing cries: *Chris'mus gif', Marse! Christmas gift, Shade. Chris'mus gif', Miz Gerda! Christmas gift, Densey. Pokey, stop those boys from stuffing themselves blue in the face before they even sit down to the breakfast table. Christmas gift, Bonapartt, it seems natural to have you here. Chris'mus gif', Marse Bruff!*—every one trying to get ahead of the others with the glad greeting. Then, after the feast-day breakfast, the giant holly tree before the parlour fireplace quivering under its bright burden. Every one crowding for a place from which to see amid the expectant silence. Then Yarbrough, trying hard to find among his rusty Bible words the right ones to make a prayer, and at last his commanding voice lending the rhythm of reverence to the phrases, at the end of which all mumbled: "Amen." A cough, a squeak of cramping brogans, then a released wild medley of delight and greed and gratitude for the gifts being dealt out or grabbed from the scarlet-spattered boughs of the holly. *Christmas gift!*

3

Lucinda's house party was in full swing three days after Christmas. Bonapartt bemoaned the fact that it was not as uppish as her other one. Since the inauguration of Bruton Academy she had made Top Hill more of a liberty hall for the young people's pleasure than any show place for herself as a hostess. Very early in the school's régime Danley had made it clear that he was not abashed in the slightest by his poverty as an English youngest son or by her ownership of the property. "I," he announced, "am bringing to the venture something quite as valuable, and I will not tolerate a petticoat government." She saw clearly to what a fine-drawn point his aristocratic penury had schooled his ambition, and she realized its inflexibility. Whenever she tried to act with a hoity-toity magnificence, he took her down with the greatest good humour, which left her feeling as if the joke was on her.

However, they had been looking forward to this gathering, for they both enjoyed entertaining and liked to give their imaginations full rein in devising new diversions. The evening the company arrived, instead of the traditional dancing and card games, they held a " picnic " in the large drawing-room. They banked the walls with shocks of cornstalks and sugar cane; they had the food brought in in baskets; and they even barbecued a very young pig in the fireplace beneath the Carrara marble mantel, which had been disguised by boughs of evergreens. Every one fell into the spirit of a crop barbecue. Gerda, at the little Walthour boys' instigation, snuffed candles when they were held before an open window; and later sat on the floor with a group of them, playing William-a-Tremble-Toe. Joby joined in, and was the best one at not cracking a smile or showing a tooth when tickled unmercifully during the forfeits. They soon had drawn a half-dozen peeking piccaninnies into the game, which made it twice as hilarious, for the small white boys were not accustomed to playing without their little negroes.

Down at the other end of the room the belles and the beaux had started a country-breakdown dance, with Lucinda and Bruff heading the two rows, and Danley and Lutie Caraway at the tail. They turned it into a noisy performance, more like follow-the-leader than a dance, with every one cutting wild capers. At the end of the last figure Joachim caught hold of Lutie and made her come away into the dining-room with him. " I have something pretty for you," he told her.

" What is it?" she asked, cupping her palms to hold fast to all he gave her.

" It's my extra Christmas gift for you. It'll be becoming to you with your red hair. Here." He dangled the ornament before her. It was an amethyst and silver rosary that Gerda had once given Pokey, who was a Catholic though so few remembered it. Innocent of this knowledge, Lutie let the beads trickle into her palms and saw the violet lights of the stones. " Ooh, pretty! But—but, Joachim, I can't. Not jewels from a gentleman when we aren't——"

" Who says we aren't betrothed? You're the one to decide."

"But——" she began to protest, when Tom Two came through the folding doors, his shoulders bulky.

"Lutie, I'm sorry, but you'll have to give that trinket back to him. And I'll have to take him outside and whip him good."

Lutie's fingers fell open and the rosary dangled rather foolishly from one of her fingers. "W-why?"

"He took it from a mulatto woman."

"Ugh!" she cried in disgust, dropping the trinket to the floor with a slight clatter, and dusting her fingers clean of it. "How *dared* you, Joachim Whetstone?"

"No," cried Joachim lividly, "not *that*! Not what you think about a mulatto. It's from ol' Pokey that I took it!"

"Oh?" Lutie left off dusting her hands, confused at her own remarks, which now seemed inexcusably bold in their implication. She felt hot around the roots of her hair.

Still the brothers had to have it out some way now. Tom Two was leading the way outside, with Joachim striding along after him, not looking very worried about a whipping. She picked up the rosary swiftly and tucked it away. Then she peeped out the window and saw Tom get in a couple of blunt blows before Joachim struck him with one swoop and Tom fell straight over backwards without bending his knees. Joachim leaned over him quickly and held him carefully so his nose could bleed without dirtying either's clothes. Lutie shook a little and sat down on a chair to pull herself together after the excitement, but the contention had been more pleasurable than otherwise for her. Now she heard footsteps coming through the Little Parlour and then Yarbrough asked her: "What foolishness have you put my boys up to?"

She tried to raise her chin pertly, not to betray how she was shaking.

"Why, you poor child," he said in a kinder tone, thinking her trembling was from nervousness, "were you scared by those young ruffians?" He walked over to the sideboard and began nibbling at scraps of ham. "Don't give it a second thought. A fight over a gel never amounts to much, especially between any two of my brood. They set too much store by each other."

She flounced about in her chair. So he didn't think she counted to his old sons? She'd show him, if he didn't watch out, what she *could* do to men. He was continuing indulgently: "Why don't you choose one of them? I'd be right pleased to have you in the family." He came over to her and began studying her, taking in her top-knot of reddish curls, her funny half-yellow eyes, her wispiness decked out in receptive ruffles. "You're just a mite, aren't you?" he teased.

She dropped her lashes in feathers on her cheeks.

"Minx!" he said, pulling her to her feet by her wrists, causing her to seesaw from one slipper to the other. In a way she was a little taken aback by all these importuning Whetstones, but her whole training had been to please the gentlemen, so her instinct now was to enhance this moment of intimacy. She let herself lose her balance in Yarbrough's direction, and when he caught her with a grab at her funny-bone, she giggled.

He glanced down at her, where she was tipped against him, and thought she made rather a silly picture. Then she raised her eyes, which were starting to glaze with moisture from her giggling, and he thought she was having a crying fit. "Don't feel bad," he coaxed, rubbing the drops off with his fingers because he could not find his handkerchief. She stayed quiet while he finished, then pulled loose and sat primly on her chair again.

He gazed down, not noticing her face with its drilled expression of coquetry, but seeing the thinness of her throat cords, her sweetly narrow body. He stooped over involuntarily, resting the elbow of his arm on the back of her chair, until as she leaned back to look at him her head nudged a warm spot against his upper arm. He thought with a feeling of rejoicing that was almost young: "Maybe this is that thing I wanted to go on a quest for . . . when I was a lad . . . the will-o'-the-wisp. . . ." His head felt too light suddenly.

He said aloud when he could speak: "You make me feel—*fine*!"

Then he went outdoors to make sure his two sons were peaceable again. He found them sitting on a wood-pile, laughing about something else entirely. He walked away and left them. As he roamed about he wondered if there could be any harm in his smiling at this child of a girl. He didn't want to possess her. He would simply like to stroke her curls, to take in that sweet newborn smell of her and try to catch from her the shape of a memory of unreality, of the dream that had never been dispelled by fulfilment.

4

The next afternoon most of the ladies gathered in the Little Parlour to chat over fancy-work, while the men were out quail-hunting. Nettie had cornered Dolly Walthour and was trying to turn that new-comer against Lutie, whom she had never forgiven for Nat's temporary defection before their marriage. "Just watch her, how every chance she gets she'll butter up to the men, even to Mr. Whetstone, trying to put him in the humour to give Joachim a big wedding settlement. She's finally set her cap in Joke's direction. He's the awfully handsome one, but I don't think he has right good sense. At least there's something queer the family's always trying to cover up about him."

"I could forgive plenty of queerness in him myself, he's that handsome. Are you *sure* they're engaged?"

"We-ell," Nettie hesitated, "I'm not certain sure, and I'd like to see someone give Lutie a run for the money. Look! There, didn't I tell you?" Both turned to watch Yarbrough, who had come to the doorway and was looking around.

"Where's my wife?" he inquired. "I wanted her to ride with me over to the Stand on an errand. The fresh air would do her good."

"She's out after quail with Willy and Mr. Walthour," Joby said. "She had a wager with them about who could bag the most."

Yarbrough started to turn away with a disappointed expression, then his eyes lighted on Lutie. "Here, sorrel-top, why don't you come with me?"

She glanced out at the heavy sky doubtfully. "It's not a very pretty day," she objected.

"Come, now," he gibed, "you're not a rheumatic old woman yet."

At that she scrambled up. "I'll go if we can use a gig so I can keep covered up warm."

When she joined him at the carriage block she was snugly hooded, but he tucked a robe around her also. "There, you ought not to perish now," he laughed.

"Don't make fun of me," she pouted. "I hate cold."

The sky was a dead slate colour, with the pines like a fortress. All the coloured leaves from the other trees were gone; only the road made a raw bright streak in the bleak scene, and the trotter tossed up sienna scoops of clay with his hoofs as they clopped along. Yarbrough had not much to say and his profile, knifed out by the cold air, seemed very remote. He acted almost unaware of Lutie's presence. So she gave a pitch now and then as they went round a bend, in order to land against him; then she would pull back apologetically. She kept it up until finally she managed to subside in a small bundle burrowed into his side. Then she felt him lean his shoulder over in a way that gave her more protection from the cold.

When they drew up at his front wall, he apparently dismissed her again as his eyes surveyed the scene for any laxity on the part of his negroes during his absence. He scarcely helped her out, and he led the way rapidly into the house calling for Pokey. "I must see how Foolish II is weathering her snuffles, then go over to the south patch about those seedlings. Pokey, you have a fire built in the parlour for Miss Lutie and bring her some refreshment." He glanced back at the girl, who had pattered after him. "You go right back into the parlour, missy. I'll be in for a dram before we start back."

Lutie returned to the parlour rebuffed. The place was dismal from being shut up, and she couldn't tell now what had possessed her to come. Pokey returned with a boy to lay the fire. Towering witch-like in the dimness, she merely bobbed her head silently at the girl and addressed all her attention to the little darky, giving him needless directions. After they had gone, Lutie moved closer to the fire, but it was slow in driving out the dankness. It seemed a very cheerless room to her, accustomed as she was to all the little feminine things with which her aunts cluttered the Caraway parlour. She thought all of Whetstone Stand was too big and bare and plain. How could any woman endure it? She supposed it was all very well for men and boys, but for a girl it was dismal.

Pokey re-entered with a tray holding cake, wine, and some biscuit, with chicken breast sliced between. Pokey remarked disapprovingly: "We don' keep much fittin' for visitin' ladies around when Miz Gerda ain't home."

"No, I reckon not," agreed Lutie uncomfortably. Then a sudden cunning thought struck her which she felt would allay Pokey's censure of her unseemly presence here. "I came to bring back something of yours to you."

"What's that?" demanded Pokey, unconvinced.

"Well, you mustn't tell on Joachim; he only took it because he thought it would become me." She whipped out the rosary from where she had secreted it in her petty-skirt pocket, and thrust it into Pokey's unwilling hand.

Pokey was taken aback and plainly at a loss for a moment. Then she pulled herself together and said almost haughtily: "They ain't nothin' to tell on Marse Joachim *about.* He knowed he was welcome to it. I tol' him so. I just wasn't handy to give it to him when he wanted it in a rush," she lied grandly. "I hopes it gives you pleasure, Miss Lutie." Thus she refused to take it back. There was no use of that snippy miss trying to pull the wool over Pokey's eyes about the reason she'd come gallivanting here to the Stand while Miz Gerda was away. Pokey muttered as she left: "I trust you'll be comf'table awaitin'."

"Comfortable!" echoed Lutie, pettishly, looking about at the forbiddingly shadowed room. She nibbled at the cake and biscuit, but they were dry and she didn't like wine. That mulatto woman had made her feel like a fibber and a thief, when it was all Joachim's fault. She felt of one of her ankles that was beginning to itch. Then, slapping at it, she killed a *flea,* of all things! What else could you expect in a place where they allowed the hunting dogs to have the run of the house? And Mr. Yarbrough was staying away from her all this time seeing to a *dog*!

She turned towards the window at an uncertain soft sound and saw it was rain coming down. It was pounding by the time Yarbrough swept open the door of the room, whistling as if his mission had been a success and carrying a carafe of spirits by its neck. He set it on the tray. "Chicken in the biscuit? Why in thunder didn't Pokey bring sausage? Oh, I reckon she was trying to cater to a lady." He measured himself out a tot. "Why, you haven't touched your wine, and your hands are frozen blue. Here, swallow this taste of brandy down, it'll warm your blood."

"It makes my ears sing," she protested, but in a moment her cheeks began to feel pleasantly roasted there before the fire; and the rain which had sounded so depressing a while ago was drumming like music now.

"We're all to ourselves here, with that outside," he nodded at the downpour. He had settled into a big chair with his booted shins stuck out before him. She flicked the crumbs from her skirts, and as she did so he took one of her hands and drew her nearer to him until she was backed up against his knee. He pressed her down so that she was half-seated on it. "Don't be afraid," he murmured; "I'll not harm a hair of your head, but I like to touch you because—there isn't very much to you." He leaned his head against the back of his chair and gazed at her musingly as he might have stared into the shift of the fire's flames, as if at something not corporeal.

Gradually her shoulders relaxed their stiffening. She swung one of her slipper-toes back and forth. He shifted his head and nuzzled his chin idly in the hollow of her shoulder. She pressed back against him. His forefinger came up and began tracing the outline of her bodice, then stopped over the sheer part of the mull. She could feel its hot line across her thinly covered chest. She felt as if she had to stop something that was about to happen to her from that touch, she felt that she was maybe going to have a spasm! It began to go through her like shudders, from her breast to her waist, to her knees, jerking her. He held her gently, and no closer. It passed, after one queer instant that hurt her heart so much it made her happy and she called out his name. After that she was limp except for a twitch or two. He patted her soothingly. "Such a little girl that you don't understand."

She stood up and began tugging her hood on feverishly, feeling embarrassed resentment flushing all over her now. But he said in a matter-of-fact tone: "We must try to make Top Hill before supper; the rain has let up." He was completely Joachim's father both then and while driving back. "I believe January's coming in warm," he prophesied, looking at where the late sun had come out before setting, making a jagged yellow tear in the clouds.

CHAPTER THIRTY-EIGHT

JANUARY did come in mild, with thick fringes of Ronald's snowdrops about the gate-stumps, and Yarbrough sat almost constantly wrapped in a cloak under an old deerskin robe in some sunny spot in the yard. Gerda made him take egg-flips laced with brandy, but saw that the colour they put into his face lasted only a short while. Also whenever he felt he had to go to oversee some project, which was seldom, he had Shade drive him instead of riding his stallion. He accounted for this by saying that he was taking things easy until the real summer sun came along to bake this lingering cold out of his chest. Still Gerda was alarmed, never having known him to coddle himself before. Yet sometimes when they argued over some farming method, his eyes and cheeks grew so bright that she told herself she was a goose to worry over any one so lively.

Before long the cares preceding planting-time were beginning to take more and more of Gerda's attention, making her welcome visitors who took his mind from its restlessness. Lutie Caraway, she noticed, came often and made a pretty fuss over him, but Gerda put that down to the chit's interest in Joachim or Tom Two. She thought nothing of the fact that Lutie usually prevailed upon Yarbrough to go into the seclusion of the parlour with her, and she never guessed at the petty intrigue of frustration the girl was playing.

But the absurd paradox was beginning to madden Yarbrough. He had drifted into an incipient intimacy because it gave him back some taste of the withheld folly of youth. Her skin was thin the way only a girl's is, and there was that manner in which her little thighs failed to fill out the volume of her skirts which pleased him, made him want to hold her, very lightly. Then when she grasped his coat, pulling at it insistently, trying treacherously to rouse him to an urgent hunger, it was one that he would not satisfy if he could. That was not what he wanted, satiety. No, he wanted something more impossible: to upturn the hour-glass of his life again, so that there would be a steady yellow trickle of its sand remaining to be run.

Inescapably an afternoon came soon when he refused to be enticed inside the house where her hands could have the chance to torment him with unfulfilling caresses. It was a craven game they had been playing, and he was determined to withdraw them both from the quicksands before they were lost. Therefore he sat stubbornly on in the yard in the paling sunlight and meted out his words sternly: "We have to make an end of these passages of spurious sentiment between us. They end only in distress for both of us."

"Who said they distressed me?" she demanded. "I'm happy if I can be near you, touch you. I have to have that much! It's so little, pressing myself against you. But then I feel—why, I feel like I'm growing right out of you, like a vine, sort of." Her eyes widened at him, asking him what this meant, this dependence of hers upon him.

He thought of the mistletoe, fragile and cherished, a parasite upon the oak, and of how some of the sturdiest trees decayed under it. "A virgin's hold is a vicious one," he told himself, "because it is all fine tendrils you think you can brush loose, until you find yourself strangled by the tentacles." He could not explain this to the dwarfed mind in her Columbine bit of a body. But, adamant, he would not go inside the parlour that day with her.

2

The rains, setting in again after the unseasonable warmth, continued without let-up until Gerda was worried about the early-planted seed rotting the ground. She had come in bedraggled and stood in the doorway of the dining-room, her eyes fastened on Yarbrough with an expression half-tender, half-chiding. "I think we'd better get a better doctor for you than that old Grand-daddy Caraway, so you'll pick up faster. Because I declare I don't know what I'll do if anything else goes wrong in the fields before you are back on your feet."

He looked at her standing there, gritty and dishevelled, but withal so ripened, so completely sufficing by reason of her own generous vitality, that he wondered what possible need she could have of the fatigued shell he had become. And an alien antagonism to her vigour took shape in him, with a venomous entity which was beyond his governing. It made him contradict her flatly. "Oh, you'd make out somehow, no matter what happened to me. Even if I were gone for good!"

"Don't say such things!" she cried in a terrified tone, crossing over to him swiftly to put a rain-moist palm over his mouth and stop his words. He felt somewhat mollified at her gesture; still, when Willy came saying he had brought a special treasured bit of venison for him, he would not enthuse over it especially. Instead he sat gloomily rolling two pecans on the table, listening to the hollow rattle. Poor Foolish came out from under the table, wakened by the sound. She put up her muzzle against his knee and stared worshipfully, but her eyes were so old and sad that she depressed him all the more. "Poor old girl, and to think I raised your mother before you, from a pup! Too much time has passed in my life." The bitch drooped, sensing that the sight of her had made her master unhappy instead of bringing him comfort.

That night all Yarbrough's resentment at Gerda vanished as he watched her moving about their chamber, her long plaits of hair swaying down to her knees. Now and then as she performed some small bedtime rite she looked into his eyes with a look of sharing in her own. At last she buried the fire in its ashes and blew out the yellow light of the candle, leaving the room filled with the softness of dark. She was still for a space, probably saying her odd, practically worded prayers to a God she wished for more than believed in. . . . During her silence his thoughts began to fray off towards the edge of sleep, until when he felt her length at last there beside him in the bed, although desire cast a glow in the dimness of his consciousness, he could not rouse himself to move towards her.

3

He woke some time in the night. He had just learned that he would not live long now. He did not know how the conviction had come upon him, except that it had not been through a dream. It was simply a full knowledge, filling him more completely than his blood or his breath, more immediate than the moment in which he now lived. Before, death had been but a vague superstition in which he did not put much stock. Now suddenly the threadbare phrase "All men must die" had ceased to be a shibboleth that was not even particularly true, and had become an *act* that he would be performing soon. The deed, almost the manner of its accomplishment, had somehow become as familiar to him as the process of ploughing. He understood now how one did it. And he wished he had not learned.

It left him lying like a stone at Gerda's side, not touching her, for she could not comfort away what the night had done to him. Nor did he look forward to the dawn, for its light could not release him from his dark pact.

CHAPTER THIRTY-NINE

With the coming of spring Gerda saw that Yarbrough was not improving, but going downhill fast. During the winter she had been able to read hope into little rallies that he made, but now when the sun was finally as bright as buttercups, and his cough grew yet more constant and drastic, she knew they had to face the fact that he was very ill indeed. She decided then to override any protests he might make and call in some doctor better informed than diddling old Dr. Caraway. Yarbrough made no protest whatever. Instead he looked up eagerly. "We'll send for Dr. Gadsdenn from Tuscaloosa, that's our man. He'll cure me if any one can."

He looked forward to the famous physician's coming as a schoolboy looks forward to a rare treat; for in spite of his strong prescience of the end, he still felt the human impulse to leave no stone unturned to go on. Also he was impelled by the desire, typical of the ill, to break the monotony of lying in bed by erecting a goal of some event in one of his day. He counted the time until the doctor's arrival, grew cranky about the appearance of his room, and surprised the household by the drama he was developing around the hour of welcome. He ordered Patt to be on hand to lend any help needed, but he said off-handedly to Gerda: "You go on out and look after things around the place the same as usual, till the doctor's gone. Else you'll make me feel already dead and buried." She went, leaving Patt posted like a sentinel in his doorway.

While Yarbrough waited he drew himself up tall against his pillows. He had looked in the looking-glass to make sure his hair was slicked and his moustache pointed, for he had certain strong notions of how he wanted to meet any blow. When Dr. Gadsdenn was shown in he greeted him as if his only concern was with courtesy and hospitality, and after that with the latest politics. The physician's keen eye was not to be easily deceived by any debonair pose, and very speedily he was making a minute examination of his patient.

At first Yarbrough watched Dr. Gadsdenn's expression eagerly, with small involuntary stabs of hope, but these grew less frequent as he saw the other's features composing themselves into a non-committal blankness. Then as he watched the doctor prolonging the putting away of his paraphernalia while searching for tactful words, Yarbrough's dim hope for recovery, towards which he had directed his thoughts for the past week, flattened out and vanished. He smiled a sorry smile. "You needn't try to fool me, doctor, I know I'm done for. You'd better take a stiff dram, though, before you break the news to the others. They'll be quite a handful."

He reached out for a dram himself, without asking permission, and drank it neat, like any ordinary before-dinner toddy. "Do you mind telling me the name of my plague? Since I'm to be on such close terms with it. Consumption, you say? I thought I recognized the trollop. Heigh-ho, not very pretty bedfellows, though, any of them, are they?" He spied into his empty tumbler a second, then, finding it empty, set it down with a clack. "Marm Pokey is in the ell, she'll tell you where Miz Gerda is."

After that Yarbrough lay with his arms folded, his lips compressed. So this was it. That had not been a hallucination that night. Well, what to do?

The first thing was not to let it alter his manner. Those close to him, who cared, must not lose his person one whit before the end. "I can accomplish that much," he mused. "What's to stop me from seeing to that? I'm alive to-day, and the wellest man on earth can live only one day at a time. I'm as alive as any man I know. Any one of them might be thrown from his horse and have his neck broken, putting an end to him before ever my time's up. There's no reason for any one to feel sorry for me, when none of them is a single jot more live flesh and blood than I am now!"

The conviction welled up, filling him, that his remaining days were not to be doled out to him by Fear, in any miserly fashion that reduced them to a tag-end scrap of time, and himself to a beggar cadging for alms on the outskirts of existence. No. Instead he would contain, within the circumference of each hour, the whole rounded-out sphere of this world—of dawn and dark, the seasons, the seed, the harvest, love, birth, the dreams for which his mind had fashioned itself into the thing man calls a soul. He must own a universe in which were stored all the years and feelings of his life, in one gigantic sum that would envelop him in such a state of being that it would obliterate for the present—which after all was the only time any man had—that annihilation that was Death, thus encompassing his sphere like Eternity.

His eyes, ovor his compressed lips, studied the outlines of his folded arms as if their pose held a deep significance. He threw his chin up. What was a gentleman good for, if he could not treat Death like a servant holding open a door?

2

When Dr. Gadsdenn asked Gerda's whereabouts, Pokey motioned him out back towards the scuppernong arbour. Gerda was standing there picking little pieces of green moss from the scaly grey posts that propped up the vines. She was recalling that other hour when she had lain on top of the arbour at the Home Place in South Carolina waiting for Yarbrough to settle her fate, scarcely daring then to hope that he would himself choose to woo the raw girl she had been. It was both strange and fitting that now she should be waiting in an arbour again, when once more the question of whether she was to have him and happiness was being settled. For a moment she was dwelling in the old joy of her hour of betrothal; then she turned at the sound of the doctor's voice, and her heart closed up with dread.

As soon as Dr. Gadsdenn saw her terror he knew there was no way of making it easy for her. "Your husband is dying of consumption," he told her. "I doubt if he will last out the spring."

She stepped towards him as if she were going to strike him to make him take the words back. Then a scream got loose from her throat and tore out with an animal yowl that made a sickening thing of the air. She felt its hideousness, its hateful humiliation, and tried to suck it back. But she was far, beyond any decency or dignity, she was wallowing in the worst shame of all. Sorrow. For a space she sank deeper and deeper, polluted by grief. Then from somewhere outside herself a dim warning came to her, that this abandoned rage of feeling would never do. At first she scarcely heeded the warning; but finally, labouringly, harshly, she lowered the scream to the tone of groaning, and after more struggle to occasional dull moans.

Then she steadied her gaze until she could make out the doctor's features. She did not want to see them, but she had to call him up clear again, so she could tell him: "I'm sorry." She felt horrid at having had another person witness the nakedness of her grief, holding as she did that grief, like prayer and passion, should be cloistered. The face she turned to him was as blanched as that of a cadaver, and her eyes were so blank of all hope that they looked like the vacant dark holes of the sockets in an ancient mask of tragedy. She said: "I had better walk off by myself for a while, till I'm fit to let him see me."

She moved away through a thicket, without feeling the sting of its thorns. There was no way for her mind to turn. No path out, no reprieve, no time after this stopped hour of all ending. In any direction that her thoughts tried to go they were blocked.

She quit trying to reach out.

She walked a long way, and saw nothing of what was around her. She did notice the coarse stitching in the tongues of her house-moccasins and marked how they protruded from under her skirts as she took steps. Also there was always the surface of the ground passing beneath her feet, and the sensation of hill-rises and gully-declines.

Much later she looked up and saw that she had come around by the pasture bars, and that the sun was coming down rather close to her. The sky was a wild primrose that even she could tell was a pretty colour. She felt it sort of wash over her face, and she held her cheeks up into it more. It seemed to calm down the few moans that were wanting to come up. It spread into her, soothing some of her brutal turmoil, leading to the first stage of composure.

She opened her eyes once more. A cowbell came on the air with its usual meandering music. She thought: "The evening world is still fair to look upon . . . the air that stirs in secret spring moisture is still sweet to taste . . . the starlight will thread through the dark. . . ." She must stay steeped in all this, so that if he thirsted for any draught of any beauty he had ever known, he would find it in the cup she held for him to quaff.

She looked a little longer at the sunset until it had deepened into umber over the hills, then she turned back home. "I must," she vowed, "feel only that he is *alive* now, that he will brim with power, to the last." And then there came upon her the bewildering knowledge that she was almost happy in some way that could not be told.

Something pleased her; her heart felt uplifted high above the ground as she went stepping towards the house, the dew making tiny wet lashes where the grass struck her ankles above her moccasins.

When she entered their room, Yarbrough saw none of the troubled lines from her pain, for her face was rich with the vigour of all her senses merged into one transcendent splendour. Later had he glanced up from his supper plate, on the tray Patt had brought him, he might have thought that she looked as if she faced an impenetrable wall, but that by sheer force of staring she was bound to pierce through, to see what Infinity was like.

CHAPTER FORTY

THE OTHER MEMBERS of the family received the news about Yarbrough each in a different way. The younger boys sat huddled on the back steps in a group with their negro boys, feeling scared the way they did about ghost stories. Tom Two and Joachim became friends again, gripping each other's arm, as much as to say: "We've still got each other." Wayne became scared of the dark and tried to behave well to the others, so they wouldn't leave him by himself.

Hans came to speak to Yarbrough, who was so much more than a father, being his only parent. "You can count on me to help Ma'am."

"I know," Yarbrough told him. "'And some seed fell on good ground and brought forth an hundredfold.' You're 'good ground,' Hans."

The lad gulped and went out to shake his fist at his land. "Yield! You better had!"

Joby, when C. D. fetched her, was so distrait that Gerda shooed her out of the room as soon as she could, for fear of making Yarbrough feel down in the mouth. Gracey fluttered sympathetically, but did not linger, as she was timid about illness. Guy and Ven, looking very low, left of their own accord after a short visit. They could not keep from remembering how much older they were than Yarbrough and wondering when it would be their turn. Willy acted exactly the same as ever, which was a relief to Yarbrough, yet puzzled him and made him wonder irritably if Willy grasped the gravity of the situation.

Lucinda came in very angry and paced the room, kicking at anything that happened to get in her way. "I don't see any *sense* to it! Why couldn't it be some old goat like Uncle Ven or Uncle Guy? It's a mighty sorry mess the way this world is run!"

"It appears to me," her father remarked dryly, "that you've had your good share out of this world. So don't go back on it. I'll warrant you'll enjoy yourself again after I'm gone. Many and many a time."

At that she cried out, shaking his shoulder in helpless wrath. "Don't, Papa, don't go out of *reach*!"

His eyes went wet. This daughter had one spot in his heart that no one else could come near, and her cry shot through it like a sweet-pointed arrow. She made him feel so human for the moment that he had nothing in common with a doomed man.

2

The negroes took the news with wailing and moaning, continuing to carry on so badly that they had to be taken in hand, to keep their racial revelry in sorrow within bounds. Bonapartt came over from Top Hill and refused to budge from Rock Wall. He and Patt carried on their old feud, trying to outdo each other in Yarbrough's service, which tickled their master.

Bruff came hurrying home from New Orleans as soon as word reached him; he could complete his few remaining studies later, but right now he felt that his place was at his father's bedside. With his recent training he could carry out Dr. Gadsdenn's instructions and not only make his father as comfortable as possible, but help to keep the scourge from attacking other members of the family. Old Dr. Caraway was in a fine huff about the newfangled notions and predicted dire results. He was most incensed when Bruff told Joby and Gracey, whom he considered frail, to make few calls in the sick-room and then not to hang over the bed. "It's unnatural," Dr. Caraway growled, "to keep them away from the side of a loved one in distress. I'd hate to have to answer to my Maker for such an inhuman act."

"That's my look-out," replied Bruff. "*I'd* hate to answer to another human being for the careless spread of a disease." To bolster his confidence against the older man, Bruff reminded himself that the Whetstones weren't in the habit of letting other folks run their affairs, and that they usually managed to turn even their mistakes to their advantage in the end, like Hans's parentage, or Guy's Indian marriage, and Lucinda's refusal to mourn for Malone.

Yarbrough, watching his son's face after this set-to, remarked: "I reckon you'll do."

"For what? A doctor?"

"Yes, that too. But I mean you will do to take my place, in the next generation. Your mother will fill my shoes now, raising cotton.

That's not my point. Each new batch of a family has to have some *one* person out of their *own* lot to turn to. I know I didn't think myself fit for that job when my father turned it over to me. All the same I've managed somehow. The only difference between the hero and a live man doing the best he can is that the hero's dead. After I'm gone, if you want to look back on me as someone bigger than human, that won't hurt, as long as you're willing to stretch your own measure up to the same size. That's mostly how leaders come about, anyhow. *You* can amount to as much as any man that ever lived, and you might have a son who will be great to the whole wide world! Who knows?"

Bruff stared at his father hard. Why, Yarbrough was talking as if he, Bruff, could be somebody for them all to look up to! And beget a great man. "All right, sir," he promised, "I won't be scared by anything just because it looks big."

"That's it," Yarbrough praised him. "I'm turning the reins over to you now. Try not to have a runaway, though that's hard with a headlong lot like the Whetstones." He reached for his son's hand, and the grip held strong between them, a bond that had already held through generations.

3

As the days went by, Bruff saw that although he wanted his father to rest as much as possible, the neighbours claimed a certain amount of his time, and that it had to be so. Not only did Yarbrough mean much to them, having built protection for them in the wilderness, shaped their rough land into comfort, showed them how to garner their crops into riches, but they also were to him a symbol of tremendous value. For what was a leader without followers, a ruler without a country? Bruff saw that it was a great treasure that they brought as they came with an air of loyalty that lent pomp to a pot of gruel, or grandeur to a gritty bottle some man had dug up out of his wine ground-hole. They tried to say things that might bring Yarbrough cheer, and one or two succeeded.

Duncan MacDuff rolled his great barrel of a stomach around until he was settled more comfortably in his chair and spoke in the Scotch burr that had overtaken him afresh in his older age. "I tell you, Yarbrough, we're gain to miss you a great lot. The way you could hot-foot it wi' the devil, yet sit with the Laird Justice. I'm glad I hae'ed no pretty lasses in my family. Else I'd have to've stopped at home more, to keep you out, instead of roamin' after my own pleasures." He winked a Trojan wink.

Miz Lydia Screws came in one day and remarked tartly: "I can afford to tell you now how mad you made me back in Egton when I was a girl before I was all pock-marked. I tried to catch your fancy, but you looked clean through me. You were too entranced with Miss Sabine Lou from Charleston. You couldn't tell then that she would end her days behind lock and key, with her wrists tied down to keep her from choking herself. No one would have guessed it then, when she had a face like a seraph and a laugh like a bell. I reckon it was that laugh that made me catch on that she was going to turn fey. I heard it once ringing and ringing out on the night, like glass being continually broken."

"Do you call this cheering me up?" Yarbrough queried humorously.

"No." She grinned her snaggle-toothed smile. "I call it revenge." But her raillery picked him up immensely. He liked her to stop by, for she brought him the whole county picked up on the sharp point of her tongue. She was not vicious, but she was ruthless at peeling off pretence. One time when she was there and Lutie Caraway pried her way in, Miz Lydia hissed at him in leaving: "I should've warned you, that gel lives for mischief." When she saw him shut her off with a polite uncomprehending look, she sniffed in parting: "Go ahead and act deaf-and-dumb polite about the chit now. Well, too bad you were so anxious to feel skittish, for she's a pest."

Yarbrough didn't wish to see Lutie, not because Miz Lydia had ridiculed her, but because her fluttery ways irritated him now. She had been asking for some time to be permitted to see him, but Bruff had not thought her robust enough to be allowed in. This day, however, when Bruff had not been on hand, she had slipped by. She stood uncertainly by the post of his bed, looking at his sharp cheekbones, which made his face look so spare. This was not the man she had been so proud to stir. This sickly gentleman, whose face was as transparent as paper held up to the light, was so austere that she would not dare perch on the edge of his bed, or let his fingers touch her wrist.

She plucked her wraps about her, coughing breathlessly in her anxiety to be gone. "I mustn't stay. I can see you're very fatigued," she told him with thoughtless cruelty, hurrying over to the door. After she was outside she peered back with a childish curiosity. He had raised his head half up and pulled the corners of his mouth down in a quizzical way that mocked her. She was startled to see suddenly how compelling and gallant that sharp-limned head was, and wanted to rush back and fling herself at him once again, but he dropped his head to dismiss her. She remembered then, moving away, that he had never liked her flinging herself at him. He had preferred to hold her off and watch her. "But he doesn't want me even in his sight now," she whimpered, incredulous that any man could be so indifferent to her.

She could not, of course, comprehend how he had progressed to that stage the very ill reach, when they are imbued with a limpid purity amounting almost to asceticism. Though the messages of his senses, many times refined, coursed rapidly through his veins, all sin, by mortification, had been distilled out of them. Unaware of his motive in any articulate way, and having no faith in the kingdom of heaven as such, he was yet by his immaculate present endeavouring to reinstate himself with some lord of the living. All his understanding of other people's needs and foibles, all his denial of his baser hungers, all his brave way, were a part of his battle to yet escape the punishment of death in some miraculous way, and live and live and *live*!

It was not an unworthy thing that he was undertaking. It was the simple thing that all men would do: *Escape final defeat.* So he lay, controlled, valorous, his arms stretching down at his sides beneath the stark sheets, his mind musing: "I am doing right now, for I am doing nothing wrong." The afternoon air as it lay across his face felt like a swab of absolution.

The days of the belated spring drifted ahead out of the veiled grey that winter had tried to keep drawn over the countryside. The perpetual raininess had ceased, and the second planting was thriving. Yarbrough could crane his neck about and see out of his side window to where a scattered line of hands, like a fence of scarecrows, were chopping their way up across the rise of his high field, where the cotton plants first flourished. But he did not look in that direction often, for he knew it was doing well, and he was tired of having his mind burdened with care. He rested.

One day Danley and Lucinda and Bruff came in and looked first at Gerda, who was carding cotton in a rocker, then at him. Danley sloped his hand happily along Lucinda's shoulder, then spoke, "Lucinda and I are going to have a child."

"And you mustn't worry," Lucinda assured him, "because it's been going along several months, the worst ones, and I feel fine. I thought you'd like to know."

Bruff, her twin, put in: "You can depend on me, sir, to take the best care in the world of her. And she won't cut up this time. She'll be safe."

Fright, nevertheless, clutched at Yarbrough unreasonably, and he reached out for his daughter. "Promise me you won't do anything foolish, pet. Promise!" She gave him a saucy tweak on his cheek. "Oh, I'm trained to the bridle now. I'm not such a colt any more."

Yarbrough found himself clapping his hands for Patt or Bonapartt to bring the finest bottle on the place. Bonapartt fetched it, together with the good goblets kept up on the top pantry shelf. "Marse," he whispered, "I trusts you all don' feel called upon to shatter dese goblets after drinkin'! 'Tain't de real christenin' yet a while."

Yarbrough gave him a wink; he was glad to find one of his darkies acting sensibly, not desiring destruction.

The field-hands were somewhat demoralized by their master's illness, and not disposed towards anything so commonplace as steady work while the excitement of trouble lurked in the air. They were all loud in their protestations that they would cut off their right hands to save Marse Yarbrough, but they were not so willing to get callouses on those same hands chopping cotton. When they did, they were apt to be careless of their method. As it had been a rainy spring, the grass was growing faster between the rows and needed more hoeing than usual. Yarbrough reckoned it would take at least six times over the whole crop. Therefore Gerda spent her days plodding through sucking mud, trying to spur negroes on to activity, while all the time, each precious minute, she was thinking: "There are so few more moments left to share with him, and I want to be there."

Hans and Tom Two tried to help her all they could, but that

amounted to little out of the whole. Besides, there was no satisfaction for her in coming to see Yarbrough if she brought him no news of progress. Stoically she stayed in the fields each day until she felt she had something encouraging to report. Then he listened to what she said, judged it for himself, praised her, or dropped a word of caution. "Don't let them chop too close to the plants while they're still so young and tender. Remember the 'sore shin.' Later, by early June when the plants are sturdy, they can go so fast they'll double the amount of rows in their tasks. But now care is the main thing. I'll tell you how to manage them differently in June." He stopped abruptly.

A pain gnarled her face. In June he would not be able to tell her one single thing! In June she could never hear his voice, ever again! But this was the very thing she had vowed not to give in to, this looking forward to that empty time. There was no room for being sad now, not in any one of these precious days that were still his.

She rose and went over to the hearth after the brush-broom, to sweep some of the mud off her boots. He took his fill of her as she stood there, her habit looped up in a twist about her waist, her cheeks bright, her eyebrows glistening with beads where the mist had caught in them and condensed. She came back and leaned down over him, to get the touch of him that she was never complete without now. He caught the spring damp with which she was saturated, seasoned slightly with brush-smoke. They both felt eager in the cool freshness her face dispelled about them. "My beloved!" he called her.

That became one of the most beautiful nights they had ever given over to love, for it had about it the spell of immortality that danger can cast. It was like legends of old passion, magic with the beauty of desperation. There was no desire in them at the time for more of life after this, or break of day, or any future—only surrender to the oblivion of consummation, the doomed hour of completion. . . .

CHAPTER FORTY-ONE

As THE DAYS left to him grew fewer, Yarbrough liked to spend them more and more with Gerda. She made him feel, in spite of his increasing weakness, most vital, most aware of the pleasures in his world. With her tending to some small chore there near him, he could lie happily, his gaze roving out the front window to where the yard was overrun with blossoming. The chaste blades of the bulb flowers were gone, and the roses had burst forth with their profuse woman-sweetness. He watched them each day, their white elegance, their cadence of scarlet, their scarce and secret yellow spiciness like the perfume of ginger.

His days went serenely in an arch shaped like the time marked on a sundial. The acts of sleeping and waking became large adventures significant with mystery. Eating was a ceremony, the sense of smell an elation. He was filled with the wonder and the richness of his simple days.

In a slate and chalk-blue hour Gerda would rise from the trundle bed where she had slept beside his great one and fetch him a basin of water. She would keep silent while he revelled in its scooped-up freshness, then she would smooth his sheets and pillow and go away.

He would rest there priding himself on his victory over one more night. He would watch the copper side of the tree-trunks where they stood in the path of the sunrise; then presently the burnish would spread over the whole floor of the yard and pour up into the sky, becoming daylight. Gerda would come back bearing his black coffee and other breakfast, smoking hot. He would relish it deliberately, while she cleaned his room, with the wide-open windows freshening the night-staleness out of every corner. After this he always felt greatly restored and his mind perked up with curiosity about the doings on the plantations and in the county. Pokey and Patt and Shade looked in with messages from quarters and stable. Duncan MacDuff and John Screws and Willy came with news from the towns. Bruff seemed so pleased with his appearance that for an hour Yarbrough felt he might yet live to be a hundred. He was renewed to life!

He took each hour of his day apart, as a child divides the sections of its Christmas orange, to taste its full delight. One morning Miz MacDuff sent him a bouquet of flowers pressed together in a pattern as intricate as embroidery, and he spent much time marvelling at its cunning artificiality, and built his consciousness around the pleasant feast it gave his eyes whenever they roved across the bright spot it made on his table.

Another afternoon late, David Walthour stopped by with a small stone pitcher of eggnog he had concocted for him. Walthour and Gerda sat and watched expectantly, while Yarbrough spooned some into a tall glass and admired its foam, as stiff as a queen's ruff. He held it up so its golden heart would glow in the firelight, and he could catch the whiff of nutmeg off its crest. Gerda passed Walthour something tawny in a small glass, and the room, with its brown puncheon floors worn into slight grooves, the core of heat in the fireplace, the clash of colour in his quilts, seemed to enclose a world of cheer for Yarbrough. Walthour told a joke; the dog Foolish gaped at a flea. Gerda raised her head, which looked like a black drake's arching above a stream, and Yarbrough felt his heart jump a little at the sight of it. He gulped down a rich portion of his eggnog and gradually felt a glow like its colour suffusing him. This was a pleasant hour, and the boundaries of an hour seemed wide now, when a day might be all that was left of his life.

2

This day had dawned with a very thin pearly light; Yarbrough could tell that with his eyelids, before opening his eyes. It seemed to be a day of all air, the earth just a flat line below it, great fans of air sweeping across his face. That had been the way it was at dawn.

Later it was all sunshine.

He had slept lightly off and on since, feeling rather dreamy and floating, even when he roused to drink his coffee. He waved the rest away and sank his head back on the pillow, closing his eyes. But he could hear wherever Gerda moved in the room. He knew when she threw open the window wider to bring in the April air. He could feel the sun dappling him. He opened his eyes slightly and saw how clean the room had become; everything looked polished. The air was bright with clear prismatic tints. And though he could touch the smoothness of his sheets, he felt buoyed up as if he were not touching anything heavy like a bedstead. Gerda was standing between him and a window, so that the light sprayed out all around her, showing him how her waist was shaped in smaller than her hips and shoulders. He kept feeling that swaying sensation beneath his covers, and kept letting the smell of the roses come and staunch his nose with their sweet tea-scent.

Then he opened his eyes full and smiled at Gerda so that she came towards him without his calling. She leaned down near, and he murmured as if he were giving her a secret: "The day lifts me . . . so airy . . . sunny . . ." Her mouth met the corner of his lip, which had a skin as thin as a grape.

It made her so happy she had a bubble where her chest was. She turned towards the window to hold it, blown big. She saw a redbird wing up across a path. You could make a wish on a redbird. She turned to tell Yarbrough to look quick and make his wish.

Then she saw Yarbrough was gone. . . .

His lids had closed, but only in a sheer way that seemed to curtain an eager look. She thought: "Why, I can lean down and kiss him and still touch a warm cheek. Or else I can stand here and speak and he will answer me, and fall into a half-laughing cough. Then everything will go on. I will bring him his milk. All I have to do is—make him *hear* me."

She took his hand, the fingers still flexible. She leaned down to push his hair back with her mouth, and cherish the secret scent that was like his name. Then she rose. She stood there for a little while, smiling in the sun, with him near. This would be the last she would look at him, now. While his face was still aware, with his quick going.

"Dreams," she mused. She had not had much use for them because she had had him. And he stood for the breath men draw when they call up the myth of courage, the tinkling sound of folly, the ache that despoils a woman of content. And, though he must leave, his footsteps were all across the land. . . .

CHAPTER FORTY-TWO

Grief, Gerda discovered, was a slow thing to depart, while Time was swift to race on, leaving the last year of Yarbrough's life abandoned to the past. For a while everything throughout the family was related to him. No undertaking had any worth unless it accomplished some purpose of his, no one's mind seemed complete without some thought of him, no day closed without that forlorn hour when he did not join them. . . .

Yet on the very day after his death Gerda had a premonition of how the compactness that had constituted Yarbrough would be dispersed by the insidious treachery of memory.

She had borne with remarkable composure a stream of callers who in their well-meant condolences made free with his achievements, his jokes, his wisdom, his foibles, until she felt that they were making conversational carrion of him. Irrational as she knew it to be to object to their attempts at tribute, she could not quell the wild fear that by laying such neighbourly claim to him they were removing her husband from the custody of her love, leaving her an incoherent babel of praise in his place.

To escape from the strain, she retired to her daughters' old room, there to come upon Gracey and Joby discussing with shocked disapproval her plan to bury him in the front yard within view of her window instead of in the knoll burying-ground they called Holy Hill. "Why," Gracey was expostulating, "it will look just like putting him to bed, right out before people's eyes!"

"Never mind about people's eyes!" cried Gerda, startling them apart. "*I* want him close by—the only part of him that's left."

"But, Ma'am, his soul——" began Joby.

Gerda stopped her. "I don't want to hear any more palaver about his soul. It's a sickly word. Besides, he'd dress you down properly for meddling with his." She stalked out of the house, full of helpless anger at every one's readiness to belittle his beloved body in their eagerness to use the picklocks of praise to pry into his spirit—a spirit over which, living, his pride had kept such high guard. His heart she had had, save for a few wild errant throbs, and his name in all its honour to share with his children. To men he had given his deeds, for them and the altering years to interpret. But that shred of immortality that was more Yarbrough Whetstone than the sum of all these others, he had kept undisclosed to any one.

His *person,* however, had had an exact and evident shape. No one could change that actual man now, by any reminiscence, or meanness of resentment, or by sanctification. Nor even by the numbness that would cure their woe in time.

Pondering thus, Gerda turned back with an appeased heart, to listen with renewed calmness to the litany of traits his friends had salvaged piecemeal from his character, according to their own needs of him. Now she rested secure in the comforting thought that to her, his wife, was reserved the privilege of putting his tangible form to rest, there in the spot he would have chosen, beyond the front porch, by the copper rosebush he had favoured.

The next sore task had been that of ending his dog's misery. From the time of Yarbrough's burial Foolish II had lain under the house, refusing food and water until her tongue hung like a pouch outside her jaws.

Finally Gerda had agreed with Bruff that there was nothing to do but shoot her. Yet when Shade crawled under the house to haul Foolish out, despairing as the bitch was in life, she instinctively stiffened her forelegs to resist being dragged to her doom. The only other sign she made was a faint dry whine as they carried her past her master's grave. Neither Bruff nor Shade had the heart to do the shooting, so Bruff ordered Pint to do it. Afterwards Bruff involuntarily cuffed Pint on the side of the head, and Pint gulped: "Whup me good! I sho' feel low-down."

To Gerda waiting up on the porch the sound of the shot smashed like a fist across the white silence of the first hour after dinner. She flinched as if she were a young girl who had never heard gunfire before; something strange was happening to her. She rose and took two light, firm steps across the planking. She skipped the porch steps in one long bound and began to run across the yard, away from the sound of that muffled echo. She loped at an undignified pace that left one of the yard boys gaping. Outside of the back-lot gate she struck out around the ploughed land, but at the top of the rise back of the field she knew there was no use going farther.

Already, with the summer barely begun, the hot sun had brought the tall stiff grass to its height, and in that green bed Gerda sank down, glad that the hardy blades grew high enough to conceal her face, to make a green-slatted wall before her eyes. Now she was really hidden. Now she wept.

Not for many months to come would she know it, but the period of her womanhood had come to its end. What was left was very like what she had started with, on that day so long ago. Or was it really only yesterday when she had swum far out in the Mountain Lake and tossed her arm in a purely zestful gesture to Pokey, knowing that she had been *one being,* self-sufficient. That had been the time of her girlhood, a time for being single. Then had come Yarbrough to teach her another completion, and he had almost served out his time of husbanding her—almost but not quite. Yarbrough had died a month, a year, perhaps five years too soon, leaving her unmated, while yet she was at an age where she felt the need for being coupled. Desolation engulfed her now, knowing that there would be no time ever when his absence would end. Her eyes and ears and nose and mouth were stopped by the black blot of Never.

All she could do was weep.

2

But not often did she sink into a morass of sorrow, and always she did it in secret, so that no one could shame her dignity later, recalling her weakness. In the county many marvelled at her stoicism, while some condemned it. The truth was that in spite of spasms of realization, such as that springing from the shot that was his dog's knell, she could not yet sustain any grasp upon the finality of Yarbrough's departure. Her senses still held his shape, the forces of his actions had not yet run down. Involuntarily she went about the plantation expecting to encounter him at any turn, perhaps around the corner of the smoke-house, or up by the lightning-blazed cotton oak, or maybe down where the grist-mill churned the Big Branch waters.

She never knew exactly when that phase of loss-alleviating expectancy left off. Yet presently she was at the next stage, where she kept wanting to write him a letter to tell him how well the crops were doing, and how proud he would be of the way they were bearing their trouble. She caught herself wondering often by which mail-coach she ought to post such an epistle, before she realized what an impassable distance of infinity separated them. Also, she noticed that, whereas a month ago she had constantly envisioned him as appearing on any scene, now she had to pause and shut her eyes to bring him up before her. She was never to have any warning, though, of when some odd hour would seize her and rack her through and through with a fresh onslaught of agony.

Still, more and more later events were crowding in, taking up her attention, distracting her from her constant train of memories. Gradually, day in and day out, the shifting in the balance of the scale of her life went on. Slowly the weight of her loss lightened, as the accumulation of daily duties bore down. Bit by bit the months, rounding upon themselves, brought her mornings in which she rose up to look upon a world that once again seemed quite natural. As the year wore on, things broke loose from the pattern of which Yarbrough had been the centre, and took on new dimensions of their own. A day here and there belonged almost solely to the person who lived it, with little or no relation to the former master of Whetstone Stand. His children, his seed that had taken root in the land he had cleared in the wilderness, were making their own flourishing felt. Now, for all their clan-closeness, Yarbrough's sons and daughters were beginning to loom as separate men and women on the county's horizon, to have a bearing upon its oncoming destiny.

3

A day came when old Dr. Caraway cast aside his dotard's scorn of Bruff's professional knowledge and called him in to attend Lutie, who had been stricken with galloping consumption. Gerda knew, with a belated pang of jealousy, that it had been contracted from the girl's association with Yarbrough; but she had no time to brood now, for Tom Two was demanding to accompany Bruff to Lutie's bedside, and his mother knew what that portended. She could only trust that his robustness would stand him in good stead.

The Lutie Tom now saw was no longer the least bit pretty, with her garish red hair scraped back from a thin, crone-like face. Yet he insisted she had to marry him straightaway. He carried his point, although coughs were racking his bride until she could scarcely speak her responses. In between she looked pathetically arch, hanging on to his hand.

From then on, Tom Two settled down to nurse her, more faithfully than any old mammy, telling her she must get well in time for some of the cane-grinding fun. Often he made Joachim accompany him into the sick-room to divert her with some of his cajoling tomfoolery. Thus it happened that the two brothers, who had been rivals for her favours, were alone with her the night she died, pacifying her sense of coquetry to the last. Joachim, though squeamish-natured about all unpleasantness, stayed by his brother the night through, without calling any of the Caraways in during Tom's first stark hours of loss. At dawn Bruff, coming in on the situation, had taken charge, and sent them off with instructions that Joachim drink his brother into a stupor which would make Tom sleep.

The next episode of family significance had been Cinda's confinement, which had gone hard with her in spite of her good health beforehand. However, she had not harped on that, once it was over, had only asked sharply: "Is my belly scarred from all that stretching? Lord knows I made Pinky rub it with mutton tallow often enough to keep that from happening. She'll catch Hail Columbia if it looks like a zebra."

Then she had said they could show her the baby, whose looks she pronounced nothing to brag about.

After the others had gone out, leaving her and Danley alone, he had suggested they name it Yarbrough, magnanimously waiving his preference for Danley. To that Lucinda retorted: "I'll do no such thing. I have too much respect for my father to name any bastard after him. We'll call him Whetstone Bruton, my name and your name together, which is all he has any real right to."

Danley's pallid mouth rippled in a supreme effort at control, while his nails dug into the polished mahogany bedpost, to keep his hands from flying at her throat.

Lucinda merely lay there shunting off his unbelieving look, her restored narrowness making a hard line under the covers.

No hint of this scene was conveyed to Ma'am Gerda by word, but she divined that Lucinda had committed some cruelty concerning the naming of this first grandchild, upon whose birth Gerda had counted for the softening of his headstrong mother. Evidently that was still not to be through any such medium as the baby's helplessness; Danley, Gerda observed, plunged grimly into his work once more.

Spurred by him, the three younger sons—Will Bee, Daniel, and Turber—were setting a standard of excellence in their studies that was to outlast two generations of country-school scholars, and to equip youths of a far-off blighted era to cope with a still harsher, larger world. These three boys were a great solace to Gerda as she took account of her children, cataloguing their strengths, weaknesses, and tastes.

Joachim, strutting his unabashed way through card games, reels, tap-rooms, and ladies' hearts, was fast becoming part of that symbol, "the Southern blade," in this blustering realm of the Cotton Snobs. Hans and Tom Two, labouring steadily, were a part of that other typical class, the small farmers who constituted the firm if hidden backbone of the cotton-raising world. And Wayne? Wayne was one of those ugly scars that gashed across the serene land, a defacement more deplored by his intimates than he could ever be denounced by his critics, the Abolitionists. What stream, Gerda wondered, had crossed with hers and Yarbrough's to curdle this son into enmity towards mankind?

It had ever been Yarbrough's custom to give over the charge of their inheritance to each of his sons on his eighteenth birthday, to accustom them to the responsibility before they took true title at twenty-one. Wayne alone thus far had so abused his premature authority that Gerda would have liked to revoke rather than confirm his power when the time came. He was for ever scheming and conniving against his brothers, cheating his negroes out of their just rewards, and driving them beyond capacity unless prevented by one of his elders. A climax of his viciousness came on his twenty-first birthday, when he felt free of any further restraint. He had beaten a sick hand into insensibility because the poor creature stopped work against orders, unable to drag about any longer. Gerda, hearing of Wayne's brutality, commanded him into her presence. When he saw the whip she was going to use on him, he told her in surly defiance:

" You can't lay on to me with that. You forget what day this is. I'm my own man now."

" I know it's your legal age day," she told him, " but you have failed to grow into a *man,* and until you do I'll punish you as you deserve, to teach you the taste of the abuse you heap on dumb souls you hold in slavery."

She had hated meting out to him this punishment meant for beasts, she had hated worse the way he tried to dodge the lashes. Later she had silently handed over to him the deed to his land, which she had hoped to give to him at supper with good wishes for his prosperity. Now the bestowal was a sorry act.

Up at Yufala, Joby, in a milder way, somewhat baffled Gerda nowadays; for since she and C. D. had effected some semblance of a peaceable union, they had had a daughter born the year after Cinda's son. It was a pale little mite with a fretful face, its scrawny body decked in prickly embroidery-encrusted garments. Joby was now emulating the showy ways of the Melburnes, turning up her nose at the Whetstones' plain comfort, and boasting of how the Melburne grandparents had sent all the way to England for the infant's silver mug and porringer. She was already trying to train the baby's duck-down fuzz into curls and prophesying complacently how she would take her little darling back to relatives in Charleston one day, to attend the St. Cecilia Ball, where she could meet proper suitors. Gerda, eyeing the sallow little tad, privately thought she'd better stay here where women were scarcer, where she might manage to make a match with some son of a small farmer, some boy now working barefoot alongside his father's lone negro hand. There was no doubt about it, Joby was becoming a precious prig, but Gerda held her tongue because she knew that this smugness grew out of a new security induced in her by C. D.'s belated decency.

Aside from that she felt that Joby's stickling for the niceties had a certain value to the county's development at this stage and should be tolerated along with Gracey's faded airiness. Gracey was for ever traipsing to Tuscaloosa or Shelby Springs or Montgomery, to be present at some much-touted social event. She came home bringing the latest in highfalutin fads, a bilious stomach, and perishable favours to be squabbled over by the girls at the Bruton Academy. Yes, Gerda chuckled to Danley, it was a good thing for his school to have Gracey to teach parlour manners and be cranky about the table linen, so that it didn't become mildewed in rainy weather.

Danley, in high amusement, had shown Gerda the letter stating the school's aim of character-formation, which Gracey had prevailed upon him to send out to prospective patrons. It read: "Passions should be restrained, obedience to parents enforced . . . deference to authority, subjugation of the will insisted upon. . . . Reason and religion should control in everything."

"What a hodge-podge!" pronounced Gerda.

"'Subjugation of the will' is slightly in conflict with the 'control of reason,'" agreed Danley, chuckling. "I fear it's a stiffer order of social discipline than we can achieve."

The flighty Gracey saw nothing incongruous in the fact that her lofty aims dwindled down to the teaching of "raised and palace work, linear drawing, pianoforte, tissue flowers," and some vague advanced thing called "calisthenics," which left her tight-laced young ladies out of breath after a lot of aimless arm-waving.

Danley's attitude towards his male pupils, however, was quite another matter. His curricular requirements were severe, endeavouring to apply Oxonian standards in this hit-and-miss environment. He was aided by the rare gift that marked him as a true teacher, that knack of imbuing learning with a sense of adventure and challenge. He had perfected that trick with the first of his forest-bred lads at the Stand, and thus far it had never failed him. Pioneers all, they could not miss a dare.

It was in Bruff that Gerda centred her untempered pride after his father's death. Impetuous, forward-looking, he made a persistent leader in the fight for more stringent ethical demands among Alabama medical practitioners. Deep in the movement to establish a state medical school, he yet had time to support Dorothea Dix in her struggle for an asylum for the insane. In addition to his lively interest in public health problems, he had a fine patience for the tedious side of his country practice. He could work as tirelessly as any mother over a baby with croup; he was not afraid to go into the thick of an outbreak of typhoid; he could take a scared child on his knee and feel with kind fingers for the seat of pain; he knew how to make a woman in labour feel brave; and he was not above lending a hand to a mule with colic. He rode silent miles into the dark pine woods where some

" poor white " lay dying, up clay banks with yellow jasmine scrambling, then home again, fagged out, to the stable lot where the grey wood chips had been powdered into silver dust by the restless hoofs of stock.

Gerda felt content in her bones at the part he had borne in the years that had turned two since his father's death. She knew him for a son fitted to be that father's namesake.

4

At last as the third year since Yarbrough's death commenced, Gerda felt herself less washed by waves of womanish weakness, not so much in need of his advice at every turn. A confidence in handling her crops on a par with any man was growing in her. Last year she had worked hard over her cotton, preparing the seed for planting by soaking them in brine to the point of fermentation, then drying them off in ashes. When the cotton had begun to make, she had insisted that her hands pick as clean as possible. After drying on a scaffold, the bulk had been packed away to wait a spell before being ginned, until the lint could draw some of the oil from the seed to give it a rich creamy colour that would bring two cents more to the pound. In the end she was not ashamed to stamp the Whetstone name on her bales and ship them out to compete with the best of any man's on the market.

Aside from her cotton yield, she was gratified at not being " cotton poor " like so many of the other big planters. When she went to the County Fair at Yufala and heard the speaker of the occasion pleading with them to practice " diversification of crops," she could nod her head in proud agreement. For she raised enough provender and stock to keep her people in good and varied food if they spent not a cent in the outside markets. They made their own syrup and sugar, as few planters did these days; they wove most of the cloth except for party clothes; tanned their leather for brogans; and besides all that she had another trump: her grist- and saw-mill, which kept them in meal and could saw six thousand feet of lumber a day even with a lazy crew!

She could not help feeling covered with glory at the Fair when she took first prize for the best corn-and-cob-crusher, manufactured on her own place. She interested the other planters, and embarrassed Willy, by telling how she occupied some of her field-hands in the slack season, making barrels of oak staves to be sold to the tavern-keepers and merchants for whisky-kegs. Willy also flushed when she openly derided the trotting-horse prize's going to a beautiful creature of Nat Screws', because, she claimed, it "gobbled biddies." "Why," stated Gerda, "he nibbles the little chicks up alive, almost from under the hens' wings. They make a terrible *ch-eep* as they go down."

Later she would not pay one whit of attention to Willy's trying to coax her over among the ladies for dinner. Instead she had settled down at a trestle table with the men, where the barbecued meat had been served up in thick slabs among their tumblers of whisky. There she had alertly discussed the merits of the fine-saw gin, while poor Willy fidgeted. She had not guessed what ailed him until that evening.

That night she had gone walking down in the bottom land. It was the full of the moon, and the second picking of cotton was bursting out of blue-washed bolls. The corners of her mouth lifted in the start of a smile, the way it did when she felt she had acquitted herself well for Yarbrough's sake. Then suddenly, without trying to evoke his presence, she felt as if he were right there! Or rather that she was somewhere with him.

It wasn't remembering. It was simply like *being* back with him on a certain rock ledge below some spruce trees, climbing after dewberries. The bush growth was tough and so brambly her hands were snagged by the briers, but still she filled his hat with the glistening black fruit. She held it up to him and he plunged his mouth into it. When he lifted his face again he was blue-blobbed about the nose and lips. She leaned back against the red side of the ridge, noticing how the berry-stain smudged where his beard was sprouting.

Then abruptly, right while she was catching sight out of the corner of one eye of the first dancing yellow rag of a fall leaf . . . abruptly she lost the smell of sun on dirt, and felt once more the damp of night about her ankles, and Yarbrough had left her. But all the way up the path to the house her steps glanced lightly over the ground. Once again she knew the glad feeling of having just parted from him the moment before!

It was that same night that she found the missive from Willy waiting for her, embodying his formal proposal for her hand. In it he addressed himself to no woman aged by the fact that she was the mother of grown men and women, and a grandmother now thrice over. Instead he restored her beauty to her, feature by feature, and begged her to accept his long-cherished tenderness, which had tormented him for years.

The words of his proposal jolted her into an acknowledgment that no part of her was dessicated even by her loss. She was grateful for the liveness the shock gave her, but in achieving that Willy had served his purpose. Now she thrust the letter out of sight in the escritoire and went over to grip hold of her great chest of drawers. Everything of hers was massive, her two-poster bed, the great quilts, the heavy jewellery, representing the lasting solidity of her matronal years, the solitariness of her widowhood. Let other women have the weak-water happiness of remarriage, she felt the whole fortress of her and Yarbrough's life strong about her. Now she was upborne by the lust for work, roused by the thought of the victory to be wrested from the soil and seasons, the drama of politics and laws, shaping of sons growing, and a clan founding!

The next day, near its close, she went where she had not gone for a long time, up to the family burying-ground. She turned her eyes in a circle. This was a fine place, where she could see far and wide. There was nothing meek about their dead. They were all dressed up in their Sunday best, with rings on their fingers and stick-pins in their shirt bosoms. There were no willows for them either, but the prickle and scarlet of holly, until she felt more like wishing "Christmas gift!" to company than saying prayers for the dead. And here in their midst she felt like Sister God indeed, standing on a piece of high ground!

There she let the hours pass by in her power.

Later she saw where a curtain of gold had been lowered over the sky, and the yard bell began to toll with its pure sweet call across the fields, to stay the hands from their labour. While she watched she saw them coming one by one, scattered. Then the separate figures joined in a lingering row, plodding along the rutted road, a brown procession making its way towards the temple of her home. The last note of the bell fell away, broken apart by quiet.

BOOK FOUR

The Cotton Snobs

CHAPTER FORTY-THREE

THE DECADE of the fifties opened with a shout in Alabama. The harsh days of pioneering and Indian-fighting were over, now came a time when its broad half-cleared lands were under the golden reign of King Cotton. The river boats creaked with it, the market-places resounded to the cries of its prices. A black race laboured and white lords prospered. The earth burst forth with it, and the sky was filled with clouds upon clouds of white, obscuring all else. It was a time of *Jubilate!*

In Montgomery, the new State Capitol stood on Goat Hill above the sprawling town, unkempt, but bursting with its new political importance. Tuscaloosa, the former capital, remained serene behind its high-pillared porches, like some widow that had once known the favour of a robust mate. Mobile was a rowdy water-front town, with its open square used as a horse and hog pasture, although to the men who came down with their bales for sale it was a colourful place for a fine holiday.

And what of the men who dwelt in this land, called her their mistress, and gave to this time its flavour, its tone, its shape, its reality?

They were not minted from any single well-worn stamp of high degree. Lordly and humble, they shifted and intermingled, until, without waiting for the passage of a single generation, they became a freshened breed, more vigorous than any of the stocks that went into the making. Virginians, New Englanders, Carolinians, Dutch, Scotch, and even the mercurial Irish strain, mingling in a common conquest, made a high-spirited, stubborn, ruthless race, building prosperity on the foundations of a wilderness. Worrying about malaria and ground itch and schools, knitting their brows over the state of their slaves, visionary about the textile uses of their one staple product, cotton. Dashing, generous, crass perhaps, questioning, bombastic. But whatever else they were, they were not of a worn-out vintage of blue blood, past the best year for its consumption by life.

They included all manner of folk: conscientious and astute professional men and out-and-out quacks; small farmers owning a patch of land, with one slave and work-toughened sons to help them grow rich overnight, to turn them into " planters." There were a few courtly aristocrats like Mr. Lucas at Mount Meigs with his formal gardens tended by a score of negroes under a white gardener, but there were numberless poor whites in the piny woods who counted themselves lucky to have a pallet on the floor and side-meat and cow peas to exist on. However, it was a multiplication of clans like the Whetstones that determined the dominant caste of Alabama. Families blended of a Cavalier strain and some slower, steadier blood, the parents having known the hardship of blight and flood and sickly slaves, no matter how they pampered their offspring into a show of idleness or coxcombry. And their stronghold, while frequently a veranda'd frame mansion, was more often a house like Rock Wall, buttressed in part at least by logs, with a breeze-swept centre hall through which a visitor could see the hens scratching in the back yard as he mounted the front step. A domain set in a clean broom-brushed, oak-shadowed yard, penned in by snake-rail fences festooned with Cherokee roses.

But it was at such a gala holiday gathering as Lucinda was wont to give in her impressive establishment that every one came together, and the crazy-quilt patches of all sorts and kinds showed the whole colourful pattern.

2

It was the eve of the New Year that would usher in 1850, and the house at Top Hill was being put in final readiness for the party that would see the old year out. Before early candlelighting time, when the day had not quite waned outside, Danley, who had made his careful toilet early, was strolling in the gardens. The bitterness of boxwood drifted, making him indulge in an unearned sadness. It was a gentle winter evening with a peach after-light suffusing into a fading upper sky, while below, the horizon was edged with trees as soft as the breast of quail.

As Danley turned his steps back, the looming bulk of the house began to be pricked out by first one spangle of light, then another, until it lost substance and became a fairy palace moored to the sky by a constellation. When he went inside, he felt how pristine the whole edifice was—waxed, gleaming, sweetened through and through with the blooms and ferns from Lucinda's new conservatory. He hated, almost, to have its garnished and expectant emptiness ravished.

Yet he bounded up the stairway eagerly enough, on his way to supervise the completion of Lucinda's toilet. Whatever antagonism they felt over other matters, he was almost foolish about her splendid looks and on every special occasion worked over her like a masterpiece. It made Cinda laugh to hear a man giving Pinky finicky orders and tugging her garments about, but it also fed her never slumbering ego. He was very dictatorial about certain of his decrees, insisting that her hair be dressed in a crown of braids in order not to hide the fine shape of her head; and he was partial to high combs or bandeaux set with jewels of as fine a water as those in her other ornaments. He agreed entirely with her prejudice against wearing anything save velvet in the winter, and he was never content with a commonplace colour for her. Above all, he had not one vestige of false modesty concerning her, for he wanted to display her charms very clearly. Let other men look, he told her, all they pleased and know him for a lucky dog in possession of the prize.

To-night she was ready for the choosing of her top petticoat when he came in, and Pinky had two spread out. He chose the plainer, saying that nothing must be bunchy beneath her gown and destroy the fall of its folds. She was to wear a violet velvet worked in gold fleur-de-lis. After she was gowned he shook his head, dissatisfied. Then he walked up to her. " Here, Pinky, let me show you. You'll have to relace her and push her bosom up higher." Placing his hands below Lucinda's breasts, he pressed them up so they showed in beautiful half-mounds above the gold-encrusted stuff. " You need to be very voluptuous to offset the richness of the fabric—to show yourself up more than the gown.

" Well, get at it, Pinky," he ordered. He watched the process of seeing Lucinda's breasts bared, then tucked scantily into the corselet. When it was done, his prediction was right. Any one would glance first at the romantic colour and gleaming gold embroidery of the frock, but after that his eyes would feast on the beautifully exposed bosom that seemed scarcely able to contain itself in its casing. " Now," he decided, " I wouldn't wear any jewels, except those cuffs of diamonds at the wrists. Not even a high comb to-night. So that from there *up,* it will be all you." He laughed slightly, but impersonally. " It's so beautifully shocking, that coronation robe, and your nude Highness." Pinky cackled appreciatively; she was a lewd wench and enjoyed Marse Danley's brazen sallies. She lifted up the train for her mistress, and Danley led Lucinda down to the head of the large drawing-room where they would receive the company. They had not had so gala an affair since their union.

Shortly the creaking of carriage-wheels sounded and the guests began to alight. Those who had come a long way and were to spend the night bundled their children off in charge of little Whet's mammy. Soon the company was swarming past the Brutons in greeting, gentlemen in maroon or buff-coloured breeches and Marseilles waistcoats, ladies in pink and blue *glacés,* striped faille, embroidered net, and saffron and rose brocade; Captain Melburne with his fluted shirt and gold snuffbox, speaking in a high discontented voice to lawyer James Pugh about Southern Rights; his wife lace-bedizened and gushing, just behind him; Miz Lydia and dry-witted John Screws, passing a wink at Cinda at the expense of their son Nat and his pushing wife, Nettie, who was jingling with too many ornaments. Then several demure girl pupils at the Academy, ducking curtsies and casting sheep's eyes at Danley. Tom Two, right after them, was squiring his lost wife Lutie's sister. The girl had returned home from a Northern boarding-school because her grandfather, the old doctor, had got mad at the Abolitionists. Her hair missed the brightness of Lutie's, but her eyes were not so shallow and corner-wise, and she glowed under Tom's attention.

As the guests, from bowing dandy to small merchant, went trooping by, the musicians began playing a medley of equally assorted tunes: *Carnaval de Venise, The Low-Back'd Car, The Caliph of Baghdad,* and *Jim Shuck Corn.* When the crowd had thinned down to a trickle, Danley turned to welcome John Upshur, the former preacher, now a man of considerable means but not grown purse-proud. He was accompanied by his peaked wife, Miz Della, who had never witnessed such magnificence as this, though she had Crown china to testify to the manor-house her mother had come from in England. They had brought their daughter Nan, on whom they doted. She was a slight child of nine years, with a level mouth, but eyes that snapped like cinder-sparks with mischief. On her head was a curt-cut cropping of her curls that failed to make her look like a boy. She wore a simple white mull with a prim locket over her chest on a blue ribbon. As they moved away from their hosts, Bruff spied them and came over to exclaim about Nan. "Why, here's my little pet! And she's about to turn into a young lady behind my back."

The child replied in an unflurried manner: "You could have seen plenty of me without going to any trouble if you had stopped by at our place some of all those times you've been tracking up to that Emma Will Willis's."

Bruff started and glanced about uncomfortably. He didn't want his jaunts in that poor-white quarter broadcast, but Nan persisted: "She brags you're paying her attention. *I* told her you were just fooling her." She looked his face over. He had, she thought, a little too much beauty to his mouth, and pride in the nose. That merely caused her chest to give a quick squeeze inside, as it always had at the sight of him from babyhood.

Her mother, not knowing what Nan might say next, spoke nervously. "Now, Nan, Whet's mammy is beckoning. You'd better run along to bed with the other children."

Obediently Nan made her manners to her parents and hosts, then with a composed air took Bruff's arm, to be seen to the stairs. At her quaint gesture he looked down at her amused, once more at ease. She pinched his arm where her fingers lay. "I told Emma Will too that you were just waiting for *me* to grow up."

Upstairs she wouldn't join the pillow-fight, but slipped off into one of the ladies' retiring-rooms and undid her frock to see how much growing she had done lately. "Very little," she concluded glumly, "I'm not a very flush girl."

Downstairs the dancers were choosing partners for a figure. Joachim, very vain in his new satin-revered coat, was being beset by the coquetries of a bevy of girls. In Jerard Malone's old office Duncan MacDuff was leading the serious drinkers in Rabelaisian stories, with Ven ahead on the drams. Over whist tables in the Little Parlour the players were expressing their views on current politics in that sharp tone that card games engender. "These Abolitionists," fretted Melburne, referring to the new pest that might easily put a blight upon cotton, "these Abolitionists ought to be hung." Said Guy: "They ain't as bad as the

Free Soilers. Besides, they cain't do us any real harm, because one thing's certain, they cain't free our slaves from us till kingdom come. But now you take these here Free Soilers; what they want is to keep us out of the territories, so's they can get more new states comin' into the Union on their side."

"Yes," James Pugh backed him up, "the Free Soilers aren't concerned like the Abolitionists with the 'bondage of the Africans.' What they want is to bring in new states with their same interests. With men who will vote for high tariff, the United States Bank, and every measure inimical to our planting system, who will protect Northern mills that batten on cheap free white labour. And believe me, gentlemen, they do not undertake to care for that 'free' white class in the way we protect our 'poor chattels,' as they term them!"

Several men clapped their cards against the tables in applause. Danley, entering, sent Bonapartt to fetch some special bottles, and the players relaxed behind the vapours of fine cheroots to discuss their favourite topic, Cotton.

Across the hall *Rosalie, the Prairie Flower,* had given way to the increased excitement of the *Herculean Quickstep* as the last hour of the old year drew near. Upstairs in the nursery the children began to make Indian war-whoops; outside Turber had the other big boys set off a sputter of firecrackers.

Far off in the backwoods Nathan, the second stroke-setter of Top Hill hoe-hands, stopped and sat down on a bank because he didn't know which way to turn next. *He was running away. He wanted to get to Freedom.* But he had run and run and gone as far as all get-out, yet here he still was on Miss Lucinda's land. That was something that Yankee inciter hadn't told him, how far it was to Freedom. Looked like that white man, who'd pestered him with all that talk that day, when he was coming home in a hurry to make it before curfew and the Patrollers, looked like that inciter ought to have explained to him about the distance. Or maybe Nathan should have taken a mule to ride, except a hand got whipped good for stealing stock. Anyhow, Nathan guessed he'd lie down now and sleep a spell. He'd need that rest before he lit out good to-morrow. He rolled over, tucking his face and shins under a fallen log, to shut out the daylight when it broke. It shore felt good to be free!

Back at Top Hill a pair of piccaninnies were drumming on a brass fire-shovel with tongs, marching ahead of Bonapartt, who bore a giant bowl of eggnog for the drinking of ceremonial toasts before supper. Lucinda and Danley took their stations beneath a girandole mirror. After every one had been ladled out a cup, the brazen gong went twelve slow times. "I give you," cried Danley, "I give you the year *eighteen hundred and fifty!*"

"Happy New Year!" they shouted back in chorus, after which every one quaffed.

Gerda stopped before she could drink the toast. It set another milestone between her and Yarbrough, took her away, out of even the last decade which he had known. "What of these ten years coming on?" she asked herself fearfully. "How will they use us?" Someone was drumming four wild notes on the new piano, over and over again: *Eighteen-fifty—Happy New Year—Eighteen-fifty——*

Then Tid bolted in, his eyes rolling. "Miz Lucinda, Marse Danley!" The white people let him pass through. "Nathan done run away. Mammy Lizzie jes' found his partin' signs, an' dey show he got a long start. But Lawd save him, Miss Cinda, he done took Marse Malone's silvah toofpick whut you gib Bonapartt!"

A bedlam of unbelief went up, crossed with the discord of denunciation: "Not good steady Nathan . . . the snake poison of Abolition . . . and mind you, filching silver. . . . Soon the country will be destitute of slaves . . . or worse, aprowl with a black menace. . . ."

Danley said to Tid sternly: "Tell our people to all stay in their own cabins. And, Bonapartt, you will be in charge here, with the house servants to help you attend the ladies." He turned to his guests again. "I trust you will forgive this disruption of our entertainment, but I suggest the ladies repair upstairs for the night, where some supper refreshment will be brought them. You, gentlemen, I should like to confer with all of you at the stables, about the immediate recovery of the runaway. Again I wish you all a prosperous New Year."

"Happy New Year!" the ladies answered uncertainly as they trailed off to the stairs, voices chattering. With all this runaway business, the next thing might be a slave uprising. In some other places already it had happened.

Cinda stayed a moment holding Danley's arm. "We sort of fell off our chalk-marble pedestals, didn't we?" she grinned.

Up in her room she found Gerda. "I don't like the looks of it," frowned Gerda, "when any one as reliable as Nathan can be stirred up to such a trick." But Lucinda was surveying herself in the glass. "This is a truly handsome gown," she remarked, to which Gerda replied: "Shows too much meat." Then Gerda leaned out over the window-sill as if it were some barricade to the future. She heard the bloodhounds far off. *1850?*

CHAPTER FORTY-FOUR

GERDA's foreboding of a shadow to be cast across the brightness of the new decade soon appeared to be well founded. Nuisances instigated by the anti-slavery people began to crop up on all sides, rousing many hot-headed Southerners to a desire for instant Secession. Gerda, however, in common with many other large slave-holders, was against such drastic action. She felt in her bones that that would be bound to cause trouble with the rest of the Union and might even end up in fighting. And if the fighting did not turn out their way, they might suffer the complete loss of their slaves. At the very best it would stop them from profitable working of their land for a season or so.

Heaven knew Gerda was as anxious as the next one to see their "institutions preserved," nor was it in her nature to submit to any outrage against her property by an alien hand. But she was against trying any hasty high-jinks; she put her faith in the power of the planters to carry the day in Congress as they had many and many a time.

One particular day there was a subdued pleasant activity in the ell that certain rainy days brought about. Pokey was supervising a monkey-fingered piccaninny who was learning how to wrap head wool into pigtails fit for Sunday go-to-meeting. Little Whet, over from Top Hill with Miss Cinda, was riding horse on an overturned splint-bottomed chair. Miss Joby's eldest girl was sucking her finger in placid hauteur.

Miz Gerda herself was grading dried peas for planting, sorting them according to whether they were intended for table use, the quarters, or cow feed. The batches were heaped in mounds spread fan-wise about her chair, and as they mounted high enough, one of the piccaninnies piled them into her apron-skirt and carried them over to the proper crokersack. Marm Pokey called sharply to a tyke who was gobbling some stray ones like ground peas: "Don' you know they ain't goobers? Yo' gizzard'll swell up and bust ef you eat many of them things."

The rascal went on nibbling on the sly.

The rain drove down heavier, until a wash-kettle had to be set beneath the leak that had rotted through a joining in the roof. Immediately little Whet went fishing in it, with a pole of dried sugar cane and a line of carded cotton. Lucinda eyed him absorbed in his activity for a bit, then shrugged and turned to her mother. "Ma'am, did Bruff tell you how bad Nathan came down with pneumonia after his New Year's didos?"

Yes, Gerda knew all that, so Lucinda went on: "Well, he hasn't been worth two shakes since we got him back. I doubt if he can manage to hoe to the end of a row. And worse than that, he's acting uppity, because he thinks he's been free for a while. It's upsetting the other negroes too." She jerked her head impatiently. "These plagued Abolitionists!"

Gerda scooped some cow peas into the palm of her hand and studied them as she answered slowly: "Somehow I feel inclined to put the main blame for this growing exodus on the owners. Except of course for hands that run away regularly twice a year to escape heavy pushes of work instead of coming down with 'misery in the back.' Those always show up again on the dot when work lessens. But don't you think you're somewhat at fault, Lucinda? About Nathan? Don't misunderstand me. You treat them fine, leaving out the tantrums you have against your house and yard negroes. And they admire that, think it shows your dander. But I mean you don't keep a regular watch over them, know what's happening all along. You leave their care too much to Mr. Dicks. Now, how in time did a good steady one like Nathan ever have the chance to listen to any inciter or agitator? If you send them into town on an errand, you ought to see that they attend to business, then check back home. And under all circumstances they ought to be home, *without fail,* before curfew! Mine all are." She dribbled the peas back into her lap, knowing that she would have to sort that portion all over again because she had been distracted.

Joby, hearing Ma'am's last statement, remarked to Cinda patronizingly: "Not a Lord's blessed one of my people would leave me."

"Hnh!" snorted Ma'am Gerda. "Hardly! Living right in town at Yufala. Wearing shoes the year round, and nothing to do but keep from stepping on each other's toes while bowing and scraping." She started to turn back to pursue the subject with Lucinda when she caught the wail of Joby's new baby girl. "Better send someone to tend it. Sounds like it's messed itself."

The rain was letting up enough to see it falling in steady strings. Tom Two and Hans came out of the boys' room, where they had been taking some sleep while the heavy downpour lasted. Tom Two looked brisker these days than he had since Lutie's death over two years ago. He cracked a hickory nut merely by crunching two together in his powerful hands, and as he picked out the meat he announced: "I'm going to be on my way up to Yufala." Gerda knew that meant he was calling on Lutie's young sister, Hannah Lee, which she thought was just as well.

Hans stopped beside Lucinda. "I made up that shakedown bed in the little far room for you. I thought maybe all this commotion might be wearing you out." He looked about at the scramble of white and black people pursuing a conglomeration of activities all over the room. It wasn't much like the ordered ease of Top Hill.

Lucinda, out of sorts at Gerda's lecture on her runaway Nathan, answered: "I'm much obliged. Is the fire lit?"

"No, but it's laid. I'll start it." He went with his quiet woodsman's step, so like the man Hans who should have fathered him instead of Yarbrough.

When Lucinda joined him in that odd little room which had been added to Rock Wall, he had the fire sending out a sweet smell of dampened smoke. She coughed from it, holding out her hands to the almost obscured patch of warmth. Gradually the fire beat the damp back up the chimney and blazed tawnily. She sank down before it tailor-fashion, saying: "It was chilly out there in the ell all right. I don't see why Ma'am doesn't have doors made for both ends of it."

As she sat with her knees squared, hands clasping her ankle-bones so that her skirts fell slightly away from her limbs, Hans could see how much richer-thewed she had become since bearing Whet. When the heat of the fire increased, she pulled her frock impatiently open at the throat until it rolled away widely, then she pushed her sleeves up. "I declare, it's already too late in the season for velvet."

Hans could hardly bear to watch the white pit inside her elbow, but when he tried to shift his gaze from that, it fell on her exposed chest, which made his palms cup involuntarily. Lucinda rose from the floor yawning logily, careless of the feast of flesh she was displaying to him. "Get me a quilt," she commanded, "I'm going to take a nap."

He brought one, clean, yet with the camphor-smell of being packed in an unused chest. She crowded her shoulders under its protective clamminess, making a little hollow on the edge of the bed for him to sit. He took his place gingerly, shaking inside at the light pressure his back made against her, where her thighs joined her belly. He stayed very still for a long while, then irresistibly he found himself shoving the hardness of his backbone against her yielding softness. Now, now he was so close against her that she must be aware of his obsessing importunity!

But only an even sigh responded; she had fallen asleep. He wanted to pull aside the quilt and look at her breasts, but he rose instead and tipped toward the door, careful not to jar it as he shut it behind him.

When he passed through the ell, Ma'am was listening to Bruff, who had come in with a *Montgomery Daily Messenger* in his hands. They seemed to want Hans to stay and join in their discussion, but he went on, headed for his cottonseed bin, where he could work through his agony in his own way. "Oh, Lucinda," he moaned into the smothering softness.

Back in the ell Bruff was slapping at his newspaper angrily. "Look at it! It's broken out like smallpox with a rash of notices about runaway slaves." He spread it for her to see the all too familiar picture of a negro running and carrying a bundle, the sign used with printed notices of runaway slaves. "About all I do in my practice is go to answer the call of some planter with a broken-down fugitive back on his hands. Sometimes I almost wish that every last one of them would land up in the Abolitionists' laps, so they could have a taste of what it's like to try to care for negroes."

Gerda was picking at the remaining peas, trying to think of some way to smooth down Bruff's ruffled cock feathers, when Joachim came tearing up the side steps shouting: "Bruff, Willy just stopped by the wall steps to tell us to make haste to Yufala. They've called a mass meeting to back up Postmaster Lanforth in his stand against the Government about not delivering those inciting pamphlets to the negroes."

Gerda quit even pretending to sort peas. She knew what a ticklish proposition this was. Lanforth had been refusing to deliver incendiary pamphlets from the Abolitionists addressed to some of the slaves hereabouts who could read and write. The printed matter was meant to stir up a slave rebellion as it had in some other states. Now the Federal authorities at Washington had got wind of Lanforth's refusal and were out to punish him by removal from office. "No telling," she thought, "where this will end."

"Do you hear that, Ma'am?" demanded Bruff. "Now even Washington has gone too far! Come, Jake, let's saddle up and all go to take Lanforth's side."

Watching them ride off, Gerda shook her head dubiously. She was in sympathy with the postmaster's stand against such mischief-making literature, but she didn't want to see the county go off half-cocked over any one incident. Besides, so few of the negroes could read and write that pamphlets couldn't do any great pack of harm.

She cleared her lap and went to judge the weather. Darkies, she snorted, loved any tall tale of a Promised Land, where they could ride on a carriage cushion and eat all the pork they wanted.

It now being full dark, she ordered the new kerosene lamp to be lighted on the dining-table, to brighten what had been a drear day, and ordered a new cake cut to satisfy the youthful sweet tooth. After supper they gathered in the ell again. The children, black and white, spread on the floor the paraphernalia for playing stagecoach, with little Whet as the driver of the churning-stool horses. There was a great bustle of portmanteaus being packed with doll rags and pecan hoards, then stowed on the rack amid whip-cracking and a general contagious excitement. Every child lost his breath clambering aboard. Presently Lucinda entered into the game, unable to resist its lifelike dangerousness. Joby's older coddled darling raised a wail at the way the coach lurched, and her Screws cousin, now a passenger, pinched her nose to shut her up. Whet wanted to hit him for that, but instead drew his cousin India over and petted her sore little nostrils. Her tears dried immediately, but she kept on with her whimpering from time to time conscientiously.

Gerda rocked, contented at the sight.

2

Towards morning, when the household was deep in sleep, the men could be heard returning home from the postmaster's rally, yowling a Non-Submissionist political tune. Hans and Tom Two were trying to steer the others, who were roaring drunk, safely to their beds. They all came to a late breakfast supported by pick-me-ups of Ven's concocting. Bruff announced triumphantly, in spite of his hollow-socketed eyes, that the people of Yufala had backed Lanforth to the hilt in his risky stand against the Federal postal laws. In fact, the citizens had passed a resolution that they would permit no other man to take Lanforth's place if he were removed from office.

"Last night was just the start of it," bragged Joachim. "We're sending delegates to the convention at Nashville to demand slavery in New Mexico and California. Either that or we're going to secede!"

"You all are going to land us in a peck of trouble, that's what," predicted Gerda. "There's always some fracas being stirred up around here to give an excuse not to stick to regular work. If 'tisn't Indian wars it's conventions. Those things are a worse plague to cotton-making than caterpillars or the scalds."

She stirred her coffee with grumpy digs of her spoon. Hearing her sons' protests grow audibly, she was filled with foreboding and longed for Yarbrough's reassuring presence, then realized that he more than any of them would have slapped the dare into an opponent's face. Yarbrough had been the first warring king-errant, seeking a throne on horseback.

The clatter of her sons' knives and their foolhardy boasts rose raucously in a challenging din. To dismiss it Gerda left the table and went about her day's business.

But the disturbance for Southern Rights still continued at that breakfast table, as it did at many another throughout the South, all spring. Calhoun stirred his supporters with *On to Nashville!* In June a jubilant hoard congregated there to demand recognition of their sectional institution of slavery in some of the coming new states. And, if refused, to rally the South to bolt for its freedom. They were met by Henry Clay's diplomacy, and before they quite knew what had happened, they found their wings had been clipped by the Compromise of 1850. They were still firmly fenced into the Union.

Bruff arrived back from Nashville in a vile humour. Gerda was glad enough not to take verbal issue with him, now that a crisis was past and they could go ahead with the peaceful task of raising crops and employing a quiet winter to be ready for another more settled year. She was even willing later to humour Joby, when her younger daughter began to fret about how every one of any elegance except herself was travelling to Mobile to hear the concert of the Swedish Jenny Lind, now touring under the management of Barnum. A country, Gerda sighed with relief, was safe from war when its women were putting on airs.

Certainly it proved a flourishing epoch, with something to suit every one's taste: circuses, lectures on Women's Rights and Temperance, Chaufran Booth playing Shylock and Richard III to Danley's satisfaction, and low burlesque more to Cinda's taste. There were dog-and-bear-fights that roused Will Bee's enthusiasm, and the choicest horses racing for Ven to pick. Dancing-classes, serenading, and fashionable watering-places flourished. It was a time for gallivanting in one's best clothes, and for gabbling constantly of Southern Rights. In fact, it was a high old time to be alive and boast tunefully:

We live in Alabama,
'Mongst the noble and the free!

In spite of all the reassuring hullaballoo of good spirits, Gerda noticed, though, that the agitation for Secession had not ceased in Turber County. 1851 opened with a stamping of feet and the boast:

The Southern cause is gaining ground,
On right, on left, from far and near,
The Southern skies are getting clear!

Soon a bitter election campaign was under way between those who wanted to gain the planters' interests by exerting power in the Union at Washington and those who were rabid for Secession.

As June came in, the campaign boiled up hotter, with rallies and counter-rallies, and every known device for stirring up hysteria. With July Fourth approaching, big preparations were being made for a political barbecue at Blue Springs, which was to be the final wind-up of the campaign. Horses and carriages were groomed and polished till they shone blinding-bright. Children were made to obey for weeks ahead, by the threat of being kept at home from the big treat. Every lady and young girl in the county had a new frock, and the more up-to-date were fitted out in picnic gloves, which was quite the latest cry. Joby was sure hers were more effective, owing to her fine-boned hands, than Nettie's, which had cost more. Young Hannah Lee Caraway, whom Tom Two was now courting steadily, had none and felt completely disgraced. However, Tom took her bare hand tenderly as he helped her into the Screws' carriage, in which they were guests along with Joby and C. D.

Hannah Lee felt even more reassured later when she had gone to repair her hair in one of the dressing-marquees and Joby had whispered: "Don't be so taken up with the speeches and goings-on that you can't give Tom Two a chance."

"What do you mean?" gasped Hannah Lee.

"Why, don't you know that he's already bespoken you to your grandfather?"

"What? And what did Grandpa sa-ay?"

"Well, of course," shrugged Joby, "first of all he 'most popped because he thought it was a sacrilege against your dead sister Lutie. But he wound up by thinking it was the sweetest tribute Tom could pay to her memory, to want to marry her sister."

"Oh." The sound Hannah Lee made was very small. She felt like a bunch of flowers being put on a grave.

Even that regret was lost very soon in the hum of the crowd, the stinging smell of the barbecue sauce, the intermittent spasms of negro laughter. So presently, when Tom Two took her for a quiet, determined stroll up the paths that had grown chocolate-coloured in the shadow of the pine trunks and asked her to be his wife, she felt no sad ghost between them as she answered: "Yes, if you want me." Afterwards she sat very proud beside him while they watched Willy and Bruff up on the speakers' platform; and she thought: "They're my kinfolks now, the Whetstones."

The rhetoric resounded up into the arch of the trees, a July fly skimmed the surface of a pool, some of the people were in a mellow drowse, others were loosely stirred by words hurled into their state of surfeit from whisky and barbecue. The sweat swam down the backs of gentlemen under their coats, palm-leaf fans waggled in front of ladies' faces, children itched. And all were warned that unless the South defended her rights, the lives of their people, their liberties, their lands, their negroes, all would be lost. Still, it was believed, with great eloquence, that "the people will sense this danger, and then they will strike for independence and establish a Southern Confederacy, and the gates of hell shall not prevail against it!"

3

In the end Cochran, the Southern Rights contender, lost his seat in Congress owing to the conservative sentiments of the big planters like Gerda. For a few days her offspring were inclined to blame her personally for their candidate's defeat. They recovered from that quickly, however, when the tide turned in their favour with the election of Pierce for President and they regained every point they had lost by the Compromise of 1850. After that they thought of their private concerns once more.

Bruff's was medicine, and he deplored a laxity in professional ethics in some parts of his state. He had been earnestly working for a law to admit only those holding diplomas from reputable medical schools to practice. He had also led in the movement to discredit the Thompsonians, who believed that "life is heat and death is cold," and who did disastrous things sometimes in administering stimulants both internal and external.

Bruff reported to Ven, late one night, a discouraging case where he had not been able to save the patient when called in tardily. The "heater" had already practically blistered the patient to death with everything including red pepper.

"A leetle mite of whisky," opined Ven, "and a heavy quilt is enough heat, to my mind, for any mortal."

"Yes," replied Bruff, feeling tuckered out, "and I'll take a 'leetle mite' now, if you'll pass it to me. It helps me to sleep instead of moping." He sat brooding into his toddy-glass for a moment. "You know, I had just about quit drinking while I was studying at Tulane." He reached over suddenly and tossed the remains of his glass into the fire. "Reckon a doctor can do better without that."

"Here, here," cautioned Ven, "whisky's for startin' a fire, not puttin' one out!"

But Bruff sat up relieved at his self-denial, his face so lighted that Ven moved back a notch or two at its resemblance to Yarbrough's do-or-die look. It gave Ven the jumps, as if his brother's ghost were addressing him.

Suddenly at that very moment a string of little piccaninnies came howling up through the ell on the way to find Miz Gerda. Bruff caught one by the wrist and asked what was up. Aunty Pheaby, gasped the wall-eyed child, Aunty Pheaby had gone and died. She looked a lot like ashes in the face. "Fo' Gawd, Marse Bruff, I was scairt of bein' rode off in de witch-wagin wif A'nty! I gwine beg Marm Pokey to keep me on a pallet close to her to-night, so no ghos' kin catch me!"

Gerda came out quickly, gathering the piccaninnies in a comforting huddle. "You can all sleep with someone grown up and have a crossed stick sprinkled with sweet water nailed across the doorway; then nothing can get at you. For didn't you know that Aunty Pheaby was a good Christian? She's gone off in a big gold chariot with an angel, the way she believed. The Lord promised it to her. She never had any truck with witches. Now here's Lessie, and Sal. They'll boil you up some syrup candy in a kettle, and you can have a candy pulling right here in my kitchen while I go to see about things."

A yipping and a *hi-yeee* went up from the little nigs as they fetched the molasses-keg and kindling.

Gerda was already half-way across the yard following Bruff to the old crone's cabin. A moment or two later, gazing down at the dark-skinned rack of bones, she said: "Well it's so unseasonably cold we can wait a day or two to bury her if we put saucers of saltpetre under the trestle we rest her coffin on. I think she'd like to be buried slow and fine, with a big preaching." The negroes were already gathering in a slow drooping group outside Aunty's sweet-potato patch. *Mmn . . . ummnnn* . . . the mourning sound was still closed in. *MMMNN-U-U-UUMNNNN—ooahm—O-o-oOAAHMMN!* Now it was opening their wide mouths or swelling deeper in their bellies. In an hour it would rumble in a rich roar, with now and then the stab of a proud cry for the departure of a Christian woman who had yet held their ancient African life in her scrawny hands.

Up in the house Ven sat rubbing the crack in the bottom of his cowhide chair . . . numbering his days by hers, recalling how he could remember when Aunty Pheaby had been just a young serving-wench . . . a long time back.

4

These days Bruff began finding himself a stronger outlet than whisky when his spirits sagged or his nerves became knotted too tight. It was women, or at least that girl Emma Will in the backwoods barrens.

As a boy at home, his hunting and fishing, his leadership of his younger brothers, his scholastic ambitions fostered by Danley, had all combined to keep him unaware of the little misses he knew. Then in New Orleans his medical studies had been so stringent they acted as a check-rein on both drinking and any possible philandering. Besides that, the fact that that city offered a predominance of mulatto or quadroon paramours to the young bloods of the day went against his grain.

Now, back home in practice, and in the maturity that had come upon him since his father's death, he could not rest so easy. He needed the comfort of physical contact. Yet he could not take up easy ways, for there had to be some meaning, however imperfect, attached to any body that came to his. Thus for a while he was balked, until he came upon Emma Will up in the malaria district and saw something sharp and decided about her that bit through her coating of sluttishness. Her family had been all scrambled together, a whiny lot, whipped and no-account. Emma Will had stood out from them, not because of any fineness, but because of a certain hard definiteness. On his first sick-call he had asked her if she, being the oldest girl, would stand by to help him with his ministering. But she had shaken her head and jerked a thumb at a smaller girl. " She will, she's right spry. I'm goin' fishin', and anyway 'tain't a bit of use tryin' to cure Pappy. He won't stay well no length of time." Then she'd gone off and not reappeared.

Next time she had sat around for a while, watching Bruff's motions over the patient's bed. " You're set on wastin' your time, ain't you? Doctors and preachers, they do that way. Well, I expect it must give you some pleasure to act smart."

He looked at her more closely this time and found that he had remembered her point by point. Hair yanked back into two loose plaits, with a natural corkscrew curl over each ear; sharp hazel eyes behind sunburnt lashes; nose nothing much; very full, coarse mouth of a pretty colour, but showing one side tooth gone when she grinned too wide; a skimpy body with a remarkable bulging of lush breasts. His eye for anatomy dwelt on them speculatively, wondering how she had achieved them. She saw his gaze upon them and moved closer, as if pushing them up to him. He said nothing and turned away to close his bag.

Then one day after her father was over the attack, he came up to their cabin just the same. Emma Will was lying spread out on the empty porch, flapping at the flies if they tracked across her face. She raised to a half-sitting position. "Pap's in the patch; no need for doctorin' him. Kids are all out aberryin'. I'll keep you company." She looked down at her calico frock, falling slack across her thin legs. He looked too, then stooped down to pull her up to him. They stood there looking mad at each other for a second, then she asked him laconically: "Want to come off in the woods with me?"

He almost snatched her down the porch stepladder by her wrists. And they went into the woods.

Afterwards he said slowly: "You seem to guess, to know, what a person is thinking without him telling."

She shrugged and put her calico back in place, paying attention to nothing but the leaves making grey shadows over both of them. "Reckon you'd better be goin'. It's late and you've a far piece. Besides, I got to fix supper." She would not allow him to soften the situation with any phrases.

All his way home Bruff was able to keep the idea of the keen, plain thing it had been; but the next morning he recalled her grubby hands. Still, he went back there often enough, and when he was with her he never felt foolish, simply because she did not herself. He did not always manage to go off into the woods with her because she had other things to do—berries to preserve, weevils to sift out of the meal, or she simply wanted to go fishing—always by herself. However, when they lay together on the scraping brown leaves, her eyes lit up, and the cushion of her breasts couched his weight easily. "Don't take on over them so," she told him, "they're a bad sign. I prob'ly wouldn't be able to nurse a young 'un. What I eat would go to bust, instead of makin' milk. You ought to know that, bein' a doctor."

He lay back on the dead leaves and began to note the bright ones that were starting to drop from the boughs. He wished she were somebody different; that is, that she had been born in the right sort of house, and wore shoes, and washed with soap instead of scrubbing with sand. If she had, and if she could read and write—but that was all nonsense when she didn't even want to be that way. He sat up with a shake and began picking the trash out of his hair.

On his way home, going down the wagon-road that led past the Upshurs', he saw the little girl Nan seated on the lot gate. Her posture even on a fence-rail was erect. She lifted a hand to him with quaint stateliness.

He drew rein suddenly and came back. "I wonder if your mother would let me take supper."

"It would tickle her to death," replied the child. "But will you go tell her? Because I'm waiting here for the new moon."

CHAPTER FORTY-FIVE

THE FEVER for fervid devotion to Southern institutions spread to Lucinda. Whereas formerly she had left all arduous duties in the hands of Bonapartt, Mr. Dicks, her overseer, and Danley, now she endeavoured to superintend all three departments of her property: the Top Hill mansion, her outlying plantations, and the domestic end of the Academy. She went about her latest household régime with a pomp that appealed to her darkies' love of grandeur. She made no fatiguing daybreak rounds of her kitchens, as did Ma'am Gerda. Instead every morning after the dining-room had emptied, she drew herself an extra cup of coffee from the Sheffield urn and summoned Pinky and Bonapartt, while she sipped the beverage lazily. Bonapartt stood at her left elbow, trying to clasp his hands obsequiously to keep from carelessly popping his knuckles, a trick left over from his early dicing days.

First Lucinda checked the lists Cousin Gracey had submitted for the scholars' fare, usually adding some treat to what she deemed tasteless menus. Then she consulted about the damask for her own head table, the replenishing of the company cake-chest, and the state of the luxury larder. The cellar was Danley's concern. Having ordered some rich dish for her own indulgence, she rose and, flanked by the two servants, made a cursory tour of her household. If her domestic observations were not very astute, at least her mixture of impulsive sympathy for ailments, peppery rebukes, and badinage about courtships marked her entrances and exits with drama.

Her house attended to, according to her lights, Lucinda donned one of her riding-habits with the new-style vests and separate skirts and set out on horseback for whatever quarter-section Mr. Dicks was superintending.

When Mr. Dicks saw her bearing down on him he took off his sunhat and laid it on a stump, in order not to forget and put it back on. He was not one of those numerous untrustworthy overseers who tried to cheat their employers out of the very eyeballs, and he had been devoted to Jerard Malone.

Dicks's one shortcoming was that, lacking all cajolery, he could not manage the negroes in their life in the quarters as well as he could direct them in the fields. He had hoped for a solution of this when he'd heard that Mr. Malone was going to marry Miz Gerda Whetstone's eldest gel, but he had soon discovered that she was more of a charge than a help. Many things she had done that first year had provoked him; still, he had remembered that she was mistress. Besides, something about that restless girl, urging her mount to gallop across furrowed fields, to leap slippery branch-banks as if she were trying to gain that ledge of land that met the sky and break through the very bars of the horizon, something about it made him pity her in his crabbed heart.

Oh, he had hated her hard enough for a few hours after seeing the master, Malone, humbled in a fashion that sent him away! However, he had felt he had to obey those last mumbled injunctions of Jerard Malone's: "Keep care of your mistress, do you hear me, Dicks?"

Watching her to-day, cantering across the fields, with no regard for the tiny plants not yet showing plainly above the ground, he shook his head tolerantly. He saw the hands step back and lift their hoes in salute at her greeting. There was no use denying that they worked up more sweat these days when they thought she was paying attention to them.

Another thing that pleased Cinda's negroes was that she had adopted one of her mother's methods of allowing the smarter hands a private profit from certain small patches allotted them as their own. But whereas Gerda had seldom paid the negroes the cash from the sales, providing them instead with reasonable and scrupulously supervised credit at the Screwses' store that ensured them real profit from their extra toil, Lucinda carelessly tossed out the coins. The result was that the more thrifty buried their booty sterilely in the ground, and the more spendthrift wasted it on some cheap-John bauble like a plated watch or a fancy jack-knife. None of them had anything of use to show for it in the end, yet all felt puffed up with pride for a time.

Her recent assumption of full responsibility in running their domestic arrangements freed Danley for educational purposes. His interests were now reaching out far beyond his own Academy, towards establishing public schools. He was in fact becoming so rabid on the subject of making education a public rather than a private enterprise that Lucinda grew bothered, afraid that the Bruton Academy might go downhill from neglect. So, hearing him talk wistfully for a new schoolhouse more weather-tight, and built with the Lancastrian seating-plan, she made him explain to her what it was. He told her that, instead of having the pupils seated on benches in a hollow square about the edge of the room, with only himself at a desk in the centre, the Lancastrian plan seated the students in parallel rows at smaller desks, with himself at a large one up front. He ended by dismissing it all as a pipe-dream that would cost a thousand good silver dollars!

On his birthday she surprised him with a draft for the thousand, and the statement that it would pay them in the end to have his school top-notch.

He felt amazed with gratitude, yet somehow uneasy over taking as a gift something he had not earned. As the new edifice drew towards its completion, he still could not take it for granted. He marvelled over each smoothly planed board, the bright glazed windows, and, above all, those neat ranks of desks. When the last bit of carpentry had been finished and the key to the wrought-iron lock was in his hand, he made a special pilgrimage to survey it on a November afternoon. Leaves fell in gold flecks, leaving the boughs stripped to grey. Blue weather was in the sky, and a pink in the dry clay. He fitted the key and opened the door. There was a clean new hush to the unused room; everything in it was straight and perfect. Yet he felt a trifle wary, as if he must make Lucinda's lavishness keep its distance from his own fenced-in restraint.

The room was all complete, and all a little hollow.

2

A week later John Upshur came driving his daughter Nan over to the Academy to enroll her as a pupil. As they arrived at the last mile she removed the peppermint lozenge from her mouth and put it frugally away. "I'm so excited," she told him, "that I might swallow it all at one gulp, which would surely be a shameful waste." The only remark she made as they passed the lofty mansion was: "I expect I shall feel like a chicken on its roost, sleeping two stories above the ground. You don't suppose I'll become dizzy? I couldn't tell that New Year's because of worrying about that runaway slave."

She sat in one of the visitors' chairs holding tightly to her own fingers to steady herself while her elders were discussing her scholastic ability. She was interested in a map of Italy drawn on the big slate blackboard, with towns and rivers dangling in tiny tassels of print all over its wrinkled riding-boot shape. It was labelled: *by Turber Whetstone.* Another side of the wall was flanked with such formidable study-books that Nan was glad when her eye lighted on a rear desk where a forgotten rosy pomegranate were perched all lop-sided, reminding her of their own familiar fruit-yard.

Meanwhile Danley Bruton was unobtrusively studying her, in an attempt to discover her potentialities. He saw immediately that her natural composure was enhanced because she had been deferred to by parents who had begotten her after their hope of progeny was gone. But there was nothing of arrogance about her, only the fearlessness of complete candour. He surmised that she had not the Whetstone tendency to ride roughshod over others, simply a sure ability to extricate herself from any encounter where she might be trampled under. He also felt, irrelevantly, that whereas Lucinda, even as a child, had welcomed the combat of physical attraction, this girl was too selective to tolerate easy personal encroachments.

Presently he summoned her, saying: "From what your father tells me, I judge the only place for you is in the boys' Upper Form."

"He has drummed the classics into me, and no mistake!" she agreed.

"That makes an odd situation for all concerned, a lone girl in that class. I'm afraid you will find it stiff going among those lads."

Not feeling like boasting, Nan said nothing.

Danley pinched his upper lip reflectively. "Perhaps you would find it pleasanter among the girls—learning accomplishments?"

He couldn't mean that, decided Nan, not answering again. She spoke few uncalled-for words.

In a moment he threw up his hands, laughing, and declared: "Yes, it will be the Upper Form for you, Nanny. Come, let us see Miss Gracey now, about where you are to be quartered."

On the big-house veranda they came upon Miz Lucinda slapping the dirt from her riding-skirt, while a yard boy cleaned her heels with a flint arrow-head. The damson colour of her velvet skirt was so rich that Nan could hardly keep from rubbing her palm over it. Cinda greeted her with a grin: "So Bruff's little short-haired favourite is coming to us to school? Tell somebody to fetch her a piece of cake, to put a good taste in her mouth to start with."

After the cake Miss Gracey, who had been waiting in the hall, led Nan up to a room given over to a small group of girls older than the primary department, yet not quite young ladies. "I thought you might prefer it in here, with the least number, if you're shy at first."

"I'm not shy," Nan told her. "Still, I shouldn't like being pushed about by a pack of little girls, so I thank you." She surveyed the beautiful large room with its long front windows opening like doors on the upper gallery. Passing through one of them, she leaned over the railing to take in the wide landscape. Staring at the distant margin, Nan thought that no matter how far she gazed, she would not run the risk of seeing her idol, the young doctor, passing by on his way to that low-down white Emma Will's cabin. This would be a blessed relief.

Then Miss Gracey was calling her to take off her cloak and saying she would send someone to unpack for her. But Nan, in a spasm of remembrance of her mother's careful packing of every cranny of her boxes, begged off. "Please, I'd rather do it myself."

Thus it was that she was surrounded by a muddle of her belongings when a group of girls came in. "Lawsy me!" exclaimed a sly dark one. "The pedlar is back again!"

Nan catalogued the girls carefully, especially two contrasting ones. The older was Dolly Walthour, a candy-pretty towhead who rushed up to her bubbling: "Goody, you're even younger than I was when I entered the old Academy!" and gave her hand a friendly squeeze. The other was the sharp dark one who had tried to tease her about her traps. Her name was Veda Polk, and, as Nan learned later, Veda's father over in Mississippi was as rich as Crœsus, but her mother was too sickly to raise her right. A lot of the pupils couldn't abide her, but others swore by her staunchly, and she would go to the wall for them.

Now after the instant of meeting, Veda turned away to take a dip of forbidden snuff. The monitor went over and snatched furiously at the tin box, but Veda tucked it out of her reach, jeering: "I expect I'll stink of it at table. Then you will catch the mischief for not controlling your charges properly, which will serve you right for walking the littlest girls so fast their heels blistered."

Something about this unequivocating creature drew Nan's admiration. She wanted her for a friend.

There was one other striking person that Nan encountered that night. It was Turber Whetstone. True, she had met him several years before, but she had not seen him since he had become so nearly grown up. To-night she was struck by the extreme likeness to Dr. Bruff that had developed in him. Of course Turber was fair of colour, with hazel cat's-eyes, where the doctor was dark. Yet there was that same look of being nourished more on pride than on bread, and that tension of living the moment before it slowed down into an hour. In a way the similarity disturbed Nan, as if something were being filched from her early idol by a changeling. It was a little like having her dream change its face in the middle of the night.

Presently Turber caught her gaze travelling over him, and snapped his fingers at her as though shooting knucks-down in a marble game. Directly the meal was finished he came over and took hold of both her hands, swinging them gaily. "Bro' Danley has assigned me to be your special tutor, so you'll have to mind me. Do everything I tell you."

She snipped her tongue out at him. "That depends!"

"Here!" With a quick motion of one hand he squeezed her mouth open and nipped her tongue. "I'll teach you to sass me!"

The morning of Nan's first day in the Academy went by like a riddle that she was curiously delighted not to be able to solve as yet. The rows of pupils were not playmates now, but adversaries in the contention of learning, superior strangers who unwound the roll-call glibly to the tune of the Latin *adsum*. Slates were passed out, children even in the lower forms rose and recited according to a rehearsed rote that overwhelmed Nan, who scarcely noted what simple bits of information they were mastering under the impressiveness of their class-room etiquette.

During the afternoon session Nan felt less hypnotized by strangeness, yet somehow regretful to see things emerging from a charmed haze into clarity. For the next stage would be their settling down into that unnoticed state of the customary. However, she was proud to find herself answering a difficult question correctly. It was very like suddenly being able to speak in a hitherto unintelligible tongue. Turber gave her a pleased salute. At the close of the classes he collected several books she would need for study, and steered her out the aisle. "On the way through the grove," he told her, "I'll try to clear up that matter of Hannibal's tactics that confused you this morning. You see, Bro' Danley cares as much about your *understanding* the times and the customs as he does about correct translations."

As they passed by, various girls darted glances or made pointed remarks, which he parried by plunging into his subject. Succinctly he analyzed Punic warfare, while they strolled through the grove. Her ears gave close attention to his words, and before she knew it, she was putting forth logical opinions, changing his tutorial summary into a joint discussion. "I see," he exclaimed, pleased, "where I'll have to pull in my horns and not try to bait you for being an ignoramus. And to think I balked when Bro' Danley assigned you to me, for fear you'd be a dunce, though I confess I liked your looks on the instant."

He leapt into the air and snatched a tatter of Spanish moss from an oak branch, then attached it to his chin as a goatee. "Does that make me look more learned?" Next he divided it in two parts and hung them over her ears. "That's how you will look when you're a granny, only you must see to growing out that thatch of yours first. Look here, I've a mind to show you where my private hickory tree is, if you'll vow not to tell." He held out his jack-knife for her to spit on the blade and give the oath of steel.

His hickory grew in a hidden cove, shut about by a screen of dense growth unlike the spaced grove they had left. By the time they had made their way into the isolated opening, Nan's curls were stuck full of burrs, her hands scratched, and her frock torn, but she did not care as she viewed the cove. The air had a wan blue wash, like the pale indigo water used in laundry-dipping tubs, and the nut tree was so dark and polished a green that it might have been fashioned of some semi-precious stone growing in the nether world. The occasional pelting of the nuts to the ground was a ghostly sound.

"Suppose," suggested Turber gutturally, "I hold you here a captive, all through the fall, all through the long winter, if you eat of this tree's harvest?"

She gave a happy shudder at his playing the mystic game of ancient danger.

Then they began to gather his nut crop, he using his book-bag as a knapsack, she stowing her hoard in her skirt pockets. When finally they were laden, she noticed that the light had faded almost entirely in this gap in the thickened forest. They were walled about by so impenetrable a blackness that it seemed in truth some underworld dungeon. A mourning dove moaned like a lost soul crossing the Styx. She clutched Turber's elbow. "It's scary!"

He secured her hand tight about his elbow with his other palm, and they were very close. His chin dented down into her hair. She stood quite still. She was not used to touches, but in this duskiness, loneliness seemed to be the one thing to keep at bay. She could hear his voice coming down in a low tone from above her head: "I'm glad you are in *my* charge. I like to keep care of you." He lifted his chin and dropped down to where he could take hold of the hem of her skirt and raise it to his mouth. Nan could feel her pocketful of hickory nuts banging against his ducked head. . . .

When they came into the open grove she was astounded to find that they had not been lost by night. Here between the widespread trunks the air was lambent with that early gold that fills the time beween full day and sunset. They said no words, so companioned were they.

At the top of the front steps they both turned at the same time and gazed out into the sky that went far away beyond the world. Turber said: "If ever something feels too big to take in, like that, the world rolling off into the sky—remember I can manage whatever ache is left over from yours."

Then he sent her in.

3

It was summer now and the year of school had ended, leaving the Academy as familiar to Nan as a well-thumbed book. Jogging homeward from Top Hill with her father, she let a panorama of recollections pass through her mind: the cane-grinding picnic over at Miz Gerda Whetstone's sugar-cane mill, the mules that pulled the lever plodding round and round the press, stalks being fed into its maw, juice spurting out to the dull, strong hum of a cloud of greedy yellow jackets. Then the ride home clasping her share of ripe stalks close, the tune *Nellie was a Lady* spreading out in a blanket of song over the fields, and afterwards the school yard littered for a month with the white pith of spat-out chews.

Then came Christmas-tide, which should have been dismal for herself and a handful of others, marooned at school away from home by the flooding of Pea River. But it was a holiday that had proved a festival of festivals. For a week, with Top Hill sheeted in rain, Miss Lucinda had seen to it that they lived one continuous party, mostly in the Little Parlour, telling stories, acting charades, playing out-to-old-Jack's-house, stuffing on candy and nuts, with golden oranges galore to suck. Then came the night of the Big Storm when the window-panes shook like oiled paper and winter lightning was a weird green-white. Miss Lucinda had had Mr. Danley call the group into her own apartments, where they brewed tea, and Mammy Lizzie read their fortunes from the leaves in the cups, distracting even the most cowering from the elements raging outside. When the lull had come at daybreak, they were fed milk, and ham wedged between slices of light-bread, then tucked into the various beds by Miss Cinda, who joked about their being big babies but gave each a kiss nevertheless.

All that morning they had slept, with blinds shuttered and a tiptoe hush over the mansion. Nan, half-waking once, had eyed the stripes of eleven o'clock light on the floor matting and lain terribly still, alone in a big room in the middle of a silence as deep as the hundred years' slumber of the Sleeping Beauty, the whole world barred out by a charm.

There had been many other weeks of usual tasks, knotty lessons, and petty grievances, as the rainy season kept pouring down upon them. Then suddenly over the hills came a spring uncertainty of clouds; after that the gush of roses and sun smiting down so hot that everything lagged.

At last there had arrived this day of orations in the schoolroom packed with parents, of creaky new clothes, and faces swabbed blank by decorum. Also Turber taking final honours with a swift drawing up of his chin, while county dignitaries and furbelowed misses pressed their congratulations upon him. Then a moment he had saved of good-bye for her alone, where the May light flashed through the fig leaves. . . .

And now here she was, riding once more beside her father, watching the swish of the horse's tail, and the sorrel dust settling over the white-spangled bloom of wayside berry bushes.

That evening she was at first elated by her homecoming, seeing her mother's sparse figure waiting in greeting, illumined by a kerosene lantern, while her two negro house women waited solemnly at either elbow in imitation of Miz Gerda Whetstone's greeting ceremony. The steps showed how they had been scoured down white with sand in honour of her daughter's return, and Nan sprang up them to her mother, squealing and jigging.

But after breakfast next morning, left alone with her mother, the monotony of domestic routine began to wear on Nan. Had she never before noticed how Miz Della fussed apprehensively over each detail, accompanying her actions with exasperated *Pshaws* and *Mercy me's*? Had she not minded before that her mother gave her questions the barest replies, then branched off into domestic dissertations she had reiterated from time immemorial?

Finally unable to endure further cluckings and dabblings, Nan escaped to the front yard to lie under the black cedar, chewing on some of its fallen spicy burrs, *homesick, of all things, for her schoolmates!* The dinner bell when it clanged sounded tiresome. In the afternoon she went tree-climbing and had the good luck, while perched in the topmost crotch of the china tree, to see that old Emma Will gal tracking down their log road. Nan grabbed a handful of chinaberries and began shooting them viciously, hearing them hit with sharp plunks on the other's forearms, head, and bare tough shins.

Emma Will whipped about and, spying Nan's head among the foliage, lashed her fishing-pole at her furiously. Following a few blows, Nan managed to catch hold of the tip, and after a moment's tussle snapped it off by several notches, then sent it spinning, tangled in its line, down in Emma Will's direction. She followed this with another hail-storm of chinaberries. Emma Will scarcely noticed these, so beside herself was she over the ruined pole, vainly fitting and refitting its severed notches together again.

Watching her, Nan grew still, feeling suddenly a shamed pity for the older girl scrambling about on a rich farmer's log road, fumbling aggravatedly with the poor broken contrivance. Nan called down: "Look here! I'll have Nate cut and dry you a good new pole."

"You'd better!" responded Emma Will. "But that don't do me no good now, about gettin' that mess of crokers I had my mouth set on to be fried fo' supper. Ef'n you was one of our young 'uns, I'd lay on to you with what's left of this." She whacked the cane across the logs, making the old crumbs of bark fly.

"Would a good sugar-cured shoulder of ham tempt you?" asked Nan. "Because I'll go get you one."

Before the other could snap her up, Nan was scurrying for the smokehouse; she knew how to pry open any warped lock. Miz Della saw her scooting away, hugging the meat, and called out to stop her, but Nan vanished through the wild-plum thicket. Holding her peace-offering out to Emma, she advised: "Better soak the slices before you fry them, to draw the salt."

"I know how to cook good victuals," retorted Emma Will with asperity, snatching it. As she vanished up over the hump of the road, Nan sang out in an effervescence of goodwill: "Maybe you might let me have some of your next catch of crokers."

"And maybe I mightn't! High time you was learnin' to ketch yore own fish."

When Nan came into her back yard again, stepping spryly because she'd at any rate had the fun of sparring with a fairly young person, her mother met her accusingly. "Associating with trash! And running barefoot in the late afternoon, after having been sent to a genteel school!"

Nan giggled, thinking of exactly how genteel the Academy was. Her mother continued: "Let me tell you, if I ever catch *you* leaving off your petticoats like trash, just because it's a hot day—why, I do believe I'll switch you good."

Nan skipped into the house and leapt on her bed, where she bounced up and down, up and down, landing at last in a glorious flump, her bare legs sprawled. "I s'pose," she addressed them, "you'll have to wear *pantalets* to-night, pore things." She waved her legs about, enjoying the current of air they blew up. "Our seminaries of the Southland," she mimicked Miss Gracey, "turn out young ladies of the most elegant deportment."

CHAPTER FORTY-SIX

On and on that kaleidoscope decade kept revolving, making bright, sometimes clashing designs with each new twist of the times. To the eyes of those viewing it close, it seemed a lovely era that need never end.

For two years now following the death of C. D.'s mother, Joby had been mistress of the Melburne home in Yufala. At first she had been timid, shunted between the old cook and the children's mammy. But gradually she had grown in confidence, until now the entire household recognized the inflexibility of her gentle routine. She rose early and, dressing, sipped a cup of cambric tea as had her grandmother Miz Lisbeth. Then she toured her house, noting what needed to be put to rights, and wound up in the kitchen, where she meagrely doled out supplies for the coming day. When company came, the board was loaded, but everyday fare was on the skimpy side, served, however, with an eye to elegance that made a chance unexpected guest feel he was partaking of a choice repast.

Joby was always at her place behind the silver table-bell before any one else appeared for breakfast. Each of her children, numbering three now, including a fretful little boy, filed by her chair to be inspected and to parrot some rule of etiquette. Once they were seated, a different one each day asked grace. After that they were allowed to eat, watching each other for faults that they would tattle to their mother later. In cool weather the little girls were instructed by an inept governess. To-day, being the height of summer, all three children were allowed to follow their mother out to the grape arbour. The yield was large this year, so Joby had ordered old clean sheets spread beneath the trellis, and put a group of light-weight piccaninnnies on top to toss the clusters down to negro men below, who placed them in bushel baskets for wine and jelly-making. Joby was very proud of gathering her grapes so fastidiously, though Gerda had snorted at her that she'd have to wash off the bird-droppings later anyway, so what did a little dust matter?

Presently buggy-wheels sounded at the front, and Joby went in the side door and freshened her palms and finger-tips with rose-water before going to greet her visitor. It was Hannah Lee, Tom Two's young second wife, with their pudgy baby at the year-old bumbling stage. Hannah Lee thought Joby perfection and came often to see and, if possible, to imitate her ways. "How do you keep cool-looking?" she panted.

"Oh, it's no trouble at all to me," murmured Joby, who had a fallacious pet theory that no lady perspired, which necessitated her dabbing her skin constantly with some sort of cologne to keep it dry, and to carry her point.

She led the way into the second parlour, which she thought plenty good enough for family. There they settled themselves for gossip. Hannah Lee plunged into the account of how Joachim had got himself into a pretty dilemma between that Walthour girl-child and her cousin from Tennessee. Next she reported that she had seen Nettie Melburne Screws driving around the Courthouse Square to check up on how many people were trading elsewhere than at the Screwses' store, and she had been wearing the tenth new bonnet since Easter! Another bond between these two young women was their common resentment of the more prosperous Nettie. Presently with guiltily lowered voices they began discussing the possible paternity of that low-down Emma Will's brat. They'd heard she'd vowed point-blank to Bruff that it wasn't his. Well, it certainly looked too poor-folksy to belong to any man with a decent connection. Hannah Lee was just remarking that some said it was "got by a cousin," when a sound of footsteps in the hall silenced them. C. D. came in to find two pretty women digging demurely with their needles at their embroidery, and to have Joby half-way put her cheek up to him.

That same afternoon, after her company had departed, Joby in a clean pale lawn frock was seated in the hall to catch the river breeze when Armand Petit, reincarnated from her former life, descended from a carriage at their steps! She could not quite believe that it was he, after all this long stretch of time, but was thankful her attire hadn't had time to muss even the least bit. He came up with the sharp step that she found she had not forgotten, and bent beautifully over her hands. Flustered, she called out for a servant: "Bats, come here for my keys and bring Mr. Petit some of that good brandy that's open. And mind you, some *cold* water from the spring-house."

She led Armand into the first parlour, which had a ghost of pot-pourri behind drawn blinds. He crossed over to the front shutters and swung them open on their hinges, showing the late light hovering on the river. Fronds of cool air came in quickly. "Ah, that suits the hour more, and the occasion."

She felt like a girl again, flitting about uncertainly for a chair, having someone with her to watch the sun setting, while smelling tea-olive coming up by way of the garden paths. He chose to lean against a table and face down at her. "So of what are we to speak to one another, after all these years of my going away? Of love, no? Of regret, yes?"

She bridled. How dare he talk like that to her, here in C. D.'s house? "You forget yourself, Mr. Petit."

He gave her no apology, but studied her. How soft and virginal she appeared in this shadowy room with the enchantment of playing light! But he could see how her first faint girlishness had become smothered by prudishness. "*Quel malheur!*" he said to himself. "And I drove a long way round, to stop for a sight of her, *Moi,* who long ago learned better. *Eh bien,* I have at least the satisfaction of learning that her husband now cherishes her, and that she has no more need of me, except in her reminiscences. She can rest in tedium."

He stood upright now. "I think I will not delay for the brandy. Make your husband my regrets." He did not say for what. Formally she replied that C. D. would be sorry to have missed him, and learned that Armand was going to take train at Montgomery for Washington. "May I send your *bébés* some trifles from there?"

"They are not such babies now," she boasted. "The two girls are learning to read, and our son can count up to twenty."

They walked together down to his carriage and stood a moment smelling the lemony odour of some browning magnolia-blossom cups. He entered his equipage. After she could no longer hear the whir of his wheels coming back to her, she felt the sharp fatigue of having taken part in a disappointment. Yet somehow she was almost at once wrapped in the satisfaction of having been seen by him at last in the honour of her own home. She wondered vaguely why she had not shown off her children before him.

The river was quiet now, under the thickness of dusk. Only white roses showed on the bushes cool and undisturbed. She walked back to her veranda.

2

While Joby was changing the distorted shape of earlier married life into a presentable pattern, Bruff was letting the strands of his professional and personal life dangle somewhat at loose ends. His intensity about his work was causing him, during his brief reprieves, to bog down into careless relaxation. That might have been all very well had it not affected so directly two young people, Turber and Nan, who had set him on a pedestal—two young people who also held some nascent charm for each other.

In the dimming day after Sunday supper those two had strolled up towards John Upshur's high pasture. On the way they heard the sound of hoofs making off by the log road into the backwoods, and there was no mistaking the loping of Bruff's stallion, or the sound of his own high keening whistle when he felt in high feather.

Nan swerved towards Turber, her teeth caught over her bottom lip in a tight tuck. "To Emma Wills's, that's where he's going!"

"Don't, Nan!" Turber began pressing her hands.

After a while she noticed the twist of his fingers locking hers, and thought: suppose she had been all alone here when those hoofs pounded by. She very likely would have ducked down and hidden under something like a bush, feeling crushed. But with Turber there, she could keep standing and encompass the pain within herself instead of being browbeaten from without.

They moved on, to the pasture where the rail fences were so prickly with the rose thorns that they could scarcely find a spot to lean against without Nan having her dimity folds catch and pucker.

Later that night Turber waited up at Rock Wall, in the back yard near the smoke-house, for Bruff's return, though he thought many times longingly of his comfortable bed. Along about moonset he heard Bruff drop off his horse and lead the animal to the stalls. After bedding him down, Bruff came houseward, with the springy stride of a man who has felt the force of his maleness recently released, whiffing out the pungency of whisky as an accompaniment to his lowered half-whistle. His voice was wholly good-humoured when Turber stepped out to stop him. "What's the trouble? Anybody sick?"

"No."

"Well?" An edge of command for a younger brother crept into his tone.

Turber marked Bruff's face and its measurements as if he had never seen it before. He had not, quite. It had always been Bruff's. Now he saw that it was the visage of a man that would brook no interference, but he could not let that stop this thing he had to say. "Don't use the Upshur's log road the next time you want to turn off in the wrong direction toward *trash!*"

Whack! Bruff slapped Turber's cheek as if he were still a child. Then Turber leapt at him, both fists striking out. They locked, and went down in a silent roll. They fought with what sounded like controlled breathing. Occasionally there was a dull thud. At the end Bruff rose and helped Turber to legs that buckled under the lad. "Come on, Bub, brace up. I can't carry you, after the drubbing you gave me." He rubbed the youngster's tousled head.

Turber looked into Bruff's face and was glad it was not one whit less dominant.

Then the doctor steered the boy into the office of his sleeping-room. "Better not go in with the others just yet, till I patch you up."

Lying limp while Bruff swabbed him with arnica, and did not guy him, Turber said: "Reckon I cut up like a meddling fool."

"Now don't back down," Bruff replied sharply. "That'll land you nowhere. You did right to call me for my bad manners." Bruff threw down the swab. "There, that fixes you, and now for myself." He looked up chuckling from under his welts. "What I don't understand, Turb, is why *you* want to whitewash me with Nan, when you feel the way you do about her." He stood up, closing his medicine-bag. Then a curious look came into his face as if he were intent upon the strange but pleasing new thought of Nan as a courted girl. A smile played in creases near his eyes.

"Lord," groaned Turber to himself, "now I *have* thrown the fat into the fire, all by myself, by calling his attention to her." He lay beside his older brother all that night bound by a double loyalty, unable to ward off the sacrifice to come, of his own courtship. He fell asleep given over to nobility. When he woke, though, and heard the roosters, he swung his feet over the side of the bed with a jerk. He would do as he pleased. None of the night's unselfish mawkishness about Bruff and Nan counted now.

Outside the house he shouted for his boy, Wright, and raced him to the swimming-hole branch. Wright won and turned a handspring of glee before catching Turber's nightshirt. The negro stood admiringly on the bank, watching his young master do somersaults in the muddy water, while keeping an eye out for water moccasins that might bite. "You dive bettah than a fish," the negro declared.

Turber came up and lay spreadeagled on the bank. The morning cool was heightened by the water on his limbs. Wright started drying him. "You'se almost fleshin' up. But just a little bit. No Whetstones evah gets ovah bein' rangy."

Turber shoved him away, hearing some jays quarrelling, and feeling a kinship, since his fighting with Bruff, however inept, had won him the right of manhood, to woo where he chose.

3

Back over by Pea River, Nan was ashamed to think that her feelings about Bruff and Turber had become the cause of trouble which she heard their brother Joachim had dared twit them about. To-day she was seated moping in the rope swing hung from the gum tree when Dr. Bruff drove up in his buggy.

"Where's your father?" he asked, scarcely noticing her, and when she had called John, announced: "I'm off to Montgomery, to help out with that yellow-fever plague."

"You know," Upshur reminded him, "that it's dangerous. Dr. Guild says that though it's probably not infectious, it's in all likelihood portable."

"What kind of coward do you think I am?" demanded Bruff.

"All right, all *right*," conceded Upshur; "still, I don't want you forgetting what a help you are in this community, before you go hunting trouble."

"I've got to go," growled Bruff. "I can't stop at just curing a few folks around here of a bellyache. These scourges, yellow fever, malaria, and hookworm—there's no sense in letting them sweep over us! I'll give a pretty to get to the bottom of any one of them. Seems to me sometimes that the stripe-legged mosquito must have something to do with yellow fever. Since you always find them close together, mosquitoes might cause it."

"Or bedbug bites," chuckled John.

"Maybe! I tell you the bites of bugs and insects have more to do with illness than you reckon."

"*Whoosh!*" John waved it all away. "You're riding your hobby too far and fast. *I* say ease the sick, born the babies, bury the dead. That's about all a doctor can do."

Bruff rose. "That's not all *I* hope to do." He was moving towards his buggy when Nan came to ask him to stay to dinner, but he hardly seemed to hear her. "I must move along. To Montgomery, and roll up my sleeves."

Nan watched him off in the September dust that blurred about his wheels.

Later John had a letter from him, which he read first to himself, then only partly aloud to Nan as it was too blunt for a girl's ears:

It proves worse than we had heard, sixty-two deaths in October alone. The best people have fled the town in all directions, until we speak of the "absent treatment" for preventing the ailment. As for me, I belong to the "Can't Get Away Club." Am only sorry I did not arrive here sooner, since even the humblest is of some assistance.

Much to the chagrin of all of us hot-headed Southern Rights men, New York *has contributed $1,300 to our relief!! Must close and snatch what sleep is possible. Would appreciate it if you would send me any paregoric you have available, as the bowels of some are running off too sorely.*

Yrs. Truly,
Yarbrough Whetstone Jr., M.D.

Shortly after that, Turber came cavorting up on his horse, waving another letter from Bruff to his family. When he let her have it, she sat poring over its pages, to see if Bruff was in any danger he had not mentioned to her father.

Turber raked the sand with his heels. "Nan, you're a plumb idiot! You took to Bruff before you could crawl, and you won't even look at me or any one else. You had better, though, because when a heart beats, all Bruff hears is a pulse."

Nan held her face still.

What neither of them could know was how Bruff in these plague-ridden days could scarcely drag from pillar to post. Nor how the coffins were piled in stacks at the graveyard wating for decent burial, how the whole town of Montgomery stank with a peculiar putrescence. When he lay down at night with his knee-sockets jumping spasmodically from tiredness, his mind buzzed like a swarm of those mosquitoes that interested him so. His thoughts were trying to dodge through to some one thing causative of the whole epidemic. With the sleep-sand in his eyes he recalled how he had meant as a child to travel the world over, but now he knew that this state of Alabama was his country. And not because of any fame to be attained in the capital, Montgomery, but mainly because of the sick in the backwoods cabins. . . .

CHAPTER FORTY-SEVEN

THE CAMPAIGN of 1855 had been an orgy of mixed issues in Alabama, with much clashing within all parties as well as between opposing ones. But one phrase had been on every lip whatever the man's political allegiance, whether he hoped for its realization within the Union or vaunted the threat of Secession for its sake. That phrase was "Southern Rights." And *Southern Rights, Southern Rights,* the refrain rolled off into the years, from which it would one day echo back as loud as thunder.

In 1856 Ven turned eighty, and suddenly was obsessed with the importance of having been born in the famous July of 1776. "A year fittin' for a *man* to be born!" he bragged. He could no longer keep his horse-betting straight, and his toddies did not set well. Cudge, now too feeble to stand behind him at table to pour them, sat on a stool pulled up close in back of Ven. In fact Cudge, who was terrified of the Patrollers catching him if he got out of his master's shadow, dogged his heels in a way that kept Ven eternally bumping into him whenever he turned abruptly.

It ended one day when the negro failed to catch his balance after such a collision and fell against a rock, where he lay still. Ven hollered at him to get up that instant, but Cudge did not obey. He lay a poor old black bag of bones.

Ven's scared, cracked yells brought all the household running. He ordered Cudge carried into his own bed, where he called Bruff a liar when his nephew pronounced Cudge dead. "Why, that boy's worth eight hundred dollars any day! Many's the time I've been offered that by the packet card-sharpers, just for the way he can palm an ace." Irascibly he sent them out, to be alone so he could try to bring the old darky round with "some good strengthening whisky."

Within the hour they found him fallen where he himself had died of heart failure beside the spilled jug.

At his burying, which included laying his "boy" to rest at his feet, Gerda found herself not praying for Ven, but begging, for the last man of Yarbrough's generation: "Please, O Lord, spare me at least Guy, for a little longer."

2

The next year was a hard one in some ways, a victorious one in others. In March the United States Supreme Court handed down its decision in the case of the slave Dred Scott, remanding him into slavery and declaring that Congress had no power to prohibit slavery in the territories of the United States anywhere at any time.

"There," Gerda told Bruff and Joachim and Will Bee, "I told you our rights would be protected *in* the Union." A hot discussion ensued, with many wild statements made by Joachim in particular. Pokey, who was winding up her chores in their hearing, took it in avidly; and something about her pompous air as she set off for the quarters made Gerda stop her a moment. "If you're going down to speak a piece of your mind to our folks, don't scare the spry ones so bad I can't coax them to do an errand off the place for fear of the paterollers."

But Pokey gave no nod of agreement as she stalked on.

It was warm enough for the mulatto to set her chair outside, while one of Lessie's piccaninnies scratched her head for her. Lessie had been made the mammy of the negro orphans, which included all without acknowledged fathers. It was about this brood that Pokey commenced speaking. "Lessie, you don't lay on the switch enough. The least ones cry fo' too many mo'lasses tits, and the bigger ones is lazy. And—I hearn that Gaby gal askin' what's the use of learnin' to sweep de yards, 'cause when they was growed up they'd all be free an' not have to work. *I* whip her, so she sweep dat yard clean as a tablecloth!"

She ordered them all out. They came scurrying like ants, with the older women shoving eagerly behind them, knowing Marm Pokey was on the rampage and not wanting to miss any excitement.

Pokey looked them all over scornfully. "Y'all ain't nothin' to brag about. But Miz Gerda has you on her hands and got to keep care of you best she can. Bee-cause, an' mark my words, they ain't nevah gwine to be no place else fo' you all to go! De United States Gov'mint jes' send Miz Gerda word to-day that niggahs is goin' keep right on belongin' to the mastahs and the misstises, an' the Pres'dint tell her if she have any trouble jest let him know. She thanked him kindly but say she don' look for no foolishness from her folks. Still he sendin' her an' the MacDuffs an' Miss Lucinda all a lot more paterollers hot-foot."

She watched them shuffling uneasily, trying to decide between fear and a thrill of pride at their mistress.

Pokey squinted. " But that ain't all I got to say. I want you all to know what this North they call Freedom's Land is like. I *know*. I *been* there!" They gaped. Pokey's New York life was hidden under such layers of years that she had come to almost disbelieve it herself, and it was past comprehension to these young ones. But now she launched in with all the potency of a prophet of old.

" You know what hit's like? *Snow* all the time. You know what snow is? Hit's white frost piled up above yo' knees! How you like dat? Then 'cause it's cold, you got to wear yo'r foots pinched into *shoes* all the time. No fried chicken, no yams, no greens cooked with fat-back. Stingiest folks you evah see. Scrapin' the left-overs victuals off'n plates and usin' 'em again fo' *white folks!"* She could see them begin to flinch at the pinch of such meanness. " No other cullud folks to pass the time of day with neither; no company at the big house to cross yo' palm with a little present. White womens pesterin' you to scour the tasty grease-coatin' out of yo' pots and kettles, an' to sweep under the dressers."

" Fo' Gawd, Marm Pokey," ejaculated Sal, " what white ladies doin' scrouchin' down on they hands an' knees to *see* ef'n you *didn'* sweep clean?"

" I'm tellin' you, gal! An' they tries to make you wash yo'self wif alum water to keep down yo' body-smell!"

" Whut a passel of folks—whut a place. . ." the murmer grew. " Why don' they leave it an' all come down heah?"

" Friz up in de cold," piped one excited piccaninny, " an' cain't break loose!"

But Pokey settled that. " 'Cause they ain't been *in-vited."* She rose with deliberate stateliness and turned back towards the house path, leaving a pall settling over their good spirits at the thought of such grimness going on up north.

" An' I thought dey had gold street," mumbled Sal to Gaby.

" Dat's hebben," Lessie chided her.

" Well, leastways parasols fo' nigger gals." Sal sat down disconsolately. Sal had never had any notion of running away, but it had been pretty to think about—having a parasol. . . .

3

Almost before the county ceased rejoicing about the Dred Scott decision, a financial panic burst upon the country. Gerda's sons tried to cheer her by belittling it, but they could no longer minimize it when two of their own, Tom Two and Hans, were among the number of panic victims. Hans himself would never have been in such a plight had he not, unbeknownst to Gerda, gone on Tom Two's notes up at the Melburne bank. Guy was no longer associated with that concern, and Willy's other affairs left him as little more than a figurehead. Melburne, a notoriously selfish man, had been all too willing to heed Nat Screws' advice to press Tom's notes when they became slightly overdue. A number of them were for supplies bought by Hannah Lee at the Screwses' store, in an attempt to keep up with Joby's Bluff House airs.

The job of finding a solution for the tangle without letting her boys lose their inheritance almost drove Gerda distracted for a spell. In her anxiety she launched a rush of activity to catch up any possible slackness on her own plantations; and besides took refuge in every omen that she or Pokey knew, binding each charm with the wish that she would find some way out of trouble for her children. In the end she did, with Guy's shrewd advice, manage to straighten out the muddle satisfactorily. Tom was sheepish, but not loath to accept her help promptly. Hans, however, was so stubborn about not becoming further obligated to her that she had a hard time bringing him round. It was only when she finally asked him bitterly whether she had bestowed her maternal favours grudgingly that he succumbed. She could never forget his man's voice choked up like a child's while he clutched her apron-skirts in the old way. "It's just that you've been exactly the opposite, giving me a *rightful* place in my father's house! Always."

"But, Hans," was all she could find to say, "you were such a good little mite."

Shortly afterwards Gerda had the whole family come to spend the day at the Stand, feeling the need to find out if any of the others like Tom Two and Hans had strayed beyond her reach in any disastrous way. The result of the day was to set her mind at rest about all of them except Lucinda and Danley, or rather about little Whet. She could tell that they were making him a bone of some contention, as she had often observed them doing, ever since his birth.

He was a high-strung little chap, given to alternate fits of shy day-dreaming and rather desperate displays of mischief timed to upset some social occasion. Not very robust, he yet drove himself to try to excel his mates. He was downright beautiful to look upon except that the measurement between his temples was distressingly narrow, and his eyes often hollowed by fatigue.

Danley, with Dr. Bruff's approval, tried to help the boy form quiet habits, even to devour books only within reason, but most of all to avoid the hysteria of competition. Lucinda pointed out that Danley encouraged that very thing in his other pupils, so why coddle his own son into becoming a dullard? He tried to explain the necessity of providing Whet with a sound foundation of health to forestall his over-keyed sensibilities from running away with the formation of his character. But Cinda always cut him off with scorn, leaving Danley with a baffled but strong urge to shelter his son from any hurt his mother might one day deal him.

The child perversely adored Lucinda. And while he was often grateful for the spells of recuperative quiet provided by his father, he seemed to use them only to renew his energies in order to impress his mother with his prowess. It must be admitted that Cinda spared no effort to make life enjoyable when it came to amusement. She had always had that attraction for children that a daring figure possesses, and since her wealth made indulgence of their appetites easy, it was small wonder that she had a troop of admirers among the small fry. She had never lost, either, her own childish love for the excitement and trappings of elaborate games.

The result of the combined, or opposed, proclivities of his two parents was that while Whet relied on his father's every word, he hinged his actions on his mother's every whim. He could rise leadenly of a morning and find that by evening the day had opened out into a clear brilliance, all because of not having had to shrink from any scathing on her part. If he could go out on his favourite hillock and say: "I didn't cry to-day when the game rooster spurred me, so I made *her* proud," why, then he could hug his knees in delight.

The point was that he was a *physical coward*. Never afraid of ghosts, of fatherly authority, or of a far-away God, he was always sickeningly in fear of pain. This was his shame, which he tried to hide from his mother by frequent exhibitions of bravado.

One day she had been down at the stables confirming the points of a colt she meant for Whet's use, a beautiful but unsafe creature. Tid had managed to work a bridle on him when she called: "Here, Whet, here's your chance to be the first to mount him."

Before he could control himself he had made a prayerful gesture of terror. She slapped his hands apart, saying: "I won't have a sniveller for my son. Get up on him or I'll put you back in pantalets."

He mounted, and the attempt was over in two shakes. The colt gave one agile writhe that slung Whet across the lot, landing him with a jolt that he felt to be the end of the world. He lay there in a fatal calm, bewildered because the hereafter appeared to be only a stunned version of the old world. He could not hear Tid's or the stable boy's words, could only see their mouths yammering at him. After a while he saw his mother's face join their faces at the edge of his vision; and he did hear her command: "Pick him up, if he's going to act the baby." Then her face and neck receded.

In the yard his father met Tid carrying him, and took him over himself. After Danley had laid him on his bed and felt over all his bones, he had closed the blinds and sat beside him while Whet fell into a half-conscious drowse. He could feel his father sitting there quiet beside him and know that he leaned over him from his chair watchfully now and then; but nothing disturbed the sense of the hour's solitude and blessed remoteness. Slowly out of his lassitude Whet thought: "Oh, wouldn't it be good if I could stay still in this room forever . . . have all my meals brought . . . and a book to read each day. . . ."

But they had been broken in upon by Lucinda, announcing that the carriage was waiting to carry them to the Stand, and before his father could voice his objections, Whet was scrambling up with nervous eagerness, anxious not to affront her with any further puerility.

It was natural that Ma'am Gerda could perceive upon the boy's face that day the ravages not only of being made a battleground for his parents' diverse ambitions for him, but also of his own conflicting strains of heredity. She longed to help him towards union within himself, but felt that her hands, heavy with years of authority, would bungle if she tried to lead him. There were times when one had to leave the young alone; those were the times of real fear for the women who had created them.

But at least there was always work on the land waiting to occupy her when she had to stay her efforts on behalf of humans.

It was on the fresh late spring morning following that evening that Gerda, making her way out to her fields, pondered some theories about possible cotton textile developments in the South that she had heard Guy expounding. He had wound up by pointing out: "All that water-power spillin' down the mountains in both the Carolinas ought to be enough to run a heap of mills. Why, we could beat the North all hollow at its own manufacturing game."

"Sounds sensible," Hans had agreed, "only I'd rather farm."

"Well, that's what most of us down this far south would keep on doin'," Guy had assured him. "Grow the cotton, and let the seaboard states and folks up in the Tennessee Valley do the millin'." Gerda, listening, had thought his idea sound. Lord knows the South needed to look ahead, to see cotton from its beginning to its ultimate uses.

Now, on her tramp, she had come far out into one of her best fields and had seated herself on one of Yarbrough's old "coin" stumps that had held the prizes for those who completed their tasks first. The swirl of the ploughed rows had dropped their state of being earth for this newer thing of green plants growing hesitantly, plants so tender they might have been in flower-pots. Before long they would take on a stubborn stockiness of stalk, and the chopping about the roots would become incessant and deeper. Later, when everything felt pressed down under the heat, all would grow mortal tired of the fields. Then one day a white flower would pop out on some plant, and the field-hand who first saw it would feel freshened, thinking: "It'll be pickin'-time befo' long now." Then there would be a quickening in the air, now that the time of toil was shaping toward its end.

There would come later yet the end that the cotton factors knew, of bales packed solidly in the holds of ships . . . the end that the mill workers of the North and of England knew, of cotton being spun and woven . . . and the end of the counting-houses weighing its worth to the world in a minted coin. That was what cotton seemed to the rest of the world. But that was not what cotton was to the South, not what it was to Gerda.

No, she could feel the dogged picking going on, as pulp on pulp of tender white left the boll for a black palm, then for the dun colour of a croker-sack. She could feel this being done by rows of negroes as far as her eye could see, and then by more rows that she could not see. And so she saw the South as if it were acres of this act of gathering, of field upon field and state upon state full of fecund white roses spilling a cloud of white down over the land.

"I'm crazy as a loon," she told herself, "carrying on like that in my mind." Yet she reached down and took up a handful of soil, felt the almost organic richness of it grating in the crevices of her fist. And she carried it almost back to the house with her before her hand gave it up slowly.

CHAPTER FORTY-EIGHT

As THE LAST YEAR of the decade drew to a close, two members of the family paused to take stock of the momentous years now ending: Danley Bruton in the sanctuary quiet of his schoolhouse, Gerda in her bustling ell.

Ever since the death of Yarbrough this season had induced in Gerda a nostalgic pondering of the past, a recurrent foreboding for the future. This December the thought of yet another new decade weighed down upon her mightily. To-day while she superintended the making of an extra batch of fruit cake, she was taking stock of her family, studying over the county's condition, facing the national situation, while keeping a sharp eye on her culinary process.

Hannah Lee, who had lately drilled herself into a model of domesticity, was slivering citron rind into bright lime shavings. A half-grown mulatto was chopping raisins. A piccaninny was cracking pecans with grinning white teeth and nibbling up far too many. Gerda herself was grinding spices in the spice-mill, placing them afterwards in carefully graded mounds of brown or buff powders. As she ground away, she was thinking of how the Government at Montgomery had warned all owners to keep their slaves close at home during the approaching holiday to avoid trouble, when so much unrest was abroad and so many young bloods would be roistering about, too full of the Christmas bowl. She scarcely needed to give the order, for her people were already huddling close to the Stand as if for protection. This very condition, however, made for a cooped-up feeling. She was continually aware of them mumbling conjures against falling afoul of the paterollers, bickering for the favour of the white folk, disrupting regular work habits to perform some preposterous service in hopes of gaining good repute, moiling with jealousies and tattlings, and constantly cowering under the shadow of Rock Wall. This fear, she knew, was not good. If it continued unabated, it would rot their faith in their mistress. She had learned too well from Yarbrough that essential lesson that *trust bound together, where fear rent asunder.*

Staring now and then out of the back door, she searched in her mind for some way to leaven this heaviness, at least for the Yuletide. But it would take more than the usual issue of best clothes, the shower of ribbons, more even than the barrel of whisky. It would require some of that old heedless happiness in the hearts of all the white people before the cry could go up gladly from the blacks: *" Chris'mus gif', Miz Gerda, Chris'mus gif', Marse.* That rejoicing was a hard thing to come by this year, for people of her sober bent of mind in the midst of a world verging on war.

Her musings had been accompanied by the stately progress of the beating of batter, the conglomeration of fruits into the sucking tan mass, until before night the cakes were in the oven and the house enriched by the incense of spice. Then she thought she would rest herself by taking a turn in the open. Inevitably her steps headed in the direction of the quarters. There the cabin windows showed orange squares of warmth that somehow cast a nimbus over the surrounding walls. The house servants' cabins could be distinguished from the field-hands' by the glare of their whitewash in contrast with the soft dirt-colour of the other plain weathered logs; but almost all had plumes and brushes of flower bushes about the door, that in the spring and summer lent a beauty not incongruous to the most squalid of the cabins. Now the two streets of the quarters lay in a plus-sign where they crossed, and shafts of sparks were pricking their way up from the stick and clay chimneys.

Not so much laughter as usual came issuing forth from the half-swung doors; instead there were rather more full sighs and glum mutterings. Gerda glanced into this cabin and that, not spying, but observing quietly, with a deep sense of responsibility, the state of each group. At last she came to Shade's place, marked by the stench of the stable, and saw him bent over some harness-mending. His woman, Rinda, was moving about like a shadow cooking supper, and the children instead of playing were huddled on a pallet watching their elders warily. Shade let the patched harness fall and mumbled: " Wish trashy white folks wouldn't meddle wif us niggers about freedom. Jes' makes fo' trouble wid de paterollers. I'm scairt to drive into town come Sat'dy fo' a new plug of chew. 'Cause worse'n hants they'll creep up on you."

The piccaninnies walled their eyes and their mother said: " Hush, Shade, you'se about to give the chillun fits."

" They ain't the only ones that's jibberin'," he declared darkly.

Gerda stepped up and flung the door clear open, sniffing the supper. "Smells good, Rinda, like cracklin' bread."

"Yas'm." Rinda's grin came out of a cloud. "Aunty Pheaby taught me yo' way. Heah's one smokin' hot." Gerda munched the pone, blowing her breath to cool it. The cracklings were as plump as plums and as buttery as nuts to bite. The salty tang was fine after the over-richness of the fruit-cake aroma. She said nothing in particular, except to ask after a new mule she'd purchased that Shade was teaming to pull stumps, but she felt a little comfort grow in the room. Presently the creeping baby sprawled his way over near enough to play with her shoe and spatted it with his grey-pink palm, gurgling up at her between spasms of slaps. She tickled it absently with her toe.

"Shade," she said, wiping crumbs away, "you're good at seeing to it that the plough-hands never abuse the mules, never ride them to death nights till the critters aren't fit for work next day. I wonder if it would be a good idea to put that new mule up as a prize on Christmas Day, to be held each month for riding by the gang that have worked the smartest and kept their own work team the best."

Shade's eyes rolled at the importance of her proposal. "You kin count on me to tell you fair, Miz Gerda, whichuns don' shirk. But 'deed that's a mighty fine mule to be lettin' niggers have use of it."

"Well, no ornery ones are going to get astraddle of it, I can tell you!" she said, and went out feeling a little better. Still the shadows seemed to her to loom large and uneasy in the row of cabins.

The sick spot in Gerda's heart, the thing that ate like a wormhole, was the revulsion caused by her son Wayne's behaviour. At best he was taciturn to the point of surliness, and at worst he was many hideous things that shunned the decent light of day. He did not merely whip his negroes, but added always some touch of torture, such as ordering a recalcitrant's friendly chopping-partner to lay on the lashes, while he himself stood by with another whip to flay either or both if the punishment fell short of vehemence. Or he deprived a negress's children of holiday spoils, or shamed some courting buck in whom he fancied he detected a trace of sassiness, by making him wear a woman's wrapper instead of overalls. And he kept two black paramours, who had hated each other from birth, cooped in the same cabin, where he not only lay between the pair whenever he passed a night there, but insisted that they perform every disgusting personal service for each other.

It was hard to account for the fact that in spite of his maltreatment of his negroes he yet managed to get his full stint of labour out of them. In all likelihood it was because he was ever present, driving himself to set a merciless pace behind which they dared not falter.

Gerda could seldom obtain positive proof of the monstrous cruelties he inflicted, for he was diabolically clever about perpetrating them on his own holdings, behind a screen of terror in his slaves. And whenever she or Bruff undertook to take him to task, to go beyond his sneering refusal to answer, they bogged down in the close-mouthed mumbling of sullen negroes who had lived too close to brutishness to dare look justice in the face.

Perhaps because Wayne could gauge the antagonism he had invoked in his brothers, he seldom risked ostracism by coming to table with them. On those rare occasions when he could not time himself to miss them, or when his absence from a special family dinner might be construed as providing a chink in the carefully wrought armour of his sadism, he sat among them beady-eyed, unflinching in his vindictive observation of any lapses on their part into their numerous foibles. For he had no intention of letting any one of them off lightly if ever he managed to have the upper hand and could call the card.

Small wonder that Gerda turned from the sickening twinge of thoughts about Wayne to an amused aggravation induced by the roistering of Joachim and Will Bee. The latter, who in younger days had been paired with the shy Daniel, had since gravitated to Joachim, acting as henchman to the other in his careless proposals for devilment. Gerda had hoped fruitlessly that as they neared thirty they would outgrow their rambunctiousness, yet they still continued to precipitate escapades fostered by idleness and propelled by drink. The town square made a public frame for their days. There Joachim and his coterie whittled, made bets, and kept up a reiterated discussion of their latest cavortings. They never grew weary of their community quips.

In this group Joachim was a marvel of favoured worthlessness. He could not do one single thing that men deemed important more than passably well. He was one of the most haphazard shots in the county, but he could recount the details of other men's prowess, sparing them the bluntness of personal boasting. He could act in a mannerly fashion around the staid older ladies, while in the very act of spitting their fruit nectar out behind his hand over their piazza rails. Among the belles he threaded his way with a blade's spurious deference for, and a natural horror of, innocence. As for mulatto wenches, his dandy's body felt a distaste for them, and whenever driven to them, considered them as no more than a bedstead on which he lay himself down seeking rest.

He cared for all people, since they formed a mirror before which he could posture, having early in life perceived his own beauty. He drank, not because he was a drinking man like his Uncle Ven, but because it gave him a sense of appropriate swagger. He felt no loyalty to anything except the becaped figure he desired to cut. And he revelled in his own slapdashery with a contagious merriment. Gerda sometimes toyed with the idea of the quandary he would find himself in if time and hardship robbed him of his vanity of person, for she wondered how his beauty-accustomed eye could adjust itself to the paltriness of his personality.

There was another care that weighed on Gerda at this passing of the decade; it was a dubiety about her grandchildren's force of character. Joby's brood, now increased to five, had not improved in quality along with quantity. True, the eldest girl, India, was achieving a certain distinction of bearing, and the older of the two boys could be winning enough when not in one of his pouts, but there had not been a coarse enough grain in Joby to counteract the devious opportunism of the Melburnes and strengthen it into true robustness. And robustness, Gerda surmised, was the one trait that would be sorely needed in the ensuing decade, whatever befell.

Tom Two's three children did have a good amount of physical solidity, coupled with forthright good nature, yet there was in them none of the potential capability for dominance that she demanded in the Whetstones. Hans, if he mated with a girl of sharp enough temperament, might well leave strong heirs. And something really fine would come of any alliance between either Bruff or Turber and Nan Upshur, if the three-cornered situation ever resolved itself into a marriage. Somehow she longed for that ill-lost son of Lucinda and Jerard Malone. Whet could not make up for him. There was a strange lad, Whet, one of whom much could be expected if something were not first warped.

2

This day, Danley observed, was not cold. A warm smokiness hovered in the air, the ground had been gentle to the footstep, peace was in the sky. But he mistrusted these placid portents, for the ten years had been fraught with too much turbulence, marked by heedless impatience of each section of the country with all others. In Massachusetts in 1857 Wendell Phillips had called for disruption of the Union and separation from the slave states if Abolition were not accomplished, while in the South the threat of Secession if slavery were not extended had never wholly died.

It was a curious thing, ruminated Danley, how down here the high and the low, industrious and unworthy, worshipped the fetish of a feudalism that comparatively few could ever enjoy. The impressions on the North that all Southerners owned enormous chanting slave-gangs was scarcely the truth. In Alabama there were nearly ninety-seven thousand families, and of these little more than a third owned slaves; of those who did, many had only one. There were of course a few with a roster like Lucinda's of over one hundred, and Ma'am Gerda's varied from thirty to forty; still, the rule in Turber County was about eight to a dozen. Yet the obstinacy in the South about preserving and spreading slavery was enough to give rise to the notion elsewhere of countless bondsmen and to feed the Abolitionists' responsive fear.

He supposed that the widespread Southern espousing of the planters' aims was the result of the articulate leadership of that group. But of late other sections of the country had grown restive under the dominance of the slave-holders, had felt a counteracting power rushing out toward other goals—after Western gold or Northern steel. Cotton was no enshrined idol to them! In fact they had begun to growl insurrection against its disproportionate sway.

Danley rubbed his forehead wearily with two pressing palms, trying to clear it of a beating sound.

He went to the door to survey the placid descent of dusk, and there saw Whet strolling towards the horizon. At fourteen he was easier in his gait, gradually having gained something of an acceptance of his limitations as those of a spectator. He was shedding cowardice by avoiding those activities that had induced his fear. Danley thought:

"If I can only help him to maintain his outer reticence until he has built up inner safeguards, he may strengthen into real manhood." And somehow suddenly, watching his son pass from sight, he felt convinced of the kindliness the day was trying to wrap around the earth like a mantle.

3

This afternoon Whet had been very happy walking across the jerky terrain of the bare fields, watching the look of winter in the sky. For all its mildness, it had a pale, far cast, as if the gold had been blanched out of the sunlight by some northern light too distant to appear black, but too powerful to have its cavernous cold altogether vanquished. He felt the remote chill, where his father had been baffled by the lingering insidious tenderness.

Gradually his mood shaped itself into an austere cadence of words, drawing heavily upon Greek sources. He began to stride evenly, planting each step one cotton row apart. His head was raised, his eyes wide open against the pale dazzle of the sky.

"So they spoke; and I in soft words made answer," he declared aloud; then he left the *Odyssey* and began to add words of his own extemporizing. They rang clearly, without faltering, so that he had to quicken his homeward treading to write them down. They had to him a sound worthy of treasuring.

The house, as he approached it, loomed with dignity. He was glad it was before candlelighting, so that no relief of coloured warmth marred its majesty. He went in softly, unstopped by any spry servant's attendance. The stairway, as he mounted, curved dimly silent. At the last bend he paused and surveyed the lovely dark well below, the white glimmer of the spokes unreeled with a moony fascination. He bent his head far over into the spiral and felt floating away. Then he continued upward.

Closed in his own room, he laid out paper and took up his pen. The ink was a trifle gritty and had to be watered before it flowed smoothly. The light from the high windows lasted him out, while the lines formed into stanzas. The last slender row of lettering was perfect across the paper just as the sunset began to suck the light out of his room back into the hills. He sighed. His father would be very proud.

He rose and began to pace his room out of sheer restless happiness, putting to rights small objects that appeared suddenly out of order to his new sense of perfection. Then he went back to the window by his escritoire and stared at the colours on the clouds, catching all the while, out of the corner of his eye, the stitched precision of his stanzas on paper.

A sketch of a knock sounded on his door, and his mother entered without the ceremony of permission, her riding-habit grandly awry. She joined him by the window, her eyes also dwelling for a moment on the piled rose in the sky. Then they dropped down and saw his sheet of foolscap. Idly she perused the verses, starting with indulgent casualness, ending in high-handed scorn. "This is all just aping your father's notions of the classics. Why don't you write something that has happened to *you*? Or hasn't anything—ever? Are you any part my son, or are you to go on and on in the shelter of echoes? Help yourself to the high-flown sound if you want, but I'm disappointed," she ended brusquely, "at your not going forward, but lying down worn-out at the side of the past."

She shook out the trampled skirt of her habit then and laughed at him in a way that made the whole room recede into a collection of shadows huddled about her knees, from which she emerged as the only live thing.

He saw her to the door, then came back and sat down to read the poor patterned prating which he had such a short time ago deemed a poem. He could not show it to his father now, for any measured commendation. He tore the foolscap sheet across, and his forehead felt weary from one temple to the other. He buried it in the pillow to bring on the shelter of sleep.

4

On just such another December day, up in western Virginia at Harper's Ferry, where a high ridge of azure mountains hunched against the sky, the Abolitionist John Brown was hanged from the gallows. It was not much of a hanging, not held in the town square, and the militia jostled awkwardly as they deployed in the death manœuvres. But Colonel Preston's voice had rung with a dread enough authority as he pronounced the words: "*So perish all enemies of Virginia, all enemies of the Union, all foes of the human race!"* The fact that the man being executed felt a fanatic hatred of that section of the country that was most willing to disrupt the Union, the fact that he had embraced too early the humanity of a chattel race, had little or nothing to do with the legal case of treason. And it was hard to say which section wanted most to repudiate his action, the North or the South.

The people in the North, except for a lot of women who prayed for Brown, wished to high heaven his slave rebellion had never happened. The Republicans denounced it as "the gravest of crimes," and even the lawyer Lincoln termed it a foolish thing that had unfortunately resulted in the death of Brown.

Somehow, though, the incident of Harper's Ferry rumbled through the land, echoing and re-echoing. Over and over in the mild, dying year, through the warmth of oven fires scented with holiday baking, under the voiced wishes of children approaching Christmas, in home, in church, in store, in any group paused to pass the time of day, the clangour jangled again: *John Brown the traitor, John Brown the martyr, John Brown, John Brown,* resounding in the million throats. Ominously.

CHAPTER FORTY-NINE

By the year 1860 Turberville was no longer a huddle of shacks, but a proper county seat. The log-hut courthouse, once so dear to Yarbrough's sense of justice, was gone; in its place was an ample, columned building before which the main pikes of the county met. Flanking it were the other sides of the town square in suitable formation of stores, hotel, post office, and newspaper print-shop. In the centre of the square was a grove of grave, tall trees fenced by rustic benches, where certain town sages and jokesters forgathered hour after hour, day after day. Immediately up the Yufala road were the cotton warehouses giving out their damp, linty smell which was the breath of life to the community. And from north, east, and west on alternate days the stages came jangling up, carrying the post and disgorging passengers at the welcoming steps of the Veranda House.

To-day it was the stage for Montgomery that held the attention of every one. It was packed chock-full of shouting, singing men bound for the steam cars that would carry them on to the Democratic Convention at Charleston. All about its wheels swarmed men, unable to go, joining in the farewell rumpus. Shouts of "Down with the tariff!" or "No ship subsidies and no national banking!" were alternated with the clamour for "Slavery in the territories!" and "Strict enforcement of the fugitive-slave law!" while through it all rang the chant: "Don't give an inch to the North! Don't back down on the South!"

Crowded in one corner of the coach Danley Bruton shook his head dubiously over their cocksureness. It was apparent that the rulers of the cotton kingdom, having tippled so long on power, were now too deafened by their own eloquence to catch the rumbling of the tumbrils. Besides, there were no cobblestoned streets here to rattle beneath the wheels of the death-carts, only slow, lazy clay roads spreading easily across their acres, culminating in pleasant town squares, where every one met as a neighbour, parted as a friend, and swept off his hat to the ladies. Danley sighed.

In the jostle outside the coach Bruff Whetstone's face stood out from the jovial pack because of its mark of frustration. He had been chosen as a delegate, but here he was kept at home by an outbreak of diphtheria, and after he had worked like fury ten long years for the cause of Southern Rights! He had cut no fancy figure on the rostrum, challenged no opponents to duels, jingled no words into campaign ditties. Instead he had risked rebuffs to his own free-handed disposition by canvassing for funds, had spent tedious hours drawing up resolutions for other men to round out into rhetoric. While as faithfully as he made his sick-rounds, he had spread his gospel of Cotton, to wealthy intrenched Whig and poor white, over rich bottom-land and pine-barren, in frame mansion and log cabin. For this belief was his birthright as Yarbrough's firstborn. As surely as it had been his father's task to wrest a stronghold from the wilderness, so it was his lot to hold that fiefdom intact, for all the heirs to that way of life which sanctioned the leader, protected the thrall, and sang its song on a trumpet!

Now he turned away from the last volley of farewells and headed to where his horse, Grey Ghost, was tethered; but Daniel hailed him from the print-shop doorway. "Come in and see the new motto I'm flying from my mast-head: *Separate Nationalities for Antagonistic Peoples!*" he read proudly.

"That's it!" declared Bruff. "Secession! That's what I'd pull for, if only I could have gone!" He clenched his hands.

"I hated like poison hearing you couldn't go," Daniel said. Rabidly Secessionist himself, but timid except in print, he had strongly banked on Bruff's barbed demands for dissolution of the Union, should the Southern Rights group fail to carry the convention. Now he nodded towards the new young doctor from North Carolina, who was at that moment progressing towards them from the drug-shop he had acquired as a back-log of income while he was establishing a medical practice. "Bruff, couldn't you have had him tend your ailing folks?"

"I tried to, the worst way. Wanted to give him a boost, as well as get away. But they were all scary, then some of them became too bad off."

By now young Dr. Fenway Cox had entered to make it known to Daniel that he wanted a professional card announcing his practice in the columns of the paper, where it was then the custom for all reputable professional men to advertise. He spoke with a hesitation that gave the false impression of shyness and resulted in his being interrupted often.

Bruff grinned at him in welcome. " Piecing out a living here some way, eh?"

" I'm used to scuffling," Fenn Cox announced, then told them calmly that he had come here to get away from his family, who were no-account. Also, he added, to have a chance to court the daughter of a wealthy Mississippian who visited friends here. Figured he'd stand a better chance than tackling her at home, where maybe her pa might interfere. He stopped short at telling her name in public, however. " Besides she might not know me—from the side of a fence next time we meet. I've only laid eyes on her twice—and one of those times she jogged me out of her way—with her elbow—to get past me in a push." He chuckled.

Bruff rose, restless now at hearing trifles, with his political career so recently bashed. He went out and jumped on his horse.

" Skittish chap!" remarked Fenn Cox.

" No such thing," objected Daniel. " His dander's just up."

Meanwhile Bruff, having reinforced his evil humour by a nip from his flask on the fly, was streaking by short cuts in the direction of Emma Will's. He had gone there very seldom since Turber's reprimand, though he had not attributed it to his younger brother's reproof, but to the knowledge of her alien offspring. Occasionally, however, when things went criss-cross, his perversity sent him there.

As he came into the Willis's mean little clearing, Emma Will shoved the cluttering children down the step-ladder of the shanty porch and moved aside from its top slat to let him mount. With no more greeting than a hitch of her shoulder, although she had not seen him for months, she pushed the sagging door wider open for him to enter the one room. She had long since abandoned their wood meetings and taken over rights to the house when he appeared, an innovation he regretted. For though his donations had added to its comforts, they could not detract from its slatternliness.

After she shut the door she asked: " What are you mad about now?"

" I didn't say I was mad."

" I can tell. Anyway, you never come my way unless you are mad. Not that I mind. In fact, you fetch me more excitement when you're frashed."

He jerked to a stock-still stand. Her out-and-out talk did not set well to-day, with his thought on far goals of statecraft.

She was loosening the stringy rope tied about her waist, and with one swift shuffle dropped her wrapper, the only garment she wore. He made a protest in his throat and turned his head sharply away. He could hear the corn-shuck mattress rustle as she stretched out on it. His eyes burned with a sudden shamed scorch.

"Emma Will," he commanded, "pull some cover over you."

There was silence and a stubborn absence of motion on the bed.

His head hung down, and he condemned himself for criticizing, but he could not go over, near.

He opened the door gently to let himself out. A long while he stood at the top of the step-ladder, waiting, in case there was anything he could do for her. Presently, when he heard her clattering the iron cooking-spider and cursing the new kitten litter, he called out in relief: "I'm going now, if you're all right."

"Well"—her voice was shrewish—"you'd better send me some sort of pretty, to make up for *this*. I never was treated so!"

He jumped to the ground and swung upon Grey Ghost. His last look back showed her lumbering cousin swinging out of the woods towards the shanty, and the door sagging open on its one hinge again. But Bruff's thoughts were moving away from there, following the route of the stagecoach laden with delegates headed for Charleston.

He took the Upshur's corduroy log road for his return, walking his horse softly. When he came to the end of it he halted and gazed a long while back at John Upshur's house. Their dogs, knowing him, had not barked, so he could watch in quiet. He could make out Miz Della lighting lamps in two rooms, then calling Nan from somewhere in their orchard. Nan's figure separated itself from the thicket of fruit trees and moved with something of the silent, effortless dipping of a kite across the clear space to the house. It went up the steps the same way, floating as if unimpeded by the use of feet.

After she was gone his mind still held the stir of her wavering white frock. . . .

2

In these momentous days Nat Screws in his store had kept careful tab on events, and instituted a *Buy Southern* campaign. He never ignored a trend or failed to placard his wares with a self-assumed stamp of popular favour. During the convention he had advertised in the *Trumpeteer* under the grandiose title:

THE GREAT CONTEST

To those who are not called off to Charleston, I wish to announce I am compelled to stay home myself to receive the largest assortment of goods, strictly from the South or those countries sympathetic with our section. All of which I am anxious to sell to my friends on the very best terms.

After the delegates had returned home from nominating their champion against Northern industrialism, Nat had made a shrewd bid for patriotic patronage by offering a minor partnership in his Emporium to that hotspur Joachim Whetstone. The profit to himself being a percentage of Joachim's cotton bales, and the main inducement to that young peacock the promise of unlimited finery at less than cost price. Every one had been surprised at the idea of Joachim even pretending to work, and Ma'am Gerda had been disgruntled beyond words at his poor bargain.

Joachim soon displayed two traits that fitted him for his new occupation of merchant: an intimate pleasure in handling tempting stuffs, and an aptness for putting his own covetousness for them into catchwords. His gift for plagiarism made it as easy for him to pilfer topical phrases for their advertisements as it had once been for him to "borrow" the possessions of others.

To-day as he was returning from his noon meal at the hotel, to keep store during Nat's own dinner hour, he was planning a series of announcements that caused him to snap his fingers and whistle. He liked his thoughts and the job that lay ahead so much that he liked everything else, including the heat not yet grown stale from repetition, the lizard matching its skin skilfully against a post, and the Yufala road taking its deserted siesta beneath a screen of boughs. But best of all he liked the Emporium after he had entered it, with its multitude of boxes and barrels into which he could dip freely, and their seeping scents of spice, salted fish, calico, coffee, and pomade.

When Nat returned, Joachim whistled for Will Bee, loafing in the livery stable, and proceeded to the *Trumpeteer* office. Life was returning by degrees to the square. Darkies were stalling about odd jobs, the chronic whittlers had returned to the benches about Centre Oak, the urchins' eternal mumblety-peg contest had resumed itself in a patch of mossy turf, and in a nook of the courthouse portico Judge Dormley and Willy had lifted the silk handkerchief spread over their chessmen and lapsed into cunning silence. At the bend of the Turber Pike a buggy could be seen making a puff-ball of dust, a buggy he knew to be heavy under Ma'am Gerda coming to outbargain Nat about a Weed sewing-machine.

Joachim entered the print-shop and was soon deep in confab with Daniel over the notice: "To Patronize Home Industry. Brogans! Brogans! 3,000 pair all the way from the Turberville Tanyard!"

"That ought to satisfy the old goat," said Daniel, "smearing even those rawhide clumpers in red clay, as if 'twas as enticing as gold-dust." Then, "Holy Hector, what's this puking one?"

Come and Buy
Come, Friends and fellow citizens,
Come gather at my store,
Come every one that hates the North
And loves the South still more!

"Hey, I wrote that one," remonstrated Joachim, "and people like this doggerel. It scratches them in the place where there itching now, the sting from the North."

Joachim, stepping out of the greasy-aired shop, noted that the square was arustle with freshened tree-tops and lively with carriages careening full of girls. Their treble voices fluted through the buzz of tired flies. At the Emporium he found the expected babel of pleasure. Young ladies toyed with furled parasols, children shoved towards the tub of iced lemonade, women thumbed judiciously at eight-pound blankets for field-hands. Presently some of the girls surged over to shoo the children away from the lemonade treat, to pass the dipper daintily among themselves.

"There's Nan Upshur, sashaying right on past us," exclaimed Dolly Walthour. "Yoo-hoo, ho-oo! She didn't hear me."

"Pooh, she hardly ever shops. Kind of sniffs at clothes."

"She always looks a perfect picture, though," championed Dolly.

"With *that* plain face," scoffed Claudia, "and that funny short hair?"

"Still, she has her pick of some of the best catches in town. Or half of the Whetstones!"

"Clannish family, the Whetstone tribe. Always picking on the same girl to court, or even like Tom Two marrying a couple of sisters in succession. Downright clannish."

"All the same, they have *more fun* among themselves," insisted Dolly. "Why, one of their everyday dinners raises as much racket as a barbecue."

"Oh, they're rumpusy, all right," sniffed Claudia. "No company manners, except Miss Joby."

"And Mr. Joachim," added the nettled Dolly. "Besides, they don't need to show off, like some prissies I know."

Just then Nan returned, hopping like a jumping-jack with joy and towing a skinny familiar-looking girl.

"Why, Veda Polk!" squealed Dolly at the sight of her old schoolmate. "What are you doing here?"

"Bringing my baby sister to put her in spring term at the Academy. And tormenting two of my prospects," she answered, as glibly outrageous as ever. She nodded over her shoulder at Fenn Cox and the antagonistic Wayne Whetstone, standing in the doorway. Wayne's face was livid for all of its supercilious smile, and Dolly glanced anxiously at Nan, but Nan's voice was controlled as she announced that she and Veda could not linger, with such a long way to go. Wayne was waiting surlily with Turber to drive them, but Fenn Cox, having had his fill of Veda's antics, had quickly departed.

The crush was thinning perceptibly. Dolly's group drifted back to the counter, where Joachim was winding up the muslins and the *point d'esprit,* as each girl wistfully conjured up a bedecked vision that was herself. Now the store had become an echoing cave, coloured lilac from the dying sun. They sauntered towards the exit amid Joachim's parting pleasantries, and Dolly turned to him with a covertly pleased glance that drew a special sally. The others, ahead of her, were laughing at some joke Will Bee had popped. Dolly started to flurry after them, whereupon Joachim slid her arm against his side, then assisted her to the door with it strapped close to him.

Outside, the girls told Dolly's pa's coachman to wait at the square while they took the evening stroll that was a veritable good-weather ritual. The box-boy hopped down to walk behind, close enough to keep them in sight, as they traced up College Lane, so named because it joined the road leading after many miles to the Bruton Academy. Here it rose towards a high look-out viewing the whole township. The branches of its trees were remote over their heads, the panel of space where the sun had hung was dyed a deep crêpe-myrtle hue. A cowbell tinkled with the listless note of after-milking.

As they turned back, the path under their feet had become a spooky white. They walked abreast, arms entwined, fancies of future fairy-land happiness bemusing their cheeks with the twilight breezes. When they reached the carriage the sky had let the night drop out of its hold, to fall over the earth.

CHAPTER FIFTY

In the martial month of July the favourite lines quoted from the *Trumpeteer* were those relayed from the Macon *Telegraph* : " The last words spoken from the floor of the House of Representatives prior to its adjournment were uttered by Mr. Z. B. Vance, a member from North Carolina, and they were singularly appropriate to the whole history and condition of the last House—appropriate to the state of political parties and party politics—appropriate to the whole disorganized and unhinged condition of public affairs. They were these :

'I call for the reading of the riot act !' "

Secession, with very little opposition now, pervaded the air of Turber County. The militia, which had been organized in a desultory fashion during the past several years, began to take on disciplined shape. The approach of Independence Day found the community companies numerous enough to endeavour to form a regiment. Danley had recently consented to replace the sick captain of the Turberville Guards, since so many of its members were former pupils of his and he felt he could continue a sort of guardianship over them. All the other men of the Whetstone connection were members or officers in the various companies. Even the Academy had a company of cadets, of which Whet was second officer and rather in love with the dash of his uniform and the notes of the assembly bugle.

This summer patriotism began to tattoo like a drum, until Danley, urged by Lucinda, had sent out invitations to all companies to meet on the cadet's drill-field on the Academy grounds, there to organize into a regiment. The various units agreed to assemble at the courthouse, to make the march together to Top Hill. Nothing had caused such turmoil in the community for years. Boots were polished till they gleamed like dance-floors, sabres and pistols were put in duelling condition, cockades and bright silken sashes were presented by sweethearts.

Bruff, never scot-free of his sick-bed people, had several typhoid victims who had recently caused him some anxiety, but now seemed well on the mend. However, since the wife of one of the poorer ones was panicky about her husband's condition, he had decided to wait over one day to ease her mind with a last-minute visit. He knew he could easily overtake the militia's march by riding Grey Ghost over a short-cut bridle path he knew. "The Ghost can make it as fleet as his namesake," he told Turber out in the stable where he was currying his favourite mount. "Besides he'll be strong as turpentine after his rest. I'm not going to ride him on my rounds to-morrow or next day. I'll use the buggy so as not to risk spoiling his coat." He was grooming the grey horse to a pewter shine.

Turber, admiring the Ghost's sheen and his elder brother's assertiveness of gesture, said: "Won't you feel proud when they choose you colonel?"

"Colonel! You're overreaching yourself with such fool talk."

"No siree, Bob!" declared Turber, rocking up off his spine in surprise. "That's the bet that's going the rounds."

Bruff clapped the currycomb between his palms rhythmically, weighing the worth of a brother's word, but Turber leaped up in convincing vehemence. "Didn't you know that? Besides, who else *could* they pick? They've been used to following your lead ever since they were in apron-shirts. Then, since you've been a doctor, they've all depended on you twice as hard. Why, I thought that was the main reason you were prettying up the Ghost, so as to take charge of the parade!" He laughed in joyous disbelief of Bruff's own doubt.

Bruff stared at the manure-crumbed floor a moment to hide a hope he had harboured all summer, while rumours of a regiment and talk of a colonel had been going the rounds. Now he raised his chin and blew a big breath up out of his mouth past his nose, to cool off his whole face, before he answered practically: "You're *Whetstoning* again," which was the term Ma'am used for their bragging of the family among themselves.

"Jupiter, no! Who do you think can hold a candle to you?" exclaimed Turber, pommelling the air about his head as if calling on the gods to uphold him. "Or have you got to be *coaxed*? *Colonel* Whetstone?"

Bruff chucked the currycomb away and lunged into a happy wrestling-match with this youngest brother.

2

The three local companies gathered in the square late on the afternoon of July 2nd. They set out from the speeding laughter of onlookers just as the slow evening cool began to come through the heat. The Light Horse trotted sedately ahead, followed by the other companies in mule-drawn wagons, all winding off in a twisting line. Bruff, watching their plodding, looked forward with much relish to the fast canter he himself could have the next day.

He had reckoned without knowing that one of his typhoid patients would take a turn for the worse during the night. The last dark hours when he had counted on slumber found him and Grey Ghost racing in the opposite direction from the militia to a remote and meagre farm.

The horse had waited quietly, as it had learned to wait when his master disappeared into a cabin. After a while a white boy came out, wiping his eyes and his nose on his naked arms, dangling out of his overall galluses. He bedded down Grey Ghost for what was left of the night. The next morning the stallion munched the fare provided, politely, after which the day droned on, with heat and more crazing flies than the animal was accustomed to.

Grey Ghost lived in this bare stall-pen for several days, getting on amicably enough with the other stock, because he was trained to strange pens.

Once, on the second day, his master did come out and call to him, but seemed scarcely to notice when the Ghost nuzzled his lax-hung palm. It was the next day that the long box was carried out of the house on people's shoulders, and the woman behind it could be heard howling under her sunbonnet. Later Grey Ghost was saddled and he and his master started for home. They walked most of the way, which raised no dust. But the Ghost's coat was already spoiled. That didn't matter, now, since the muster was out of reach.

3

Nan, who had been visiting at the Stand for the militia send-off, was still there when Bruff returned from that death-bed call.

He had gone directly to his room, and it was late the next day before a tray of food was carried in to him. It came out cleared, and after that the family ate a silent early supper, then settled into a quiet which would not disturb him. That night Nan could not sleep, except in those mirage-snatches which were more fatiguing than complete wakefulness. Upon rising she learned that he was again out on his round of patients, and was warned by Ma'am Gerda not to bother him at dinner. He came to the table and ate with absorbed hunger, after which he retired to his office, announcing another nap.

Nan was ready to be nasty even, to break through his shell, but the sternness with which his sanctuary was isolated stayed her carping comments. So she went out and began throwing the first good ripe figs away to the hens.

By chance the post brought her a letter that afternoon from Turber, telling all about the mustering. Before she had read three sentences she decided that she would use it as a pretext to break in on Bruff. "It may make his mouth water with disappointment, but then it's better he let loose and holler than keep up this brooding. And *I* might comfort him," she ended, recognizing her own selfish purpose.

After one quick rap she entered his door without waiting for permission. He was awake, lying on his old leather couch, his eyes drawing a bead on his boot-toe. At her voice he rose, drew on his coat, and went to sit before his secretary, where he kept his supply of medicines. There he folded his hands, consultation-fashion, and waited. She did not know that he was noting again the springiness of her ginger-peel curls and how her skirts seemed able to carry the narrow arrow of her body without any effort on her part. She felt instead the seriousness of the room with its sombre furniture, the foreign odour of drugs in one's nostrils, and the way the trumpet-vines at the window obscured the light, as if providing a shelter against the glare of bad news for the sick. She wanted to back down and excuse herself from his presence, but that was not her way, so she said stubbornly: "I have a letter from Turber, about the regiment. I have read only a little of it, but it seems interesting. Would you like to hear it?"

"If you like," he answered, without changing his doctor's non-committal expression.

She placed the pages flat down on her lap to hold them steady as she read.

My dear Nan-cee,

We went only eleven miles from Turberville before a storm broke, and not being able to pitch camp very well, were soaked. I do hope they let us take our negro "boys" to wait on us if we really have to make a trip to war.

Why did you fail to come over in one of the carriages of visiting girls and ladies? All your companions have been here for the festivities. Your visitor, Veda is looking as sharp-toothed as ever, being mean to Fenn Cox and Wayne at one and the same time.

On the fourth we assembled to parade, and everything was so alive to martial music that we all felt the South could easily resist any interference. At ten o'clock we assembled in the old school room, packed so tight that I must admit we were sopping-hot. Judge Dormley spoke, in his usual high style; after that came Bro' Danley's speech, which you can read in the Trumpeteer. *Suffice it to say that it so touched one and all that he was elected Colonel by acclamation.*

I myself had heretofore entertained some notion that Bruff would be chosen, but his absence worked against him. At any rate, you never heard such shouting as there was for the new Colonel. Bro' Danley seemed somewhat at a loss, but Cinda looked blazing proud!

There was so much fun that night, and so many of the militia got drunk that Cinda sent Bonapartt to quiet us, very fine in his coat-tails, in which he got ducked.

This is about all I have to report, if I am to get this off so it reaches home ahead of my carcass. Nan, you should have seen the funny faces the boys made after taking off their fine new boots. All seemed to hurt.

Your Un-obedient servant,
Turber Whetstone.

Nan's attention had become so lost in the narrative of the letter that she had forgotten her listener. Now, looking up, she saw Bruff struggling to blot out from his mien any bitterness at learning the supreme honour had gone to Danley. She knew instantly he was also recalling how Turber had nicknamed him "Colonel" lately, and that he was feeling ashamed of having enjoyed the title. Scorning to offer him any pat solace about the office being awarded to Danley because he was their old schoolmaster and mentor, she rose, casting her skirts out of the way with a sharp little kick. "I'll go now and let you compound those prescriptions you've been measuring out in your mind." She studied the drug compartments of his secretary, thinking of the power they held of life over death. For a moment she forgot about soldiers, thinking of Dr. Bruff's healing powers. Her father had taught her the ways of peace, and she hated strife.

As she moved out of the room, the light there seemed desolately faded about his lone figure.

4

Bruff might have been able to conceal his chagrin entirely had not Danley made a well-meant, but ill-timed overture at their first encounter. Danley was taking a natural pride in this addition to his prestige, feeling that perhaps at last he had surmounted the barrier that before had consigned him to a lower rank than that of a born Whetstone. Therefore the taste of his authority was sweet beneath his tongue and he made the mistake of supplying himself with the audience of an assembly family dinner. His voice already carried the ring of command. "Bruff, I have given the matter careful thought and have decided that for the common good you must resign your Light Horse captaincy and accept the post as doctor of the regiment."

Bruff stared down at him incredulously. "What authority have *you* to revoke my commission as captain?"

"I had not considered that angle, I was so certain you would put your medical duty first."

"I do, during peace. But in war I'll serve as a soldier. I'll render what aid and succour I can on the field naturally. But I'll not be fobbed off with any milk-and-water booby prize of regimental doctor! In the morning"—he drew himself up with the ire of a man giving challenge to a duel—"in the morning you will receive my resignation as a captain of the Turberville Light Horse, accompanied by notice of my re-enlistment as a *combatant* in its ranks!" He snapped an angry bow at his brother-in-law and charged down the hall towards his office. But when his hand fell on the latch he jerked it away impatiently. "No, I'll be damned if I'll putter around with powders, except gunpowder!"

Back in the dining-room Danley began to fumble irritably for the frayed thread of his logic. "It's all nonsense for him to waste his professional skill as a common soldier."

"Agreed," pronounced Ma'am Gerda. "But he's been a doctor only sixteen years, compared to the thirty-six years he's been a Whetstone."

"Well, of all the crowning fools!" ejaculated Lucinda, outraged at Danley's effrontery to her twin. "You made yourself look like a bantam rooster then, trying to strut before the cock o' the walk."

The rest of the table burst into horse-play about it, all except Turber and Nan, who slipped away as soon as they could. Out by the well Nan played with the creaking bucket-chain. "I can see the sense to what Mr. Danley says."

"Yes, but he did strut like Cinda said. And somehow it isn't right for him to king it over Bruff, who's a natural-born commander. Bro' Danley seems more like—a dominie!"

"He does. He's like my father, meant for peace. Much more than Dr. Bruff, for all his healing skill."

They stood leaning over the well, gazing down into the rippling picture the dark water was struggling to show. "I know," said Turber, "that Bruff feels like this in *his* Secession. He proselyted for it continually and he believes in it like Salvation! While to Bro' Danley it used to be something to write a treatise against, and now by accident it's put epaulets as big as ham-bones on his shoulders."

Nan nodded at their blurred images in the well. "Do you suppose we could sort of go riding, and just happen to catch up with Dr. Bruff? I hate for him—to mope."

"We-ell, it's a pretty hot time of day and he'd know we'd done it on purpose—I don't know how he'd take it." However, they saddled their horses.

It was cool rather than close in the vine-hung woods, and they followed the branch beds, listening to the repeating watery clopping of their horses' hoofs. When finally they came up with Bruff, letting his mount have a short drink, he gave them a snort of anger-mingled laughter which warned them the dinner-table subject was forbidden. That left them looking rather foolish, for how could they make their presence signify loyalty if he winced from the rasping salt of understanding?

In no way did he join in with them or let the easiness of everyday chaffing relieve the strain. Finally he said, stabbing bitterly at one topic never before mentioned when all three were present, which made it impossible for the trio to continue riding together: "I shall leave you two *young* ones to your Arcadia. I find I'm in no humour to play spectator at your idyll." With that he goaded Grey Ghost into a startled departure.

They were left sitting their saddles stiff with self-consciousness, evasively eyeing patterns made by damp leaves on the bank. Nan was the first to speak, and rather exasperatedly: "He has a right to cut me off at every turn if *he* doesn't care for my sympathy, but he hasn't any right to throw me at *your* head!"

"Oh, now, pretty!" choked Turber, laying a hand in caress on her bridle. "No one can *stop* me from throwing myself at your feet. Only," he smiled ruefully, "whenever I do, you take another path to avoid noticing my supplicating posture." He tugged at her reins until their shoulders as well as their horses sidled together. "If we have any war, you won't—you won't let me go without any hope at all, will you?"

She opened her eyes in wide distress, bewildered at the thought of not having Turber for her fairly constant companion. "But I'll come visiting at your camp next time," she promised.

He was silent. No use explaining that war might not mean a row of tents during visitors' hour. He noticed that she did not answer his question. Still, as their horses picked their way downstream she kept giving him small smiles out of one corner of her mouth.

5

Gerda watched the progress of Turber's courtship of Nan Upshur with a mixed mind. She could not rid herself of a deep conviction that the girl's emotions were, and always had been, profoundly involved with Bruff. Heretofore he had treated her with the raillery accorded a favoured child, but lately he had shown a guarded tenderness, as if he himself were still too unfamiliar with the shy face of so incipient a love to risk startling it into escape from the heart.

Then at quite the wrong moment had come this regimental humbling, mixed, she knew, with some notion of Turber's defection from his camp to Danley's at the muster. The double jolt had resulted in a feeling of thwarting that permeated his entire manhood. Coupled with his refusal to play military understudy to Danley was an iron-hard determination not to play second fiddle to his younger brother, who had hitherto been his lifelong vassal. As a result he seemed bent on spurning the girl into Turber's arms. But whatever Gerda's misgivings about the increased romantic cast to the young pair's relationship, they were a pretty sight to watch, in their tentative gropings after a surer bond of more trustworthy feelings.

There was another instance of emotional sparring going on in her family circle, which engendered neither hope nor approval in Gerda's thoughts. That was the testy attraction between Wayne and Veda. The girl was making an endless round of visits in the community and now at the close of the summer had been bid to the Stand. Gerda did not dislike her guest, but she was wary of her. Veda was a trouble-maker. Not in the rampant manner of Lucinda, but in a sly way, hard to lay hold of and combat. She and Nan seemed ill matched as friends, yet Veda, for all her orneriness, was devoted to the demurer girl; while Nan passed over Veda's tricks with amused tolerance or abrupt impatience.

Their intimacy was no concern of Gerda's, but Veda's and Wayne's relationship presented an ugly problem. For one thing, the girl spared time to torment young Dr. Fenn Cox, who was no moon-calf to endure it without a reckoning in the long run. Then the fascination between Wayne and the sallow Mississippi witch was based on a mutual perverted mockery, a callousness toward inferiors, a creed that cruelty was a basic trait of human conduct, which a clever person never discarded but kept as a trump.

Gerda's own simple sternness recoiled from this malformation of her own code of honourable authority. She thought now that she comprehended why God had been forced to banish Satan to hell.

To-day in the ell she had been watching them dourly, disgusted by the feints they made in each other's direction, and horrified at the snatches of remarks she overheard from Wayne concerning his recommendations for dealing with delinquent slaves.

For all the Abolitionists' inciting efforts there had been no slave uprisings in the county, nor any slain masters, as there unfortunately had been in some other places. So it seemed to Gerda that it ill behooved any owner here to speak of such heinous punishments as Wayne's maggotted mind had conceived. Finally, unable to endure it longer, she towered up over their chairs. "*Faugh!* You make me want to spit my own tongue out, because it speaks the same language as yours."

Wayne made no sound, though his eyes beaded venomously, but Veda inquired pertly: "What's so dreadful about a master making an example of a nigger caught armed? Before any white people are murdered in their beds?"

Gerda studied her contemptuously. "What's wrong with a master treating his negroes, not *niggers,* so they won't want to draw guns against him?"

"Oh," began Veda, so rudely that Gerda was about to order her to her room like an incorrigible child, when Bruff entered and regarded them with such gravity that all three were silent.

He came over in front of Wayne and clapped a hand down on his shoulder in a grip at once steadying and restraining. His tone was cautioning: "Two runaways were found in a cave at Jonases' mill, with pistols. They said some strange white men, inciters probably, had given them the firearms. One of them was your Jed, whose rib you broke the last time you brutalized him. I brought him back to his cabin. But now let me warn you, those ribs haven't knitted good yet, so don't risk doing anything that will leave you with a dead hand."

Wayne sucked in his breath in a sound like ecstasy, and a fantastic light leapt in his eyes. He cut through the door like a knife.

Veda's shoulders contracted in sudden jerky shudders of aversion at the naked viciousness she had just witnessed in him.

"Now, you *see,*" Gerda told her ominously. "I hope you're proud of your work, helping to roil up the devils within him."

Veda's fingers ran one sharp tattoo against Wayne's deserted chair-back, then swiftly she left the ell, headed in the direction he had taken.

Gerda stood heavily. Bruff said doubtfully: "She might overtake him if she's quick."

"What good will that do?" asked Gerda. "You yourself could do no more than warn him not to injure Jed beyond repair."

The last hour before noon hung sickeningly hot—in the doldrums.

As the dinner was being put on the table, the dishes sluggish with their steam, Gerda saw the two returning, marching bleakly apart. She halted the clapper of the dinner-bell.

Veda came up the steps and passed on into her room, and Wayne said sullenly: "I let Jed alone *this* time." Then he took his place at the table and began spearing slices of ham, which he ripped with his teeth without looking up.

After the meal Bruff laid his hand on his mother's arm. "I expect you ought to go thank Veda."

Gerda went to the girls' room door and knocked. Inside she perceived there was no welcome, but said nevertheless: "We are indebted to you for saving an abused hand from harm and for sparing our family making its name bad."

When Veda finally replied, her tongue seemed knotted about the words: "Then, since I am making my departure early in the morning, I don't feel I have imposed upon your hospitality beyond forbearance. Oh—what I almost *couldn't stop*—what I almost *saw*!" She made a frantic motion towards the door, and Gerda departed before the distorted laughter rifted loose.

6

It was the next Sunday that the Reverend Mr. Pollock preached his sermon on the kindly relations between slaves and their masters that justified the institution. Gerda knew he was right on the whole, but if one blot could seep so far and so black in her own well-assured mind, how could a number of them fail to spread like a dark sea over the consciousness of Northern Abolitionists?

As was her custom of Sunday afternoons, she went down to the quarters visiting the sick, carrying a basket of first-table dainties to be distributed according to their ailments. Everything was pollen-golden with August. The children were all starched out in their Sunday best, many of them walking conscientiously hand-in-hand to keep from getting dirty before her rounds. And all were courting the favour of the lucky piccaninnies with sickness in their cabins, in hopes of sharing in the spoils.

To-day Gerda made unusually generous bestowals, and her voice was more inclined towards gentleness or merriment than towards the tartness of admonishment that so often accompanied her bounty. Pokey, walking the customary piece-way back up the lane with her, said in parting. "Now there's nothin' for you to be frettin' youself about down here, Miz Gerda. Our folks knows when they's well off."

"What would I do without you?" asked Gerda doubtfully.

"Well, child," remarked Pokey briskly, "you wasn't studying 'bout sellin' me off into de canebrake, wuz you?"

They chuckled together over this good old joke, and Gerda continued on her way, after one more reassured backward glance at the cabins among their bloom-laden bushes, hearing the rocking of released merriment easy on her ears.

CHAPTER FIFTY-ONE

THE LAST WEEK of October the regiment held its first encampment at Turberville. Hundreds of people visited the camp by day, and the nights were noisy with entertainments provided by the citizens for the militia. With tents and bands and torches, it had the carnival air of a circus.

Shortly after the camp broke up the election for President took place in the nation. And somehow, because of the split-up of the Democrats, those Black Republicans won by the skin of their teeth and Lawyer Lincoln was elected. Since, however, he had only a minority of all the votes, showing his weakness in the north, and since the county was strong for Secession anyway, folks were not downcast but jubilant in the extreme. The middle of November a great military demonstration was held in Turberville, and the young ladies who had attended the Bruton Academy presented Colonel Bruton with the flag they had made. The ceremony was accompanied by explosions of the "Little Hotspur" as they called the cannon belonging to the Dragoons. The Judge, who had adjourned court, made a speech; the regiment passed a resolution by acclamation in favour of Secession and offered their immediate services to the Governor. The affair wound up in a torch-light parade after nightfall.

Now they were getting somewhere, thought Joachim in his yellow sash, Bruff in his plain enlisted man's garb, and Turber in the mirage of a knight-errant's dream. "And now," wondered Whet, gazing at his cadet's uniform, "if they call even us boys out, how shall I prove my mettle, how can I hide my fear?" Then he remembered his father and took comfort. His father would be there to shield him, his father was in charge of it all.

The torches snuffed out.

2

Owing to the wet weather and the approach of Christmas, all encampments had been temporarily abandoned, so Joachim was once more back at his duties in the Emporium. To-day he was keeping store alone, while Nat was at a meeting of lawyers, convened for the purpose of resolving to refuse to take the cases of Northern creditors trying to collect debts from county debtors. Presently the sun burst through the clouds in watery radiance, lighting up the gaudy wares of doll babies, striped stick candy, penny whistles, beaded fans. Before long there was a fair-sized crowd: matrons pricing, girls longing, children coaxing. This woman ordering a bolt of satin, that one skimping over an extra yard of calico, and baby's ill temper being bribed with a button of sugar candy. This was the way Joachim liked to see the store, as zany as a circus, as jingly as a calliope.

But speedily the holes of sunlight were swallowed up again by grey, and the bright fair-ground crowd vanished, leaving the store to the square loungers driven indoors. To-day they were not chewing a cud of gossip, but debating how soon they could count on Secession. Alabama was whooping it up, just waiting on South Carolina to follow suit.

Suddenly Fenn Cox injected a mild objection: "But my state, North Carolina, ain't *bound* to secede. Up there, we little farmers don't exactly hold—with you negro-owning planters."

Somebody mocked: "*North* Carolina! Are you all claiming to be a Yankee state?"

But Fenn Cox was too stolid to fight. All he did was answer: "I don't see why those in the *South*—without slaves—should go to war for the rich men's field-hands."

"Pshaw! There ain't going to be any war to speak of. Just a good big rally of all the different states' militia. Why, I'd engage to drink all the blood that's shed in any war between the North and the South."

Cheers greeted this, and requests for Joachim to pass the cup of free whisky. He turned the tap, and language grew more oratorical, or more homespun with each gulp, according to the profession or trade of the braggart. One thing though, they all agreed, was that their regiment would have a big time at the "rally."

In a lull they noticed the sky was letting up a little, and they'd better all scoot for home while they had the chance. Joachim was left deserted in the store just as the next downpour hit. Cut off by the rain, he turned glumly to shrouding his shelves. He called for the negro porter to sweep out the mud tracks, then realized the darky was caught out on an errand. For an hour, and then another, he waited in the grey sepulchre for the rain to let up, but still it came drilling down. When a third hour got under way the sluicing was commencing to bring night in its streaming strands. So, lighting a lantern, he started wading through the thicket of water that had replaced the atmosphere, even under the sidewalk canopies. He had forgotten to fortify himself with another dram, so his spirits as well as his boots bogged. He felt clotted with mud all over, and the sensation fouled his gentlemanliness. He lost the sharp silhouette of his caste. Suddenly, abandoned as he felt himself to be, in this quag of filth, he wondered if war would be muddy. Something queasy scrooged his vitals at the prospect. "Maybe we'd better not fight," his teeth chattered. "Maybe we'd better go on wearing brocaded waistcoats instead of uniforms."

3

In Columbia the South Carolina convention met on the 17th of December. On the 20th the cause that had known the disappointment of compromise ten years before, succeeded. And to the wild acclaim of onlookers from Alabama and Mississippi, South Carolina seceded from the Union.

"Hooray for Dixie!" yelled the once more irrepressible Joachim, and a group of men in the street struck up whistling that jig-tune:

Away—A-way—
A—way down South
In Dixie!

Thus jocularly was a battle-hymn born.

4

Christmas had come to the Stand once more, with the rabble of grandchildren's laughter while the cold bright stars gleamed in the pitch dark of the winter morning. Silly fowls in the hen-roost, hearing the noise, thought it daybreak, so flopped their wings sleepily while cocks crowed in the hour after midnight. In no time blazing fires were lit by house darkies, bobbing and chuckling the old greeting of "Chris'mus Gif'."

Whet, old as he was, gazed at the tree in the ell, bewitched by its sorcery of tinsel and sweetmeats and heart's desires pendant from its branches—a tree from which the Christmas fairy might speak in a sleigh-bell voice.

Now the hallway was showing window-panes of Madonna blue. He stumbled out from the happy babel into the clear, cool air, chanting to himself: "Oh, Star of Bethlehem that bringeth peace and goodwill." It was more a charm than a prayer.

Not again could he know the protection of quilts during his slumber on the Eve. Nor rise up with children, to claim his lumpy stocking. Nor have his eyes hoaxed by a popcorn-festooned tree into belief in fairyland. Not again could his heart be blown into an iridescent bubble holding all the perishability of innocence and illimitable immortality!

"Oh, Star!" he called again. But the white-grey of day had shut out the cerulean sight of the heavens.

5

It was the night after Christmas and the house was filled with a desultory satiety, broken now and then by some child trying to tug a disputed possession away from its owner. The servants loitered over half-done tasks, scratching their pates in woolly distraction. The floor of the ell was gritty with crunched nutshells; the air was stale with the over-sweet scent of fruit, causing the sudden rancid smell of a kerosene lamp to be a relief to the nose. Gerda thought how heartily every one would welcome plain fried bacon to-night.

She had reached the stage in life where she liked the day after Christmas best, being grateful for a chance to sit down to rest. Now, listening to the sizzling cooking from the kitchen, she was glad the men were still away in South Carolina. Supper would be quiet, with only the drowsy children spooning grits and batter pudding slothfully about their plates.

She could not hold her eyes open for long after the meal, and the house scarcely had been blanketed in the slumber of the children before the heavier rhythm of her own breathing had thickened it.

That night, the night of the 26th of December, while Gerda slept with peace for a bedmate, the Federal troops tramped in Charleston. And morning sent the news broadcast over the land that the South had been betrayed by Washington. That the Federal troops now occupied that symbolic heart of the planters' section, Fort Sumter!

6

It was one of those flighty days that had turned into spring before winter was gone. The blades of jonquils could scarcely shield their buds, and one lemon-yellow narcissus had shivered into premature bloom in the noon warmth. Gerda told Roxanne, Veda's little sister, to go pick it. The child had paused on the way though, and squatted to gather a clump of first violets. "They make a Southern Blue Rosette," she chattered, stuffing them up her nose to smell.

"What did I tell you to do?" demanded Gerda.

"To go get that Lone Star State flower yonder," replied Roxanne obediently. "That one's for Texas."

"Everybody's gone crazy on the subject of a Confederacy," sighed Gerda as Roxanne trotted off, her pantalets showing cuffs of dirt. The big chestnut oak above the child was displaying its first fuzz.

"It's going to be a mild year," prophesied Gerda, thinking of her planting, while she watched the child holding a fistful of flowers and trying to catch a downy chickabiddy that had wandered from its mother hen.

The sky was chalk-water blue overhead. And suddenly, for no reason at all, it reminded Gerda of the shadows cast on the snow of her childhood New York home. It made her long to see once more the resistant purity of a Northern snowbank.

7

The news that Alabama had seceded reached Turberville about three o'clock that afternoon, while the Guards were drilling and Bruff's company, the Light Horse, only watching. It would have to happen that way, he thought, with the others taking all the show and Danley, as their former captain, standing near, supervising. Then Bruff checked these hateful thoughts, listening to the great news being announced from the courthouse portico. The new captain of the Light Horse caught his quick signal, and their own company drew up in formation beside the Guards. The people on the sidewalks stood still too, facing the speaker.

Judge Dormley, who had received the message, was declaiming sonorously: "As you know, there was no hope for our Southern institutions to survive in the Union. The independence of our people required a Southern Confederacy. And now to our everlasting glory as a sovereign state, Alabama has not lagged behind. She has chosen on this 11th day of the year of Our Lord 1861 to secede! And to help *form* that Confederacy!"

Carriage horses shied at the shout that went up; darkies yipped: "*Hi—eee!*"

Then suddenly a hush came as Danley said in his old sweet willow-whistle voice to those he had taught before they were men: "Let us pray."

They remembered not to go down on their knees in their uniforms, but they heard him just as clearly, saying things for them all that yet left each of them room to ask the boon he most needed. Many of them, like Bruff, recalled their tutor's voice of old in a log schoolroom, declaring: "*Thus the gods wrought. They spun the thread of death for some, that others in time to come might have a song!*"

Then Danley gathered their separate prayers back together with his own words: "This we ask, O God of our white fields; let us shelter them and the black men that toil therein. And in His name I ask you to protect and bless these, my boys. . . ."

It was only a small Courthouse Square, long plastered down by rain, now beginning to give up the first false-spring dust. There was no real flag as yet for them to raise their eyes towards. Still, the two companies slanted all one way, reverencing the only emblem they knew, their courthouse.

Nothing moved in the square while Danley prayed.

BOOK FIVE
Cotton Militant

CHAPTER FIFTY-TWO

THEY HAD EXPECTED Secession to be something like a convention followed by a parade. They had, it is true, anticipated an outbreak of numerous duels and fracases if they came face to face with the Yankees. After that they had looked forward to a flourish of pens on parchment, and a victorious resumption of the old life under a new untrammelled Confederate Government. They had not expected Secession to come riding in the chariot of Mars.

Yet within less than a week after the fateful day of Alabama's leaving the Union, companies of militia were leaving for Pensacola to seize the Federal forts. In spite of the panoply of Blue Rosettes, vaunting tunes, and emergency romances, the county felt as if it had had its breath knocked out of its vitals. One hour the Yufala Road would be choked with wagon-loads of uniformed men, then an hour later it would be a tunnel of emptiness.

Before the first departure, that of the Guards, Danley had sent an urgent plea for Ma'am Gerda to come over to Top Hill and give counsel; for Lucinda's spirited scorn was driving Whet into resignation from the Academy Cadets and enlistment in the Guards. As yet his father, as Colonel, had not formally passed on the enlistment, but if the boy continued to insist, there was no way to refuse him.

In the schoolhouse on this chill day when winter had its grip upon them once more, Danley paced, because his military boots bore him to and fro against his wish as a scholar for seated contemplation. Unlike other more sanguine minds of the community, he could not conceive that this break with the Union would be effected peaceably. He expected a certain minimum of real battles before its conclusion, and aside from danger to his son he foresaw that there would be much coarse privation that would go hard with so sensitive a boy. It was not that Danley wished to pamper his offspring, but neither was he willing to see him wantonly marred or destroyed. He feared acutely that if Whet were thrust into the fierceness of battle before his thin outer skin had been tanned into a hide, he might retreat into the only protective guise he knew, cowardice.

Danley's boots halted before his desk and he sank down wearily, linking his fingers in his old judicious teacher's gesture. His eyes sought surcease against a rectangle of window-glass, behind which the flick of twigs reduced his weighty gravity to a minor personal anxiety once more. Still, he wished Ma'am Gerda would arrive.

In his own upper room Whet stood before the mirror, admiring the white blousing of his shirt above his well-breeched legs. He was loath to don his tunic in spite of all its trickery of insignia, for he preferred the soft swaddling of the sheer linen about his delicate shoulders. Smiling at his image, he caressed the shirred curls at his narrow temples.

He did not glance out the windows at the wide bald wintry land. Nor did he let himself contemplate not being here when shortly the scene would give way to real spring. For he preferred to believe that he could return every evening to this chamber, dip into his dish of fruit and walnuts, muse in his slipper chair, low and graceful like a lady's, awaiting him before the hearth. He was so absorbed that his room was but a stage-setting; he had forgotten that its windows gave on a world to be whipped by elements.

He made his way to his mother's room for approval. She was wearing a cream mull dressing-sacque over a mulberry velveteen petticoat, while Pinky brushed her hair. Because she refused to sit for this ministration, the maid had to hobble about on a milking-stool to reach the top of the tresses, which resulted in much yanking of Lucinda's scalp and smacking of Pinky's fingers.

Lucinda eyed Whet critically. "You don't look very spruce," she told him, and he saw with shame in her long cheval glass that he wore soft house moccasins instead of his boots.

Then suddenly his eyes jerked towards the window by the sight of a bluejay lighting on a limb. He felt pounding in himself his power over beauty that made him expect others to acknowledge a certain supremacy in him because of his sovereignty in that realm. He need not wait any longer upon even his mother's whims. He retired with a distant air to his own room. There he skirted unseeingly around his packed knapsacks to pass through the French door of his small side gallery, where he could survey the hills. He decided he would *not* go away from this domain of his, held by the right of his sensing each change in the creation of its varying ecstasy.

Later down in the drawing-room Whet found his father with his uniform spotless, each notch of his spurs sparkling; and his mother, her braids coroneted superbly above her straight brow. Also there was Ma'am Gerda's impressive presence. He rather regretted having had to return to a lounging-suit, but his uniform in view of his negative decision about enlistment would be no more than a paltry pretence now. He drew himself up, though, until he could feel the lean wick of his personality feeding through the basin of the world's crude oil, coming out into a flame! *He would not be browbeaten into going off to this war!*

He was eyeing his father's spurs with hostility just as Danley spoke. "Son, we all hope, and many expect, that any military unpleasantness with the Union will be of short duration. But should it drag along for a half-year, it seems to me advisable that the cadets of the various academies occupy the interim with perfecting themselves in tactical skill at home, and leave the rough-and-tumble fighting to the militia."

Whet peered at him, mystified about whither this oration-like blandness was leading.

Danley continued: "You will be of inestimably more service to our Confederacy if you remain here drilling and preparing yourself properly than if you dash off pell-mell into this first skirmishing."

Gratefully Whet grasped that his father was providing him with an honourable reprieve. Quickly, in his relief, he responded with a jaunty gesture of simulated protest at being held back from combat, but before he could complete the challenging thrust of his chin, Lucinda spoke, her tongue darting out first to attack her own heated lips.

"Oh, so *that's* your trick, is it, School-marm Danley? To fool him into staying home, riding on a hobby-horse! Coaxing him into the belief that in the end it will grow into the great wooden horse that will pass inside the walls of Troy, to overcome the foe!"

Father and son stared at her nonplussed, hearing her quote their own classics to confound them, but her wrath was running like a torrent now, not heeding glances. "And you, Whet? I can't call you *Whetstone*. You're snatching at every measly straw he tosses you, to build yourself a nest in which to hide your head under your wings, till the war-hawk passes!

"Well, twirl your toy tin sword like a drum-major, here on the parade ground bordered by the hickory-limb school swings. And halt your manœuvres whenever the school-bell tolls you in, to con your Greek and Latin by the warm sputter of a stove. But don't you *dare,* don't you ever dare to scan one *certain* heroic stanza! Leave that one alone!

Arma virumque cano
Troiæ qui primus aboris."

She shook now. "For *Arms and the man* you can never sing!"

"Stop!" Gerda's voice commanded suddenly. "You're beside yourself, Lucinda."

Her daughter flung about in Gerda's direction. "Oh, *you* can stand calmly and tell me to be quiet. He's only a grandson to you, a baby. *You* have your many strong sons to go wage their part. But this, this is my *only* son. *All* of my flesh that *can* fight." Her face had a fierce whiteness now, of the creature thwarted by its femaleness from wresting its own spoils of victory. Then surprisingly she hardened herself into a semblance of composure, which made more bitter the ensuing denunciation. "It is my fault though, Whet. Your nature came from my linking myself with a pedant. Likewise it is my fault that my other son was not birthed, who would have been brave." Whereupon she turned her back upon them, below the Malone girandole mirror, to thrum noiselessly on the mantel.

Danley had been seized with speechless rigidity, but Whet, advancing towards his mother's velvet-sheathed back, said: "I will thank you to retract that inference. Quickly."

She thrummed on.

He glanced at his thin-boned fist as if determining its striking-power, then he spread it out into a taut palm which he studied carefully, and ended by dropping his arm stiffly to his side. He faced about towards Danley. "Father, shall we ride? Have my mare brought around with your mount at once. I trust, Ma'am, we may stay this night at the Stand." His haughty voice dismissed his mother, but Gerda saw that the tight control of his lips came from the hysteria of a courage spawned by fear. She walked lumberingly towards the front door with him. There she stopped and let him move on alone. He had become unaware of her while he watched the smoky blue that had succeeded the slight rain. All she could catch of his murmuring was: ". . . Only this one world do I know . . . do I see . . . with the mists parting a path for the light . . . or autumn's pelt of loosened gold-turned leaves . . . the spring shoots stabbing through the hard-packed top ground . . . Only this *one* time do I know I will be here . . . have *life*. . . ."

Then he drifted out of her earshot, his thin shoulders hunched like a jack-knife.

Gerda went back to Lucinda. The drawing-room had darkened and was cold. "You will live to regret this, my daughter."

Presently two riders could be discerned threading their way down the drive. The rain had started again dispiritedly. "I would not choose to be you," said Gerda.

2

With bitterness in her mouth from Lucinda's forcing of Whet, Gerda returned to Rock Wall to bid her own sons good-bye within the month. Pokey and she saw to the packing of vast hampers of food, stomach remedies, bedding, and other home comforts. Each Whetstone man was acompanied by his own servant to cook, polish boots, and generally look after his well-being. As each unit left, these body-servants came up to the house to bear away the loaded hampers, and Gerda charged them briefly: "Attend your masters faithfully. If you can't be worth your salt there, return, we can put you to good use at home." It was not like many of the high-flown farewells that passed from owners to slaves hereabouts, but their negroes took her seriously.

The Guards were the first away. Joachim the most dashing, wearing his cockade like a lover's knot, while Dolly sucked her finger childishly, watching him. Other girls contrived to draw him off for sheltered good-byes, but she bawled openly like a baby. To cheer her he presented her a bag of candy lozenges from the Emporium, and the last he saw of her showed her cheeks bulging with the sweets as she waved the bag after him.

Will Bee was jovial, Daniel mild, and Tom Two grumpy because he had been excused from going for a few weeks until Hannah Lee could bear the next child, which she was expecting shortly. Wayne had evidently had some fresh falling-out with Veda, for she avoided him assiduously. Her father, who had arrived from Mississippi, came to Gerda for enlightenment. Brusquely Gerda told him: " The pity is that my son Wayne has a streak of evil in him; and your daughter has enough capacity for cruelty to be quickly corrupted by him. I abhor something dire that I foresee should there ever be any union between them. There, I have said it, spoken against my own kith and child." Veda's father understood that she wished to end this painful interview, and walked off.

Hans, the other one of Gerda's boys to leave straightway with the Guards, was heavy-hearted at the thought of Lucinda being left to herself without a man to handle the check-rein she so chafed against. He begged Ma'am: " Keep care of her. Even when she flails out at you. Keep care of her most of all then." He spent his last night camped in a flower-bed below her window, feeling as if keeping watch one final time would ward away harm from her while he was absent. Whet had refused to see her again, and Danley had been ostensibly too busy for more than the briefest of parting words.

As this group departed to join their command assembling in the square, Gerda took her last look at them from her own steps, where they were wont to see her on such occasions. She tallied these off: four sons, one foster-son, two sons-in-law, and that lone grandson. Eight already, a goodly number from any family.

Entering the house later that evening, it seemed swarming with girls or very small children recruited from Joby's and Hannah Lee's flocks, and some of Cinda's school protégés. The game in progress was a miniature of the send-off they had witnessed in town that afternoon. Tom Two's stocky eldest, Tomas, was doing the Judge's solemn speechifying, while C. D.'s first one, Charles Dillard, responded as the Captain. Joby's second girl, the flighty Maude, was trilling: *" Farewell, Brother Jonathan,"* from steps improvised out of chairs, and meant to represent those of the Veranda House. Veda's little sister, Roxanne, walked about distributing her inevitable violets, as substitutes for the ubiquitous Blue Rosettes, thrusting them among the " men in the ranks," mostly girl piccaninnies with peach-tree switches for muskets.

Pokey chuckled to Gerda: " Puts me in mind of when our fust ones was chillun. Except these don't know about such early hard times."

" I wonder," amended Gerda.

3

Now the first planting was over, now Hannah Lee had been brought to bed with yet another son, and now Tom Two was free to join his company. He sat beside her clasping her hand for her comfort. " You'll be well taken care of here with Ma'am. It's a load off my mind to know you'll stay under this roof till I come back."

" Oh," she snuggled her face into his palm, " I couldn't bear to stay in our little house, empty of you. I'll be fine, now my milk's come in all right. But you must promise to keep your feet dry, you catch the snuffles so easy."

" Then," he grinned, " if I stay well, I won't have the chance to use all that goose grease you gave me for my chest."

" All the same," she warned him, " don't you give it away, because you know how you hate the smell of makeshift mutton-tallow."

Their hands folded within one another's surely. Fear did not make them clutch, though they would be lonely apart.

Out in the plum orchard Turber was walking with Nan, pointing out how the buds were already knobby on the thorny branches. " It's too bad it turned mild again so soon after that last sharp spell. I wanted them to ripen late, so I could have my share when I came home."

" Oh, maybe you'll be back for them even if they are early."

" No," he protested, " I don't think our fight will fizzle out too fast. And I want," he bent her hand back at the wrist, " I want the chance to strike one blow, not so much for the Confederacy, like Bruff, but for you. And don't tell me I ought to be ashamed to put it that way. It's been a dream since school-days, the chance to fight for you. Remember the hickory tree in the cove?"

" I'm not ashamed of anything about you, Turber."

" Nan, will my leaving make you find out that you can't do without me so easy? Listen, try to make believe I'm in danger while I'm gone. You can, if you try hard. Use your imagination, as if it were history, all about cannon and Waterloos. Then maybe you won't be able to stand the thought of never, ever seeing me again. Maybe you will ' get ' love like people get religion. The kind I've always had for you." He placed his mouth down gently on her wrist.

" Turber," she pleaded, " don't talk like the end of the world."

" There," he laughed happily, " it's beginning to work already, my playing dead dog. Why, you're actually shaking, Nan-cee." He smoothed her hands till their trembling grew less.

In Bruff's office he and Ma'am Gerda were going over the account-books one last time. Things looked pretty prosperous for all of them, in spite of the cost of uniforms and equipment, and the forty bales of cotton Gerda had already donated the Government as a free gift. Bruff warned her: " Don't sell any of the negroes without asking me first; not that we're any of us much given to selling our people. But these will be unsettled times when you might need cash bad, yet more unsettled times in which to send any of them off into strange places." He cogitated a moment. " Though there are several doubtful ones on Wayne's holdings that I hate to think of you having on your hands."

" Do you think you are speaking to a Joby by any chance?" asked Gerda sarcastically. " You know better than to coddle me. I was running plantations single-handed almost before you were bed-broke."

He laughed and closed the books, then handed her the keys to the remainder of his drug stock. " Be stingy with that stuff. I'm taking right smart with me, but I may have to send home for more. Then you'll need to doctor some of my patients among the poorer ones from time to time. The county will be left bad off for doctors, and too full of dosers. Thank the Lord you and Pokey don't have the notion that you can blister every ailment out of a sick person."

They passed over the touchy subject of his refusal of the regimental surgeon's commission and adjourned to the porch. She saw his eyes searching for Nan and Turber, but he made no reference to them; instead he swept a hand towards the rock wall.

The eyes of each studied it. The stones had grown coppery with age and deposit, yet there was scarcely a crumbly one among them. Solid, it bent slightly to the natural curve of the land, holding back a lot of wasting down-wash. Then as they looked over its firm brim they saw how it bulwarked their land, until not even the sky could swallow Whetstone Stand!

Bruff said: " As long as that wall holds, the family will last."

" We will outlast any wall!" Gerda told him, " anywhere. We will build new ones if the old ones have to fall. Our family holds that wall firm, more than it guards the family. No year can come and go with its four seasons that will put an end to our race. I say this who thought I knew death, with Yarbrough."

He put a hand, in faith, on Gerda's shoulder. "I give you my word, Ma'am, the family will go on. Somehow. Through some of us." The young pair came from the plum orchard, glancing up at the duck-down clouds dispersing before they could form in the light sky.

A metallic rattle of empty stirrups sounded as the negro "boys" brought their masters' horses around to the front.

Turber was at the steps now, releasing Nan's fingers, and Tom Two had emerged from the house. The hallway entrance overflowed with grandchildren, behind Pokey, who held them properly dammed back. Yard negroes and some field-hands had edged about the porch. Turber was mulling his mother's neck. "Be a good boy," she told him, her voice roughing a trifle.

"Patt," Bruff addressed that ancient relic of their South Carolina days, "you must take good care of all, with Shade's help. Pokey," he held his old nurse in a hug, "take care of Ma'am, especially."

"I been doin' that since befo' she was born, much less you."

The three brothers were on their horses now. "Good-bye, all!" A deep chord of negro devotion responded, punctuated by the white children's calls.

Gerda watched them canter straight down the yard path, and clatter on the stone steps between it and the wall. Then they turned over the hill towards town. One, two, three more. Making eleven of hers, making all. She saw them breast the brow of the hill, then go down in eclipse behind it. She wondered which of her sons would not come back from that rack of war being constructed stroke by stroke across their beloved domain. She turned around to reach for Pokey's hand and caught sight, out of the corner of her eyes, of the pale scrap of skirt where Nan still stood in the lower yard watching the way to town.

Pokey asked: "Hadn't we better coax her in?"

"No," said Gerda, "don't spoil her sorrow."

CHAPTER FIFTY-THREE

THE CONFEDERACY organized itself rapidly. A provisional Government was set up with Montgomery as the capital, and Senator Jefferson Davis from over in Mississippi was elected President. Although still but a provisional President, Mr. Davis appeared in Montgomery to make an inaugural speech, and Danley was lucky enough to be present *en route* to Pensacola. The roar of cheers acclaiming Davis seemed fitting; previous words of Mr. Yancey sounded splendidly prophetic, declaring: "The man and the hour are met!" Repeatedly the cheers volleyed, like the voices of cannon.

Swiftly things moved towards that April week when General Beauregard up in Charleston demanded the surrender of Fort Sumter from the Federal General Anderson, and the latter refused. The sound of cannon came then not from the throats of hurrahing men, but from steel monsters. From the housetops along the Battery the citizens watched the two-day bombardment. Finally flame belched from the portholes of the Fort, and the Stars and Stripes fell, were raised, were shot from their mast once more, raised again. Then lowered carefully to allow the white flag of truce to be run up. And on Sunday the 14th of April the Confederates took possession of Fort Sumter, to raise a new and untried flag.

More swiftly yet did events move following the fall of Sumter. Virginia, so long deliberating, threw her lot in with the Confederacy, and shortly thereafter the capital was moved from Montgomery to the more strategic Richmond. North Carolina, Arkansas, and Tennessee followed suit, and for the moment the South was realizing itself as a whole, was conscious of a fierce nationality. Now was the time, this was the opportunity, forged if need be on the anvil of war, to set it apart once and for all as an impregnable autonomy. Soon, so soon, they thought that land would be giving their children their birthright of peace and plenty and placid years of endless acres of cotton.

2

Although Lucinda had had terse messages from Danley during their stop at Montgomery on the way to Pensacola, the first truly enlightening letter any member of the connection wrote from Pensacola was a loquacious one from Turber to Nan. When Shade delivered it, Nan knew what it was and sought Ma'am Gerda. "Here is word from Turber. I promised myself I wouldn't go home until we had heard something from them."

She read aloud as much of it as she could. It spoke of their handsome treatment all along the way, and also of having had to trudge forty miles through mud. He was much impressed by the floridly tropical scene around Pensacola and the handsome welcome accorded them. Near the end he said: "Our troops are in possession of all except Fort Pickens, which is reported to be indomitable. However, they had better look out when we get started, as war such as never swept over land before is going to break loose. And may God protect the Right. But remember, Nan-cee——"

Nan ceased reading. "He's teasing me again," she remarked of the flustering lines of endearment she would have to take away and read alone.

"Well, don't let him hack you," replied Gerda. "And I thank you for giving me this news." She plucked a moment at her lower lip. "Still I would like to hear from Bruff," she wound up, abstractedly.

Nan pulled her own mind away from that idea of Bruff's being the final word and went outside, to try to summon up the sight of Turber. The paper crackle of his letter gave her the essence of his feelings, but changed his reality into grammar. The figure she was limning out evaded his familiar contours, took on the composite vision of all guerdon-bearing knights, resurrected from centuries of buried romances. As she looked at the March scene, the unformed climate of spring came to her aid. She was loved at least, even if she could not yet return it.

Thereafter Bruff wrote regularly to Gerda, reporting on the health of his brothers, but otherwise confining himself chiefly to inquiries about the conduct of the plantations. Hans wrote seldom, but methodically, sending her concise information about the number of troops on hand and the capacities in which they were detailed to duty. The others wrote in varying degrees of patriotic fervour and disgust at not being allowed to fight, but forced to drill, dig entrenchments, and perform other distasteful camp duties.

Her sons, being attended by their own "boys," could escape the more menial tasks; but before long they discovered that even they could not be waited upon hand and foot, since able-bodied negroes could be used to better advantage at hard manual labour. Presently it turned out that while many other negroes were put to digging, their own more skilled servants were portioned out for general camp duties, according to their aptitudes: Tom Two's was made cook, Joachim's Duke did laundry-work and polished leather, while Bruff's Pint, accustomed to going on sick-rounds, was used as a nurse. Gradually the regiment's surplus servants were shipped home, where they could be of more practical use, but these three stayed "in the army" to the end of the war.

Will Bee wrote Gerda that it was a rare sight to see Duke currying Joachim's hair. "Did you know that His Elegance brought a looking-glass he unhitched from one of your old bureaus? On fine days he sits out in front of his tent to do his primping. The other day his men presented him with a bouquet, as if he was a belle. He took it in good part and made a vase out of a whisky jug, then called for a square dance. Shortly we were all cavorting as peart as if we were at the Veranda House, though those of us meant to be ladies were a little left-footed."

One thing that Gerda was sorry to learn was that, while Danley wrote punctiliously to Lucinda, including tactful references to Whet's well-being, the lad himself never sent her a line. Gerda broached the subject of Whet's silence to Cinda one day. The latter merely shrugged one shoulder. "He'll come out of his pout in time. I never pay any heed to him when he's in a pet—that brings him around quicker. He can't stand being in my bad graces. He'd have been out of his sulks long ago if he were home around me."

"Yes," replied Gerda, "*if* he were at home, where he ought to be."

Lucinda turned away, apparently unperturbed, to join the game the children were playing. It was Inaugural Speech and Cheering.

Not long after that, though, Cinda decided to find out what, if anything, ailed Whet. She could not believe that he would hold out this long against her good favour, so presumed he must be slightly sick or in some difficulty that Danley obstinately avoided mentioning. She could not bring herself to eat humble pie before the boy's father, and she knew Bruff to be out of sympathy with her on her treatment of Whet. So she picked on Joachim as being a rogue too, to whom she could speak of the matter under the guise of flippancy and without fear of unsolicited censure.

She despised writing letters and had to brace herself for this one with a stack of raw sliced sweet potatoes to munch on while she composed it. "Bet my belly will bust," she remarked ruefully as she finally arose from her literary labours and her chomping. Fairly well satisfied with her efforts, she went back and drank a whole dipper of good greasy pot-liquor to soothe her complaining stomach.

The reply from Joachim came with gratifying promptness. He had invited his nephew to a special supper alone in his tent, to give him a chance to talk; but they had said good-night no better friends than before, even after Joachim's regaling him with the best that was left of his home hamper. A few days later Joachim had noticed the boy going off on a solitary walk at the time for mail roster and had recalled that Whet rarely received any mail although he was eternally spending his spare time in his tent writing. At first his uncle had concluded that he must be composing some literary fiddlesticks.

Then quite by chance Joachim got to the bottom of it. Joachim's Duke, having a cleaning fit, was endeavouring to shine up the whole camp, when he came across some of Whet's papers mussed and hidden in a corner. Being scared to throw them away, he had given them to his master, and what Joachim learned from them showed him the boy was in a bad way about his attitude towards his mother.

Each letter was addressed to Cinda, but remarked that as usual it would never be posted. Apparently he wrote to her almost every day, then destroyed or hid the letters. Part of each sounded as if he loved her to death, then the rest showed he was as mad as all get-out with her for "condemning him to death," as he put it. Joachim was both sorry for the boy and mad clear through at his impudence to his mother. His own letter ended:

Ought I to whip him for speaking of his Mamma so? Any way

I will take the first opportunity to tell him his notion of being killed in this so-called war is all tommy-rot. His trouble is he has always hollered before he was hit. In a way I don't blame you for lashing out at him, except that has never been the way to cure a gun-shy dog. You might tell some of your schoolgirls to write him.

Lucinda jumped up laughing from where she had sat reading, and brandished the letter gaily in the air. So! Even if Whet was sulking at the things she had told him the day of his departure, which she had meant from the bottom of her heart, he hadn't been able to shake off the fact that he was her son. He felt that tie, strong to the point of hatred.

Suddenly she stopped her dancing about. Yes, he was fired with anger at her, but then this other business of writing day after day and withholding the letters. . . . She didn't like such mooniness. That wasn't the kind of action she wanted from him. That wasn't action! That was pulling away. The slight his silence put upon her vanity might have been allayed by Joachim's letter, and her spontaneous anxiety about the boy's health appeased, but now she was goaded almost to distraction by a greater fear. Suppose *her son*, away off there from her, under Danley's influence, weakened in the knees? And hid, tucked off in some safe coat pocket of his father's, out of all harm's way? What could she do?

Nothing.

CHAPTER FIFTY-FOUR

THERE WAS confidence everywhere in the Confederacy during the late spring of that first year of the war. Every one expected that Mr. Yancey, who had been sent to England, would gain recognition for them abroad shortly, which would result in foreign loans and foreign shipping directly to Southern ports. Then before long the whole unpleasantness would be brought to a triumphant close.

Meanwhile things were going very well in Turber County. Gerda, used to running her own acres, found it little additional trouble to attend to the adjacent holdings of her sons; especially since Hannah Lee, now residing at Rock Wall, could relieve her of many household duties. Guy and Willy kept an eye on Joby's Melburne lands outside of Yufala, after C. D.'s departure. The chief concern, however, of Joby's limited feminine mind was that of irritability at having the war interfere with the social triumphs she had planned for her daughters from birth. When she ventured to complain of their plight to Ma'am, she was met with complete indifference, and when she turned to Lucinda, the latter scoffed: "They're too young to take on about beaux yet. And if the fighting lasts till it's time for them to be brought out on the carpet, why, they'll be proposed for as quick as you can say Jack Robinson. Because men who think war will prevent them from being tied down right away aren't half as skittish of the marriage halter."

Lucinda had her hands full enough with Top Hill and the Academy without taking Joby's plaints seriously. Mr. Dicks was a capable overseer of the land, but the school was in a shaky state with headmaster and all the male teachers gone, for Miss Gracey was no more than a mincing sort of chaperon. However, Lucinda had hit upon an opportune thought when Veda Polk came to pay one of her frequent visits to her small sister Roxanne.

It seemed that their situation at home was almost intolerable since the advent of their stepmother, the woman even influencing their father to the point where he skimped them in money and clothes.

Lucinda knew better than to mention this to the thorny Veda, but one morning of the girl's visit she addressed her offhandedly as she poured coffee from the urn in an amber stream.

"With the Academy Cadets for ever drilling, the rest of the school is reduced to a sewing-circle under Miss Gracey. Now I need someone who can at least drum the three R's into the young ones' heads. If you want to take a try at it during the spring and light summer term I'd be pleased. Though what Mr. Dicks will feel I can spare to pay you, above yours and Roxanne's accommodations in these times, I don't know. What do you say?"

Veda clutched a hot biscuit, scorching her palm. "I can't thank you enough, Miss Cinda" No one knew the wormwood it was to her soul to traipse around permanently visiting, living on her friends' bounty, because she must hoard her slight store of cash for Roxanne's schooling. She could have fought it out at home with her stepmother on her own score, but she would not subject the sensitive little Roxanne to the spasms of terror that shook the child whenever any ire was loosed.

Lucinda finished the bargain without taking any apparent notice of Veda's intensity. "I don't expect more than the simplest teaching from you. It's more a question of keeping the biggity ones in hand and pounding in some plain facts. Mr. Danley will have to straighten out the scholarship when he's back, in the fall. Just try not to cross me, though, for, as you know, my fur flies, and so does yours, rather easily."

"Oh, I know," chuckled Veda, "but I've learned something about being picked on, since I was such a varmint here at school."

"Well, it's agreed then, is it?" asked Cinda, stretching her shoulders and rising from the table. She halted a moment before leaving the dining-room and added rather offhandedly: "I want you to feel something else about this, that you've a home here, so you needn't pair off with either Wayne or Fenn Cox. Though I'd never lift a hand to stop you. But you seem to have a knack like mine for curdling men, and it's not much help in marriage, let me tell you. I'm no one to advise you, though. A pretty one I'd be to set myself up as a model when it comes to choosing husbands and steering a proper course in matrimony." She indulged in a sardonic laugh at her own expense for the other's benefit. "Well, I can see that you won't let anything *down* you. You're like me that way too, you'll always be up and kicking, even if you're but kicking up more trouble."

Then Lucinda whistled *Whrrt!* out of the side windows across the range of the yard, to summon Mr. Dicks. She had no wish to linger and grow embarrassed at having shared with another woman any of the hardiness of her own attitude gained after mistakes towards men had been perpetrated.

2

The whole South was jubilant over the victory at Bull Run, but down in Pensacola the summer was hot and bad. A typhoid epidemic fastened on the camps, and Bruff was able to help very little, being stricken himself. He endeavoured to give directions to Danley, who followed them as meticulously as possible, but Bruff, like all doctors then, was still too much in the dark about it to combat this pestilence effectively. Fenn Cox had not had much experience with it either, though he was uncannily clever at administering drugs, thus inducing a maximum of comfort for patients in the sultry, logy climate, and Bruff's Pint was adept at nursing, which was a help, but the number of seriously ill mounted.

Out of the family, Turber, Daniel, and Tom Two, in addition to Bruff, had come down with it. Bruff was slower recovering than he should have been, since he was for ever rising from his cot in an attempt to attend some nearby patient. Turber was up and down by turns, and Bruff could exercise no control over him, yet Turber had a hardihood that lessened Bruff's anxiety. Tom Two's bad spell seemed to drag on the most unremittingly and he had Bruff the most worried. In the end it was none of those three, but Daniel, quiet Daniel, who died.

He had scarcely troubled them with his illness, as he had scarcely made any mark on the family while he lived, except upon Will Bee. He had used, as a child, to be paired with that robust brother. Now Will Bee acted crusty towards the others for not recognizing his deep loss, though he was well aware how he had long neglected the timid one, in his later allegiance to Joachim. Will went the whole long journey home, sitting by the coffin-box. Often he put his hand down on the pine planks to steady it, saying: "I wish I hadn't forgotten you for so long, Bub." He hardly thought of his other sick brothers he had left in Pensacola. They could take care of themselves. "No one ever took special care of Dan'l, after I let up on doing it." Will Bee accused himself and the whole tribe glumly, feeling himself to be to blame for his brother's end.

The pine oblong was transported homeward on schooner, cart, steam-cars, and the Yufala boat. And Will Bee was relieved when at last it was placed on the stripped-down litter of four slow-moving wheels drawn by their own mules and driven by Shade, who would see that Daniel wasn't bumped about. The lights were on at Rock Wall for this homecoming, with Ma'am Gerda waiting on the top step as usual to welcome any son. Somehow then Will Bee did not feel funny about Daniel lying in that box. He simply said: "I think he'd feel more restful, Ma'am, if he could go right to sleep in his place on the hill, without any more fuss. The chaplain's already prayed over him back down there."

So Ma'am told the negro boys to carry him on up.

The place was clear and almost cool by night, and seemed more peaceful for Daniel than any blunder of battle that might have followed.

3

The typhoid plague had not yet taken its full toll of the Whetstones. Bruff's case proved so severe and lingering he had to permit himself to be invalided home on sick-furlough. He submitted to Danley's orders listlessly; lethargy held him throughout the journey, and even after his arrival. There was no juice of elation welling in him at the sight of home, nor pleasure in endeared faces and voices. He simply asked to be left alone, to lie under his mosquito-netting staring vacantly. The only strong sensation he felt was one of scorn for his former acceptance of illness as all in the day's work. Having never before experienced more than childish distempers, doctor though he was, he had had a spectator's viewpoint. Now sickness penetrated his very bones.

Gradually he improved enough to forsake his bed for a portion of each day, though his weakness still kept him idle and fretful. When he had a letter from Turber saying he was back on duty, Bruff fumed to Gerda: "Now, he needed a sick-furlough as much as I did. I can't think what has come over Bro' Danley to put him back to work in this weather. Turber's so quick to wear himself out over anything he does."

Gerda was silent, unable to reassure him, since she too knew her youngest son's intensity of action. Besides, the sky was brazen with heat—she could only put her hope in the Gulf breeze.

Bruff continued to act like a pettish child around Ma'am and shocked every one by being peculiarly irascible towards Nan whenever she attempted to alleviate his convalescent tedium. They did not realize that the thought of the romance he was convinced had sprung up between her and Turber was well-nigh unendurable to him; and that at the same time he kept thinking it ironic that the younger brother had not been invalided home to the girl who was waiting to be courted.

In his extreme irritability he lashed out at Nan time after time, and her continued mild refusal to lash back discouraged him in a way incomprehensible to one who did not share the full flush of his violence of nature. Nan did not grasp his dire need for some adversary that would require strength from him and so restore his vigour once more into being. It was inevitably his own twin who got under his hide and goaded him towards recovery.

He was lying on a pallet in the shade of his small enclosed office yard when she came noisily up, progressing by some half-hopscotch jumping.

"For the Lord's sake," he rasped, "can't you even behave grown-up? Even if it is beyond you to act like a lady!" Having started on that tack, he continued to upbraid her. "I declare, Lucinda, I believe you were cut out for a slut from the word go."

She grinned. "If you weren't flat on your back, I'd whack you hard for that. And now don't you try to trounce me, you're not strong enough to match me yet." She dodged out of his fist's reach, and he shook with exasperation at being weak as a ninny.

"I can see where I have to get well enough to take you down a peg before I go back."

"Better get well enough," she advised succinctly, "to go back and put some ginger into the rest of them at Pensacola." She sat down near his pallet and began making small haystacks of dropped pine needles. "Appears to me when they aren't down ailing, all they do is dig around and make mud pies. Doesn't seem to me our men down in those parts are getting very far with this war, though we were mighty anxious to start it. Now we're leaving the fighting to Virginia mostly, who didn't want it in the first place."

He glowered: "Do you mean to call us yellow-bellies?"

"Fit the shoe yourself." She shrugged and, rising, dusted her hands off on the back breadth of her skirt.

"Don't you dare," he shouted, "call me any coward's name. You might think you needed to flay a half-grown boy like Whet into the shakes, so he ran away from you even if he had to run towards war. But you know full well how I aimed for the thick of it from before the start!"

"I do, brother." She came over and stroked his prone shoulder affectionately with her slipper-toe. "I was only pestering you. Then I guess I'm cranky on the subject of thrashing this war out fast, so our fine times can come back."

"Me too. I hate this trifling around." He patted her slipper reassuringly. "Never fear, I'll be up and hopping soon. Reckon I needed you to put some starch into me at that."

"Well, you don't show off as well as a patient as you do being a doctor," she chuckled, "and you really have been making the most of your distemper for a while here."

"Go 'long." He gave her a friendly smack.

4

Although Danley wrote Bruff shortly that Turber had suffered a grave set-back and was being furloughed home, the family was in no way prepared for his condition when he arrived. 'Fenn Cox and Pint brought him on a mid-September day. Gerda and Bruff had not gone to meet him at the Yufala landing because they wanted to have everything in readiness for his convalescence at the Stand, including Nan Upshur's presence.

As the carriage rolled up, the late sun was more brightening than burning, and in its light Gerda saw he had shoved off his cap, so his hair had that shiny look she remembered from his childhood, different from all her other dark-haired children. He was not reclining as they had expected, but sitting between Dr. Fenn and Pint, who was soothing his hand. Turber almost sprang down, though Pint managed to lessen his exertion by half-lifting him.

Then he called out gaily: "Now, Ma'am, you needn't try to put me to bed before supper. I want to help gather the eggs."

Gerda started to chuckle, then she noticed how his blue eyes did not quite settle on anything; and how when Nan stepped forward holding up her face, his glance lighted on her with polite brevity as if she were a total stranger at whom he must not stare. The two doctors saved him from tripping, and Pokey took him from their arms, the mammy in her speaking, resuming the past: "Now, Turber, they's no use your tryin' to fight off the sandman. You'se asleep on your feet, but I'll give you some bread and jelly befo' you drop off."

Roughly Bruff asked Fenn Cox, as Pokey led him away: "What's happened to him, man?"

"Sunstroke on top of typhoid, from too much drilling. He'll doubtless improve some in time—get to know people other than those he was accustomed to in childhood, but beyond that——"

"He'll be simple-minded?" finished Bruff harshly.

Simple-minded? My brightest boy! Gerda felt as if her heart were buckling, sagging. Then she wrenched her shoulders about from following her youngest son and surveyed the county for which he had been named. Turber County had seemed, to her high hopes for him, but the bare beginning of his realm! And in his own bright mind she had sensed that his princedom would extend far beyond counties, and centuries, and all courage—in his once bright mind.

Now Nan said to her: "He looks very beautiful," and the wind rippled through the water oak.

CHAPTER FIFTY-FIVE

EIGHTEEN SIXTY-ONE was gone, with its April gaiety of the fall of Sumter, its continuously tuneful departure of the militia, its pounding victory at Bull Run; yet the end of the war was not in sight. They had heard that Mr. Yancey was on his way home from England without recognition of their nation, in spite of his cordial reception by the British peerage. It seemed that the English mill-hands had been so against slavery they had given Parliament pause about coming out in favour of the Confederacy. Still, cotton was indispensable to the world, and by refusing to export their bales, the Southern planters felt they could create a European famine for it and simultaneously raise the price of their product. Yes, Cotton was still King.

It was too bad, though, it had to be raining on President Davis's second, and authentic, inauguration day in Richmond; for to people with wet feet, waiting to hear the defeat at Roanoke Island denied, his words were not comforting: "The tide for the moment is against us, the final result is not doubtful." That far-off promise was not enough for them. Turning away in the dankness, they could not help thinking that a war that had lasted a year could last almost any length of time. Then they tried to remind themselves that possibly they were looking on the dark side of things because of the rain.

Before the second year was ushered in, Turber County had abandoned the preliminary festivities of war and settled down to the long task of winning it. Situated remote from seaports, it early felt the pinch of the blockade that was choking Southern commerce with Europe. The county's problem came home to Gerda full force one day when she was in the Screws Emporium bargaining with Nat for a barrel of flour. She grinned at his scantily laden shelves. "I see you don't need Joachim to help you get rid of all this."

"No," he replied glumly, "and the store hardly needs me. I shut it up on the days when I'm off tending to my duties for the Commissary." He had just wangled an appointment as Quartermaster, which exempted him from military service.

She eyed him suspiciously. "While you're 'keeping store' for the Government, don't cheat its customers in the ranks of their fair share of victuals." Returning to her bargaining, she was appalled to learn flour's standard price and refused to make the deal. "Time was when Whetstone Stand made all its bread from its own cornfields. It can do that again," she declared, and tramped out to her buggy. All the way home she harassed that lower lip of hers with worried fingers. Something would have to be done to impress upon her daughters and others the need for making their places self-subsisting. "And even I," she gloomed, "have slacked off about making cloth and shoes since stores have been handy."

Straightway she sent out a summons for a group of them to meet with her at Rock Wall to take counsel about coping with the increasing shortage. Speculatively she studied the group when it gathered: Guy so feeble if still shrewd, Willy having his usual twitchets, the grandsons all too young, and Turber not even putting in his uncertain appearance. Bruff of course had been five months back at Pensacola. No real men, but women and girls galore. Petticoats, petticoats switching everywhere, liable, she thought, to trip them in the kind of work she had in mind.

She had also summoned her old stand-by servants, and each other mistress had brought one trusted one. Now Ma'am Gerda addressed the negroes first. "The times coming down on us will be harder than any we've ever seen, harder even than the pioneering days."

"Come now, Gerda," chided Gracey, "we may have to turn our frocks more than usual, and coffee is very dear, but after all, we don't have to use greased paper for window-panes! We aren't reverting to barbarism."

"Aren't we?" demanded Gerda sceptically. "Don't interrupt me anyhow, I'm trying to impress something on the servants." She turned again to them. "Two things must be changed. First every one will be used where most helpful, and no one is to put on airs about who is a house or a yard or a stable negro, rather than a field-hand. We've all, white and black, picked cotton in our time, and will be glad when there's plenty of it to pick again. Meanwhile if it's hoeing corn that's most pressing, we'll all hoe corn. The only fine manners to be tolerated are the ones of stepping smart and doing as told." She knew she would find in their faces no mutinous pride, for the pride of all of these lay rather in the trust imposed in their loyalty.

"Now the other new rule is that if, in spite of all, supplies do run low, the field-hands who labour the hardest will have first claim on the bulk of the food, shoes, and clothing, even before the white people."

"Aw now, Miz Gerda, white folk's victuals always is helped fust—ladies cain't go barefoot." A hum of disapproval went up from the negroes that caused a burst of laughter from the whites which allayed their first amazed displeasure at the prospect outlined. Gerda silenced both, then spoke with finality: "We all appreciate your devotion, but the work in the fields must go on before all else! You will have to learn now to obey each day's orders instead of old customs. It's up to you head ones to back us up, as you always have done. Now go pass the word to the others." They strutted as they went kitchenward.

"I'm through with my speechifying," she said briskly to her company. "Here's what the situation amounts to. We have to grow grain like all get-out. To supply ourselves and the army too. Then we must raise stock wholesale and cure meat. Yet we can't feed the stock on much grain, because our men need it. That means finding substitutes for fodder. I don't know what will turn out best, we'll have to try around. Right off I'd say cow peas should be good."

Every one nodded agreement, all thinking, however, mainly of the fact that their idle cotton land could well be filled with corn and wheat. They were now allowed to plant only one tenth of their acres in cotton, partly to create that shortage that would start a sharp demand for it from England, and partly because food was sorely needed. Gerda's voice startled them out of their complacent acquiescence. "How we'll thrash and mill wheat is a problem, but we'll manage. Next, sugar is going sky-high. Instead of leaving sugar cane to the small negro patches for crop-barbecue pleasures, and to children for a school snack, we shall be forced to grow it in plenty and make our syrup and sugar."

"Go back to brown sugar!" hooted Lucinda. "The day won't come when I can't afford white sugar for my table."

"You," warned Gerda, "most of all need to worry about making sugar, with your school full of girls."

"Poppycock!" retorted Cinda good-naturedly. "Do as you please, you've been making sugar, at least for your quarters, ever since the county began. And you're set in your ways. But that's not our newer way over at Top Hill."

"You're the one, missy," snapped Gerda, "who's *behind* the times.

I look ahead." To Lydia Screws she remarked: "Cloth's the next item. Lydia, reckon we can teach these young ones to weave? The few textile-mills that are being built around here can't fiddle with us, they're for the soldiers' benefit. I haven't let my loom go to rack and ruin, thank fortune."

"They'll catch on spry enough, I dare say," cackled Miss Lydia, "and good homespun wears like iron."

"*Homespun?* You mean for *us*?" gasped India. "Why, even the trash wears store calico now."

"You children," ordered Gerda impatiently, "may be excused from the room. You'll be surprised at what you'll be wearing before long." She shook a stray lock out of her face. "I never was much good at persuading."

"Don't grumble," said one MacDuff sister, "they'll make a fine frolic out of it when the time comes."

"We had some mighty fine weaving-sings, didn't we?" sighed the other MacDuff as the older women moved out to the porch where Gerda's loom used to stand in fine weather.

"I'll put it back," she promised them.

In the ell Lucinda chuckled: "To hear Ma'am talk you'd think we were on the brink of starvation."

"Do you think," Joby whispered cautiously, "that—well, Daniel's death and Turber's condition—that they might have upset her—her common sense?"

Lucinda laughed derisively. "Ma'am's mind is as strong as hickory and will be when yours crumbles like cake. No, it's more likely she thinks we need to be taken in hand, with the men away. Lord knows, I could do with the sight of a man who fills out his breeches."

"Ssh, Lucinda!" warned Gracey as Willy fussed with his fingers to assume deafness, and Guy broke into a bawdy guffaw.

Lucinda smote her hands impatiently. How she hated having her share in winning the war confined to the tame domestic! For a moment she almost hated Whet for not appreciating an opportunity to fight that she would give her eye teeth for.

The girls in the side yard shivered a little in the waning February day, and India said petulantly: "It's high time we spoke to Mamma about our spring wardrobes, Maude. I think we look downright tacky. It's all right for Ma'am Gerda to talk about what they wore in log cabins, and, after all, Rock Wall is partly log; but we live in Yufala on the *bluff*."

Hannah Lee's little Lutie burst into tears. "Pleathe, I don't live in a cabin like piccaninnies."

Veda reached impatiently for a handkerchief to mop Lutie's eyes; teaching seemed to be mostly nursing.

On the front porch Gerda, now alone with Lydia Screws, was discussing carding cotton for thread, when she caught sight of Turber wending his way towards the steps in the rock wall. "I'll tell him our plans before supper."

"Will he catch on to what you're driving at?" asked the other bluntly.

"Oh, he's a heap better now," insisted Gerda. "Everything he does or says makes some kind of connection." She floundered under Lydia's kind scrutiny, but added resolutely: "Be sure to speak to him as you go out. You'll notice the improvement."

He was walking in a curious pattern, painstakingly dropping bright pebbles to mark his tracks, chanting in a high sweet tone:

"Now I will not be-e
Lost in a maze,
These coloured jewels
Will mark my wa-ays."

A moment later as the visitor passed him Gerda heard him say plaintively: "Miz Lydia, Nat doesn't give me any candy when I visit his store, like he used to when I was last home from the Lower School. He tried to tease me by telling me it was because of the war, but the Creeks have been driven out ever since I was born. Tell him not to be so stingy," he coaxed.

"I'll tell him," she promised kindly.

The shade of despair was on Gerda's face, but she droned stubbornly to herself: "Nan told me that she had him up through the Third Reader again."

2

Gerda was resting on the piazza in the mild falling twilight. Her outdoor work on the plantation was done for the day, and her household regime could wait till after supper. Turber sat on the steps at her feet, where he could reach out and squeeze her ankle in his old way of teasing her. They had little to say, but these days there was a very evident improvement in him. His remarks were fitting replies to hers.

"I planted quite a lot of rice," she told him.

"Where? You haven't much swampy land, and I thought sugar cane was to go there."

"Sugar cane's in all of it," she agreed. "I planted rice on some uplands. Thought I'd try it there."

"May turn out," he giggled dubiously, "because *you* planted it. But ricefields go in marshes . . ." he ended dreamily.

"I know, that was the South Carolina way," she answered. There was a satisfying companionability about sitting here with him, talking over her experiment. A soft dampness was mixing into the air. Good rice weather. The distant creaking of a wagon far down the road came pleasantly to their ears, meaning the passing of home-going neighbours. A child inside the house cried out: "I kicked my shin." The wagon-wheels squeaked in a turn against the rut-dirt at their lot gate instead of passing on, then a hullabaloo went up, with white men's voices drowning the outcry of the stable boys. "Ma'am!" It was Bruff calling to her. "Ma'am, Ma'am!" the others echoed, even Wayne. She counted them as they all came in sight, no more missing.

"Furlough, after re-enlistment! We're leaving to really *fight* this next time," bragged Joachim. "Hey, Turber, are you clear of fever, so you can join up for the fun?"

Turber's face looked as if a cloud had been lifted from it. "I'll go put on my uniform. I've been saving it to go back in."

"You'll do no such thing to-night," Bruff objected. "We'll see about it to-morrow. Now we all need a rest out of our uniforms."

"Come to supper," Gerda called them in.

3

In Yufala the Melburnes sat about their board, with Willy present to help them admire C. D.'s new Captain's gold braid, which made his older Lieutenant's share show its tarnish.

" You should have had all new, I think," suggested Joby.

" My dear," he reminded her, " it doesn't grow on bushes."

" It's a shame," exclaimed India, " that people have to make out with left-overs. Look at our 'new' spring frocks," she mocked, " turned till the seams are pulling apart." She sent a spiteful glance towards her mother, and Maude pouted.

" What's this, Jobyna?" inquired C. D. " Why don't you take them to Nat's and outfit them in style for Easter, especially since we're all on hand for some entertainment. I'm sure Nat will be agreeable to terms."

Joby laughed shortly. " Now it's you who thinks finery grows on trees. Nat's stock covers barely half of his shelves, and the poorest calico is three dollars a yard."

C. D. frowned until his moustache trembled, then he resumed vaguely: " Perhaps some runner will slip through the blockade before long, up the Chattahoochee; then the girls can be properly frocked."

" Tell us," blurted Arthur, the jovial but belligerent one, " tell us about the battles." At which request his humorless elder brother, Charles Dillard, corrected him: " Papa hasn't been in any battles in Pensacola," causing C. D. to regard him with disfavour for this disparagement of his military actions. He changed the subject by bantering Willy: " Looks like they'll be conscripting high enough to enrol you before long."

Willy replied haughtily: " I'll volunteer before long. After all, I'm not senile and don't have to wait till they call men in their dotage."

" Please," implored Joby, " let's not talk as if this dreadful thing were going to last much longer. Surely it can't." And C. D. agreed: " Quite likely not now that we're showing them we mean business up there in Virginia, and over in Tennessee."

Her fears subsided at that reassurance. How thankful she was that Virginia was so far away, and Pensacola so quietly inactive! Her husband was very impressive as *Captain* Melburne. She planned to call him that hereafter, beginning the next time she asked him for a helping of meat.

4

It was late at night when Danley and Whet rode up the drive at Top Hill, and Lucinda could not tell who it was, except that their voices were male and not feeble with age. Rousing Pinky from her alcove cot, where she now had her sleep, Lucinda ordered her best wrapper brought.

"You ain't goin' down yo'self, is you?" cried Pinky in terror. "Might be Yankees."

"My God, aren't Yankees *men*?" demanded Lucinda excitedly, loosening the plait of her hair so that it fell in an intimate mantle. Out in the upper hall she could see Bonapartt below shuffling cautiously to answer the bang of the knocker. Before she could descend, Veda and an alarmed Roxanne were at her elbow, Veda saying crisply: "Miss Lucinda, you may be risking your life going down." She pushed them aside. "Back to your room," she ordered, not wishing to subject girls to a danger she herself courted, but they tagged along stubbornly.

Half-way down the curve of the stair she saw who it was. Danley, and her heart took a dip of disappointment. Immediately, however, she saw that the familiar scholar was lost in a soldierly rogue. His cape swung, his visage was sun-blackened, and his eyes taunted as he suggested: "You were expecting *us*? Attired in your most becoming dishabille."

She swooped down the rest of the way, scarcely noticing the boy beside him as she locked herself in Danley's arms. After a deep kiss she reared her head and shoulders, letting her waist remain clamped close to him. Their glances knit together, then his dropped to her shoulders, stark in the frame of dark velvet and fallen tresses. This time when their mouths joined, it felt like tugging at roots.

They were roused by a cough of embarrassment from Whet on behalf of the girls who were witnessing this uxorious scene.

"Oh, yes, Whet, here you are too?" Cinda recalled, while he bent over her hands formally.

"So? Grown up?" she pronounced lightly at that. He went to greet the two sisters now, with: "Veda, how are you? I dare say Roxanne doesn't remember me, being such a baby."

"Oh, yes, sir, I do. You showed me how to make a moss box once that kept wild flowers fresh for ever so long."

In the Little Parlour by now Bonapartt had had the fireplace darky start a blaze, and wine and biscuit set out. Cinda told the girl to amuse Whet, while she withdrew to a sofa with Danley, watching him with a smoulder as he took his refreshments. She buried her nose in her own wineglass, swallowing the wine in two gulps. Under her wrapper folds her knee caressed his breeched one with slow insinuation. He darted a glance in the direction of the young people, but Whet was trying not to allow Veda's sardonic attention to lapse and wander towards the tableau on the sofa. A spirit of paternal concern caused Danley to say: "I tried to induce the boy not to re-enlist this time. He's still under age for conscription."

Anger crackled in Cinda's eyes for an instant, then died like the gleam from a broken ember. "I take it you couldn't coax him into cowardice even away off from me."

He sighed. "He's back in it, and it's your doing, if that pleases you."

"It does." She displayed triumph, yet it seemed less related at the moment to her son than to his father. Something male in Danley exulted in the fact. Her knee started that stroking against his once more. Danley's hand that lay along the back of the sofa slipped through the cape of her hair, parting it to grasp her bare collar-bone. She sucked in her breath in a half-whistle and shuttered her eyes in abandonment to the sensation.

"Come," she spoke. They rose entranced. As they passed the trio, Lucinda blinked, some fragment of an alien idea intruding into her desire. "Roxanne," she directed, "you stay and play propriety for that pair."

"Mother!" cried Whet violently, offended beyond endurance for the child, not for that sharp young lady Veda; but his parents had passed on, leaving him humiliated by the revelation of their uncovered emotions.

As they ascended, Lucinda leaned hard back against Danley. In her chamber she scarcely gave Pinky time to "make her manners" to her returned master before banishing her for the night and loosening the belt of her robe. Danley was searching his clothes-press. "I left a dressing-gown behind among my citizen attire."

When he returned, a single low candle sputtered, and she lay on the bed in her splendid hair.

5

The next morning Lucinda tried to make up for her neglect of proper welcome to Whet and in a high good humour sent for him to attend her in her own quarters. He came with a hauteur of manner that in her eyes added manliness to him. "You look very fine," she complimented him, "now that the bleach of the schoolroom has been taken off your face, and now that your uniform has become your *clothing*, instead of fancy dress."

Her blandishments, however, produced no softening in him. He continued coldly polite even when she went to the trouble of whisking some soil from his shoulders with her own clothes-broom. Nor did her concluding kiss mollify him.

Rebuffed, she slapped the broom back on the toilet table and addressed him in an astringent tone: "Still acting the martyr, aren't you? Now I claim you ought to be grateful to me for making a man out of you!"

"Why," he asked her with fatal calm, "should I undertake to form the habit of gratitude towards you, under the existing circumstances of war? A 'man' can't continue to show much gratitude once he's dead."

She was stunned for a space by the finality of that truth.

In her robust self she could not comprehend Death. Even her father, Yarbrough, was still so very alive in the conduct of the family that now that the grief of being denied his physical appearance had passed, he seemed still here. Thus she had escaped the toll of death in even that instance. It was a factor to be discarded from her scheme of things.

"Have it your way, then," she upbraided him. "Shiver in your boots all the rest of your days simply because you are scared of pain! For that's what it amounts to, you're squeamish with fear, and blood makes you vomit. Good Lord, you should've been Cousin Gracey's child!"

She flung the door open to be rid of the sight of his sudden uncontrollable trembling.

CHAPTER FIFTY-SIX

THIS WAS A PAUSE in war. This was a celebration of such glories as Manassas and the valour of their leaders. This was a toast to early victory and final homecomings. This was Happiness, before Danger could snatch it away.

The Veranda House blazed with the last supply of Nat's store candles, the floor of the General Parlour was covered with crash, much seamed where the rips had been mended. Urns dripped springeria, mantels were piled with garden blooms, trestles in the dining-room creaked with the county pantries' last hoard of fine food.

Joachim was sweet-talking Dolly, who looked fetching in something she had concocted, a cap of delicate lace sprigged with fresh live rosebuds. She didn't care if the lace was out of her grandmother's scrap-bag and as old as all time, now that Joachim was admiring her in it. From a corner Wayne, watching Veda egg Fenn Cox on, thought: "She's as mean as I am, and she'll bite to the bone before she'll dodge." In spite of their unmended feud over his runaway Jed, his assumption of the ultimate acceptance of his suit was unperturbed.

Out on the floor, Fenn, speaking to Veda in his deliberate, divided syllables, said: "You listen—where do I write your pa? You'll end by marrying me—and bein' of some use. Not frail yourself out—on that ornery Wayne. Yes, I know he has—a queer touch on you—but I won't allow it. I won't go off—to the next part of the war—with you puttin' me off—with those two sticks of fingers. I'll break them off like twigs—and fling them back into your face! Unless you give me—your promise." He tramped down heavy on his heels and bowed to his next partner in the figure before she could get mad. She saw Wayne watching, his eye polished hard as hazel-nuts. Suddenly she realized with closed finality that the shell of his cruelty neither she nor any other could break through.

On the next swing of the music she swayed gladly back to the kind, butt-headed Fenn, who could keep her out of harm's way. "As soon as you can swap a furlough, I'll marry you," she told him briskly. The other couple in the figure heard her, and—so did Wayne.

He stood there trying to turn his eyes into magnets, to draw the iron filings of Veda's gritty personality towards him, but she had already gone towards that other sure pole, the bluff young doctor. Wayne teetered badly and went out to the side hall towards the private entrance. He hit the door trying to open it. Gerda across in the office, recognizing his fist-fall, came out and said: "Here, control yourself," and lifted the door-latch for him, knowing she could help him in no other way. He went down the steps and across a plot of mushy mud.

Lucinda was wearing her first new spring gown, which had run the blockade. It was a grey satin that gave her eyes a huckleberry colour, and she wore her hair as sleekly braided as ever, in derision of others' flucey curls. Contrarily she carried a fan of home-reared peacock tails, but had each feathered eye studded with a semi-precious stone sewn in by Pinky. The fan was a yard tall and almost half again as wide, and she relished the thought of her Paris satin behind its barnyard glory. Still she waved it slower and slower, tickling her nose in puzzlement. Whet still had not bestowed one glance of his accustomed homage for her in ball regalia, and now was in the hall playing games with Roxanne and other children, forgetting completely both his manners and his soldierliness.

Nor had Hans stayed near her to hear her tale of things that had amused or aggravated her. He stood with his arms folded, his shoulders squared bigger than ever, and made jolly remarks to those who jostled him. When she beckoned to him he glanced elsewhere; although whenever she was occupied with stupid people she caught his old look of sombre devotion. Ill-naturedly she flapped her fan, longing for Danley to return from his whist game and attend upon her.

All evening the main attention of the company had gravitated in the direction of Nan Upshur and her two escorts, Bruff and Turber. Her frock, plain and butter-yellow, fell in soft mull folds with no hoops to hold it out in a hard bell. Her shoulders had the faint sweetness of sparing young flesh, and as usual her only adornment was that locket of her mother's mother, pendent upon a narrow black ribbon to-night. Bruff watched both his younger companions, but his brother, more than the girl, for Turber walked as carefully as glass. He wore his uniform again, clayed clean. Every one had heard the astonishing news that in spite of his illness he had re-enlisted, to fight once more in the war under Dr. Bruff's care. Every one wondered.

However, Turber was giving a good account of himself, appearing very military in bearing. His boots were glossy; his light hair brushed as close as silk about his skull, showing the fine shape of his head; and, if he held his chin too anxiously far forward, at least it betokened strength. People stopped him all along, heartily, as if he, more than any of these others, had but recently returned on furlough from danger. While he gave out his hand to the men or bent over the ladies', they failed to notice how he looked, not into their eyes, but above and beyond their heads, into some unguessed territory. Before he returned their salutations in words, he measured his impulse to prevent it from rippling out in foolish phrases that might mark him as unfit for service.

Insisting that Bruff should have the honour of Nan's favour for the first dance, Turber carefully chose for his partner his young niece India, who, being used to him, would not shy away. They were paired with Joachim and Dolly, two other deft dancers, and the figure worked out its intricacy to the proper concluding design, which made him cluck his tongue in childish pleasure before he recalled that such mannerisms did not become a man. After his gaucherie he studied his uniform buttons a moment for reassurance; then leading India off the floor, he abandoned her rather abruptly, to seek praise from Nan for his conduct.

By ill luck, at that juncture he saw her receding from him out the door, tightly clasping Bruff's arm. Then he felt his heart spilling out of the glass vessel of his body, and noticed people walking around him at a distance, as if to keep clear of a pool of lifeblood. He closed his eyes to create the protection of a void, then slowly, painstakingly, poured his trickling spirit back into the narrow vial that could contain his self, if kept unshattered by a harder fate.

Bruff and Nan were strolling down the dip in the Turberville Road. Bell anemones showed in a shawl pattern along the path, the sky had a young and rainy look in back of the quarter-moon. The air chilled Nan's breast-bone beneath her cloak until she felt an ecstasy within. She wanted to cry out to stop the world from shedding one petal! The drink of spring went down her throat and passed through her very soul before it slaked her thirst.

Now Bruff was lifting her towards him by the waist, high enough for her to reach his lips, while her slipper-toes were barely scraping the ground, and he was saying: "Our wedding must be within the fortnight, before I leave." Then he set her down, and they saw the flowers they were stepping on.

2

The following morning Nan and Veda, huddled over the fire in their room at the Stand waiting for it to catch, repeated frequently that it was odd they should both become betrothed the same evening and to doctors. "They'd better form a partnership," decided Veda, "so there won't be a feud. And so Dr. Bruff can tell the sick 'uns what ails them before they die of suspense during one of Fenn's *pa-aws-es*!" she giggled.

"Mmn," replied Nan abstractedly; then, "Veda," she blurted, "Veda, you don't think that Bruff is just taking me over as a—well, a sort of sentimental legacy from Turber? He's so set on carrying the whole responsibility of putting things as right as possible for Turber, not letting Turb's life go to pieces, that I'm afraid he's trying to take care of me too just for Turber's sake!"

Veda took hold of her and shook her hard. "Now come to your senses! Sometimes I've been clear out of patience with that three-cornered romance. Why people have to go play-acting about being noble, like your trio, beats me. You only turned to Turber because he was the nearest you could get to the elder, when Bruff was tracking after that Emma Will, and later huffy about losing the colonelcy. It's a God's blessing Turber's sunstroke put an end to your namby-pamby sacrificing. I've known for years that you and Dr. Bruff were eating your hearts up raw for each other." Suddenly and amazingly tears broke loose from Veda and her nose ran. She stood there hugging Nan, using a wrist to wipe her tears away, thinking of something beyond Nan's ken, of her own blind loss because she could not mismate with Wayne.

The breakfast table was clattering with talk about the night before and all the conquests, and Joachim started teasing even the child, Roxanne. " Missy, I saw you hovering around with Whet a plenty, and you not yet out of baby pantalets."

" Oh," Roxanne's eyes met his with candour, " that's because he's promised to send me a real china doll the next time a ship comes from France to fetch Miss Cinda's frocks. She'll have pink cheeks and blue eyes, and nostrils you can pinch. I never had anything better than a rag baby before; and their noses lie flat on their faces. I'll love Master Whet for ever, and pray for him next to my dead mamma." The whole table subsided abashed into a scraping of forks over plates at that.

After breakfast Nan and Bruff stepped into his private closed yard outside his office, and he took her chin tight. " Happy?" he queried. This time she knew before the kiss what the shape of his lips would be like.

As they sauntered out into the main yard she stipulated: " I have to tell Turber before you speak of it to any one, even to your mother."

" He *should* know first," he agreed, " and no doubt you are the one to tell him."

Turber was seated on the wall steps, shuffling some pebbles, when Nan approached and spread down the piece of sacking she'd brought to sit on. They stared at the road. " Turber, I want to tell you about Bruff and me," she began.

He tilted the pebbles over into his other hand. " You don't need to," he said in his old knowledgeable voice. " He was always your *one*. I couldn't truly ever believe otherwise. Be happy. That's all I want." The pebbles spattered on the stone steps, and he gave her that childhood face again. " Do you know, Nan-cee, I'll have to go back to school after the fight is over and learn again." For a long time they sat, with her soothing his twisting fingers. Finally he clambered up. " Anyway I don't need Greek now, do I?" he asked anxiously. " Soldiers don't parse."

Up on the porch Bruff had seen their talk and knew that now he could tell Ma'am and Cinda. Ma'am was in her usual chair by the loom, Cinda was half-sprawled across the top step, batting at a waving post-vine tendril. The sun was coming towards the lowest step, and there didn't seem to be a war anywhere as he told them of his impending marriage.

"That satisfies me, son," Gerda told him. "More than enough. I have always wanted Nan for one of you."

"And Fortune be praised," exclaimed Lucinda, sitting up, "that it's the right one that gets her! I was almost beginning to be worn out at the misalliances this family's been making. Now this will be almost as good as having Papa back with you, Ma'am." Her words went to her mother, but her fine glad glance went to her twin brother to give him her joy in his new happiness.

He swooped her up on his way to embrace his mother, and they all three stood sharing the same conviction, that their blood was going to blend truly after this with another right blood. The stream would go on in all abundant strength.

Then Nan and Turber rose to saunter towards them, and Danley with Whet and Roxanne rounded the corner of the house. Curiously the three on the porch felt a resentment at having to break their strong interlocking for even these other dear ones, for there was a closeness of blood kin between twins and mother that existed nowhere else throughout the clan.

"Time we came down to earth, anyway," laughed Cinda, and rushed off awkwardly to try to use her good news as a way of winning over Whet at this eleventh hour.

However, he kept swinging Roxanne's arm as if they were playing London Bridge.

3

That same afternoon Nan, accompanied by Veda, went home to Pea River to make ready the things in her hope chest. Upon her arrival she learned that her news had preceded her, since Bruff had ridden out in the morning to ask her father's sanction for her hand. Her mother was all atwitch with pleasure and plans, but her father drew her aside, cautioning: "You know that Bruff's already like a son to me, but I've watched you seeming to shilly-shally between the two brothers, until I began to doubt my convictions about the elder having been the real man for you." He searched Nan's eyes as if they were the sky and might have clouds; then, satisfied, he dropped his arms across her shoulder in comfort.

She wished she could tell him how all the happiness she had forced under lock and key for years was pushing her heart open. But she could not tell him, though she might have spoken of it to Turber once on a time, having always been at home in words with him, infrequently though she was in the habit of conversing, because of her loneness.

Miz Della was in her element. Besides the linen, quilts, and laces hoarded almost from Nan's birth as a dowry, she now disclosed a store of china belonging to her own mother, marked on the back with crowns, proving the makers had served the kings of England. Awed, Nan ran timid fingers over the baked-cream surface of the porcelain. "Why, Miss Lucinda, even, doesn't eat off of anything so fine."

"I should say not," sniffed Miz Della. "Hers were new-bought. These have been kept in castles since time out of mind."

Even Veda was subdued by their beauty, and Nan kept recalling the tale of how her mother, who owned these treasures, had yet, when a poor itinerant preacher's wife, once been overcome by a gift of a hen and a setting of eggs from Ma'am Gerda. *Alabama,* what a place! Nan shook her head over it.

Cayline was fidgeting to make her young mistress submit to fittings of her costumes. They were not as numerous or handsome as they might have been, though the materials had been purchased long before the blockade; but neither Nan nor her mother had ever fussed over personal adornment to amount to much. However, there were some breadths of rich cloth that had been cherished from Miz Della's own bridal outfitting; and Cayline's nimble fingers had been busy on it night and day. Its satin, turned topaz with age, was resplendent in its lustre—like sauterne translucent in a crystal goblet. With the ginger of Nan's cut curls above, it would give the picture of a princess garbed in gold for her wedding. Nan was startled at her bright looks at the fitting. It seemed too much like telling her heart to the world.

After she was once more in her calico wrapper, her father came with some bulky papers in his hands to make his marriage settlement: He gave her Cayline of course, with her husband Honest, just purchased from the MacDuffs for the purpose of marrying his brood wife, and four toughened field-hands. All the land would be Nan's some day, but Upshur would not saddle her with that now, when her husband was not around to manage it. "I wish I could give you more cash silver, but you know how 'tis now with our Government. Still, here's twenty dollars in hard coin, just in case. Then I've tacked your name on fifty bales of cotton I'm holding. It ought to be a help some day. Now bless you." He pressed his palm down on top of her head, the way he used to after a baptizing, and her eyeballs thickened with tears.

4

Nan sat by herself on the old teeter-board under the big pine, musing. Her wedding was to-morrow, the war was day after to-morrow. In the meanwhile she would marry Bruff, as her dreams had begged her all her life. She sat scuffing her slipper-toes on the bare spot beneath the teeter-board. Now and then she would stamp them down hard and the board would bounce her. She would not go in till she pleased. She would stay here all night if she wanted to, where she had been a child. Then she found her cheek resting on the board, and it felt hard. She rose and walked in to find the comfort of her bed, even if she could not sleep. . . .

When the first excuse of daylight had come, Nan rose glad that she could now occupy the hours with activity. Veda obligingly slumbered in the other half of the bed, while Nan scuttled into her clothes. One thing Nan wanted to do to-day was to act quite as usual, as long as possible. Not tarrying for any ceremonial breakfast, she paused in the kitchen meaning to poke fun with Cayline, but her sewing-maid was scandalized at such carefreeness on a wedding day. Old Reba, the cook, gave her a small try hoe-cake, sizzling in bacon fat, and Nan had to dance her fingertips around its hot edges to hold it for a bite. It had a satisfying salty-mealy taste. "No cracklin' bread, huh? With hogs so precious to the Government." She helped herself to another more comfortably cool cake, and two eggs fryed hard and as yellow as sunflowers, to take with her.

Outside, her feet made clear prints in the grain of the damp sand, and the walking was easy. She reviewed spots where she had played as a solitary child. Next she came to the clump of their negro cabins, where all the slaves' best clean clothes were hung out on the line to air-dry for the big event to-day. "Don't put them on too early and dirty them," she warned.

The peart Rezzy called: "Set down, Miss Nan, an' le' me curl your hair over willow sticks like I used to. I promise to leave it jes' as soft."

They all clustered around to admire how her hair came out in bright scrolls from the willow sticks. She chuckled at their grotesque postures and grinning black faces, thinking: "I'm Nausicaa being attended by her handmaidens, slightly dusky." When the last curl was perched in its place, she waved back at them, after she left, and two little gals flopped into a twist-and-turn dance to honour her.

On the log road she came across Emma Will for the first time in years. There was a new toddler at her heels and the inevitable fishing-rod over one shoulder. Under the peculiar circumstances of the day Nan would have given a pretty to be able to walk by, but Emma Will slapped the pole across the road in a friendly signal. "I hear you an' Dr. Bruff're plightin' at last. That's good, though I never thought *I'd* say so. But now I'm losin' my teeth, and that 'un there's my youngest chile of six by Cuzin Neb, so I don't mind. Git the doctor out'n this old war though, for keeps. Folks need him." Then she added with sudden generosity: "I'll send your niggers up a good mess of fish for a fry to-morrow, to take the taste of marriage sweetenin' out of their mouths. I owe you one from a long time back, recollect?"

Nan did remember, with shame, the time when she had broken the other's precious fishing-pole that filled the Willis' poor cabin larder so largely.

Emma Will waved her rod once more in leave-taking, and Nan watched a spectre go out of her life, leaving in its stead a homely woman hitching along on lean thighs. Nan recalled with more difficulty that Sunday when Turber had had to comfort her to dull the stab of Bruff's hoofbeats pounding past her to that shanty. All that seemed far away, and about another person.

Then for the moment she forgot them all. This was the last time she would wander over this place while it was called home, and her name unchanged. She sat down on a stump warted with fungus and clubbed her heels against it. She stared at the sky, feeling the involuntary self-pity of approaching homesickness.

5

Unknown to the Upshurs, late the night before, orders had come to Rock Wall that the Light Horse would have to make its departure within two days for the Virginia battlegrounds. The messenger found Ma'am Gerda and Pokey polishing Bruff's uniform buttons with lye and ashes, to shine them for the wedding; Bruff was looking on with almost as much childish curiosity as Turber. When the news was imparted, he stared at the messenger's mouth, as if he could not quite catch the words it was forming, but Ma'am Gerda had risen, stroking her forehead to think, leaving streaks of ashes across it.

"Then we can't," she decided, "waste all that time going clear to Pea River to-morrow, nor have long-drawn-out jollifications there, with the journey back besides. I'll set things in order here and send the message around for folks to come to the Stand instead, close to the point of departure for the front. Then I'll have Shade drive me to the Upshurs', to acquaint them with the need for the change."

"I'll be ready to go with you to fetch her," announced Bruff, coming to life from what had seemed like his doom.

"You'll do no such thing!" declared Gerda. "It casts a bad omen for the groom to see the bride beforehand on the day. Besides, I want you to look to it that your two rooms are made welcoming like a home; Pokey will have her hands full running other things."

Bruff spread his chest at that, the thought of preparing his wife's abode.

Then Turber stepped forward tentatively between the two. "Could I ride along behind you, Ma'am? It seems as if some man of the family ought to escort—or do I count as a man?" his voice died down.

"The very thing," exclaimed Bruff. "Nan will like that. Also I want you to stand up with me later."

"Me?" queried Turber unbelievingly. "Not Joachim, with his sash?"

"You," said Bruff. "Haven't you always been my closest Bub?"

Very shortly the slumbering household was roused and every one fell in with the fun of doing things in the black of night. It seemed like an old-time Christmas, waking before day, except there was no tooting of toy horns. No *toy* horns sounded in these days of brass bugles.

Driven by Shade, postilioned by Turber, Gerda set out long before daybreak. By the time it grew first-light they were well on towards the swampy lands, and by the time it was full morning they drew up at the Upshurs'. John Upshur and Miz Della came to welcome her, the latter frittering the tiny company apron she had donned hastily. "We are surprised to see you here so early," said John. "I trust nothing ill has befallen Bruff."

"No," answered Gerda, "except what has happened to all of the Light Horse." Then she explained how brief a time was allotted them, and broached her plan for having the ceremony pronounced at Rock Wall.

John gazed at her steadily. "I had expected to give my daughter from my own house."

"These are war times," Gerda reminded him simply.

"I know. But all I can do is send for Nan and let her decide. She's out roving, as is her habit."

Turber spoke with a quick light rush. "I'll find her. I know all her places."

Her father nodded and motioned Gerda towards a rocker, then directed Miz Della to see that breakfast was laid for company. The latter retired to the dining-room, calling to old Reba and Cayline. She waved at the extra trestles that had been put up for the feast. "Take all that truck down," she said pettishly, "there'll be no use for them. As usual we all have to kowtow to Ma'am Whetstone." Then she began to cry, peeking through her fingers to relish the effect of the shock she had caused.

A pert young head in a mob cap poked round the corner of the door, and Veda inquired: "Has the *grand seigneur* sent to fetch the sacrificial heifer? Well, we'll have to bustle to have her garlanded, if we can catch her in from the fields in time."

"Yes," added Miz Della crossly, "Nan's every bit as bad as they are about doing upsetting, out-of-the-way things like running wild on her wedding day. She scandalizes me, since she's been half-living over there for years. About time she married one of them." Her pent-up jealousy of Ma'am's influence vented itself against even her cherished daughter.

Out by the stump at the log road Turber had come upon Nan. She glanced at him almost as if he were expected. She saw that to-day he appeared tight-knit and self-contained with some unusual honour.

He lifted her from the stump by her two hands. "Our Light Horse company's regiment is moving on the morrow for the battlefront, hence Ma'am and I have come to fetch you for Bruff. You will want to spend your time with him at home, not merry-making here."

"Yes," she said. Then with her face sure in a very new brightness that had come upon her since her morning encounter on the log road, she confided: "Do you know, there is *no* one any more for him or for me—except *ourselves*."

"None!" Turber's voice rang from out some selfless space. "*Your love* is *whole*."

6

Those whose affection counted to the pair were present, yet the house was not crowded, for many of the soldiers had farewell hours of their own that claimed them. This was the way Nan had wanted it. She was dressed in the room where she had stayed for so many happy visits, with Veda teasing her, and Miss Lucinda adding touches that gave elegance to her array, then undoing them laughingly. "No, let's not spoil you with jewels, Nanny." The girl was relieved to resume her familiar simple locket, on a blue ribbon to-day for the bride's charm.

It was just at early candle-lighting time that she came out to stand by Bruff. It seemed very right to be looking into her own father's face while he read the vows, as if she were listening to some new lesson of his teaching. Then she anchored her hand in Bruff's.

It was good to hear someone laugh as quickly as someone else sobbed, then have all the sounds and voices mingle musically.

At the table afterwards the healths had to be drunk in home-made scuppernong wine or kegged corn-whisky, but the good wishes were as fervent as if given in vintages. The food was savoury, though not elaborate, and the guests could not linger interminably, in view of the departing troops. One by one they wished the pair well and drove off towards their own homes. Nan and Bruff waved them off, listening to the neighbourly good-nights called over their shoulders through the crisp April night.

Some of the young people of the family connection were strolling in the gloom, their snatches of song trilling with the marred joy of youth. It seemed more like a house-party than—leave-taking.

Gerda's form could be seen lingering near the palings about Yarbrough's grave. "Let's go bid her good-night," said Bruff. After they did so, Ma'am touched his shoulder and Nan's cheek. "You have his name, son. Now your wife has mine. Guard them."

The two then passed back along the side of the porch, where Nan's mother was murmuring to John Upshur. Nan leaned up, as was customary, to kiss her, and there was something serener than usual in the "Good-night" Miz Della gave her.

Bruff guided Nan around to his office steps. "We will enter by our own door," he said. When he had lifted her up and set her down on the opposite side of the sill, he regarded her deeply. "Do you know that war comes back to-morrow?"

"Yes." She searched carefully for her words. "And others may have a long wall of years, like a fort to protect their homes . . . while we are sure of only one whole-blown bubble of magic like a golden moon. Still; I could die without a hurt after that. Only—I would rather death took place before morning."

In his gloomy office he saw the new moon of her face . . . and the white clumps of flowers he had plucked for her bouquets . . . splashed like milky puddles. . . .

CHAPTER FIFTY-SEVEN

THIS SEEMED a bright unclouded time for the South, the six months that started with the furlough frolics of April. True, there were perils: McClellan advanced so far up the Virginia peninsula that Richmond was threatened with evacuation, the great port of New Orleans was lost, sending the county its quota of lady refugees. But McClellan was driven back after the Seven Days' Battle before Richmond, while Lee pressed forward towards Washington! His rising star shone ever more effulgently, and faith never faltered in the stubborn strength of Stonewall Jackson.

Bruff, with C. D., Whet, and Turber, had become part of Jackson's brigade in Lee's army, and wrote with unswerving admiration of his commanders. Nevertheless Bruff's letters were more taken up with the discussion of a trade he was driving, to purchase Nan a house on the edge of Turberville, than with even the details of their victories in Virginia. As for Nan, she was still so encompassed in that completely bright space of fulfilment that as yet the greyness of separation had not seeped through to overcast her days. Memory could transform the immediate past into the present for a length of time. Everyone else entered the summer cheerfully, having feasted his eyes on beloved features so recently.

Late one clear hot afternoon Ma'am Gerda was tramping over her grain-fields, trailed by an assortment of her grandchildren. She was immensely gratified at how well her farming experiments had turned out. At first she had been extremely puzzled as to what to feed her fowls and stock as a substitute for corn; but soon she had hit upon the idea of planting the interstices of her orchards with chufas, a tuberous plant with a kernel to its roots about the size of an almond—called earth-almonds sometimes. The fowl had pecked away at them contentedly from dawn till roosting-time, and never had their flesh been firmer or sweeter, while the hogs had rooted with gusto on the tubers, fattening succulently. With most of her stock grown accustomed to new fodder, she had been free to concern herself with growing the much-needed cereals to capacity.

Raising corn was an old story with her, it having been their chief crop in the thirties, and an abundant one ever since; and her grist-mill was in excellent shape to provide all grades of meal. Rice she did not attempt to produce in large quantities, since it would not prove so generally useful to the army. However, that which she had planted on the uplands, against Turber's judgment, had flourished; and already she had devised her own primitive mortar for garnering the grains. It was nothing more than a huge hickory log, hollowed out by charring with fire; with a heavy wooden pestle to pound the rice free from the husks, it completed the mill.

However, threshing her plentiful wheat, she foresaw, would tax her ingenuity to the utmost, it being a foreign crop to her. To-day, tagged by her grandchildren, she paused at one especially rich hummock of land that her eye calculated would probably yield fifty bushels to the acre. Shoulder-high it stood, burnished and staunch. "That's good wheat." She waved a triumphant arm.

Suddenly Maude, Joby's giddy one, snatched her broad-brimmed sun-hat off and sailed it over the field. There it came to rest flat on the surface of the sturdy grain, without so much as bending the stalks! Quickly all the others copied her, skimming their headgear out likewise. And there the hats all lay, as secure as if resting on a shelf, while Gerda swelled with pride. "I'll thresh it some way!" she vowed.

Next year she was to recall her first clumsy method with scornful indulgence; but this year, bunglesome as it was, the process was pure joy.

She had chosen for it a clear spell, with a lot of air stirring, and invited not only all her own family but the neighbours as well. In the ell and the yard were spread old sheets and fresh-washed quilts. On these were poured measures of wheat, and each person was given a home-made flail to pound the kernel from the hull. The young were put to work in the yard, while their elders occupied the ell and porches.

But Lucinda, being caught short without a flail, had a barrel placed before her, over which she spanked sheafs of wheat with force enough to send the grain flying out. Presently the children, hearing this jolly commotion, set up a hue and cry to be allowed to play this game! The result was that Cinda increased their output with their flails by letting the one with the biggest pile at the end of each quarter-hour take a turn at "whipping the barrel," as they dubbed their new pastime. Hilarity and energy both waxed, till it sounded like a frolic for fair.

After the bulk of the kernels was freed, Ma'am Gerda called for the children to file up to the stoop with the grain in peck measures and, standing on the highest step, pour the contents down on a sheet. The draft of the air blew the chaff away. Before long several of the more venturesome ones insisted on climbing the roof-shed to pour, arguing that this would make the wheat cleaner. The performance lasted till Tomas, Tom's eldest, tumbled and sprained his wrist, after which they were willing enough to be herded to a back corner of the yard, where their simple supper was spread out of doors, turning it into a picnic.

Then Lucinda, passing some nectar she had brought to the young figures crouching about the sheet that glimmered below the down-coming blue of evening, suddenly stilled, and lifted her face baffled. What was it she recalled? Where had she had this experience before—of a small child breaking bread at a white cloth in an out-of-doors ringed about with danger? Oh, yes, it had been when they paused to make camp, entering the Wilderness. Back then she had raised her eyes even thus, hunting out the first star to make a wish on, for safety.

Her gaze now, having encountered the silvery prick of one in the stretched silken tent of the sky, came back instinctively to hunt out Whet. Then searched in the press of shadows surrounding these children at their supper-cloth. What dangers lurked beyond the pale of that white square? And how far away from its protection was her only son?

She moved over to put her hand on Ma'am's arm for refuge. "I wonder where Whet is to-night. You're right, he *ought* to be here."

"There, child," Gerda comforted this woman daughter of hers, who had ever scouted fear.

"But," Lucinda whispered dry-throated, "he was always afraid—of the outdoors dark."

"Bruff's with him," reminded Gerda.

"I suppose so," agreed Lucinda dully.

2

With McClellan backed off the Peninsula, and the cry of the Confederate Army now changed to *On to Washington!* Bruff's letters dropped the placid subject of his and Nan's house, to take up the war-cry. C. D. filled pompous pages to Joby, never failing to mention if he were so much as jostled in passing by some hero of the hour. And even Turber finally managed a spilled little scrawl to Ma'am. "They say we will 'sack Rome' soon. I wish Bro' Danley were here to put me straight about where this ruler Lincoln fits into the Succession, and if an Emperor or not. I fear to ask others, since Bruff urges me to keep my thoughts about history, etc., to myself, saying it best not to try to show off my education away from home."

Gerda cherished this epistle in the key-pocket of her skirt, not sharing it even with Nan.

Lucinda had no letter from Whet, not once did a missive from him come her way. However, after what Joachim told her of his unsent letters, she lived with an edge of expectancy about her thoughts of her son. Of his whereabouts and well-being she lacked no possible news, for her brothers kept her posted, but those reports were merely a picture of him pencilled against a distant horizon. That was not the boy she had been aware of here at home, engrossed in his remote gravity, or raucous spasms of bravado, or showing his delight at a layer of wind across his face. She found that she missed him now when it was borne in upon her that she could not terminate his absence by her own summons. She even missed his habit, after they had offended one another, of staying still behind his door, hoping she would pass it by.

While the Army of Northern Virginia moved forward under Lee and Jackson in the sultriness of the summer, the blockade tightened on southern Alabama. Not only did prices soar beyond belief, but flour, coffee, and sugar were scarcely obtainable at any figure. By the end of the summer term Lucinda discovered her stores of these staples had all but vanished; yet she was faced with feeding, in the autumn, a school full of girls with a craving for sweets. Ruefully she recalled spurning Ma'am's admonition to plant plenty of sugar cane, realizing that even if she now stripped the darkies' small patches it would not supply the shortage. She was sitting in a rocker on Whet's little upper back gallery, pondering her uncomfortable straits, while Roxanne combed her head for her, digging at her scalp with a light but satisfying scratch. The child had a knack of performing trifling disagreeable services shirked by others, with an absorption most children devoted only to play. "Miss Cinda," she remarked interestedly now, "do you know I can see the *skin* of your scalp, instead of dandruff like in most? I expect you wear Pinky out with washing it."

"No, she wears me out at it," responded Lucinda absently, her eyes on the dark columns of shade cast by the tree-trunks across the back-stair yard. She felt very cranky inwardly at the thought that she would not be able to indulge her scholars in the usual toothsome goodies this fall. Too bad they weren't here now, to enjoy at least her gigantic crop of prime watermelons. That would be about the last sweet the place would yield.

Suddenly she leapt up so violently that a rocker of her chair dug Roxanne's knees. "Watermelon sugar!" she cried. "And pray why not?"

Roxanne, who was nursing her barked knees, gulped: "I couldn't help being in your way. You mean watermelon *pickle*?" Her mind seldom grasped innovations.

"No, ninny! I mean I'm going to *make sugar* out of my fine juicy melons." She went scooting down the gallery steps, her hair at full sail, headed for the patches.

At supper she explained to them what she planned. Miss Gracey said: "Fiddlesticks!" and chipped with the tines of her fork around on her plate till it made Roxanne's skin crawl. Veda said sharply: "It'll be a sticky job."

Roxanne had never seen so many watermelons as were unloaded in the kitchen yard the next morning. They were stacked up like logs and were hacked open like carcasses. Pretty soon scooping out the pink pulp made Roxanne almost sick-stomach, yet she kept on even when it began to remind her of hunks of human meat.

When several tubs of it were ready, it was packed into big wash-pots and boiled, and skimmed and skimmed of scum. While Milly and Pinky and Mammy tended the kettles, and Miss Lucinda pranced around overseeing it all, Roxanne still had to continue scooping the pulp. To make it worse, all the bees in Christendom were now beginning to swarm about, and the air had that sickish watermelon odour half of sugar, half of cucumber, that always made Roxanne want to belch. Suddenly she did, and just missed vomiting into the trough of one fine half-section of fruit. But Veda snatched her quickly behind a pomegranate bush and put her head down between her knees. After a minute of watching the ground spin like a top, her head slowed down its whirl to where she was able to stand up, though wobbling. No one else had noticed. Roxanne asked permission to take a nap, a thing they were always forcing on her other days to rid themselves of her childish pestering.

When she came out again in the cool of the evening, the bee hum was gone. She peered into one of the pots and saw a glorious rosy well of juice. It reflected the play of leaves overhead like blossoms. " What a pretty way to make sugar," she murmured now, " kinder like growing a garden!"

After the sugar was finally finished somewhat later in the week, it was the whitest they'd ever seen since the bought barrels were gone. Miss Lucinda felt very frisky about it. " We'll have a tea party in honour of it and serve some of the real coffee the ladies from New Orleans gave us. Come on, chickie," to Roxanne, " we're sashaying out to pay a 'sugar-call' on Ma'am Gerda. I confess I didn't like being left out of all that rigmarole last year."

It was all the fashion these days for folks to take little packets of their home-made sugar with them when they went spend-the-day visiting and offer samples of it to their hostess to be praised or criticized helpfully. Very little of it except Gerda's had amounted to much in '61, since she was one of the few practised in its making. Moreover she had iron rollers to crush the full juice out of the cane, rollers she was planning to lend around to the neighbours this fall.

As the Top Hill vehicle rolled over the hills Roxanne sat very proud, holding the little basket of sweet morsels, each wrapped separately like French bon-bons, which no longer seemed to exist since the blockade. " Won't it be a treat to show them?" Roxanne crowed.

" Can't tell," said Lucinda shortly. " I recall how rich and crumbly

Ma'am's is. Really better tasting than white." Then she chuckled. "Anyhow, Joby's last year was boiled too long and turned out to be nothing but a barrel of rock-hard caramel. It had to be chipped out with a hatchet—what they called 'hard sweetening' in the Indian days. Now, don't you tell them how we did it till we hear their opinion."

Gerda, seeing their approach from midway of the ell, called for Pokey. "Here comes Cinda switching her fan-tails nearly off about something. Wonder what she feels so uppish about."

However, after her daughter had spread one of the packets open in Gerda's palm and she saw the texture and the colour, lambent as light honey, she flumped down in her chair and granted honours. "You'd better take up the sugar-making trade. But the cane's not ripe yet! How did you do it?"

Cinda told her.

"Well, frash me standing!" cried her mother enviously. "Here I thought I was one jump ahead of everybody on scheming up ways." She poked her fingertips into it and tasted. "Mmmm. . . . Here, Pokey, what's this remind you of?"

Pokey rolled her eyes in spite of the wrinkled leather of her lids. "Yankee maple sugar, 'ceptin' 'tain't got that tree-glue taste."

They sat dipping and sucking their fingers till the last smidgin of the sample was gone. Then Pokey ordered her mistress: "Don' waste this on chillun. Heah, give me." She took the remainder from Roxanne's basket to hide for some special celebration. "Now that Doctah Bruff's weddin's ovah," she pronounced, "we'll save this for peace-time high-doin's."

3

They had heard the good news of Lee's victory at Cedar Mountain, and his routing of Pope at the Second Manassas on August 30th. Now he was at the very gates of Washington, or perhaps he had even entered it! Any hour the telegraph instrument might click out the news of victory. Every one went about smiling at every one else, or into vacancy if no one else was handy. Consequently Lucinda decided it was time for her sugar party, for, aside from everything else, another box of luxuries had somehow crept through from France. Not a large box lavishly filled, but containing at least a few bright symbols of the outside world, reassurance that they were not completely consigned to oblivion. Most precious of all was a parcel containing a present Whet had commissioned her to obtain for Roxanne. She did not open that; instead she laid it gently on the pillow of his empty bed, for safe-cradling.

To her festivity she invited as many as she could reach, including the New Orleans ladies who had supplied the coffee. That would be the greatest delicacy on the table, for the other refreshments would be little more than nourishing. "I declare," she snickered to Pinky, "I never thought I'd feel like bragging about filling stomachs instead of tickling palates."

"Well, leastways," Pinky reminded her, "they's the Frosted Cake."

The Frosted Cake had become a legend with them long before it was baked, using the last scrapings of white flour. Now that it was an accomplished fact, in all its creamy glory, no wedding tiered confection of other days seemed to equal its deliciousness. Roxanne wreathed it with smilax, and the dark leaves around its base enhanced its near-whiteness.

"Ma'am Gerda's goin' to git us," predicted Pinky, "for wastin' all that sugar on icin'."

"She would indeed," grinned Lucinda, "if we hadn't just about finished the war."

The first guest to arrive was Joby, breathlessly gulping: "General Lee has *crossed the Potomac* into Maryland."

"There, didn't I tell you, Pinky?" Then: "I suppose," Cinda twitted Joby, "that C. D. was riding saddle to saddle with the General, helping him raise the tune *Maryland, My Maryland,* eh?"

"Now you know," protested Joby, "that C. D. isn't in the cavalry like Bruff."

"Ssh, if you don't tell, who's to guess from hearing you read his put-on letters and watch your airs?"

Joby moved away stiffly. Lucinda could call her for bragging all she pleased. Joby was only too grateful for having arrived at a stage where she felt C. D. deserved it. Lucinda had never had to put up with bodily terror, torment of mind, and degradation of her fastidiousness—as she had in those hazed-over early cruel days. Yet she had stayed it through, hanging on till she felt—well, as if her wrists might snap in two. Yes, she had *stayed*. And found, if not quite peace, a certain face to put on before people; until gradually she had come to feel she need show no shame in the company of other wives, had even achieved a thought of grace about it all.

C. D. valued all of that now, however poorly he had helped her at the start. Now too she thought of him with a decent conjugal regard—and she *loved* her house, her children, her estate as mistress on the bluff. Loved with an intensity that had formed a core in the tissues of her being, that could only be carved out by her own extinction.

She had not so much as thought of Armand Petit in years. Now his shape surprised her on the surface of her mind. She considered it curiously a moment; then it had not been banished, but simply vanished, having no way of attaching itself to her concerns. There was no regret in her for him, since there was no interest.

The New Orleans ladies came, lolling their eyes, and slurring their soft Creole voices. Gerda came, grumping about the waste of icing, but pinching Cinda affectionately to make up for it. Nan came, placid in the state of being with child. "Perhaps," she confided in Cinda, "Bruff will be home in time for me to have our son in our own house. If that disappoints me, surely we will be under our own roof for Christmas, the way things are going now."

Lucinda said oh, yes, it certainly looked that way. Then Nan added: "This may not be the right moment to show it to you, but I had a letter from Whet which I think you ought—that I think he wants you to see."

Lucinda jerked up her head. "Be careful how you show Whet's letters around. He is very chary of his confidences." She started away, but Nan stuck the letter into her fingers. "Take your time about reading it. I'm giving it to you, because you *need* it."

Characteristically, after once giving in, Lucinda did not postpone perusing the letter, but skirting behind a shrubbery-tub devoured it. He wrote:

It's all glory and winning among the other soldiers now. But don't they ever stop to think what they have to trample down first to gain it? Seems not. Seems they think the guns are no more than a lot of

Christmas firecrackers. Yet most of them have been in real combat a deal longer than I have. Still they don't seem to mind the jumble of battle. They holler their way through it, while I can't utter a peep. I never did like bashing against things, always preferring to walk around. Well, there, my sweet Coz, you have a confession of my cowardice, but preceding that is a true question of doubt in my mind of our ultimate triumph. Or mayhap I just don't like being jolted about. For your own good cheer I will tell you that the cry is now, not only "On to Washington," but "Home before Christmas."

Tell me, is there as much space down there as ever, with so much room that even the hills do not seem crowded in the sky?

Your faithful kinsman,
Whetstone Bruton.

P.S.—Has the blockade strangled you all entirely in its coils? If not can you ascertain whether a certain gimcrack I requested for the child Roxanne has ever come through, in any of my mother's parcels? Or did she overlook it in the press of important things like frocks?

Lucinda winced, as if slapped by a hand she had deemed soft. "Serves me right, though," for suddenly she saw how even her spasmodic indulgences of him during his periods of favour with her had been prompted by the whim to make him dance to her piping.

"Well, at least right now," she determined, "he's going to have the credit before company of playing fairy godfather in a princely way." Revelling in such rôles herself, she felt she was thus atoning somewhat for her slights of him.

When the party had whipped up to its gayest froth, she produced the parcel and tinkled the bell for attention. Then she summoned Roxanne, who stood biddable and good awaiting some little task to be required of her. Veda watched, straining her lips, fearful of some discipline to her sister. Instead Lucinda was ordering Bonapartt to place a chair for "Miss Roxanne." When Roxanne was settled with her slipper-toes striving towards the touch of the floor, a long bundle was laid across her lap.

"Now you must open up and show your prize. It came all across the sea from France, all through the blockade just for you! From someone you were sweet to when he was home on his furlough. It came from my soldier son, Whetstone!"

"Whetstone?" Roxanne's puzzlement at the full name sounded stupid.

"From Whet!" exclaimed Cinda with a small rush of impatience at having her fine speech destroyed.

"Oh? From *Whet* to *me*?" repeated Roxanne, awed; then her fingers began strumming the strings of the parcel delicately, as if it were a harp.

Lucinda had to hold back to keep from ripping the wrappings off herself. But gradually Roxanne's fingers set about undoing the knots.

"Wind the string carefully, to save," admonished Miss Gracey, "it's so precious scarce."

Painstakingly the child rolled a little ball, while Lucinda felt gusts about to explode in her. Presently the wrappings fell rustling away. Then there was the doll! China and perfect. Gold as to hair as a fairy queen, gowned like a lady of the court of Napoleon III, aloof yet consenting to love. "Why," choked the child, "why, she's wearing—*little blue kid boots*!" And she turned the slippers up to view the soles, before she began to cry.

4

These days Lucinda discovered she was less restless than she had ever been before the war. "It's because it will soon be over," she told herself, yet she sensed there was something more. It was due to the fact that she had an aim, to take the pointlessness out of the passing hours. Never one to care much for purposeful accomplishment, still she could not abide the lack of zest that came from waking into a day that held no prize to be anticipated. Now she was engaged by a novel sensation, the surprise of finding that she was enticed into a vivid interest in her son. Not a weighty settling into maternity, but the sharp discovery that his moods, his sallies of mischief, his crankiness peculiar to the *exquisite,* could catch her fancy, could put a tang into humdrum hours.

She was strolling around the carriage circle by herself, without even Roxanne, one late September evening. The fall term of her school had opened against all odds, since she felt her achievement would gratify Danley upon his return, thus paving the way to enlisting his aid in her reconciliation with Whet. Secretly, though, she scoffed at the idea of her needing any other than her own presence to effect that, now that she wanted to turn the full force of her interest towards winning his affection. Still, she wanted no bickering with Danley to set Whet on edge.

She smiled at her new concern for Whet's aversion to strife. "If I don't watch out," she warned herself, "I'll become a doting mother." Then she fell to wondering why she had overlooked his engaging qualities so persistently before. "He hasn't changed much, except to act uppity toward me lately. Was it that piquing me? Not entirely. Also he's grown an inch or two, so I can no longer look down on him. No, that's not the reason either. Couldn't I *see* before what he was like? Yes, I did. Only those qualities of congeniality of wit and prejudices didn't strike my fancy then. I wanted——" Her impulses leapt reminiscently towards her oft-kindled desire for the male in men.

She sighed: "I guess I wasn't old enough to appreciate what a son meant then. . . ."

The evening was serene. Small puffs of sweet smells stirred among the shattering rosebushes and left wrinkled petals in scraps by the path. Then a rider came in sight, shaping a soft curve along the road. Shortly Willy swung down at her feet and lifted his hands under his chin. He told her of Antietam, of Lee's defeat—and that Whet was dead.

5

That first day afterwards Pinky turned all who came to Lucinda's chamber away at the door-sill. There was Roxanne wanting to lend her the doll for comfort. "Hide that thing!" commanded Pinky grimly, and the child hastened off, trembling, to put her treasure out of harm's way.

There came Nan stepping deliberately under the burden of the unborn. "I wish I could do something, and I know nobody can, not even Bruff if he were here." Pinky patted her shoulder-blades. "You keep care of yourself, child, so's to add another gran'son now."

Gerda came and warned Pinky: "I'll have you whipped if you're barring me out when she needs me in."

Pinky shook her head. "She don't."

"I'll be staying a spell all the same. Fix that room for me next to hers, in case she calls."

"She won't call nobody," said Pinky, as Miz Gerda followed the chambermaid Milly.

That evening Gerda sat in a rocker by the window-sill, her chin gripped hard in one hand. Clouds knocked back and forth around the moon's head. "I have never," she said sadly, "been much good to my elder daughter. Somehow, some day I must open up a path to her."

Lucinda remained in her room, speaking into her mirror. "You did it. You slew him." Until Pinky came and led her to her bed for the second night. "Tell me," she pleaded with her servant then, "it won't be quite so bad when I wake up on the second morrow?"

BOOK SIX

The Land Scarred

CHAPTER FIFTY-EIGHT

LUCINDA discovered that autumn of '62 that one could learn an emotional bravery as one learned how to read, by study and practice of outer symbols. Physical courage she had been born with, along with her quest for excitement; but this learning not to mourn for a treasure she had lost just as she discovered it was a new task for her senses. Behind the discipline of the strange custom of fortitude which she was imposing upon herself was always the ghost presence of her own sin of having sent Whet to that destruction he had so keenly dreaded. His eyes, opaque with his effort to hide their terror, were for ever appearing before her, grey and bleak.

Yet she knew that she must contrive some semblance of natural composure, to go through the coming days and nights. Her method was, from the second day after news of her son's death, the simple one of pretending that she felt no sorrow, of not countenancing any over-display of sympathy from others for her trouble. She had discovered that if she acted unafraid of bereavement, and of the long self-accusing hours alone, presently the reality of their terror receded a bit from its sharp closeness to her and became bearably dim. As she continued the process of assuming a superiority over grief, she discovered that she was in truth achieving it. Before long she appeared to every one to be her usual buoyant self, without any having guessed that she had passed more than a few days in dismal loss.

Eventually she began even to distil a certain exultance from the victory she was gaining over pain. Now she felt because of that personal conquest an almost vicious goading towards the larger triumph of their Southern purpose. At last she had found in the war something she could get her teeth into!

2

The day had become chilly though it was scarcely October, and Ma'am Gerda was closeted in her room, trying to think out the letters about Whet's death that must go to the men of the family fighting in the West.

Even Danley she feared had not yet heard, since no word had come from him; and the burden of the telling devolved upon her. She chafed her hand that held the pen, since her fire had died. Then she called for her grandson Caraway, or Car as he was nicknamed, to fetch an armful of firewood. "One thing we haven't given out of yet is firewood." She dabbed her pen into the ink-basin and it came out mucky. "Tomas," she called now to that prudent boy, "I'm out of ink here. Will you fetch me some?"

"Reckon I'll have to mix some new," he told her; "the little jug's empty." He enjoyed dabbling with the indigo and soot and water from which the ink was concocted.

"Well now, mind you don't fritter too long," she cautioned. "Just let me have this saucer full for I must send these letters off first chance possible."

When finally settled, she evaded her obligation to Danley no longer. She wrote him that he had lost his son, and that his wife had been in a bad state of mind, though now she was going about her duties once more. "Precious lot he will care what Lucinda's state of mind is, upon hearing these tidings, if it's the first word he's had. He surely ought to have some warning of his loss," Gerda brooded. So then, as a bad omen, she inked a dark border around the edge of the sheet.

Closing the letter, she decided she needed the relief of the outdoors in spite of the inclemency. She would take a look at the leather tanning for brogans. Leather was worse than scarce, and while it mattered less what the whites and house negroes who stayed under shelter wore, the field-hands, labouring under exposure, need stout shoes. Her tanning-vat was in the same place that Guy had pointed out to her the day after her arrival in Alabama, near a stream beneath a covey of red oaks. She climbed down the bank to inspect the coppery ooze. Her nostrils received the tan-yard stench hospitably, for she was thinking of the care that had gone into the process that thus fouled the air. She stood calculating. "I'll give that batch another month and a half of curing, if the rains don't become too heavy. Don't want the hides raddled around and scarred by the bark." She stood making a squeezing gesture with her palm and fingers, the way a tanner did when testing good leather by the peculiar soft noise it made when rubbed.

She meant, when she reached the side yard again, to tell Pokey to see that the "ropery" was cleared of all finished ropes. That was one thing that exasperated her, the fact that nearly finished ones were often left to grow saggy and uneven for the mere lack of a few final twists and the cutting away. This time, however, she saw that Veda had taken advantage of the rain's let-up to lead the younger children and some piccaninnies in a game of rope-twisting.

The "ropery" was a crude frame so arranged with a windlass at one end that by proper twisting a fairly strong product could be made from cotton lint. The children turned out a passable cable if allowed to play their game of "touch-and-run," beneath the rack. They chose a person to be "it," and "it" had to skip beneath the whirling rope at just the proper instant, touch the rope, then duck through to the other side free; failing, there was the forfeit of turning the windlass.

Gerda sat on a sawhorse, appraising the symmetry of the rope in progress. The white children and darkies ran in a hoop around beneath the upswing of the rope, leaping and touching, or missing and being relegated to the group of forfeiters. The damp yard splayed crumbs of red dirt up from their flying heels, while the mouldy grey of the lot fence set a boundary to their pastime, and the rope tightened.

Abruptly a wild yell cut the air! Maude, Joby's prettiest, had been caught in reaching for the last tense twist. Her uptossed curls had somehow become entangled and were being almost scalped from her head. She dangled there, neck jerking one ghastly instant with the windlass still grinding in a hypnotized piccaninny's clutch before Veda and Ma'am Gerda swooped her body up in the air to relieve the strangulation. Thereupon the windlass was released, and the rope began to unwrap, snarling her curls into a worse tangle. In the end there was nothing to do but shear away a great many of the curls to free her. When she was led into the house, Joby screeched at her moulted appearance, while Gerda pacified the girl's vanity by wrapping her head in a turban and ordering the other children to call her Aunty Maude and mind her like a mammy.

Joby, not realizing her pet's neck had been in danger, continued commiserating: "Everything's at sixes and sevens, even for my pretty one. And how I'm going to bring India out on the carpet without a new dress in sight I don't know."

"I can teach your gels to spin and weave," offered Gerda flatly, "but I can't supply their other lack, which is that there's not a new young man in sight."

3

After Antietam there had come that proclamation given out by Abraham Lincoln at Washington concerning the emancipation of slaves. The county had wondered what he expected to accomplish by his statement. True, Lee had fallen back, but he would go forward again, the war would still be won by the South. They derided the idea that words from Washington could change the life of the negroes down here in their quarters. Some people were angry, while Guy chuckled, Willy pursed his lips, and Gerda said merely: "I venture none of us will find any difference or have any trouble."

She was right, though she had not counted on such a special display of loyalty as was tendered her not long after. Somehow in that strange way in which news always in the end crept through to the blacks, they learned of Linkum's Freein'. There was a moiling about among them for a day or so, as there had been after the John Brown outrage. Again they lost their unison of effort in attempts to provide themselves with exceptional favour at Rock Wall. Gerda felt inclined to show her shortness of temper, yet realizing the source of their disquiet, bided her time.

One late afternoon she was out cooping hens that seemed broody when she saw the file of negroes advancing towards her. It was early for them to be in from the day's work, the yard bell had not even been tolled. Stuffing the last hen into a coop, she stood to see what was the matter. Pokey had come from the kitchen to take her place behind her, as she always did on occasions of tribal state, and Patt stepped forward as spokesman for the slaves.

"Miz Gerda, we come to hear if you was goin' to turn us out. To shift for ourselves."

She looked over their solemn attempt at a straight line, shoring itself about the lot, with straggling toddlers squeezing in among the legs of their elders. Yet the whole number made a formidable pattern against the falling bosom of the field beyond. She could see faces standing out from it. Could recall croup-beds of infants, whippings, feastings, ploughs furrowing, the first impudent plant springing up, baskets billowing with white lint, the days that were gone with Yarbrough, and the days to come. . . .

They would still be planting and raising cotton in the end . . . a long time from now when the war was silenced, whether they were bond or free . . . when she lay once more at Yarbrough's side through that eternal-long night.

She passed the back of her thickened wrist across her eyes.

"My people," she said, "nothing has changed here. Hard times and fighting have passed over us before and left us one band. Work is your share, and care for you is my share. The Stand will always be your home place. Bless you."

"Amen!" they praised her and God.

Then they started crowding up and laying down at her feet "jes lil things we prize:" sling-shots, lumps of beeswax, rancid bacon rind on which babies had teethed painlessly owing to some conjure, one good knife even, clumps of black figs cured to sugar dryness, a pair of stockings stolen from her. . . .

She called a halt. "Pokey, tell them to gather up their belongings. I'll remember their loyalty without all that."

Pokey whooshed out her breath in a way that always commanded obedience without any other signal, then she beckoned them to take back the things they had laid down. A hubbub of grabbing, pushing, and shuffling like cattle's hoofs chuffing in a branch-bed rose; for most of them were bent now upon retrieving something of more worth than they had given.

After the final scuffling departure, Gerda sank down on a step and leaned against the boards of the one above, pressing her weary shoulders. "I must keep them from any fear of Emancipation. It's a boogy, to them, like the fear of being orphaned, after the way I've always looked after them."

4

The problem of procuring salt became one of the most acute that confronted the county, as it was painfully scarce everywhere. There was no substitute for this elemental ingredient, nothing was "just as good," as in the case of soda, for instance. In place of that staple they had quickly discovered that the ashes of red corn-cobs could be used in everything requiring alkaline properties, including even the raising of bread-dough. But salt could not be duplicated, any more than gold, and salt was not a symbol of barter, it was an essential for life.

Every effort was made at Rock Wall to conserve it, down to the re-evaporating of that used in its vats for curing; yet even so the supply was dwindling alarmingly. Nan noticed that Ma'am Gerda guarded the key that locked the salt-box with vexed fingers. Finally one day when Pokey came to request a small portion, Ma'am grasped the whole bunch of keys as if she were going to bend the metal in two, and cried out: "What do they *do* to waste it so fast? Do they lick it up like livestock at a salt-bed?" Then with a volcanic burst of choler she hurled the keys jouncing across the floor to Pokey's feet. "Go unlock the box yourself! Go throw it *all* over your shoulder—like a silly charm to stop a fight!" Then she caught up a pewter mug to send it banging after the keys, her empurpled cheeks bursting with blood.

Pokey stalked over, keys in one hand, and with the other she gripped Gerda's arm with a power that took control. "Child," she warned Ma'am in guttural tones, "you'se courtin' a slappin'. Shame on yo'self for actin' thisaway, and before Miss Nan, drawin' close to her time. Now you *mind* me!" She stuffed the keys back into Gerda's pocket, signing for Nan to vanish.

From the centre hall, as she left, Nan gazed back at Ma'am Gerda standing very still, holding her head neither high nor low, simply level. Then she saw that Gerda reached her hands up to smooth the sides of her face and, after resting them there a space, drew them down in a motion as if folding the garment of her dignity about herself once more.

Sitting in Bruff's office, Nan kicked off her shoes and rubbed her tired feet lovingly. She basked in the belief that the child she was carrying must surely be a splendid strong son, to weigh her down so heavily. Gradually her mind forsook her absorption in her coming child, to mull over the salt problem, a thing which could drive Ma'am Gerda to such a display of frenzy.

All that night long, whenever Nan waked to shift her odd bulk about, she cudgelled her brain for some new method of finding salt. Eventually her half-waking musings began to retrace their path to the smoke house, where meat still hung in an abundance that had employed salt lavishly in its curing. Finally on one of these mental errands her mind paused and she lurched her body bolt upright. "Salt in the *soil!"* she exclaimed. Why, of course, there was bound to be a great deal of it wasted in the dirt, there below that richly encrusted meat.

Forgetting her melon-thickness, she swung down out of bed and grabbed an old cloak she kept handy for rising in the chill of night. She could not find her crocheted slippers, but her feet were fairly warm as she hurried quietly out, skipping the squeaky boards and padding down the steps out through the yard. The texture of the grainy ground felt to her bare soles glistening and cool like that of salt. She knew how to pry the old lock, which had rusted and not been replaced, owing to the scarcity of metal; she had done it on innumerable hasty kitchen errands before, unrebuked. Inside, the cavern had that rank and musty scent of the fresh animal petrified in the timeless captivity of salt.

She crouched down and applied her nose to the earth, cupping her hands about it to shut out the aroma of the meats above. The smell came strong of itself, the dark odour of earth, not fertilized by sun and seed, but permeated through and through with the sharpness of that precious substance. It gave off a monkish stench. She scratched up a pinch or two to test outside in the open air. It was still there, that dried-sweat whiff of saltiness.

Back in her bed she fell off to sleep quickly, not caring if she ached.

Before she arose the next morning Nan had planned how she would extract the prize. She would wait till Ma'am was safely away on her plantation rounds, then she would proceed with Cayline to the smoke-house, to scoop up several peck measures of the dirt for trial. If any one like Pokey accosted her curiously, she would play on their concern for her condition not to cross her, and let them assume it was some conjure.

Luckily every one proved too busy that day to take notice, and she and Cayline with a little yard boy, Neddy, arrived at their secluded spot unchallenged. They set the measures down, Nan grateful to be free of hers, for she felt a stitch in her side such as she had used to get from running too hard as a child. This spot she had chosen had a particularly free, clear outlook pleasantly open for their odorous task. It was perched away from the lowering shed of the scuppernong arbour at the rear and hanging above a new-run gully. She felt glad to stop a moment, to have her eyes come to rest on the opposite side of the sky without striving upward to see it. When she felt she had finished washing her eyes in space, she turned back to the bins of scraped soil.

They had collected several old hoppers, used formerly to leach ashes for soap-making. Now they placed the soil in them and filtered water from the gully stream through, catching all of it in vessels they had lugged here earlier. It dripped slowly and they grew tired of simply watching, so Nan suggested they all go down to the branch and up through the ravine to see if there were any persimmons yet. They found one bush, with its fruit ravished by frost into luscious wrinkles, and ate greedily.

Climbing back to their own site, Nan felt a reluctance in her limbs. She wished Cayline were older and knew more midwife lore, or that Neddy were large enough to carry her. She heaved up over the last ledge of the cliff with a sigh and lay flat on the earth. She felt as if the sky was coming down and spreading itself like a giant handkerchief over her face, smothering her. After a while her breath came back into the bellows of her lungs, and a scared Cayline helped her to her feet, saying they'd better go in. But Nan said she didn't care if it did bring on labour, she was so anxious to see Bruff's child. Besides she certainly meant to finish the easy part of this salt job now.

When they examined their filters again, they saw that the vessels were full to the brim with a greenish-dark liquid that tasted sharply bitter. They hauled their spoils to the boiling-pots near the wash-house and boiled the liquid all through the afternoon, watching the crust thicken like hoar-frost over the welling contents of the cauldrons. Before sundown they had set aside to cool one pot of crystalline fluid, beautiful to behold.

Nan sat back on her haunches unexpectedly, then tried to get up; but her head knocked against her knee and she caught hold of her own ankles instead. "It's come, Cayline, too early," she gasped as the pain receded.

"Now hush," soothed Cayline as she and Neddy made a basket chair of their hands to carry their young mistress in to her child-bed.

5

The baby lived a few weak days, long enough for Nan to study his small face. " He wasn't very big after all," she whispered over his faint respiration. "Or maybe I wore all the flesh off him the other day." She lay feeling dead level with depression, wondering what had happened to that full, rounded world she had inhabited with Bruff. She roused herself from this dazed dreaming to measure the scope of the room, to discover why she felt—not suffocated—but almost obliterated. Then she glanced down and saw the suddenly pinched face of their baby, from whom all the breath had escaped.

6

The next day her room was in complete quiet, all the noises seemed to have been shunted off to a distance. She lay with a finish of calm over her features, praying: " I hope I never quicken again. Then my senses will remain deserted by pain."

Late that afternoon she heard a certain pattern of footsteps leaving the parlour, crossing the porch, treading the steps, and moving towards Yarbrough's spot in the front yard. " They're going to bury my baby, under some dirt!" She plaited her fingers over her eyes. She kept them that way all night long, so that her arm could not search at her side. Once she did think numbly: " That was nice of Ma'am to put him safe by his grandfather."

She did not know that Gerda had done it because he seemed so puny he needed the protection of the man whose name he should have borne.

CHAPTER FIFTY-NINE

AT FREDERICKSBURG in Virginia on December 13 the Union forces under Burnside had suffered a severe loss, yet the toll on the South had been so great during the fall that their spirits were scarcely revived by this victory. There had been no attempt at Christmas celebrations in Turber County that year. The land lay shrouded.

To-day was another dismal one of a winter when there seemed no end to the rain; the bushes and trees outside looked more like seaweed than anything that grew on land. Every one was huddled in the closed corner of the ell, as near the fire as possible, with Nan, who had been out of bed only a few days, protected by a quilt screen to shut out the drafts. She was making thread, a tedious task, since the fine tendrils broke so often; but it was something to take up her attention and required little strength. The smallest girls cuddled at her feet, watching as she wound it in balls, soaked them in warm suds, then twisted it on to a bobbin made of corn-husks. When the bobbin was placed on the spindle and began to whir, a miniature fountain played from the moist ball. The children pushed their cheeks into the fine spray, squealing happily even if soap got in their eyes. Their cries sounded the one lilting note in a place weighted with work and anxiety.

Nan's eyes strayed around the scene as she rested between bobbins. Hannah Lee had a group of boys methodically weaving baskets from willow switches, none of them apparently noticing the brightened colour of the willow shoots, which was almost winter's first hint of spring coming on its hidden way. Joby, with India and Maude, was stirring some dyes, while India fretted. "The same old things! Brown from walnut, grey from myrtle, garnet from pine-tree roots. I wish to heavens I had something fresh and gay!"

"Hickory bark," offered Nan mildly, "makes a very pretty bright green. We must go to the woods on a dye hunt when the weather breaks." Then her eyes wandered to Ma'am.

Gerda had gone to stand by the door, leaning with one arm upflung along the jamb, in a gesture as if she were about to break away from the house and make for her fields.

"She misses her cotton," thought Nan. "These house chores, and even her food-production, can't take its place with her. She feels *widowed* without it."

In truth Gerda had felt these days much the same sense of desolation she had endured after Yarbrough's passing, when she could hunt their land over, yet not encounter the proportions of his body. So now to walk out, however far across her acres, and not find miles of cotton troubled her more deeply than the struggles for corn and fodder and herbs for drugs. Grieved her more in some ways than the news of the battles, for she had grown familiar with the alarms of war, but with cotton no longer in the ascendancy, she felt as if she lived in a rulerless land, with a vacant throne.

From the mistress Nan's glance moved to the slave. Pokey was hunched over some vials, straining out a cordial brewed for dysentery from blackberry roots. She gave out none of her usual cackling at her own wit. The only punctuation to her work was an occasional leaning backward to scrape her cramped back against the slats of her chair. Finally when Pokey had measured the last bottle, with a grimace that was a caricature of her ordinary grin, she popped her walnut-shaped old knuckles with a sound like pistol-shots. That semeed to break the spell of concentration in the ell, and every one flexed tired muscles or said something silly.

Into this atmosphere of slackening, Lucinda, accompanied by the inevitable Veda and Roxanne, entered, tousled from the downpour, yet oblivious of any discomfort. Passing towards the fire, she shook her cape hard on purpose, to spatter Joby, who was a tabby in her distaste for moisture. On the hearth Cinda sat down where she could lean her head against Pokey's knees while she poked her feet out to have the sodden shoes and stockings pulled off, showing feet with patrician insteps but shamelessly wriggling toes. The younger children immediately started to tickle them, but she pounced on a couple and sent them into paroxysms of laughter themselves.

Righting herself, Lucinda asked: "You've not got any real coffee, I suppose? All right, those slops will do, if you'll drop some spirits into them. I brought a brand-new letter from Danley. Not very hilarious, but at least none of ours were killed." Her statement passed calmly over any catch of remembrance that her only *real* one *was* dead, once and for all.

While Lucinda rattled open the paper, Nan summed up her sister-in-law's abundance of vivid pigment, of fine-pressed flesh cleaving close to strong bone, of breath that blew vigour through her lungs, and eyes that claimed any scene they beheld for her own assimilation into that process of action and sensation that constituted Lucinda's living.

Nan had no need to drop her eyes to her own attenuated lineaments to draw the concluding contrast. Instead her mind went directly to the point: "I may recoil from her rampant vitality at times, yet I must admit that she came through in two short days a more fatal loss than mine. Her sons are all behind her, both of them shuttered away from her by reproachful deaths while mine await borning, all but that one, and he was tenderly succoured. Yet here she is, only a little more distant from a greater grief than mine, making the air of this room beat with the pulse of promise, while I sit closed in a cocoon of martyrdom."

Nan straightened her shoulders. "Preaching myself a sonorous sermon, like Pa," she snickered, and the snicker broke into a good giddy giggle, at which Cinda flashed a hand at her. "Reckon you're frisky enough to stand the gore now, eh, Nanny? Because then I'll read my latest letter."

The letter was a description of the Battle of Murfreesboro in Tennessee, which had been fought in December. It had been a welter of blood and mangled men, but except for a little nick in Tom Two's thumb none of theirs were scratched. Wayne had comported himself with ferocious valour, and Joachim and Will Bee had joshed their company along in high style. The privations of the enlisted men were past words. Yet they bore them with humorous fortitude and were determined to stake all on this vast struggle. "In closing," wrote Danley, "I might say that the poorer ones worry more about the state of their loved ones at home who are in want than their own hardship. In line with that, may I charge you to deliver the enclosed note to your mother, who, because of Bruff, will feel a certain stewardship in regard to this particular family."

Lucinda handed the enclosure over to Ma'am, biting her tongue in sudden chagrin at having failed to omit the reference to Bruff, for she had caught Nan's jerk of attention.

Gerda read the note with deliberation. Then Nan approached her,

her feet still a trifle hesitant from her prolonged confinement. "Could I see?" she asked, steadying herself by a chair-back.

It was written by Emma Will's oldest brother, who had tilled a fair amount of subsistence out of their unkept acres during peace. It said:

Please see Gran Paw Ograw and tell him carrey my boys and Emma Will's young sprout to Turberville for safety. The big ones can work for keep. I wish you wood see Mr. Screws about shoes and clothing for them and my nigroe. The note Mr. Screws gave specified clothing on the face of it for my wagon and mules. $400. is the amount agrede if not mistaken. If Mr. Screws holds the cash shut out on them, giv my respecks to Miz Gerda Whetstone. And ask her to get after that sharp trader. She will hav to take it on herself since Emma is to biggity to speak for favurs. Giv my respecks to all & receav same yourself. Oby Willis.

Nan gazed down so long that the lines of writing jiggled like ragged notes on the staffs in a pianoforte book. It would be easy to be dissolved by a freshet of pity for this pathetic epistle, it would not be easy continually to prevent the rasp of old jealousy of Emma Will if in frequent contact with her; still, a charge had been put upon her as Bruff's wife. The execution of the matter required guarding her manner with matter-of-factness. "I'll attend to delivering these things," she said, "if you can make terms with Mr. Nat. I meant to go up that way to see the folks, as soon as this flooding stopped and the swamps were passable. If you'll settle with him shortly, I'll be able to give Emma Will some satisfaction."

Ma'am nodded. "Soon as he comes back from his commissarying."

"You know, Nan," remarked Lucinda, yawning with her open mouth the size and rosiness of pomegranate, "your being in a family way made you lose scarcely any of your hair, and none of its springiness." Thus casually was Nan's bereavement consigned to common conversation, not left embalmed in unnatural silence.

The remark brought Nan a sudden wonder, though, as to whether any sorrow could ever go deep with Lucinda, until later that evening she spied her fishing in the dining-room sideboard for something. It was Whet's worn baby napkin-ring, and Cinda squeezed it fiercely in her fist, with grief like anger runnelling on her face.

2

It was quite a time before Nat Screws was at home long enough for Gerda to see him. In order to tackle him about Oby Willis's note, she had finally to track him to the loading platform of his warehouse farther down the street than his Emporium. Here he had his headquarters as the local Quartermaster of the Commissary, presumably merely to take in supplies collected and ship them on to a central depot. However, there were rumours of a certain share that was never moved that he claimed for his own profit.

It was beginning summery to-day; the earth in his team area was dried to a bright tan, and some stinkweed flourished, virulent green with robust burrs. The sun dazzled Gerda's eyes pleasantly, and the mules hitched to the drays eyed her well-known figure with a stolid stare of greeting. She examined a galled spot on one, the creature standing tolerantly still under her touch, while she told the driver what to do for it. Finally she mounted the steps. The platform planks were grooved grey, worn by the thudding of cotton bales, cleaned by rain and this thorough-going sunshine.

Nat, hearing her measured gait, hustled out, hoping his cordiality would stand him in good stead in whatever bargaining came up. She said: "Stob bobbing and scraping. I came here to give you all-Hector about Oby Willis's note for clothing, and the price agreed upon for his wagon *plus* the increase from the inflation of currency." She could see him trying to scheme up some shifty evasion about "uncertain wartime conditions," but she cut that short. "I don't want to come to grips with you over this *small* matter, Nat," she said significantly. "I'm saving my thunderbolts for a bigger issue with you, if you don't mend some of your Quartermaster ways that I hear about. Now about this, if you'd been smart you would have settled it before goods went so sky-high. I'm not going to let you off too light about that wagon price, either. You'll have to up it considerable. Also *I'll* do the picking of the clothing and supplies that go on that note."

His neck went up and down like a turkey gobbler's as he grew mad, then swallowed back his bile. He wasn't anxious to cross Miz Gerda on top of her references to his illicit Commissary profits, yet he never knew how to give in graciously, so now he remarked bitterly: "Naturally you can select whatever you see fit from my stock, which is very low. I'd forgotten your *family* interest in the—uh—Willises."

At that she tramped down hard on his foot with her heavy heel. "Don't you speak so to me! Or I'll thrash you the same as if you were still little enough for me to take down your breeches."

"I didn't mean wha-at you think," whined Nat. "I was referrin' to Joachim's part in the *Emporium*."

"Humph!" snorted Gerda. "Don't try that on me, for I know what you meant, and I hope I struck your biggest corn. Now come on to your store, I'd like to do my own choosing."

When she had finished, the Willis family had their money's worth, and some to boot for the delay. Nat's expression was sour as a lemon following her back to his area, to see about loading her wagon. There they found Guy and Willy waiting while Shade and one of Nat's porters packed. She marched down the steps huffing and directed Shade to meet her at the post office.

Guy hitched along after her, and Willy touched her elbow tentatively. As they reached the square he said: "I've been meaning to tell you I've volunteered, and they've taken me, though I'm over age. They say that they can fit me in somewhere, since I can surely ride and shoot.

Gerda stood stock-still. *Willy gone?* The last blood kin of her generation. Nothing but little boy grandsons left about her? Her eyes ran around the square as if seeking a way out. For a moment it seemed but the shell of a forgotten world, then she blinked, as if to dispel a bad dream. This place was a fortress of their life! The four sides of the courthouse would be a boundary to protect the contents of the county for generations to come, whatever the encroachments of war.

"The Grove trees are a sprucer green because of all that rain in early spring," she remarked finally, then leaned over and idiotically kissed Willy.

"That," he stammered, "makes up for the time you slapped me, for pressing you into a corner after a kiss when we first met at the Home Place."

Old Guy, squeezing at an ear-lobe, was trying to recollect what these children were hackling each other about. He seldom saw them as grown up any more, since his eyes had grown far-sighted peering into the past.

3

Now that Ma'am Gerda had procured full value for Oby's note, and the weather stayed clear, Nan set out with Cayline and Honest on her visit home to Pea River. They travelled in a light fast-moving vehicle that was rather like a buggy set over a small wagon-bed; this gave them plenty of room for their own traps and the goods from the Emporium, yet could be pulled by one strong-shouldered horse.

Ma'am Gerda was sending the Willises in addition two cans of syrup and a small poke of meal. "Tell them," she charged Nan, "that I'll be on the look-out for places where the older boys can work for their keep, but I don't think there's any war danger to them up there any more than to us here—though the Lord only knows when it'll strike down from the northern part of the state."

The trip went easily, with a light whipping-whir to the wheels and an almost constant trotting of the big horse. Birds had to dart out of their way, and mock-orange blossoms snowed in the strong breeze they made.

It was almost supper time when they arrived, but there was no cheerful bustle to be heard. One wan light showed kitchenward, while the rest of the place had that peculiar ghostliness of a house open but apparently untenanted. "Yoo-hoo!" Nan called. "Hoo-o!" That brought her mother on tiptoe out of the kitchen through the hall, finger at lips. "Ssh, your papa's resting." She pecked at Nan abstractedly, glancing towards a closed door apprehensively. "He half kills himself these days, so be as quiet as you can bringing in your things."

Silently Cayline and Honest unloaded and brought the things around the rear way to Nan's own former room. It looked both cramped and bare to her now, after the amplitude of the Stand, a place to contain a few pieces of furniture, but no joy, or dreams, or a human girl. It was neatly uninteresting and she began flinging her wraps and some of the smaller parcels around in an attempt to break it loose from its inane emptiness.

She had no chance to greet her father until they were sitting down to supper; then she saw that his gauntness had gone into utter emaciation, that weariness saddled his shoulders. She understood that he had been endeavouring, born farmer that he was, to lend a hand on almost every place for miles around. Still she was shocked at the listlessness into which he had to retire by evening, in order to recuperate somewhat before the next day's toil. It saddened her that he was too tired even for affection towards her, after months of separation.

"I'm not as brawny as I used to be," he admitted with a weak grin. "Leaves me pretty worn-out." He crumbled his cornbread into some drippings and worried them around with his fork, but ate little. He was fatigued past any appetite.

"Now, John," admonished Miz Della, "you know you won't be a bit of good to anybody if you don't keep up your strength."

"What's that? Oh, that's right." He scraped up a forkful and swallowed it without any relish, his eyes watering weakly.

Nan stared down at her plate to avoid shaming him with sympathy.

"Have some of this nice fresh fish," urged her mother.

Nan selected a delicately crisped one. "You're lucky to have such a good fry so early. How come?"

"Oh," murmured Miz Della vaguely, "that Emma Will keeps us supplied pretty well, early and late."

"Emma Will? Well then, no wonder, for she's the best fisherman anywhere around. Better than Ma'am Gerda. By the way, that's the main thing I have to attend to while I'm home. I have to deliver all that goods Ma'am sent her from the Emporium."

"You," exclaimed her mother, horrified, "are to take stuff up to *Emma Will's*? And Miz Gerda Whetstone sent it? Well, I never in all my life! I won't have you setting foot in that shanty. You hear me, Nan Upshur!"

"You forget," Nan pointed out quietly, "that my name is Nan Whetstone now, and that you can't forbid me to carry out an errand I'm sure my husband would want me to perform."

"Well, I never . . ." Miz Della could manage no more than that, though she kept half-opening her mouth hoping for words.

"You seem," pursued Nan, "to be able to *accept* favours from Emma Will without a qualm. Eating her fish right this minute."

"She takes the fish to the cabins of course," protested Miz Della, "and our negroes bring a share up to me. She'd never dream of coming to my own back door!"

"I see," said Nan evenly, rolling her napkin into its ring and rising. "May I be excused, please?"

"Me too," spoke up John irritably. "You've driven away what little appetite I did have. Quarrelling always does."

"I'm sorry," apologized Nan for herself, brushing past him, "but I couldn't help that. I hate hypocrisy." She had to go for a walk, fast. She could not trust herself to stay here near her mother right now.

Funny how tame and meek she herself seemed over at the Stand, hiding so often behind a shield of stillness from the family. Yet the minute she came home she burst out like a regular Whetstone. She supposed that was the way that strong line was carried on, by their absorbing other strains in spite of everything. It was still Whetstone blood when you'd done with mixing in the others—still red and rich. The blue only lent it a purple cast. "I'll wager," she chuckled, already so sure of all the other children she would have, "I'll wager that none of mine will inherit a single trait of mine except my stubbornness, which the breed already has in plenty. I do wish though," she mused wistfully, "that one, just one of them, could keep his own counsel like me. That would be a very strong trait. Maybe, between Ma'am, who weighs her words, and me, who uses them out loud so seldom, we can manage one with some silence in his make-up. He could be a very great man, with that added to the Whetstone."

She found that she was calmed down now, out in the open and the slow-shifting sounds of evening.

The next morning Nan went whistling up the log road in the direction of the Willises', with Honest trundling the large hamper on a wheelbarrow behind, while she and Cayline swung a big basket between them. It was a gay day that made Nan step three logs at a time in spite of their burden.

"Feelin' mighty fresh, ain't you?" observed Cayline.

"Fresh as mint!" agreed Nan. "But I sure felt old 'omanish back there for a spell this winter." A bluejay scolded at them, and flirted some trash down on them from his tree limb.

The shanty, when they reached it, appeared about ready to fall to pieces, with the step-ladder so snaggle-toothed Nan could barely climb up. Emma Will, emerging from the shack door, said: "Howdy. What's all that?"

Nan explained briefly.

"Well, no use your niggers tryin' to clomb the ladder with it, they'd jest break they legs. I own a right strong piece of rope I keep hid, so best to use it to make a pulley-like round that post, and h'ist it thataway."

Honest and Cayline and some assorted Willises followed her directions, with the result that shortly both baskets were resting on the shaky porch ledge. "I don't reckon it'll cave in yet awhile," Emma Will decided. "There's one good shade tree," she told the negroes, "where you can rest without the ants eatin' you up alive. Now," she invited Nan, "let's set and catch our breath." Then to her flock of children: "You young 'uns *scat*. I ain't openin' airy a thing till I've visited with Miss Nan here." They dodged her flaying-switch and skittered into various nearby hiding-places.

Emma Will motioned Nan to sit down where there was a post to lean against and where she could dangle her legs comfortably over the edge. When they were settled she said formally: "Be sure to pay my respecks to Miz Gerda and thank her kindly. But spit in old Screws' tracks next chancet you get." She scratched her back then and requested: "Give me some news of the fightin' if you hearn any. Or any tale they're tattlin' around about Turberville. It's all entertainment to me."

Nan regaled her, therefore, with everything she could think of, from the newest word from Richmond and the battlefronts to the oldest backache in Turberville. The other nodded appreciatively at it all. "I never could abide bein' shuffled up that close to other folks' houses; still, bein' in town has its p'ints." She hesitated, then added: "'Twas kind of you to set with me so sociable."

"It's no more," declared Nan, "than I ought to do, after the nasty way I broke your fishing-pole that day, 'way back. I couldn't seem to help it though—I hated you so."

"Is that a fact?" exclaimed Emma Will. "I took it you was just scornin' me because I was trash. I didn't take it personal. Now I somehow always had a 'miration for you. I held you was the nicest little gel I ever seen. Why, you know, I was so took with you wearin' that locket of yours, till when I had my first young 'un I found a two-cent piece and bored a hole in it, so it could be hung around her neck by a ribbon, but she used to get that ribbon so slobbery, chewin' on it while teethin', that I had to put string through it in the end. Know what come of it?" she demanded with a laugh and a slap on her knee. "That ornery Mr. Screws cheated her out of it one day with a pep'mint drop. I frashed her good, I can tell you, to teach her how to mistrust rich folks. I don't mean any of the Whetstones. And that reminds me." She sprang up. "We'd better unpack these things. Then you can holler at your niggers to wake up and fetch your baskets down."

"You're supposed to keep the baskets," Nan told her.

"Dunno what I'd do with them." Emma Will regarded them dubiously. "Still, I thankee, and the young 'uns can prob'ly have some fun or other outer them."

Nan had noticed the children creeping back. "You must be anxious to unpack, I think I'd better be getting back. It's almost dinner-time."

"You sure won't stay and have some fish with us?" invited Emma Will, as her brood began to tear into the contents of the baskets. Then she herself pitched in. "Snuff!" she exulted. "Lordy, my gums have been plumb achin' of' some, for the longest!"

They had clean forgotten Nan in their jubilation, but she managed to scale down the wobbly ladder without mishap. When she had aroused her two servants with their wheelbarrow, she waved back at the group at the shanty, but nobody saw her. Trudging home, she thought how it had not been at all hard coming here. She knew, though, that it was because Emma Will was as grotesque as a witch—that the perky cabin girl whom Bruff had known had been destroyed from the face of the earth. There was simply no woman left to arouse her jealousy.

She threw pebbles up at the sky. "I do wish Bruff would hurry home to me now. Here it is spring again."

4

Gerda and Nan had been packing more baskets for general distribution among the dependants of needy soldiers, since it devolved upon the women of the well-to-do plantations to provide for those on the small barren farms. The contents of the baskets were scanty, owing to the long-division, and their quality was makeshift—substitutes that had become a byword throughout the Confederacy: the nauseous parched giblets of sweet potatoes that passed for coffee; home-made earthenware to take the place of vanished pans, since metal had all to go to the army; cough syrups made of mullein plants, globe flowers, and wild cherry bark; something like quinine produced from dogwood berries; a few pounds here and there of rice or meal or meat; a scamped length of homespun cloth, and slippers with soles of their domestic pasteboard.

Gerda picked up a flimsy slipper. "What good those will do any but the bed-bound sick, I can't see. Maybe we ought to be thankful to have some sick who can use them and the home-brewed medicine," she snorted. "Wish I could send out some of my brogans. But stock's too scarce to slaughter much now. My own field-hands are wearing through their shoes beyond repair. It's a good thing summer has about come. I know I won't have anywhere near enough to go around this fall. Besides shoes, I wish I could send out a little more meat." She shook her head.

"One thing," Nan put in with an odd pride, "Emma Will's outfit doesn't suffer much for lack of meat. Not with her knack at fishing, trapping and bird-hunting."

"That's true, and fine as long as the Yankee raiders stay out of this section; but if they swarm over us the way they have the northern part of the state, they'll soon clean the country out of even jack rabbits. There's another thing that bothers me, almost more than Yankee raiders, and that's the no-account white-trash men, who have kept out of the army by hiding and keeping on the move. 'Disaffected men,' President Davis calls them. They prey on unprotected women and children, especially the refugees, and take their spite out on faithful negroes whose masters are away. No wonder women and children travelling, or refugeeing back and forth, go by night, do anything to escape a run-in with those varmints."

"Don't let's talk about it," shuddered Nan, "at least not till after the Union forces have passed over us and left us helpless carrion for such vultures." She laughed half-heartedly. "We sound like the Book of Job, don't we?"

They continued packing baskets, Gerda aware without words of a vicious circle about this provisioning, of home people starving themselves to provide food for the army, while the army was being slaughtered to help the home folks to survive.

They were about to sit down to rest when they heard the sound of a strange wagon pausing in the lot to let some people out. Going to the stoop they saw Roxanne scurrying towards them, with Veda at her heels, and an assortment of women and children tagging behind. The two Polk girls had been home on an emergency visit to their sick father, and Gerda had heard from Lucinda that they were forced to take a circuitous route back because of the movements of the Yankee troops. Directly behind them, among the unfamiliar women, came one woman Gerda had known somewhere, and well.

At the foot of the ell steps Veda spoke. "These people have done us a great kindness, Ma'am Gerda, and we told them they could rest here. We are all too exhausted to reach Top Hill now."

"Besides," shrilled Roxanne, "some of them are acquainted with you."

That older, familiar woman stepped forward. "You may not call me to mind, but you and Mr. Yarbrough stopped once at our cabin, up near the Tennessee line."

"Maria Somers!" cried Gerda, grabbing her hands. "Come in, and gladly welcome." The way she clasped Maria's palms made a covenant between them. Under the fan of shadow from the chinaberry tree they saw, after one instant of perceiving each other's weathered cheeks, only bright eyes with lake-mirrored scenes of long ago . . . a high hill yard, and a moon, and a man making fiddle music. . . .

They dropped apart.

Then all made their way inside and settled on chairs or floor, while Pokey sent the darkies about the business of providing some food for the visitors. Gerda explained: "We have plenty of waiting-on, and a fair amount of the plainest of victuals. I trust it will prove nourishing." She knew that she was making talk, for once in her life, to restore this heart-disturbing event in an everyday sequence. Maria said: "It will taste like heavenly ambrosia to us."

CHAPTER SIXTY

THE SUMMER OF '63 was a long dull back-stretch, marked by rather monotonous mile-posts of unpleasant pieces of news or small local occurrences. There was the fact that Nettie Screws, owing to Nat's mysterious prosperity, went often to Montgomery and spoke of spending nearly a hundred dollars on a meal at a good restaurant. There was the time when a ship finally did run the blockade up the Chattahoochee and Uncle Shylock Screws, as Veda dubbed him, spread the meagre assortment of inferior goods out over his shelves in an attempt to sell them to people who had almost forgotten the shape of money. The younger women and girls of the Whetstone connection went to see it in Cinda's carriage, which had been spared when a large number of wagons had been commandeered for the army.

They entered the Emporium curiously, not having been inside in two years. Recalling the firecracker gaiety of childhood visits there at Christmas time, Veda exclaimed to Nan: "I can almost smell the sawdust in the dolls' bodies!"

"Doesn't smell like my doll," objected Roxanne, sniffing the mustiness. "Stinks like a stable to me." Veda pinched her wrist to make her behave.

Their tour of the store was one of inspection only, except when India, long coached in vanity by Joby, broke down and bought a length of calico at twelve dollars a yard, the total cost being well over a hundred dollars, and Maude paid eighty dollars for a quire of small notepaper to write elegant letters to young officers whom she scarcely knew.

In the dead heat of July they heard of the reverses of Gettysburg and Lee's retreat from his second great offensive, but the great gravity of this failure was not borne in upon them. The main outcome of that seemed to be that because of the loss of C. D.'s major, he was promoted to a majority and as a field officer had to have a horse. So he wrote Joby to raise the price of it by selling a wench, Ella, adding: "The farther away from Yufala you sell her, the better I will be pleased, as she once bit my hand."

After the fall of Vicksburg in the West they heard from Will Bee that in spite of everything he was well satisfied for the moment as he had had some meat for a change. Also there was news to cheer them from the North occasionally, such as that of the anti-draft riot in New York City. It tickled them to hear that the draft headquarters had been wrecked, some homes of Unionists burned, and over a thousand people killed before the troops could quell the three-day fracas. So the Yankees weren't so whole-heartedly behind old Lincoln after all?

Meanwhile the summer and early fall were a pleasant time for the young folk to go on dye-hunts in the deep parts of the woods, coming home laden with the makings of a rainbow. Another thing they enjoyed was having an "indigo-mud" churning, deriving a heavenly blue from the indigo weed when it was in full flower, and after the Confederate victory at Chickamauga they settled down quite contentedly to a winter of weaving and spinning. Although few were as expert as Ma'am Gerda and Miz Lydia Screws, the loom had become part of the furniture of every plantation. Throughout the county the hum of the spinning wheels and the clang of the batten sounded; the beat of life in any household kept time to the *tramp, tramp, tramp* of the looms.

For pleasure the children could parch ground peas and make syrup candy as their parents had done in their pioneering childhood. Lucinda showed them how to place two Dutch ovens in front of the fireplace, one sprinkled with clean white sand in which the goobers were scattered to roast. In the other they had poured syrup, into which as it thickened they dropped fragments of nuts. The best fun came later when they had let the mess cool and pulled it out in hempen twists, knobby with jutting nuts. Thus hilariously engaged with their Aunt Lucinda, even Joby's eldest were inclined to wonder why she fumed so at their lack of pleasures.

The encouragement to the grown-ups induced by the victory at Chickamauga was short-lived, however; 1863 closed with a succession of defeats in the West, where Grant and Sherman had formed a menacing alliance. Joachim's description of the Battle of Missionary Ridge, in a letter to his sweetheart Dolly, made no pretence of covering up their confusion with glory. "Don't pay any heed," he admonished her, "to this claptrap brag we used to make about how any Southerner can whip ten Yankees. Because, believe me, the blue-coats can lick their weight in wildcats."

They also heard that criticism of President Davis was growing, that in many parts of some states, populated by small farmers who had never cared much one way or the other about slavery, people were talking of returning to the Union. Everywhere there seemed to be springing up secret Peace Societies, bound under oath to encourage army desertions, harbour escaped prisoners, and give information to the enemy of the movement of troops.

The tales of such traitorous Peace Societies seemed not only vile to the county, but remote and unreal. For here every one was gritting teeth and slaving to win the war. What was real to them was news such as that from Will Bee, that the soldiers were living mostly on parched corn, with now and then a rasher of sorry bacon the width of a pocket-knife. This, he said, they cooked holding over their corn-bread in order not to lose any of its drippings. Sometimes, he reported jocularly, they stole some fowl or even a poor skinny shoat, as pilfering was no longer frowned upon by the superior officers; in fact, it was encouraged. He supposed that robbing the hen-coops of Tennessee was partly responsible for the growing unpopularity of their cause up there. He ended by inquiring if there wasn't some way under the sun for Gerda to send some provender direct to them. "Or don't you all make the good crops you keep writing us about? Whatever it is, if the situation doesn't improve all around, a lot of the men will be making tracks for home, to raise a mess of food fit to fill our bellies."

Gerda groaned, thinking of his husky appetite that had welcomed the plainest pioneer fare even as a baby. It made her sick-stomach to think of his hunger when she sat down at table next; she shunned her own portion of food, preoccupied with the general problem of provisioning the troops.

Now the letters came less frequently and were opened with dread. In March Ulysses Grant was made commander-in-chief of the Union forces and, leaving Sherman in the West crossed the Rapidan into Virginia. There followed the long Battle of the Wilderness in May, about which Bruff wrote: "Our dead were so numerous, it looked as if we had ploughed up a graveyard." By mid-June Grant had set himself and his heavy forces down, like some prehistoric behemoth, outside Petersburg, to camp before that shallow crevice, which served the other gaunt, besieged creature very poorly as a lair in which to remain at bay.

2

The summer came down on them like a pestilence, and the hogs on which they depended so strongly sickened with cholera. At night Gerda, with Shade, would count the well ones, then the next morning an unsuspected number of them would be stretched out stiff and lifeless. There was little to be done with their diseased carcasses, till Gerda hit upon the idea of flaying the hides and curing them for shoes.

The prospect for the girls of the family having new leather shoes after two years of crocheted slippers was entrancing. They went chattering gladly to the bench before Clump, the cobbler's cabin and tried to hold their feet without squirming while he took their measurements.

"Now mind," he warned them. "Don't try to squinch yo' foots to make 'em small, 'cause I fits shoes like gloves fo' ladies. An' hit's nice workable leather." After his injunction they planted their feet down with dainty precision. None of them could foresee that after a short wearing the leather would stretch and spread so ridiculously that the girls would have to give them away to big-footed negroes.

"I don't see, though," puzzled Roxanne now, "why if leather's so scarce, they don't let little'uns like me go barefoot during the summer, like we did during flush times."

Maude bounced a succession of shrivelled chinaberries over the quarters street. "It's something or other to do with *Pride Goes before a Fall.*"

"It has to do with just plain and simple pride," corrected India severely.

"Oh well, I mean," shrugged Maude, "they're trying to make us grow up like ladies against all these odds. The chances surely are against us monkeys."

India stopped short and rapped her foot on the ground. "Now you listen to me, all the rest, including myself! We may not grow up to be mistresses of great plantations with lots of wealth. I don't pretend to know what's become of all the money. We may not be able to sit still with a silver-clappered bell to tinkle when we want a fan or a drink of cold water, but watch what I say. We'll be reared up right, the rest of the way, in manners if nothing else! That's one thing we won't lose, no matter what else the war takes away, and no matter what hard things we have to do. Now mark me! And all of us young ones will wear what shoes we have, even if they make our toes sweat, and we'll comb our hair right too. That's the least we can do."

She flounced her skirts about and marched briskly towards the house, expecting them to follow obediently, which they did. Maude whispered to Roxanne: "I never cross India when she high-tails it that way." To which Roxanne remarked: "And well you mightn't, for she could put all of us in our places in two shakes."

That night India pinched at the joinings of her bones and thought: "I'm not much to look at, and I'm spiteful. But I insist on not ducking my head for anything and I'm going to always take care that I don't. My, I'm homely. I never knew quite how homely before. Yellow as parchment when I'm scarcely seventeen. Well, Maude can be the pretty one for us, and Laurie. I'm the one where the rosy colour of the blood ran out. But never the blue thread. No one will like me much, because for one thing I won't palavar. What a face!"

It was an odd face, plain as clabber, yet with a studied formation of bones beneath, so that if she lifted it a certain way, a rarity in its fine structure gleamed like an odd quick light, something that would never be doused by wind, or wet, or woe.

"No, I'm not much," she repeated, "but I can be a thin true old maid. Admit it, not fake like Cousin Gracey." Yes, she could stand stringy and strong, letting the others' little girls play games around her. She could be a reservoir for the family's outpourings, hold herself as a cold, clean basin waiting for their overflow. She saw with great clarity that she was a vacancy, in which there was no life except inasmuch as it was received from others.

3

In spite of her daughter's growing adaptability to the blockade and the dearth of masculine attention, Joby continued to scheme fretfully to create about them the aura of being belles. She nagged them ceaselessly, about the care of their complexions, and the gait of their steps, which was becoming too free for her mincing notions. She concoted a succession of would-be bits of finery that were tackier than the ragbags from which they emerged, and she chattered with incessant archness about an almost wholly imaginary number of suits that had been made for their hands, especially for Maude's. Lately India had curtly dismissed such hypocrisy when her mother attempted to fasten it upon her. Maude, however, going on sixteen now, and possessed of a burgeoning beauty with no vestige of thoughtfulness, enjoyed her spurious popularity as spontaneously as a new game or a pocketful of sweetmeats.

When Roxanne asked her in childish bewilderment where and at what time her numerous romances had taken place, Maude was stumped for a moment and looked as if she were going to cry under India's sharp scrutiny. Roxanne, distressed, patted her cheeks. "P'raps 'twas while Veda and I were off in Mississippi. I didn't mean to be Miss Pry. I reckon I am too literal-minded, like Whet used to say I was, and I haven't an iota of imagination about anything but how to arrange flowers." She poked an index finger into the centre of Maude's cheek to coax her. "Where's that dimple that's usually there? Come on, show it to us."

The mottled raspberry in Maude's cheeks faded down to its more usual blend of peach-petal and risen cream. "Anyhow," she announced, "I *will* be addressed by scads of young men as soon as we quit this old war."

"Well, missy, we aren't going to *quit* it," declared Lucinda, who had appeared at that moment with Joby. "We're going to *win* it!" She tacked about on Joby. "You and your continual triviality about frocks and attention, you wear me out! You act as if the war were a mere nuisance. Don't you know yet that war is the arithmetic of Death?" She strode out of the girls' room and sought Gerda.

Ma'am was with Pokey in the ell, brewing opium out of poppies. She glanced up as her elder daughter came in storming.

"Lord above!" cried Cinda, "Joby gives me the pukes with her fuming over her gels, when all any of us ought to think about is our men. And how to back them up, so we can hurry and win. If we don't hurry now——" She stopped, she could admit no other alternative than victory. There had to be in all minds and hearts a sublime, blind ignoring of the factual road of defeats leading ever downhill, and a fanatic insistence upon the sharp upshoot of valour and hope. "We *must* win!" There was grim grandeur in her voice. "Defeat—defeat would be a tomb. The South would be sealed in the dungeon of the dead." Then she raked her arm across her sight as if to clear away a macabre vision. Light glinted quickly in its wake in her eyes. "We'll win, as sure as cotton ripens!" She gave a half-ashamed laugh. "My, how I carry on! Here, show me how to help to do that."

It was a slow process making opium, but they heard how horribly in want of the precious drug the hospitals at Atlanta had been. It was unendurable to think of the men in their own family, or of their neighbours, lying in pain with no relief. It was worth it, Gerda felt, to spend day in and day out extracting mercy in tiny drops from the poppies.

4

The first direct news they had received of the Battle of Atlanta had been Danley's letter to Lucinda, telling of the terrible cannonading, the demolition of New Hope Church, and the pity of the droves going by to the graveyard. What distressed his kindly mind the most appeared to be the incident of the poor woman and her two children who had been killed in bed one night and not discovered for several days.

The next word came in an epistle from Joachim.

We have good quarters, and the wood we burn for cooking is from the finest residences. Having no other, we are compelled to stew in such luxury. The troops are in fine spirits and will whip Sherman if he attacks us.

"There! What did I tell you?" exclaimed Lucinda triumphantly.

"Ssh," commanded Gerda, resuming her stilted letter-reading.

However after one engagement I had to set out over the battleground to hunt for Will Bee, who had been reported wounded. Oby Willis from the Pea River company, caught up to me and stated he would help, as he owed Ma'am some favours.

Ma'am, it was pretty dark poking about the field, but we made out well, and were close enough to recognize Will Bee when a Yankee sentry discovered us. I probably would have done just the thing to warrant us all being shot, but Willis dropped behind a splintered cannon wheel while I was brashing it out with the sentry. He was nowhere near as nice as most Yankees I have come up with, had no notion of a joke or a civil tongue neither.

Well, just as he was about to fire, Willis, who had sneaked around behind, clapped him a good one with a stick of lightwood from where a tree had been blown to pieces, and the sentry keeled over fine. That gave us time to fetch Will Bee off the field. We spliced his splintered shin up pretty fair and the surgeon says he won't need to more than limp afterwards. However he hurts till his veins bulge and we have not a thing to relieve his pain since he is not bad off and opium too scarce even for the sickest ones.

Gerda's voice, towards the close, rasped into a natural anger at such suffering being endured by one of her offspring, while right here in this house she had distilled a pain-killer. She felt a sort of bear-love for her cubs rising to a dangerous pitch. If this kept up, she would lunge through whatever barriers the enemy set up, to reach her young, with food and comforts and anodyne!

CHAPTER SIXTY-ONE

SHORTLY AFTER THAT the news came that Atlanta had been evacuated by the Confederates and burned by General Sherman. After leaving a portion of his army to watch Hood in Tennessee, he started on a march of devastation through Georgia towards Savannah and the sea. The county was conducting a correspondingly grim campaign to transport produce to sustain General Johnston's army, which was trying to stop Sherman's swath of destruction. At first Gerda was bent only on donating far in excess of her share, but then she suddenly saw her chance to convey medicines and supplies to Will Bee and others invalided outside of Atlanta. For if Sherman was drawing the bulk of his forces seaward, the prospects of reaching her goal were not too remote. She must, she argued, in any event make the effort.

First she approached Nat Screws, seeking the co-operation of some of his Commissary convoy facilities; but he was harassed by a none too veiled reprimand he had lately received from the Government concerning the disposition he had been making of the produce he had collected hitherto, so he was making a furious show of beating the record of any other quartermaster in his vicinity in this desperate emergency. Also he thought Gerda might have been partly responsible for his reprimand; consequently he was very short with her. "No time to grant any personal privileges," he barked. "Got my hands full, meeting Gov'ment's demands. Working the living daylights out of every teamster, every mule, every-——"

"That's enough," said Gerda gruffly. "It's a pity you let your stores *choke up* on you so. *If* you'd been moving them right along, you'd be able to spare me a little help now. But never mind, I'll manage. I always do." She left his warehouse, cross as two sticks at letting him get away with his prevaricating talk. Still, her first concern was to get help through to Will Bee and other invalids who needed her succour.

Gerda was in a disheartened mood when she arrived home. The day was a slothful September one, and the yard seemed infested with the numerous children of her combined families and the no longer itinerant refugees. She could scarcely walk for fear of treading on small bare toes. In the ell the various women of her colony appeared packed too close for either comfort or capable work, and the discordant screech of rocking-chairs set her teeth on edge. She wished heartily that peace had come, and that these others had all gone home about their affairs, leaving her to a profitable pursuit of her own.

Instead of staying in the ell, she went to her room and was thankful to find it empty of those who now shared it with her. "Yarbrough," she said aloud unconsciously, "tell me what to do! How am I to make it?" Her hand held on to the bedpost in imitation of his old gesture when he was hard put to it by a problem. She wanted him back dreadfully, as she had not for many a year while his sons had stood her in such good stead. But now his sons needed help, and she knew not how to give it. *"Yarbrough!"* He must counsel her in some way, here in this chamber where the floor had been worn by his deliberating footsteps, where the bed had bolstered him during many a midnight communing concerning obstacles and surmounting them. She bent her forehead against the smoother grain of the post. It reassured her. A wash of confidence flowed through the room with the hyacinth shadows of evening.

Lucinda, after rapping on the door, came in, followed by Maria Somers to advance an idea. "We heard Nat Screws turned you down, but we knew you wouldn't give up and Maria here has a plan that might work. I stand ready to help you push it through."

Gerda gazed at her daughter, startled. She so strongly resembled her father at that moment that Gerda had trouble focusing her eyes. Even after she assembled Lucinda's woman's garments and heavy braids in her vision, she could not divest the face of Yarbrough's imperious purposefulness. There was none of Lucinda's old expression of indulged womanhood; instead her whole head was cleft stone-clean, face honed fine by the knife of determination against defeat.

Never before had Gerda felt the true accord of admiration for her daughter. Now she gave it in unstinted measure.

Maria was speaking. "Miz Gerda, it's been on my mind ever since the hard fightin' moved from Alabama to Georgia, to suggest I be herdin' my crowd back home. Then the news kept on comin' in so bad, it was kind of a comfort to huddle close. But lately, since the fall of Atlanta, looks like I just cain't stay put. I want to track out and see what's goin' on. Maybe that's because Jacob taught me his teamster ways. Anyhow I have to be movin'. Then this evening when I saw you come in, so down-in-the-mouth, it came over me that maybe I could help you *con-voy* your personal donations."

Lucinda cut through the other's colloquial loquaciousness. "Maria thinks that if they packed up their belongings like any other refugees, they could conceal a fair amount of food and medicine among them. Then instead of heading straight back for Huntsville, they could take Miz Vally and her baby to Gainesville, Georgia—Miz Vally could tell us some Gainesville gossip to use among ourselves, to throw anybody who was suspicious off the track if they stopped us. And with Gainesville north-east of Atlanta, we'd have a perfect excuse to be going in that direction. That way we'd have a good chance to reach the hospital camp."

Gerda was already falling in with the plan. "I'll leave Pokey in charge here, so Joby won't make an unholy mess of things; and with Nan to help, things ought to run smoothly. Now let's see what we had better take. What is most needed besides medicines and all the lint and bandages we can get together?" The three settled themselves to plot out their course, as well as to list supplies.

2

The line-up they formed when they set out reminded Gerda a great deal of the Whetstone cavalcade migrating from South Carolina, though perforce on a much smaller scale. It was more like Yarbrough's first scouting trip, except for the preponderance of women and children instead of men, and the presence of the carriage. The carriage had been Lucinda's inspiration, to make them appear truly "refugee." The few wagons had their quota of meal, bacon, and other food hidden under tattered quilts, tired women, snivelling cranky children. But Gerda had been at a loss how effectively to conceal the precious opium, bandages, wine, and spirits until Lucinda hit on her scheme.

"We'll take my big carriage, with an enormous feather tick in it—anybody would try to save one good tick. A fine feather bed will convince the Yankees we are only refugees, if nothing else will. We won't have much provender where they can find it easily, and I hear that now

Sherman's gone on, unless they're awfully hungry, the Yankees don't pilfer the pitiful little belongings of the refugees."

"Yes, I'll take my chances on the blue-coats," declared Maria, "now that that Sherman Satan is headin' away. It's our own ornery tramps, like those that molested us coming here, that will mulct us of every last bit they can find."

The morning was hot and still even before daybreak, when they left. The rickety old wagons looked as if they might fall apart at any plod of the bone-poor mules, for it had been thought wisest not to substitute better Whetstone equipment for fear of arousing roadside cupidity. The refugee women had sour faces and sagging shoulders as they started jogging away from the house where they had been comfortable for over a year. The children scratched at their night's mosquito bites and tried to nestle to sleep again in the straw, it being too early to peer excitedly out at what they were passing. The carriage, with the feather bed sticking out like a white rabbit's ears from the two side windows, came along at a hearse's pace. Within, Gerda, Lucinda, Maria, and Miz Vally with her baby were huddled, all so weary from packing that it was easy to slumber over this familiar way. Lucinda had her legs propped up across the feather bed, to cushion the jolting. Ma'am Gerda contained herself sternly in her allotted corner even while she napped.

They had driven a long way, they had rumbled over the river bridge at Yufala into Georgia, they had eaten under fans of tree shade, they had come upon roughening red roads on a hidden back way to Columbus. They had made bed and slept that night. They had risen up cheerier somehow on the second morning, perhaps because of progress. Whatever it was, they had pushed forward into the day.

This road, so like the old one over which the Whetstones had come, induced in both Gerda and Lucinda long-ago memories. For Gerda it had meant then the blessed nearing of rest in Alabama, though Alabama had proved later all effort. At that time she had been weary under the burden of her unborn child. Now she was more wearied by the burden of her many born children, and the heaviness of years. She felt rather poorly.

Lucinda was recalling how excited she and Bruff had been at reaching the real Indian country at last, where there might be fighting. Now she was thinking that she was heading back in the direction where there might be other fighting. Little she cared!

As that day wore on, though, the successful culmination of their travelling seemed very far away. It was not something that could be accomplished in a day or two with mule-teams. It was a matter of *trudge, trudge, trudge,* over a dour terrain. The ending of the second day saw them following a rusty ridge of unfriendly hills, with rain drooping half-heartedly out of low clouds.

By bedtime none of those in the wagons were able to keep completely dry. The children snuffled under quilts soon sodden, the women latched their shawls closer and twisted their scrawny frames about, attempting to shelter the young more. No one dared disturb the careful covering over the cornmeal and other food. All prayed that it was not being rained upon. In the carriage Gerda shuffled about uncomfortably for a long time after her companions were asleep. Finally she rose stealthily and let herself down its step. "Several of the least children," she murmured, "could be put out of this weather in my place. And I'm hardy." She bundled the three most snuffling ones up into her arms like a load of kindling and tucked them on top of the feather bed. Another two she scrouged into the space she had occupied, shoving Cinda over, who grunted in her sleep but never woke. "Now that," thought Gerda, satisfied, "takes care of the puniest." Then she found herself a place in the wagon. It felt like a hog-wallow, and the wet quilt only made her bones shake. But finally she fell asleep, gratified that she had not let the little tykes stay out and suffer.

When the next day broke, slow and late because of the cloudiness, she could not seem to care about what preparations they were making for breakfasting and starting the convoy on its way again. She lay stupefied in her damp bedding, huddling her head under a corner of cover to shut out sounds. When Lucinda and Maria located her, between them they lugged her back to the carriage. They had made a good bed for her, by propping the feather tick level over the middle part of the carriage floor-space. They chafed her limbs and wrapped her in one of the best quilts, meant for Will Bee.

There was little else that Gerda remembered for several days, except that she saw the sun come out in stabs of red for a while before the day was over. She was told that none of the children were ill, having been all toddied up with hot whisky, and that the wet straw had been taken off the top of the wagon-beds so nobody else would catch cold. After that she was willing to lie still for several vaguely blended days and nights. Finally, on the fourth day of her illness, the sun burst through with a late September flush, and everything everywhere was warm and bright, with vivid colour replacing dreariness.

Gerda was thinking, while she still lay at rest, that as soon as she got on her feet to-morrow, they could make up for lost time. She had no idea how rickety she would feel when finally she did essay a standing position. She almost pitched over on her face, but Maria caught her arm in time. She was willing enough to sit down on the carriage steps, to let the pins-and-needles pass out of her feet and legs. She was dubious about whether only one more day would strengthen her enough for them to move on, yet she did not quite care. She was more concerned at this instant with the fact that her head was settling back down on her shoulders where it belonged, instead of spinning around among the tree boughs.

She was grateful when once more she lay on her feather tick, and felt the evening air sliding through the apertures across her face, soothing, not chilling her. The encamped children's voices sounded pleasantly far off as they chased after grasshoppers to make them " spit tobacco." This was restful.

By the time she was able to walk again in a shaky way, she saw that Lucinda and Maria had salvaged all their supplies, rearranged them, and made ready for further progress towards their goal. Nothing of importance had been lost. They had even dried out the soaked straw, and had fed the company sparingly, not to run short of their own rations. Gerda was gratified by their method, and decided that she was now strong enough to sit out in a wagon where the sun could warm her through. She summoned Lucinda from where she was fiddling with a mule's bit, and told her: " I believe I'll ride in a wagon in the sun for the next day or two."

" Ma'am," answered Lucinda earnestly, " you'll realize, as soon as you think it over, that you mustn't continue on with us. We're going through night-driving and Lord knows what hardships now. It could be the end of you!"

Gerda growled angrily at this daughter who dared defy her about so grave a mission: "I have tackled death before, and it has not bested me yet. I shall ride with you."

"*Please,* Ma'am." Lucinda's voice rang with the ardent strain of entreaty. "*Don't!* If not for your own sake, then for the good of Will Bee, lying there thrashing with pain. And others far worse off. They're waiting for this relief, though they don't know it's on the way. And we must not fail them! If you come along, you will cumber and slow the whole train. Even now we may not get through, at our fastest pace, for we have—already—been too long delayed." She stopped talking and walked over to the road's edge, where she began plucking the tops of weeds off by their necks and throwing them down desperately. Her shoulders she kept implacably backed towards Ma'am Gerda. She had begged her best.

Gerda rose to move towards her daughter, to express her decision, but her knees broke unexpectedly. She felt the first ghost-touch of her successor—laid but lightly on her shoulder, yet her throne trembled. Or rather, *she* trembled on that throne with the ague of age, which is the courier of Death. A far-off Death, yet discernible on the horizon. She might have wondered how many twists there were in the highway he was travelling towards her, had she not been so balked in this one bitter moment of being thwarted. Gerda was not skilled at giving ground. She raised her arms outspread for a moment towards the hills for help. It was not easy for her to abandon power even for so short a span.

When she reached Lucinda she said: "You are right. I cannot afford to hold you back, to the snail's pace suited to my sickness. So now I must count on *you*! Do manage the convoy."

"Oh, Ma'am, you can do that!" declared Lucinda. Then she dropped her voice to a talking tone. "I sent some messages back along the way, fixing it the best I could for you to stop at Richland and other places. You won't have to sleep out of doors unless you want, and Honest will drive you, so my mind will be easy."

"Well," said Gerda, ending the discussion of her weakness, "I want to see you all start now."

"We're ready. I was only waiting to settle this with you." Cinda looked over her small tight-packed drove, knowing what bounty she had concealed so skilfully, by a joggle of women and a scramble of children.

"Keep still!" Maria ordered them sharply, and they subsided into manageable laxity. "It's best to keep them logy. They cause less trouble on the road."

Gerda tested her feet against the ground before she rose again. They were firm. "I suppose, Lucinda, you have that feather bed, with its contents, in a safe place in the train?"

"I put those articles from it out of sight," Cinda assured her, "but I left the tick in the carriage for you."

"Then I won't budge a step toward home till you move it into a wagon. I'm sleeping at houses all along the way, and I mean that tick to go to Will Bee!"

Lucinda beckoned for Honest and Ambrose, the other negro driver, to pull it out of the carriage where she had it so cunningly tucked down. It took a deal of manipulation to find the right place in a wagon where it could again be concealed. By the time the job was finished, Gerda had slumped inside on the carriage seat. Her cheek-bones rose gauntly from her physiognomy, and for the moment she felt totally disinterested in the whole project. Not for thirty years had she been weakened into such lassitude—not since that sterile wilderness birth.

Maria came and poked her hand out to shake Gerda's, which grew tired before it could grip back. "I do thank you, Miz Gerda, for putting up with the whole push of us for so long. And I promise I'll bite my own hand off if I don't finish this job right. Thank you a thousand times."

"You know you were more than welcome, and a godsend as it turns out. Good-bye, Maria, till peace time." Peaceful days, they would be good.

Lucinda scarcely knew how to speak her farewell to Ma'am under the circumstances and flapped about the carriage in embarrassment. Finally she ducked in at the carriage door and nudged Gerda's cheek with her nose in something meant to be a kiss. Then rushed off.

Gerda saw her step up into the lead wagon and crack the whip to start the team. It flicked through the air in a quick dark curl, then subsided. The teams strained forward; the faded boards of the wagons looked strong enough for the haul, while the women and children retained their proper balance over the hidden supplies.

Lucinda surveyed her outfit from the first mules' nostrils to the last pair's tasselled tails. She spun the quirt of her whip through reflective fingers, then dropped it. This outfit would pass. She would manage it somehow! She stood letting the wagon sway her from one side to the other, bracing herself easily.

Gerda saw her going that way. "It would take something awful," she knew, "to make her quit!"

Lucinda turned her head about once more at that moment and saluted with her whip against a high-hilled sky. "We'll go through!" Her voice keened with the cry of victory. "We'll win!" it screeched. The sky behind her tossed head and wind-blown skirt was bright.

Gerda, in the dread act of turning back for the first time in her life, felt suddenly dragged forward by the power projected from Lucinda in her progress. Then she fumbled down upon the carriage seat, her limbs turned to deadwood. "I am old," she agreed with the years, then fell suddenly asleep with her chin stuck over an elbow like a child's. Her driver saw to it that she was properly covered.

She slept through the rest of the day and all the night, intently, less like the old than like the very young. When she awoke the next morning her mind was loaded with disappointment; but she was revived by her deep rest and anxious to arrive back home. She did not trust Nat Screws to push supplies through to General Johnston.

CHAPTER SIXTY-TWO

LUCINDA and her convoy had not been long on the road that first day before their spirits began to lift. It was cool for September, the staleness washed from the air by the rain. Even in the middle of the day the heat did not hang like its usual suffocating blanket over the earth, and the sky seemed like a high wall through which the wind could blow.

Under Lucinda's vibrant command the occupants of the wagons began to show the tang of their individualities. Miz Vally divulged a drollery behind her demure delicacy that delighted them when least expected, and the cackling, good-natured Essie Somers hopped in and out of the several wagons starting games among both the women and the children. She had a special gift for " making faces " that convulsed the most dispirited with laughter. Said her mother, Maria : " There's been times when I've wondered if I was scared by a hobgoblin 'fore she was born."

As the afternoon passed in what Miz Vally called a " peachening glow," they all relaxed in their seats, and someone began to hum. Voice after voice came in on the tune, and presently they were all carolling away like courting couples on a sugar-moon ride. Lucinda and Maria tried to supply the tenor, and from the back in the hind wagon black Ambrose rolled forth a grandeur of bass. The others hummed the missing harmony.

I-know-a-girl-with-eyes-so blue,
Ask-for-a-kiss and she'll-give-you-two,
Good-by, my lover, good-by,
Good-by, my lover,
Good-bye-e-eee.

The notes made a trail of sweetness back over their shoulders that them all happy. It brought them closer to those other times they had known, of pleasuring.

That night they made a fair fire to sit about after their bit of cooking and eating was over, and Ambrose, lumbering up with a final arm-load of fuel, asked: "Miss Lucinda, like you, I should tell 'em a tale about how come niggahs' hair wuz crisped to wool?"

"Surely-sure," encouraged Cinda, and the circle drew closer, hugging their knees in anticipation. The white faces one and all turned with childlike faith toward the dark beaming one, knowing that its tongue would not fail them for an hour of fable that had the good spice of ginger-cake. There never were, thought Cinda, story-tellers like the older negroes, for they lived in the kingdom of gullibility and shook and shivered or rose to glory-be along with the victims of their imagination. They were the greatest tellers of tales in the world because they made truth of their outlandish lies.

The story ended, and Ambrose quit being a molasses-voiced spell-binder and became a help-out coachman grinning and wiping the black grease off his face, while they all told him how good the story was or demanded what happened next.

With shuffles and nuzzling about in the wagon-straw, they settled down for the night, except for one or two of the small boys who had leave to camp on the road bank. After Lucinda had inspected each group and counted noses, she set out with Ambrose to reconnoitre in the adjacent woods for any possible danger of Yankees or, what was more likely, some of Sherman's "bummers." The latter, also called "coffee coolers," trailed along in the wake of his army; yet because they were not exactly in it he was not held responsible for their acts of depredation. It was they who wrought the worst havoc after the fighting had passed.

The glade showed nothing but quiet, and now that the leaves had fallen a little, the sky sent a pattern of light down that made the woods look not too mysterious. Lucinda came out of it satisfied that they were safe for the night, and she whistled a few bars much as a sentinel might proclaim: "All is well!"

Ambrose shook his huge woolly head. "Don' you know *how* to be scairt, Miss Cinda? I'clare I don't think you does."

"What on earth is there to be scared of here?" she demanded. "It's nothing but a piece of wooded ground."

"Nev' mind me," he apologized, not wanting to disturb her, but unable to stop worrying about Yankees.

2

The next day they set off in the same lusty spirit, all the more cheery for having chucked off war worries for a spell. However, before they had gone very far they began to see signs where Sherman's march had laid waste. At the end of the morning they happened upon a place where a woman was sitting on a kettle and holding an empty gun, her eyes even more empty, except when they filled with stark-mad visions. Lucinda tried to ask her what had occurred, in order to see if they could help in any way. She answered in tones alternately mumbling and screeching: "They tried to take my kettle away—this one I tried out our lard in when we settled here. They didn't get it, though. Then they went into the wardrobe my son gave his bride in '52, and they slashed her wedding dress to pieces with knives! Yellow ribbons—that's all . . . all's left of being a lady. No ladies any more. But I kept my kettle! Don't you dare touch!"

Her eyes went mad again and she cocked her empty gun.

Lucinda made motions that brought Maria, and quietly they managed to leave the old granny a piece of pork and a bit of meal to put in her pot, if she could ever come to her senses enough to fix a meal. Lucinda patted her shoulders, and she seemed to like that, sagging for a second against Cinda's round strong arm. "There, there," said the younger woman, "you'll be all right now. The Yankees have all passed by and won't bother you again."

Can I count on that?" queried the old lady cunningly, as if she were holding the other responsible for her well-being.

"Indeed you can," replied Cinda easily as she turned away.

When they were once more on the go, Maria asked in a grudging tone: "Why'd you give that old loon those good victuals, to lie there till the rats and crows eat 'em?"

"Is that any concern of yours?" demanded Lucinda. "I don't see that it is." She couldn't speak of how it had hurt the other day to see Ma'am age before her eyes—and this was a pioneer woman, too.

It was toward noon that they met up with the "bummers." They could see that roystering lot coming from a long way off, and could hear their noise before that. They were sweaty-looking men in odd garb, though a few wore some piece of uniform that appeared to have been rightfully earned. As they approached they began joshing one another about how to divide the spoils of the convoy, and Lucinda felt her stubbornness swelling up to bullfrog size in her chest. She did not give way to them one whit on the road, but blocked them squarely, so that they had to split their squad in a way that dispersed them as a unit.

"Good day, 'coffee coolers,'" she greeted them disdainfully, deciding that scorn was better than the shudders.

"Good day to you, ma'am," answered the most hulking one, who seemed to be their leader. "I 'spose you're bent on the regular errand of takin' a little food and spirits to some pore dyin' relative of your'n?"

"And what if we are?" she inquired with asperity.

"Dunno, except our job of hell-raisin' is to put a stop to all that. Won't lick the South till we whip you women folk. That's what ol' Tecumpseh says! Break the women, and the South's beaten."

"Then you're a long way from winning, 'coffee cooler,'" she sneered. "Better start your war all over again."

He ruffled his fingers through his chestnut thatch. "Seems almost a fact," he admitted.

"Well," she said sharply, "are you going to move out of our way and let us by? I'm tired of this."

At that tone the pseudo sergeant turned about and looked over his men. Something not flinty but dogged made him reply: "No'm, not yet."

Lucinda sprang down, holding her whip and caressing its tip, but not viciously. She looked up at him in a way that men want. "Oh, you are going to let me by, aren't you?" she asked, with a suggestion, however, that she hated for them to part company.

He stood half-diffident, half-aprowl. "Your crowd *could* go right ahead, if only *you* would come off first——"

Lucinda's laugh broke loose, and she jumped back into her wagon, leaving him at a loss for an instant before her mirth. From her position of advantage above him she said quickly: "I know what you were going to ask as a forfeit, but don't hold us up thinking of that as punishment." She peered down into his eyes a moment. "For *that* wouldn't be a forfeit to a woman who has gone manless these past years." Then she jerked her team up and with a lash sent them down the road.

His roar of involuntary laughter followed her for a second, and before he could feel any chagrin she waved back at him with her arm that held the whip.

They gestured once or twice again to each other, framed against their separating horizons. Hail-and-farewell was what they meant, between two road-robbers. Lucinda went on in a high good humour for several hours after that, and Ambrose's chuckle kept gurgling up. "It do beat all, the way Miss Cinda treat them Yankees lak a jollification."

3

The afternoon began to cloud over strangely, and the remaining daylight took on a dreary cast with something uneasy about it all. Lucinda tried to convince herself that their lowering of spirits was due only to the landscape. The brighter-coloured foliage was being dulled by too much moisture, and bushes looked like beards of age that the earth had grown. She felt a cantankerousness coming upon her, and her abusive good humour towards the "bummers" departed, to give way to a lurking sullenness.

As they came round one bend in the nearly lost road she caught sight of a skulking figure, and Maria Somers half-coughed at her: "That's one of them tramp men. The 'disaffected' *scum* of the South. Watch out, 'cause they're mostly weak-wits from back in the piny-woods and don't know where to stop when it comes to meanness."

Lucinda nodded, and drove her team as if nothing had happened, while the figure slithered back like a snake up the damp bank and they no longer saw it. "I don't like that at all," she grumbled. "Something's up."

"'Fraid so," agreed Maria.

They had not jogged far before they fell into the ambush. An array of tramp men straggled across the road, weevily-looking varmints with rat mouths or rheumy eyes, and every one of them degenerated below any state of manhood. Lucinda recognized real evil in them, and sickened at the thought of that pallid worm eating from within at the vitals of the Confederacy.

However, she continued driving forward.

A squirty little fellow shambled out and yanked at her mule's bridle. She halted before injury could be done her critter. "What do you mean by bothering my team?" she cried with plenty of power in her angered tone.

"Wants whut you might have—eat or drink—with youh." He spat through two slits of his teeth and kept his fingers twined in the thongs of the harness. She cracked her whip handle down on them so that they jumped away to the sound of his cussing.

"That's how you ack, huh?" he snarled. "Must have plenty booty." His raggle-taggle group brayed with discordant laughter, then they swarmed about the wheels of the various wagons and started tearing at the contents of the straw after the prizes, without any regard for the humans huddled upon it. They slapped children right and left, they poked women out of the way, while pitiful animal noises of alarm rose from the wagons. Lucinda felt a rage churning in her that would bring brimstone, not butter, to the surface.

So far, in spite of their panic, her charges had resisted the efforts of the marauders to discover the secreted stores, which merely infuriated the latter further. Suddenly one of the worst ones leaned over into Miz Vally's lap and took hold of her baby's leg. "You betta tell me where's all at. Else I'll brash you' brat on wagon wheel."

Miz Vally sat tranced in the finest fervour of complete love that was conceivable, an absolute rigidity that could not be shaken even by terror. Stillness alone could save her child.

Then Lucinda hollered out: "Great God, what are they doing to Ambrose!"

The man dropped the baby's leg and whirled to see what the others were up to. The main group had fallen on the fine old tar-barrel, and, dragging him from his seat, started pommelling him, in hopes of a confession of how to find things more quickly. He had stood their blows as long as he could, then he had started banging back at them, hitting down several who called themselves "white" men. One squinchy rat he picked up again in his great hands and broke his back over the nearest wheel. None of this trash would live to touch Miss Cinda's stuff whilst he could fight!

The group tore the carcass from his pounding grip and flung it like offal at the roadside. Then their whole number made a lunge for him, their multitude of scrawny claws pinioning his greatness.

Lucinda, on the hurry toward him, saw what happened, and before she could come anywhere near reaching him it was over. They didn't even bother to kill him first! His body stripped, they struck him down with their knives and hatchets. The blood burst from him almost in spurts as he was drawn and quartered!

She sucked her own sickness back into her mouth, then took aim and fired. A man dropped. Maria and Essie were shooting over her shoulders, too, with good mountain sight. The creatures were falling thick now, and suddenly Miz Vally's little pistol cracked and got the one that had touched her baby. In another instant the rest were skedaddling. Soon they were all gone, scattering into the frayed trees far over the hills and out of sight.

"Essie," sobbed Lucinda wildly, "you go hide the children's eyes from *this!*" She was picking up the pieces of Ambrose and trying to put them together again. Maria lent a hand. Back in the wagons they heard Essie and Miz Vally telling high-sounding tales of gibberish to make them laugh, even if it was only a weak squeak.

Finally, Lucinda rose up, her hands swathed in blood and dirt, and faced Maria. "Well, we at least covered him decent."

"Let's get on from here," answered Maria gruffly, "before we go crazy."

There wasn't any creek to bathe their hands and arms in, so they used swabs of grass, which left caked streaks. As they drove into the night that had come down Lucinda thought: "Now we have *nothing* to fear! For the worst thing that can happen to us *has* happened."

Now she knew by all her gods of Courage, and by all the devils of Disaster, that she would win through.

CHAPTER SIXTY-THREE

Gerda had made her return trip by easy stages, arriving home feeling fairly restored, a fact for which she was truly grateful when she discovered the conditions awaiting her. The first concerned Nat Screws' chicanery. He had, as she had long suspected, been playing both ends against the middle, which was his personal aggrandizement. As quartermaster he had collected produce, then as a conniving merchant he had deducted portions of it to secrete to sell later for his own profit.

When Guy told her of this after her return, Gerda sat gnawing her thumb knuckle. "I'll do everything in my power to help him push our good supplies through this time, because a green quartermaster would be worse than the sorry piece he is, right now. I'll let him off for the present. But when I think of the way I slaved over that wheat, only to have that *weevil* get into it! Well, I'm not through with him by a long shot!" Her face was so criss-crossed by intent, frowning lines that even old Guy could no longer think of her as a young woman. But it was strength that sawed into her face with finality.

2

The other catastrophe with which Gerda had to cope was the care of a number of sick field-hands. Seven of them had come down with bad chest colds and high fever, and could not remain in their now leaky cabins. The ell was too much in use, as well as too draughty, so the only suitable place left was the "boys' room," with its lean-to. She moved her grandsons into Bruff's office, with Nan's eager permission.

The seven negroes were very sick she saw, as she had them brought in. Yet sick as they were, they tried to lean upright against the board wall of the room, waiting for her to speak. "Put them to bed quick," she ordered, "before any of them can topple over." She and Pokey and Nan, with Shade and some boys to help, ranged them on pallets of quilts scorched hot before the fire, and placed over foot-thick mattresses of corn shucks. Their sickened distress seemed immediately relieved by the protection of the house.

"Ma'am Gerda," suggested Nan, "couldn't these spry boys who are helping us sleep in snatches? Then let's leave them with buckets of water to doze in the corners of the room and bring drinks to the sick whenever they twitch and cough too long. They could sleep far enough away by the windows so as not to catch this mizry."

"That's a good idea," Gerda commended her. "Drinking water handy means so much when you're feverish."

"I'll have some cherry-bark syrup ready, too, for coughs," said Pokey. "I'm goin' to watch over them myself to-night, so neither of you needs to worry. Later in the week you kin take yo' turns, but not now."

Gerda started to quarrel with this, but at that moment one of the sicker ones woke, sure his heart was quitting on him and that he was dying that very minute. His antics were arousing the others from their torpor when Pokey dosed him with corn-cob soda, and after belching resoundingly several times, he flopped back on his mattress, his chest congestion relieved, to slough off into sleep.

Gerda and Nan, as well as Pokey, stayed watching them for a while. Nan was intent upon proving herself a good doctor's wife. Gerda was fatigued, but accustomed to being ready with aid and reassurance. Pokey was simply waiting to swab their mouths, or hold a basin, or tuck a cover. Pokey was born a nurse.

3

Lucinda returned one afternoon alone in a wagon. She reported simply that they had carried the major portion of the supplies through. "Will Bee sent you a message, ma'am, that he had eaten his fill of good victuals once more. He didn't need the drugs any longer, so he gave ours over to, of all people, a Yankee surgeon! I give you my oath. Will Bee has a little knob on the front of his shin where the break is mending, but he'll have only a slight limp, so that Yankee surgeon said." Cinda sat down suddenly right where she was in the yard. "Do you know I'm kind of tired? Dro-ove all—night——"

Pokey and Gerda lifted her by the armpits and knees and carried her the rest of the way, refusing to let the yard boys take her. They laid her on Gerda's own bed, without her stirring. They drew the blinds and ordered the household to be quiet.

She slept the clock around, then woke wolf-hungry, and at the fullest meal available. Sitting propped among the pillows, she spatted at the covers impatiently. "I have to get to work to start better crops next spring and to cure what meat we have the right way this fall." She tossed the cover back. "I must get up from here. There's such a lot to be done."

"Keep quiet a minute," ordered Gerda. "What you need is more rest. You've been up aganist too much." She rocked slowly in her chair beside the big bed. "I hate to tell you this right now, but somebody else might at a worse time. We've lost badly up in Virginia and Maryland. Turber was with General Early on his last raid on Washington. They almost could have captured the capital, if it hadn't taken them so long to draw up their companies. But before they could get into formation, that Grant sent the Yankees reinforcements. Well, I reckon we'll live through that, too. The only thing is"—her voice slowed—"Bruff writes that Turber's mind has slipped back since that defeat. And that's hard, because Turber himself wrote Nan one of the finest letters you ever read about the attack. Maybe, though, we can put him on his feet if they'll only send him home."

She peered over at her daughter to see if this long-drawn-out account of other family worries had helped to distract Cinda's attention from her own inner turmoil. Gerda saw that it had not.

Instantly Lucinda began again: "There's such a lot to be done. I hope you don't mind keeping my pitiful few schoolgirls here, for a while anyway. Top Hill is too remote to be safe till—till *all* vandals pass for good. But I must be on my way, to plan with Mr. Dicks about garnering every smidgin of crops we have left. I'm planning on planting and raising some really big ones like yours, Ma'am, after this. You never saw such famine as there is up that way where the armies have passed. Oh, the things I've seen! Things you'll never know. The only thing I can pay any attention to now is the fact that we need more and more and more for our armies!" She started to stagger out of the bed, but Ma'am steadied her back against the pillows.

"You had better have another good night's rest before you go. Now it's your turn to listen to me."

Lucinda turned one cheek over gratefully against a pillow and drew a long, tired sigh.

CHAPTER SIXTY-FOUR

A PALL of bad times had settled everywhere over the Confederacy. Abraham Lincoln had been enthusiastically re-elected, and the Union had admitted a thirty-sixth State, Nevada, rich in silver mines. Farragut had run the forts at Mobile. On land, after defeating Early on his retreat from Washington, Sheridan had laid waste the Shenandoah Valley, which had long been Lee's granary. And now that formidable general had joined Grant outside of Petersburg, to increase the grimness of that siege.

From closer home, word came to the county that on December 12th Sherman had reached the sea, in spite of the valiant resistance of Johnston's army and the redoubled efforts of productive counties like Turber to ration the troops.

Gerda, standing in her depleted barns, shook her head. They would go hungry here this winter. And their men? The hardships they endured had long since passed the point of comprehension. Their habits of living bore no resemblance to the customs of civilization. The wonder was that they had not reverted to beasts, that they still retained a frayed aspect of gentle breeding. Reality spoke from their letters now, unvarnished by artificiality, yet their salutations and farewells kept the cast of courtesy. "I'm afraid," Gerda admitted candidly, "that I'd not remember to 'pay my respects' if I were scratching body-lice and starved to the bone."

Angrily her eyes travelled about her bins once more, and she called out Nat Screws' name like a curse. Mildewed wheat! She wanted to skin him alive; she had sent in her complaints, complete with affidavits, but little good it would do now. A veritable case of locking the barn too late. She would not forget, though, in the future. She felt like a baulked beast in a cage, not to be able to bear down on him till he howled for mercy. She fumed: "I don't like this letting up on my aims the way I've had to do twice lately. I will be in my dotage for fair if I let this namby-pamby caution become a habit." Still, she knew that all strength of purpose had to be conserved for the more feasible projects, that the time had come when everything had to be considered, not only in the light of steps to be gained, but with regard to preventing total annihilation of all to which they still so stubbornly held.

Things had in fact finally reached the stage where the Government was openly considering conscription of the slaves for the army. They had come a long way from their first hot-headed attitude that it was "against all codes of chivalric warfare." Now faced with the accumulation of defeats and the fact that the North boasted more than two hundred thousand of escaped Southern slaves among their troops, they realized the gravity of the situation and the probable necessity for availing themselves of the help of their own negroes before the enemy could further convert that strength to its own use.

"It seems like," concluded Gerda in her thoughts, "we're called upon to swallow a lot of bitter pills. But I for one won't care if they'll purge us of strife in the end and let us settle down to work in unharmed homes once more."

2

Lucinda had ridden over alone to the closed house at Top Hill to gather another handful of jewels to contribute to the Treasury. While there, she first made the rounds of her quarters to see how such winter work as could be accomplished was progressing. She liked being out on horseback, though it was beneath a cold sky that showed no piles of clouds, simply a cast-down dimness. The house, when she entered it, echoed with that utter hollowness of the empty. Up in her own room she unlocked the drawer that held her jewel-box and began scraping up the remaining trinkets. "I'm touching bottom," she said aloud, recalling how she had formerly been able to bury her fists in a regular Aladdin's treasure-chest. She studied several of the more inferior pieces, then dropped them with a little clink into the box. "Pretty sorry stuff, that, which would do the Government no good. So I'll leave them for keepsakes, though I don't know what for, with Whet gone." She pocketed the rest.

"Cold as blue blazes here," she shivered, and walked over to the window to gaze out at the weather again. "Must be what they mean by 'feels like snow' when they say that up north."

Suddenly she saw a gig containing a lone man rounding into the carriage circle, the wheels rattling over the frozen earth. She went quickly down the staircase and towards the door, expecting his knock, but it did not come. Peering out the side light windows of the door, she saw how he had alighted from the buggy, but was standing with his back towards the house, on the lowest step, in an attitude of one accustomed to surveying this horizon from that particular vantage. His eyes swung in a deliberate circle, tallying each detail with a half-critical, half-approving manner.

"Not a Yankee! Coming to take up headquarters here," Lucinda told herself, convinced by more than his lack of a blue coat or a staff of aides. "Not a new quartermaster, for he's looking the gardens over and in no haste about the fields. Who?" He half-turned about then and began to mount the steps sideways, with feet so sure of the steps that he did not even have to look down.

She opened the door, and he swung full towards her. *"Cinda!"* he greeted her in a great, deep voice, and she saw his face, florid with full-bloodedness, beneath a tough short beard as grey as frost. Deep, dancing blue eyes had laughing wrinkles skipping about them, and his one word of salutation: *"Cinda!"* broke bounds and went into a merry roar.

"Jerard Malone!" Her voice cracked in her throat like the squawk of a goose. She plunged towards him to grab him with her hands, to hold him there in solid flesh and not let him vanish as he always had in her dreams of their re-meeting.

They both pumped and swayed each other's arms, grinning all over their faces and shaking their heads in happy disbelief. Finally she exclaimed: "I'm so thankful you didn't die of that typhoid!"

"Saving the pleasure of killing me with your bare hands, eh, chick?" he chuckled. "Don't mind telling you now that you'd liked to've done it—that night—here." For a moment their eyes were sombre with the load of tragedy buried in silence, and all breath was held. Then he dropped her hands and motioned in the direction of their gardens. "You've kept them up well, 'specially for such bad times."

"Well, you left me with plenty of negroes, and they've multiplied. Though I'm afraid I don't get the real good out of them at farming, since cotton hasn't been the crop and Mr. Dicks has been off following the fighting since Atlanta. I'm not handy that way, like Ma'am, but I can learn."

He regarded her curiously, never before having heard her speak of work for herself.

Suddenly she remembered her manners. "Come on in. Though, after all, you don't need to be bid into your own house."

He followed her, his eyes roving over every detail. They entered the Little Parlour, where a fair amount of fuel was laid on the hearth. She began kindling a blaze, while he poked his head into the dining-room, and then ejaculated: "What in time!" amazed at the addition of the scholars' dining-hall beyond. She explained, and he chuckled: "That's right, you married the schoolmarm, so I heard." He saw her stiffen. "Don't mind me, Cinda! I didn't mean harm. Why, great Jehoshaphat!" he changed the subject to another tone of greater surprise. "You've built a fire all by yourself."

"That's not all I've learned to do lately," she laughed. "I'll fix you as good a meal as can be had in these parts after a bit. After all, I don't want to call up from the quarters any servant that would either question a stranger or—recognize their master. Remember, the older ones, especially, are scared of ghosts." She chuckled. "Too bad you can't have a look at your handsome gravestone."

"A vixen still, ain't you?" he admired. "That's the thing that I hankered after the most about you, after I was gone."

She was bringing out as decent a bottle of spirits as she had, and, pouring carefully, measured drams. "You taught me to drink, 'member? And you did a careful job of it. It has never gone to my head. But tell me how you came here. And what's your name now?"

"Mallory Fitzgerald. Irish and near enough to the old one. Funny thing, it seems as much my own now as the other. Kinder like a left shoe is to a right shoe, its mate. I did well in Texas. Plenty of opportunity there, and I had money to start on. Then I seem to have that knack of making it. I've been in Richmond considerable since this ruckus started, finance and farming being my specialties. Next to fighting, which they wouldn't let me do. Lately old Jeff's been hopping mad about the graft going on in the Commissary, and one of the *beauts* down in this section, that's been gouging the farmers' eyes out and cheating the Government both, is Nat Screws. Ma'am Gerda sent in a complaint, so I was told to put the screws on Screws. He didn't recognize me, being too busy trying to cover up his own tracks. And I steered clear of Ma'am.

"Well, while here, naturally I had a hankering to come out—home." His big voice died quickly on a lonely tone.

Lucinda put a hand over his and gave him the only comfort she could: "Danley knows you didn't die, but he thought—and so did I—that this way was the best way for me. Even though *I have never rid my heart of you.*" She stared down, for the moment unseeingly, at the gnarled shape of his once vibrantly fleshy hands. Hands betrayed the years, when a laugh could wipe them from the face. She stood up. "Want to look over the rest of the house?"

"Nothing except the big double drawing-room," he told her heavily, and she understood how he flinched from encountering any signs above stairs of the household and pupils that had replaced his ways. As they walked across the wide hallway, he glanced up the charmed curve of the stairway. "I can still see you, Cinda, sweeping down it, with your skirts spread like a queen's! I had my share of happiness from you."

The Double Room, always kept bare, did not have such a war-stripped appearance. It might have been merely closed while they were absent on a pleasure jaunt to New Orleans. Also it was mildly fragrant with the pot-pourri of Miz Lisbeth's that Gracey had somehow concocted out of each June's honeyed roses. The girandole mirror shone like a vast crown jewel above the marble mantel, and the pianoforte queened it over this throne-room of elegance. They each stood with unconscious stateliness before the gleaming hearth, as if awaiting a host of guests, invited not by the inscribed word, but by the five senses startled into memory.

Next their glances lingered over each other with the appraisal of two accustomed to former intimacy. He saw a woman of fulfilled magnificence, but not the girl as wild as a thunderstorm who had struck his home like lightning and destroyed it for him. This woman took pleasure in dispensing generously instead of pirating at every turn. He half-lifted his hands, then let them fall as if they had spilled something from their grasp that they had long held close. This woman was more like a splendid mother of the Cinda he had known, and yet . . . and yet . . . she was by no means done with the full-charged forces of living, while, for all his bulk, he felt sapped of the juicy fluids of vigour there beside her.

Lucinda saw a man still greatly robust, but none the less old—like—"Why, like Gran van Ifort!" she exclaimed with inward dismay. "Like my *great-grandfather*!" Her head bowed a moment before this blow of Time, and she had to suck her bottom lip to hold back a sob.

Then they lifted blank faces towards each other, bereft because no longer anywhere in the world did there exist those two people who had once so loved each other.

"I am going now," he said, "for ever and ever! This is our end." She nodded and stood where she was. Before he quit the house, she heard him turn his steps back towards his small office-room and open the door for a last look. He would not find that changed. Then once more his steps sounded in the hall, and the big front door opened. And closed.

Presently wheels creaked, turning against the cold dirt.

Standing alone, in the cold tunnel of the ballroom, Lucinda felt the first shadow the years cast across her own conception of herself. A war. A son dead in that war. And forty years upon her. . . . She was no longer young.

She tried a prayer: *"O Time, pass not so fast! Let there be Love once more!"*

CHAPTER SIXTY-FIVE

The briefly nurtured hope of effecting a peace with independence by a conference with the North had died still-born in the cabin of a steamer at Hampton Roads, Virginia. Now the South knew where it stood; it must be war to the bitter end for its independence. The South was indeed girding up its loins for one last powerful stand, to turn the enemy back and hold its land whole unto itself!

There was one problem, however, that was becoming ever more serious, that of desertion from the ranks. Nor was it now the desertion instigated by traitorous Peace Societies, but rather a defection caused by the plight of the families of soldiers at home. You could not blame the men for stealing home for a few months, in an attempt to remedy such dire conditions. The "crop deserters," one and all, intended to return to the army after starting their crops in the making, to return with minds free to continue the fight even more fiercely.

Yet the drop in the muster-roll was alarming. Even General Lee admitted: "Parts of the armies melt away before my eyes." The number grew till it reached one hundred thousand known deserters! Gerda, hearing of that total, felt dispirited. As a planter she knew that food was elementary necessary to a campaign, yet that soldiers were even more necessary to war.

2

Lucinda had moved her household, including her scanty number of pupils, back to Top Hill, since it was now imperative that she start her planting. Nor was that an easy thing for her to plan and execute, on a place that had so long been completely given over to cotton-growing. It had come hard for even Mr. Dicks to switch the fields over to the grain and other produce required for the Government. The vast majority of her large holding had perforce lain idle. This year, with even old Dicks gone, Lucinda felt she was indeed floundering in a mud-hole of hopelessness, like some of the ones she had traversed to-day.

It was a real spring day in spite of the sucking soil about her ankles. A peach-pink haze was coming into the atmosphere, which was always a forecast of blossoming fruit trees. Also branches and twigs had that fresh-peeled look they took on prior to the first green quirks of leaves. She was standing in a fallow field far from the house, wondering if she could make an easy crop here, when something made her listen. Over by a boundary that fuzzed into the brush, she knew something human had moved, then hidden itself in immobility. "Who's there?" she called loudly.

The brush quivered, then broke, and a man's bulk came out of it. "It's me—Hans!" the call came, low with caution even in this remote place.

Pell-mell she raced towards him, losing her brogans in the mud. "What's the matter, Hans? Is there fighting near here? We've had Sherman's 'bummers' all around over the state, and we never know about the Raiders, but there's no real engagement, is there?" By now she had reached him, they had kissed quickly, and she was satisfied that he was not wounded.

He took hold of her shoulders with his quiet hands and warned her: "Don't make so much fuss. I don't want even a stray negro to hear. No, there is no battle. But I heard you needed a man's help who knew farming. And I was not so much good where I was. Other men fight better. So I told myself I would come and do that for which I was fitted. Do it for you." Then he said calmly: "I have deserted, for a while."

"A deserter?" She dropped back. "No, Hans!"

He nodded doggedly. "Food they need. You don't know how. And so much can come from this good land."

"But, Hans, you can't." She searched for a way to tell him the unforgivable thing he was doing—in their family! "You can't desert the army," she ended flatly.

"I am not deserting its needs," he persisted, as if by rote. "Food must be had."

"Ma'am will never forgive you."

"*Ma'am* must never know," he told her.

Lucinda's eyes shot all over his face, trying to solve his mind, and the problem. "You mean I have to hide you, not only from the Yankees, but from the family? That's all wrong, Hans. For one of Ma'am's sons not to be able to face her—why, even Wayne brazens out——"

He stopped her. "You forget I am not one of Ma'am's sons. Now let me make it plain." She could see he had something he was striving earnestly to make clear. "All of you have been kind to me, Ma'am the most kind, who might have been the least. Still I have always felt I was the kitchen churl, in my own mind. Not one of the blood royal. Yet now this thing I can do." Lucinda noted the slow half-inverted Dutch to which he oddly recurred, like Gran, like Marta, whom he could not remember. "I know, believe me, the way of the soil, not as a planter, but as a ploughman. And you, not even you can turn me away from my task. Well, can I count on your mercy to give me the working of these fields far from the house and to keep me hidden while I sleep? Then will I give you a planting, and early cultivation, that will bring in such a good harvest! I cannot stay so long as that harvest, that you know, but I will get it under way."

Seeing Lucinda still hesitating, he laughed harshly. "If you wish to notify the military provost——"

"Hush that!" she clapped a palm over his mouth, and the sandiness of his unshaven chin sent a sensation of his actuality through her fingers to her mind, as nothing before had. Suddenly she smiled delightedly. "Why Hans, you're really here! At home! And I've been fussing all the time instead of telling you how *good* it is to have you. Hug me tight, so I'll know it's really true and not just one of those fancies we women have." She was almost jigging with delight, now that her dislike of his desertion had been discarded.

She started leading him around the field, along the edge where the brush would make them indiscernibly blurred. "The place for you to stay, Hans, is in that old boys' dormitory near the schoolhouse, where the trees grow high above the dip, and even your chimney smoke if seen, can pass off as a bush-fire smudge. I keep school, such as it is, entirely up at the mansion. I'll pick you out a number of hands that can be trusted. And, while I know good and well that after a while most of my negroes are bound to suspect something, they won't dare breathe it to any white folks. Pinky and Bonapartt will see to that, without my ever mentioning your name. And what a crop we will make! Funny," she was spilling out words now, "I was worrying myself sick about crops, right at the moment I saw you. By the way, how would you have communicated with me if I hadn't happened to come down there?"

"I have been watching for you for two days," he told her. "Sooner or later I should have found a chance to let you know."

Their way was roundabout and long—she had insisted upon leading her horse instead of riding ahead and awaiting Hans. But they enjoyed every step, stopping to sniff the loamy smell, to point out old county landmarks for which he had been homesick, and presently, after night fell, to watch the stars that were shiny after so much rain. Neither one grew tired before the end.

Finally they reached his hide-out. "I won't trouble to bring you any bedding to-night, for they must be missing me by now. You'll be dry in there, and after the army I don't doubt that's comfort enough. But here," she added impulsively, "this will help." She took off her cloak and the skirt of her dress. "Now I'll have to run, not to catch cold."

He could not answer before she was gone, her petticoat flashing like some ghost through the old school-yard clearing.

3

March sailed in on a high wind, and the world could once more be felt tugging at the leash with its vigour. Lucinda was keyed to a continuous pitch of optimism. There was Hans' hardy male presence, the promise of a gigantic crop, and the surge of hope that, if Petersburg had withstood the winter's siege, their troops could somehow break through as the spring had and confound the enemy.

Lucinda knew little of actual outside events these days, since she had enforced what amounted almost to complete isolation in order to lessen the danger of exposure for Hans. She had handpicked the field-gang that worked with him on the far holding, and by tacit understanding not even Pinky and Bonapartt allowed his name to cross their lips. On her visits to his hide-out she was accompanied by a deaf-mute little darky to fetch for her, and left even him on the schoolhouse steps, where he saw nothing.

She had spent much care in making a room habitable for Hans, after its long disuse, while retaining an outer appearance of abandonment, since they had the ever present fear of detection to contend with. The windows which had been boarded up in '62 were now arranged to permit one board to be cautiously swung back for air and light, yet quickly closed at any alarm. A feather bed was kept rolled up in a cubby, and when in use spread in an obscure nook at the rear of the chimney. A Dutch oven and some simple cooking equipment were stowed out of sight. Lucinda herself had seen to it that outer signs of absence of habitation were preserved, should there be any inquiring eye. Ant-hills along the door path, and wasp nests beside the door jamb, were left undisturbed. Hans had good naturedly fallen in with her small deceptive practices, even while deeply preoccupied with bigger problems.

He had set about the tilling and planting with an astounding proficiency, considering he had been unused to husbandry for over three years. He went to the fields before it was light, since in that way his passage escaped being marked; and he returned after nightfall for the same reason. Midway in the morning Lucinda made her inspection of his place, tidied it, mended his few clothes, and left new supplies of the best available food in his secret cache, accompanied by some note of instruction, greeting or such scant news as trickled through with Tid and the mail. It was discouragingly meagre for she was living in virtual exile now; however, the comfort she drew from her solitary hours in his room was sustaining.

There was a hush over the place to-day, in spite of the lurch of the wind outside. The room was chilled, since she could risk no chimney smoke at this hour on a clear day and allowed herself only one bar of light from the window. Still it fell through fresh from the sky, over the unspoiled bareness of the floor. The tasks she performed were simple, a bit of patching or darning, sweeping, or the mixing of some hoe-cake batter. Once she paused with her fingers clotted in mealy mush, and thought: "It's kind of like our childhood, praise be, when we lived in our own safe world, and the whole tribe of us would set up housekeeping under the grape arbour, with a little batch of dough from Aunty Pheaby to bake over stones, and Bruff and I would always lord it over the others as mother and father. . . . This seems as simple as that . . . making me hurry to wake up each new day, to be back at the game, and forget."

She paused. "Yes, it is as simple as that, but more lonely now, for there seems to be no one else in the wide world except Hans and me. It is as empty as Eden. . . ."

On some days when the rain decided to pour, Hans stayed in; then he had time to report to Lucinda the progress he was making in the fields. It sounded Trojan to her after her inadequate attempts, and she sang a song of victory to be harvested for the South. Hans did not join in, he had come home simply to keep her from going hungry.

Along about the middle of March they had one of those long grey days, which she spent with him. Early in the morning she heard the drumming rain on her window, and was glad, for she knew she would find him in his hide-out. She packed food, including a precious last hidden packet of coffee and some nuggets of two-year-old watermelon sugar. She added a small bottle of corn whisky that had become a decent amber by now. All this she placed in one large basket so she could dispense with the mute's services; then she had Pinky wrap her feet in old sacking.

"Ef'n," Pinky instructed her, "you scrape the mud off of these when you git there, and spread 'em out, they'll serve you good comin' back. But put them out of sight from prowlers." This was the nearest Pinky ever came to referring openly to Hans.

As she went through the woods, the rain was sifted into drops that plashed in beads, rather than a shawl that washed over her shoulders and she could lift her face to it without being blinded. But when she came into the clearing, it had increased till a blanket of rain almost hid the house and she had to breathe as if she were swimming. She pounded up the nearer front path, knowing the wash-out had obliterated all trivialities like ant-hills. It took a moment or so for Hans to open the unused lock and admit her by that door. Then she stood gasping through streams of water, after spinning the basket over the floor towards him. He mopped her eyes and nostrils in some alarm before he shut the door; then he turned back to her in anxiety. "What ever made you venture out in this flood, Cinda? It's as dark as doomsday, and as dangerous, with the wind tearing trees up by the roots."

She had flung herself down before his hearth, where a small spot of fire was burning, and had given up to panting. The bellows sound of it could be heard in here, even against the roar of the rain and wind. He waited till her breathing quietened, then he unbandaged the croker-sacks from about her feet. "Any whisky with you?" He prodded through the basket. After poking a dose of it between her gibbering teeth, he set about making the cherished coffee. By the time its good smell was toasting the air, she straightened up full of life.

"That dram," she told him, "hit clear down to the bottom of my soles."

"All the same, you're not going to help preparing the meal." With a forager's skill he went about frying the rashers of side meat and hoe-cakes, finally dropping the eggs into yellow blobs that formed as beautiful as daisies in the sizzling grease.

They ate with the devoted hunger of animals, crouching over their plates protectively, as if to fend off a predatory foe. When finally their stomachs felt glutted in a way they were no longer accustomed to, they stretched their arms back from their shoulders and grunted rather than sighed in repletion. The kernel of fire was still red and Hans managed to rise and put another chunk of wood on it. Then he dropped heavily back into his chair, grunting: "What food! I haven't gorged so since '62—not since furlough. . . ." His voice faded into a vacant state of beatitude.

They sat while the rain never parted its curtain at the window, and the fire clucked like a red mother-hen. Presently he rose on his quiet-moving woodsman's feet and took the bottle down from the chimney-shelf to mix them a real toddy. They sipped it with slow relish, their limbs lounging, and well-being trickling like a sweet syrup through their veins. They had no desire to move and nothing to say, sequestered from strife in a space of slothfulness. Though it was barely noon, it was as spellbound as twilight. The rain came down. . . .

As the day wore on, he gave her an accounting of his overseeing of her fields; and they computed bushels against acres, each feeling profound gratification at the promised plenitude. Once or twice the rain slackened, and she spoke of going, but always the hurry of a new freshet delayed her. She stayed on until they were finally casting about among the scraps of food for enough to make supper for two. Lucinda was arranging some titbits in a pan to concoct some "cush" when they heard the sound of boots sloshing stealthily about the house. They were a white man's, there was no doubt about that. The two stayed absolutely still and blessed the last burst of rain down the chimney that had obliterated the smoke. Lucinda called the roll of threats that could fall upon Hans: Yankee scouts? No, for they would have been upon him by now. Also they would have heard some echo of trouble at the mansion, some emissary would have come scurrying. One of the family who might carry word back to Ma'am Gerda? But any such would accost him first and hear him out. Quartermaster? Her thoughts buckled sharply. Could it be that Nat Screws was attempting some reprisal upon her household because of Jerard's censure? Her body petrified with wariness, and her raised finger kept Hans motionless.

Finally they heard the gushing that mud makes about the boots of a man no longer cautious who has decided that no one hears, that he can now make his progress noisily, being out of sound of human ears. Whoever he was, he had not discovered their presence. And he was not tarrying here to seek cover from the storm.

When the squelching steps had been sucked away into the rain, Lucinda whispered shakily: "He didn't find you, thank the Lord!"

They reached across the foot of distance between them and closed their arms about each other in deep relief. Whatever it was, danger had passed. Still, their elbows felt as weak as a picked chicken's wings.

Much later they found that their limbs had ceased to shudder and instead were shoved steadily close to each other's. She could detect his thigh muscles rippling slightly against her own in silent communication of his nearness. Very gradually she slid her chin up along his chest until, with one cheek laid flat against his shoulder, she could watch his face staring over her head, as if in some supplication to old Greek gods.

He released her inertly.

4

The next day the rain had slackened some, and Hans went for a walk to ponder that crisis of discovery he had escaped. All unwarned, he stumbled upon a ghastly sight; it was Wayne's body on a branch bank with a voodoo sign stuck into it! Hans sat down ill and covered his face from the shame before him., He had long known of Wayne's intention to come home and dispose of his negroes by trade and sale before negro conscription could result in their manumission. Now—he had returned! Hans wondered what atrocity he had committed in secret on one of his negroes that had sent him skulking away from his holdings to Top Hill in a fruitless attempt to escape vengeance from the wronged. Here, none the less, retribution had overtaken him. Hans buried him, trying to recall some conception of his half-brother that would replace this distorted memory of him. At least he could choose a spot with a little thorn-apple bush at the head, and he mumbled a prayer. Ma'am would ***never*** know. He returned to his shelter heavy with the secret he must hide, even from Lucinda.

As his instincts had foretold, she was there waiting, performing trifling housewifely tasks. She did not seem to distinguish his present profound preoccupation from his usual taciturnity. Swiftly she moved to him, linking her arm through his with a little squeeze. "My, how I've worked to freshen this place up! After yesterday's complete shut-up 'twas as musty as a chicken-house." She had let in a lot of clean air, and he saw that she had his water-pitcher filled with glossy clumps of rain-washed rhododendron. She pulled him towards his chair.

After he was seated she dropped down where she could lean her head against his knees. "I have your dinner about ready, but rest a spell first." Her head squirmed, seeking a comfortable spot, then was still, her eyes browsing in the sparseness and isolation of this room. In some strange way its very meagreness reassured her against war's horror, gave her a conviction of ultimately bringing about the fruition of her life-desires for bountiful plenty, untrammelled laughter, furious passion, careless giving. A living that, whether pared down to the momentary penury of war or on the rampage of extravagance, would refuse to be hindered by the lack of functioning of even one of the five senses, and would trumpet the triumph of the total human!

She shook her shoulders to cast off such far-fetched grandiosity of thought. Right now all her pleasure lay in this one room, where she sat with her back propped against Hans's shins. "I feel absolutely at home here," she told him abruptly. "More, in a way, than I do up at the house. There I feel like a paper doll or some image of a plantation mistress kind of faded from careless use. Here I feel more like Cinda, scrabbling after things I want, as I did when as a girl I wanted plums or sunflower seed or the fattest pecans. The years, with their layers of manners, are shed; it's as if I were out walking early again—above the big gully, barefooted and holding my apron-frock up around my shanks to keep its hem from becoming scalloped with muddy water——"

She broke off with an embarrassed laugh. "I don't know why I'm going on this way. Except something makes me feel awfully young and happy again. Here."

She switched about towards him, sitting in her characteristic tailor fashion with her elbows propped on his knees. In the filtered light her features wore an amazing gleefulness. He poked his palm under her chin and pushed her face back till he could bend over it closely, to study its shifting whims.

Under the load he carried of battles and desertion and Wayne's death, he thought, because there is no way a man can guess at a woman's burden of withheld trouble: "I'm older than she, for this hour—as a man always is when his shoulders are full-weighted. When men play truant and the women are bearing then the rôles reverse . . . but when men are labouring, their sweat and their muscles have an age that no woman has ever reached! Man must have been on this earth first, with woman coming after as his first offspring. She is weaker now than I—I who have always wanted only to crouch down at the bottom of her skirts."

Lucinda was moving her cheek against his, knowing that he felt himself to be in possession of more gravity than she could plumb. Then she placed her mouth beneath his and held it in shape for an instant before mashing briefly into his lips and receding with a laugh.

She rose with an easy stagger and looked out of the window, where sunlight had broken apart the rain. "If I hurry I can reach the Hill for late dinner. I hope yours isn't all dried up."

Standing near the door, swathed in her cloak, her eyes darted over his features, ending in an imaginary imprint upon his lips. Hans could feel her taking pleasure in their touch once more. "She will return again and again, as long as I distract her from the tragedy that is filling her other, larger world. She is curious also about a new quickening. But I must beware . . . if I am not to be destroyed. She is, for all her brief display of tenderness, the queen of the bees, giving a deathly fate to those who serve her."

Lucinda walking through the woods was happy again. The water drops on the boughs were opal.

5

One day soon after that, when the wind was swift, Lucinda rode over to the Stand. Her horse raced almost as fast as her spirits, which were freed at last from the nightmare of her catastrophe with the convoy. She was hastening to give vent to her jubilance, sure that the

South could reap the tall stack of replenished fodder for its armies out of the snapping jaws of defeat. Surrender! She twirled her tongue in a whistle.

At the Stand she could not gather a group together long enough to make them listen to her talk, for they were all going about their chores, without fervour, yet without despair. And when Nan stopped her shuffling of the parching ground peas that made the best "coffee" nowadays to ask Lucinda some civil questions, the other felt as silly as if she was Joby "taking on" about Maude's frocks. She went in search of Ma'am after that.

When she found Gerda she hadn't much to say, except: "I feel like ten kinds of a fool, charging over here to tell about the sprouts I've seen coming up in my fields. Only, Ma'am, didn't your first farming get you excited too?"

"Lordy, yes!" Gerda's voice rolled out of reach, back to that time when she had first found out what could happen to an acre. Cotton or corn, it took hold of you.

As they went circuitously back to where Lucinda's horse was hitched out of sight, Gerda regarded her daughter. Lucinda stepped so lightly on the stones that kept her feet out of the bog that the stones were scarcely pressed down into the mire, and Gerda wondered what it was that buoyed Cinda up so high.

Lucinda rode off into an invigorating wind that almost tore her unhatted hair out by the roots. Triangles of cloud sailed high and wide over heaven, and her horse's mane was like a torn shawl flapping. She leaned over his neck towards her goal.

Having taken the abandoned mill road on purpose, she came around to where Hans was leaning in a far fence corner surveying the fields.

She dismounted and came over beside him to look at the same thing, at parted shoots of green, at something fresh springing with renewal out of their ground.

This was a sweet chill hour of hope. She took hold of his hand in a union of endeavour.

CHAPTER SIXTY-SIX

AFTER THAT, Lucinda did not stir away from Top Hill, feeling that she had no energy or interest to spare elsewhere. The show-off in her had learned its lesson; now she was always at work. In such isolation, naturally, she heard little news, and all bad tidings she discounted as rumour. She pinned her faith in Johnston's stubborn army and the great size of crops like hers coming forth.

At Yufala and Turberville and at the Stand they knew that the ceaseless calamities must be given credence, though they could not comprehend their import. One day word came that Grant had at last drawn his lines around Lee's right flank and the next day that Sheridan had won the Battle of Five Forks, which compelled the evacuation of the long-held Petersburg. On the third day of that first changeable April week Richmond had fallen, dragging the hopes of the Confederacy down in dust.

Still the fighting went on, for the South did not know how to quit. So Grant and Meade and Sheridan pursued Lee and surrounded him. Then there, in a small unknown country courthouse whose name of Appomattox was henceforth to go down in history with Waterloo, the incredible to all Southern minds, the utterly impossible, took place. General Lee surrendered.

It was not true, it could not be true. Denial would come soon. Soon! Many defeats they could endure and never falter from their goal of victory. But to lose their bright star? No, it was not true, for then the heavens would have fallen, to end this earth!

So the fighting still went on, in the Carolinas, where Johnston struggled to thwart Sherman. The war was *not* over. The South had not yet surrendered.

But now the war was moving into Turber County. Word had come that Federal troops numbering four thousand, under General Grierson, were on their way to confiscate all obtainable food, livestock, and valuables. As soon as word of this reached the Stand each woman reacted in her own particular fashion. India strung the last of the family trinkets on a locket chain and flung them into the lower part of the copper rose bush, where she trusted to the blossoms to help hide them. Maude donned all four of her dresses to keep them from seizure, and looked worse than a toadstool. Joby, accompanied by Hannah Lee, went post-haste to Yufala to make sure her children's christening porringers were secreted. On their way they passed various other equipages driving headlong in diverse directions to escape the Yankees. The most comical was that of Nettie Screws. She was seated in her carriage with the rolls of her turkey-red carpet protruding from its windows. "She'll wind up in the piny-woods probably," laughed Hannah Lee, "scared pea-green, but with her rugs safe."

When they arrived at Joby's house they decided the best thing to do was to put the mugs into a sack and anchor them in the river, tying the bag to a tree root on the lower bank. After they had finished the task they sat rubbing each other's shoulder-blades to bring relief to their tired muscles. "Do you remember," asked Hannah Lee, "when we picked scuppernongs into clean sheets? My, you were festidious then."

"Can you remember peace at all?" asked Joby. "I seem to have forgotten what it was like, though I've hugged its keepsakes closer than any of you."

Back at Rock Wall, Nan had methodically hidden some of the smaller sides of bacon in the ash-hoppers and lowered pails of lard into the well. "I don't doubt," she remarked to Cayline, "that the Yankees have learned all these tricks twice over while raiding other counties. Still, we have to try."

Meanwhile Ma'am had gone about conserving their larger supply of food, allowing her people very little waste motion of fear. She made Slade supervise the digging of trenches in the early vegetable garden. Then they laid away more bacon, dried beef, meal, hominy, brown sugar, syrup, and wine. After that they rapidly raked the soil over it all and set out rows of hardy young cabbage plants, puddling them down to make them take root quickly. Before nightfall of the next day they were growing spunkily, as if nothing were below them except solid earth.

The hard part after that was the waiting. Even Joby and Hannah Lee were back, so there was no diversion of speculation about their whereabouts. Gerda herself had one more important duty to perform, but the others had nothing to do now except await an armed enemy.

She could sense their fear was inside of them rather than outside, where it might have been shaken off. She longed for tasks to occupy them, but could devise none.

Finally the news reached them late one day that Grierson was crossing the Lower Bridge. Every one gave up all idea of sleeping that night, and the negroes gathered close about the house. " At least they can rest their limbs," Gerda said to Pokey, " for the ground's dry, which is a blessing. And I'm counting on you to keep their skittishness in hand to-morrow."

" What you goin' to be doin' that you ain't told me yet?" barked Pokey.

" Hide my livestock in the swamp," answered Gerda. " I'll take Shade, because he can stop them from whinnying and mooing."

" How about you catchin' cold in that damp swamp? You're not so young you cain't get rheumatism now."

" But it's the only good place," pronounced Gerda. " Let's worry about my aches when they happen. Besides, I'm not going before sun-up."

There was solace for Gerda in having her negroes banked about the house as that night waned into the next morning. There they were, solid and obedient, shifting their weight when necessary in a quiet fashion, like cattle in slumber. Yet there was no sleep in them, only a still watchfulness as they eased the cramps in their bodies at the end of the night without any murmurs of protest.

Gerda came out from the ell just at that time, ready for her trip to the swamp. She wished she had real coffee to give them, but there was nothing but that parched ground-pea brew. Still she said: " Let's ask a blessing for the night having passed without mishap." They lowered their heads while she made her grace. Then Lessie came from the kitchen with the big pot and commenced passing dippers of hot drink around. They took the swallows gratefully, each in proper turn under Pokey's watchful eye.

Faint and grey the morning was waiting for one wan moment, then the sun rose in its bronze wonder. Gerda watched it. Why was it that after all these thirty years and more of Alabama it looked so beautiful? How could so simple a thing as one more plain day breaking from under cover of night always be a miracle? She did not know.

Splendid shone the gold!

CHAPTER SIXTY-SEVEN

Lucinda woke early to the skirling morning notes of birds and lay awhile trying to catch the calls of those she knew by name. Somehow they failed to come through clear, because of another, a thrashing sound, very like the coarse crying of magpies. "The darkies," she thought. "They can't stay out of the yards since those rumours about the Federal raiders. They want to hang on my skirts. Well, I'll pacify them later."

She lay an instant longer, stretching her arm back above her head, her toes down towards the foot of the bed, feeling narrow and strong and exultant in this early hour. Outside of her wide-open windows the whole world stood tall; there seemed to be no limit to her county or to her own sway over it.

Rising, she went quickly to her dressing-alcove, where she leaned out to survey her people. They were all there except the shift that Hans worked in those far fields, and all were dressed in the best clothes they had, wearing a holiday manner. They acted as if it were a Christmas morning, the way they gyrated with expectancy or broke out laughing at nothing at all. They appeared more gleeful with excitement than frightened about Yankees. She heard one of the negresses cackle. "Now then, them folks up arounds Huntsville cain't brag so big 'bout their raids, 'cause we'll have one of our own."

"That's speakin'!" ejaculated a buck. "To hear them, you'd think this wa'n't our war atall." Happy hooting cheered him, and some piccaninnies commenced to jerk their joints in a capering dance.

After regarding their effervescence, Lucinda wished she had something special in the line of extra rations to give them. Her eyes dwelt appreciatively upon the bright pattern their patched garments made among her shrubbery in the glisten of the bright-come day. She flung out an arm possessively over them before turning back to her ablutions.

A moment later she was absorbed in making her toilet. "My skin," she observed critically, "is showing more than a trace of grain. Needs rosewater glycerine like it used to have." She was interrupted by a bustle outside of her door, and she called impatiently: "Come on in, Pinky, but why in time are you making such a fuss?"

There entered then, not only Pinky, but Milly and another extra maid, with their white turbans banded smoothly, their clean palms hanging like slices of pink ham at their sides. Lucinda inspected them, noting the exaggeration of their usual mannerisms of courtesy. These house servants, equipped by training to ape their mistresses, were aping her profoundly to-day.

"I haven't finished washing yet," she told them, "but as soon as I do, Milly and Dewberry can start brushing my hair. It's flying all over the place after yesterday's laundering. I'm glad it's clean again, though, for it surely was rank." She sudsed her hands up and down in the basin, watching how the bubbles from the home-made soap dried in grey beads on her forearms and had to be scraped off. However, the morning's elaboration of service compensated for this makeshift.

None of their negroes were acting the way many of them over in Georgia had—deserting in droves in the wake of Sherman's army. The slaves here were as immovable as the land itself. However much their volatile black minds shifted about, they still retained an axis of loyalty through the centre of everything, just as they counted upon protection from their owners.

This elaboration of luxury that they accorded her this morning was of their own devising. Apparently they felt that stateliness should be preserved in the face of the enemy. Moreover, to them this was a special occasion, when some climax of the war was expected in the county. Thus a certain regalia must be donned, a certain ceremony observed, to ward off the trampling of the idols they held dear in their white folks, symbols of bounty and arrogance, humour and testiness, and above all an easy-going grandeur.

Lucinda went down to a breakfast that tasted better than usual owing solely to every one's high spirits.

The pupils rose to greet her with a spring, and she saw that even Cousin Gracey's cheeks were perked with pink. At her own table Veda and Roxanne stood formally behind their chairs, while Bonapartt held hers out for her. She waved them all to sit down. Seeing that Roxanne and Veda wore their good new homespuns, she commented mischievously: "Everybody seems to be dressed up to-day. Is it to welcome the Yankees?" Then she added in ire against any Northern interlopers: "But just wait till they run up against Johnston's army. They'll find out that the fighting has started up fresh!"

Roxanne was inquiring anxiously: "Ought we to have buried our good dresses, Miss Lucinda, with all the other valuables? I thought maybe so, but Veda said we ought to show them what ladies looked like. Only I'm scared they'll cut our frocks to smithereens with their sabres, like you said they did over in Georgia." She poked forkfuls of food hastily into her mouth, as if to make sure of secreting at least that much from the Yankees.

"Don't fret, little biddy, I've heard that it's mainly horses the Raiders want to get here, to help stragglers leave the state. If that's all, we'll speed them on their way, to the Carolinas, where General Johnston can take a whack at them. They haven't licked us yet by a long sight!"

The light touch of anticipation that had bidden her rise this morning was still intact as she glanced out at the general sunniness of the day.

After breakfast Lucinda went to the garden maze, trailed by Milly and Dewberry, to cut flowers that grew between the hedges. She freighted her willow basket with blooms and, taking one cluster out, let her nose dive into its perfume. When she saw how she had crumpled it she was sorry, and shook it out the best she could before replacing it on top of the pyramid of flowers in the basket.

As she entered the side yard she noticed that the negroes had consolidated into a more compact group. The men had settled down from their cavortings, the skirts of the women no longer flirted in the air. Yet there was no stolidity about their massing, rather a concentration of intensity. She felt that the excitement which had eddied like a spring breeze earlier was now heading in one direction, carrying the scent of fear.

She surveyed the whitewashed blaze of her plantation yard-houses, wondering if they could possibly be split apart shortly by vandal blows. She shook her head, regarding the plain, calm blue of the ten-o'clock sky. Then she looked back at her negroes. "They're like a herd about to stampede before a storm. I see now that I've kept them too shut off from the outside these last two months. They're in the dark about what's been happening. Well, if I can't give them extra rations to-day, at least I can shake off their fears by sending for news. Then probably by nightfall they can laugh it all off—this scariness they have been fomenting out of rumours. Besides, I must know myself!" Suddenly she felt a hungriness for tidings of late events. It may have been necessary lately to stay shut off, with Hans here, but no ignorance had become insupportable.

"Tid!" she called, and he came forward, his whip tilted like a lance. "Ride over to Rock Wall and bring me back the news from Ma'am Gerda." She spoke as if asking him to fetch another part of her family inheritance, a portion she had not needed till now, but suddenly felt she must have, to dole out to these dependants for reassurance. "And hurry, because I don't want to fritter away any more than this one day on such a commotion. After all, it's not crop-barbecue time," she half-laughed, and their chuckles echoed her. "This is the work season."

Tid scraped his left foot politely, and passed his carriage whip over to his youngest boy to put away. "I'll ride my fastest. An' I'll fetch you news that'll put all these back in harness. They've been actin' as skittish as stock turned out to green pasture after being shut up all winter." Now he scraped his right foot in proper request for dismissal.

2

At first, after Tid left on his mission, Lucinda occupied herself with her usual rounds, but after dinner, when the girls were performing their lessons in deportment for Gracey, she was at a loss. It was her usual napping-time, yet she could not force herself to lie still on that broad bed. Folding her wrapper about herself, she began to tramp back and forth across the room, like an animal that for a long time has been hypnotised by some strong hidden power and now is feeling a quiver of outside shock trembling through its state of mesmerism. Restively she picked up objects from tables or mantel, worried them a second or so, then dropped them indifferently, to move toward the window as if drawn there to watch for Tid's return, though she knew he had as yet barely reached the Stand.

Leaning against the armoire at one point, she exclaimed desperately: "*I wish I had Hans here!* He wouldn't let me go out of my mind this way." She folded her forearms about her head to form a retreat for her thoughts. She recalled the last day she had been alone with him. It had been very quiet there, and peaceful. She had been content to help him work tallow into his shoes where they were cracking. The day had passed almost wordlessly.

Now she dropped the hood of her arms from her bent head, and her eyes sought the window again. Her shelter was being shaken by the events taking place over the landscape outside of her haven. She found herself walking over to thrust her head out the window, then going to tinkle her bedside bell fretfully for Pinky.

When Pinky came she led her mistress back to her couch in the dressing-alcove, saying: "You better rest." She straightened Lucinda's wrapper carefully, then propped her head up so she could see the drive.

For a while Lucinda controlled herself by a pretence of gossip with Pinky, but presently she quit pretending. She alternately knelt on her couch or flounced back, letting her eyes skitter from corner to corner of the alcove. "I want Bonapartt up here too," she announced.

"You jes' rest and I'll got fetch him," Pinkly placated her, moving with smothered steps into the Hall, vowing she would never let Miss Lucinda babble to anybody else the foolish things that were about to drive her wild. "She's taken this war on herself evah since Marse Whet died. An' it's too much for her to carry by herself. I pray to the Lawd she keeps lyin' down while I'se gone."

Lucinda herself had determined that she must not move, that some tax was being put upon her to maintain an outer calm. She straightened the plaits of her hair, made precise her interlaced fingers, and raised her eyes only at decently-spaced intervals to watch the road.

She could not, however, stop the rustle, the mumble, the clapping of the darkies waiting in the lower yards. Finally she grew really nervous concerning Tid's whereabouts. "He said he'd be back before nightfall, and here it is almost that time. He ought to have been back before now, if there wasn't any trouble." Her thoughts ran wild. I wonder what's going on? Are they really raiding the county? Has Tid been caught? Are any members of my family hurt? What is going on out there, beyond my sky-line? Have guns been firing—and I not hearing? Why hasn't Tid returned? Why? Surely Ma'am would never keep him . . . for nothing . . . when she knows how I need him here . . . I have a house full of girls with no protection. I need Tid to keep guard; the others would all scurry into hiding at the first crack of a rifle . . . Tid must come back to give us protection—but no, I can take care of that; the thing I want in the worst way is *news!*"

She braced herself on her wrists and peered out at the sky, where a prismatic arc of colour was clashing in a way that put her teeth on edge. She wanted to snatch that gaudy sky off the earth, as she might have torn a bandana from the head of an impudent kitchen negress.

Then she heard the hoof-beats of Tid's mare coming at a wild pace up over the rise, swerving madly into the curve of the circle, then stopping—dead!

She hung dizzily far out of the window to ask him what news he brought.

But before she could call out, she saw the yardful of darkies running toward him, as if sucked into a storm centre; then she witnessed them scattering back from what he told them like leaves before a cyclone. In a few instants they had vanished to the rear, into hiding. Tid was left there alone, quieting his tethered horse before he came to mount the front steps. His use of the front steps meant the dignity of tragedy.

Lucinda had taken her stand at the head of the staircase by the time he had swung the door back beneath its fanlight. A black silhouette he stood against the pinkened piece of air that the evening showed through the door.

"What tidings?" she asked low.

"They've won! The Yankees!"

"No! What of General Johnston? In North Carolina?"

"He surrender too. To-day."

Lucinda held her balance. She did not fall forward into the stairwell. She stood upright, wondering if a bruise showed on her cheek, where the blow of defeat had struck.

The war was lost. Why, then, were they not all dead? And gone?

3

The path to Hans' cabin lay well worn. Even in the dark Lucinda knew each turn and how to let her face pass through unscratched. Hans was in the doorway as if expecting her, and stated without question: "This must be the end."

He led her to the hearth, which was stone-cold, and he offered her no words of comfort. He simply passed his hand over her forehead to smooth off the moisture, then let it fall again. He went to the window and pried another plank loose, to lean out, now that discovery meant nothing.

Lucinda was intoning behind him: "I have lost all. Jerard, my son, the war. Now if only I could lose myself—in oblivion——" Her voice dropped into a pit.

Hans stayed with his eyes buried in the night a little longer. Then he turned toward her. All the shapes were shadows, yet he could divine her where she stood at the corner of his spread feather tick, her head cocked sidewise as if knocked askew. Then she sank down on the floor, all thought of comfort spent. He saw how her curved body flattened against the boards.

When he came and lay down beside her she seemed in a swoon.

The splinters pricked his hands as he reached for her. Then his shoulders crowded over her bosom, and his mouth made deep search of hers. "Lucinda," he begged her to understand, "you do know how I love you?"

"Yes, Hans."

"Do you want that—idolatry?"

"Hans, yes!" Her voice rose for one instant of resurrected power.

"It is a sin."

"No matter," she groaned, "when all our world is damned. . . ."

His lips murmured along her forehead and down the cheek to her throat. "I will be glad to pay by death," he pledged, "for you." Then he was tracing the slope towards her breast.

4

At about dawn Hans led Lucinda back to her high-placed house. It was against her will, for she wanted never to emerge from the hidden dimness of his cabin. "But you must go," he told her. "Your house needs its mistress, during danger."

Even through her stupor she could understand that—how she must stave off havoc when the defeat rode over to Top Hill. So finally she stood with her head as high as a swan's, there in that doorway beneath the fanlight. Hans, taking in the whole look of her, saw the stunned shape of her features gathering a hard-summoned arrogance. Then he prayed silently for some penance, for his immolation, to restore her ravaged ascendancy, since his worship had been her bane. "Lucinda!" His voice was a votive cry.

But she did not heed him, for from far off she could hear the confused noise of the raid heading their way. And in another beat or two upon her ear-drums, it turned into the pounding of the Federals along the road that flanked her grounds. They would be here in a brace of minutes.

She stepped one pace back over her door-sill and hurled her voice up the stair-well. "The Yankees! Bònapartt, Pinky, tell the girls. Get ready for the Yankees!"

She could not know what went on behind her. She could not even see what Hans was doing right before her, except that a certain squareness of his frame shut out part of the swerve of the men curving into her drive.

Then behind her one sound scurried into her hearing, starting at the top of the staircase and running its scared way down step after step, almost tripping in its panic. Lucinda flung her head around and saw Roxanne poised on the bottom step headed towards the Little Parlour. Her puny arms were holding Whet's gift doll. "I can't let them get her! Not my china doll!" Then she raced to the fireplace and laid it on the kindling sticks. Lighting the fire, she pressed her small breath out as if from a bellows, to blow the flame up. Lucinda's eyes were spellbound by a whole childhood going up in a blaze.

Then a clamour tore her gaze away, out towards Hans, standing between them and the Raiders. "Hold them off," she beseeched, "till Roxanne is finished with her baby!"

But the men had clattered down from their foraged mounts and one had started up the steps. Lucinda saw the joint scenes—the Federals come to pillage, and Roxanne fanning a lightwood fire with a rag rug.

The man was almost up the steps now, ready to shove his way in. Then Hans lifted his arm to bar the way across the entrance, and he had put his other hand on his pistol. "You can't come in yet!"

"Step aside, Reb!"

"No, sir!" Lucinda heard him command the other as the final flames wrapped up around the doll.

"I'm coming in!" threatened his foe. "After whatever 'tis you're hiding from us." He levelled his musket. "See?"

Hans jerked the trigger of his pistol at the same instant, and the two shots sounded as one. The Federal dropped back down the steps, with one foot dragging, while Hans fell forward, bumping his head. Lucinda dodged forward even before the smoke cleared away like a grey ravelling. Her knees broke beneath her as she reached Hans, and her face almost fell against his. "Hans!"

But he was dead. His solid arms would never be able to work again. She played helplessly with one of his big hands.

Then another Raider began clambering around on the steps. "Excuse us, we didn't mean to shoot before ladies. But can we pick up our Bud?"

Rising to her feet, Lucinda answered: "You can go in there now, the dolly's dead."

They supposed she had gone out of her head like so many of these women down here, but then suddenly she was speaking composedly about their needs. "You could carry your companion," she directed them, "over to my family's burying ground. It's a good distance off, but any of my negroes that you see will show you the way. Now let me see after my own."

They shuffled back down, picking up their comrade while hearing her call out: "Bonapartt!" to a very old darky who was coming out into the hallway blowing on his fingers as if he had burned them.

One of the Raiders felt obliged to ask her: "Can we help you any way?"

"No. Just leave me."

Before they had gone far on their uncertain way, they were overtaken by the clumsy cortege of that shot-down Southerner. The bier-driver, who was called Tid, directed them to fall in behind. "I'll lead you to the restin'-place at Miz Gerda's."

They followed, promising among themselves not to pillage anything from this family in reprisal.

At the end of the ride there was a commanding old woman waiting, standing in a place that looked like a garden except for the headstones. The driver Tid said: "Reckon our word git here in good time that we was bringin' Mister Hans."

"It did, thank you," was all Miz Gerda said before she went and laid her hand against the square cheek of the son, where its jaw-bone shone sure and bright. Then she turned to the cavalcade, remembering she had strangers to attend to. "I've sent for some old quilts to wrap them in. And there'll be tree-splits aplenty to prop the earth back—inside. We don't have any nails now, to use in coffins. So see that you fold him decent."

They watched her as she laid Hans out, and copied her. The darkies dug a full-size space for their Bud, not skimping him, and all treated him as religiously as the dead son. The old mistress spoke the prayers gruff and quick over each grave.

While all this was happening, the Northerners were amazed at the way the holly trees showered blossoms down. They had never known anything about holly before, except red berries on small bushes. They had never smelled that incense of sifting, creamy bloom.

5

Lucinda climbed the stairs after sending Hans on his way home and after quieting her people. As she climbed she had to hang to the bannisters because her eyelids felt scorched from Roxanne's charring fire, her eyeballs bruised by Hans' downfall. Also her mind droned that now it was truly done, not even danger demanded her presence. Now she could seek surcease.

She opened the door of her room. It was in gloom, for which she was grateful. It was very silent too. Slowly she went about shedding her garments, then walked towards her alcove to wash, to try to cleanse herself for some final sleep.

She felt deathly as she filled the basin. Her head hung down towards the bowl. *Dead and gone*, drummed her ears. *Dead and gone are your loved loyalties. Now you should die, Lucinda.* Her head dipped into the dim water. But the cool laving braced her face, making her straighten up again. Numb she stood that way, but no longer expecting instant destruction.

As she went toward her bed, she paused a moment at the alcove window to see the western tints across her garden. She had forgotten, because of the shadowiness enveloping her, that it was not late afternoon. A wash of dark swabbed over everything, as if evening were falling. Well, that was right, she thought, and went to bed hoping never to wake again.

She did wake, however, to the sound of Cousin Gracey *tat-tatting* at her door. When Gracey entered, Lucinda saw her figure as if it were bordered in black. Lucinda wondered if her own memory could be playing her tricks, by going back to Gracey's spurious widowhood. She half-chuckled. Still the black border did not disappear from Gracey.

Some while after that, Roxanne tiptoed in, wanting to comb her hair for her. When Lucinda raised her lids to see how the child looked after her loss, Roxanne's face appeared as dusky as a mulatto's. Swiftly Lucinda swept her palms across her eyes to clear them.

Roxanne remained dark.

"Could you go away please, child? And let me rest," she requested, and Roxanne did as she was told.

Lucinda saw now that there was no daylight in her room although it should be the yellow part of the afternoon. She lay still in her acre of bedstead and let the rest of the day pass until the real evening came on. Then Pinky and Bonapartt entered, but that was not so bad, for they were supposed to look all dark.

They brought supper for her, on a plate with a soup dish turned down over it to keep it warm. Both dishes appeared to her as black as frying-pans. Yet she ate what Pinky forced into her mouth with a spoon, and remembered not to babble before Bonapartt again.

After he was gone she told Pinky: "I'm going to die. I'm not fit to live!"

"Don't act up so, Miss Cinda."

"But I tell you," she screeched, "I'm already in a place as dark as doomsday! *I'm going* BLIND!"

"Want I should put a compress ovah yo' lids?"

Lucinda felt her head being bound up by one of the last of the white cloths left in the house, and over that pads of spring-chilled compresses. This would be a cool, blessed death. Yet even while she slept, she knew she was still alive.

BOOK SEVEN

Rock Wall

CHAPTER SIXTY-EIGHT

IT WAS regular Maytime weather that day when C. D., the first one back, rode up to Rock Wall and delivered epistles from Bruff, who was still on the way with Turber. Ma'am Gerda gave C. D. a great hug. "Isn't it good to be home again, son?" she asked, calling him that for the first time and trying to clear the fuzz of tears out of her voice.

He patted her a long time. "Yes, it is—good," he said in hesitant tones. "But," his gaze moved slowly about, "of course the damage down here is nothing to compare with the way it was in Virginia. Yet somehow I hadn't thought—of home as changing. I guess Joby's kept back most of that." His face puckered for a moment like a schoolboy's deprived of his prize for good conduct. "I always thought of coming home into the hall where the floors would be *all shiny with wax*!"

Nan laid a timid hand on his arm. "Still, Joby has you back safe, C. D. And it didn't last long enough to take your boys."

He looked down at her wonderingly. "That's so. I never thought of the little fellers as growing fast enough to get into that inferno."

Gerda slapped her apron, to shake them all out of this state. "At least, C. D., a rubbing of wax can cure your disappointment in time." They let that pass as a joke and laughed.

"Here I am about to forget," he said, handing over their letters from Bruff. Gerda opened hers at once, and after a quick glance began reading it aloud. It told of how before Appomattox Lee's officers had made him the proposal that they never surrender, but drag the contest out in relentless guerrilla warfare until the fighting classes of the South were exterminated if need be, rather than accept defeat. Lee, Bruff stated, was proud, being so stern a warrior himself, to hear of his men's choosing death. Yet his warrior's code also counselled him to abide by the outcome of battle. And being a wise, far-seeing man, he felt that his finest men had no right to obliterate from the future such splendid posterity as they might beget, the generations that could remould their broken world once more to the shape of life.

Gerda's voice stalked on to reach the words Lee himself had spoken to them, his soldiers, at the last: "I need not tell the survivors of so many hard-fought battles, who have remained steadfast to the last, that I have consented to the result from no distrust of them; but feeling that valour and devotion could accomplish nothing that could compensate for the loss that would have attended the continuation of the contest, I determined to avoid the useless sacrifice of those whose past services have endeared them to their countrymen. . . . I bid you an affectionate farewell."

C. D. had his head down and bare, and said in a prayer-like voice: "Yes, he spoke to us that way. He said an 'affectionate farewell.' He knew we all loved him."

2

They heard once more from Bruff before he arrived. The letter said he had to take things slowly, not only because of the uncertainty of transportation, but because Turber was in a bad way. Bruff told them that he hoped none of them would act odd, or shy off from the boy. Turber had slipped back still more since the failure of Early's last raid, and the surrender had utterly fazed him.

When finally the pair did arrive and Gerda saw the pitiable figure Bruff was helping from the dray, she had to pray rapidly to God, to Gran, and to Yarbrough, all three: *"Now you must help me, now and for ever after. Amen."* Then she started to hurry down the path, but stayed herself in time, recalling how she always welcomed her returning sons from the front porch, with Pokey standing behind. A snap of her hand signalled clear to the ell, bringing Pokey to her usual place.

Bruff did not attempt to hasten Turber's steps, but let him putter his own sweet way up among the bushes and clumps of border stock-flowers, or scuff at twigs dropped from the great oak tree. Turber paused once, baffled, abreast of the palings enclosing Yarbrough's grave. "That chicken-house hasn't any roof," he remarked. Then on moving closer and peering down into the enclosure, he puzzled out the name on the stone. "Lordy, Bruff," he laughed in a high key that sliced eerily through the morning, "they have you mixed up for dead and buried. Maybe I'd better go ahead and break the news gently that you're alive—to Ma'am and to—to——" His mind could not quite reach the other name of "Nan."

Then he looked up and saw Gerda waiting, and shot forward, home. Gerda rocked his face in her lap. After a little, with sly mischief he began to plague her as of old, by twisting the fingers of one hand about her ankle-bone.

Roxanne rounded the porch corner, holding a May fly cupped against her ear, listening to its strumming. Seeing him, she flung it out of captivity, and rushed towards him. "Uncle Turber!" she hailed him gladly. "I think I know more about things that grow in the woods than you do now! And I can make ink, and bluing, and thread!"

"Catch your breath, Roxanne," chuckled Gerda, elated over the child's giving Turber a natural welcome. "You'll have time aplenty to tell him, and to show him. He's home for keeps."

"Yes," said the child soberly, "and I wish Whet was too."

Nan had this moment now, while no one looked, to go into Bruff's arms. And all life was a long view ahead, where no spectre straggled.

3

From far off Top Hill looked to Danley like the house of the dead. And as he drew nearer, the cemetery scent of the boxwood assailed his nostrils with the bitterness of negation. He saw also how the windows of Lucinda's chambers were shuttered.

The steps leading up to the veranda were like white chalk. "The House of the Dead," he said aloud, regarding its sepulchral appearance.

He chose not to enter it yet. Tethering his sorry mount to a tree, he made his way to the one bit of graceful laciness left on the scene, the summer-house with its matting of vines. There he found a strip of seat that had not rotted, and sat where he could see the mansion through an opening in dangling tendrils. The ominous look of the house still overwhelmed him.

He knew there was something dread here. He wondered if he could master it.

He rose and walked from the summer-house towards the steps. Once he paused in a particular place. "*Whet!*" he cried before he knew it, for he had come across a spot where his child had played, where the lad had stood to dream . . . where the plants were still a trifle stunted from his restlessness, and—where the boy could not come again. He was suddenly bereft because of some broken bushes, as he had not been when dwelling on a young hero fallen at Antietam. "Whet?" he spoke again, this time softly as if to beckon his child home. Then he walked on, knowing that he had access to this nook always, to his son, whom he had not betrayed.

"His poor mother," he said, pitying Lucinda, recalling the alien farewell between the two. Yet he sensed that her shortened motherhood was not her greatest tragedy. Again his glance darted at the house and again was struck away by its blankness.

He tried to muse awhile, to gain courage to advance towards the house where no wife came forth with a welcome home for him from war. He reflected detachedly: "After all, I was never her real husband. Only a consort, a tutor to explain instead of make history. Perhaps," he exclaimed bitterly, "if I could have truly mated her——" He knew that however often their senses had flared for one another, there had never been that culmination of being wedded beyond the body.

His eyes went in hatred up against the walls of that house, built for a cruel bride of another man and shunting him off like a pretender. Glance by glance he dealt it blows. Of condemnation for its waste, its wanton owners, its vaulted beauty.

He made his legs bend at the knees, to walk up the white steps. For one moment after he had reached the top he turned around and stood at their head, not as if he owned this place, but as if he laid claim to a far-stretched landscape beyond. Out there were high hills, and after the hills the sky. "Free sky," he called it.

"They cannot take me now, the Whetstones. Not with my son gone. I shall remain an odd off-piece from their pattern, though even that will add to their form by giving it contrast." Then he saw how the enduring hills reached up and took hold of the free sky. And he wondered bitterly if people would remember his last name, once he was gone. Yet perversely as he turned and went in, pleasure at the doorway's grace descended on his spirit.

Suddenly the stairway looked like a staff of music and his steps scaled up it rejoicing. His mounting stopped at Lucinda's door, and he held silent and whole that moment of belief in the glory of returning. Then he swung her door open.

He did not cross the sill. Her voice told him not to enter. He saw, in the dark of her room, how her hands lay crossed like those of a corpse. Her eyes were blindfolded, only the jut of her chin and the band of her forehead showing.

"Go back," she told him.

His hope snapped off, like the cold breaking of a dropped icicle. It made a tiny mocking tinkle.

4

Nan and Bruff had driven into Turberville early to inspect their newly purchased house. "We'll want to walk around over its town land before it grows too hot," Bruff had said, adding a statement of which he was never to tire: "You know we can, if we choose, walk all the way from our house out to the plantation without once setting foot off of Whetstone land."

"That's a good thing to know," Nan answered, "but don't forget you promised to let me have the say-so about how to use the town land."

They drove up into the lot and unharnessed the horse, as if it were already home. The lot was grown up in weeds, and such fences as there had once been were decayed; while the one or two yard-houses left were slanted from abandon to wind and rain. After a glance at the side, they walked around and entered the front gate. The small house had been built sturdily enough to withstand both war and disuse. It was no mansion like Top Hill, no Bluff House like Joby's, nor even as spaciously roomed as Rock Wall. And perhaps it was set too close to the Turberville Road; still, that would be neighbourly for a young doctor's wife, who would be alone a great deal.

"The first thing of all with us," she insisted, "is to procure some real medicines and some new instruments for you. Others can hoe and dig, but you are supposed to cure."

"That seems all so far away," he sighed. "I've been killing too steadily."

None the less, they went into the house, to inspect the right front room. It would do for an office, because its morning dimness would soothe the ailing people who had not slept, and its later westering brightness would cheer others out of fear of the dark-falling night. Bruff surveyed his probable quarters carefully. "I believe I can fix this up pretty fair."

"I liked staying in your old office while you were away," she told him. "It made it seem as if you were near, especially during my bad time."

Softly he held her in a kiss, with his eyes open so that the tumble of her curls dazzled him. Then he laid his arm across her shoulder, propelling her into the chamber opposite. "This is where all our other children will be born," he told her. She gave up mourning then for the child that was the ghost of a war now ended.

They were standing in the back yard, ready to leave, after having set out orchards, planted garden patches, and even constructed a scuppernong arbour, in their minds. They were examining an unkempt pomegranate bush, poking at the hard knobs of the coming fruit, when they heard someone slow a horse to a stop in the soft dust and dismount quietly. After that they heard Danley's careful steps coming around towards them, and they had their first sight of him since peace, but they were stopped from any rejoicing because they could tell he had come on a grave errand.

"Bruff," he said, "you will have to attend Lucinda, I can do nothing for her. She shuts me out. And she has gone blind! Blind, there in her room alone."

Bruff turned to Nan, speaking as a doctor. "Nan, you must get back to the Stand as best you can."

"All right," she answered.

Bruff and Danley spoke seldom as they rode towards Top Hill.

"It's wiser," said Danley in a colourless tone, "for you to observe her state unprejudiced."

CHAPTER SIXTY-NINE

GERDA was sitting in an hour of unwonted ease rocking on the front porch, waiting for her family to gather for dinner. The shade fell in an unbroken sweep without a single stipple of sunlight, but far beyond the cape of her trees the summer heat held the earth in complete fervour. The sky above was a mighty blue. It was good growing-weather.

Below the corner of the steps Roxanne and Turber had drawn a circle on the ground and were shooting marbles. At times he won. With each of their shots a powder of silver sand spouted, and the game went on with interminable pleasure.

Gracey came chirruping out of the house to flounce herself down on the top step like a girl. "I declare this reminds me of soon after the Creek War, only a lot happier."

"We had more to eat then," Gerda reminded her, forbearing to speak of worse things.

"That's true," murmured Gracey, "but I don't feel so much grief now. I was too young to be left a widow. Still, I mustn't take on so. I'll be going to rejoin Ronald soon, no doubt. And I'll have the satisfaction of being able to face him in all fidelity." She primped her faded hair as if she were speaking of being his partner for a cotillion measure. Then her eyes strayed towards Roxanne. "That child is as clever as a monkey with her fingers, but she hasn't one vestige of sense. I can't teach her any French phrases. I wonder sometimes if she's quite bright. She always takes up with the queerest people, like——"

Gerda cut her short before Turber's name could be disparaged. "Never mind about throwing off on Roxanne; she can use every-day sense, which is more than I can say for some members of this family."

Gracey took no offence, merely nodded brightly and burbled on. "Well, I'm not so proficient at French, but no one can question my talent with the pianoforte. And, do you know, I've hit on a splendid way to teach the pupils to carry a tune. I'll draw a great big staff on that slate board over in the schoolhouse, and picture the notes on it shaped like mouths; then make the scholars go over and sound each note, holding their own mouths over them, in a sort of bite."

"My Lord," groaned Gerda inwardly, "and she's talking about common sense." However, Gerda did not stop her, for the babble did no harm, and Gerda felt kindly towards weaker ones, watching Turber at his game of marbles. Presently she asked Gracey: "Do you know whether your father and Willy are coming here for dinner?"

"I expect so," replied Gracey lightly. "They haven't anybody who can cook up left-overs into a meal. My, I feel musical! I never knew the birds to keep on singing so hard when it was this hot."

Gerda lost the thread of this conversation, listening to a comfortable domestic squabble taking place between Tom Two, Hannah Lee, and their offspring. It was compounded of affection, ways of reassembling farming implements, and the question of where the children were to sit at the table to-day, when a large gathering would force them out of their regular places.

"Tomas," objected Car excitedly, "shouldn't always sit where the fullest plate is dumped. No wonder he grows bigger for his age than me. Anyhow, we'll both be big enough to pick cotton the first crop that comes."

Gerda chuckled to herself. They would pick many and many a bushel, for the new cotton farmers would have to learn like their parents in pioneer childhood. Yet whatever else their problems proved to be—drawbacks of scavenged countryside, rotted buildings, raided stock, lack of metal, vanished currency—one trouble they would not have in Turber County was the problem of negroes gone too free. They might not own them as something to be sold, since Emancipation had turned them into the "coloured people," yet the negroes would still hold their nurse-like sway over their white folk, and trust to their folk for a roof overhead, food to swallow, and land to chop with a hoe. The dark ones would hover, giving succour in sickness, scoldings for faults, and a chant of praise to the family's name

A spring wagon drawn by two spindly mules halted out front. It was driven by Fenn Cox, with Veda, his new-wed wife, beside him on the driver's plank. They waved hands at Ma'am Gerda, but shook their heads at her invitation to stay to dinner, claiming they had a fry of fish that would spoil if left over. Gerda sensed that Veda knew this was a family dinner, and that for an instant something dark darted in the back of her mind about Wayne. They had once been two dark gnome-like creatures, not fathomable by others. Gerda wondered what road he had gone that led away from the war with no returning. In a cavern of her mind, marked by his name, dwelt her one undenied grief.

Now Joachim was helping Dolly down from the corn-shuck cushion in the back of the wagon. Her skimpy skirts caught on the wheel, which switched them aside, showing that her ankles were not encased in the traditional white stockings of a pre-war lady, but in the home-dyed black ones useful to a young woman who had to tramp about a sooty kitchen hearth or in polluted pig-pens. Gerda could see the freshest of colour staining the girl from forehead to neck as Dolly caught the fastidious Joachim's eyes staring in startled fascination at this homely apparel. "My," thought Gerda, "I know she's mortified, and palpitating for fear he'll quit courting her."

As usual the pair was accompanied by Will Bee, bumbling good-naturedly at their heels, spitting tobacco juice with profound relish from a compact quid and complete disregard for where it fell. "Lord a mussy!" he exclaimed in sudden dismay. "I hit your hind ruffle that time, Dolly, as square as if I'd aimed at it!"

She whirled in a frenzy. "I could wring your neck," she cried, clutching the ruffle and shaking it in awkward despair of ridding it of the filth. "Don't you realize," her voice rose piteously shrill, "how hard it is to look even half-way decent these days? Dressing out of scrap-bags, and wearing hats made out of bulrushes! It isn't much fun trying to be a lady in such raggle-taggles. And then to have to endure *spittle!*"

Will Bee ducked his head, trying to palm his precious quid out of his mouth without her seeing it, while Joachim took hold of Dolly's hands and said: "Listen, sugar, you're as pretty as a picture in anything, and don't forget that none of us are dandies any more. It would hurt our feelings if you ladies showed off before us, when we look like scarecrows."

"Oh!" Dolly blinked the tears from her shallow eyes. "I never thought of your side of it."

"Our hide, you mean," muttered Will Bee. "You must have forgotten about the body-lice."

"Talk polite, or do you want me to take you out behind the barn?" demanded Joachim of him.

"Not unless you have a buggy whip to help you out," answered Will Bee, unperturbed.

Roxanne and Turber broke up their marble game to approach the steps with the trio. Gerda continued to rock easily, and instructed Roxanne: "You show Miss Dolly to the bowl and pitcher. Hannah Lee is somewhere around back there. And you boys," she told her sons, "wouldn't hurt yourselves if you took a lick and a promise at the well basin."

They all went inside, leaving her to the stillness of midday and its somnolent quiet. It was so silent that she detected the approach of Joby's and C. D.'s vehicle from far round the bend, while the whirring spin of its wheels was still muffled in dust. She stopped fanning her palmetto to watch them alight. They accomplished it in proper order, C. D. turning the reins over to the buggy-boy who had been crouched in a corner of the wagon and who now hopped down to stand as alert as a footman at the head of the irascible team. He stirred only to hitch his galluses where they galled him over a flea-bite; otherwise he was as immobile as a servitor attending Jupiter's chariot.

C. D. helped Joby down, while his two sons performed the same courtesy for their elder sister, then indulgently swung their pretty pet, Maude, out in a fine skipping swoop which landed her laughing between them on the top stone step. She nudged each one's arm affectionately and still hung on to their hands, now and then raising her weight on them to skip on her very tiptoes. Arthur twisted her uneven curls once, but then Charles Dillard admonished: "For goodness' sake, don't spoil Ma'am's temper by taking on over her so!"

Ahead of them walked India. Even in walking up a path she placed her feet precisely and held herself erect. Her face was slightly saturnine in its indifference to her present shabby apparel, and her grandmother approved her carriage.

Half-way up the path Joby was gesturing at C. D. to call his attention to Yarbrough's continually flowering copper rose bush. "It looks like a regular ball-bouquet, doesn't it?" He pressed her elbow in response.

Gerda appraised their little group, conceding them their proper importance. For behaviour needed to trace a pattern through impulses, and shape must mould content, while Purpose, that ultimate deity of both the formalist and the procreator of power, compelled the final result. Watching them loitering along, passing an unpruned flowering bush, overblown in its beauty, and bandying compliments about the blossoms, the weather, and one another, she conceded that they were a courteous group, however wanting in other respects. Their good manners had a value like loyalty. It could protect behind frail fences plants that flowered fragrantly, while leaving to the trees the labour of dropping fruit.

Gerda wrenched her shoulders to bring herself out of her day-dozing as Joby came up the steps. Joby fended herself from tripping over her skirts by the deft use of her finger-tips, remarking: "Papa's rosebush looks like a nosegay, doesn't it?"

"Yes, it does," agreed Gerda, "but come on in. They're waiting dinner."

2

All during the meal Gerda kept looking for Bruff and noticed that Nan was trying to control her own expectancy. Several times others in the family started to address him before they recalled his absence, and finally Joby asked: "Ma'am, is Cinda real sick? With Bruff staying over since yesterday, I worry."

"If she was, he'd let me know," Gerda answered shortly. But right after dinner Gerda walked down towards Pokey's cabin, turning to the one person who never failed her. The path was the colour of nutmeg and it bent around in careless curves that darkies' feet had trodden. Some piccaninnies lay sprawled napping under bushes, not minding the flies that crawled over their legs. It had grown hot that day. Summer had burst.

Pokey's cabin, Gerda observed, needed a new coating of whitewash, but the crape myrtle bush shook its rosy ruffles out luxuriantly beside her step. Pokey was pulling the door open wider for Gerda and trying to pretend that she had on her shoes. Gerda went into the cabin for a moment out of politeness, but she could not stand its sweet stuffiness for long. After she had appreciated how well Pokey kept it, she came back into the air and sat down on the cabin bench.

"What's fretting you now?" asked Pokey.

"Lucinda."

"That gal!" grumbled Pokey.

"This is a lot worse than usual, with Bruff staying there so long."

"When you get ready to go to her, I come along."

"I'm afraid you can't help," replied Gerda heavily. "I have to take care of this myself."

"All the same," said Pokey, "I'll come too and carry Roxanne home. An' some other chillun to keep her company. It's time Cinda was up again." She pulled up a ground-pea vine and looked at its clotted roots. "Them goobers ain't so big this year."

Gerda stared at the crape myrtle clusters which withstood the sudden heat without wilting. "I'm not as young as I used to be," she sighed. "I like to just sit."

Pokey laughed hard at her and pulled the knot of her hair. "Child, you do sound funny sometimes. I'd whip you for such talk as that if you wa'n't too strapping big."

Gerda laid her head down in Pokey's lap to let her comfort her.

3

It was the next evening before Bruff returned from Top Hill, and Gerda, restless beyond measure, had gone walking while waiting. She sought her favourite part of bottom land. "Next year," she planned, "I'll plant this from my best saved cotton seed. By that time England ought to be trading with us again." She had no idea of how the carpet-baggers would come, the worst scourge that ever befell cotton. She uprooted a scalp of crab-grass and shook out the dark loam from its roots. Then examining the rich cup of soil from which it had been pulled, she thought: "Maybe I'd better start killing out this crab-grass right now, only we don't have the salt to spare to do the trick."

It was at that moment that Bruff came walking down the hill towards her. As he approached he noticed the clump she had plucked and dropped, and he tossed it about with his toe. "Good crops will come from these fields again," he said.

"Yes," agreed Gerda. "This soil crumbles as rich as a twelve-egg cake."

"It will be a long while," he predicted, "before any of us will prosper much without the aid of cotton, in spite of the surrender and the North. I expect we'll have to raise my children on its nourishment."

"That's true," she nodded, "only I wonder if some day you mightn't have a granddaughter who'll think of it as no more than a starched white petticoat?"

"If she does, I'll wring her neck!" he growled. "No, I think she'll be fond of the stuff, whether she wears it next to her skin to sop up the sweat or raises it in a parasol over her head."

"You dream like your father," said Gerda.

They stared at the saucer-dip of their land, with the fading blue plate of sky over it. Rich land still.

"I want to talk to you about Lucinda now," said Bruff, coming to the point.

Gerda answered in a slow voice: "I knew something went wrong with her at the close of the war. But I never could find out because she shut herself up and told me not to come over."

"She has gone into hiding," said Bruff slowly.

"The way she did after Whet's death?"

"No. This is not the same. That was grief. This is a shock beyond description. She is almost *blind*."

"Blind? Your sister blind! Look me full in the face, Bruff," Ma'am Gerda ordered, "and tell me, because I have a right to know the straight of this."

Bruff shifted about towards her, and the afternoon rays of light lanced across his cheeks. "It's a hard thing to tell you, Ma'am, because I don't grasp it all myself. But I know I felt that there was something wrong there, in that house, that would always stay untold. And Lucinda's eyes are as blind as her secret, though I could find nothing wrong with them physically."

Gerda sat down on a rock. "Do you mean she really can't see?"

"Ma'am, she can't distinguish more than a blurry shape of any one close to her, and that's a strain. She doesn't suffer much now except that her head aches in 'sort of bursts,' as she calls them, whenever things are forced on her sight, or if the light in the room becomes too bright." He paused, then continued reflectively: "The trouble first started the day after Tid brought her the news of General Johnston's surrender. People, starting then, all looked black to her, I've learned. And she has been alone in her room since, shutting out every one except Pinky and occasionally Bonapartt, because they are meant to be black and so don't frighten her when they have to lift her bandage."

Bruff turned his worried face away a moment, then went on with his account. "When Danley returned she wouldn't even greet him. She hasn't permitted him over her door-sill even once, which was a hard thing for him." Bruff stared at the measured sweep of the fields.

"It's strange," he ended, "that she cannot stand sunlight, yet when I took her outdoors last night and made her face the sky in the dark—her eyes didn't flinch. She even started to count the stars."

4

Gerda ascended the white flight of steps to the Top Hill Veranda. The heat was white also, a shimmer of silence. Danley awaited her, and with one accord they turned to regard that silver fire.

He said while they had the distraction of scenery: "Ma'am, you know my love for Lucinda has always had a guardian quality, yet I have never been able to discipline her. Any guardian is worthless who cannot control his charge." A calm gave dignity to his admission of inadequacy. Something rendered him invulnerable. It was a scar he was displaying, not a wound. "You are the only one," he ended, "who can help her, Ma'am Gerda, since you are the only person with authority over her."

Now the heat hovered as if it would consume all the earth to ashes, but Gerda did not shrink from it, she stood there while it smote her. When she was ready, she turned about and entered the high hall, with its coolness.

5

Gerda didn't sidle into Lucinda's room as if it were a death-chamber. Instead she opened the door amply and greeted Pinky as usual before she settled herself in a rocker and untied her sunbonnet to fan with. "Hot!" she whiffed. Then to Pinky: "You'd better wet that cloth on Miss Cinda's forehead. It looks dried out." Thus she passed over the blindfold as a simple headache remedy.

While Pinky was wringing out the bandage in fresh water, Gerda saw how Lucinda's hands groped, with no help from her eyes, trying to resettle herself among the pillows. This blindness was actual enough right now. When Pinky had plastered the cool cloth down over Cinda's lids, Gerda dismissed her, then asked: "Do your eyes ache bad?"

"Not very, any more."

"Bruff said he didn't think you suffered much pain now, and that your eyes were unharmed, no matter how your sight seemed blighted for the present. Do you run a fever?"

"Not now. Only I feel the heat terribly." She scarcely knew how to speak of her strange affliction.

"No fever, hum? Then why don't you try getting up a bit each day?"

Lucinda's bitterness brewed up at such matter-of-fact talk about something that was as dread as Judgment Day to her, something that was shaking the soul inside of her loose from her senses, until there seemed to be no person left called Lucinda, merely a tabooed form lying swathed in a shaggy sheet.

Ma'am's voice was going on, while her rocker made everyday squeaks. "I would have come over sooner if I'd known you needed me this bad. But at the same time I heard you were ailing I had word from you not to bother. And with your brothers coming home, those that were left——" her tone quickly skirted away from sorrowing for the lost and took up the practical—"I was kind of run ragged. Then I've been trying mortal hard to spare our few horses and mules all the labour I could."

"That's right," gibed Lucinda, "spare your critters before your daughter."

"You know good and well," retorted Gerda, "that I'd have been over here as quick as lightning if you hadn't warded me off. But you were ashamed to see me, for some cause. Put me off. Couldn't look me in the face."

"That's not it. I really *can't see!*"

"True, but Bruff says you can make out the stars in the sky. So why not folks? Why not try? Take away that cloth."

"Don't touch it!" Cinda mashed the compress down frantically.

"I won't snatch it." Gerda scorned that way. "Besides, what I want you to face is facts more than objects. And to stop your cowering."

"Don't you dare call me a coward! I never was one."

"Not about blows. But you're almighty scared to look back on how you've played hob with other folks' lives. You mussed Joby's into a pretty snarl. You tormented Jerard Malone to——"

"To the point of destruction," wailed Cinda. She knew about that, and also how she wantonly lost his son. She knew too how she'd tried to fray Danley Bruton to pieces, merely to show her power. However, he had managed to cloak his mind in self-control, away from her preying instincts. Yet—she had killed *his* son, too!

She shrank from this thought as if thrashed.

Ma'am's voice was continuing, meting out a measure of even more awful guilt: "Last of all, somehow—I don't know how—you wronged Hans to death. You might have spared—him. . . ."

A groan blurted out of Lucinda's throat. She knew, without being told, what a pariah she'd become. Men and women wouldn't speak or eat with her if they knew of Hans. She interlocked her fingers wildly, as if to clutch at any string that might tie her to the human race. The very violence of her gesture stirred up some defensive anger at her lot, and she lashed out at Ma'am.

"Oh, you're righteous, and I'm sinful! You help people, while I bang them to pieces. But you never gave me a chance to *do* anything because you were always too busy doing a lot more than your share. I wasn't taught how to take over my part, like the boys were by our father."

No, recollected Gerda, she hadn't tried to instruct Cinda much. Simply whisked her out of the way, to tend to her own next task without stumbling over the child.

"Well," cried Cinda, "I ran wild!"

Yes, wild, after being shoved out of the bounds of duties by her mother, grieved Ma'am.

"But mind you"—Lucinda's laugh rang sardonic at herself—"I learned to revel in my wildness. I despised the tame. Ran over them, rampant. Like I did over poor Joby." The mocking dwindled out of her words. "No wonder you dressed me down to the bone at that bad time of Joby's."

Gerda recalled how on that day her heart had sickened for both her daughters.

Lucinda resumed: "In spite of all, I thought on one other day that I could retrieve myself. It was on my wedding day. I wanted to promise you I'd behave better, and hear you say you knew you could count on that."

The time and place came back to Gerda. Cinda had hunted her down where she'd been standing, worn out from preparations, near the scuppernong arbour. She had been breaking off the bare fig-tree twigs because she was worried about this day, which she didn't think she'd met right.

"That day," Lucinda reminded her, "I tried to tell you that maybe Jerard and I could copy you and my father. But you wouldn't allow me that. Wouldn't even let me speak of anything approaching your love. I can't exactly blame you for tearing its very name off my tongue. But I do blame you," the charge sounded loud, "I do blame you, from the bottom of whatever heart I could have had, for taking no notice of my *wanting* to be a wife, and my asking your help to *grow!*"

Gerda gazed aghast. She, Ma'am, had shut her daughter out from womanhood!

Lucinda's voice dropped to pieces in a whimper. "And you didn't—even come in—to see my wedding——"

"Child, child!" Gerda said deploringly, moving over to lay calming hands on Lucinda's frail arms. "You ought to rest now. I've taxed you." She called Pinky to swab Lucinda all over. "Ma'am will be close by," she promised. Presently when Cinda dozed, she went into the small adjoining room where she was supposed to lie down herself.

6

After Gerda had reached that corner room she could not nap. She tried it for a quarter-hour, stretching her limbs solemnly. Still her thoughts kept working. "My mind's worse than yeast," she grumbled as she rose and put on her grey wrapper again. She tied its apron-like strings firmly, as if girding herself. While doing this she studied the room. Three times she had occupied it: first when Lucinda lost her unborn child, next after Whet's death, and now. Each other time she had failed Lucinda. That must not happen again.

The room was a narrow one contrived out of a handy corner, with only a back window to give air and light. Its single advantage was that it was handy to Cinda's.

Gerda took three strides from her cot to that lone window. From there she gazed abstractedly down at the yarb garden, which was all burnt to straw; then her eyes from force of habit began roving over such land as she could see from here. It was limited. Just as well, since she meant to confine her thoughts to Lucinda.

Right here and now she knew she had to take stock of herself before her Maker, tax herself with her sins of omission and commission. She had omitted to train that daughter, who might easily have sown instead of plundering. She had committed the constant sin of battling that daughter out of her path into outlawry, because she had feared her as her supplanter. And had tried to ward her off by declaring her own self supreme, vowing that there never need be such a thing as her successor, since she, Gerda Whetstone, could last for ever!

To-day this window narrowed her gaze, sliced her hold over the earth down to a fraction of former grandeur. Through the heat of the slowing summer day there seeped a conviction of her own mortality . . . but vaguely hinted at once before on that rain-traced road to Gainesville. Now there came upon her also a sense of being like something cut, harvested, stored away against the winter hunger of others.

Yet it didn't come easy to her to resign her person to a general immortality. She wanted to stay and watch over her own, to guide them on and on. But that was not the way of it now. She had to call for help from another. Someone to whom, as Pokey had told her was done in the African tribes, she could pass the torch. Not throw it away in a wild blaze, but hand it over like a beacon passed from one side of the altar to the other.

Her mind sombre with abnegation, her body begging for rest, she lay down on the cot, grey wrapper and all.

7

A slight breeze was licking through the upper hall when Gerda entered Lucinda's room again. Lucinda was sitting up against smooth pillows, her braids coiled evenly about her head, and wearing no bandage, though she had to hold her lids low. She looked very thin and young that way.

At the first sound of her mother's step she flung out an arm, in a plea to be allowed to humble herself in the confessional. But Gerda tucked the arm back down at her side. " Don't frash. 'Tisn't good for you. I want you to stop having fits, even fits of repentance. You've got to improve fast, so you can do your share in the family. As you did in the war."

" Do you mean," asked Lucinda painstakingly, " that you still think that after all the evil I've done—after Hans—*and oh, Ma'am, you don't know how evil*—do you still believe that I can help?" She held her fingers across her lips after that to ensure asking no pity. She heard Ma'am rise and move to stand at the foot of her bedstead, as if that were the most suitable place for this deliberate speech.

Gerda spoke.

" I have some things to say to you, Lucinda. I know I don't share my thoughts enough. Are you listening?"

" I am, Ma'am."

" All right. I'm talking to you this way because I think *you're* the one to bear my part after I'm gone." She let that sink in.

"I don't belittle what the others give, it is all important." They both thought of Joby's courtesy and Nan's fidelity before Gerda continued: "Still, somehow I feel as if the fire would die out of our children's veins if 'tweren't for having you to kindle it into a fine flare."

Lucinda understood what Ma'am meant. It had to do with her peculiar attraction for children. For in spite of the fact that she had cut short her own child-bearing, she wasn't unfertile like Gracey, or a too carefully domesticated wife like Joby. She was *quickened*, which drew children to her.

"Little folks," continued Gerda, "are never cast down around you, Cinda, because you don't frown on their misbehaviour. In fact you make common talk of your own faults and tempers. That makes them feel the warmth in you, and the fun."

Cinda pushed back her braids, straining to hear every word. Why, Ma'am was pouring life back into her!

"Of course some would like to look up to you, like Whet. He stuck you on a pedestal, and you scuffed it out from under. But most of the others, like Roxanne, want you to be just the way you are. They'll always follow at your heels."

Slowly Lucinda began to realize that whatever her sins had amounted to, she couldn't creep off and hide under a cowl of black. Because the young would poke slits of light into her oblivion with their demands. She noticed now how the drawn wooden shutters at her windows were creaking against their metal hooks, trying to let in the outside air.

Ma'am was forgetting to pay attention to Lucinda. She was peering into the future at her picture of the kind of man she wanted to come from their family. He would be kind but terribly stern, and his face would be cut from all time, so it could never be destroyed from people's memories.

She sighed over her prophetic hopes and spoke again. "Somewhere out of the next lot I hope we'll have a man to equal Yarbrough. Because women, at best, can only grip hands to bridge the gap. Our family will have another such, if *you* hold fast with me, daughter."

She looked distressed at not being able to rend her garb of reticence asunder and make a reckless union between her thoughts and her speech. She wanted to let her voice ring out like a pæan. To cry out: "You aren't the tree-trunk that I am. You're more like two spliced pieces of wood called a cross. Still you will remain upright and high on a hill! A signal!"

She didn't mention a word of that grandiloquence, however. Instead she summoned a dry chuckle that went with the creaking window-blinds and the plain summer day that was taking place outside. "You know, Lucinda, somehow you remind me of myself a little. Long ago, when I went trampling. Pokey used to get after me about it, tell me that I acted like the sister to God. Well, you remind me of that same high-stepping creature. 'And you, Sister God, are my favourite child!'"

So saying, Gerda swung over to a tall French window and barely parted the blinds, but that one cool green crack split open the gloom. Through that margin she could see Roxanne and Tomas and Maude. They were flying June-bugs on long threads, as children loved to do in the summer time. Gerda half-turned her head to finish what she had to tell Lucinda. "Do you remember how the steps in the Rock Wall look?"

"Yes, there are five."

"It takes five wide solid steps to pass up through the thickness of that wall. They mount solidly, and it holds the land firm around our house. Your father, Yarbrough, built it strongly, to hold back any gully-wash that might threaten the family. To keep it unharmed." Gerda gripped both blinds. She heard the big bedstead give out a creak behind her. Then there was the fumbling of Lucinda seeking for the ladder, where she placed her feet cautiously to feel her way down to the floor.

At the bottom Lucinda was dizzy for a moment and had to brace herself. After that she parted her eyelids and felt another sick heave. That passed. The outlines of the furniture blurred and moved, she stood still till they came to stopped bulks. Then she commenced making her way through them. Once she struck her shin on a stool. At the window she took hold of the shutters and pushed them far apart. A wide wall of light assailed her eyes and she could see nothing else as yet.

Ma'am Gerda held an arm behind her shoulders. The brightness stayed there, and the free smell of day came into the room. Lucinda listened to the sounds of play from the children in the gardens. "You must have brought the whole pack over here with you, judging from the noise."

"Pokey did. Look! Look, Lucinda! That's the next part of our lives!" Gerda herself could see the children weaving in the boxwood borders below, and Pokey flapping the white tent of her apron after them, to summon them in. Then she could hear the early supper-bell jolting in a subdued way as old Bonapartt carried it out to the spot from which he always rang it.

Lucinda's eyes were wiped over with a haze of brightness, in which the June-bugs' wings looked as big as birds against the glare. Still she held her gaze on their fanning without blinking.

As the supper-bell clamoured loud and sweet, the children let the June-bugs go free!

THE END